I0582748

A FLAME

OF THE

PHOENIX

SHE WILL REIGN

A
FLAME
OF THE
PHOENIX

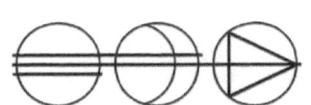

CHLOE C.
PEÑARANDA
NEW YORK TIMES BESTSELLING AUTHOR

LUMARIAS
PRESS

A Flame of the Phoenix
Copyright © 2025 by Chloe C. Peñaranda
All rights reserved.
This is a work of fiction. Names, characters, places, and incidents either are the product
of the author's imagination or are used fictitiously. Any resemblance to actual persons,
living or dead, events, or locales is entirely coincidental.
No part of this book may be reproduced in any form or by any electronic or mechanical
means, including information storage and retrieval systems, without written permission
from the author, except for the use of brief quotations in a book review.

Published by Lumarias Press
www.lumariaspress.com

First Edition published April 2025

Map design © 2025 by Lila Raymond
Cover illustration © 2025 by Alice Maria Power
www.alicemariapower.com
Cover design © 2025 by Lumarias Press
Edited by Bryony Leah
www.bryonyleah.com

Identifiers
ISBN: 978-1-915534-10-1 (eBook)
ISBN: 978-1-915534-09-5 (paperback)
ISBN: 978-1-915534-08-8 (hardback)

www.ccpenaranda.com

ALSO BY CHLOE C. PEÑARANDA

READING ORDER

Dear reader, I am a fantasy nerd to my core, and the idea of multiverses has always tickled my brain. We've seen mentions in prior books of Nyte not being in the realm he's supposed to be, and the concept of the Nytefall trilogy transpired from my fantasy series, set in a different world, An Heir Comes to Rise. There are vague mentions of people in the final book of the Nytefall trilogy, The Dark is Descending, which could potentially spoil for An Heir Comes to Rise series. And an appearance in this book, A Flame of the Phoenix, which could spoil for the Nytefall trilogy. If you desire to read both for the full crossover experience, my recommended reading order is the order my books have been published which is as follows:

An Heir Comes to Rise, A Queen Comes to Power, A Throne from the Ashes, A Clash of Three Courts, A Sword from the Embers, The Stars Are Dying, The Night is Defying, A Flame of the Phoenix, The Dark is Descending.

However, if you discovered me through Nytefall, reading as follows will have the same effect:

The Stars Are Dying, The Night is Defying, An Heir Comes to Rise series in full, then The Dark is Descending.

Though I also stress, you do not need to read An Heir Comes to Rise series to follow and enjoy the Nytefall Trilogy. Nor vice versa. It can be read completely on its own with no missing information.

Happy reading!

DEDICATION

For those who've walked through fire and kept turning the page.
You are the ashes, the flame, and the rise.
This final flight is for you.

THE BEGINNING OF THE END

The heir of souls will rise again,
Their fate lies in her palms.
With rings of gold and will of mind,
She'll save the lives of men.

For every evil born,
A way to destroy it is conceived.
When the chosen join as one reborn,
The fire of fate is finally achieved.

In Ungardia's darkest hour,
When all shall burn and fall,
Only the Phoenix Queen can find a throne from the ashes,
And rise it true for all.

To see the end the Mortal Gods must stand,
It is not without them that power is true.
Fall one, fall all,
Find friend in foe to see it through.

Come the return of the lost first son,
The end will fall at last,
For only if the heirs unite,
Can they right the wrong of the past.

Bound by strength, her fire will burn,
Shaped by darkness, with no return.
Spirits will clash as the fates demand,
And the cost will be life, torn from hand.

PROLOGUE

Approx. 500 years ago

It took seven Gods to create her, and one mortal man to break her. One might find her tale tragic, but she would come to make it her legacy. They would not win.

In her cursed immortal fae form, she had two paths of fate: submit to the dire choices she'd made and allow herself to succumb to a desolate, piteous existence; or take back all that had been stolen from her.

She stared down at the man she once loved. The man she'd given up her divinity for. The man who was nothing more than a pretty lie…

Her choice was already made, with the dull heart that had become a dead weight in her hand.

His hair, as dark as the black soul he'd parted with, was spilled like ink across his face. Strands touched his eternal glass eyes of horror, still echoing with the scream from when she'd taken her revenge. He should have known what was stolen was always bound to be collected. Nothing in this world was without a bargain. Though he'd reaped far more reward than she this time.

This was the last time she would lose.

From the gruesome sight of what was left of him, she felt nothing.

It wasn't enough.

Not enough revenge. Or solace. Or triumph. Maybe nothing ever would be. But her choice wouldn't end here.

Despite all the ways he had wronged her, hurt her, in such deplorable ways, never did she believe a mortal to be capable of conspiring…

She mourned for him.

For herself.

Unable to tear her gaze away, all her mind could torment her with was, *Why?*

Why, why, why couldn't it have been real? Their love…it had once felt so *real*.

There was nothing more despairing than being fooled by one's own weak heart, which she considered ripping out in the same manner.

Yet she couldn't even if she wanted to. She could not die. She could not be killed by mortal means.

"You did this to me," she whispered, letting the cold organ slip from her grasp.

Even in death, he'd won.

Her tears were hot against the ice that began to embrace all that she was.

Though it was his heart that lay torn from his chest, it was hers that would pay the price for his betrayal. For eternity.

Love was damning. Love was cruel. Love was weakness.

All she had now was time.

She looked down at the thick black stone bracelets. Pretty shackles to her power. Whatever dark magick they'd used to bind them, she would find a way to break them. That, she promised their damned souls.

Swiping up his sword, she found it was heavier than she antici-pated with her weak muscles. She made it to the door and listened. She didn't have her power, which could kill everyone in this wretched place in minutes, and she knew little of how to use the weapon tightly clutched in her grip. It was in that moment she dedicated herself to learning. To becoming death incarnate to track every one of those in Ceaser's band who'd basked in the glory of capturing a Goddess and made a mockery of her name.

Then she would break her chains and save the world too. Of weakness; of human greed.

The scraps of fabric that covered her body were drenched in blood, but she wore it proudly as she left that room that would haunt her for the rest of her immortal days. Where she'd spent years in captivity. Used for her blood.

She'd *made* them what they were. It was her blood that Transitioned humans into fae.

"Marvellas."

Her name had never been said in a breath of such horror and fear. She was used to hearing it chanted with laughter and triumph. The great Spirit of Souls, conquered by once mortal men.

She turned slowly, but her rage and her sorrow were like adrenaline coursing through her, so she couldn't see the odds of three fae being a real threat. She recognized each one of them. Her hatred and her revenge flashed in her eyes, and she didn't feel her steps advancing toward them, sword gripped so tightly her knuckles were white.

Steel sang as they armed themselves. Whatever they saw on her face widened their eyes, and wariness slowed their movements.

"How did you escape?" one she knew as Harris asked cautiously.

They didn't see her as a threat. Of course they didn't. Regardless, she was ready to cut them down like timber through sheer determination to be free.

As soon as she was, in her quest to find the key to break her manacles, she would spend every waking moment training to master the weapons she'd seen—the ones that had been used on her. Harris's sword. Jaquard's bow. Leon's daggers. And many more.

"I told you I would kill you all," she said, not even recognizing her own voice. For so long she'd used it to plead in cowardice; to beg with mercy. She was used to her words being empty.

The chuckle that came from Harris was a violent trigger. With a cry, she lunged, and his wide-eyed horror didn't get the chance to take root before the slick feel of blood and flesh met with the end of the heavy blade she wielded. Right through his throat.

She let go and stumbled back. Harris choked, spraying blood from his mouth before he fell. Her pulse sprinted, surprised by her own swift movement, as her blade clattered to the ground. The two fae behind him stared down at their friend in bewilderment before anger firmed their faces. She'd seen their anger before. *Felt* their anger before. Fear took over, and she had no weapon now. Her trigger response to cry and plead burned in her throat, but she swallowed it down, determined not to become that frightened, captured prey again.

Never again.

Her instinct told her to twist and run. Run as fast as she could despite her frail body. Yet for the first time in her tragic fae existence, it was as if the Gods had finally heard her apology for betraying them so long ago and had allowed her to come to land.

The fae on the left barely managed a strangled cry before someone approached from behind, locking into position, and swiftly snapped his neck. The sound shuddered through her. Sickness rose in her stomach, but there was nothing to bring up.

Her savior twisted to the other fae, about to plunge his dagger through his neck.

"Wait!" she called, trembling to intervene when she might be next on his kill list.

He halted his attack, pinning the fae to the wall.

Hesitantly, she took steps toward them despite her desire to flee the opposite way now the opportunity had been granted.

She needed to know...

Her bare feet stepped through the cold blood pooling out from the one she'd killed. Her stomach was so painful with hunger and the need to retch.

"Tell me," she whispered, her voice hoarse and afraid. Stopping a short distance away, she spoke to the last of her captors, lifting her wrists. "Tell me, how can I be free of these?"

The fae snickered, but it was cut off by the one who pressed his dagger tight enough to his throat to draw blood. She tried to catch a glimpse of her savior, but his mask concealed his face, and his hood cloaked him in shadow.

"You'll never be free, *witch*," he sneered. She wondered what she'd done to earn such a name. "What you are should never be let loose on this world."

She found the courage to step closer. Her anger and embarrassment were as cold as they were hot, battling an urge to submit and agree or to prove him wrong. "Then you should never have brought me to your land." Her voice was ice. She hated him so much. She loathed them all for what they'd done to her. "Whatever happens next...*you* made me into this."

Then her savior slit the fae's throat. She flinched at the gruesomeness of it but felt nothing for him as he choked on his own blood, slowly falling to the ground before he stopped jerking.

Awareness of the dangerous assailant and his sharp blade returned. Fear struck her as her eyes locked on the lethal tip that dripped crimson to the wood floor. Her breath shuddered as she took a step back. She tried to catch a glimpse of his face, but it was futile in the dim hall.

She decided he was male from his height and broad build, but she couldn't be certain he wasn't just another person out to capture the ultimate prize while she was vulnerable. He held up his hands, but it did little for her nerves.

"I don't wish you harm." His voice held a smooth, silvery note.

She swallowed hard, but her throat remained dry. "You're not the first to have claimed that," she said, cursing her wavering voice as she took another step back. "They were all liars."

Instead of answering, he flipped the dagger. She flinched with a gasp, anticipating a sharp plunge into her flesh. Yet the blade didn't soar for her. She blinked at the leather handle—extended *to* her. A weapon offered, not used.

Having lived as long as she had by the rule of cruel hands, a broken piece of her wondered if the fear that had grown roots down to her very core, grown vines over every fiber of her being, could learn to trust again. She craved it. The trust of friendship she'd watched stem through all walks of life as a Spirit of the Realm. The trust of lovers who fell so surely for each other that they would bind their lives together. The trust of blood; family. The trust of neighbors and allies, and even the trust of enemies—equals.

All she was left with was the trust in herself.

The stranger took slow steps forward, and she locked eyes with him, not his blade. "I promise you, from this day, I am yours. To protect you."

She could have spluttered at the blatant lie.

The male pulled down his hood, and he was striking, with hazel eyes and dark raven hair so long it was half-tied in a knot. It didn't stop the strands from framing his firm face, his jaw shadowed with coarse hairs.

She shook her head. Having only just broken out of her cage, she couldn't allow this male to fashion new bars around her before she'd tasted freedom.

"There is always a price," she said.

"May you ask mine?"

"No."

Her hand lashed out for the knife, slicing through his glove, cutting flesh. He clenched his teeth but made no sound or movement. Her stance was clumsy as she slipped through blood in her backward stride, angling the blade with false bravery.

He didn't react in anger, though her pulse thrummed to brace for his wrath. He didn't do anything but watch her steadily.

"What is your name?" he asked calmly.

She blinked. It didn't seem arrogant to assume he would know who she was. Everyone did, or at least...

It was in that moment her world shrank so small that air became nonexistent. She had once been all-powerful. Her name had been a prayer; a blessing. Then she'd taken flesh, and when she'd been tricked and trapped here, the world had slowly forgotten about her.

"Marvellas," she said, but her own name made her swallow with regret.

"Let me rephrase," the male offered gently. Everything he did was in consideration of the spooked deer she clearly was. "What would you *like* your name to be?"

That question crumbled her anger. Stole all her revenge and pricked her eyes.

It was a chance to be free. To leave behind the tragic, fallen, humiliated Goddess she was. To be someone else entirely. Yet she couldn't let go. Her failures were as much a part of her as her triumphs.

"Marvellas," she repeated, sure now.

She wouldn't let the vile greed of mankind make her shun her identity. Hide from it. No. She was Marvellas, the Spirit of Souls and Goddess of the Stars. And she would make the world pay in that name one day.

"Marvellas," he echoed as though testing it against his tongue.

"And yours?" she asked with a confidence she could only credit to her defiance.

"Mikhael," he said, the name accompanied by a twitch of his mouth that if held might have passed for a smile.

It was just a name. Just a word. Maybe it was the unhesitant way he offered it to her that made it settle like a token of trust as sure as his dagger.

"Mikhael Ashfyre."

PART ONE

Ashes
of
Dawn

CHAPTER ONE

Reylan

There were infinite ways to break a person. Flesh was fragile, easily torn, and fear was a relentless accomplice, twisting the mind until it fractured.

But for Reylan, there was only one way to truly destroy him—one weakness that could shatter his soul completely.

And she was safe.

For now.

Every shift moved the metal tearing the flesh of his wrists. So he kept still. Arms splayed and bare-chested, kneeling in dried pools of his own blood. He tunneled far away into his mind. He didn't care how much time had passed. He wasn't wishing for it to be over.

To keep Faythe from Marvellas, Reylan would kneel there and bleed until the final darkness claimed him.

There were times a part of him hoped for death, if only to keep his mate from the path that would lead her to him. He prayed to every damn God that was still out there she wouldn't find him. And that Marvellas wouldn't find her.

A cobalt fire blazed at his back, but the warmth hardly reached him from the far end of the quaint home. The chill still seeped into his bones, and he figured the fire was only a measure to dull the sharp cold from killing him.

They began his test of endurance with lashes. The scores across his skin were familiar, if distant, from a past that made him able to tolerate them now. They left hours in between lashings so he'd heal enough for them to start again and not have him bleed out too much.

Marvellas came frequently, attempting to slip into his mind each time he got close to the limit of his pain tolerance. Reylan would forget every slice of flesh, every ounce of blood spilled, to delve into his mind and block her violation with everything he was.

He couldn't lose Faythe—the memories of her that Marvellas tried to pluck from him one by one. He didn't want to live should she succeed in erasing Faythe entirely.

She won sometimes.

Faythe's smile…it was gone.

Though not entirely.

He couldn't remember the image, as Marvellas had gone straight for the things he treasured most about her. She'd been unrelenting in her attempts to erase Faythe's smile this past week. Reylan bowed his head in defeat at the triumph she'd gained.

He remembered how it felt. That when Faythe smiled, it awakened something within him and cast a light through the shadows of his mind. He knew what a smile looked like on another person. Marvellas's mouth curled often, but her smile was one of cruelty and amusement.

Faythe…her smile was a token of liberation. A streak of light breaking through angry clouds. It was his beacon home.

Yet when he tried to picture it, all he found was her mouth firm. Often troubled and frightened, and though she masked it well, it spoke to him in her eyes.

He'd been suffering worse than any physical pain since her smile was taken.

The hut door creaked open, and he squinted at the brightness flooding the dark. Outside the wind howled and flurried the air with snow. They had to have taken him somewhere high—a mountaintop, perhaps—for the snow to be so thick and the air so bitterly icy.

He knew her by the scent that triggered the first inkling of any feeling in days—or weeks—of deserted misery.

Rage.

"Not so mighty, White Lion of the South," Marvellas drawled, taking steps so slow and predatory toward him.

She crouched when he didn't lift his head. To lock eyes with her golden irises made him conflicted with heartache and fury. Though they couldn't contend with Faythe's, the color never failed to slice him with yearning.

Marvellas gripped his chin. With the Magestone shackles draining his strength daily, he had to preserve what he could, so he focused on his breathing and allowed the repulsive touch.

It left him with no choice but to meet her gaze. He'd seen the ethereal brightness before, when Faythe harnessed her powers and became a breathtaking spectacle. The same glow was ever-present in the Spirit's eyes, indicating she was a force to be reckoned with even in her perfect calm form.

"I wondered for a long time if I should have come for you sooner. Killed you back then. But I believe in the Order, Reylan, and now I see it has brought you right to where I need you."

"You're going to fail, Marvellas," he said, his tone dripping with venom.

Her head canted while two fae unlatched his chains from the wall.

"You're not going to let that happen," she sang.

Reylan remained in his shackles but gritted his teeth against the burning sting when his arms fell, shooting fire up his stiff muscles. The cold had numbed him enough, and with her so close...

His hands had barely risen a fraction to lunge for her when she invaded his mind and halted his movements—an impulsive error as the damn Magestone stripped his resistance, leaving him to her mercy. He channeled the heat of his vengeance through his eyes.

"It's too perfect, us being together now. I believe there is a God on my side to have granted this alliance. Your reluctance only makes this painful for you."

He remained still when the Spirit unfolded something in her lap before draping the material around him. Threads caught in the scabbing wounds of his back, and his teeth clenched at the itch. She clasped the cloak, and despite his lacerations protesting at the friction, it gave him relief from the frozen chill circulating the cabin she was keeping him in.

Her hand lingered, and she fixed her sight on his chest. He didn't move at her touch, which felt so vile and wrong, fingers tracing his right collarbone, down over his pectoral muscle.

"She remained with you this whole time, yet you never remembered," Marvellas said distantly, but he didn't understand. "She was powerful then but succeeded in erasing your memory, while I can't, only because your mind and soul were entwined with hers. That trust you yielded, the heart you surrendered, she used it against you. Don't you see? Love will always be betrayal."

Marvellas straightened, and Reylan tried to calculate her words—what she meant. More games, trying to make him surrender his mental barriers enough that she could slip inside and steal more of Faythe. He guarded her fiercely in his thoughts.

"Come. We have much to do."

Though he was weak, he shrugged off the guards who closed in to haul him up. Reylan forced his stiff legs to rise from the position he'd been kneeling in for so long. It was like standing with broken bones. He didn't give any of them the satisfaction of seeing his agony as if glass shards sliced through his muscles with every movement.

Outside, his body tensed against the brutal beating of the weather that seemed to be in alliance with his enemy. Ice chips carried on the sharp wind to cut his flesh and lasso his body, dragging him back as if the thick snow weren't enough to slow his miserable trek.

Against possibility, Marvellas was nearly untouched by the winter storm. She glided ahead, a flame against the ice.

His punishment from the weather eased when they entered a cave. He followed, because there was no merit in fighting while weak and outnumbered.

Instead he mapped everything. The way Marvellas moved; the way she talked. Every habit and quirk. He searched for weaknesses should he get his moment to end her. He observed the cavernous walls: warped and winding but with no alternative direction. Getting out would be a one-way sprint. That was the easy part. Stealing the right moment would be the challenge.

The cave opened to a wide, cylindrical space, and they wound their way down a spiral staircase attached to the wall, with no railing to protect them from the fatal drop.

Down and down.

On the ground level, through the shadows, Reylan understood where she'd taken him.

The familiarity of the door made dread clench in his gut. He'd seen it first in High Farrow, adorning Aurialis's mark. Then on the Niltain Isles, in the cave, adorning Dakodas's mark.

Now…

"A bond is the key to touch the sky." Marvellas recited the poem just as he found it in his memory.

Faythe had shown it to him: the locations of the Spirit Temples.

He knew she'd been containing him on some high mountain

range, and now it seemed foolish he hadn't thought of this sooner. They were in the Sky Caves of Lakelaria.

Reylan's spine straightened with foreboding.

Muffled cries carried down a passage before two forms were dragged in. A fae male and a fae female.

"It used to only require a true bonded pair to visit my temple. They had to be willing to draw blood from one another," Marvellas said, so detached and distant she wasn't really speaking to Reylan.

The couple were brought to the door before being roughly pushed to their knees. His body stiffened against the instinct to intervene.

"But I needed to be sure no one would make it through those doors, so I added my own protection. Blood is not enough."

With a dip of her head, the guards reached for a dagger. Reylan got one step before the invasion in his mind stole his will to move. His teeth clenched, fighting the ache that amplified to a drum in his head, trying to defy Marvellas's control.

"It now requires the life of one mate from a true pair, and you get to choose, Reylan Arrowood."

The Spirit came around to stand in front him, leaning in close. Her flaming red hair spilled over her shoulder with the elegant tip of her head up to him. Her red-painted lips curled with cruel amusement.

"Which one shall we allow to live?" she coaxed.

Marvellas slipped a hand around his arm, leaning her head against him to watch the tragic souls on their knees as though she owned him. Reylan had never experienced a touch so revolting his blood boiled beneath his skin. He wanted to tear her arms from her body to be rid of it.

"I'm very patient, Rey, but when the solution is only one small decision away, I can become very impatient."

There was nothing small about what she was asking of him.

"You want blood? You'll choose it yourself," he snarled.

Marvellas pushed off him with a bored groan. "I expected your refusal, of course," she crooned. "It only makes it more satisfying to craft you into my willing soldier so very soon."

She lingered a twinkling gaze of admiration over him before turning to the guards. They gave a nod of obedience, both dropping a dagger. Metal clanged against stone, declaring a challenge that taunted death.

The two fae on their knees glanced with terror between each other and the blades dropped in front of them. Reylan's skin began to crawl.

"Love is only a delusion," Marvellas said, standing beside him and waiting. "You'll see."

The male lingered a longer look at the dagger closest to him, contemplating. The female could hardly contain her sobs. He reached for his.

"Stop," Reylan snapped, realizing what was about to happen. "You prove nothing by having them kill each other."

Marvellas turned her head to him curiously. "I am giving them a choice," she said.

The female reached for her blade with a choked cry, and they both stood with trembling balance. They clutched their weapons, ghostly stares targeting each other.

"They can take the blade to their own heart or each other's."

The choice seemed easy. As barbaric as this portrayal was, Reylan waited for the point of steel to turn from each other toward themselves.

"In their minds, I have shown each of them a life of wealth, of finding love again, if they choose to save themselves. Being mates is merely a recognition of equal power and potential."

Reylan's head shook vacantly. It didn't matter. There wasn't a single thing in this realm, or in any, he could ever want more than Faythe. Every material thing, every living being—it all became insignificant and hollow in a world where she didn't exist.

Yet to his incomprehensible horror, the pair didn't redirect their blades from pointing at each other.

She had to be tricking them with something else.

"I may be wicked in my methods." She answered his desperate, disbelieving thoughts. "But I am no cheat. Why should they sacrifice themselves when their dream life is one act away?"

Reylan wanted to avert his gaze from the scene he couldn't fathom. He pictured Faythe, his Phoenix, and perhaps Marvellas was right. Love *could* kill, for there was nothing he wouldn't give for her. Even himself.

They moved in unison, lunging for each other, but the female seemed to waver in her choice right before they met. It became her end when the male's blade plunged into her chest. His arm circled her as they fell to their knees, and Reylan witnessed their wide stares turn to regret in an instant.

"The action can be hard to bear in the moment, but time will bury the guilt," Marvellas said.

"What have I done?" the male whispered.

Reylan tried to find pity for him through the outrage at what he'd chosen over his own mate. He wanted to believe Marvellas was a liar and had orchestrated this play.

"You proved nothing," Reylan said coldly.

Marvellas sliced him a bored look before her hand rose and a sickening crack cut off the male's sobs.

He stared at the two tragic fae, watching their love spill in a crimson pool around them. It might have been selfish only to think of Faythe as the devastating scene changed from two strangers to him and Faythe. It slammed into him, the gravity of what Marvellas was capable of. If she broke his mind, she could force him to do something unforgivable toward Faythe.

"You don't have the Riscillius," Reylan said vacantly.

Marvellas liked proximity. Perhaps she felt a person's emotions more intensely with physical touch and she loved to manipulate them.

"Do you want to know a secret, Rey? One I have not even exposed to my sister," Marvellas said with a note of pride. "It will remain just between us. I had the Riscillius once, and when I came here, I made sure I would never need something so easily stolen to get to the only weapon in this realm that can kill me. You see, Faythe has been told I can be sent back to the Realm of the Gods and face my penance there, and that can be done. So all I have needed is to find someone with enough strength to break a ruin."

The Spirit glided over to the fallen bodies, bending to swipe her finger through a pool of blood before reaching the temple door. "It took three oracles to break the binding of the Riscillius and forge my own. I haven't told my sister, because when it becomes a matter of life or death, one might find betrayal lies in the thickest blood. I want Aurialis's ruin because it is a powerful tool on its own, but more importantly, I have been searching endlessly for *you*, Reylan. I commend you for keeping the extent of your abilities from me all that time ago, making me believe you were like any ordinary Mindseer. It took seeing you in action with Faythe to realize how wrong I was."

After her blood tracing, the door groaned inward with a familiar, daunting crawl. Marvellas looked to Reylan expectantly, and the uncanny resemblance to the first time he'd followed Faythe to the Light Temple in High Farrow made his heart race.

Gods, he missed her with such agony there were days he thought it could end him.

The chain between his wrists clanked as he braced, pushing the stone door with more exertion than it should take in his feeble state.

"I am a Goddess. A true immortal. I cannot be killed by mortal weapons or means. There is only one way to kill a God." Marvellas passed him inside, heading straight for the podium. "With something from which they are made. I couldn't risk Dakodas finding out that when she could attempt to use you or Faythe to break her ruin first. When you achieve this for me, there will be no portal to open to the Realm of the Gods, and no weapon that can kill me. It is a peace I have been waiting a millennium for, and only then will I be able to right this world one mighty continent at a time, starting with Ungardia."

They knew Marvellas wanted to conquer their realm, but it was horrifying to discover her ambition stemmed beyond a single continent.

"Come," she commanded. With the word, she forced his movements.

Reylan shook with a growing, palpable resentment. When he was standing in front of the arrow-shaped slate slotted into the podium, his hands reached for it.

A hum raked over his skin, pricking him with heat, and whispers of power and destruction twisted like wind around him. The first pulses of strength he'd felt in weeks were too tempting to answer, but there was a counter voice in his mind that reminded him how deadly this power was.

He craved it. How could he not?

His fingers hooked under the metal, and he lifted it from its place. His chest flooded with warmth in response to the magick trapped within the slate, calling to merge with the well that resided in the core of his being.

"Addicting, isn't it?" Marvellas said, admiring it with him. "The essence of power. There isn't a being in any realm that would resist the pull. Yet power can corrupt as fast as it can lift. It invites the impossible into the minds of men too weak to balance such a privilege."

His breathing came clearer. Something primordial and goading whispered within the gray rock. He became spellbound to it, and the symbol of Marvellas started to glow. All he had to do was open himself—

"This is necessary for now."

Reylan had become so entranced by the magick coursing through him he didn't hear the approach from behind. He hissed through gritted teeth when a thick collar of Magestone slammed shut around his neck, and another two around his ankles. Whatever beckoning he'd begun to feel was now silenced by the additional suppressing material.

"For my own protection, as I hope you can understand." She glided toward him, pausing just shy of pressing her chest to his, and tilted her head elegantly to observe him. "I will break you, Reylan. And when you think I can no longer hurt you, remember that the broken can be shattered."

CHAPTER TWO

Faythe

The curves of the small wooden butterfly dug into Faythe's palms as she clasped at her chest. She awoke with the beats of her heart struggling and a tightness expanding behind her ribs. Every time she tried to Nightwalk to Reylan, she was slammed back to the cold truth of their distance.

She couldn't find him.

As she rolled onto her side, tears slipped silently. She unfolded her tight grip to trace her fingers over the carving he'd made for her.

Forcing back her heartache, with a deep breath Faythe pushed herself up in the small makeshift bed inside her tent. She'd refused anything that would grant her more comfort than the rest of the Rhyenelle soldiers in the war camp at the edge of Fenher.

Faythe drove her hands through her hair and clenched tight, pulling at the roots to inflict pain. Her sleepless nights were only adding to her frustration and anger.

She had found Reylan once before without even trying. Found him through a dream, as an untrained human unknowingly reaching for the other half of her soul. There was no road too long; no mountain too high. She just had to figure out the direction.

Dressing swiftly, Faythe slung on her cloak and headed out of tent soundlessly. She remained as stealthy as an assassin so as not to wake Kyleer in the tent next to hers. He might reprimand her for what she was about to do to release the anger that wouldn't stop growing in her bones.

Out on the streets, the wintry night air bit at her cheeks, and she rubbed her gloved hands together. Her frosted breaths were steady in her focus to extend her senses while she strolled the deserted streets of the small town, pretending she was oblivious to the darkness that had been tracking her from the moment she set out. It didn't take long, sauntering with her distinguishable golden eyes fully exposed, for the vultures to pin her. This outskirt town was crawling with dark fae. They had begun to seep through her kingdom like a black plague, and she was riled and ready to eradicate them one by one if she had to.

After a moment of peace, Faythe Ashfyre took off in a sprint and did not falter. The pace drummed her pulse. She didn't feel a single beat of fear after breaking her act and becoming the bait of a chase with four dark fae.

She raced over rooftops, hopping seamlessly between buildings with her laser focus. One of them she was tracking took a leap to the skies, and at that, Faythe began her descent.

Dropping into a slide on the ice near the next edge, she twisted as her body cut the air, fingers catching on the harsh ledge, and she dropped, meeting the ground in an elegant brace that scattered the vibrations of the impact throughout her body.

A scream ripped through the air, and Faythe's attention latched onto it. The terror from the civilian pumped her blood hotter, spotting her vision with rage, and she ran *faster*.

Faythe found the victim in the clutches of her attacker—a dark fae with his teeth sunk into her neck, determined to drink her dry like the other human man already dead at their feet.

She saw white.

Dark fae minds were a void, some more depthless and demoralized than others. Slipping into this one almost forced her right back out with the ripples of bloodlust coursing through it. Sinister chants to *kill, kill, kill*.

Instead of retreating, Faythe embodied his merciless, cold detachment, letting it become instinct that seized his mind and shattered it in a breath. She wouldn't have outlasted him in combat with the amount of human blood heightening his physical strength.

Those who'd been chasing Faythe closed in behind her as the one she'd killed slumped to the ground. The woman fell too, but Faythe was too far gone to check on her survival right now, and the threat wasn't over.

Three rushed in at her back, one in the sky.

"Nowhere to run now, *Heir of Marvellas*."

They taunted that title, and Faythe's fists flexed, ready to unleash all she'd built in the ten minutes she'd been entertaining their chase. The only luminance to break the pitch-darkness they cornered her in was from the glow in her palms.

One dark fae took the lead, chuckling in mockery of the display of magick.

"I only need one of you alive," she said. "Though death might be kinder."

"We can't kill you. But we can certainly have fun with you before taking you to her."

Faythe only focused on the one closest, and as he stepped forward, she slipped into his mind. The surges of negative aura circled her, pushing back. It had taken some practice to remain inside against the nauseous force.

With a strangled sound, he crashed to his knees by her influence.

Keeping him there, Faythe thrust a hand skyward. Her ability was manifesting stronger every day, able to grip the hovering creature with a lasso made of burning gold essence. When she felt her snare around him, she poured in all her strength, amplified by the anger shaking from her, to bring him careening to the ground.

His wail cut off with a quick, revolting crack, and Faythe wasn't immune to the note of disgust at what she'd done this time. But she never felt regret.

Another advanced, and her head pulsed to split her focus, but she seized his mind too. Then shattered it. The exertion was catching up to her, laboring her breaths and slicking her skin with a dangerous warning.

"Where is Marvellas?" she asked the one she held at her mercy.

"Burn in the Nether," he spat.

The third dark fae charged for her, and Faythe twisted around the vertical swipe of his blade. Her own dagger plunged through his back in the same maneuver. She yanked it free, letting his body drop.

One less obstacle to Reylan.

One less creature to pose a fatal danger to her people.

It was all she could console herself with. Grappling with threads of humanity that were fraying with each passing day.

"I'll meet you there," Faythe answered. She took a fist full of dark hair, yanking his head back, and he gave a venomous hiss. "Where is she?"

Silence.

It was a cold calling to her volatile rage. Every beat of silence darkened in her soul. It felt like wasted sand in an hourglass measuring Reylan's life. Faythe didn't know herself in his absence, while they were hurting him. It was all she could think of, and she didn't know the limit to what she was capable of anymore as she approached every barrier to him not only with a determination to knock them down, but to make them suffer just as she was.

"Valgard?" Faythe prompted, flipping her dagger.

Turning back to her kneeling victim, she pressed the slick blade against his cheek.

The Niltain steel clawed a shriek from the dark fae's throat.

"We don't know where Marvellas is," he hissed through clenched teeth.

Faythe cut from his cheekbone to his chin, collecting beads of black blood against his pale complexion, before pointing the tip to the hollow spot of his neck.

A headache cleaved her head, twisting her thoughts and warping reality as she delved into his mind for answers. If she wasn't careful, Faythe thought it could drive her to madness if she lost herself too far. Their minds were always so, so desolate. Part of her wondered, maybe even hoped, she would come across one who didn't seem like a lost cause.

If she had to annihilate them all—achieve what had been failed in history to eradicate them—she believed she could.

Faythe was their villain. And she was losing patience.

Retreating from his mind, her teeth ground together.

Nothing. They all knew nothing.

They were merely mindless soldiers ordered to capture her and take her to Dakodas, who must be the only one to know where Marvellas had taken him.

"Send this message to her for me," Faythe said.

He jerked, seething with a string of profanities as her hand reached for his shoulder. She'd learned to tune out the ear-splitting cries. Gold dust crept in behind him, shimmering beautifully over his wings, until it began to devour the flesh and cartilage like flame. His eyes bulged and his mouth tore wide-open, but she could hear nothing.

Feel nothing.

When his wings had been burned to nothing but serrated stumps, she let him go.

The dark fae curled into himself, trembling on the ground. Every time she watched the vicious creatures turn from her foe to her victim, she wondered if any would ever make her feel regret.

Faythe crouched to him as she said, "I will burn flesh, I will burn cities, I will destroy anything she tries to claim if I find him harmed."

When all turned silent, Faythe bottled her scream against the torment every still moment opened up to. With a deep breath, her exhale shuddered from her in the aftermath of her brutal vengeance.

"Phoenix Queen."

Faythe's shoulders locked, only her head twisting back to the woman she thought had been killed.

"They say you turned on us. Abandoned us. That Malin Ashfyre is our savior king who will bring peace again. I didn't believe it." Her voice croaked with pain. A hand clutched the bleeding wound on her neck. "It's not true, is it?"

Words scrambled her mind, most of them vicious and self-deprecating. Faythe only lifted her hood.

"Get somewhere safe. Find a healer. They won't get the chance to harm you again tonight." She didn't look to the woman again, disappearing as a shadow of the night.

Faythe took more caution to remain hidden now. On the rooftops, she tracked the injured woman until she found her way to an inn, where a group of humans immediately came to her aid.

Observing the moon spilling a glow over the cloudless sky, Faythe wondered, with a bleeding wound on her heart, if Reylan could see it, or if he was chained somewhere dark and lonely, robbed of day or moonlight.

Faythe crouched, gathering her hands together, and honed her focus on her task. Phoenixfyre had a distinct feeling in its magick. It wasn't ashy or hot like Firewielding; it was like growing a heartbeat. Millions of tiny vibrations crawled to her fingertips and began to draw across the air in front of her. When she was finished, the form it took would never fail to entrance her. She watched the tiny Firebird fly away.

It had been six agonizing weeks without Reylan. Two of them, she'd been in and out of consciousness from the effects of her burnout and Niltain steel-poisoned wounds following the Battle of Ellium they'd lost and fled from. Since she'd been well enough, they hadn't remained idle for a moment.

Kyleer had taken her to one of the army camps in Fenher. Most of

Rhyenelle's forces who had been told to retreat by Reylan—his last command as general when he knew the city was lost—would be around the many camps in Rhyenelle, waiting for their next instruction. As Reylan's second-in-command, Kyleer had become the leading general.

There was not a day, barely a moment within each one, that Faythe wasn't thinking about Reylan. They had a kingdom to take back and an evil to rout out, but she didn't know if she could do it without him.

Faythe had been too distracted to detect an intrusion sooner, but she freed her blade, lunging up to attack...

Her body relaxed from a braced pose of combat as her eyes trailed the length of the Ember Sword as it clashed with Lumarias, finding a disgruntled Kyleer peering down at her.

"If you're heading out for some fun, it's only fair you extend the invite," he grumbled.

Faythe huffed as their blades slipped off each other, and she sheathed Lumarias. Watching Kyleer do the same, an ache clenched within her, catching the glint of the ruby pommel that mocked her.

Every time the light caught on it, her pulse would skip, but never did it glow like she hoped, indicating the direction to Reylan. She'd slipped the twin Eye of the Phoenix around his wrist before they were parted.

Perhaps Agalhor's tale about them had been a fable.

"At least one of us should be well-rested," Faythe said. It certainly wouldn't be her.

Kyleer folded his arms, but his expression was all-knowing. "I'm not having much luck with sleep either."

Faythe ran a hand down her face. She was exhausted, but it wasn't often by choice she didn't find sleep. Most nights she braced to meet horrible nightmares in the darkness, and this time she didn't know how to tame it.

"Perhaps a drink might help," Kyleer suggested.

Faythe nodded, trying to reciprocate his smile, but her mouth refused to pretend.

Kyleer glanced down the alley, where quiet whimpers of the wingless dark fae still echoed.

"That's the third you've done that to," he commented as they turned from him.

"I won't have her forgetting for a moment that I'm coming."

There were days she felt her world crumbling. She would walk and walk until her steps stumbled, as if she'd come to a cliff edge, about to collapse. Times when she would wake and gravity no longer felt like an anchor. Moments air refused to fill her lungs, and her mind was convinced she was drowning on land.

Every time, she would remember all over again that Reylan was not with her. That her father, Agalhor Ashfyre, was dead. And her mighty kingdom lay in evil hands.

"Still no luck reaching him through Nightwalking?" Kyleer asked.

Her fists tightened. "No. It's like he's…gone." Her throat tightened with pain. "Or she's taken him too far for me to even reach a small essence of a clue as to where she might be holding him."

"It seems our obvious choice is Valgard."

A chill swept over her at the conclusion they'd circled before. It seemed the most viable option, but her gut couldn't settle on it. They'd sent spies to try to reach the enemy island east, but none had returned. Faythe had tracked down as many dark fae as she could while they were actively hunting for her, trying for *some* reassurance it wouldn't be time wasted if she went to Valgard herself—a path that, should it be wrong, could cost her Reylan.

At least in remaining here until they could find something to give them hope for a way to him, she was training, leading, helping to keep their armies strong, and strategizing tirelessly for ways to take Ellium back. It soothed a small part of her to be productive in a way Reylan would be proud of until she found a course to him.

"Maybe we should split up," she suggested.

"That's not an option," Kyleer said firmly.

It was a weak suggestion, but she was so tired—and terrified—of choosing wrong.

"We'll try to hunt more darklings tomorrow for information," Kyleer said, with an inkling of hope she couldn't muster anymore.

She gave a nod regardless.

"I miss him," she said, realizing another absence, a more permanent one, also softening the ground her own grave was being dug in with every footstep. "Both of them."

The hopeful future she'd dreamed of in her father's company had always been painted in watercolor, but now it was drowning, washing away scene by scene what would never be.

Her absolute determination not to lose her mate too had become a powerful suppressant for that anguish. The will to do her father proud kept her active and engrossed in battle plans for the kingdom.

Kyleer shared her grief in tangible waves as he said, "Me too."

There were two halves to the heart of Rhyenelle since she'd laid her claim, and without Reylan, she feared it might be forever lost.

"I would feel if he…? I mean, you said you did—"

Gods, how could she even ask that of him? Her selfishness silenced the thought, but Kyleer knew what she'd wanted to say.

"Yes," he answered. Kyleer gave a smile to shadow his hurt from the past. "Even without a completed mating bond, you've been forging a tie to him since you met…again," he added with a quirk of amusement. "I felt it when Greia died. With your bond to Reylan having been formed over more time and stronger, I can't imagine you wouldn't, even being so far apart."

It was the relief she needed in her time of turmoil. Reylan was alive.

"Maybe we should go back to Ellium ourselves," she said.

"We checked a week ago. He's not there."

"The others are."

She watched the lines on his face firm. Though she didn't mention Izaiah, she knew it was he who struck him in that moment.

"Marlowe couldn't tell me why, but she told me she created the Phoenix Blood for Malin, and that he plans to have her spell the others."

"Then they're traitors."

Faythe winced, but she couldn't blame his observation.

"Her gift is a heavy burden. She can often risk harm more than help should she make the wrong move with what she's seen."

Faythe's heart was split, trusting her two friends while also carrying a sting of resentment. She had to see them and had mulled over the idea of infiltrating the castle again, but their scouts had strongly advised against it with the forces of the dark fae and the new defenses they'd implemented.

Malin knew she was reckless enough to think of attempting a return too soon.

"Why wouldn't Izaiah have told me?" Kyleer said.

Faythe had no answers, only the fleeting recollection of Izaiah's last words, which hadn't been very reassuring.

"Tell Kyleer, for once in our lives, I was one step ahead."

What was Izaiah planning?

They entered an inn, keeping their hoods up.

The bustling establishment lingered little attention on them as they headed to the front to order a drink. It was exactly what Faythe needed to curb the sharp edges of her anxiety.

They'd barely had time to deeply reflect on all that had happened before they fled Ellium. Kyleer had been as closed off as she these past few weeks.

"What happened——?" Faythe tried carefully. "In those cells, before everything went to shit. Zaiana made me believe she'd killed you."

The air threatened to choke her at the mere recollection of that grief.

Kyleer gave a twitch of a smile, a wince of his pain, staring into the ale-soaked wood of the bar. "You were right," he said, detached, but his hurt weaved through her. "You were all right. Dead hearts can't beat, and I fell for the foolish notion she would yield something different to me."

Faythe leaned on the bar with him. Her head fell to his shoulder.

"For what it's worth, I think she did."

"You don't have to try to make me feel better about my lapse of judgment."

"I'm not. When we took to the skies, even through my rage, I believed her true self had surfaced in those moments we were both preparing to go down. I think——"

"Don't," he said softly. "She betrayed us all. I won't forgive that."

Faythe sighed with the weight of sorrow they both carried.

She straightened when two tankards were placed in front of them, but as she reached for hers, Faythe's back curved with a strike of alarm at the prick against her spine. Kyleer hissed with a similar reaction at the threat behind them. Bold, in an establishment so packed. Who would risk confrontation here?

"Please state your name and business."

Every sound in the room was stolen completely, leaving only those words on repeat. Ones from a distant memory. In a voice she would treasure until the end of her days.

Faythe's eyes stung.

She couldn't move. Even when the blade was removed from her back and she knew who she would find. The impossibility of it taunted it was only a trick.

Her heart thumped so hard it stole her breath.

Grief, heartache, yearning—it all threatened to bring her to her knees before she could turn around.

"Faythe," he said gently.

A hand encased her upper arm, and she released a whimper. It guided her, and the moment she met those emerald eyes, Faythe broke.

Shattered.

Tears slipped from her eyes when she blinked hard to clear her vision, but she smiled with such elation that it broke through her resistance to feeling anything at all since having been torn from Reylan.

"It's really you…" she breathed. His smile was a piece of treasure given at her most dire time. "Nik."

They embraced tightly, and she didn't care for the ugly display as she sobbed into his hood. Faythe breathed his scent to calm her. Her human senses had never been able to detect the notes within—hints of vanilla and meadows, then deeper. It had a smoky essence, not like fire but a storm. She committed it all to memory.

Faythe shut out the questions of this chance meeting. Why he was here; how he'd found her. All she clung to was the impossible gift that consumed her.

"I suppose I should order a few more drinks," Kyleer cut in when she was beginning to come down from her high.

Faythe pulled back, lingering one last look on her dear friend before she was alerted to the fact he wasn't alone.

She let Nik go in her shock.

"Nerida?"

The healer beamed brightly as they stepped for each other and collided.

"I knew we would meet again soon," she said in that beautiful, melodic voice of hers.

Gods, Faythe felt in another realm with this reunion. It was lifting her from a dark pit she hadn't thought she'd be able to claw her way out of. There'd been no light until now. But as she scanned the others, it shone brighter, reminding her not everything was lost.

"It's so good to see you, Your Highness," Lycus said, smiling knowingly, and Faythe choked a sob.

She also found a breathtakingly beautiful fae female with auburn hair by his side. The fae offered a timid smile of greeting, then the person who'd crept close to Nerida…

Faythe blinked at the Prince of Olmstone.

"We have a lot to catch up on," Nik said, but his tone wasn't all cheerful, and Faythe acknowledged their reunion might hold heavy tales on both sides for him to be here without…

"Tauria," Faythe breathed, whirling to Nik.

She'd never seen such desolation overcome him in an instant. Nik flicked a look to Kyleer behind her and gave a quick survey of the group, noting Reylan's absence too.

Her face fell, as torn as his.

"A lot to catch up on indeed," he said sadly.

CHAPTER THREE

Izaiah

I zaiah drifted through the halls with confidence despite the many dark fae tainting them. One hand in his pocket, he didn't care to give any of them his attention.

These halls closed in with judgment, eyeing him like a traitor, but he blocked that out too. He was no stranger to the feeling of being outcast, and he didn't surface the urge to defend himself to anyone observing his actions.

On time, Jakon rounded the next corner. Izaiah knocked the human's shoulder, turning to him with an unfazed smirk, while Jakon blazed.

"Watch yourself," Izaiah warned.

Jakon paused, debating whether or not to engage. He didn't, and Izaiah relaxed, not dropping his arrogant swagger down the rest of the hall.

Now he was heading to the king's study.

Over the weeks, he'd attended meetings with Dakodas, listening in on tedious outlines of the city and their new defense measures. Of course, he never expected those meetings to divulge anything of real secrecy that could be used against them.

His goal was to appear compliant. Irrelevant, so they'd ease up on the close watch they were keeping him under. It was working—slowly.

He couldn't fathom Faythe's grief and was somewhat surprised she hadn't stormed back already, healed physically and furious in her vengeance. He shouldn't have doubted her. While she was often hotheaded, and he feared the world for what could become of her wrath, she was also smart. Reylan wasn't here, and her being caught on Marvellas's terms would waste the subtle advantage they still held to counterattack.

The only real twist of guilt in his gut was the occasional times he wondered what Kyleer thought of him. Reflecting on his impulsive, secret decisions, he came to realize his brother's opinion was the only one that could truly impact him.

He shrugged off the notion. It only served to distract him.

Izaiah had been watching the shift of court closely. How the new false king, Malin Ashfyre, was unraveling to the most frighteningly unhinged he'd ever seen him in his desperation to fit into the crown he'd stolen. Faythe's human friend, Reuben, was near delirious in his search for the ruin, and Malin only added pressure to whatever influence Marvellas had plagued Reuben's mind with, as though possessing the ruin would prove Malin worthy, and people would yield once and for all.

In his boredom, watching the prince's downward spiral had made Izaiah *very* curious. He was a male with a desire for power, but it was like there was something more. Something hidden. So he'd made it his own risky trial to scour places he never would have been able to before. With the disarray and lack of order, he thought he might never get another chance.

Nearing the king's study, Izaiah shifted into a black panther. He quite liked to frequent this form. The powerful jaw and lethal claws made tearing through bodies like tearing through a field of wheat.

He kept to the shadows, spying the two guards posted outside the place he wanted access to. Izaiah growled low, and they snapped their heads toward him. He eased out, lips curled back over his teeth, braced low in a predatory stalk.

It was enough to get them to back away in fear, unsheathing their blades. They might have tried to challenge him, but Izaiah pounced with a roar that sent them scattering with cowardly shrieks.

Izaiah shifted back to his fae body outside the study door, chuckling to himself. They made it too easy.

He dipped into his pocket for the key Jakon had slipped to him expertly in their collision. Marlowe had made the copy he'd asked for.

He sauntered inside, observing the miracle that it wasn't a wreckage like the other rooms of the castle. Many parchments littered the table, but one caught his attention from the name scribbled out angrily in black ink.

Faythe's legitimacy.

Malin should have all but signed his own name under it from the bitter, childish act.

Angry little prince.

It didn't matter. There would be several other copies in existence.

Izaiah sighed lightly, treading quietly with the awareness the guards could return to their post at any minute, likely with others, alerted to a wild beast roaming the halls.

He opened various drawers and filtered through boring court documents until he came across a locked chest. Izaiah had become rather skilled at lockpicking from his time in the mines. He and Reylan would evade the patrols to get extra food and water to pass around to those far weaker than them.

Inside the chest, he filtered through the more important decrees within it. Another of Faythe's legitimacy, one of Agalhor's marriage to Liliana. He was surprised to find Malin hadn't torched the whole chest to ash. At the very bottom, Izaiah found the bastard's name on something at last.

Malin's legitimacy.

Izaiah could relate to him for his lack of parents at least. Sometimes Izaiah wished he could tell the easy tale of his parents both dying before their time, rather than the tale of abuse and abandonment, but he didn't think of his past at all. It was vaulted. A side of him he didn't ever want to touch again.

He skimmed over the name next to Ashfyre that had annoyingly been smudged over with ink. It was no secret Agalhor's brother had died near the start of the war, though a body was never recovered. His name wasn't known to any of them. Malin's mother, however... Interestingly, she'd died first.

It made his betrayal to Agalhor far worse when he'd practically raised his brother's bastard.

He stilled. Read the document again. Then he lifted it next to Faythe's legitimacy document. He was no expert in these things, but he knew someone who might be able to confirm or deny his suspicions.

Izaiah leaned against the desk, scanning the words again and again as though they would reveal something new about Malin he could use.

Mumbling sounded outside the room. Izaiah swore, folding and pocketing the documents, before dipping behind the door as the handle turned.

When it closed again, he lunged, but his intruder was swifter than he hoped.

They caught Izaiah's wrists, and he was spun around and slammed, his back to the wall.

"Pathetic," Tynan snarled.

Izaiah's mouth curled. "Or purposeful."

He twisted his wrists, gripping the dark fae's and earning a curse as he maneuvered, swiftly switching their positions.

"Still no guards?" Izaiah observed, since they hadn't come charging in at the commotion.

"When I heard of an oversized black cat, I wanted to hunt it myself."

Izaiah reached, twisting the key in the lock. "Good."

Their mouths collided, as hateful as it was passionate. Both of them despised the desire they craved, but like all drugs, they were hard to resist once within reach. And *fuck*, was this one insatiable.

There was something thrilling about the forbidden. Delicious about the taste of an enemy. It was a war with feelings as knives, not knowing who could take the most cuts. Bleeding and bleeding, until they were both sure to fall.

Tynan's hands knew where to touch and where to squeeze. The hand Tynan slipped between them wrapped around his throat. Izaiah battled for that dominance. Tynan hissed with the drag of Izaiah's claws up his chest, shifting to his preferred black panther form and growing lethal nails that spilled his skin with dark ink.

"Hardly fair," Tynan muttered.

"But you like it," he said thickly.

With a primal growl, he pushed Izaiah back, slamming him against the table. It was so deplorable where there were, but neither of them cared. Finding a moment out of sight wasn't easy.

To everyone beyond, they were perfect enemies.

"Want to tell me what you were doing in here?" Tynan growled against his lips, undoing the buttons of his jacket.

"Want to tell me where they've taken Reylan?"

"I've told you, I don't know that."

Tynan helped him out of the sleeves while untucking his shirt.

It was all Izaiah had to keep his intentions plausible. He'd stuck to that excuse for his reckless roaming since the dark fae had first caught him rifling through the drawing room four weeks ago. It was the first time they'd broke. The maddening tension that had built between them while he'd been captive in the cells months ago couldn't be contained any longer, and that day was one Izaiah thought about. Often.

"You're going to get yourself killed," the dark fae promised.

"Hmm," Izaiah mumbled, brow pinching at the lips Tynan dragged across his bare, toned torso. "I wouldn't be doing this with you if I didn't think that."

Tynan's brown eyes flicked up from halfway down his body.

Gods, he was a devastating sight. With dark blond hair, which he'd fantasized running his fingers through too many damn times, and irises that lured him in with a mere flash of attention.

"I won't be your savior if that happens."

Izaiah chuckled. "Trust I won't shed a tear even if you're the one to wield the sword."

That caused Tynan to straighten, arms trapping him against the desk.

"What are you hoping to achieve?"

Izaiah groaned, tired of the talking, and reached to grab a fist of Tynan's shirt.

"Are we doing this, or are you choosing to be loyal to your side and rat me out?"

Conflict furrowed Tynan's brow, but he folded out of his shirt. "I am loyal to Zaiana," he said firmly.

Izaiah's teeth dragged over his bottom lip as he felt up the hard contours of Tynan's abdomen.

"So while she is unable to give orders in her...current state, she can't command a thing," Izaiah said.

Zaiana had been mostly unconscious all this time, and too sickly in the moments she was awake enough to drink. She had people concerned for her, Tynan being one of them. Maverick being the worst.

Tynan gripped Izaiah's throat again. The fight waging in his eyes twitched the ache of his length. The anticipation drove him nearly to the brink.

"Make no mistake—should she order you dead, I won't hesitate."

"You're a male of commitment," Izaiah said. "Now fucking commit."

The flash cutting across Tynan's features was the unleashing of that pent-up battle, and Tynan's fingers hooked around Izaiah's waistband before he dropped to his knees.

It would have been poetic, if twisted, to say he'd taken the risk of staying with the dark foes for Tynan. A person who could be his. He tried to imagine war in his name and burning the world for him.

But that kind of love...Izaiah didn't think it existed in his heart.

CHAPTER FOUR

Zaiana

Z aiana stood in void without memory, but the peace it offered left
her with little desire to question it.

She wasn't alone.

From the dark depths, Maverick eased out. Her breath caught at
his shirtless chest, eyes mapping the scars he wore. She tried to find
her own within them, and where their paths of cruelty joined.

"What are you—?"

He hushed her with a kiss to her neck that tipped her head back
on a breath. His hand cupped her nape. It was then she realized all
she was wearing was a dainty black silk nightgown. She couldn't stop
her desire to place hands on his abdomen.

"What's one more night of *fantasy?*" he murmured over her skin.

She almost nodded; lust clouded her senses to drive an immediate
agreement.

"Why didn't you kill him?"

Zaiana's fluttering eyes snapped open at the question. She racked
her mind for a name teetering right at the edge of her thoughts.
"Who?" she asked, though a coil tightened in her gut.

"Me."

Her breath drew sharp when Kyleer pressed into her from behind.
Large hands dominated her waist, and his *scent.* Zaiana's eyes pricked.

"I couldn't do it," she whispered. Gods, she hated herself for the
weakness, but more so, she was overwhelmed with need for him.

Her back curved into him, her body turning to clay that was his to mold.

Kyleer's soft lips planted to her shoulder, and she bit back a pitiful whimper.

The heat from him—and from Maverick—encased her in two conflicting yearnings. She couldn't push either one away, giving in to the greed of wanting them both.

Her hand reached behind her, and her head inclined sideways against Kyleer's bare chest while two sets of hands explored her. Maverick's kiss met her chest; Kyleer's breath trickled over her ear. She was melting in the press between both of them.

"Why did you do it?" Kyleer's hurt vibrated across her neck.

When she angled her head back to look at him, she came apart inside. The betrayal he pinned her with smothered her lust.

His moss-green irises swirled to hatred so fast. Both his hands wrapped around her throat, and she clawed at the vise grip.

"Ky—"

Darkness peppered her vision.

"You will always be cold and alone, Zaiana. Always lost and wandering with the choices you've made."

A spear of air sliced her throat. Zaiana's whole body jerked with a pain that shot through every nerve and clenched her teeth. She panted, snapping her lids open when it eased, but her breathing wouldn't tame as she recalled her dream—no. It had turned to a nightmare twisted from her reality.

Her skin was slick and hot, and one glance to the side stilled her at the person she found in the chair across the room.

"You mumble in your sleep, you know?" Maverick drawled, flipping through a book.

Zaiana tried to prop herself up, but her movements were agony.

"Here," a soft, feminine voice said to her on her other side. Amaya.

Zaiana's senses were stuffed with cotton—she could hardly detect a thing. The fright caused another wince Amaya shared. The darkling extended a glass of water, which Zaiana immediately reached for. Her throat ached with every gulp.

Wiping her lips, she dreaded to ask, "How long have I been asleep?"

"Six weeks," Maverick said, thumping his book shut in one hand. "In and out, but I'm going to guess you don't remember any moment of consciousness when you were hardly present."

She couldn't have heard that right. No—it wasn't possible she'd lost that much time since the Battle of Ellium. Her breathing picked up. Scanning outside, glimpsing the crimson peaked mountains, confirmed she was still in Rhyenelle. They'd won. Except...

Zaiana flung back the covers, but she couldn't twist out of the bed as quickly as her mind wanted her to. Her entire body seized tight, with sharp pain shooting through every muscle like she'd never felt before...because she'd never lain so still for so long in her life.

They weren't lying.

Maverick stood from the chair, lingering his eyes on Amaya expectantly.

The darkling rose from her crouch by the bed Zaiana was in, obeying Maverick's silent order. Zaiana's thoughts were too scrambled to even object.

Her memory came in flashes.

Trembling, terrifying slices of vision that almost could have been mistaken as movement in her dead chest with how fast the adrenaline coursed through her.

"Kyleer," Maverick said. That name was like a whip that drew her bewildered eyes to him.

"What?" she breathed. He couldn't possibly have found out what she'd—

"You said his name a few times over the weeks." Maverick stared her down, and Zaiana had never before felt her cheeks heating, flustered over how to explain that. "Did he hurt you?"

Zaiana blinked, not expecting that would be his conclusion, but she supposed it was her own guilty conscience that had thought it was evident why the commander was plaguing her mind. "Something like that," she muttered. Her thoughts were frayed strings trying to find something to tie onto.

The battle. Faythe had *wings*. They'd fought in the sky.

Zaiana had lost.

No—they both had.

"What happened?" She tried to recall, but all that stunned her mind was a final bright flare before the impact of power she should not have survived.

"There were moments when..." Maverick trailed off as though he were tormented by his own memories. He paced away from the bed.

"We didn't know if you'd pull through. But I shouldn't have doubted. You're far too stubborn to die."

Zaiana tried to study him, and while she would usually want to cast him out, say something wicked as the language they'd crafted between them, she was momentarily caught by how vulnerable he looked.

She'd fallen from that sky, her wings…

"You caught me."

A muscle in his jaw flexed, but he didn't meet her eye.

"You're not in the clear yet," he said vacantly, heading for the door. For the first time, a calling for him to stay lodged in her throat. "I'll let Dakodas know you're finally awake and lucid but still recovering."

The mention of the Dark Spirit sent a chill down her spine.

"Did anyone…?" Zaiana shouldn't care, and she hoped it came off as an inquiry about their triumph. "Did everyone make it?"

Maverick paused with his hand on the door. "For now," he confirmed. His black eyes lingered on her like he was yearning to stay and explain, but something was dominating him to leave. "Faythe escaped, Marvellas has the general though. Truthfully, I don't know what they're planning for now, but I think we should all brace for the Nether that's about to be unleashed by that one."

Zaiana's gut twisted at the notion. If they captured Faythe's mate…

A dizzy spell threatened to collapse her back down, but Zaiana couldn't rest another moment.

She'd wasted too much time.

"They don't expect anything from you until you're fully recovered. If you were smart, you'd consider drinking human blood to heal faster despite your long abstinence."

Zaiana's mouth fell open with a denial she didn't get to voice, because Maverick didn't look back as he left. How did he know she hadn't indulged in human blood for a long time? Or was he merely guessing, since she'd refrained on their quest together?

It didn't matter. She had far bigger problems to face, and she would prove she didn't need the help of human blood.

Zaiana clenched her teeth, maneuvering to sit with her legs off the bed. Bracing a hand on the headboard, she forced stability through the sharp pains to stand.

Her footing stumbled at the tilt of the room. Zaiana caught herself on whatever object she could. The bedpost. Then the dresser. Where were her clothes? She only wore a black silk nightgown.

She decided to try the closet. Within it, she found suitable combat attire and had to wonder who'd left it for her. Now her mind had started to come back, she gathered the right sense to be irritated by Maverick watching over her like he *cared*.

He'd saved her. Zaiana's fists clenched with the notion it could hang over her, a life debt owed.

If he'd let her die, she would have been out of his way as the most favorable dark fae in the ranks. She didn't want to believe it was out of his own will, his want. No—she couldn't allow him, or herself, to fall into a trap of caring whether the other lived or died.

With the world cracking into war, and with their fates to lead on the front lines, entangling their emotions with each other would only get them killed sooner.

Fully dressed, she found her metal guards on the nightstand and slipped them onto her middle and pointer fingers. Her body ached, adjusting slowly with small movements she hardly had the patience for, and she despised her short, lethargic breaths.

Zaiana's brow slicked as she paused to lean her back against the wall. To distract herself, she watched her fingers flex, adorned with the metal weight that felt more natural than her fingers did when they were off. Though she didn't have much strength right now, she had to feel it—her magick.

She reached within herself, touching around for the hum that would rake over her skin in answer.

Zaiana felt…nothing.

She quelled the spike of panic before it could waver her focus. Reaching again, she searched, diving deeper for the vibrations of her lightning, but it was so still. Zaiana retreated in horror.

Her skin was pale and cold yet beaded with sweat. Her chest remained as silent as always. Her magick…

"No," she breathed, clamping her eyes shut.

Zaiana braced on her thighs with the sickness roiling in her stomach. Then, with a groan of frustration, she straightened, though it was painful to do so. She walked a few paces and rolled her shoulders.

Her exhale shuddered from her as she felt the weight of her wings expanding from her shoulder blades. Relief flooded her, though it exerted her of far more energy than it should to release her glamour.

She still had her wings.

Zaiana dropped to her knees, clutching a hand to her chest. Her magick couldn't be gone.

She was just recovering.

Even as she chanted the assurance this had to be a block, a temporary torture, clouds of anxiety filled her mind and taunted her existence. Who would she be without it? It didn't bear thinking about.

Zaiana was her lightning. Its strength, its unique beauty. If she didn't have that...

She would be nothing at all.

CHAPTER FIVE

Faythe

They gathered around a table in the main room of the inn, but heavy silence lingered, with no one knowing how to begin their tale.

Faythe swirled fingers around the rim of her tankard until Nik, seated beside her, placed a hand over her other on the table.

"We heard news in some of the towns that Ellium has been invaded," he said gently, trying to ease into the story she couldn't bring herself to explain.

Her lips parted a few times, trying to arrange the words and be able to deliver them without breaking down again.

"The king—"

"I know," Nik said, and her brow pinched, unable to meet his gaze.

"I couldn't stop them. I couldn't save him or Reylan. She has him, Nik. Marvellas took him, and I haven't been able to figure out where."

His fingers squeezed hers. "You will. The war isn't over yet."

"It's barely begun," Kyleer muttered.

"Where is Tauria?" Faythe dreaded to ask, still clinging to the hope the fact Nik was here without her didn't mean something awful had happened.

But it seemed they were both walking in their worst nightmares.

"Mordecai has taken her to Fenstead."

Faythe sat back. "Mordecai," she repeated, the name uncoiling something dark and foreboding in her spine. "Then why are you here?" she asked.

"We were looking for you," Lycus answered.

Nik said, his shoulders deflating, "Our resources are limited. I have High Farrow's armies ready to march, but it will not be enough. We've always known this."

That caused her to flick an expectant glance at Tarly, who sat silently, close to Nerida.

"You have Olmstone's army too?" she inserted, figuring now it made sense why the prince was with them.

"No," Nik said.

Faythe's head whipped back to him, confused. He dove a hand through his inky black hair in exasperation.

"We came to ask you for help, actually, hoping you might be able to assist knowing what is left—and what has been rebuilt—of Fenstead's armies is in Rhyenelle too. Then we heard what happened. We were already close, and I had to see for myself you'd made it out."

Faythe's gut sank with his explanation. She couldn't help him. She couldn't help anyone. "What's the plan now?"

"I'm going to Tauria regardless. I've been able to Nightwalk to her, but I won't leave her with Mordecai no matter what she was planning in going with him."

Her relief at that enlightenment quickly faded at her sorrow. Nik could still reach Tauria through Nightwalking, but Faythe had failed to reach Reylan that way. He knew exactly where she was, while Reylan remained lost.

"She is well then?" Faythe asked.

Nik gave a bittersweet smile. "They haven't harmed her, and she's coping just fine given the situation. I shouldn't have had any doubt. She's come up with a clever way of keeping me informed. Though it's not the same as when you and I meet each other in Nightwalking. Tauria can't interact with me that way."

"She hasn't told you why she went with him?" Kyleer cut in.

"Tauria has always been fiercely spirited, especially when it comes to her people. She hasn't been hiding in High Farrow—she was biding her time. When the opportunity came to be taken into the heart of her kingdom, I'm not surprised she took it. It kills me she's in the arms of the enemy, but strategically, it's smart. She can learn a lot within those walls. I believe in her."

So did Faythe. As long as Tauria wasn't being harmed, they had time.

Nik drummed his fingers on the table, staring at nothing in particular as his thoughts turned.

"Did Rhyenelle lose many warriors in the Battle of Ellium?" Nik inquired.

Kyleer answered. "Not enough to severely dent our numbers. Given that it was an inside job, it was over before it began. Rhyenelle doesn't earn its esteemed military reputation merely for effective training. Our city may have never fallen, but our kings have never been arrogant enough to believe it could never happen. If the city ever did fall, our armies and our armadas know where to go to await further instruction."

Nik mulled over that information for a solitary moment.

"You're a great leader for your people," Nik said to her. "I must be a leader for mine too, and that includes Fenstead now. I don't want to take away from what you need, but Tauria's army is among yours, and I must call for them to join me in taking back their kingdom."

"Then we won't be enough to take back ours," Faythe argued.

"I'm sorry, but they're not yours to command anymore."

"Fenstead would have no army if it weren't for my father. You would make them abandon Rhyenelle in its worst moment when it gave them everything during theirs?"

Nik sighed deeply. Faythe hated this tension. In this conversation, friendship had to come second to the monarchs they were.

"There has to be a way to help each other," he said in a grumble of frustration.

Kyleer said, "I hate to admit this, but Rhyenelle isn't under immediate threat right now. With Malin still alive, and with no one knowing of his role in the battle, our kingdom has a reigning Ashfyre, so the civilians should be safe. We don't need our armies right now, but I'm not in favor of sending them to Fenstead without any sure strategy we're a part of either. You're both motivated by grief for your mates. Much as you are the queen and king of your respective kingdoms, you have to lean on our judgment for this."

Lycus said, "I agree. Though I want to call upon every army I can to storm Fenstead for Tauria, that's an emotional response that will lose us precious resources. Our best course of action is to continue on alone, to scout and keep checking whether she's managed to discover anything pivotal from the inside."

Nik wasn't pleased with the idea, but he knew the generals were right.

Nik said, "If it's all the same to you, we'd like to sit in on your next meeting with your generals. I figure they must be frequent while you're figuring out your next movements."

Kyleer nodded. "Of course. I think we could all benefit from keeping track of each other and figuring out a plan to join together again once we have Reylan and Tauria back."

Nik slung an arm around Faythe, defusing some of the tension building in them.

"How are your abilities coming along?" Nerida asked.

"Firewielding is easy. I can somewhat Shadowport. And I think I can summon lightning now, but it's the most unpredictable."

"Lightning, huh?" Nik hooked a brow toward her.

Faythe twitched a smile. "A lot has changed. More than just pointy ears," she said.

Nik's smile widened as he flicked the tip of her ear. It triggered a smile long forgotten on Faythe's mouth too as she batted his hand away.

"You met Zaiana again?" Nerida inquired, her interest brightening.

Faythe nodded, wondering what Nerida saw in Zaiana to think of her so fondly despite having traveled in the dark fae's company against her will.

"The dark fae?" Nik inquired. She'd forgotten the glimpse of Zaiana she'd shown him in a memory of the fire mountains. "She's a Stormcaster?"

Faythe supposed his wonder was justified since the ability was rare. She nodded in answer, and Nik seemed to travel somewhere with the knowledge.

"How do you harbor so many talents?" Lycus asked.

"When I feel someone's ability, I can learn them. Some are far harder than others."

"Like Reylan?" Nik asked.

"I can...*keep* the ability," Faythe admitted.

"Well damn," Tarly said. "You're a whole arsenal."

Faythe didn't know much about the prince, having only seen and not interacted with him during the kings' meetings in High Farrow that felt in another lifetime now. He seemed changed from that prickly prince. Not entirely, but as though layers of him had shed since then.

"Not to be rude, but why are you here?" Faythe asked him.

His expression turned guarded, as though he regretted speaking at all and wanted to remain a lurking shadow. The smile Nerida cast him over her shoulder seemed to ease some of the tension squaring his defense.

"Olmstone has fallen too," Nik said.

"It has not *fallen*," Tarly objected.

"It's not exactly in Wolverlon hands now, is it?"

That hadn't changed. The stand-off between Nik and Tarly was the only familiar aura.

"Do you think I don't know High Farrow was close to finding a new reigning name too?" Tarly bit back.

"Close to and being taken are not the same, *prince.*"

Tarly shifted until Nerida's hand eased over his.

"You two have far more pressing battles to focus your attention on," she said with an edge of vexation that told Faythe it wasn't the first time she'd had to defuse their bickering.

Faythe shook her head, thrilled to see every person in Nik's company, but one by one the ensemble became confusing. The unlikely group that had found her.

"How are you all together?" Faythe asked plainly.

"It's quite a long story," Nik said as he took a long drink and then set down his empty tankard. "We might need refills."

Half-sister.

Faythe couldn't stop stealing glances at Nerida with the stunning revelation. It seemed so glaringly obvious now. The resemblance Nerida shared with Tauria opened a new clarity, and most of all, Faythe felt it the healer's eyes. The color and shape of them tugged on a string of yearning for Tauria.

Though that was all the explanation Nerida had shared, Faythe couldn't settle knowing there was far more to her tale she was still keeping guarded. After parting from Faythe months ago, Nerida had crossed paths with the runaway prince beside her, and they'd kept each other company while Nerida sought out a particular book she suspected could hold answers about the Spirits.

The fall of Olmstone clashed with Faythe's own memories of Ellium. On that level, she thought she could come to find common ground with Tarly Wolverlon despite his clear reluctance to open up to anyone as he held back most of the time.

Then there was Lycus. His presence was the least surprising considering the circumstances surrounding his queen. But hearing of the events leading to Tauria's willing capture strained Faythe's urgency in two opposite directions.

Her mate and her dear friend.

"How have you been sleeping?" Nik asked quietly, and she realized he was the only one who could relate to her type of unrest.

"I combatted the nightmares once, but maybe I'm not strong enough anymore."

"Or you're punishing yourself. Not accepting your failures since you haven't fixed them yet. I know…because I can't allow myself peace until Tauria is with me again either."

Faythe's eyes pricked with tears, and she nodded, leaning into his side-embrace as it opened.

"I miss him," Faythe whispered.

He gave her a gentle squeeze. "I know. I wish there was something I could say to ease your torment, but there's nothing anyone could do to soften mine."

Faythe was so damn grateful to have him here. After all that had happened, his presence and those he'd come with was enough to tighten the straining seams on her grief, and she hoped it would be enough to hold her together until she found Reylan.

"Can you still reach Tauria through your bond as well?"

Nik dropped his gaze, and the others seemed to pause their idle chatter at overhearing her question. Dread sent a chill over her skin.

"Marvellas broke our bond," Nik said, his tone hollow.

Tarly shifted closer to Nerida. Lycus tensed. Kyleer turned wide-eyed, and Faythe… It impacted her like something had slammed into her gut, and hands choked her throat at the same time.

Then a heat of rage slowly crawled across her skin.

Within her, the tether to Reylan that ran through her *pulled*. It had been so quiet and distant, but at least it was still there. Her bond to Reylan wasn't claimed, and though she may have been able to find him quicker if it were, the risk of Marvellas being able to break it made her glad they hadn't had the chance to tie it yet.

"Faythe." Nik said her name carefully.

Following his line of sight, she caught the gold essence diffusing out from her under palm, which she'd flattened on the table.

When she lifted it, the mark she wore was branded into the wood.

Marvellas's symbol, flaring brightly for seconds as if it were laughing at its presence here.

Faythe had become more and more sickened by the thought of being of her bloodline. The only time her disgust quelled was when she focused her determination enough to remember, through Faythe, Marvellas would be her own downfall.

"I'm going to kill her," Faythe said, locking that promise tighter within herself. Then her attention turned to Nik. "I'm so sorry."

He shook his head. "We gave it willingly, knowing neither Marvellas nor Mordecai would trust her with ties to me. We wanted to get Dakodas's ruin, but it seems that was all wasted planning."

"What if Dakodas left it with Mordecai for safekeeping in Fenstead?" Faythe suggested.

"I wouldn't be hopeful about her entrusting the one thing that could kill her to anyone else's hands," Kyleer chimed in.

Nerida said, "Technically, it can't truly be in her hands either. The Spirits can't hold their own ruins. She would have someone close to her guarding it."

"Do you think it's in Rhyenelle then?" Kyleer pondered.

Faythe blanched. "That would mean two of the ruins we need are there."

"And they have the one person who knows how to use them," Kyleer added gruffly.

"Zaiana," Faythe said in answer to the questioning glances of the others. "She's unparalleled with the amplified power."

"She's the only one who can wield them?" Nik asked.

"As far we know. I don't think she lied about that," Kyleer admitted reluctantly. He asked her, "I'm trusting you have the Light Temple ruin well-hidden?"

Faythe had hidden it well, but now she was doubting. "I only entrusted one person with the knowledge of where it is, in case anything happened to me." Faythe's stomach knotted. "Izaiah."

Kyleer swore, settling his flash of upset and anger in a castaway glance.

Faythe went on, "He might not have told me his plan, but I don't believe he's truly working for them. It doesn't make any sense. I was barely half-conscious when he took me to the courtyard after the battle was lost, but what he said—"

"That he's one step ahead? Hardly a soothing statement that it's not for the enemy. He could have shapeshifted and come to explain it to me by now," Kyleer muttered bitterly.

"They'll be watching him far too closely. I don't know what he's planning, but I trust him."

While he was still dealing with the sting of betrayal from his brother, Kyleer wouldn't admit Faythe's declaration eased his tense shoulders.

"Just one ruin grants a powerful upper hand. Right now our greatest enemies are circling around them all. Perhaps we should be devising a plan to infiltrate the castle ourselves to retrieve the Light Temple Ruin," Faythe said.

"You can't wield it. Best leave it secured if you're confident in its location. Marvellas is hunting you, and if she gets you and the ruin, it'll lose us the war," Kyleer countered.

"I can use it—I just…don't have control with it." She cringed at the memory of such devastating power coursing through her.

"You mean it's a huge risk to your life to try it," Nik said. "I remember it nearly costing you your life in High Farrow. There's no way you're exposing yourself to that."

"I was human then."

Kyleer said, "You could easily become too overpowered in your fae body too. You need someone to teach you how to wield it, or you're at more risk of it killing you than helping you."

Someone to teach her.

A memory unlocked in her mind so clearly then she couldn't believe she hadn't thought of it sooner. Or perhaps she had, in some part of her subconscious that had always known Zaiana was important. That it was crucial they secured her to their side.

"Find the teacher who tames the storm."

Aurialis had told her that.

Her vacant stare had settled on Kyleer as she'd pieced together that riddle, and he was becoming far too in tune with her thoughts. His pinched brow of concern smoothed out as if Zaiana's name had been pushed from her brain and was scribbled across her forehead.

"We could *never* trust Zaiana on our side. Even if we kidnapped her, forced her, she's far too cunning and would find a way to turn anything we tried to learn from her against us," Kyleer protested, his voice so torn with hurt under the firmness.

"Taking back any kingdom means nothing if they use Zaiana and the ruins to destroy them. Worse, Marvellas's goal is to destroy her own ruin, and then we have *no* hope of ridding the world of her. None."

Faythe's daunting dread grew the longer she pondered the options.

"We all need to get some sleep. This kind of decision on where to move next isn't going to be solved in a night," Nerida advised. Her eyes turned to pity, casting over Faythe. "I have a tonic, and with my magick, it'll send you into a deep enough rest that your Nightwalking shouldn't be able to surface."

"It works," Nik confirmed, giving the healer a smile of gratitude.

Faythe nodded. "Thank you."

Kyleer stood after draining his drink and wandered over to the ensemble in the corner who had paused their music for a break. Faythe's gaze caught on the quiet fae in their company. Samara—she'd learned her name. Her elegance and poise almost seemed out of place among them, but it was clear she was trying to fit in, and Lycus whispered occasional assurances to her.

Kyleer returned as the small band took up their playing stances again, and soft music began to fill the space.

"I'll be heading back to the camp for however many peaceful hours I can get," he announced.

"We'll get some rooms upstairs." Lycus spoke, guiding Samara out of the booth.

Faythe gave a nod to them, wanting to finish her drink before she attempted sleep.

The song the players wove grew on her drowsiness, and she leaned back against the booth as the words began.

She was so exhausted in her mind. Every thought was misery. Every step was hollow. Peace would never find her until she found *him*.

Nik slouched down with her and lifted his tankard. Faythe huffed, clinking hers against it—a cheers to their matching heartache—before they drank.

"I always pictured we'd be meeting again under far better circumstances," he mused sadly.

Faythe leaned her head on his shoulder. "As Faythe and the fae guard in the woods?"

Nik's light chuckle was a brightness bursting against the clouds of darkness around her heart.

Tarly and Nerida stayed with them in the main room, which had quietened in the small hours. Faythe's lids fluttered even without a tonic. They should retire for the night, and at least with the healer's help, she didn't have to fear it.

Still, she wanted to bask in this moment with Nik, and she tuned in to the song as the bustle began to fade away.

Come fly the Phoenix, come soar the sun,
Fall a monarch's reign, another will return.
Come fly the Griffin, come rally the night,
Answer all and stand as one, together they will fight.

The song kept going, and some lines would repeat. Faythe nestled in closer to Nik as she felt herself drifting with it.

"How long has it been since you slept?" Nik asked.

Faythe couldn't be certain when the fleeting hours she'd captured here and there were riddled with unrest. But with Nik here, his scent soothed the ache within her just enough to want the deep sleep.

"She needs it more than any of us," Nerida said.

"Come on." Nik pulled her gently with him as he left the booth.

Faythe groaned, almost reaching to grip the table in a childish display of protest. Nik was swift, hooking her around the middle until she stood. The song wasn't over, and she was enjoying it.

Come fly the Phoenix, come soar the sun.

Nik steered her toward the stairs.

Fall a monarch's reign, another will return.

"We're going to get them back," Nik said to her.

Faythe nodded, though he didn't see it.

Come fly the Griffin, come rally the night.

"I have something I need to tell you," she mumbled sleepily.

How would he react to the revelation of her soul's long past when she didn't even hold the full memory of it?

"Save it," he said. "I'm not disappearing through the night."

This was it. The sound of war that had always been background noise now came to terrifying life as a crescendo of pounding drums she felt in her chest.

Answer all and stand as one, together they will fight.

CHAPTER SIX

Zaiana

When Zaiana's eyes flew open to a crack of lightning, she knew immediately her consciousness wasn't awake in the real world.

No. This can't be happening again.

It had to be a nightmare. A cruel punishment plucked from her worst memories. She stayed down, curling into herself, since she couldn't stand to find the face of King Agalhor that would come out to taunt her after infiltrating her mind.

Even with him dead, and whatever he'd discovered about her burning with him, she was unable to forget the violation of his intrusion into her mind. Even awake, she carried a new shame as if the world now knew her twisted mind, and nothing of her was safe anymore.

Zaiana whimpered at the presence that grew stronger. Approaching to stalk its feeble prey, submissive on the ground.

This wasn't her—she didn't yield like this. Yet in here she didn't have to pretend she wasn't afraid and tired. So very tired.

"How are you awake?" the male asked with a fascination she didn't expect, in a voice that wasn't familiar.

Zaiana uncurled herself, raising a hand against the stormy wind that dragged her hair across her vision. She could barely make out the tall figure cloaked in the darkness of her mind and concealed in an oversized hood.

"Who are you?" she asked.

"More fascinatingly…who are you?"

Zaiana knew this game. He spoke in taunts she was all too used to parrying with.

"You already know that if you're here."

"You got me there. Though knowing of you and wanting to *know* you are two different things."

She tried to squint through the darkness of his hood, but his face was completely erased, lost to darkness, and she came to the conclusion that was his manipulation.

"It's rare to find a colorless mind," he said, pacing away. "More so, this aggression… Your own mind is rebelling against you. Torturing you. It's almost a miracle you're sane."

"Thanks for the compliment."

He chuckled smoothly.

"Have you ever tried letting go of what it is you're fighting against?"

If she knew what that was, perhaps she would consider it.

"What are you doing here?" she diverted.

"I was curious," he said simply.

Zaiana found the sensation of him odd. Unlike Agalhor, he didn't feel so daunting and vicious. She watched his hooded form with his back to her. He reached out a hand toward the strikes of lightning that slammed into the ground violently. Her chest ached to feel it coursing through her veins instead.

The next jagged purple line touched his fingertips. Zaiana drew breath sharply, as if it had been absorbed by her own body. The male tensed with it, but it didn't hurt him like it should. Instead he seemed to *play* with the last of the snapping bolts across his hand.

"How did you do that?" she asked.

He lifted a shoulder. "It's your mind. You could make it hurt me if you wanted."

"I don't know how," she confessed.

The male twisted a fraction back to her, but his head was tipped down. "I can teach you how to use your Nightwalking."

"I'm not a Nightwalker."

"Are you in the habit of denying what is right in front of you?"

His hand moved elegantly, and her dark clouds answered him. She cupped a palm to her forehead, dizzy with the movements that weren't in her control, but part of her thought they should be. That this male should not have this kind of power in her mind.

This is a dream.

It was all she could do to make sense of this twisted illusion.

"Are you…a Stormcaster?" she wondered.

Zaiana's ability was beautiful, but this…it was the ugliest, most untamed side of it. Yet the male didn't react with any disgust or pity—not like Agalhor had.

"I don't think I am," he said, reaching out a hand again, and it was as if the bolts were attracted to him.

"Then I can't teach you anything in return."

"I didn't ask for anything."

"No one offers help without something for their own gain."

His hood tilted, and Zaiana was growing irritable and uneasy that he could see her, fully exposed, while she couldn't be sure where his eyes were at all.

"I can understand why you believe that."

"You don't know anything about me."

"I want to."

"Why?"

She should be afraid, like the terror she'd felt with the King of Rhyenelle's invasion. But she wasn't. This male wasn't targeting her memories; he didn't seem to care to dive deeper when his power radiating through her warned he was more than capable.

"I want you out of my mind," she said. Only then did a trickle of fear ease though her. If she provoked him, she didn't know how to cast him out. His power was as dominating as the king's, perhaps even more powerful, and she knew she would lose in here.

She didn't know how to protect herself.

"I can help you."

"Why would you do that?"

Everything came with a price.

He took a long breath, swirling fingers that shifted the dark mist.

"Maybe I like the challenge."

On the tip of her tongue, she wanted to demand he show himself. But maybe she preferred not having a face to this presence. Without it, she could pretend he was only a ghost of her own conjuring, not a real person trespassing in the most private place.

"Why don't you search my thoughts?" she dared to ask.

"Why would I do that?"

"To gain some advantage? To make me fear you or force me to help you?"

"What has happened to you to make that the first assumption about anyone you meet?"

She cursed the sting that pricked her eyes at the question. *What happened?* Zaiana could almost laugh.

Her emotions were too volatile and exposed in here, and suddenly, her defense was rising, wanting to cast him out before he didn't have to reach for a damn thing to get to her vulnerability.

"People want power—it always requires an upper hand."

"Not always," he countered. "What about gaining it through respect and loyalty?"

"Values that can be overthrown in a second," she said firmly. "They can be betrayed, and you wouldn't know until you were staring into the eyes of the one plunging a dagger into your chest."

"That is a fair precaution," he agreed, pacing a few steps. "But I believe there are bonds we can forge that will make such a fear not a lone burden. You become a force of many who would protect each other against anyone who threatened them."

Zaiana tucked her knees to her chest. She didn't fully agree with his poetic notions, but she was intrigued about him.

"How do I know you won't just kill me in here?" she asked.

"Because our first lesson will be how you would stop me," he said. "Deal?"

Zaiana was cut with memories of Agalhor. The helpless way she'd been overpowered while he'd feasted on the darkest parts of her. How he would have killed her within the prison of her own mind.

This space, it was so furious and ugly. Part of her didn't want to spend another minute here. She would rather never awaken in her subconscious again. The only way she knew how to survive against herself was to never confront the demons that lived between the cracks.

"I have nothing to gain from this," she said.

Her cheek met her knees. So tired.

"There's something detached from you. Your ability, I assume."

Of course he would know that.

"I'm not searching your thoughts for it," he added quickly, perhaps picking up on her rising defense. "But I can feel it."

"Is it...gone?"

"No, but something is blocking it. You won't want to hear this, but it's you. A little more complicated than that, for sure. Getting it back won't be as easy as wishing for it, as I'm sure you've already tried."

"Wishing is for children," she mumbled.

"Wishing is for souls with dreams," he responded. "And dreams are powerful to keep us moving."

Zaiana deciphered his words. They were naïve. Weak.

They were *beautiful*.

She shook her head, expelling her contrasting thoughts.

"How do I get it back? My ability."

"You still have your power, otherwise we wouldn't be here. Or at least you wouldn't be. Your lightning has been your armor. I understand hiding behind the identity of your ability."

"I don't hide."

Light streaked across his jaw to reveal the hint of a jesting smile. She wanted to claw it off.

"You don't know anything about me," she repeated.

Then she was awash with the fear that might not be true. That he could have infiltrated her mind at a time she was oblivious—

"No. I don't. But there are things about a person that can been seen only if one cares to really *look*."

"Why would you care?" She couldn't stop the bitterness of her tone. Her claws that formed to scare away any shred of attention.

"I…don't know," he said.

The uncertainty seemed to confuse them both, and maybe *he* was now bracing to retreat with the enlightenment that he shouldn't be here. She was nothing to him.

"Do we have a deal?" he said.

This wasn't a selfless venture for him. It couldn't be. She would be an absolute fool to agree to let him back into her mind…but it dawned he may be her only chance to recover her lightning.

"I don't even know who you are," she pointed out.

"I don't know exactly who you are either."

"But you've heard of me?" she recalled.

"Sort of. I have no preconceived opinion of you, Zaiana. That, I would like to find out for myself."

His use of her name shouldn't have come with the uneasy tension it did. He was in her mind after all.

"It's only fair I have your name," she tried.

He shook his head. "For this, you'll have to be willing to give something you really have a hard time with. Trust."

She could have cast him out with the force of her irritation alone. Her face folded into her crossed arms. This was pathetic. She would wake up and scold herself for the dream she'd let go on for far too long.

"I don't suppose I could stop you if you returned," she said.

"Probably not."

"Then do what you want. I can't promise a welcome reception."

"I wasn't counting on it."

"Can I sleep now?"

He was in the habit of laughing in soft, barely-there sounds. Its friendliness was beginning to unnerve her.

"Yes. I'll even send you off before I slip out. I can also feel that you don't manage a deep rest on your own very often. But you can. We'll work on that too."

That sounded desirable. She wouldn't tell him that.

She allowed the weight pressing down to pass over her. It was gentle. So very peaceful, like an embrace she'd long forgotten the comfort of until now.

CHAPTER SEVEN

Tauria

Tauria Stagknight had been imagining this moment for more than one hundred years. Now, living it, she couldn't organize her tangled feelings about being back on Fenstead soil.

Staring up at a banner hanging at an angle, Tauria resisted the urge to bow in sorrow with the stag emblem of her kingdom.

The lands were not the same. Casting her sight out the window, it tore her soul-deep to see the vibrant hills and the thriving city she once knew so lifeless now. It may as well have been wraiths who roamed the streets. Many dark fae—but also many of her people who hadn't been able to make it out—still lived here under a dark, disorderly regime.

These halls she walked were foreign now. She'd dreamed of the welcome embrace they would offer, but all she'd been met with was the shunning of a betrayer. While her kingdom remained overrun by the enemy and destroyed of its beauty, she felt no better than the dark fae invaders. She was here in the arms of the one who'd taken everything from her.

Mordecai had been suspiciously subdued, leaving her alone for the most part while she came to terms with being back on Fenstead soil. Tauria had been allocated a guest room in her own castle as one of the few that wasn't ransacked and torn apart. She had yet to face what had become of her old rooms.

The walls bore eyes of judgment. Sometimes, she even thought they whispered their shock.

How dare she come back as a compliant hand to the dark fae high lord?

Tauria didn't dress in her homeland greens. She wore black. Until she reclaimed the kingdom on her own terms and killed the evil that grew like poison, she would continue to mourn on these lands.

Mordecai had requested she join him for supper this night.

She didn't attend his summons. Instead she made her way to the library—another place she'd been avoiding until now, since it held too many fond memories, and she was afraid to face what state it could have been left in. She wasn't afraid of Mordecai's wrath at dismissing him.

Tauria had saved the high lord in Olmstone against Tarly's arrow, which might have struck his chest true. It had been a reckless act of fear when Mordecai was winning against them, and she'd acted on impulse in an attempt to gain his trust after he figured out Nik had been trailing them all the way to Olmstone despite their broken bond.

She'd done it *for* Nik, yet her heart ached at being so far from him, and she couldn't subdue the guilt that her ruse was to keep trying to convince Mordecai she wanted to be with him.

Her nerves about Mordecai dissipated when she approached the entrance to the library. There had never been a door to this space, as the long line of Fenstead monarchs had believed knowledge and stories should never be restricted to anyone. In their free time, the castle staff were allowed to wander and consume as much of the literature as they liked, the only strict rule being no piece was to be removed without the knowledge of the king or queen.

Tauria had slowed in the hallway leading to the open library, taking in the real tree trunks that had been crafted and preserved to create a wonderful archway. Already, she was met with the wounds of war that had defiled the space. She reached out to brush her fingers over some of the deep wedges that had been hacked out of the once perfect artistry. It wasn't beyond repair, but still, her heart ached, and the sounds of fighting filled her ears as she imagined the Fenstead warriors that would have fought until their dying breath to protect their land and the castle.

With a deep breath, she pushed herself past the entrance. Fenstead's royal library was not the most expansive—that was the Livre des Verres in Olmstone. Still, here was commonly known as the most beautiful library to exist on the entire continent. Tauria stopped before the balcony crafted of entwining branches. Her knees almost buckled where she stood. Right here was the most at home she'd felt since being back.

As a child, she'd always thought this library must be what it would be like to stand in the middle of a giant, hollowed-out tree, where within, it lent mankind its flesh to scribe the infinite wonders of life, death, and imagination.

The bookshelves were perfectly imperfect, with the artisans having preserved as much natural form as possible. The balcony circled around an ancient silver oak tree this section of the castle was built around. There were many legends about it. Its roots were deep, and they spread so far even Tauria couldn't feel where the finer veins ended. She could press her hand to it and focus her Florakinetic ability to feel the threads of life running through her kingdom like a heartbeat.

Some of the stories her mother would tell her claimed this tree spread far beyond Fenstead soils. That the strongest Florakinetics could trace the finest threads of the roots to other kingdoms.

Tauria's bright memories started to dull as she came back to the ominous state of neglect the library had been left to. There wasn't too much destruction, to her relief. Some bookcases had been toppled, and books littered the ground, but she could fix that; was already making her way toward the first section.

What made her spirit wander the library in sorrow was how lonely it was. This had always been a place of shared joy and wonder, filled with smiling faces, enthusiastic young people, and eager scholars. Now it was just her lone soul among the ghosts of her people.

She didn't know how much time passed as she immersed herself in stacking books back where they belonged and using her wind to help right the bookcases on the third level she'd entered onto. It brought a spark of hope to watch the library slowly be put back to order.

Book by book, stone by stone, tree by tree, her land would be restored. On her life and lineage, she swore it to the great silver oak tree that remained a proud beacon of her kingdom.

Tauria Stagknight bowed her head to the ancient tree in promise.

When she slipped the next book onto the shelf, Tauria stiffened at the presence that had crept in silently. Mordecai had gotten so close before she'd even detected him, and he took the last book in the pile out of her hand. She held her breath when he leaned in, her instincts screaming for distance. He fixed the book back onto the self, his front brushing her back.

"You missed supper," he said, so calm, but with an edge of discontent.

"I wasn't hungry."

"Still, I expect you to join me when I ask. I do not like to be left waiting."

"That was not my intention."

"It matters not. When I call, you come, princess."

Her nails dug into her palms with the title.

I am Queen Tauria Silverknight.

"My apologies," she said tightly.

With Mordecai, she had to choose her battles. Provoking him over a missed supper would only set her back with him.

Tauria didn't want to turn around, wishing he would leave now he'd had the chance to chastise her.

"Don't you want to know why I invited you to dine with me?" he asked with a note of impatience.

"It wasn't simply for my company?"

"While it is cold and empty, your company has not been desirable to seek thus far, no."

After what had happened in Olmstone, she'd hardly left her rooms in her turmoil. Nik had suffered a near-fatal wound...and she'd left with the enemy before she knew if he'd pull through. In all his Nightwalking to her since, she'd awoken with impressions of Nik's unwavering love and devotion. It had slowly been killing her that she couldn't give it back in the same way.

She missed him so terribly. A piece of her soul was decaying in his absence.

"It's been a lot to process," she explained. "I didn't know what to expect, being back in Fenstead."

"Which is why I have been gracious enough to give you time and space, but I cannot wait much longer."

Tauria's teeth slammed together when his hands on her arms guided her around. She couldn't look anywhere but at his depthless onyx eyes. His firm jaw had grown a darker shadow, and his black hair was longer and unbound.

Dread pooled in her gut.

"Wait for what?" She put every effort into keeping her voice from wavering.

"I have long set aside a needed visit to my kingdom—Valgard."

The air released from her lungs. It wasn't what she'd expected him to say.

"Was the supper your farewell for a while?"

"No. I wanted to ask you to join me."

Tauria didn't know what to say. The suggestion shocked her, only because in all her life, she'd only known their eastern neighbors across the sea in the whispers of nightmares. The kingdom responsible for the Dark Age that wanted to suppress humans and have the dark fae dominate. Then, in this age, they were the face of the centuries-old war still waging.

Now there were new truths to their current war. Mordecai was the resurrected dark fae king of nightmarish legend, but it was Marvellas who'd brought him back. The Spirit of Souls and the Goddess of the Stars had been behind the war this time, and Mordecai was as good as her puppet.

Tauria wanted to figure him out. She was here by his side and playing a very risky game in getting close to him. But she couldn't shake the feeling there was more to him. How could one as powerful and legendary as Mordecai be content as the foot soldier of someone greater? He had a child in this life—something that sparked her curiosity wildly. They could be a weakness to exploit, or if that wouldn't work, she could at least discover who the child was, so they could eliminate the threat of his spawn before it became one.

"I only just got to come back to my kingdom," she said.

Tauria weighed the options in her mind. Staying in her kingdom while Mordecai was preoccupied across the sea would give her freedom to start strategizing here. Find weaknesses in the dark fae forces, go out to speak to what was left of her people, and get all of this information to Nik.

But no one had been to Valgard, Mordecai's stronghold. What secrets or revelations could she uncover in the land more elusive than Lakelaria? It was a highly tempting curiosity.

"It will still be here after a week or two, depending on my business over there."

She made up her mind.

Tauria couldn't pass up an opportunity to gain intel with a ticket straight into the heart of the continent's enemy territory.

"You would trust me with you?" she tested.

"You came with me despite your dying mate. I've been thinking I was wrong about you."

"What did you think before?"

"That you had conspired with Nikalias against me. But that would be a *very* foolish thing to do, and you are no fool—are you, Tauria?"

"I warned him not to follow, but I knew he would anyway." It killed her how easily the lies about Nik had started to flow.

To slither away from his close proximity, Tauria resumed her work, bending to scoop more books into her hands.

"I will assign staff for this."

"I would like to do it myself, or—" Tauria swallowed her resentment to have to ask *permission*. "If you would allow it, I would very much like to recruit my own selection to help restore the library. And hire staff. Discover what noble houses might still be alive to resume an orderly court here. I was hoping to venture out into the city."

The capital city of Calenmoore had no high walls like in High Farrow and Rhyenelle. Fenstead was a peaceful nation that had upheld its values of peace and acceptance when the war broke out. Even now, Tauria would not wish any barricades to be in place, nor would she build them. She would fight for what her people believed in.

"It is not safe for you. Fenstead has long been left to a state of anarchy, I'm afraid."

"Then why usurp my father's throne and slaughter all those people to let a great kingdom fall to ruin?" she snapped.

It was rare for Mordecai to show any sympathy, but he did right now, even if only a flicker before he looked away.

"Eventually, Marvellas wants you back on the throne—as dark fae. You would not have been killed all that time ago when your kingdom was taken. The instruction was to capture you for Transition."

Tauria stiffened against a shiver at the alternate fate that could have easily been hers.

"That's really her end goal—for all of us to reign as dark fae?"

"We are the strongest species."

"Because you feed on humans," she said, unable to hide her disgust.

Mordecai came closer again, and Tauria's grip on her books tightened.

"I have already told you, the dark fae are not all cruel, and humans can enjoy being fed from. At the end of this war, only resistance will be cut from humanity's weakness."

His certainty that he would achieve his dark fae reign grated on her nerves. While he wasn't forcing her to change now, and she'd been adamant against it, she wasn't such a fool to think she was safe from the Transition forever.

"When do we leave for Valgard?" she asked.

"In a week."

Her heart skipped a beat.

"Then I should like to enjoy my kingdom before we leave," she said to excuse herself from his company.

Tauria didn't wait for a response. She placed the pile of her books onto the shelf, forced a pleasant smile to the high lord, and left.

Her thoughts were a storm, and her magick could hardly be bottled in her restless state. She played with wisps of wind between her fingers, which helped soothe her emotions all the way to her guest room.

Inside, she headed straight to her desk, opening her well of ink and hastily pulling out a sheet of parchment. With her quill she began to write out what had happened today. So little, yet so much with where she was about to venture. Once she'd got it all out, Tauria finished her note as she always did.

The moon is half tonight. I love you. I miss you.

Standing with her letter, Tauria made her way over to the fireplace that was kept ablaze. Flame caught at the edge of the paper, and she watched it devour her words like she did every night before she slept. For Nik. It was how she communicated with him without their bond. He would Nightwalk to her and be able to find the memory of her writing the note to know what it had said before she'd burned it. Then he would create a beautiful dream that left his lasting impression when she awoke, so she'd never feel alone.

Dressed for bed, Tauria sat at the mirror for a moment. Since he could only see from her perspective in her memories, this was the only way Nik saw her face. Her hand reached to the glass as she thought of him, but the cold surface turned her sorrowful, and she hugged her knees instead.

"I'm a little frightened," she admitted, knowing he would feel her emotions anyway. "But I'm even more determined."

Tauria hoped to dive deeper into the history of high lord Mordecai—to find weaknesses to exploit—and there was no place that could have more knowledge about him than his own kingdom from ages past. But there was no telling what else she might discover on the land of the continent's roots of terror.

CHAPTER EIGHT

Faythe

Faythe stood around the table in a war tent littered with maps and figures. With the commanders and generals gathered, her concern for Commander Livia Arrowood came back to the surface of her thoughts. They hadn't seen Reylan's cousin since the Battle of Ellium.

In these past weeks, Faythe was focused and determined to learn all she could about Rhyenelle's armies and strategies, and to get to know the leading commanders and generals at each war camp she traveled to with Kyleer.

Knowledge that would take years to learn had to be crammed into as many hours as she could spare for the battle efforts now. It kept her mind on two tasks at once, so as not to be idle or hopeless while they searched for Reylan. He wouldn't want her to waste time focusing solely on him. This way, they were making plans to take back Ellium, possibly pivoting to aid High Farrow and Fenstead now, and all the while they had every resource on finding any information on where Reylan was being held.

"Our legions in the east have been discovered despite our diligent efforts," Commander Leon informed them.

A map of Ungardia spanned the table in the camp's meeting tent, with various figures placed to mark their legions, armadas, and potential threats that had been scouted. Faythe was becoming familiar with all the terms and strategies for movement, defense, and stakeout.

"How is that possible?" Kyleer said, leaning his hands on the table and observing it as if the enemy would pop up and tell him where they were coming from.

Another commander added, "They weren't prepared. We lost half. It's like they knew not only exactly where they were, but also our entire protocol for ambush and defense."

Faythe's spine stiffened. She whispered, "Like Reylan would."

Everyone's attention snapped to her.

She didn't want to be right. She added quickly, "He would never give it willingly."

Her throat tightened until she could hardly draw air, but she kept still and poised, hands clasped behind her back to keep her composure. But thoughts of what Marvellas would have done to him to get that information from his steel-guarded mind racked her with tremendous fear and pain.

"Shit." Kyleer straightened, keeping his sights on the table, and Faythe could practically hear the cogs working in his brain to figure something out.

How to outsmart their best.

"If that's true, we have no chance of moving our forces anywhere General Arrowood wouldn't know," Leon said, dread now surfacing.

"High Farrow," Nik interjected. He stood beside her, observing attentively but patiently. "Rhyenelle and Fenstead forces would be safe in High Farrow. If Reylan's knowledge is compromised, that won't be a strategy they'd find out."

"You mean to harbor the entirety of our armies within your borders?" another general asked.

Nik nodded. "It will be a stretch of resources, but in times of war, we have to adapt."

"And when those resources run out?" Kyleer asked. "As soon as they discover that's where our forces have gone, they'll attempt a siege, locking us all in there and starving us out of food and materials needed to fight back."

"It's not a foolproof suggestion, or even a favorable one for anyone. But the alternative is risking more attacks on unwitting legions and losing invaluable warriors for nothing," Nik said.

"I'm in favor of this plan," Faythe agreed.

She could feel a shift in the tent. A brewing disagreement infused the air with dominance and frustration.

A Rhyenelle commander named Cale spoke. "With all due respect, Your Highness, we need to consider this more carefully. Our army positions right now have been carefully considered over centuries. There are many strategies that hinge on retaining these positions for our best chances of reclaiming the kingdom if it ever fell."

"You'll address me as Your Majesty now," she said calmly. "You're right. I don't know as much as any of you here, but I am the Queen of Rhyenelle."

"Not while Malin Ashfyre sits on the throne as king," someone said.

"He's a false king," Kyleer warned. "If anyone in this damned camp has even the slightest disagreement with that, you'd better make it known now."

The tension grew thick enough to cut. Faythe might have buckled, were it not for her pillars of strength: her friends. She wasn't born into this, had barely had the time to grasp what being a ruler meant before she was thrust into a war—not just for her kingdom, but for the entire continent.

She knew there was resistance to her sudden status. In the wake of the king's death, no one had been given time to grieve or to adjust to the shifting crown. So Faythe understood, but what she wouldn't tolerate, like Kyleer, was doubt about her right to rule over Malin.

"We will not win against Dakodas." Faythe's voice rose. "She is the real threat in our kingdom, not Malin. But we are not enough to consider any advance on Ellium."

"So we hide," Cale said sourly.

"Better to wait and gather a bigger plan than lose warriors out of pride that gets us nowhere."

Her stare-off with this commander turned heated.

"I agree with our queen," Leon said.

Though it pleased her to hear this, she didn't allow any relief to quell her nerves.

Cale said, "Aren't you supposed to be powerful? How can we follow a fable? A *Phoenix Queen*, who was there as the kingdom was invaded and did nothing to stop it."

"What use is a mind ability to an army?" another remarked.

A line of lightning shot from her fingertips, cleaving the table but not splitting it entirely apart. Everyone in the tent backed away from it.

Faythe said, "Power doesn't make anyone invincible. Including Marvellas and Dakodas."

"Maybe Malin was right," Cale said. "You may be powerful, but you are untrained and volatile in this role."

Steel cut through the tent. Kyleer pointed the Ember Sword at the commander's chest.

"Sounds like you're declaring a side," he said like a warning.

Cale's face twisted in anger. "You would order me cut down, *Your Majesty*?"

Faythe debated the order for the mockery dripping in that title alone. "Depends on your answer," she said.

His glare felt warm over her skin.

"I have been loyal to King Agalhor Ashfyre for longer than you've been alive," he said through gritted teeth.

"Yet in questioning me, you question his judgment to declare me his heir."

"I do not. I'm merely saying you have a long way to go to learn what it takes to lead our people."

"Watch yourself," Kyleer said in a deceitful calm.

Faythe's fingers clenched against the wood, and with a groan, the table pulled back together, the flare of her gold magick filling the crack before dying out, leaving the table and the map perfectly untouched by her violence, save for the knocked-over figurines. Everyone looked over it with confusion and awe.

"Send the order to every general to retreat to High Farrow. They'll aid in securing the borders and protecting the citizens there," Faythe said.

"So we abandon our own people?" another commander asked.

Faythe despised what she had to admit. "No. Rhyenelle is still under the rule of an Ashfyre, rightful or not. So long as he's kept alive, I have to gamble the citizens of his kingdom are safe for now. Malin's only goal has been to discredit me to the council lords and take the crown. He'll need the people on his side. So we must shift our defense toward High Farrow, as it's the last kingdom not infiltrated by Marvellas. If we lose that, we have no stronghold left."

Faythe exchanged a look with Nik, assured by his single nod.

Kyleer sheathed the Ember Sword but lingered his threatening stare on Cale for a moment longer.

She'd expected resistance and questioning when she asserted herself, and she wouldn't let it shake her confidence. Agalhor believed in her, Reylan believed in her, her friends always stood by her, and most of all, Faythe believed in herself. It was a road that had taken her a long time to reach, but now she was here, she was not backing down for anything or anyone.

They stayed another hour discussing the finer details of moving the legions one by one inconspicuously, predicting where they might try to infiltrate next and staging their obliviousness to give others a chance to make haste toward High Farrow.

With each movement of figures across the map, the sound of the war drums heightened.

Faythe smiled to Commander Cale before she headed out, but he retained his sour expression.

"You did well in there," Nik said, following her.

She breathed in the crisp air as they climbed a hill.

"Sometimes I miss delivering apple tarts."

Nik chuckled then rubbed his stomach. "Marie's tarts were the reason I started stalking you. Training you was just a cover-up to visit the stall."

For the first time in weeks, Faythe genuinely laughed, pushing him.

Snow had begun to fall. Faythe reached out a hand, watching the white flurry land and melt against her leather glove with a sense of foreboding she couldn't explain. She became entranced by the weather, but not for anything good. That was when she stopped walking, recalling the word of the Dresair she'd freed from the mirrors in a Rhyenelle town.

"When snow falls, it will not end until the war is won."

Faythe sighed, wondering what had happened to the creature…if she'd unleashed another monster onto their land. She couldn't think about that when she had three more imminent ones to slay.

Marvellas. Dakodas. Mordecai.

"Agalhor would have been proud of you," Kyleer said gently, catching up with them.

She spoke her gratitude in a heavy smile. "They have a right to be wary of me," she said. "I have a lot to prove, but I'm ready."

Pride twinkled in Kyleer's eyes, and she leaned into him when he slung a large arm around her.

"Where are the others?" Faythe asked Nik.

They'd tried to convince Tarly to come to the meeting, if only to be another allying monarch to their cause, even without an army to contribute. He'd declined, and it hadn't felt right to insist after his look of reservation and defeat this morning. Tarly had lost his father, was separated from his sister, and had fled his kingdom with no ambition to go back. She didn't know him well, but she ached for him.

"Lycus was helping Samara figure out our fighting attire. Nerida went into the nearby woodland to find new herbs, and Tarly claimed he needed materials for arrows, so he accompanied her," Nik informed her.

A large white wolf stalked up the hill behind Nik. Her name was Asari. Faythe had found it amusing how the beast often followed Nik though he had little desire for its companionship. Her twin wolf, Katori, was always by Tarly's side. A wonder, really, how the sister wolves had chosen two people who could barely tolerate each other.

Between Asari's teeth were two rabbits, reminding Faythe she'd skipped breakfast this morning.

"She's useful sometimes, I guess," Nik grumbled, reaching out a hand to scratch behind her ear. He may voice his dismay, but he couldn't hide the small hint of endearment in his eyes when he looked at the beast.

They headed back down the hill, deciding to walk into the forest and try to intercept Tarly and Nerida to share their rabbit meal with them.

An hour later, they'd made a fire, cooked and eaten the rabbit, and been found by Nerida, Tarly, Lycus, and Samara.

Faythe gave over to a punishing exertion in her sparring against Nik now.

"I must say, it's thrilling to finally have you somewhat match my combat ability now," Nik quipped.

She scoffed, clashing Lumarias to the Farrow Sword, pushing off and twisting right before they could lock still.

"Somewhat?" she goaded. "I'm about to hand you your ass."

It was the perfect distraction they both needed. While she appreciated Kyleer was always eager to release their anguish through a session, she was rejoicing at the memories being with Nik stirred up.

So much had changed.

Her fae body allowed her to rise against him, and he didn't need to hold back. No longer did she feel like something was missing.

Faythe tracked his movements without the use of her ability, wanting to expend her full combat abilities to beat him fairly.

"You could have ended this with various maneuvers from Kalsain Seven and Kajac Nine," Kyleer said to her over their clamor. They were highly effective battle sequences. He stood leaning against a tree, eyes trained on them by habit, assessing the fight.

Faythe only smiled. She didn't want it to end so soon.

"Don't pretend you're going *easy* on me," Nik chuckled.

Faythe ducked under his vertical swipe, turning in a crouch, with both hands clamped around the hilt to block his next move. He was fast. *Very* fast.

"You seem particularly tired today, or were you always this sluggish?" Faythe gibed.

Though she was taunting him to distract him, she had noticed when Nik joined them for breakfast that he looked half-asleep.

"I have to check on Tauria as much as I can," he answered coolly.

Before she could say anything else, she had to hone her skills when he came at her with more force.

Kyleer was strong, masterfully strategic, and knew her ways; beating him took outsmarting him, which she had yet to achieve. With Nik, her speed was tested like with no one else.

They parried for another minute until Faythe stumbled in her focus because of a pressure in her mind. She tried to shake it off, thinking a headache must be forming from their unrelenting efforts. It grew like a gentle prodding, turning more forceful, and it was then her eyes snapped to Nik's, forgetting their battle. He anticipated it with a wicked smirk before he disarmed her swiftly and kicked her legs out from under her.

Faythe hit the ground, wincing at the impact, but she didn't immediately peel herself up.

"Do I want to know how you're doing that?" she said incredulously.

She partly hoped she was delirious, yet the impression was too damned familiar, and Nik's hooked brow confirmed what she expected.

He had conscious mind abilities.

"You were right," he said casually, thrusting a hand to her.

Faythe accepted the help to stand, her thoughts reeling, while Nik dipped inside his jacket. The vial he produced immediately stole her attention for the hum of energy it gave off. Shaking the vial, her eyes widened on the glittering crimson liquid.

"The Phoenix feather was real," he clarified.

"From Atherius," Faythe breathed.

"You're sure it's from that particular bird?" Nerida chimed in from where she was sitting by a tree, organizing various herbs she'd spent the day gathering. Tarly tied them together, slipping them into a neat pouch, while she scribed what she found in a small journal.

"It's her... I can feel it," Faythe confirmed.

"That bird is a myth," Nik said, but when he met her flat look, he seemed to drop his skepticism. "Well, damn," he mused instead. "Want to enlighten me as to how you can be so sure then?"

"She's the bird you saw in my memory when you last Nightwalked to me. I...bonded with her."

She slid her gaze from Nik's surprise to the healer, whose smile was knowing, and then to Lycus, who gave a smirk from where he was leaning against the tree. Samara sat at his feet by Nerida, disconnected from their conversation as she was fascinated by Nerida's plants, forgetting the pretty flowers of her own she was assembling.

"Want to tell me how much you've taken of that to give you conscious abilities now?" Faythe asked, motioning to the vial.

Nik pocketed it. "One dose. Months ago in Olmstone. I only did so for the threats we faced. It was necessary."

Faythe pained at the wince he gave.

"Fascinating," Nerida said, standing now and brushing the snow from her skirt. The way she examined Nik was like she'd found an unsolvable puzzle. "You said neither of your parents had abilities?" She mulled over this. Faythe half-expected her to start scribing her findings about him in her journal too.

Nik confirmed with a shake of his head, sheathing his sword.

"You really are an anomaly. It's not common for those without magick to produce a child of one, never mind with the strength of it you possess."

"So I've heard," Nik brushed off, but there was a note in his tone that revealed he'd never settled with the knowledge either.

They were all shocked by a presence dropping from the trees, and they spun, turning their collective attention to the intruder. Faythe's fight faltered completely at the brilliant auburn hair she spied.

"Liv!" Kyleer was the first to close the distance in a few long strides before enveloping the commander in his large arms.

"How did you sneak up so easily?" Nik admired.

"A particular catlike talent," Kyleer answered for her with the brightest grin, reaching to tousle her hair.

Faythe smiled at their playful jostling. Her chest lightened a fraction to know Livia's safety was accounted for when they'd been trying to track her.

"What took you so long?" Faythe asked.

"I've been scouting," Livia explained. "Trying to find what I can."

"Have you found anything about——?"

"No." Livia cut Faythe off before her hope could spark. "Nothing about Reylan yet, but there's an enemy legion heading toward Fener, and I predict it will settle by nightfall. We'd be wise to move this camp before they get here. They outnumber us two-to-one."

Faythe asked Kyleer, "Do you think it's the same one that attacked the other camp?"

Kyleer hummed, his expression shifting with a firm battle focus. "What direction did they come from?"

"West, it would appear. They were all in black. Valgard soldiers, I believe."

"Marvellas's soldiers," Faythe corrected. "We can't keep blaming one kingdom when they could be just as much of a puppet as High Farrow was. A nation to take the blame."

"Even in history, under the rule of Mordecai, who lives again, Valgard has always been at odds with the rest of the continent."

"Even so. I won't condemn an entire country for their history," Faythe said. Then she directed her thoughts back to the impending army. "Two-to-one isn't that unmatched."

Livia said, "Our warriors here are still recovering, and we need time to get our generals and our legions in order to fight systematically."

Faythe didn't enjoy the itch in her that wanted this battle. To be on the front line and in the thick of it, cutting through Marvellas's forces like timber. Maybe this could be their greatest lead yet toward Reylan. It was selfish of her to want to fight.

Kyleer said, "We don't have enough time to move out as one. We'll have to get word to the other generals imminently to break off and divert. Some may have to stay behind."

Faythe nodded, accepting his guidance with this. Her anger shook. She felt like the mouse in Marvellas's maze, forced to scramble and hitting dead ends while the prey closed in.

"I'm staying behind," Faythe said.

"You're our leader, not a front-line soldier," Livia protested.

"Cale was right in that meeting. I'm powerful. People are counting on me, and I haven't done anything yet to show it."

"That's not true, and you know it," Kyleer said.

"Then I've not done *enough*," Faythe corrected. "I was a fighter before I was a queen. I can be both."

"I'm staying with you," Kyleer said.

"This might not be a prime concern," Samara chimed in timidly, "but with the plans to send everything you have to High Farrow, I have to wonder if Lord Zarrius still holds power there."

Nik swore, glancing at Faythe. "Do you know if he's still in your castle?"

He was the last person Faythe had considered with all that was happening. The last time she saw the lord was when she'd rejected his dance and he'd been silently infuriated.

Faythe shook her head. "We haven't had contact from inside. Their defenses around Ellium are strong—likely anticipating I would try to return. I haven't been able to Nightwalk to Jakon, Marlowe, or Izaiah. But someone like Zarrius has no more to gain there, like my hand in marriage. It would be wise to assume he's set his sights back on High Farrow knowing you'd be absent to go after Tauria."

Nik pinched the bridge of his nose. "That bastard won't quit in his pursuit of a crown, and this has all opened up in his damn favor."

"Would your council really be so swayed by his authority?" Tarly asked.

Faythe was familiar with Zarrius's attempt to gain Nik's kingdom with Samara as his pawn. She didn't doubt Zarrius was cunning enough to try again.

"He'll have lost credibility by now, I believe, but he's cunning. With me away from my council, I have no doubt he'll try to weasel his way through their minds," Nik said. He paced a few steps in thought.

"I'll go back," Samara said.

Everyone's surprised looks targeted her, and she shrank into herself.

"You're not going back to him alone," Nik said firmly. "Not after what he's done to you."

"Agreed," Faythe said.

"I'm the only one he'll let get close to him. He'll believe I've come back with nowhere else to go, and he likes to hold that kind of power over people," Samara said, finding more determination in her tone.

"Get close for what?" Livia asked.

"To kill him."

They all knew it was what had to happen. Zarrius was too unpredictable and would always pose a threat with his drive for power, but it was unexpected to have the task posed by the gentle high-born lady.

"Much as I like the sound of that, one suspicion and Zarrius wouldn't hesitate to kill *you*," Livia said.

When Samara glanced up at the commander, a blush fanned

across her pale cheeks before she resumed picking at the hem of her sleeve. "I appreciate everyone's concern despite what I've done. But I don't have much other purpose here. After I achieve his assassination, I can flee. I want to do this," she said.

"What you've done is forgiven and in the past. I won't let you become a fugitive for murdering a lord," Nik said firmly.

He'd come to care for Samara, and from what Faythe knew of her story, she could understand her actions somewhat, even though she'd made an attempt on Nik's life. If he could forgive it, Faythe could try too. It was all Zarrius's manipulation.

"I can escort her and make sure the careful movement of our armies is on track," Livia said.

That eased Nik and Lycus's concern.

Faythe shifted a glance to Tarly Wolverlon. He was looking paler by the day. It was clear his days were numbered, and Nerida wouldn't leave his side. The healer spent all her time with her herbs and her journal, fussing over Tarly when he tried to assure her he was well. He was anything but.

She exchanged glances with Nik, who, despite his typical adverse feelings toward the Olmstone prince, bore his own concern.

"We'll leave tomorrow night," Livia settled on. She crossed the space to Nik, unsheathing a small dagger and passing it to him. "You can Nightwalk to me to stay informed about High Farrow. It's in everyone's best interests to avoid any unnecessary conflict on the inside of our last stronghold."

Nik frowned at the dagger—a belonging of hers that would allow him to Nightwalk the long distance to her—but something else was on his mind. He reached for something hidden inside his jacket, and Faythe's eyes caught on the blade he produced with a missed beat of recognition in her chest.

"He'd want you to have this now," Nik said. "He gave it to me before we parted in High Farrow for the same reason."

It was Jakon's. Faythe would never mistake the aged, worn wooden handle of the first thing she'd ever been able to afford to gift to her best friend. Faythe took it vacantly, and though she was glad to have this piece of him with her, the blade that held so many memories in its steel split open a hollow void in her. She wished then she had another dagger—the one Marlowe had gifted her before her first fight against a fae—to have a piece of them both with her while they were parted. She hoped with every ache in her that they were staying safe in Rhyenelle's castle.

"Thank you," she whispered.

Nik wordlessly slung an arm around her shoulders.

Everyone was beginning to find their role in the march toward the end of this war, and every breath was held in the hope they'd all be standing when it came.

CHAPTER NINE

Zaiana

Zaiana had slept well. It should have been a relief, but the fact kept her on a prickly edge.

Her dream had been real.

The sleep demon had promised to lull her into a deep rest, and he'd done so. She didn't know what he wanted. Worst of all, she wouldn't be able to stop him infiltrating her mind again if he truly wasn't finished with her.

Zaiana marched Rhyenelle's halls as if they were the warped, cavernous walls of the Mortis Mountains. She'd allowed herself to soften too much with the kernels of weakness that had begun to plague her. Not anymore.

Maverick turned the corner toward her, and Zaiana was torn between wanting to kill him or demand what game he thought he was playing.

Zaiana intended to walk right by without engaging, keeping her eyes locked ahead and away from him. The bastard was dancing with death by sidestepping into her path.

"Get out of my way," she snarled, lifting her eyes to his dark irises, which narrowed at her reaction.

"Where are you going?"

Zaiana placed a hand to his chest to push him, but he didn't back down. His hand wrapped around her wrist, twisting to pin her to the wall, and she turned livid.

She only realized it wasn't a wall he'd pushed her against when he leaned in and the next second it was falling away from her back. Her focus dropped from him only to spin and avoid an embarrassing tumble through the door.

Hate boiled in her. Turning back to him, she couldn't see fully, as darkness engulfed them when the click sealed them in the room. The unknown tightened in her throat—only for a second before a blue flame ignited, and Zaiana breathed lighter with the illumination allowing her to map her surroundings.

Not a tight confinement.

They were in a small sitting room.

Maverick's expression was disturbed under the glow of his flame. Then he passed her, stopping at the table, and lit the two lanterns there.

"I'm going to kill you," Zaiana promised.

"I have never once doubted you'll be the death of me," he said, so calm in contrast to her fury.

"Why did you save me?" she snapped.

It had been tormenting her—how he'd caught her in the sky when she would have plummeted to her death.

Maverick took a long, bored breath as he leaned against the table and folded his arms. "I am very adamant you stay alive."

"So you can be the one to kill me?"

"Something like that."

Zaiana's nostrils flared. What had been reeling through her mind since she'd awoken came surging to the surface to use as a weapon now.

"I must commend you for playing the fool all these years, Maverick." The energy charged between them, growing with his slow steps toward her, which she stood unyielding against. "Or should I say, *Callen?*"

His gaze sharpened at the name. She hadn't been able to stop recalling Faythe's cry of it during the battle, and Zaiana had finally remembered why it was familiar.

"That person died a long time ago."

"That *prince.*"

"Does it matter?"

"You pretended not to know." Zaiana despised the fact she *hurt* because of it. That during their time in the cave, he'd led her to believe he'd been robbed of his fae life completely.

Or had she merely missed it? Mistaken his distance and pain as lost memories, not tragic ones he reflected on?

He was Callen Osirion, the fallen Prince of Dalrune.

"They think I don't remember anything," he confessed. "They took everything from me, and remembering what they did is the only thing I have against them."

It made sense. Only, she couldn't figure out why he'd gone so long without doing anything with it.

"What do you plan to do? Take back your kingdom?"

Maverick laughed—a resentful, bitter sound. "There is no kingdom to take back. Those lands are barren and overrun with dark fae. Their monarchy is gone."

"You're still here."

"I am *not* him," Maverick said firmly.

Zaiana didn't insist. Maybe she even agreed.

All this time…what had he been waiting for?

"Whose side are you on?"

"You know as well as I do there are no sides, only a course of survival that can change like the wind."

"I don't understand," she said.

Her head grew a dull ache in her storm of emotions and chaotic thoughts. It were as if her existence had been blasted wide-open, and she was scrambling to retain any pieces that would keep her from losing herself for good.

"You don't need to understand," he said, his voice dropping soft for a split second before it firmed to say, "But I trust you won't speak of this beyond that door."

Zaiana said nothing, still mulling over what the revelation meant. To him; to her. What it could mean to the world. She couldn't figure out what his motive was. After all he'd done… Killed Faythe. Then Agalhor. Dalrune had a living heir who'd made sure there would be no redemption for him should Marvellas fail.

"You haven't shown your lightning," Maverick said.

It turned her painfully stiff. Her skin pricked, fingers flexing in irritation as if it would conjure the bolts to prove him wrong.

Zaiana couldn't hide it anymore. Not from him when he would always be on her tail, but at least now she had a secret against him to trade, should he spill her temporary affliction.

"It's been silent since I woke."

Maverick massaged his forehead with one hand. "I figured."

She didn't voice her panic to ask how it was so obvious to him.

"How is that even possible?" he said, a note of *anger* tuning his tone. "Faythe seems to have all her abilities. Shit, it's almost like she keeps advancing no matter what."

"Yeah, well, she's practically the daughter of a Spirit. I'm the daughter of…nothing."

It was all Zaiana could think of that set them apart. Perhaps her magick was gone simply because she was weaker. Unable to resurface after a burnout that had taken her ability as punishment. This new train of torment had her wondering something she'd locked away for so long.

Who were her parents? Why she wanted to know was simply practical.

The Stormcaster ability wasn't common—did one of them have it? Or had it awoken from a long bloodline?

Were they even still alive?

Zaiana's back met the wall, and her head tipped against it. She was slipping. Crumbling. Overcome with questions she'd spent so long denying. She needed the answers, but they would only serve to wound her armor. Zaiana had made herself, and she didn't want anyone to try to take a piece of that because of *blood*. It meant nothing.

"Your power isn't only in your lightning," Maverick said, so quiet her head straightened to be sure he'd spoken.

He closed the distance between them, and she didn't have the will to push him away. They were sealed within four walls, and Zaiana let the exhaustion win for a moment of relief.

"It never has been. You know it too, and you need to get yourself together. You're better than all of them, with and without magick. It does not define you."

His proximity conflicted her. She fought a certain gravity that pulled them together against an impulse to gain distance. Then guilt. Sinking, dreadful guilt as she pictured another in his place.

"Stop," she said, anticipating the hand he began to reach up to her.

"Why?"

It kept rising slowly.

She had no answer.

Zaiana allowed his palm to meet her cheek. She didn't look up. Didn't want to risk snapping out of the feelings she'd tuned in to, trying to figure them out to grapple control of herself again. If she conquered what this was with Maverick, perhaps she'd be able to fight what weakened her about Kyleer.

So she let him angle her head back as warm wisps of his breath blew across her lips. Then her lids slipped closed as their mouths met. She came alive in ways she did in the face of an enemy, wanting to slay the threat Maverick had become. The adrenaline of battle was addictive.

He was the mirror she couldn't look away from. The centuries they'd shared, every conflict, transgression, and slip of passion, would always add a new crack to their shared tragic reflection. Because she couldn't stop attacking, and neither would he.

She kissed him back with the same demand, allowing his body to mold into her against the wall, and her back curved at the trail of his hand. While desire sparked across her skin, it wasn't without unease in her gut. That swimming note of *guilt* that she was only kissing him to know if she would feel anything.

She did. There was a pulse for him that echoed in the place a heartbeat should be. But it wasn't enough. For what? She didn't know herself, and this was a distraction she couldn't afford.

With a hand on his chest, she pushed him away.

They caught their breath in a matched stare of desire and hate.

"You tell anyone of this, and I'll make sure to ruin you with the betrayal of who you are to everyone around you, *Callen*."

Sharp words, and she watched them cut but didn't stay to witness the bleeding.

What had she been thinking?

She'd promised never to get close to him again, yet she'd craved it from him. The only thing that had made her stop…was the cruel and punishing emittance of another *firmer* pulse that wouldn't stop growing even when the commander was nowhere near.

CHAPTER TEN

Izaiah

A rodent wasn't his proudest form, but he gave it a try to scuttle to the large room Jakon and Marlowe were all but imprisoned to. Old kitchens, where their sole task was to make Phoenix Blood potions. He couldn't deny the thought of such a weapon at Marvellas's disposal made him wary, and he hoped they hadn't achieved many since Marlowe's magick wasn't that strong.

A few guards passed, but he kept close to the wall and dipped out of view where he could to avoid being swatted.

At his destination, he surveyed the gap between the door and the ground. He shifted again into a smaller mouse, but his body still only got halfway. Dammit.

Izaiah tried scratching furiously, but their weak human senses didn't come to investigate the sound.

A bird it would have to be.

Flying around, he landed on the awkward window frame of the high box windows and started pecking. As he did, he realized exactly *why* they'd failed to hear him. Izaiah threw his feeble bird body at the window to create more commotion, and only then did Jakon look, mercifully before he decided to begin undressing his wife.

He was glad they weren't being thorough in their potion making, but Izaiah wished the human could see his matching sour look. He didn't want to be here either.

He shifted as soon as he slipped into the window.

"You're late," Jakon grumbled.

"So you decide on a quick affair? Unless this is an invitation, which I am not opposed to—"

"Izaiah." Jakon cut him off. "What did you want?"

Jakon's tone of distrust was mutual.

Jakon had slipped the time he should come by in a note, handing it over when Izaiah had purposely knocked into him in the hall.

Then Izaiah had gotten a little too...*preoccupied* in the king's study to remember such a time.

"Is it done yet?" Izaiah asked.

Marlowe's concern swirled in her eyes before she nodded.

"It almost killed her," Jakon near snarled.

He shadowed his wince with a nonchalant shrug. "We all have prices to pay in this war."

"And what in the Nether is yours?" Jakon accused.

Izaiah's eyes narrowed at the response.

The human went on, "So far, you seem only to be benefitting since you haven't told us what it is you plan to do with the one thing Malin and Reuben are tearing apart the damned castle in search of."

Izaiah took a second to calm himself against the desire to strike out at Jakon for his prodding. It was justified, though he had no care to share that with them.

"Where is it?" Izaiah asked Marlowe without taking his eyes off her husband.

She shifted off the counter, going over to a pile of sacks and digging beneath them before returning.

"How do we know you won't just hand it over to them?" Jakon asked.

"Because I would have killed you both and done so by now." His attention landed on the intricately carved box Marlowe held. A shadowy touch pricked his skin. His tone softened for her. "Did you achieve the transfer spell?"

Her nod was a relief. Even if a foreboding and damning one.

Izaiah had enough of Faythe's blood on him when he'd retrieved her from the square. Enough for Marlowe to use on the Blood Box containing the Light Temple Ruin, transferring the ownership and binding his blood to it instead now.

Faythe had trusted Izaiah enough to show him where she was hiding the ruin: in catacombs hidden beneath the castle.

There was only one unsuspecting and cunning way down to those catacombs. She hadn't even told Reylan of it. Smart. The fewer minds that knew where it was, the better.

Izaiah planned to follow her sense in that regard.

"What do you plan to do with it?" Jakon asked warily.

"You know more than you should already," Izaiah said. He took a step to retrieve the box, but Jakon shifted. Izaiah stifled his ire to say, "You've done your part. Now hand it over and focus on the part where you escape."

"You're not coming with us?" Marlowe asked, pulling the box back to herself as if she doubted her actions in aiding him now.

"No," he ground out. His patience was running thin. "Is there a problem?"

Jakon said, "How do we know we can trust you?"

"Simple. You don't have a choice."

He tried not to be affected by their doubt. Everything was so blasted to shit he couldn't blame them. It wasn't safe for them to know, and he didn't need to be told of the consequences.

Finally, Marlowe extended the box to him. It was heavy in his possession. Not in weight but in dark whisperings.

"You know the route out to take—"

"I'm not finished yet," Marlowe interrupted.

Izaiah twisted back from his pivot to leave. "What do you mean?"

A full explanation flexed around her features, but the words floundered on her parted lips. Izaiah figured it was her Oracle gift that kept her grappling threads of the future, but at risk of reaching for the wrong one and what it could trigger if she spoke, she stayed silent.

He chose to ask instead, "Does Faythe know?"

"I told her I had to make the Phoenix Blood potion for Malin," Marlowe admitted, torn by her guilt. "I told her the kingdom would fall and that I would have to stay here. She knew we'd be standing on Marvellas's side at the end. I don't think she'll forgive me, but she asked me to try to make sure they couldn't make any more with the feather, and that's the part I have to do."

"They'll kill you if they find out you're purposely holding back."

Izaiah glanced over at the measly half-dozen vials of potions, which might not even all be spelled fully. The Phoenix feather was clipped into many pieces, with a large part still to be sectioned. Various other herbs and powders and liquids littered the space.

"I know what I'm doing," Marlowe assured him.

Izaiah looked at her, overcome with his own accusation, which he couldn't hold back now he knew she'd seen the kingdom's fall. "The king's death—did you know of it before?"

Marlowe's gaze fell, but he caught the answer in the crease of her brow and the way Jakon shifted as if to shield her from Izaiah's wrath at the truth.

"You did nothing?" Izaiah said coldly.

"What could she have done?" Jakon snapped in her defense.

"I didn't know when." Her voice turned small. "But I knew Agalhor had to fall for Faythe to rise."

"That's bullshit," Izaiah snarled. He couldn't suppress the rage that surged. "They would have risen together."

Marlowe didn't respond. Part of him felt for her—it couldn't have been easy to harbor the knowledge Faythe would be orphaned again without being able to tell her friend. The more he thought about the consequences if she had told her, the spiral Faythe would have fallen into to try to stop the unstoppable…it would have robbed them of the time they'd had left.

His resentment started to turn to understanding for Marlowe's position.

"Shit," Izaiah conceded, running a hand down his face.

It didn't make acceptance any less like swallowing knives. Izaiah hadn't grieved for the loss of his king. He couldn't. Because that wasn't all Agalhor had been to him, nor to Kyleer or Reylan. Izaiah had too much left to achieve, and mourning only served to split his composure. War didn't wait for the wounded to heal.

"Does Malin have something against you that forced you to stay and make those potions for him?" Izaiah diverted, needing to dissolve the marble growing in his throat.

Marlowe hugged her robe tighter around herself. "He threatened our lives, of course," she said bitterly. "But I would rather die than make another elixir for him to pass around their armies to make them stronger."

Jakon's energy changed with her unwavering statement. Terror for her life. Izaiah believed her. He even surfaced a kernel of guilt that he'd assumed her capable of any true betrayal.

"We had to find a way to stop the production. If Marlowe weren't making them, he would have found another human with spell magick, and we'd have had no eyes on the inside," Jakon explained.

Marlowe said, "I've seen so many versions of this war it's hard to keep up sometimes. In most of them, we lose. This is one path that doesn't end in our favor. If Malin gets enough of the Phoenix potions, the enhanced fae abilities, along with the dark fae armies on human blood, would make them unstoppable. There is a reason both enhancements were outlawed long ago."

It unfolded in clarity. Bone-trembling clarity. Izaiah stifled a shiver that felt like a lick of death at the downfall Marlowe painted. He fixed his eyes on the Oracle, now with an urge to go to his damn *knees* for the invisible suffering she endured. He couldn't imagine witnessing the very real—and very possible—death of everyone she loved and herself.

"You haven't explained your betrayal, which I'm trusting is false," Jakon cut in.

"Like you, I can't risk my course being found out or stopped."

"We told you ours," he protested.

"No offense, but I have higher hopes of evasion if they start to suspect me. Your plan is safe."

"Thanks for the confidence boost," Jakon remarked.

Izaiah turned for the window, but just before he shifted, he lingered a look back.

"Just stay alive," he grumbled, not enjoying the care that was starting to grow roots for them. "For Faythe's sake. It would be a shame to have her burn everything to the ground if she lost either of you."

CHAPTER ELEVEN

Tauria

Tauria had been assigned a handmaiden—a timid, young dark fae she'd liken to seventeen human years. She was beautiful, with inky black hair and eyes of the darkest brown. The top talons of her wings just peeked over her head.

"How long have you been in Fenstead, Edith?" Tauria asked while she sat in front of a vanity combing her hair.

The dark fae looked up to meet her reflection with shy surprise. "I was born here," she said.

That inspired a protectiveness in Tauria. Despite being dark fae—which, in her lifetime and her parents', had never been born in Fenstead—this made Edith one of her citizens.

"What do your parents do for work?" Tauria inquired.

Edith subtly flinched, sliding a final pin into a braid crowning Tauria's head. "My mother was killed by my father. He's…not a very good male. But a very powerful one."

That slammed Tauria with shock. How barbaric the story of her parents was, even in the vaguest form.

"I'm so sorry."

Edith smiled, wandering over to arrange Tauria's outfit on the bed. "I have a good life here," she said, losing herself in the task. "I have a new purpose—even more so now." Her dark eyes slipped to Tauria.

"The winter is growing colder," Tauria said. "Would you mind fetching us some tea to warm us?"

Edith considered this. It wasn't like servants to refuse such simple requests, but her court wasn't at all in the expected order.

Tauria planned to rebuild her court—her way. She had a week before her short trip to Valgard, and she was going to make the most of her time in her own kingdom.

When the handmaiden finally agreed and left Tauria, she immediately drifted past the emerald gown and dipped into the closet. Tauria dressed in all-black: a pair of tight-fitting pants and a tunic, with a belt for her staff. Slinging on a cloak, she hurried into the adjoining small dining area of this room she'd chosen deliberately for the escape passage that linked to it. There were several throughout the castle, and her chest squeezed that it was this one she'd taken to escape the day her kingdom was ambushed.

Throwing back the rug by the fireplace, she strained, gripping the latch to the door. Pushing her wind through the gap, she pulled it open, and it came up with far more ease.

Tauria descended the steps, closing the hatch and using her wind magick again to slip through the seal and blow the rug back into place. She felt mildly guilty thinking of Edith's panic when she'd return to find Tauria gone, but she planned to be back before Mordecai would request she join him for supper.

When the bite of winter caught her cheeks, Tauria took a moment to breathe the free air. No one observed her. No one told her what to do. Tauria embraced this moment of reclaimed freedom back on her lands.

Drawing her hood, she walked casually through the streets. There wasn't much traffic to lose herself in, so she merely observed the citizens, noticing how no one paid one another any attention. It was such a bleak contrast to the bustling joy she remembered filling these same roads. Strangers would greet each other, wishing good mornings and safe evenings. Smiles would be plastered on all faces, and as a child, she'd often thought Fenstead lived in its own realm of peace and happiness, disconnected from the burdens of the world she'd learned about in her schooling.

Tauria stopped by a shop she'd adored when she was young. It sold flowers and pottery, and every year, her mother brought her here for a treat. She always chose one of the beautifully painted saucers or cups, completely taken by the talent the shop owner possessed in her imagination and her skilled hands to paint such beauty.

Her reflection in the dull, cracked window sank with sorrow at the abandoned and destroyed shop now. How many more innocent places would she find stripped of all life and joy?

She headed inside anyway, out of nothing more than a deep nostalgic pull. Tauria's boots crunched over foliage that had swept in through the gap in the door, now hanging off one hinge. Then, when she stepped and heard a break, she looked down sadly at the shattered, daisy-painted saucer.

"If you're looking to loot the place, this is hardly going to trade you much coin." A smooth, feminine voice spoke from behind her.

Tauria's back stiffened. She tugged her hood over her forehead a little more and caught a glimpse of the person over her shoulder. "Did you follow me?" she asked.

"I merely wondered what kind of bandit would be interested in pottery. Though now I'm more intrigued as to what kind of bandit would think themselves valuable enough to be followed."

The fae was little more than a silhouette with the light behind her. She stepped closer, and Tauria could take in more features. She had dark, triangular-shaped eyes and a delicate, bow-shaped mouth. She also kept her hood up, clad in leather combat attire, but her long black twin braids fell above her breasts. Tauria was quick to take note of the many weapons she carried around her belt. Between her fingers, she twirled steel in the shape of a star with lethal pointed edges. The way it spun between her hands without cutting her marked this fae as dangerous.

"I'm no one," Tauria said—a pathetic attempt to sway this fae's interest off her, but her mind drew a blank.

The fae smiled. It was the kind of smile that surged Tauria's wind to her palms before the fae had even moved. When she did move, she was incredibly fast, sending the lethal metal star spinning toward her. Tauria's wind threw off its trajectory. It would have struck her shoulder. Instead it thumped into the wall behind her.

Tauria stared at the fae, incredulous at the unprovoked attack, and braced again. But the fae didn't retrieve another weapon. The attack had been a test, forcing Tauria to reveal her ability to confirm who she was.

"We've been waiting for you, Tauria Stagknight."

Her cover hadn't lasted long.

"Though don't expect a warm welcome."

"What is your name, and where are we going?"

Tauria realized she should have asked both of these questions before she followed this fae out the shop and down several familiar alleyways. Her mind was only at ease because of how well she knew the labyrinth of Calenmoore, so she could make a quick escape if needed, and she had her magick and staff to achieve it.

"My named is Tallia, and you're going to see that even though you abandoned us, we never lost our fight for Fenstead."

Tauria's whole body flushed hot. A marble grew in her throat since she couldn't protest or deny the accusation of having abandoned them. There wasn't a day since she'd left that she hadn't thought of Fenstead and remained determined to reclaim it one day—but all this time, she was about to discover, there'd been a resistance lurking in the shadows.

Tallia approached a drain used to prevent flooding. She scanned both sides of the lane before crouching, hauling the heaving metal open, and looking up at Tauria expectantly.

This was one series of passages running below her kingdom Tauria had never ventured. She didn't enjoy being underground.

"I assume you can't be gone long." Tallia sighed, impatient. "So if you want to start proving you're still our queen, hurry up."

Tauria may hold the title, but she'd lost the respect of people like Tallia. She understood, and this was her chance to start proving that her heart and her devotion would always be with Fenstead.

She climbed down the drain ladder. Her boots sloshed in the shallow pool at the bottom. These drains were hollowed-out cylinders, dark and cold.

Tauria followed Tallia, putting complete faith in her that this wasn't a trap. It may be reckless, but Tauria didn't have the time or the luxury to play it safe.

She soon picked up on voices, which sharpened all her senses, putting her on high alert.

"Keep quiet and just observe," Tallia warned under her breath.

The next tunnel opened into an expansive space. The floors were grates of metal, with a pole as a barrier on the balcony. As Tauria eased out, tucking herself behind some people, she couldn't believe the masses of bodies gathered several levels high in this underground system.

Those who spoke came from below, and Tauria couldn't help her curiosity, slipping through the gaps between bodies to edge closer to the rail and peer over.

Half a dozen fae stood as the center of everyone's attention. A gasp left her when she recognized two of them. General Saki Corrigan and Lord Berron Lumiah. They'd both been close with her father—she'd seen them often around the castle.

"Tauria's return means nothing for us now," someone from the crowd spoke out.

Her skin crawled to have intruded while she was the topic of conversation, but she needed to hear this.

"This is what we have been waiting for," Lord Berron said calmly.

"One hundred years ago, not now."

"Perhaps exactly now. One hundred years ago, we were broken and devastated. It was not the time to fight back but to rally the force we are today—for this moment."

"We don't need her. We've done just fine without her. *You* should rule, not her. You've been here all this time, not her."

Tauria's spine locked. A spark of hope had ignited at finding Lord Berron, who'd been so kind and encouraging to her, often referred to as an uncle. But if she found out he'd led this resistance with the motive to take her throne…

"Tauria Stagknight is our queen. Anyone who opposes that should speak now, as we are not on the same side, and I do not consider you an ally of Fenstead."

Relief slackened her posture.

Tauria couldn't stand here and watch them debate her integrity. She pulled down her hood. Gripping the pole, she ducked under it, leaning her weight over the edge as she slipped her shortened staff free.

"Loyal until the very end, Lord Berron," she announced, seizing the heavy attention of the hall as it broke into murmurs.

He glanced up, and the moment he smiled she knew she never should have doubted him for a second.

Tauria flicked the lever on her staff, extending it to midway. As she let go of the rail and fell, she twisted it between both hands, unlocking the full length, and conjured the will of the wind through it to land in an elegant brace.

Before the air stopped swirling, Berron hurried his steps to meet her. They collided, and it took everything in her not to break into sobs with the welcome embrace of home. In his strong arms, Tauria realized he was the closest she had left to a father figure.

"Oh, my dear Tauria. Just as we've been planning a movement of infiltration to reach you within those castle walls," he said.

They released each other, and she was overcome with love staring into his deep brown eyes inside dark skin, which had aged with more lines since last she'd seen him.

He cupped her cheek as concern pulled between his wiry brows. "This might not be the best time for you to be here. There is much unrest with your arrival."

Glancing over his shoulder, she saw the other four fae leading this resistance certainly didn't seem pleased to see her, but Saki cast her a small smile, approaching and pulling her into an embrace.

"Welcome home," Saki said, her voice a gentle song of her homeland.

It was the first time anyone had said those words. Words she'd longed to hear for a lifetime. Once again she struggled to hold herself together.

"I found our queen wandering recklessly through the east town," Tallia said.

Tauria turned, finding her leaning with arms crossed against a pillar, fiddling a new metal star between her fingers, which Tauria eyed warily.

Someone called out, "How do we know she isn't a spy for the Nether lord?" Their bitterness wasn't subtle.

Another sneered. "She's only here as his bride after all."

Berron's eyes slipped to her with a wince. "There are many questions regarding your unexpected arrival. With all the rumors of Transitioned dark fae, your near marriage to Tarly Wolverlon, and your possible mating with Nikalias, you'll understand we have only snippets of information."

"I want to explain all. You deserve no less, and I have nothing to hide," Tauria said, loud enough for everyone to hear. She looked up, wandering around the circumference and taking in the many frightened, angry, and upset faces of her people. Those who hadn't given up on Fenstead. It was now her chance to convince them not to give up on *her* as their queen.

Tauria Stagknight told her story. No one disturbed her, and she watched many emotions pass through the people who listened to her every word. She told them what had happened the day she fled. She told them about her mate, Nik, and about their dreams for High Farrow and Fenstead. She spoke of the war far beyond the belief it was one kingdom responsible for their terror. Tauria explained as best she could about the Goddesses in their realm and everything she and her friends had done so far toward eradicating the greatest threat their continent had ever seen.

When she finished, Tauria retired from the center of attention.

"You did well," Berron when she reached him at the side of the floor.

All her tales and information had left the crowd chatting among themselves, absorbing it all and deciding whether they trusted her word.

"That's still up for judgment," she said.

Tauria couldn't be certain *she* was safe in being here. If there was even one potential traitor or someone who opposed her, they could easily put her in peril if word of her appearance at a resistance reached Mordecai.

Movements in war were never without risk.

"I need to be getting back," Tauria said.

"I'll go with you, just to the entry point," Saki offered.

"When will we next see you?" Berron asked.

Tauria's gaze slipped to Tallia, who hadn't moved from where she was leaning against the pillar. When their eyes met, whatever she read in Tauria had her straightening up, a protest lining her face.

"I don't think it's safe for me to wander out too many times, but I think I have an idea," Tauria said.

CHAPTER TWELVE

Zaiana

Her vision occasionally blurred, but Zaiana blinked hard and focused on her footing. She wouldn't lie in a sorry state a moment longer. Not with the battle won and movements being made without her.

Under her leathers, her skin was still sticky with heat, yet her teeth were bashing at the winter chill that swirled in from the open arched hall she stormed through. She should have equipped herself with a damn cloak. If this was only the beginning of winter, they'd be bracing for a long and miserable season.

Snow flurried beautifully, only light, and not enough to gather, though some of the ground was frosted white.

"You're still recovering," Amaya fussed, creeping up to her.

Zaiana's retort died when she beheld the black cloak the darkling extended with a warm smile. She slung it around her shoulders with ease as she kept her wings glamoured.

"I see you made a perfect recovery yourself," Zaiana observed, remembering the weak state she'd found the darkling in inside the cell after months of imprisonment.

Amaya nodded, and under the added weight and warmth, Zaiana's body wasn't so rigid anymore.

"Yes. Maverick found a healer. We didn't know if you would make it. At one point, you even stopped breathing, and Maverick, he—"

Amaya paused, and so did Zaiana's steps.

"He—what?"

Amaya shifted a look around as if he were lingering. Her head shook tendrils of loose black hair over her pale skin. "I'd never seen him so desperate for anything. He cast us all out, except for the healer, until you were stable again."

Why he wanted her back so desperately she could only imagine. He must be Nether-bent on making sure they were tied there together in the end for eternal torment.

Was that really what she believed?

Zaiana shook her head to expel the thoughts of him and winced with the error that throbbed an ache. She pushed forward in distraction.

"Where's Tynan?"

"He's been stationed as Malin's right hand, though I don't think he's thrilled with the *esteemed* position."

That arrogant bastard prince.

The title of "king" didn't feel befitting for a coward who had a throne stolen for him. He was nothing more than another puppet for Marvellas.

"Dakodas is still here," Amaya went on before she could ask. "Though she hasn't imposed much. Malin has been ordering a send-out for traitors—any guard or warrior who didn't make it out and refuses to swear allegiance to him."

Zaiana could admire their loyalty. Even though hollow words in surrender to Malin would keep them safe, and even though their king was dead…these fae had chosen their allegiance to Faythe already.

She could hardly think of the impossible heir without flashbacks of their battle threatening to undo her. Zaiana was so weakened, both in body and mind. From Faythe and her insufferable companion. The brother who'd fled, and the other…

"Where is Izaiah?" Zaiana asked.

She would start with him to gather what she'd missed.

He was up to something, and Zaiana wanted to be the first to figure it out.

"I'm not sure. Malin often requests Tynan to keep an eye on him, but I don't see either of them a lot. Tynan finds me before I find him, usually."

"Zaiana." Maverick's sharp tone pricked at her back.

She didn't stop walking despite Amaya's wary gaze settling on her.

"Are you trying to force yourself out of commission for six more weeks by pushing yourself so soon?" he continued, creeping up to her.

"I'm walking, Maverick. Hardly in combat," she drawled. Her body shivered at his proximity by her side. "Though if you keep antagonizing me, I'm willing to risk that."

"Must you see everything as a rule to defy?"

"When it comes to you, yes. I find it keeps me motivated."

He huffed dryly. "You're impossible."

"What do you want?" Zaiana bit out.

She didn't want his company. Not with the conflict she harbored around him.

"I came to bring you a tonic from the healer for your fever," Maverick grumbled.

"What duty has the Dark Spirit imposed on you to make you so desperate to avoid it by taking on the role of servant?"

Zaiana almost missed the flex of his eyes, a wince, as he quickly switched to match her ire.

"It's all a bit dull around here," he said blandly. "Truthfully, I'm glad you're finally up to offer some entertainment."

"What are the next movements?" Zaiana asked.

"Nothing. They took the city and placed a rather insufferable fae on the throne as king. Marvellas took Reylan away almost immediately after Faythe left."

"Where?"

Maverick shrugged, slipping his hands into his pockets, and she wondered if it was her fever making the cold sharper while he wandered around without a coat or a cloak. With them back indoors and the fire torches around them adding heat, she realized she'd never questioned before if his ability made winters more tolerable.

He answered. "They haven't told us anything. I'm hoping they're waiting to see if you'll pull through."

Zaiana shuddered at the ghost of a presence, as though death were whispering nearby.

In the throne room, she found who she was looking for.

All of them.

Malin Ashfyre reclined lazily on the throne, while three fae were on their knees before the dais. Tynan stood by him, casting a look at Zaiana as she entered, and though he remained poised, his face relaxed as if she were a ghost. Then, across the room, leaning against a pillar cloaked in shadow, Izaiah met her eye with familiar cool loathing.

"Ah, *Master* Zaiana," Malin said as he spied her.

The sharp tip of her iron claws bit into her palm at the taunt she heard in that title. Maverick shifted like a shadow turning darker.

"I'm glad you're finding your feet at last. Perhaps you want to warm up that striking ability you have to execute these traitors for me?"

Her chest hollowed out. Less than five minutes, and he'd already unwittingly upper-handed her. She couldn't let anyone know of her stifled lightning.

"I didn't come here to waste my time on your petty kills," she sneered to him.

It was a great satisfaction to rile him—one who thought he'd won his crown. It was only a matter of time before he realized it would never fit right.

"Then why did you come?"

"To find out what *king* could possibly see any advantage in murdering his own warriors, fit to fight for him in war. You'll gradually outnumber your ranks with this path."

"They had their trial. They do not fight for me."

"They fight for Rhyenelle. And perhaps their lack of allegiance says more about you."

Malin drew his sword, but all Zaiana saw was a toothpick.

Tynan remained still but braced at the threat in case she gave a signal to intervene. Maverick merely strolled casually away from her, a hint of a cruel, amused smile at the edge of his lips. Izaiah finally straightened, studying her and the false king.

He wore the crown, and Zaiana couldn't be sure why her anger surged with bloody violence, wanting to tear his head from his shoulders and watch the metal fall.

She said calmly, "Lock them up or let them go, so we might discuss matters that advance our strategy, not our egos."

"You don't make the demands here," Malin seethed.

"No." A dark voice of sin and seduction eased around the room as if it were crafted from the darkness. "I do."

Dakodas glided from a pool of shadow and stars. Zaiana bit down on her cheek at the sight of it and the unwelcome feelings it stirred within her to remember the touch of such dark beauty from Kyleer.

Malin stepped down from the dais, his sword raised, and something feral widened his eyes and locked his jaw before his blade came down without hesitation on one of the guards. It wasn't strong enough to behead them, and the fae choked on blood that echoed gargling sounds around the hall as Malin shifted his evil intent to the fae beside him.

Izaiah advanced two steps with livid fury, targeting the prince as he drove his sword through the chest of the next.

What overcame Malin Ashfyre was the snap of something he'd been clinging to the tether of for some time, and maybe…Zaiana could relate in that moment.

Being undermined.

Overpowered.

Undervalued.

As Malin killed the final guard—slitting his throat—his chest heaved, and Zaiana recognized the cloud of fury and resentment that started to disperse in his caramel eyes at the realization of what he'd done.

The ground pooled with so much blood that Zaiana shallowed her breathing against the craving to drink. She flicked her sight to Maverick, who strained with a dark stare at the fallen bodies. His lust for blood would always be a far more primal instinct than hers as a Blackfair—the insatiable curse of the Transitioned—but she commended him for his restraint when he didn't cave and seek out the closest human.

Dakodas appeared before Malin in a stroke of shadow, gripping his chin to lock his stare. Everyone stood still, unknowing of what her reaction would be at his display of carnage.

Zaiana didn't expect Dakodas to smile wickedly. She'd *enjoyed* it. Death. As the maiden of it, of course she would.

She wondered if even in this realm Dakodas might feel power from the passing of souls.

"I have been waiting for you to break out of the shadow your uncle placed you in. I knew it was not a mistake convincing Marvellas to give you this throne," she said, admiring the prince's blood-splattered face.

Malin was coming back to himself, his eyes turning wide as if he were only just acknowledging the new soul-tarnishing act he would harbor for the rest of his days.

Zaiana followed Tynan's attention to where Izaiah seemed to be restraining his impulse to lunge at Malin.

Izaiah reeled himself back slowly. Masterfully. Slipping into a mask he knew how to wear like several others. She didn't like him. Worse, she despised the fact she still owed him a debt when he'd been the one to make sure Amaya and Tynan stayed alive in their captivity by bargaining with him.

"Dakodas." Zaiana spoke boldly.

The Spirit's attention slipped to her, dropping her hold on Malin along with the smile she wore for him.

"I came to find out where I can best serve." She would take anything. She needed something to keep her mind occupied fully.

"Are you sure you are at your best strength to take on anything asked of you?"

Dakodas was almost goading her. Testing her.

"Yes," she said.

"Good. I worried for a moment you would be of no use to us any longer."

"That won't happen."

Zaiana forced down the unease in her stomach at the secret she harbored. She *would* be of no use if they discovered her magick was silent. Her fingers flexed subconsciously, as if a spark might touch her fingertips at any moment.

"Be that as it may. Your recent failure against Faythe Ashfyre has left me doubtful of your capabilities against her."

That name seemed to be Nether-bent on haunting her until one of them was in the grave.

"If you send me, I will capture her."

"Marvellas already has a plan for that."

Zaiana ground her teeth. "Then let me join."

"I think not. You'll remain here. You can oversee the legion of our army moving in from the west. They should be making their way through Rhyenelle, and their current general will be stepping down soon."

Leading a legion. Zaiana had done that before she was even Delegate of her bloodline. Being a leading general might be of high esteem in army ranks, but in her world, it was so far below where she had earned the right to be.

"I can do better than that," Zaiana insisted.

"You'll take over when they reach Fenher in a week."

Just like that, Dakodas dismissed her like a child.

Zaiana's blood was boiling, but she didn't flinch. Out of the corner of her eye, she saw Izaiah slip out through a side door, and right now, she'd only risk enraging Dakodas if she pushed for a better station.

"As you wish," Zaiana said, bowing her head.

She despised the submission, but she wanted to stay alive.

Turning, she exchanged a look with Maverick. He knew she wasn't pleased, but he didn't follow her since Dakodas requested him to stay.

He hadn't failed at all, and she had no right to the bitter thoughts that he'd likely earned a higher place in the Spirit's plans for war.

To distract herself from the ugly resentment stirring in her, Zaiana followed Izaiah out. She kept as silent as an assassin, tracking him, until he walked down an abandoned hall.

She intended to catch him unaware, but he knew she was there. Izaiah was more observant than she gave him credit for.

His hand caught her wrist, but Zaiana twisted under their arms, bending his arm behind his back. Izaiah was also stealthier than she anticipated.

He kneeled, hooking a hand behind her nape, and Zaiana braced for the impact of being thrown over his shoulder. She groaned at the sharp pain shooting up her spine but stopped struggling at the hand around her throat.

Not because she couldn't get out of the compromised position, but because she faltered in fascination.

"You're not the only one with claws," he said.

Izaiah pushed off her, and she propped herself up on her elbow, watching his skin fade from short black fur to beige skin as his five lethal talons retracted.

He folded his arms, then her ire grated as she became aware of her humiliating position on the ground.

Zaiana pushed herself to her feet. "At least I don't use them to betray my own."

This earned a dark stare from him.

"Have you come to find out what you owe me? After I made sure your companions stayed alive. Tynan might have managed on his own. The little darkling would have surely died without my help."

It was what had been lingering on her mind since waking up. That, and she hoped to gauge what he was up to in staying behind here.

"Out with it then."

Izaiah smiled, and it was a victory she wanted to carve from his face.

"I want to know how you wield a ruin."

Zaiana's face relaxed. He had to be joking. But his stern brow didn't flinch.

"You know where it is, don't you? The Light Temple Ruin your little traitor is scouring for."

It was all the poor human Reuben knew in his new tragic existence under Marvellas's influence. Izaiah had all but exposed that Faythe hadn't had the chance to take it with her.

"Can you teach me or not?"

"You don't know what you're asking for," she hissed. "No sane person would willingly want to touch the power that lives within them."

"I didn't claim to be sane."

"It is not kind—not a fantasy that will grant you an easy upper hand. To even attempt to merge with such an amplifier is a torture you think you can handle until it's too late."

"You seem to be thriving just fine," he observed.

She hated the sting within her with every mention of her magick while she couldn't wield it.

"It wasn't without great difficulty, and many times, I almost never made it. They forced it upon me without a care whether I lived or not. They've tried many others since, desperate to have a personal army of unparalleled magick wielders able to turn their abilities to something unmatched."

"You're the only one?"

"Yes."

As far as she knew at least. She'd never heard of anyone else conquering it, only of their deaths for trying.

Despite her warning, Izaiah didn't flinch. Gave no indication that the high possibility it could claim his life frightened him. It exposed a new side to the fae she didn't expect. Something cold and distant. She wondered if his companions had ever seen past the layers he wore for a crowd.

"This is my request," he said calmly.

Zaiana gave an exasperated breath.

Then a flare of *hope* erupted. What if exposing herself to a ruin could drag her magick forth?

"Where is it?" she asked with a new urgency that didn't go unnoticed.

"I'm not such a fool to take you right to it yet."

"Then how else am I supposed to teach you?"

"I'm sure you'll figure it out. There's always steps to be learned without ever lifting a sword."

Her jaw clenched. "It's not a moral weapon."

"If you don't," Izaiah went on, ignoring her, "I won't be coming for you. No. You like to pretend that still heart of yours can't feel—

make people think there's no way to hurt you, but there is. Two ways, in fact, within reach. And I won't hesitate to kill them and watch your black heart bleed for them."

His threat toward Tynan and Amaya flared a wild rage under her skin. She should have felt the heat of her lightning, and that stillness only riled her to a maddening degree.

Zaiana took a second to calm her fury, as she'd done so many times in her life when the masters had pushed her for a reaction. Only to punish her for lashing out.

She wrote deadly promise in her eyes, closing the distance to Izaiah. "You think I don't know?" she taunted.

His jaw shifted at her slow assessment of him, the energy between them charged with electric challenge, and in those green eyes he knew what she found.

"A good attempt at masking Tynan's scent—I'm sure it's working for most. You're a damned fool if you thought I wouldn't see it. Not only in scent—it's written over every damned inch of both of you in a room together. Let me tell *you*, Izaiah. If you harm him, I'll tear the heart from your chest and let the last beat of it shudder at his feet."

"You don't get to threaten me with that," he hissed, matching her standoff. "Not after what you did to Kyleer."

Zaiana almost winced. Then, there it was: a common ground she hadn't seen coming.

"Is that what this is? Your attempt to get back at me for your brother by leading on Tynan?"

"Maybe it is," he sneered.

His heartbeat betrayed his words. Zaiana had tuned herself in to it the moment she'd begun to follow him. Izaiah's was well-mastered. She'd never found one that could remain so steady even when she was sure his emotions would strike to give away anything his straight face wouldn't. Until now, with the subject of Tynan, it had sped for just a few seconds before it could be tamed.

"Don't test me," Zaiana said, beginning to walk away. "You won't like how it ends."

CHAPTER THIRTEEN

Faythe

Faythe had passed another birthday. She was now twenty-one years old, and as she stared over the thick winter hills, her cheeks nipping and an icy breeze blowing through her hair, she wondered if she would get to see the hundreds more birthdays her fae immortality should grant, or if that were a cruel illusion. A promise turned to deceit if this war should freeze her years like the winter froze any new bloom.

Nik had been the one to remind her this morning, otherwise she wouldn't have noticed the day. It didn't really matter—she'd barely been able to surface a smile for it. He'd tried to insist they enjoy a night of drinking and forgetting, but Faythe couldn't—not even for a moment.

She fiddled with the gold star necklace Nik had given her for her birthday last year while he sat opposite her. He'd shown up at her tent with a hearty breakfast and an apology he couldn't get her a gift this year. The necklace was all the treasure she needed form him for a lifetime. Something she could use to reach him through Nightwalking anywhere.

"You said you needed to tell me something," Nik said, tossing a grape up and down.

Recalling she'd said that at the inn, Faythe figured now was as good a time as any.

"Do you believe in past lives?"

"I should have known it wouldn't be something mundane."

His lightheartedness was always something she'd valued about Nik. He was the first to believe in her abilities, and just...*her*.

Nik said, "I guess in some ways I think we could come back. In a different form, perhaps only as an energy."

"What if there was a Spirit or other Gods that could meddle to bring one back in mortal form again?" She slipped him a tentative side-glance for his reaction.

"Just tell me what you're trying to tell me before I jump to the wildest conclusion."

"I think..." *Gods*, her heart was racing. She'd thought these things over, not really having whole truths, only assumptions she'd only told Kyleer so far since fleeing Ellium. "I think Marvellas might have brought me back. She's the Spirit of Souls after all. I get flashes of visions sometimes, and I think they're from long ago, around the start of the war with Marvellas. When I met you and Tauria, something always felt frustratingly missing. I would train with you as if I should be able to contend. As if I *should* be like you. I think it's because my soul was fae all that time ago."

She took slow breaths when it felt like confronting a lie—that her whole existence as *Faythe* was false, and this past she did not know wanted to shroud her in helplessness.

Nik said gently, "There are so many things that have tried to make you see yourself differently. You've combated them every time. If this is true, then what does it change, really?"

"I knew him, Nik," she confessed. Tears swelled. Her thumb twisted the golden butterfly ring on her other hand with a growing ache. "Reylan. I knew him then—I'm sure of it. I think I took his memories before I died, and I don't know if he'll ever forgive me."

"He will."

"How can you say that?"

"Because it won't matter to him. When you've spent so long waiting for that one person to take on the world with, everything that came before them becomes insignificant."

"I betrayed him."

"You saved him. If you'd died, Reylan would have followed. That, I'm certain of. He has nothing to lose, Faythe. Nothing as great as you. Then Marvellas would have carried out her plan, and he wouldn't have been here, waiting for you to return, even if he didn't know it."

Faythe hadn't considered that. Though she wanted to deny Reylan would follow her to such an extreme, she knew in her heart he would.

It killed her to be so sure of his devotion, but *Gods*, was she over-whelmingly grateful to have him.

"How are you so calm about this?" Faythe asked, wiping the stray tear that began to fall.

Nik gave a chuckle, throwing the grape into his mouth and chewing. "I found a human who could Nightwalk. Who turned out to be the unknown daughter of one of the greatest kings of our time." He cast her a gentle smile, and Faythe's chest warmed for her father. "We discovered a dark extinct species is, in fact, not so, and that they're out for vengeance with a back-from-the-dead high lord. A second almighty Spirit entered our realm. I don't think there's anything out of the range of possibility anymore, nor do I think we're done being faced with challenges. Acceptance is the only way it won't shock us beyond being able to figure out what in the Nether we do next."

Faythe absorbed everything he said. Treasured his wisdom. Her eyes slipped closed with liberation. She couldn't imagine more perfect company right now.

"Maverick..." Faythe shuddered involuntarily at speaking his name. "Callen—that's what you called him when I showed you my memory of the fire mountains."

Nik's expression fell, vacantly studying the table. "As Callen Osirion, the Prince of Dalrune, he was my friend. Not close in the ways people expect. I didn't see him often, and then the Great Battles happened, and his kingdom was collapsed completely. High Farrow, Olmstone, and Rhyenelle sent scouts to see if any of the royal family had survived, but all they found was the kingdom in worse wreckage than Fenstead. No one could have imagined Callen..." Nik trailed off, pain written in his features.

"Maverick isn't that person you knew." Faythe tried to console him.

"Does he remember who he was?"

She knew the answer wasn't what he wanted. "Yes, I believe he does, though I don't know when he started to remember."

Faythe wouldn't absolve Maverick for a single heinous choice he'd made, but she couldn't help that her heart had started to separate the dark fae from the former prince. In the end, they were one and the same, but for Nik and the friend he knew, for a prince that had his will and his life stolen, maybe she could understand just a little.

"I want to talk to him—just one last time," Nik confessed.

She couldn't be sure they would ever get that chance, so she didn't respond.

After a quiet moment, Nik said heavily, "Mordecai is taking Tauria to Valgard. She told me last night."

Faythe dropped her last piece of bread with that information.

"Have any of you ever been across to that island?"

"No. All our lives, we've stayed far away. Even before my father was compromised as Marvellas's servant, he'd never in all his battle plans or talks with the other kingdoms considered leading an attack on the county they believed responsible for the war."

"What makes them so frightening?"

Nik contemplated. "I guess their history of the Dark Age. No one even knows who's ruled over there since. The kingdom might be in disarray, and that's why Marvellas took over before bringing Mordecai back."

"Why would he be taking Tauria there now?"

"I can't be sure. I'm terrified for Tauria. It's killing me that she's alone in this, but as she said in her letter, this is an opportunity to see inside enemy territory that's never been possible before now. She's afraid but also so damn brave and confident."

Faythe was also torn with immense concern for her friend. Nik's pain and turmoil ripped through her.

"I believe in her," she said.

"Me too. I just wish I could be with her."

The somber silence left them picking at the last of the breakfast.

"While Tauria is gaining advantages, we should keep ourselves busy doing the same," Faythe said.

"What do you suggest?"

"With all forces heading to High Farrow, that's where we'll make our stand. In the meantime, we have to gain as much as we can before we head there ourselves. *With* Reylan and Tauria."

Nik inhaled, long and deep. "Agreed. I plan to head to Fenstead when Tauria returns from Valgard. If we can't reclaim Fenstead, we can still retrieve her, and maybe she'll have something valuable to use against Mordecai."

That gave them both a lift of pride and hope. Tauria was brilliant.

"While I still have you, want to accompany me on a quest the others might try to argue against?"

Nik's slow smirk of deviance was all the confirmation she needed. "Now I'm intrigued. Spill it."

"Just meet me at sundown."

"It's only sunrise—you're keeping me on edge all day?"

Kyleer called out and came into her tent. "You didn't tell me it was your birthday!" he exclaimed upon entry.

She shot Nik an accusing look, but he held his hands up.

"I didn't tell him."

"I did," Livia said, slipping in around Kyleer's dominating form. "Reylan told me. He…was planning a surprise dinner he wanted my help with before everything happened."

Faythe's heart plummeted.

Livia quickly added, "No sulking today—he'd be beside himself if he saw it. You're coming with us."

She wasn't in the mood to go anywhere, but Livia anticipated that, crossing the few short strides to her and hauling Faythe up despite her disgruntled protests.

The market she was dragged to was bustling by the afternoon. Nerida and Samara had joined them, and Faythe had to admit it was nice to be in the company of just her female friends as they wandered aimlessly through the stalls, losing themselves to pretty things for a while.

Livia lifted a pink scarf off a table, draping it around Samara. "Pink is definitely your color," the commander said.

Samara blushed, and Livia's smile dropped as if she hadn't meant to be so bold.

"Green is certainly yours," Nerida said, the savior in their spiral of awkwardness as she plucked a sage version of the same item and held it up. She was right—it complimented Livia's auburn hair beautifully.

"I'd choose gold for you," Faythe said, joining in with the light-hearted fun and swiping a golden shawl to wrap around Nerida.

She giggled, and finally, Samara chose one too, grinning brightly.

"Red for our Phoenix Queen, of course," she said, her tone naturally so polite with the elegance of court imbued in her.

Faythe accepted the deep red sheer material, glad Samara was beginning to ease into their company when she'd arrived quite reserved.

This kind of normalcy made her pine after Tauria and Marlowe a little harder, but she was trying to enjoy the day with the high spirits of Livia, Nerida, and Samara lifting her.

Nerida linked arms with her after they'd purchased the scarfs, keeping them on though they certainly didn't match the leather

Rhyenelle attire they all wore. It was more for sentiment than stylish appeal. Faythe had picked two more—a sky-blue for Marlowe, and an emerald-green for Tauria—in a silly effort to keep them close today.

They stopped to admire some brass trinkets and jeweled daggers. Samara reached her fingers up to rattle a beautiful wind chime. The sound pulled Faythe's focus, tunneling her away from the chatter of the town. She watched the small metal rods dangle.

A breeze pushed by her, tangled with a presence that pricked the hairs at her nape. Faythe's sight shifted, finding a tall, hooded, and masked figure about to pass them through the bustling crowds. Her attention tacked onto him, but she didn't know why—only that her heart picked up, and there was nothing in her senses besides this person and the gentle chime above her.

They passed by Faythe, nearly brushing her arm, and it was then her sight fell again, catching on the quickest glint of ruby where his sleeve lifted.

Her world stopped still.

It couldn't be…

Faythe was pushing through the crowd after him without a missed beat. The siren in her mind was all that rang now, maybe misleading her into thinking it was the amulet with the Eye of the Phoenix on this person's wrist.

The one she had slipped onto Reylan's wrist before they were separated.

People complained about her lack of grace as she pushed through the tight throng, but her heart was desperately reaching after him. She hadn't been able to see his eyes or much of his face at all, and now he was only flashes of dark clothing escaping her.

Faythe became more frantic, trying to push faster, but when she finally caught a clear breath, the bodies lessening, she'd come to an intersection. She spun, glancing down each path, but the figure was gone. Tears welled in her eyes out of utter frustration and misery.

Had Reylan been right in front of her, and had she let him slip away again?

She couldn't breathe. Faythe doubled over to brace her hands on her thighs with the dizzy, sweeping overwhelm and the scream she had to bottle. She focused deeply, recalling the familiar pulse of power from the Eye of the Phoenix she'd once worn herself. She searched within for her bond to Reylan. Despite it not being fully claimed, a part of him always resided within her.

"A warning before you run off like that next time."

Livia's call of outrage as she caught up to her severed any threads of the bond Faythe was trying to reach. She straightened, forcing back her whimper and tightening her fists, so as not to lash out at the commander.

"What did you see?" Nerida asked—a far more gentle reception than Livia.

She debated sharing. It would only seem like she was losing her mind in her desperation.

"Sorry," she said in a subdued voice, coming down from her high of adrenaline. "It just looked like someone I knew, but I was wrong."

"Valgard soldiers could be anywhere now—we have to stay vigilant and stick together," Livia groused.

Faythe only nodded vacantly. Nerida's gentle touch guided her again, and the Lakelarian healer wore only a smile of kindness.

"Ooh, a fortune teller!" Samara said excitedly.

Faythe wanted to return to camp after her disappointment just now, but the High Farrow lady was already making her way over to the purple tent down the market, and Livia was quick to follow.

"I'll wait outside," Faythe said, not in any mood to have some vague false foretelling of how her future would go.

"I always loved when fortune tellers came to the city in High Farrow. Many don't believe in them, of course, but I always feel a sense of…enlightenment," Samara gushed.

For the joy it brought her, Faythe appreciated the novelty.

Samara went inside, and Livia insisted none of the group should be alone and went with her. When it was just Faythe and Nerida left outside, her wandering gaze settled on the healer, who was already studying her.

"Want to talk about what you really saw?" Nerida asked patiently.

Faythe shifted on her feet. "I'm just exhausted and overwhelmed. I thought it might have been Reylan."

It sounded foolish to admit out loud. As if he would be wandering so freely in Fenher after being captured by Marvellas.

"How so?"

The fact she didn't immediately hit her with sympathy and simply accepted the delusion surprised Faythe.

"I thought I felt the amulet I gave him."

"The Eye of the Phoenix?"

Faythe nodded, and the healer's brow furrowed thoughtfully.

"It would be quite hard to mistake that unique power."

Hope skipped in her chest. Was Nerida suggesting she might have been right?

Nerida said, "Though it's likely Marvellas found it on him and threw it away. Perhaps it was found and sold."

Then her hope winked out completely. That explanation was a blow to her chest. It was logical.

Faythe gritted her teeth at the mockery. She wanted to hunt the person down anyway just to get that amulet back. It was her family's heirloom.

Samara's giggling drew their attention to where she and Livia had emerged, holding small pieces of parchment. The lady's brightness turned to a faint scowl as she read hers again.

"Not very enlightening this time," Samara mumbled. "What did she say to you?"

Livia was snapped out of her thoughts by Samara's question, and she crumpled the paper she held. Samara pouted that she hadn't gotten a peek, but Faythe observed the commander seemed...flustered. It was amusing to witness her like this when Livia carried herself so firmly most of the time. Now the commander was blushing, not meeting Samara's eye.

"A load of false promises as usual," Livia muttered.

Samara held hers out to Faythe, who took it curiously. "Maybe you could find a deeper meaning for me. I could use something hopeful," Samara sighed.

"Why is that?" Livia asked, genuinely concerned.

Faythe tuned out of their conversation to lazily scan the fortune teller's words, but past the first line, her body tensed.

Come the return of the lost first son.

Faythe's head snapped up to the tent, and her feet marched for it in a drive of impulse. She'd heard this poem before, and her adrenaline beat faster as she didn't bother with courtesy and pulled back the tent flap, heading straight through to the back, where she threw open those curtains too.

The aroma of citrus and vanilla hit her nostrils, the incense so potent she resisted the urge to recoil. A beautiful woman dressed in only a few strips of flowing fabric, barely held together as a dress that exposed most of her dark skin, reclined on cushions elegantly, smoking a long, ornate pipe. Her raven hair was voluminous in tight curls, and she smiled at Faythe—the kind that told her she expected her intrusion. A low string melody played, but there was no instrument she could find as the source.

"You're the Dresair I freed." Faythe didn't waste time in spilling her conclusion.

"I have adopted the name Presilla. This body is the fourth I've inhabited, and I think I'll keep it. Many gawk upon my beauty—it's a power in itself."

"You killed her."

The Dresair shrugged. "I've immortalized her."

Faythe's anger began to climb. "What is your goal?"

"As with all creatures, goals are an ever-shifting tide."

She would have expected her friends to have come in after her by now, but all was so quiet despite the thin purple sheets of the tent.

"So what are you doing now, here in this town?"

"Selling fortunes to make mine. It is rather entertaining to bewitch mortals so desperate for direction on their aimless paths."

"I would have thought you'd have your sights on bigger ambitions."

"Do you know what a Dresair is?" she said in a silky voice.

"I met one first in High Farrow. It said it was a keeper of knowledge, holder of precious things, and—"

"Traveler of realms," Presilla finished for her. "Do you know how one *becomes* a Dresair?"

A cold chill slithered up Faythe's spine. Presilla smiled.

"Not everyone who tries to Realm-Walk makes it through. Those who fail become trapped in an endless space. They lose their name, then their memory, then their sanity. Then they become servants to the void between all places."

Faythe shivered. "You were once…mortal?"

"Yes. I don't recall which realm I came from or why I fled it. I will never remember what species I was, what gender, what appearance I had, or even how long I was trapped in that void. Clearly, I was not equipped for—or deemed worthy of—passage into another mortal realm. It takes a grant from one of many primordial beings, and there is often a high price to pay, which is why we as Dresairs demand something, or give something unwanted, in return for knowledge or items."

Faythe found her explanation both fascinating and horrifying. "It's not a coincidence you're here, is it? You could have fled anywhere, but you're conveniently right here."

Presilla set down her pipe and shifted onto her knees. She gestured with her hand for Faythe to do the same, and she felt compelled to obey, settling down on the other side of the table, where a glass sphere hovered, held up by nothing.

"Your song has been sung since the dawn of time," she said, her voice trance-like. "Bound by strength, her fire will burn. Shaped by darkness, with no return. Spirits will clash as the fates demand. And the cost will be life, torn from hand."

Her breath held.

Presilla continued, "There are many ways this war will end. There are many where you win, but only one leads to all your heart desires."

Faythe's heart began to thunder. "I don't want to know. I can't know," she said, beginning to panic.

The last time she had been given knowledge from the Dresair in High Farrow about one of her friends dying, it had sent her into a terrified, maddening spiral. Ever since, she had been tormented by the thought things could have turned out differently for Caius if she hadn't known.

"I do not wish to harm you, Faythe Ashfyre. If I told you exactly how to win, you would fail, because you would try to prevent the sacrifices you will face."

"Stop," she croaked. Faythe couldn't bear it. She'd known war wasn't without risk and losses, but she couldn't do this again—couldn't know someone she loved was going to die.

"You have to realize that should you lose, should you fall, they will all fall. You are the *one*."

"I don't want to be," she whispered.

Presilla's features softened, her hand waved over the glass sphere, and it flooded with whorls of red and amber. "You have to be," she said.

They watched it create an image so beautiful Faythe choked on her sob.

Faythe only saw her back in the moving image as she stood between two lines of Rhyenelle soldiers holding their swords high like an arch. That wasn't the most wonderful part. It was the two small children in her arms, their heads resting on each of her shoulders, and Reylan by her side, holding an older child—a daughter with hair as silver as his that flowed in the wind. She could see none of their faces, and she wished for them all to turn around.

"Of all the infinite paths this war could take, only one leads here," Presilla said.

Her tears fell silently. Faythe understood then. She could win the war with the many other ways Marvellas could be defeated, but only this way—this one precious path—kept Reylan with her.

"That's impossible," she whispered.

With those odds, the fortune in front of her was like trying to catch wind in her palms.

"It does not mean there is no room for error, child. Fate is like the ever-growing roots of a tree. Some may seem like they stem away from your desires for a while, all may seem lost, but your path can reconnect you with the outcome you fight for. Do not be afraid. Do not stop fighting."

"What do I have to do?" Faythe's voice broke.

"Trust in yourself, and in those who have stood by you from the start. But Faythe, you must accept that not all the mortal Gods may be with you until the end."

"The mortal Gods," Faythe echoed. Some part of her knew…had been threading the pieces together ever since Aurialis taunted her with it, though she hadn't used that term.

"Knowledge, wisdom, courage, resilience, strength, dark and light as one, and you—power."

"I can't lose any of them."

"Take solace, Faythe Ashfyre, that because of the Gods who have meddled to awaken their chosen from their long bloodline and join you, those who fall will rest in an ether of paradise. Say not 'farewell' but 'see you in the crossing.'"

"It's not fair."

"Love is meant to be painful."

"Why are you telling me this?" she demanded, with the fractures of her heart sharpening.

"Because there are many ends in which you live and you triumph, but what you become because you could not accept your losses is a force worse than the one you seek to destroy. That is my gift of warning. You have a power in you this realm has never seen, and grief can make the most devastating choices. It can turn a golden heart black if you let it."

All of this was a warning…about herself. Not help to avoid anything nor knowledge to aid her. The most dangerous outcome of the war was the world in ruins not because of Marvellas's destruction…but Faythe's.

She stumbled in horror, pushing herself back up to her feet, not wanting to believe she was capable of it, but as her friends' faces flashed through her mind, Faythe's chest beat with such fierce protection over them all.

Faythe spun to leave, but Presilla called her name.

"Follow the eye, Faythe Ashfyre. Sometimes you have to lose to win."

CHAPTER FOURTEEN

Izaiah

I zaiah seized his opportunity to slip into the guarded library. He'd been here before, but never in his true fae form. It was necessary to shift back for the locked door he intended to gain access through.

"Are you trying to get yourself caught?" Tynan hissed.

Izaiah stiffened at the intruding voice. His teeth slammed together, his plan now compromised. "How did you follow me?" he grumbled, not even turning to look since the dark fae was the only presence he detected.

"The birthmark on your hip—it appears as a lighter patch on your fur. Even as a little mouse."

Izaiah's tools paused in the lock. He was caught between amusement and surprise that Tynan kept such a keen eye on his body to have noticed and translated the faint distinguishing feature. His stomach annoyingly *fluttered* like some faeling discovering their first crush. Fuck. Izaiah brewed a storm over the unwelcome feelings.

"Are you always stalking me? I'm flattered."

Tynan only glowered, but Izaiah smiled wickedly. He suppressed his ire over the dark fae following him, which was a contrast to the thrill that always broke across his skin.

Now he had to come up with another reason for being here.

"Where did you learn to do that so easily?" Tynan asked as the door clicked open.

"You don't ask about me, I don't ask about you. Don't go back on that now," he said coldly.

He would not risk spilling his past. Nothing personal could come out between them.

Izaiah stood looking into the small room. At his pause, Tynan tried to go in first, but Izaiah's arm extended to stop him.

Locking eyes with his disgruntled stare, Izaiah reached into his pocket, producing a bloodied piece of black clothing. He didn't know if it would work, so his body tensed as he reached it toward the open entrance.

A ripple distorted in front of them. Tingles crawled down his arm with the faintest resistance, but then...the ward dissipated.

"Faythe's blood?" Tynan deduced.

Izaiah relaxed. "Mm-hmm."

In the small room with bookshelves built into each wall, Izaiah tried to pretend Tynan wasn't here. When the dark fae shut the door, however, he couldn't deny the excitement that stirred in him.

"What are you looking for?"

"I should kill you," Izaiah said, hooking a book off the shelf. "You already know more than you should. What would you prefer—teeth or claws?"

"Teeth," he said, the warm impression of his body creeping up behind him. "Definitely teeth."

Izaiah turned before Tynan could lay his hands on his waist. He thrust the book against his chest. "Not this time," he said.

The rejection flexing around Tynan's eyes disturbed him. It was all the more reason to keep his distance.

"Malin's parents... I have never found a marriage certificate," Izaiah explained. It was the first thing to come to mind, and a truth nonetheless that he'd gathered from the king's study. "Odd, don't you think, for such an important royal document to be missing?"

Tynan shrugged. "Can't say I know much about royal anything. It wasn't exactly in our teachings to overthrow the continent."

Izaiah hadn't thought about that—how differently they'd been brought up to view the world. Yet despite being raised as nothing more than a soldier, Tynan didn't seem all that cold and immoral.

He found himself peering at the dark fae, who began flipping aimlessly through a book. It was then Izaiah realized by how fast he was turning, only lingering on the occasional picture...

"Can you read?"

Tynan stiffened at that, continuing to examine the pages as if he were debating whether to deny it. "Kind of," he settled on. Then irritation locked his jaw, and he thumped the book shut. "Why would you care?"

"I don't," Izaiah said, plucking another book from the shelf.

Liar. His mind tormented he did care, though not for the reasons Tynan seemed to be guarded against. As if it could be used in ridicule.

"It wasn't exactly in our regime. They told us what we needed to know," he defended.

It wasn't necessary for him to explain, but Izaiah didn't console the insecurity Tynan let slip.

"They told you what they wanted you to know," Izaiah said.

There was no telling how much of it would have been warped truths about their world and its past conflicts, painting the dark fae as the only victims to feed the thirst of vengeance in their soldiers. It was a frightening thought.

"What if I said I could teach you?"

Izaiah wanted to retract the offer as soon as it left him. He turned away from Tynan, swallowing against the burn in his throat that formed hateful words instead to fill the cracks in the wall between them.

"Why would you want to do that?"

He didn't. He shouldn't.

Yet he said, "So you can make your own judgment in this war, I guess."

The stillness that lingered for a few seconds began to tremble his hands, and they clamped tighter around the leather-bound book. He hoped Tynan would reject—

"When can we start?"

Izaiah's tension released at his response. He shouldn't want this. He should be keeping his distance.

"I'll let you know," was all he could offer for now since the storm of his mind had begun to rebel against the time together this arrangement would force. He had to divert the conversation. "Why has Malin taken a liking to you?"

It had become an irritation not to have figured it out.

Tynan slipped his sight from the book he'd splayed in his palms, leaning against the desk. "You sound jealous."

"Not even remotely."

Tynan smirked. "He's desperate for someone to listen to him. I just happened to be there. He's highly insecure. It's a pattern for people like him to attach themselves to one person to confide in."

"Yet you're betraying him."

His shoulder lifted, flicking through more pages. "I wouldn't say that. I'm as intrigued about him as you are."

"I'm not *intrigued*," Izaiah bit out. "He killed my king and turned this kingdom against my queen. I want him dead."

"Is that why you betrayed her and your brother? You hope to kill Malin alone, and she'll forgive you for it?"

"You wouldn't understand."

"Try me."

Izaiah's jaw shifted. He couldn't make sense of this frustration inside him when Tynan was around. A desire to kill him, if only to end the torment. Yet without the plague in his thoughts, the vacancy didn't sound desirable either.

Izaiah shifted the topic. "Why do you follow Zaiana? Is it nothing more than forced duty?"

"Of course not," he said instantly. Tynan thumped his book shut, not watching Izaiah as he seemed to tunnel in thought. "Zaiana was the first to ever see potential in me. I wasn't notable in my training grade, but only because I didn't want to be. Show yourself as the strongest, and you're a target. Excel at the tasks, and those around you want to see you fail. You have no idea what it was like to grow up as a dark fae."

For the first time, Izaiah didn't shy from the guard who slipped toward him. A guard who wanted to hear more. He leaned against the desk with him, folding his arms.

"Yeah, well, out here wasn't all that great either."

Izaiah tensed, unable to meet Tynan's eye.

"I don't believe that," he said lightly. "You seem to have everything. Well-respected, free to be yourself…"

"I didn't always."

Gods, he shouldn't say anything more.

He was glad when Tynan didn't push.

"Under the mountains, it was all a competition. A game of survival every day. We don't have parents, just ourselves. Some would form groups for the illusion that they had someone to have their back, but usually, they'd be the first to strike a dagger the moment you turned around. It was no secret Zaiana was not someone to contend with. No one even tried to best her. When she became Delegate, I didn't realize how much she'd been watching me. How she saw me on some deeper level I didn't think our kind was capable of. When she asked if I would be her Second, I could have gone to my knees. Not for the respect or the protection it would grant, but because it was the first time I truly wanted to *live* with a purpose."

Izaiah clenched the desk tightly at the story. For the feelings he didn't want stirring within him. And for his own past, which threatened to claw its way from the grave he'd buried it in.

Tynan's hand went over his, but Izaiah's impulse won, tearing the comfort away. And maybe it was selfish, but he couldn't go down the path that had started to emerge with Tynan.

"I'm glad to hear she's not entirely coldhearted," Izaiah said, pacing away to swallow past the tightness in his throat.

"What happened to you?" Tynan asked. It was careful, yet a battering ram to the gates of his emotion.

Izaiah shook his head. "Don't do that."

"What?"

"Care," he snapped. "Don't care, Tynan. It only adds resistance to the blade you keep aimed at my chest."

The dark fae's lips firmed. Disappointment weighted his stare, and Izaiah's hands fisted. His magick hummed in him to shift. Though he couldn't be certain if it was to kill the threat in front of him or to flee from it.

"You don't need to worry about that," Tynan said. "You're attractive, I'm bored—that's all this is."

Tynan set his book on the table as he made to leave.

Impulsively, Izaiah lashed out for Tynan's wrist as he passed. Their eyes met, and Izaiah warred with himself over letting go...or giving in to the tension straining between them. They could forget the past few minutes—all it would take was closing that distance to forget the world in the heat that blocked it all out. But every time the air cooled again, reality became a more punishing force.

"Having a still heart...does it make it easier to pretend you feel nothing?" Izaiah asked.

His heart beat faster in their silence. As if it were compensating for the absence of Tynan's.

"No," he said.

CHAPTER FIFTEEN

Zaiana

Zaiana found the wicked Malin, chasing pent-up frustration and anger she was desperate to release. At the notes of a familiar voice, she halted the urge to barge into the drawing room she'd followed his disgusting scent to.

"All I'm saying is, you have the people's loyalty right now. If they find out you've been slaughtering the strong and loyal forces of your warriors and generals simply because they were wary of a new reign, you'll lose the trust you gained from them," Tynan said.

"You're giving me a nothing of fucking use," Malin responded with cold exasperation. Then he seemed to calm. "My father would say I was destined for the crown he couldn't have. But in order to be worthy of it, I couldn't be weak—I had to show I was just as powerful in both my ability and my status to be better than Agalhor."

"Your uncle seemed to care for you," Tynan said carefully.

"Until he found a new candidate to give away what was rightfully mine," Malin seethed. "Do you know how humiliating it was to watch all my centuries of building and waiting and proving myself be dismissed so easily when his *daughter* knew nothing—*nothing*—of what it took to lead?"

Zaiana could sympathize with the prince in that moment. She didn't want to, but it was impossible to ignore the unfair hand that had switched the moment Faythe arrived.

"Then he left me," Malin hissed, but there was a wavering to it. A note of pain that made it clear he meant his father.

"Death isn't a choice on a battlefield," Tynan said. He had more patience with him that she did.

A pause of silence passed. "I don't think he died," Malin said, barley a whisper of confusion. "I searched endlessly for his body. The things I saw from that battle that they say claimed his life… I was willing to look at any shredded body I could to find him. He was the brother of the king, yet no one kept track of him? And Agalhor—" Malin huffed a resentful sound. "It spoke volumes when he called off the search and declared his death without finding his body after only two weeks."

"You think he's still out there?"

"No. I mean, maybe. Never mind," Malin grumbled. "It makes no difference to anything anyway. I doubt even after all I've done it would have been enough for him."

"Did you always want to be king?"

Malin didn't answer right away. She was beginning to think he never would.

"Want is a word of fantasy."

Zaiana slipped into the room, immediately targeting him, and the prince straightened from the composure he'd let slip in Tynan's presence. For a second, there was a broken child slumped in that seat, elbow propped on the red velvet side, with fingers digging into his temples like it would stop the battering inside his head. Until the ice froze in his eyes and his features cut to steel, ready for war against her.

Her mouth quirked, only to gain the tightening of his jaw. He knew there was nothing he could do that would make her afraid of him. Malin Ashfyre would never win her fealty, even if Dakodas herself demanded it of him.

"What do you want?" he bit out.

Zaiana's fingers traced over the long mahogany table, deliberately lingering the suspense of her presence. She noticed the few empty vials in front of him. The prince had been consuming Phoenix Blood at an alarming volume. The whites of his eyes were turning red at the edges, and he appeared as if sleep had evaded him for weeks with the dark circles under them.

"Don't tell me you forget your debts, little prince," she said.

When Zaiana was held captive the prince had visited her, recruited her, just like the traitor Izaiah. Her task was simple: to tear down the inner-city wall. Her price was knowledge he'd taunted her with, and she'd come to collect.

"Of all the things you could have asked for, you chose something so pathetic," he shot back.

His words had no effect on her. She already punished herself with worse for the information she sought. Picking up a wooden carving, she inspected the small figure holding a spear.

"Want to tell me what's going on?" Tynan interjected carefully.

Her gaze flicked up to him. She thought to cast him away, but it made no difference to her what Tynan knew. He wouldn't talk.

Zaiana threw her hand sideward. The figure sipped from her grip to pierce the wall with a loud thump of impatience.

Malin swallowed at the display. She continued around the table until she was right before him. With a deep breath, she held it, bracing her hands on the arms of his chair to lean in close.

"First, I want to know how you found out about it," she said, her tone a beautiful warning.

"One of the messenger dark fae," he said, trying not to be intimidated by her. "It seems the master's cruelty crafted betrayers."

"You met with dark fae in this city?"

Malin nodded. "Ones without wings. Not just glamoured—they were sawn off."

Zaiana pushed away from him, the disgust coiling in her stomach. She knew of the barbaric punishment. Had been forced to watch it be inflicted many times, and the screams of those dark fae were imprinted in her memory forever. It was what kept her wings glamoured often. She couldn't imagine a life without them. She would *beg* for death before that happened.

"What did they say?" Zaiana pressed.

She took up a lean against the far wall. Malin was testing her patience with a mere look of assessment that had her straining not to claw his eyes from his skull.

"That their greatest feat of control was in making you all believe you were unfeeling. That your still heart was the most cunning curse they could have placed on you for their masterful ruse."

"A curse?" Tynan echoed.

His brow furrowed, but Zaiana couldn't take his words as truth yet. Even if she did, there was no confirming the dark fae who'd spilled it to the prince wasn't doing so out of desperate revenge against the masters.

"How many times have you blamed your wicked actions on your

still heart? It makes it easier, doesn't it? I heard what you did, you know…killing a past lover of yours. Then nearly allowing that poison that leaks out of you to kill another—a certain esteemed Rhyenelle commander—"

Zaiana barely registered her movements in the flash of goaded fury, but she relished in the choking of Malin Ashfyre. Her hand squeezed tighter around his throat when he clawed at it.

"So much bottled emotion," the prince wheezed. "I don't think there's any battle you could fear more than your own self."

She pushed him, her two sharp claws cutting flesh, and his chair near toppled back with the force.

Malin struggled for breath, but he otherwise gave no reaction to her attack. As though he didn't care anymore.

The prince went on. "Perhaps that's what they're hoping for. The moment you detonate, it will be for them. In battle against all of those you care about but deny vehemently you don't."

Danger was stirring inside her. For a moment Zaiana was glad for her missing lightning since she wasn't confident it would still be contained with everything he spoke of. She wanted to kill him. It kept circling her mind, and she didn't know why she allowed Malin to keep breathing.

"Did this traitor say anything else?" Her voice was calm and razor-sharp.

"Only that you were the key. As vague as that. Somehow I think they've tied it to you. Perhaps it's why they can't kill you when I'm sure they want to. Those called the masters who raised you. I've met them too—a cold and lifeless bunch, and it's almost amusing how much they despise you."

"People hate what they cannot control," Tynan grumbled.

Malin shrugged in agreement, leaning back against his chair and hissing with the hand he placed over his bleeding neck.

"I may not like you, but those bastards need the challenge to their egos."

Zaiana could barely hear anymore while she focused on her own dissection of the claim. A curse. It didn't seem unfathomable— but why?

"Not many books exist about the dark fae anymore. Any that do only portray history. Maybe your kind aren't born monsters. Maybe you were actually a peaceful people and this was the only way to begin to break that."

She didn't know why dread began to pool in her stomach. Perhaps she didn't want it to be true. If it was something so simple, how could she accept that? If her still heart was nothing more than a *spell*...what would happen to every vile thing she'd stacked the blame on for this vacancy in her chest?

She'd been tormented by it ever since the King of Rhyenelle had infiltrated her sleeping mind and shown it to her.

A heartbeat. Hers.

No. She wanted any other truth but this. For if she came to welcome a pulse in her cold chest...she may very well rip it out for the evil that lurked within it.

Zaiana's sight pinned on the open door, needing an outlet she didn't want to display here. She knew just who she could take it out on.

"I haven't granted you leave," Malin objected.

He wasn't saying this to her, but the fact he thought he held any real authority over Tynan flared in her all the same. Zaiana met eyes with her second, who had begun to follow her. She despised what she had to do.

"You should stay," she said to him.

Tynan's expression widened in ire, but hers warned against protesting. His jaw worked, but he gave a tight nod. She would come up with some excuse for him later. Right now, she couldn't care about anything but the fury shaking her bones.

"You made sure he wouldn't come after you?" Izaiah drawled.

Zaiana found him leaning with arms crossed against a small door in the library where he'd instructed her to meet him. He was going to take her to the ruin. There was no attempting his suicidal mission to *wield* it without the real thing. Anytime they met elsewhere in her attempts to school him on what it would take, all they achieved was useless bickering.

"Why would it matter if Tynan were here anyway?" she bit out.

Izaiah lifted a brow at her tone, but he said nothing as he unlocked the door. When he waved a dark, bloodied cloth at the entrance, Zaiana spared a second to marvel at the ward, enjoying the thrill that was a temporary balm to her constant irritation.

"I don't need anyone else telling me the obvious odds of what I'm doing," he said casually.

Zaiana watched his back as he entered. A sinking anchor fell within her at Izaiah's comment. Realization that he'd become a vulnerability to Tynan, and there was nothing she could do. Killing Izaiah would only turn Tynan resentful against her even if he tried to hide it. Her fists balled with bitterness toward the younger Galentithe brother for the new claim he had—unwitting or not—over her second.

Izaiah reached the desk, meeting her eye with a gleam as he reached beneath it. As he pulled something out, Zaiana braced against the groaning of wood and stone that disrupted their silence. Then movement began along the back wall. The back tapestry sank in, then it slowly lowered, disappearing into the ground to reveal a long, narrow, depthless corridor.

A secret passage.

She chilled at the sight of it. Her throat constricted, and she swallowed against the rising nerves.

"Not afraid of the dark, are you?" Izaiah quipped. "It would be rather ironic."

"No," she snapped.

Izaiah only smirked, and with a hand slipped into his pocket, he headed inside without hesitation.

Zaiana took a few deep breaths as though they might become limited before following him. She focused on the air coating her throat. The cool temperature that began to drop. Tracking the walls, it was only her cruel imagination that tightened the space and forced her hand to occasionally brush the rock to be sure.

They descended stairs that felt endless, until light broke at the bottom, and she was eager to each it. They emerged into a giant space she hadn't expected. Catacombs. At the far end, a huge sculpture of a Firebird stood, wings splayed and triumphant. In front of it, a tall, dominant male figure.

"The first King of Rhyenelle," Izaiah said as she gawked. "And that's Atherius. We had the pleasure of meeting her on the Fire Mountains, if you recall."

Zaiana couldn't tear her eyes from the bird while her mind replayed the scene from the mountains. The gray stone torched with brilliant red fire. It was not the king she saw…but Faythe.

"You fear confinement," Izaiah diverted.

The change of topic snapped her head to him. She found him watching her with an expression she couldn't decipher, but it coated her skin with *vulnerability*.

"I'm not," she said. He wasn't convinced. "I'm merely cautious, being led down a secluded path by the enemy."

Izaiah smiled, though not with any kindness, as if he enjoyed the hostility between them. Zaiana preferred her enemies quaking at the thought of her, not *excited* to torment her back. This was going to be a long and insufferable task.

It wasn't often Zaiana was disturbed by the presence of death, but something about being in the resting place of someone so ancient and legendary pricked her skin with judgment. In front of the sculpture, there was a sunken tomb. Zaiana gravitated toward it to discover Matheus Ashfyre wasn't the only person who rested here.

"Should we really be down here?" Zaiana muttered, glancing around as if she would catch a flicker of something that would give away there were spirits around, watching.

"Probably not," Izaiah said, so chipper it contrasted with her skittish mood. "But no one else can get past the door we came through, and they won't suspect we can. You'd do best to keep that to yourself."

Zaiana didn't take well to warnings, especially when delivered in a threat. Izaiah was impressing his demand that even Tynan and Amaya stay unaware of what they were doing down here.

"So if I kill you here, no one will find you," Zaiana answered.

"Likewise."

Maybe she did enjoy the challenge Izaiah offered. It gave her something of a thrill to think she might be the one to end him first, but not before she got what she wanted.

"Where's the ruin?"

Izaiah wandered over to a sunken grave, crouching beside it.

"You're not going to—"

He grabbed a long iron rod, jamming it into the crevice before angling it to pop the stone free. Gods above, this was grim even for her. As he pried it loose and begin to slip the long, body-length stone aside to reveal the remains within, Zaiana noticed there was no given name, only the house name of Ashfyre and two dates, the occupant's end dating to around the start of the war five hundred years ago.

Zaiana peeked into the depths.

It was empty.

"My guess is it's supposed to be Malin's father," Izaiah said, hopping into the space without a care. "It's the newest-looking space here."

"No name?" Zaiana spoke the obvious.

"No body either. Got to wonder why they bothered reserving a space for him."

As he slid a small box over the ledge, Zaiana eyed the intricate carvings with a rush through her blood. Izaiah hauled himself out of the grave.

"I figured no one else would be twisted enough to go grave-robbing if they did manage to find out we came here."

"Not above your limits though."

Izaiah shrugged. "I've been trying to figure out what feels off about Malin. His father...there's very little about him. It's almost like he's been erased."

"Why would someone want the king's brother forgotten?"

"That's the wicked question, isn't it?"

She couldn't understand how he wouldn't know about such an important person in the royal lineage.

"I've felt the power that comes off this thing. I've heard it responds the most to chaos. Are you composed enough for this, little darkling?"

She cut him with a look. "You're going to die by this," she warned.

"Perhaps."

Izaiah pulled a small knife from his side, not hesitating to slice his palm. Zaiana fixed her attention on the box he set on the ground and spilled his blood onto, anticipation tightening in her gut. It had been a while she'd tasted the magnetic, otherworldly power, and all she hoped for was that once it found her, it would drag forth her damned stubborn lightning.

Every shift of the wood and glow of the markings inched her closer, *hungry* for the power that would call to her the moment the ruin was free...

The glow diminished, and she listened to Izaiah's heart quicken a fraction. His fist clenched, and Zaiana...she felt nothing. Dread consumed her. She approached the box only to drop down and knock the lid away to confirm it was inside. Only then did she feel the hum. Only a taunt, as if it knew her ability hid from her and it would offer no help to coax it forth.

"If you think of crossing me with its power, you should know I have an assassin tracking Tynan and Amaya who will act if he doesn't see me by sundown."

The rage from her stifled magick and the mockery the ruin made of it boiled over at Izaiah's threat. She lunged for him, a hand wrapping around his throat, and they crashed into the nearest wall.

"This is the last time you lay a threat before I make sure you can't speak another," she seethed in his face.

Izaiah only matched her loathing stare.

"No lightning?" he taunted.

Her claws cut into his skin, earning a hiss. "I don't need anything but my bare hands to kill you."

"I don't doubt it," he said. "Though how are you going to teach me to wield the ruin when you no longer can?"

Zaiana's nostrils flared, and she pushed off him to pace away. How in the Nether was she going to keep up her pretense that she still possessed her lightning when it seemed so damned obvious it was missing?

"For what it's worth, I only happened to overhear you and Maverick."

Her shoulder blades locked at this. The memory of being in that room with Maverick combed over her mind, everything that was said...

"The Prince of Dalrune—who would have ever guessed?" Izaiah said.

Zaiana should kill him right here. Izaiah was perhaps the most cunning of them all. He was observant, patient, and with his ability, he was the perfect spy. Looking him over, how could she deny the brilliance of his scheming? Stay cheerful, stay unbothered, and he'd become the most unsuspecting player.

"What do you plan to do with that information?"

"Nothing...yet."

She *wanted* to kill him. For the threat he posed not only to her companions...but now to Maverick.

"It means nothing."

Izaiah chuckled. "Perhaps not. When his days are numbered anyway."

Zaiana breathed steadily. She couldn't give Izaiah the impression she cared. Not about Maverick.

"Have you ever wondered why they kept who he was a secret? I hear it's rare for the Transitioned to keep their abilities. Royal blood, perhaps? Marvellas wanted to Transition Nik and Tauria this past summer."

"There's a lot to be figured out about this war on both sides. And I'd rather we started with what in the Nether you hope to achieve here," she bit out.

"I'm waiting for some instruction. Teach," he quipped.

Zaiana groaned internally. This was going to be insufferable. She was accustomed to schooling darklings in combat and keeping them in line—she supposed taking the same approach with Izaiah wouldn't be too different. Someone who was going to test her patience to murderous capacities.

She looked at the ruin with resentment, and since she wasn't volatile right now, she stormed to it without care, sticking her hand in to retrieve the broken, arrow-shaped slate. When she did, Zaiana gasped at the current that surged through her, almost believing it shifted movement in her chest. It was nowhere near the velocity of power she should feel from it, but hope grew a dangerous bud in the pit of her stomach that it was *something*.

CHAPTER SIXTEEN

Faythe

It was nightfall when Faythe met Nik, and they left camp inconspicuously. Pressed to the wall of a shadowed alley in town, with their lower faces covered and their hoods drawn, Faythe assessed the quiet street.

"I really thought you were promising action tonight," Nik complained.

"This is action."

Nik made a disgruntled sound. "Spying is tedious."

The Ember Sword weighed heavy on her hip, too big for her to wield comfortably, but it would suffice if she really needed a weapon. She'd brought it along for another reason, and she occasionally glanced at the ruby pommel as if she might miss its flare. She'd had to sneak into Kyleer's tent for it.

"We have to steal something," Faythe muttered absentmindedly. She was focused on tracking any suspicious persons.

"Sounds easy enough."

"We have to find it first."

Nik dragged her away from leaning around the bend of the alley. His flat look met her ire. "I have other things I could be doing tonight rather than goose-chasing."

"Please enlighten me."

His lips pursed, then he was distracted by Asari brushing against his side.

"She's really protective of you," Faythe mused, patting the large wolf lightly.

"I don't know why."

Faythe was about to comment again when a flicker of light caught her breath.

The Eye of the Phoenix glowed in the Ember Sword. Just for a brief second, but Faythe shot back to peer onto Main Street.

"Isn't that supposed to indicate—*oof!*"

Faythe twisted to clamp a hand over his mouth and press them both tightly to the wall. The figure with the amulet passed by the gap into the alley, and Faythe held her breath, not letting Nik go until they were out of range.

When her hand dropped from his scarf-covered mouth and she pushed off his chest, Nik stared at her in irritated bewilderment.

"Well, you've sure gotten swifter, and I don't think I like it," he grumbled.

She smirked. "The student becomes the master."

"I wouldn't give you *that* kind of praise."

Faythe spied some discarded crates and didn't inform Nik of her plans, knowing he would follow even with a series of curses under his breath. They scaled to the roofs, and she kept low, crawling and shuffling to keep out of sight as she tracked the tall silhouette through the streets.

She filled Nik in on what had happened in the market today and how this thief had her family's amulet. It wasn't without renewed anger that it had been taken from Reylan, and this unfortunate finder of the heirloom was going to feel her wrath for it even if they weren't responsible. Determination was running hot through her blood at the thought perhaps he might have seen or overheard something that could lead to where Marvellas had taken Reylan.

When they reached the last building, they watched the figure head toward a Valgard camp set up already. They hadn't attacked or caused any unrest besides the town being wary of the new forces.

"What do you plan to do?" Nik asked.

"I'm not sure yet," she answered honestly.

It was curious that a soldier in Marvellas's forces would be bold enough to steal the amulet even if she'd disregarded it. Unless he was someone high up, and it had been a token of some kind.

Her burning curiosity and anger made it a struggle to remain still. They watched him slip into one of the more dominating tents, and from their own setups, Faythe assumed it was where leading parties met.

"We need to get closer," she said.

"Are you sure? I quite like the view——"

Faythe was already scaling down with her utmost stealth and silence. With so many enemy guards in black lingering around the camp, littered with small fires in the night, she was testing her luck.

"Did you choose me to come with you because you thought I wouldn't yell at you for your stupidity?" Nik hissed into her thoughts. *"Because you are sorely mistaken——"*

"You said you wanted action."

She was darting across a dark strip with her pulse in her throat when the nearest guards turned their backs.

Faythe was really tempting fate when she snuck right up to the tent, peeking through a gap. She was right. Just less than a dozen fae and dark fae warriors were positioned around a table with a map similar to what they'd set up in their own camp.

She found her hooded bandit instantly as he strode around the group and stopped at the head of the table. He pulled down his hood and face covering then, revealing short, ashy-brown hair and a wide-set jaw. His eyes were blue, and Faythe's attention caught on them with a skip in her chest.

Those eyes.

She was distracted from them only by a new sense that crawled over her. Dark power emanated from something—or someone—within the tent.

"You have one role here, general," someone else in the tent said resentfully toward Faythe's target.

"I am in charge of this legion. Don't forget that, or it'll be the last mistake you make," he said, so cold and unfeeling.

"You know nothing of our forces when you only just got assigned here," another argued.

Then another added, "You said there would be a legion of Rhyenelle's army here for us to slaughter."

"They must have managed to spy that information from us. We have to be more vigilant," her target answered cooly.

They weren't fond of this general. Faythe's intrigue heightened. He had Reylan's amulet—and his knowledge. Faythe's skin was burning like nothing she'd ever felt before, so all-consuming with a need to confront this general right now since he had to have her closest lead to Reylan.

She could test his mind, but it was a risk. There was a high likelihood Marvellas would have warned everyone to guard their minds against Faythe.

"Our travel to this town isn't wasted," her target said. "Faythe Ashfyre is here."

Faythe froze as murmurs broke across the other soldiers.

"How do you plan to find her?"

"She'll show herself—all we have to do is start painting the streets red."

Her fury boiled at the suggestion to slaughter innocents to draw her out. She was going to kill this general before he got the chance to lead such a barbaric order.

Her target general leaned across the table, and Faythe's purpose for being here was flaunted right before her. There was no mistaking the amulet when he slipped his cuff up to expose the ruby eye. It began to glow, and Faythe sucked in a sharp gasp, snapping her sight to her hip as the sister stone in the Ember Sword flared in recognition.

Faythe swore inwardly, and a cold sweat broke over her skin. The general's eyes flicked up right to where she was, but Faythe was already darting away.

Where in the Nether was Nik?

She made it to the edge of the woods on the other side of the camp and pressed her back to a tree trunk, catching her breath and tuning her hearing in case she'd been followed. When she detected nothing, Faythe risked curving her head around the tree to survey the camp. She spotted the general from the spark of red she saw even from here, and she clamped a hand around the pommel of her sword to smother the direct beacon to her.

He ducked into a smaller tent at the edge of the camp, which had to be his own, to retire for the night. Was she really so desperate and foolish as to risk infiltrating his personal tent? If he was retiring for the night, he would surely remove the amulet. She just had to wait an hour, sure he would fall asleep. Faythe began to hash a plan in her mind. If Nik could keep him asleep with his mind ability, it would make the task easy.

Faythe squinted through the dark of the hills to try to find Nik and share her plan, but he didn't reveal himself. She ground her teeth in irritation.

Faythe couldn't last an hour. With Nik still not catching up to her, she was beginning to bloom a seed of dread. She wanted to retrieve the amulet so badly. It was right. There.

Yet with Nik and the wolf still out of her sights, her concern for him grew too much.

She hurried over the hill and kept hidden to scan for him. When a hand clamped over her mouth, Faythe almost summoned deadly magick before she was spun around to face the King of High Farrow. He let her go, and she whacked his arm with a scowl.

"Where have you been?" she hissed under her breath, aware they could still be overheard.

Nik took a hold of her arm and pulled her into a crouched jog to gain more distance. Even Asari seemed cautious and kept her body as low as possible.

"I was gaining intel in other minds," he said proudly. "You never know what the subordinates are thinking compared to their superiors. It's quite fascinating."

Faythe was hardly in the mood for humor or gossip.

"Gain anything of value?" Faythe asked.

Nik stopped walking down an alley, and they faced each other.

"Marvellas is in Lakelaria."

Her mouth fell open. She'd spent weeks trying to find that information in the minds of as many dark fae as she could capture, yet Nik had found it in a single night. She'd been racking the thoughts of rogue dark fae. It seemed her whereabouts wasn't such a secret among her armies, however.

Faythe had a destination. For the first time since she'd lost her kingdom and her mate, Faythe had a purpose to throw her all into.

"Do you think that's where she's taken Reylan?" Nik asked.

Faythe's thoughts were already reeling over that possibility.

"Her ruin is in Lakelaria," Faythe remembered, adding sense to why the Spirit would have traveled West.

"Shit. Does Reylan have the potential to wield it?"

"Yes." Faythe believed that without a doubt.

"We have to tell the others."

By the time they reached camp, they were met with the disgruntled stare-downs of everyone who should be asleep in the dead of night.

"Oh look, it's just two of the most important people on the continent, back from galivanting around the enemy without adequate strategy or persons," Lycus scolded first.

Faythe winced. It was easy to forget who she was, who Nik was, and how their friends would view their recklessness.

Kyleer pointed a finger at her. "You—I understand your lack of self-preservation, being new to your role."

Her expression lifted that he was kind of giving her a pass on this.

His reprimand shifted to Nik. "But you have no excuse. What were you thinking?"

Nik fought amusement on his mouth. Faythe knew he enjoyed being caught for his rebellion.

"I was thinking that two mind abilities are perfectly capable of remaining out of touch. A quick erasure of their thoughts, and we'd be on our way."

He was enjoying the extension of his ability. Something Faythe had once been horrified to discover she harbored, Nik embraced the advantages of easily.

"You of all people know not every mind is the same. With Faythe on the loose, there's bound to be more of the enemy training their minds against her ability, and they won't be so easily evaded," Kyleer argued.

"No one knows about Nik," Faythe chimed in. "If they focused their efforts on blocking me, he could slip into their minds while they're unaware. We make a great team, in fact."

Nik nudged her side playfully, but the others weren't so easily swayed.

Nerida and Tarly sat on logs around a small fire in front of their tents. Lycus mirrored Kyleer's cross-armed stance of disapproval until they all started to break, moving to take up their seats. Livia and Samara had left for High Farrow.

Nik and Faythe joined them around the fire.

"What were you hoping to achieve anyway?" Kyleer asked reluctantly.

Faythe hadn't been able get the Dresair's words out of her head after this afternoon.

"Follow the eye."

She divulged what she'd overheard from the general's tent, and Nik explained what he'd found out through the minds of other soldiers.

Kyleer lost himself to thought for some time, and Faythe didn't disturb him. He stared intently into the fire.

"They'll be planning an attack then to lure Faythe out," Lycus said.

"It seems so," Kyleer agreed.

Nik added, "It's masterful, really. They can lure Faythe out with

Valgard soldiers, then they'll have the Rhyenelle forces Malin still has to stop it. No one will know they're actually working together. More savior appearance for him."

Faythe could hardly stand how things had aligned in her cousin's favor while the people were oblivious to his allegiance with the enemy.

She poked a stick into the fire, waiting for a rabbit to cook. The wolves kept supplying the game as if they knew when they were hungry. Faythe kept silent while they spoke more on what to do about the impending attack.

"We should go to Lakelaria," Nerida said suddenly. All attention was drawn to her. "Me and Tarly, I mean. I know the lands, and Faythe can Nightwalk to me if I find anything that can prepare you ahead of time. We can remain hidden. And more than that, Lakelaria has the best healers in the world—we might find more answers about a bite from the dark fae."

"That would be excellent help. Any intel before we walk into enemy territory is invaluable," Kyleer agreed.

"What if it's not safe?" Faythe said apprehensively. She was awash with memories of Reuben, a friend she'd sent there long ago in an attempt to save him, but he'd fallen right into the hands of Marvellas and become her mind-twisted puppet. Faythe leaned her elbows on her thighs, holding her head in her hands.

"Look around—nowhere is safe but High Farrow right now. We all have to take risks," Lycus said.

Faythe conceded. "Marlowe figured out Marvellas's temple is in the Sky Caves. I imagine she's retrieved it with Reylan now, with the aim of breaking it."

"If she succeeds, I might have found another way to stop her from causing harm," Nerida said.

Faythe watched her pull a thick tome from another satchel. The title embossed on the front read *The Book of Enoch.*

"There are three ways, in fact, to combat God-strength power. Aetherbonds—manacles that can silence it. The Spellthief—a dagger that can steal it. And the Black Phoenix—an entity that can destroy it."

Faythe's fascination heightened. "A Black Phoenix?"

Nerida said, "The last known to exist...ended the Dark Age by killing the dark fae king."

The weight of that knowledge slammed into everyone.

"Mordecai has magick? He's never shown it. In our confrontation in Olmstone, why wouldn't he have used it if he's that powerful?" Nik inquired.

"He *was* that powerful. I might assume in his resurrection he's lost his magick," Nerida said.

"What were his abilities?" Kyleer asked.

"I don't know. This book isn't about lineage—it's knowledge on the Gods and our world."

While the image of a Black Phoenix filtered through her mind with triumphant danger and wild curiosity, Faythe had to set aside that option since it wasn't on offer.

"The Aetherbonds and the Spellthief—do we have any idea where they could be?" Faythe asked.

Nerida shifted a glance to Tarly before she answered. "I can't be certain, but a while ago, we came across humans seeking to access Hilia's Cave. It's located in the deepest part of Stenna's Fall. It would be a perfect place for a Spirit to hide something so lethal to her. There's very few Waterwielders who could reach that deep without burning out."

Kyleer asked, "Could you?"

Faythe didn't miss the tension that squared Tarly's shoulders. "Honestly, I don't know. I could try, but if I can't…no one would be able to swim from that deep before running out of air."

Silence fell between them all. Nik was the one to break it.

"Air," he said, pondering over his own thoughts for a moment longer. "You and Tauria together could reach it with her Windbreaker ability."

The solution came as a beacon of hope and a slash of despair. There were always missing pieces to their plans.

"Our strategy may be a web that takes patience right now, but it's hope, and it's brilliant. Thank you, Nerida," Kyleer said.

"So what do we do now?" Faythe asked.

"We stay the course. If the worst happens and the ruin is broken when we retrieve Reylan, we still have hope of stopping her power even if we can't kill her anymore. While we focus on Reylan, Nik and Lycus should go to Fenstead, wait for Tauria to return from Valgard, and get her back. Then you'll meet up with Nerida and go to Stenna's Fall before we all meet again in High Farrow."

There were many moving parts and people to this plan that had Faythe antsy in concern for everyone.

"If we leave in the morning, we can get to Lakelaria as soon as possible to scout for healers, gather what we can about Marvellas there, and head back to meet Nik at Stenna's Fall," Nerida said brightly.

"We don't need to go for me," Tarly protested.

"You won't last many more weeks if we don't."

"Then I won't even last the journey," he snapped.

Faythe winced, understanding his sharpness, but Nerida's falling expression was sad to witness. The healer's care for him was deep.

"You don't get to be a self-pitying hero now. You're going," Nik said, his tone firm and irritated.

"As if you'd care if I took my last breath right in front of you."

Nik's jaw flexed, and Faythe knew him. He *did* care about Tarly. She didn't know why they'd grown up with this distaste toward each other, but it didn't mean Nik wouldn't mourn the Prince of Olmstone.

Nik ignored him to ask Faythe, "Do you think you could command Atherius to take them? Would save weeks of travel, and the stubborn bastard isn't getting his wish to die this way."

"Yes, I think I can do that."

Kyleer said, "If Marvellas sees the Firebird, she'll think it's you. Best fly around the coast and land somewhere inconspicuous, if possible, but be vigilant nonetheless."

Nerida nodded, a new giddiness twinkling in her eyes.

So, come morning, everyone had a destination. Faythe couldn't think of the road ahead. She couldn't think of anything but a familiar set of blue eyes that wouldn't leave the forefront of her thoughts.

CHAPTER SEVENTEEN

Tarly

His right arm had begun to suffer a tingling sensation most days. Tarly was weighted with despair that he could soon lose the ability to use a bow. His skin was often clammy and his breaths short. He knew his ailment was becoming serious and his time precious.

Tarly had his own small tent in the camp. Each night, he longed to watch over Nerida even though he knew she was safe surrounded by warriors. As much as he was somewhat impaired, he felt at ease by her side, knowing he would protect her until his very last arrow.

He couldn't sleep with the thoughts of traveling to Lakelaria in the sunrise. Not knowing the dangers they could face. Tarly couldn't explain how this path felt like a coward's last desperate hope when Nerida thought Lakelarian healers could help him. He wasn't so certain he would even last the weeks of travel across Rhyenelle and then across the Black Sea. While everyone made themselves active players toward triumphing in this war, he was offering nothing.

When he heard Nerida's quiet voice outside his tent, for the first time he battled a will to feign sleep or cast her away. He took so long to decide that she dipped her head through the tent opening carefully and found him awake. Her small smile at seeing him sat up lit a beacon in his dark mind.

"I thought you might be asleep," she said, welcoming herself inside. Nerida carried a small wooden bowl and some new bandages, her satchel of tonics and medicines slung over her body.

"Do you need something?" he asked.

"We skipped changing your bandages yesterday, and when we got back from collecting the wood, you were gone."

Inside the bowl wasn't a salve like he expected—it was leftover rabbit and some bread he'd passed up before the meat had finished cooking. He'd needed time alone to think.

"I'm fine," he said. She didn't deserve his cold reception, but he was finding it harder to muster any emotions as the days passed by and death gripped him tighter.

He'd washed by the stream in the woods earlier and left his wound unbandaged. He didn't think the salves and cover-ups were doing anything anyway. Even the pain had stopped being a throbbing, constant ache. He didn't have long left.

"Can I look?" she asked anyway.

She didn't have to since he was shirtless despite the bitter cold, which was hardly kept away by his single lantern. He might have a fever. It came and went.

He didn't answer, but she was bold enough to approach anyway and pull down his blanket. Tarly enjoyed the sound of her gentle voice. If kindness had a face and light had a sound, she was the picture and the feeling of both.

Nerida inspected his ghastly shoulder. The entirety of his tan skin there had turned a sickly gray, which had expanded across half his chest and down most of his arm now. He couldn't feel her touch there, and that was another pang of desolation.

"Before we go to Lakelaria, I have something we can try," she whispered.

Tarly looked at her then in confusion. Nerida unhooked the satchel from her body, and he saw the new vial immediately when he'd subconsciously memorized the organization of every bottle and herb she kept. He knew what it was—had seen it before—the moment she pulled it from the tie.

"Nik gave me this... We're both hoping it can enhance my healing magick enough to give you more time or maybe even heal you."

He blinked at the bottle of Phoenix Blood.

"He really gave that up for me?" he asked, stunned the bastard would hand over such a rare thing.

"You may bicker like children, but so do brothers."

Tarly scoffed a humorless laugh. Nerida didn't know their history. He was sure if Nik heard her say that, he'd claim his precious Phoenix

Blood right back. It had to be by the insistence of Nerida or one of the others that he'd even thought to give it over.

When the shock of seeing the potion settled and the new prospect dawned on him, Tarly was afraid to believe it could work.

He was afraid…because he *wanted* to live.

Nerida had made him want what once felt impossible to desire in this cold world.

And he wanted to hate her for it. For making him fear death after the decades he'd spent making peace with it.

She uncorked the bottle. but Tarly caught her wrist before the vial reached her lips. Nerida held his eyes with question, and he didn't know what overcame him. Next thing he knew, his hand was slipping across her jaw and his lips were crashing to hers in a single deep kiss. That was all he intended, until their mouths were moving and heat was gathering. Until the stunning angel in front of him was now strad-dled over him, and nothing had ever wrapped so perfectly in his arms.

Their kiss slowed, and his hands, which had slipped under her winter cloak, traced down her spine.

"What was that for?" she asked, delightfully breathless against his mouth.

"I don't know," he said.

He didn't know what was between them, only that he didn't want it to end. He wanted to keep her, though he couldn't. He was being selfish in letting her get close to him with his days on an uncertain countdown.

"Will you let me take this now?" she said with light amusement, still holding the Phoenix Blood.

Tarly gritted his teeth against his protest. "It can't possibly harm you, can it?"

Nerida smiled teasingly. "Such a worrier."

She tipped the contents into her mouth without confirmation, and his heart skipped. Before he could panic, Nerida discarded the bottle, swallowing the contents, then her mouth was on his again.

When her tongue swept against his and he tasted the metallic sweetness of the potion, Tarly gasped at the foreign burst of energy within him. Though faint, he'd never believed any magick lived within him despite Nerida once claiming he had a kernel of healing magick —what must be responsible for keeping him alive for so long after the bite. Now he thought he felt a touch of that magick. Not enough to truly use it for anything, but it brought him closer to Nerida and reminded him of his mother from her passion for healing.

Nerida broke the quick kiss abruptly and shifted off his lap to kneel beside him. He could hear the quick, hard tempo of her heart as she stared over his gray skin and his wound with hard determination.

"What does it feel like?" he asked carefully, not wanting to disturb her focus.

She inhaled deeply, and he thought her hazel eyes swirled with a new brightness.

"I feel…powerful."

Her hand rose to his skin, and Tarly held his breath when the blue glow of her healing magick cast from her palms. He studied her focused expression, her brown skin beautifully highlighted by the magick she wielded.

He gritted his teeth, feeling her at work through his blood. It always became a vibrating intrusion under his skin. Seconds ticked by, and he didn't feel anything different to what he'd experienced many times with her attempts to slow the spreading poison or search for a way to retract it.

The hope he'd let warm him started to chill the longer she tried, and he felt nothing.

"This isn't right," Nerida said in frustration.

Tarly's eyes closed. More than his own disappointment, he hated hers.

"It's not an ordinary wound or illness," he said. "So you can stop pretending it can be cured like one."

Tarly reached for his shirt and pulled it over his head.

He found her with a wounded expression that cleaved him, but he didn't show it.

He said, "You should get rest before we set out tomorrow."

"Can I stay?"

Gods, he wanted that more than anything, but there was one thing he could control, and that was Nerida becoming more entangled with him than she already was.

"No."

Her brow furrowed—not hurt but adorably defiant at his rejection.

"It's freezing."

"You can have my lantern."

Nerida crossed her arms. "Am I that terrible to sleep beside?"

"You do snore."

Her mouth dropped open. "I do not!"

"It's light most of the time."

It was incredible how she could pull amusement from him even in his most dire moods. He didn't mention how the sounds she made in her sleep invoked such peace it sent him into his own deep rest like he'd never experienced before. That the warmth of her body relaxed his in a way he'd never found before.

Nerida huffed, crawling over his bed mat, which could hardly fit him alone. He smiled despite his back being to her—or at least he thought he did, but his sorrow weighed down anything joyous.

"You don't take rejection very well," he mused.

"When it's impractical, no, I don't. You can't tell me you haven't found the nights near intolerable in this winter."

"We have some coin for a room. I can take you—"

"Lie down, Sully."

He despised that name. And he wished she would never stop when he would run to the call of it in a heartbeat. For one so gentle and warm, she was damn stubborn and demanding. Tarly adored that contrast about her.

Conceding for this last night, he lay and let her shuffle in close, until their shared heat and the blanket covered them both.

"Maybe the Phoenix Blood needs a day to work," she said somberly.

Tarly wouldn't let his small flicker of hope reignite.

"Maybe," he whispered.

He couldn't stop thinking of his draining time. How everyone had set out with a role toward winning this war and saving their continent, whereas he planned to go in search of his own cure. To save one miserable life that didn't mean anything in the grander scheme of the world. His sister would be Queen of Olmstone, his father was likely dead by now, and Nerida…she was always a temporary blessing he hadn't done anything to deserve. She'd lived a long, fulfilled life before him, and she would after him.

Tarly thought she'd drifted to sleep with how long they lay there in silence. Until she pushed herself up gently, hovering partially over him. Her soft hand cupped his cheek, and she stared at him with such large, beautiful eyes he saw the world he wanted within them.

"What's wrong?" he asked, barely a breath of a whisper, even though she was smiling.

Nerida didn't answer with words. Her mouth leaned to his for a careful kiss. When Tarly responded, he was surprised when her leg hooked over his middle and she straddled him. His hands molded around her hips so gloriously it was torture, with his mind yelling at him to stop this before it went too far.

He couldn't.

Tarly had been so deprived of having someone *want* him that now this stunning, magnificent creature was offering herself, he'd become addicted. The taste of her overcame all his senses. The feel of her against him was so undeniably perfect that his entire being couldn't understand how it was possible.

He groaned into her mouth, flipping them in a single fluid motion until she lay beneath him.

"Where have you been?" he asked—a question that slipped from him with pain and tragedy.

He wished they could have met sooner. That maybe in a different time, they could have been everything.

Nerida's fingers tangled though his shoulder-length blond hair.

"Wandering…just like you."

He kissed her deeply. Nerida was something his soul didn't know it had been searching for until she was here. Every vacant year and every numb decade was worth a day he got to feel alive with her.

"I want you," he rasped. "So badly I can hardly stand it."

"Then have me."

Tarly's lips trailed down her neck, savoring every note and feel of her. Storing every precious impression she'd made on him since they met, so he would remember until his very last breath there was once someone who'd wanted him in the end. And more than anything before, he wanted her.

"Not tonight," he said, though it killed him to deny her.

Nerida's small flicker of disappointment sank him, but she accepted it without pushing.

As they settled back down and she tucked herself into him more intimately this time, he tried to subdue his raging thoughts. How unfair fate was to grant the one thing he'd longed for more than anything…when it was too late.

Tarly left his tent in the middle of the night to relieve himself, careful not to disturb Nerida. His mind was so wrecked, in turmoil, he'd hardly managed to drift off at all.

The sharp air cut across his cheeks. and he missed the warmth of her and the blankets immediately. Before he made his way around, he spied a form sitting alone against a tree, a small blue fire ablaze in front of them. He was compelled to Faythe Ashfyre, not expecting her to be out here so late and by herself.

Her hand moved across the air in front of her, and when Tarly got close enough, he saw lettering, glowing like thin strokes of fire, being drawn by the guidance of her fingers. He was completely mesmerized by such magick, and when she finished, the words came together, amazingly forming a small Firebird that took flight.

Faythe's head lolled against the trunk as she looked up at him. She offered a small smile of wordless greeting.

"What was that?" he asked, staring after the magick until its embers had disappeared through the canopy of the trees.

"A Fyremessage."

Tarly crouched to steal heat from her blue fire, fascinated by the concept. He asked, by way of idle conversation, "Can't sleep?"

"I can. Nerida's tonic is really effective."

"Ah. So your waking thoughts are too charged for you to let them go for a while."

Faythe's mouth quirked a little. "Care to share yours first?"

He huffed. "I hardly have anything that would interest you."

"I might surprise you."

"You have the fate of the world depending on you—everything must seem trivial in comparison."

"We're all threads in the fate of the world," she said thoughtfully, staring into the fire. "The one who hacks down the evil Spirit can't do so without the warriors who pave the way."

Tarly had to admit he hadn't thought much of Faythe when she was a human in Orlon's court. Knowing what he did now, all that she truly was, he felt guilty for how little he'd noticed or cared. He'd watched them mock her; talk about her like she was nothing when she wasn't around. It was quite phenomenal, who he was sitting beside now compared to then.

He said, "Considering what you've seen and been through, I think you deserve to take the leading credit."

Faythe's golden eyes were brilliant with the blue flame marching in them. He couldn't help but feel inspired, as if he were in the presence of something higher than he could comprehend, yet still so mortal, humble, at the same time.

"I don't want any of that," she said honestly, quietly. "I want peace like anyone else. I've made and will continue to make selfish choices like anyone else."

Tarly admired her honesty since it would be easy for her to gloat in all the power she had, and he thought she should take glory, considering all who'd looked down on her before she had any of it.

"You care deeply for Nerida," Faythe said unexpectedly.

Tarly swallowed hard at the mention, resisting the urge to glance back at the tent he wouldn't even see from here. "A mistake," he said. "All things considered."

"There might be a cure for the dark fae bite."

"I think Nerida is the best healer I could have by chance run into. Not even she can feel a resolution."

"That's why you're going to Lakelaria."

Tarly didn't answer—couldn't even muster a lie.

Faythe said, "You had a mate, didn't you?"

She must already know the answer, but she asked anyway, as if she'd been mulling over the concept prior to this.

"She rejected the bond after faking her death for decades to escape me." He huffed a sarcastic laugh. "It's quite epic when you think about it. How terrible I must have been for her to have taken such measures."

Faythe deliberated for seconds that crawled over his skin. He didn't know why her judgment weighed on him. Or why he stayed, near desperate for her to say something.

"Your father lost his mate and turned to Marvellas in his grief," she said, pondering over the facts.

"I don't know what one has to do with the other."

Faythe's eyes held him a moment longer before they flickered, and she smiled. Tarly was beginning to feel uneasy in her company.

"I'm glad she has you."

"I don't really offer her much. She might actually tell you how I didn't need to step into her path at all. She could have taken care of herself."

"I like to believe there a reason for every path crossed."

"Yeah, well, mine is coming up a little short."

"If you didn't have hope, you'd already be dead some way or another. Don't forget that."

Tarly appreciated the sentiment.

"I'm sorry about Reylan," he said, feeling ridiculous the moment he did. They were weightless words with what she was suffering.

"I'm going to get him back. That's the hope that keeps me alive."

"Your human friends...do you really think they're working for Marvellas now?"

"Yes...and no. I believe Marlowe sees things and leads by what she thinks will help, even if it's gaining for the enemy right now. She can't tell me everything, and I know that. But it's hard to accept sometimes."

There were some things beyond Tarly's comprehension, but he wanted to learn all he could. There was so much he wanted to know before he was gone.

"You don't want to go to Lakelaria, do you?" she asked.

Tarly wished he could keep his mouth shut, but there was something about Faythe that made him talk as if she might offer some answers, even if not so direct.

"I don't want to spend what little time I might have on myself. I want to help shift some movement in this war. If I'm on borrowed time, I'd like it to count for something since my life before now has been nothing worth remembering."

"That's understandable," Faythe said. "But for what it's worth, I think you've impacted more than you know already."

"I wasn't implying I need validation."

"I'm not supplying you with that. I only mean, if you don't see the hearts you lie in, you don't deserve to be in them."

Her sight flicked behind him, and he caught her meaning.

Faythe said, "You and I might be another crossing of paths neither of us expected tonight."

"What do you mean?"

Faythe inhaled a long breath, tipping her head back. She engrossed herself in the flames, but she was lost to her own mind. "I've never been fond of chess—I much prefer cards—but it's all I can see. A board of moves and countermoves. So many pieces to play, and winning cannot be without sacrifice."

"What are you saying?"

He had a growing sense of unexplainable determination, and when Faythe spoke, he finally knew what he had to do.

"That you can either stay the king, hiding behind every other piece, or take the guise of a pawn and step into the real danger of the board."

CHAPTER EIGHTEEN

Tauria

Tauria hadn't considered the means of travel when Mordecai suggested she go with him to Valgard. It made sense he would fly with her, but her skin still crawled even now her feet were on the ground and she'd gained some distance.

At least she hadn't come alone, and she was relieved when Mordecai even suggested she bring Edith along with her so she'd feel more at ease with familiar company. The dark fae had flown herself, slower than Mordecai could travel.

She had barely been able to take in the view of Valgard as dark sea turned to land beneath them, but what she did observe was how gloomy and barren these lands were. Unnaturally so. It wasn't just in sight—Tauria felt it within herself. Sinking down, when her palm rested to the chilled, dry land, she couldn't reach for any roots of life.

"It wasn't always like this," Mordecai said at her clear observations.

He'd landed them atop a parched hill, where she could see a stone city close by. It reminded her of Olmstone, but where those lands had a breath of warmth and bright beauty, Valgard was overcast with darkness, like a curse.

"When did it change?" she asked, following him the rest of the way.

"During the Dark Age. People have since whispered that because of my actions, the Gods cursed my lands to this infertility."

"How do you feed your people?"

"We still have fresh water supply, and they have learned to grow vegetables and feed for the livestock in domes of glass. There are several with your talent who inspire nature, and many others with abilities that help."

"My talent... you forced florakinetics here from Fenstead?"

"My kind can be born with abilities too, though far rarer than the fae. But what might shock you is that there are ordinary fae who have lived generations here too, and humans."

It didn't answer her question, but it was a curious enlightenment. Tauria had long believed only the ruthless dark fae occupied this island. She didn't know what it meant to discover that was not the truth.

She realized why Mordecai hadn't flown them right to his castle. He'd wanted to show her the lands and begin to teach her more, perhaps sway her mind and her heart from what it had been taught all her life on the mainland. Tauria wasn't going to be so easily convinced. She looked upon the sad soils of Valgard and stood beside the culprit of its downfall.

Edith followed a few steps behind them as they passed through his city walls. Every guard in black bowed their heads to Mordecai, but he paid them no attention. He walked casually but with a dominant presence, hands clasped behind his back and silently staring toward his black castle.

"What business is it you have here if Marvellas is on the mainland?" Tauria tried.

"You are familiar with the running of a kingdom. A ruler can only leave it in the hands of their council for so long. Otherwise we risk breeding usurpers."

Tauria felt foolish for asking when she knew this, but in her defense, she didn't know Valgard was a kingdom that still had political structure.

"Is your heir here?" she asked.

"No."

She was getting no further with her burning curiosity about his child, but Tauria had come here with the hope to discover more about Mordecai and his heir somehow.

"If you are not wed, won't your council challenge the legitimacy of them?"

"I would kill anyone who tried. They know my succession, and while it may be hard for you to believe, I have a select few who are *very* loyal to me and will make sure that if anything were to happen to me, my heir would take their rightful place."

So why are they not here?

Tauria observed his subjects as they continued leisurely through the winding path toward the castle. The buildings were as barren as the land, but not from poverty. Everything just seemed bathed in a dreary hue as if it had long forgotten the kiss of the bright sunlight.

People watched them go by with stunned stares and wary retreats. Though she couldn't be sure if it was out of fear of Mordecai or uncertainty about her. Would they even know who she was?

She saw several of the glass dome structures Mordecai had mentioned peeking over the stone buildings, and spying the first signs of any vibrancy lit her chest. Oh, how she loved the color green. Tauria had to appreciate that they'd learned how to grow plants and crops when their land itself refused.

"Welcome to my home, Tauria Stagknight," Mordecai announced as the tall, black wood doors of his castle were opened as they approached.

Despite all the darkness, Tauria found herself stunned by the beauty of his palace. Within was monochrome, but the black-and-white marble floors and pillars were crafted with meticulous artistry. She never thought she'd be walking halls lined with black banners adorning the fanged serpent of the ages-long enemy kingdom of her continent. Though there was a part of her that balked at the sight, the animal stitched into fabric was as proud as any of those representing the kingdoms of Ungardia.

"Do you know why our emblem is a serpent?" he asked, guiding her through his halls.

Tauria had read about it once.

"Your father was among the candidates who put themselves forward to be the first King of Valgard. He was the only dark fae and had no one backing his rule. Though it was decided a trial would prove the one fit to rule, not a vote of popularity. A week before the trial, Vakarys Vesaria was bitten by a serpent, and the venom almost claimed his life. A healer found him on the brink of death. Your mother, I believe. On the night of the feast before the trial, Vakarys, still recovering, attended with the serpent that had bitten him wrapped around his shoulders as if they'd become companions. People would come to believe that was his true test of worthiness, for at that feast, unbeknown to anyone, Vakarys had poised the wine of all his competitors with the same venom from the serpent. Even with healers, none of them survived."

Mordecai watched her with surprise. "Very good. Now, would you call him cunning, or a cheat?"

Tauria thought about the story again. "One might say neither. To have survived a venom no one else did…perhaps it was a favor of the Gods. Who are we, mere mortals of their creation, to question their judgment?"

"Lucky then," Mordecai supplied.

"Fated," Tauria considered.

"So what does that say about me—his son who would go on to lead the darkest age the land has ever seen?"

"I think it's not for us to question the why of fate. We are guided by infinite threads we couldn't begin to fathom. Without evil, there is no good. Without suffering, there is no compassion."

Mordecai led for a long stretch of silence. Tauria absorbed more of the decor that was as grand as any castle, but the elegance of the black and white was luring her into a sense of calm.

"I find your perceptions fascinating," he said at last, stopping outside a set of double doors with two guards posted outside. "I have something I must do, but I think you'll find yourself occupied here. Perhaps you'll discover more knowledge you can share your thoughts about over supper."

Tauria knew then he'd escorted her to his castle library, and her excitement surged. Mordecai must have read it on her face, as he almost yielded a smile.

"Do not wander from here. I will send for you later," he said firmly, not lingering for a moment after.

That left her alone with Edith, and the dark fae matched Tauria's slowly spreading smile before they entered the library.

True to the dark theme of the palace, the wood of the shelving and the double spiral staircases to the second level were coated in black. The hall was magnificent. The faint clack of Tauria's shoes was all that echoed as she moved slowly to take in the place.

"Is there anything I can guide you toward?" Edith asked.

Tauria's eyes fell to her. "You've been here before?"

"Oh yes. I spent some of my early youth in these halls before I begged to go to Fenstead."

Edith had mentioned her father was very powerful. A lord, perhaps? One that had no desire to raise a child and had let her all but raise herself.

"Honestly, I'm trying to get to know Mordecai more. He's very busy, often leaving me alone, and I would like to take some of that burden to school me about himself and this kingdom off his shoulders."

Edith hummed, glancing at nothing in particular as she considered where to direct Tauria for such knowledge.

"There are many boring books on the lands of Ungardia, and perhaps they'll give more detail about Valgard itself, but the true knowledge about Mordecai and his past is likely to be under close guard in his locked study."

Tauria's hope deflated. She might be able to catch him inside and glimpse his personal study, but being left alone to scour his books and papers would be near impossible.

"I might still have a friend here who is one of his bookkeepers. Only a very select few scholars have a key just to tend to his books. They would perish without proper care."

Edith was proving to be far more useful than simply tending to her needs. "You would really help me?"

"I think the high lord would appreciate your initiative!" She beamed. Tauria didn't know why it made her wary. Edith had been nothing but innocent and kind, but this answer to her problem came easier than Tauria was used to, and that had her searching for a trap.

"He wouldn't like me trespassing on his personal space," Tauria said skeptically.

Edith waved her off. "I'll bring the relevant books to you. Then they'll be returned. He'll only know his scholars were within the study."

Tauria nodded, uttering her thanks. For now, all she had were endless tomes of knowledge she already knew, but it would do no harm to check while she was stuck here anyway.

Hours later, and she was beginning to think Mordecai had forgotten about bringing her here. She slumped into a deep black velvet chaise littered with open books. Edith sat on the edge, engrossed in her own book.

She watched the dark fae and didn't expect to grow a protective attachment to her, much like how she'd grown a bond to Opal, Tarly's younger sister, in Olmstone. Though Edith was of an age to look out for herself, Tauria knew that wasn't enough.

"No matter what happens, I hope you'll stay by my side," Tauria blurted.

Edith blinked away the fatigue of staring too long at the text. "You're very kind."

That told Tauria the dark fae wasn't used to being seen or receiving any kindness.

"The high lord has called you for supper, Your Highness," a fae interrupted.

Tauria's stomach twisted with hunger. It was about time.

"I'll meet you later," Edith said as she stood. Their secret to retrieve the books in Mordecai's study hung in that farewell.

Tauria wouldn't hold her breath in case Edith couldn't convince her friend to slip the books from his collection. She would find another way, for what would he have to hide that he needed to keep so closely guarded?

Dining with Mordecai would always be an awkwardly unpleasant experience. They often ate in silence, but his presence always made her skin crawl as if she were in the company of a wraith, not a full person.

She slipped glances at him when he was occupied in his meal. Everything he ate was normal. The fact he was a resurrected being unsettled her. As if he should burn in sunlight or only eat raw meat, or as if he were hiding some ugly form beneath his temporary flesh.

Tauria swallowed, upsetting her stomach with her own outlandish thoughts.

"Are you not well?" Mordecai asked, pinning her with soulless onyx eyes.

"It seems I've taken a turn," she confessed.

Tauria reached for her goblet clumsily at the same time as a servant leaned in to top up Mordecai's, causing it to topple. She gasped, snatching her hand back when the thick crimson liquid flooded over the table and some of the food.

Her hand clamped over her mouth, and she stood from the table.

"You are aware the dark fae drink human blood. The Transitioned need it survive," he said, so nonchalant despite her horror.

"And what are you?" she snapped.

"Deathless."

A dark coil lanced her spine. She didn't know what that meant—that he couldn't be killed?

"Did you want to be brought back?" Tauria dared to ask.

Mordecai considered her question, leaning back in his chair while the servant tried frantically to clean the blood. It was futile. Tauria noticed his round human ears then.

"Had I the choice, I think I would have said yes. My time ended before my mission was achieved. However, had I known the condition would be slavery to a powerful Goddess, I might have declined."

"Then why do you do her bidding? What does she have over you?"

Mordecai's eyes darkened with warning. He wouldn't divulge such an answer to her, but Tauria was intrigued more than ever. He called himself a slave to Marvellas and didn't hide his resentment.

The high lord moved so suddenly she lunged back, her chair screeching across the floor, but it wasn't her he was reaching for.

Tauria's scream was muffled by her hand as she watched Mordecai grab the human and sink his teeth into his neck. The human made a few choking sounds, their blown eyes fixed on the ceiling.

"Stop!" Tauria yelled, attempting to spare the innocent life, but it was too late.

Mordecai pulled back with a groan, letting the body fall limp. The human's head turned her way, the terror of his final moments screaming at her through his glass eyes.

"You said yourself you didn't have to kill to feed!" she cried.

Mordecai plucked a cloth from the table, wiping the corners of his mouth before dropping it with careless disrespect onto the body. He stalked to her with a certain wildness in his eyes. A high from the amount of blood he'd consumed.

When he was close enough, Tauria seethed at him so powerfully she knew he could feel it. Regardless, his fingers grazed her chin, and he looked at her with a passionate desire.

To her complete abhorrence, Mordecai leaned down as if to kiss her, and Tauria's impulse took over. The resounding hard slap of her palm connecting with his face pounded the beat in her chest. Despite her throbbing hand, his face barely moved an inch from the impact.

A few beats of silence followed. As deadly as those before war.

Mordecai gripped her throat with the quickness and precision of a serpent strike. It brought their faces so close she would have retched at the scent of blood in his breath, were she not struggling to inhale her own. He was so fast, so much more powerful, with fresh human blood in his system.

His entire army would be. In even numbers on a battlefield, even with more magick on their side the fae didn't stand a chance. They'd always known this, but being in the clutches of that reality struck the daunting odds in her with renewed hopelessness.

"I'm looking forward to the day you lose your memories and indulge with me," he said cruelly.

Mordecai let her go just as her consciousness threatened to fall into darkness. She fell without the capacity to catch herself, hitting the black marble floor hard.

She couldn't hear him leave with the pounding of her pulse in her ears, but her blurry vision watched his footsteps in relief.

Tauria peeled herself off the ground on shaky elbows before hands assisted her to stand. She didn't know the dark fae guard and was surprised he hadn't just observed her suffering.

"Can I escort you somewhere?" he asked.

Tauria wondered if Mordecai would reprimand the guard's kindness toward her, but she was glad to see it. Not all dark fae were cold and cruel. Tauria couldn't let their malicious high lord and a one-sided history make her resent an entire species.

"Thank you, but I'll find my way."

With a smile of gratitude to him, Tauria breathed steadily as she left the dining hall. She didn't know where she was going, having not been told where she would be sleeping for the night.

Tauria caught herself against the wall with the wave of nausea that roiled in her stomach, because what if Mordecai planned for her to sleep with *him*?

She wouldn't let that happen.

"There you are!"

Edith finding her was a relief. The dark fae wore a cloak, and she looked around conspiratorially before flashing a bundle of books tucked under her arm.

Tauria's eyes lit up. She'd actually acquired them.

Edith giggled, hooking Tauria's arm and guiding her along the halls with memorized ease.

They came to the servants' quarters, where Tauria assumed Edith was staying. The dark fae pulled them into a small, humble room with a lit fireplace and twin cots.

"I'm not sure if they'll have what you're looking for, but this was all I could find," she said, holding out the books.

Tauria beamed. "This is perfect. You're amazing."

Edith smiled, sitting on one of the cots.

Craving the warmth, Tauria took the bedding off the second cot and sat by the fire, quickly losing herself to books that felt deliciously forbidden. Her adrenaline pumped with every page turned, as though the next could unveil the darkest secret of the high lord for them to end him.

When Tauria flipped to the next page, her fingers traced down the jagged strokes drawn on the page. "He was a Stormcaster," she muttered out loud.

"That ability hasn't been around in centuries," Edith said, now lying on her stomach watching Tauria read.

"I've never heard of it. The power of lightning is…fascinating." *And absolutely lethal.* "He would have used it by now, wouldn't he? I don't think the ability came back to him when he was brought back to life."

"I bet that contributes to his resentment about being alive."

Tauria hummed her agreement, continuing her reading. Most of it was dull and unhelpful, until Tauria came across Mordecai's family tree. It wasn't long, and not up-to-date enough to reveal the name of his heir or a potential lover.

"He had a sister, and she was a Nightwalker," Tauria discovered.

Her finger traced down the vine. Mordecai's parents had died naturally. His sister had died in childbirth with her third pregnancy. Shortly after, Mordecai had started his movement of the Dark Age. He'd lost most of his nieces and nephews during it except one—a fae male who'd mated with someone from the mainland, leaving behind their claim to Valgard once Mordecai was defeated, and ending the reign of the Vesarias. Tauria kept following until more recent times, and the family name switched through several marriages. The documentation of the diluted Vesaria bloodline had stopped around five hundred years ago, with the last being a daughter by a very different family name.

She drew a shallow gasp.

"What is it?" Edith asked.

Tauria couldn't stop staring at the familiar name, wondering if it were just a coincidence and someone else might have the same one. Because it was Nik's mother who came to mind. Leia Caeldagh…who would later meet the King of High Farrow, Orlon Silvergriff: her mate.

CHAPTER NINETEEN

Izaiah

"If you're going to pretend to read, you should at least look at the pages," Tynan said.

It jerked Izaiah from the scenes his mind had been playing out as if he were in two places at once. Only then did he realize his hand had been flipping pages while his sight bore holes into the opposite wall.

He thumped his book shut in one hand to glower at Tynan seated at the desk in his rooms.

"If you want to convince me you're making progress, you shouldn't be leaving such long stretches of silence. I'm getting bored."

Tynan's hair was disheveled from the many times he'd dragged frustrated hands through it, his elbows propped on the table. It was particularly attractive, and Izaiah only itched to be the cause of it instead.

"I think this is pointless. When will I have a use for reading? It's not like we have time to indulge in fantasies, and besides, if I'm going to die in this war, the Nether isn't going to care for my illiteracy."

He leaned back in his seat, pushing the book away, and Izaiah gravitated toward him with little conscious thought.

"I'd say we've made do with finding adequate time for *fantasy*," Izaiah said, coming around behind him.

Tynan was too damn tempting, and he couldn't help himself. This need to touch what should be forbidden. Why was it that the most sinful fruit was always the most desirable?

Izaiah slipped a hand over Tynan's shoulder, and it was like his tension melted under the tightening of his fingers. It flared dominance in him. A thought that this dark fae would mold for him. Whatever he asked.

"There's certainly some things I'd rake myself across the coals for," Tynan answered, tipping his head back against the tall seat.

Izaiah leaned in, unable to help himself with the purposeful breath he fanned across Tynan's ear as he reached for the quill. On a sheet of blank paper, he hesitated only for a second, then he scribed one line.

"If you manage to read that, you can come claim a reward."

Their heads tilting toward each other brought their lips just shy of meeting. Tynan broke first, and Izaiah gave some release to the ache swelling inside him for the few seconds he allowed the deep kiss. Then he planted his hand on Tynan's chest, pushing him roughly against the chair in warning.

Swiping up the parchment, he folded it twice. When Tynan stood, Izaiah slipped it into the pocket of his pants. The dark fae tried to step away, but Izaiah's fingers hooked into his waistband. For no other reason than his crazed need for the challenge it breathed between them, it was becoming a sadistic thrill.

"It's just a phrase about my dashing looks and stellar personality," he said. "You know how to find me when you figure it out."

Izaiah let him go. Picking up a book, he pretended the tension between them was so easily forgotten. His lust was painted in Tynan's frustration.

"Where have you been?" Tynan folded his arms with the question. His accusation was enough to smother the mood.

"I didn't know you needed tabs on me at all hours," Izaiah brushed off. "You need to find another hobby to keep you distracted. I'm afraid I have other things to occupy my time."

"You're an arrogant prick."

"Flattery won't entice me."

Tynan rolled his eyes before heading to the door. "Keep out of trouble," he grumbled.

Izaiah smiled to himself. It dropped bittersweet in the vacancy of his rooms. Bracing his hands against the desk, his head bowed at the uncertainty that flooded in during the moments he gained alone. His plan wasn't really a plan as such. Though he'd brushed off Zaiana's warnings about the ruin, he harbored them truly. He knew the risks and only hoped he wasn't the coward his father had taunted he was.

The weak, helpless younger sibling who couldn't do anything.

Didn't want to fight.

Only wanted the pain to stop, but not for himself—for Kyleer, who took the worst of it for them both.

His fingers curled to a painful grip on the wood.

He wouldn't be powerless again. Not in this war, when he had the chance to be something bigger.

He couldn't fight his father for Ky then. Now he could damn well try to fight the world for him. And for Reylan. And Livia. And Faythe. And *everyone*.

Izaiah would do whatever it took to be unstoppable for them.

On his knees, he had to question his sanity to willingly reach for the torture that reduced him to trembling and helpless on the ground. Izaiah panted on all fours, his skin hot and slicked with sweat, while he tried to blink color back into his surroundings.

"I don't care for your life," Zaiana said, crouching by him. "But I hope you're doing this knowing the wreckage it will cause your brother if it fails."

Breathing was like inhaling ash, but when his locked muscles began to ease from his attempt to merge with the ruin, he sat back.

"If? Careful—it's beginning to sound like you actually have faith in me." Izaiah's eyes slipped closed as he was reminded of his friend in that word with two meanings.

To have Faythe.

To live like death is a game.

He grinned, perhaps delirious in this state while he tempted the dark force.

Love is a prize.

Should he succeed, it would be for them. All of what he was.

And danger is desire.

There was a life he'd lived when he'd cowered from anything dangerous, but that fae had had to die to survive the mines his father had enslaved him to.

"I'm going again," he said through a labored breath.

"No, you're not."

He didn't expect her to care, but Zaiana slipped the box closed. It wasn't until the energy silenced with it that he realized how taut his body was at the power emanating through the catacombs.

Izaiah eyed the knife on the ground. He'd just open the Blood Box again.

"How do you know when you're close to *merging* with it?" he quizzed.

Zaiana paced. Something else was on her mind today, and he'd bit back several instincts to question it.

"It's like…death," she said.

"I gathered that. I've felt like it would claim me several times we've tried now."

She shook her head. "What you feel is your physical body's limit, convinced it's dying. You need to surpass that—let the mind push further."

"Aren't they one and the same?"

"No. Your mind can wholly convince your body to shut down when it is perfectly well. It is the most powerful thing alive. So if it can kill its own host just by thought and emotion, it can transcend the physical punishment magick will try to convince you is enough to kill you. Take back control of your heart that will race to its influence, cool your blood it will set fire to. Magick can't be fought physically—it has to be mastered mentally."

Izaiah's brows lifted in admiration. He had to admit, she was kind of brilliant, but not aloud.

"How did they teach you that?"

"They didn't."

He watched her, an arm folded over herself while the other propped her chin in her hand. It were as if she was in two places at once.

"Want to get off your mind what has you challenging the ground you're wearing down?"

She seemed to contemplate. They barely tolerated each other as acquaintances, but perhaps down here, they could forget the past transgressions of above.

"Your heartbeat…do you believe it's tied to your emotions?"

The question was as naïve as it was vulnerable, and at anyone else, he might have laughed.

"It's nothing more than an organ that circulates blood."

Izaiah found it somewhat tragic and ironic that someone so in tune with the mind could believe in such a fairy tale.

"I've heard it before," she said so quietly the tension in the room became as fragile as glass. One wrong word, and it would shatter and raise steel to block him out again. "From fae and mortals. They become tricked by love and give each other their hearts. I've heard the declaration before."

He didn't expect the impact that slammed into him. She believed it. Perhaps Tynan did too. All of them. That their still hearts truly meant they couldn't love.

"It's not meant so literally," Izaiah said, equally hushed, so as to walk on that glass with her.

She didn't look at him, but he couldn't stop watching her, so lost in thought he wondered what had brought on this new curiosity.

"Have you ever given yours?" she asked.

"No."

"Would you?"

He didn't know how they'd gotten here, but while they would go back to showing their claws to each other above, he kept them retracted for as long as this moment might last.

"Maybe," he answered. "Though your kind is right about one thing. To give it, to love even in friendship, it is vulnerable. It is a weakness for any enemy to exploit, and the more spots you allow, the easier you are to kill."

"Do you think I'm a monster?"

"I don't think that's what you're wondering," Izaiah said, feeling a crack on this rare pane they were balancing on. "You think you have a still heart to blame for all your heinous actions, but you don't. Regardless of whether you managed to strike a beat in your chest, everything you've done is on you. But for what it's worth…what I do think is that you've always chosen survival."

"Aren't we all creatures choosing that? Even Marvellas."

"No. Or at least not anymore. She's driven by power and greed. Marvellas sees a world not to her order, and she wants to fix it to her vision, no matter the devastation it would take to reconstruct it. It's not her own survival that motivates her—it's villainy believing it is heroism."

Zaiana was silent, with her back to him for long enough he thought their moment was over.

"They're cursed," she said. "All of the dark fae. Led to believe they can't find attachment to one another—can't love. Shouldn't mourn and shouldn't hurt. Because they have no heart to be plagued by such weakness. They're taught it's what makes the dark fae superior, that being cold and ruthless is what will win them the land and freedom they deserve. It's all a lie."

"You said you were born that way."

Her head barely shook, her voice hardly a whisper. "I don't think I was. I think my heartbeat was taken."

Izaiah stood slowly. He hadn't expected Zaiana to share this with him. Something that felt like it could shift the tide of the war. Despite this, he was growing uncomfortable with the feelings stirring between them. It didn't feel right—he wasn't the one who could hear her troubles and give a damn.

But Kyleer would. He'd wanted to be there for her, and she'd betrayed him. For that, he pushed back anything of comfort he wanted to extend to the dark fae.

"So what are you going to do about it?" Izaiah said, swiping up the knife.

He cut before she could turn around, watching the box flare to life again.

"They think they made me into their perfect weapon," she said.

Izaiah smiled without meeting her stare, feeling their thoughts align.

"Then I do hope I get to witness when they meet their maker."

CHAPTER TWENTY

Zaiana

Zaiana was plagued by an unwanted presence in her subconscious mind again. It had been some weeks since the last time they'd interacted, and she'd just about concluded she'd dreamt this place and the intruding male.

"Do you get headaches often?"

Zaiana sat in a thick cloud of her subconscious darkness, her head propped against her fist, while the invading pest paced around.

"More so since you've been showing up," she grumbled.

"You could help us both out by taming this space at least."

"I like it the way it is."

"That's a lie."

Of course he would *feel* that. Zaiana was beginning to regret the deal she'd made with her phantom.

"What do you want me to do? Speak to it?"

"Not be so uptight, for a start."

"I am not—" Zaiana stopped herself from wasting more energy on his insufferable remarks. "You're not helping at all. This was a damn foolish idea, and one I've certainly reconsidered with how long it's been."

"I've been busy, as I'm sure you have too. And I can only guide—I can't change anything. I mean, I could, but it would only be a temporary illusion. The real and permanent change has to come from you."

Zaiana fell onto her back to be swallowed by the dark cloud.

"Dramatics don't help either," he called over the next crack of thunder.

"Just send me off to sleep again," she said, closing her eyes.

The smoke around her dissipated in a flurry that forced her to glower at him.

"Neither of us can afford to expend too much energy in here, so why don't we just get a move on?" he exasperated.

She propped herself up on her hands, with piqued interest. "What might you be getting up to on the real plane of reality?"

"Nice try. Up."

Zaiana rolled her eyes, getting to her feet with disinclination.

The male stood cross-armed, always keeping his face shadowed by a hood that she thought was enhanced with darkness by his command.

"You're really not what I expected," he said, almost like a slipped thought he'd been guarding since their last meeting.

Zaiana grew defensive. "What did you expect?"

"That you'd be fighting me with vicious aggression, not juvenile reluctance."

"I guess I don't have much vicious aggression left to spare by the time you get your turn of me in here."

"Truthfully, I'm glad whatever you're doing out there is exhausting you enough to let slip the mask."

"It's not a mask," she bit out.

If she had a face for him, she imagined a hooked brow that would say, *I don't believe you.*

Zaiana didn't care what her irritating dream phantom thought. Once they both had what they wanted, she would be able to block him out for good and forget about him.

"All you've done is observe and state the obvious," she said. "It's grating on my nerves."

"I've been trying to figure out where to begin, actually. Your mind is one of the most twisted and guarded I've ever come across."

"Good to know," she mumbled.

"Everyone has their own demons," he explained. "Parts of the mind that are like a plague. When I said it was rare to see a colorless mind, this is why. Usually, the parts of the mind that fight itself and inflict self-harm are like dark spots. They can grow and linger for periods of time and then shrink back—they never fully fade. But yours…it's taken over entirely. So many dark spots have merged into one."

His tone became distant, personal.

"This is too much," she said quickly. She couldn't stand the crawling of her skin at everything he was observing, *assuming*.

He didn't know her. He couldn't help her. No one could.

"You should leave."

"Why? So you can continue to deny you need help?"

"I don't need anything from you. Or from anyone."

"I think we should start with a memory—"

"No." Her chest rose and feel deeply. "This was a mistake."

"Zaiana." He spoke her name so gently she could hardly bear it. "There is no one else here. No one who needs to know about any of it."

He would know. If she let him in, she couldn't forget he was a real person out there. Someone who could be using her and finding things in here that could destroy her.

"What if we start with me then?" he tried, so patient and calm when she was ready to do what it took to harness the storm around them and strike him with it to keep her thoughts safe.

"Are we traveling to your mind—is that possible?"

He chuckled lightly. "No, and…perhaps. I've never tried to switch minds with another Nightwalker before, actually." His hood tilted with curiosity before straightening again. "What if I give you something first?"

"Like a name?"

"No. How about a memory for a memory?"

Zaiana contemplated. It would be a clue to figuring him out—perhaps something she could have against him to track him down if he crossed her.

"Fine."

His mouth quirked before he turned, and Zaiana watched in fascination as the smoke began to shift.

She wandered closer with vacant steps at the impossibility of the moving picture before her. It remained monochrome, but it was wondrous all the same.

"I've never shown anyone this before," he said, the first hint of nerves in his tone.

Zaiana watched the scene through eyes that saw the world from a lower height. She couldn't guess his age as the memory unfolded from his perspective.

The young fae climbed over a hill before staring at woodland that appeared misty before entering. Past the tree line, Zaiana rubbed her arms subconsciously at the ominous blanket that coated her, as if she were experiencing it for the first time with this fae.

There was no sound to these woods—that was what made every one of his footfalls like a great disturbance to the silence. He stopped walking at the echo of a voice.

"What a brave little thing you are," the voice cooed. *"I'm at a loss with you since one so young doesn't know true fear yet. What it's like to love and lose. Need and fail."*

Contrary to its claim, Zaiana was overcome with a prickling terror that belonged to the young fae.

"I could simply deny you, but there is a reason you seek this place so soon. A reason you need it as much as it will need you."

"I-I just want a place to play," he said.

"Of course. Such a young heart so alone."

She couldn't sympathize with him. She'd grown up surrounded by company she'd had to shield herself from. Other darklings that knew they could end up killing each other one day.

The memory continued.

Zaiana jumped at the sudden crack of lightning. Not in her subconscious, but as part of his vision. Her hand rose to her chest as though the rapid beat were in her too. The young fae took off running when a second crack sounded. He wasn't fleeing from it—he was trying to find it.

"I'm coming!" he yelled.

"Who are you looking for?" Zaiana breathed, searching the woodland with him, but there was no form nor glimpse of the lightning she could hear.

"I don't know," he said, and she believed him. "All I remember is that someone was out there. Someone I wanted to help, and my greatest fear was that I would be too late. I'm most terrified of being the reason people die."

"I'll find you!" The young fae's last call drifted away on a wind that carried the image of breaking light through the grim woodland. One last vibrant stoke of purple lightning scored across…

Zaiana blinked at the returning gloom of her subconscious. She didn't know what to make of what he'd showed her.

"Why that memory?" she asked.

His head was more bowed than usual. "I think you're smart enough to figure out a lot from it should you need. It's vague enough to make it difficult though."

It shouldn't mean anything to her, but she was already trying to figure it out. What frightened her was that it had nothing to do with wanting his identity for leverage.

"Is that why you're fascinated with lightning?"

He huffed. "Maybe. I've always quite liked storms, but my mate does not."

Another clue. Had he meant to slip up?

"Why not?"

He dismissed her question. "Your turn."

That turned her body taut and her mind to steel.

"Don't back out on me now," he warned.

"Why? Because you could take what you wanted anyway?"

His hand disappeared through the shadows of his hood, and she imagined his exasperation. "I'm no stranger to having people think the worst of me with my ability," he said coldly. "I get it. Yes, I could take anything I wanted right now. I could hold you hostage and make you watch as I did it. You would be helpless to throw me out. But you already know that, and I didn't have to force my way in here tonight— it was like you opened the damn door and may as well have offered me tea when I arrived. Say it right now that you don't want me to come, and I won't. You were only an intrigue. You need me far more than I need you, and I know that's not something you like to hear. I can feel your protest, your defense, all from a past that has clearly taught you the only trust you can have is in yourself. I'm not going to waste my time and lose sleep convincing you of what I have offered you. Take it, or tell me not to come back."

Zaiana was stunned by the reprimand. In the real world, she might have walked away. She never wanted to depend on anyone. Help became a debt; a weakness that would be held against her.

This was different. Right now, she didn't want to walk away. She could wake up and pretend it was a dream. She had some piece of him, and she didn't know how the certainty settled in her that this wasn't a trick.

"I don't know what to show you," she said in defeat.

"If you'll let me, I can try to feel for the most prominent lead to figuring out your subconscious storm."

"What about my ability?"

"I think we need to go back further. While it may seem like it's come from some traumatic event, a block like this to take your whole ability has to be tied deeper, held hostage by something else. It won't be easy to confront, and I'll have to see it all. I promise you, anything that happens in here will remain in here."

There was no point in asking how she could trust that—she had to find it out for herself. Did she really have anything to lose now anyway?

"Do it," Zaiana said, even though those two words gripped her with a fear so great she wanted to dissipate into the storm that raged, never to emerge to face the worst of her fears...

Herself.

She turned away as if she could avoid seeing it.

"You have to be ready to face it, otherwise you could hurt us both with your reactions."

He came closer. Zaiana shouldn't be this unbothered by his company, but he was soothing the rage of emotions around them. She couldn't explain it.

"I can handle it," she said, but it was pointless to lie to him.

"Just give me a forewarning if you want us to retreat from the memory."

Zaiana could only nod, sliding her sight to him. She still had no face to mark him. Occasionally, she would catch his mouth, but it was little to identify him by.

"You'll feel me reaching. It will be like a pressure, and it might grow more intense the further I reach. This is your first chance to trust me. I promise to retreat if it's too much. Just say the word."

With a long breath, she spun around. She had faced far worse torture than this. At least, she thought she had.

"I'm trusting you."

Zaiana focused on her breathing when the first prod of her thoughts spiked her immediate need to defend herself. *Nothing to lose.* And hopefully, her lightning to gain back. Her eyes flexed at the building pressure. Deeper and deeper.

Colors flashed, as if he were touching many years, decades, filing through her memories, and she wondered how he knew what to look for. How he would know where to begin.

Farther and farther back.

Regret began to grow.

"Almost there."

"Where?" she snapped in her panic.

"The place where it all began."

Zaiana gasped as it was like a thread of her mind had been plucked suddenly.

The kaleidoscope made its final turn from a mosaic to a clear image, and Zaiana wanted to retreat. To cast him out and never come back here again.

"Him," the male said, with a low, dark edge she didn't expect.

Mordecai was the first figure in the scene, so much more dominating and taller than her small perspective, and it was as if she were right back there. They were in a woodland, and though it was all staggered trees and ominous surroundings, she knew where she was: the Dark Woods of Galmire.

"This isn't going to help," Zaiana said quietly, because the mass expanding in her chest threatened to erupt.

"There has to be a reason we're in this memory," he said.

"Come, little one," Mordecai said, but her child self was rooted. Frightened. The high lord reached out a hand, and Zaiana knew it was either take it or face punishment.

Zaiana's hand rose to her chest as the darkling's did.

"What is that?" she breathed.

It was so precious, but a building terror grew too much for the small chest it occupied.

"Your heartbeat."

She shook her head. "It's not possible."

"I think we're about to find out how very possible it is."

"I want to go home," her child self said, so timid and innocent she didn't recognize herself.

"You are so brave, Zaiana," Mordecai said, the gentleness jarring compared to the male she knew.

"I don't remember this," she said aloud.

"It was hidden, as if something has interfered with your thoughts before."

Her child self was content with her small hand sliding into Mordecai's. Zaiana wanted to believe this was a trick, a false conjuring made by the male himself, but it was so, *so* convincing.

They walked for some time, until ahead another figure emerged, and Zaiana's real breath inhaled sharply, along with the darkling's.

She was so vibrant against the misty gloom.

Marvellas.

Fire against the smoke.

Her child self knew the sight of danger, and that this creature was not a friend.

"This is an extraordinary thing indeed," Marvellas drawled, fixing wide eyes on her with fascination.

Zaiana's hand shook at the fluctuating beat under her palm. She thought she knew the language of it, except this was like no other she'd heard before. This small, untamed heart was both full and broken.

"It's not me," she said.

"This won't work if you're in denial over what you see."

The hand that landed on her shoulder as they watched shouldn't have been a comfort, but it was. The male shouldn't be extending such kindness, but she couldn't shrug it off.

"Is it really necessary to use her for this?" Mordecai asked, and if she didn't know any better, she would think he *cared* for the young version of herself.

"I only met Mordecai when I was past my second century," Zaiana said, trying to puzzle together why she couldn't remember this. "He came to watch the Blood Trials."

"What is that?"

"I won. It was to pick the leaders of the Blackfair and Silverfair lines."

"If she will be as powerful as you say, there is no better candidate to carry it," Marvellas answered.

"I have seen it," Mordecai said, but there was something detached in his tone.

Marvellas crouched to her younger self, and Zaiana's breath was becoming uneven like the darkling's.

"Such exquisite eyes," the Spirit marveled. Her head tilted up to Mordecai to say, *"A likeness we never thought we'd see again."*

Mordecai's hand tightened on her younger self's protectively. But why?

Marvellas lifted the necklace the darkling was playing with nervously. An eight-pointed star. The male beside her took one small step.

"Where did you get that?"

"I-I don't know what it is," she said honestly, unsure why that would pique his interest.

"What do you have there?" Marvellas asked.

"It's from her mother," Mordecai said.

"Where is she now?"

"Dead."

The darkling cried when the Spirit yanked the chain, snapping it from her neck. She tossed it aside, and her younger self strained to pick it up.

"No sentiments. You know this," Marvellas scolded.

Tears fell from the darkling's eyes, and her lip wobbled, but she stayed silent.

Marvellas reached out a hand to cup her cheek. *"No one is worth your tears, child. There is much for you to learn so you'll never be hurt by such pitiful things again. Starting with this."*

She tapped a finger to her younger self's chest, a dark claim on the fluttering, tiny life in her chest.

"I was born without a heart," Zaiana said, unable to comprehend this vision.

She shook her head, bewildered.

Marvellas tried to reach for the darkling, but she jerked away, *hugging* into Mordecai's side.

Zaiana stumbled back. This wasn't real. It couldn't be right.

When the Spirit reached again, with a look too frightening to the darkling, she screamed. Purple lightning expelled from her tiny body, and Marvellas hissed at it. The darkling was running before the flare of light had died out.

Running and running.

That heart in her chest drummed to a war song of defiance and bravery.

Running and running.

Lightning still shot from her in reckless, untrained bursts, cracking through the eerie woodland. She didn't know where to go, only that she hoped someone would find her. Someone good and safe.

The vision turned to flurries of color as Zaiana fell to her knees in her plumes of smoke. Her hands fisted her hair, tightening, trying to draw the pain from the inside out, but it was festering inside her too fast.

Thunder boomed more violently, and darkness stole all the light. Her subconsciousness battered her worse than ever before with a storm so thick it consumed her, filling her lungs so she couldn't breathe. Seizing her bones so she couldn't move. Ice started to coat her, until there were hands on her...and they were warm.

"I'm here," the male said.

"Why!" she cried. This emotion-filled mess wasn't her. This couldn't be her, or she would never survive.

No one is worth your tears.

Zaiana needed more pain. Something physical to stop them from falling.

"You're safe in here," he said, remaining calm despite the tantrum around them. "You're safe with me."

"Why?" she repeated, defeat hushing her tone.

"Does there need to be a why?"

"There always is."

The storm began to calm. Perhaps she didn't need pain when exhaustion could numb her being. Her entire existence. It was the only way to go on.

"Listen to me," he said, so soft and grounding Zaiana tuned in to it in her desperation to claw herself out of this Nether. "We're going to figure out what they did to you. You're important to them, and the only way to make it right is to become the revenge they didn't see coming. We're going to get back your lightning, and I think we might have discovered what it's become tied to."

"What?"

She clawed her way out of the destruction that was caving in on her, though she couldn't be certain whether the new spike of adrenaline at his next words were in terror or in liberation.

"Your heartbeat."

There was one thing she could be grateful to her sleep phantom for: a deep, silent rest. She woke early, however, needing the fresh air to dissect everything.

The emotions that had exhausted her were replenished by her blissful undisturbed sleep, and now the pressure of the bottle inside of her had been relieved enough for her to breathe clearer for now.

She wanted to beat the crack of dawn outside, but she sensed something disrupting the usually dull atmosphere of Rhyenelle's castle halls. A few lingering fae whispered closely to each other, with new gossip to spread. She thought about asking them but decided the anticipation was the most excitement she'd felt in too long.

Zaiana marched toward the throne room, figuring if someone new had arrived, they would be greeted there. Perhaps the high lord had paid them a visit, or Marvellas had returned with new instruction.

"Have you heard?"

Maverick always had a way of finding her when she wished he wouldn't.

"Are you going to tell me?" she drawled without sparing him a glance.

He chuckled low. "I think you'll enjoy the surprise of what unlikely ally just offered themselves to Dakodas. Though useless, if you ask me."

Her interest was piqued, running through several options, though his demotion of their worth made her list short. When she thought it could be Kyleer in a foolish mission to retrieve his brother, she had to clamp her fists tight. She despised the *nerves* the prospect of seeing him again so soon invoked. But no—he would be a very useful captive to draw out Faythe. The heir cared for him deeply.

"You've been absent recently," Maverick hinted.

"You must be just as bored as I am to be keeping track of me."

"Exactly. I've been craving some entertainment, and you're my favorite source."

She would have glowered, but they rounded the hall toward the open throne room doors, and Zaiana spied the figure kneeling before Dakodas, who'd draped herself beautifully across the mighty wide throne.

Zaiana didn't recognize the fae male, but Maverick had made it sound like she should.

He had dark blond hair, wavy to just above his shoulders. Over his back was a bow and a quiver of arrows.

Dakodas's onyx eyes gleamed down at him, and her smile curved with wicked amusement. "I do enjoy it when royals finally submit to order," she said, loud enough that it was a boasting announcement for everyone. "Rise, Tarly Wolverlon."

That was when Zaiana's steps faltered, and she snapped her head to see Maverick's smirk.

The Prince of Olmstone was certainly never a consideration of hers. Zaiana didn't know much about him, but she'd been informed Olmstone was under Marvellas's control and the prince and princess were unaccounted for.

What in the Nether would he be doing here now, if he'd fled when his kingdom was taken?

Tarly straightened to a tall height. His poise gave away his royal upbringing. "I fled in fear, I admit, but I've been watching and listening to Marvellas's movements, and I know I stand with her."

Spineless words of a coward out of options, Zaiana thought. She didn't believe it for a second, but Dakodas seemed pleased. The Spirit of Death stood, a shallow pool of shadows rippling at her feet as she descended the stairs of the dais.

"Poor little prince. Alone and afraid all this time, when all the others have made friends and allies. Do you resent that?"

"Yes. Nikalias and Tauria made a mockery of my father and my kingdom last summer, which led to its disorder. It is why I want to join you."

"It would be your greatest betrayal to those I believe you once considered allies."

"They abandoned me first."

Dakodas canted her head. Her hand rose to trace the prince's shoulder and around his back as she circled him. "What do you think, Zaiana?"

Her spine stiffened to be addressed for her opinion regarding a prince whose past and allegiances she had no knowledge of.

"Have you seen Faythe Ashfyre?" Zaiana asked him.

Tarly turned, and she thought him elegantly beautiful. Almost innocently so, but his brown eyes bore nothing but ice. He'd seen horrors necessary of the protection. The prince's cold look shifted to Maverick, and Zaiana stiffened at the reaction that started to widen on him.

He recognized Maverick as Callen Osirion. Of course he would. Zaiana dared a glance to her side, but Maverick kept his expression dark and neutral.

"No," Tarly said, his thoughts still trying to process what he was encountering. To everyone's knowledge, the royal family of Dalrune had all been slaughtered when their kingdom was taken. "I only saw her in passing during the kings' meetings in High Farrow last year. She was nothing more than Orlon's human pet then."

Zaiana had to keep the conversation in check before Tarly said something foolish on the matter of Maverick.

"Since you ran like a coward from your kingdom, where have you been?"

Tarly didn't even flinch at the insult she threw at him. He'd long accepted what he was, which made his submission to come here more believable.

Zaiana approached him, locking his stare as if he might give a flicker of something away that would help her figure out his motives. Could a royal really be so naïve?

His expression was so emotionless. Unafraid. Given his story, she would have thought he'd be quivering before them, desperate for an allegiance somewhere in a realm breaking with war after abandoning his throne.

What Zaiana sensed from him in her next inhale flared her eyes in recognition, and his narrowed a near undetectable fraction.

A challenge.

"Marvellas wants royals—we have one. He has no magick, and I doubt his skill to do much with a bow surrounded by enemies if he thought to play spy." Zaiana voiced her verdict.

"Would you Transition to dark fae willingly, little prince?" Dakodas cooed.

This was the first time he gave any indication of uncertainty at what he was doing. What coming here truly meant.

"Is that necessary?" Tarly asked, still watching Zaiana as much as she watched him.

Did he know who she was?

"It is a powerful gift Marvellas plans to bestow on all the royals once the cockroaches are captured. Your acceptance will make it less painful," Dakodas said.

Bored of him, the Spirit passed Zaiana, taking Maverick's hand before heading back up the dais. Zaiana's attention was stolen from the prince to track them. She didn't realize how tightly her fists had clamped until her iron guards broke the skin of her palms. While Dakodas sat again, she idly traced a hand over Maverick's forearm as he stood by her side. He didn't look up. Maverick's face turned oddly distant, as if he were no longer present in this hall.

"I would like you to oversee him," Dakodas said to her. "Interrogate him by any means you see fit to be sure his words are true."

"If I may, Maverick would be better suited for that role." She didn't know why she said it, but it was too late to stop. She wanted him out of this room, away from Dakodas. Though not for her own jealousy, and perhaps she was reading a discomfort in Maverick that wasn't there.

His sharp black eyes sliced into her. "Don't tell me you've gotten soft," he goaded.

Her teeth ground at the belittlement, but her mind was at war with his motive.

"Of course not. I just have better things to do with my time, and this is subordinate work."

"What else might you be hoping to do?" Dakodas prompted. It was laced with a warning. She didn't like her instructions being passed or challenged.

"I was hoping you might have something of greater importance for me. Hunting the heir, perhaps."

Dakodas leaned her head back against the tall throne with an arrogant smile. "You were rather proficient in that the last time, but I'm afraid that is already taken care of."

She was growing dangerously impatient. Standing here like she was no better than the castle servants to be ordered around for petty work. Zaiana was a fighter. A strategist. A weapon. She couldn't bear to be hung in these stolen halls as decoration any longer. With or without her magick, she was worth more than this.

"Very well," she said, taming her temper.

Grabbing Tarly by the arm, she pushed him toward a side door, exchanging one last hateful glare with Maverick, more out of habit than anything.

She didn't use any more force once they were marching down the halls, and the prince kept up. Even without her lightning, despite his head of height over her, she was confident she could put him down swiftly if he tried anything.

Zaiana led him down to the cells, making sure no one followed.

"I guess a real bed was wishful thinking when handing myself over to the villains," Tarly commented.

So the prince had humor.

"The pretty words of a runaway prince are not going to be bought so easily."

"You must be Zaiana."

What a fool he was.

She didn't answer. Not until they'd ventured far below and she knew no guards were lingering nearby. Zaiana opened a cell, and Tarly walked right in like an obedient dog. The moment he was inside, Zaiana slammed him to the wall.

"Exposing you know who I am wasn't your first mistake," she snarled at him. "It was coming here wrapped in the scent of the healer Nerida."

Tarly's eyes flared at her mention. He was protective of her, and Zaiana's mind was reeling with that information.

"She mentioned you," Tarly admitted.

"Last I saw her, she was with Faythe. I imagine that hasn't changed, and so your lie in the throne room was very dangerous indeed."

"Nerida spoke kindly of you. Can I trust you?"

She scoffed, pushing off him and pacing away for distance. "You'd be a fool to take my word for anything."

"In better circumstances, yes."

"Why did you come here? To spy for Faythe? You're going to get yourself found out before you can tell her a thing."

"I'm not here as a spy, and truly, it doesn't matter what happens to me."

"Noble of you."

Tarly kicked at the dead helping of straw in the corner. "How long do my interrogations last before I'm free?"

She pursed her lips. He wasn't what she expected. "That won't be up to me."

"It could be."

"Did you hope I'd be an ally to you? Whatever Nerida might have said, her heart is too soft to see kindness where it doesn't reside." Zaiana didn't want to care, but she also found herself inquiring, "Where is she now?"

"I'm not sure. Heading to Lakelaria, perhaps. Or with Faythe in pursuit of Reylan."

He'd divulged that information to her too easily. Recklessly. It riled her even though it was to her advantage.

"I'm sure they'd be kicking themselves knowing they trusted you, only for you to abandon them and spill their movements to their enemy," she hissed.

"Are you though…? Their enemy?"

"Yes," she snapped. "I almost killed Kyleer and would have killed Faythe's father."

"But you didn't."

He was prodding at dangerous nerves that would have awakened her lightning by now. Then the reminder of her silenced magick turned her emotions even uglier, and her hand itched for her knife. She couldn't kill him; the Spirits would likely kill *her* for the waste of one of their precious royals.

She stormed out of the cell and slammed it shut. Curling a hand around a bar, she fixed him with an ice-cold stare.

"I'll be sure to let them all know you're the one who gave them up when I find them."

"Doesn't sound like the Sprits have confidence in you for that task."

Her grip tightened as she shook with restraint not to open that damn door and slit his throat.

Zaiana forced herself to walk away.

Anger and torment and humiliation pulsed in every step. She didn't know where she was going, but she was done being idle. Undermined. Left to reel in the aftermath of her failure. Walking these halls, it were as if the ghost of Faythe laughed in every shadow.

They may have both gone down in that final blast, but the heir was out there, still fighting and powerful, while Zaiana was starting to feel as caged as she had been under the mountain. She had to get out of here.

She had to finish what she'd started…and capture Faythe Ashfyre.

CHAPTER TWENTY-ONE

Faythe

Shortly after everyone had gone their separate ways, Faythe suffered their absence in the core of her stomach, both fearing for and rooting for them all to be safe and achieve their tasks.

When they'd awoken before parting, one person was unaccounted for. They'd waited until midday in case he'd gone hunting or to bathe, but Tarly Wolverlon never returned. Faythe's heart ached for Nerida, who'd hardly spoken a word to anyone and tried to shield her upset over his disappearance.

They'd offered Nerida to stay with them instead, but the healer was adamant to go to Lakelaria in search of a cure for Tarly even though he'd abandoned her and the prospect. So Faythe had called Atherius, and the Firebird had taken her friend across the sea.

Faythe spied with Kyleer, inconspicuous on a rooftop with a view overlooking the enemy camp in Fenher. They hadn't sighted the general again, and the Eye of the Phoenix hadn't given a single flare in the Ember Sword Faythe chose to carry. Anxiety crawled through her bones every passing day. What if he never returned here and she'd missed her one and only chance?

"You'd better not be cheating with that intense stare you have," Kyleer said, snapping Faythe from her thoughts.

Kyleer had stolen a deck of cards from an inn and insisted they play to relieve the boredom while they scouted. Faythe eyed her fan then the rows of cards between them. He was beating her to an embarrassing degree. Usually, she was excellent at this game, but as she'd warned him, her attention was hardly focused.

She couldn't stop glancing at the ruby pommel on her hip, mistaking every slight glare of sunlight against it for a signal the other eye was close. Then she would scan over the tents and bodies they could see from here one by one, as if she might find the general anyway.

Faythe placed down a card that gained her nothing.

Kyleer gloated as he placed his next, which won him the game easily.

"I like to win, but this is just sad," he said, gathering the cards.

She hated to lose, even when she knew she deserved it.

Faythe huffed, throwing down her cards and rubbing her face. She'd run out of the sleeping tonic Nerida had provided her with, and the nights were once again restless.

"Shit," Kyleer muttered, dropping the cards so they flurried back to the rooftop.

Faythe's heart leapt, sights immediately targeting the ruby stone that finally glowed. Her hand smothered the flare, but they both scanned the field wildly.

She said, "We should go down. It'll shine in the right direction, and we can follow."

Kyleer nodded, and when they were quickly darting through the streets, Faythe could hardly contain her adrenaline. Her hands trembled. She unbelted the Ember Sword and passed it to Kyleer who caught it with ease.

"This way," Kyleer said when it had stopped glowing in the direction they were headed.

It continued to change more times than Faythe had the patience for. She was growing dizzy with the erratically changing direction, until she stopped.

"He's toying with us," she said. A cold lick of realization trailed down her spine.

He'd found them first.

Kyleer braced to unsheathe the Ember Sword, and Faythe's hand hovered over Lumarias.

"Looking for this?"

It was not the general who spoke.

They both whirled, and Faythe was overcome by a mirage of emotions to see the raven-haired dark fae beauty.

"Zaiana." Kyleer said her name, armed and disbelieving.

She smiled, a hint of a demon within. The ruby amulet shone brightly, dangling off her two metal-clad fingers as she held it up.

"Where's the general?" Faythe asked, pushing aside her fear of Zaiana that had never subsided.

"Will you ever learn to stop walking into the obvious traps set to capture you?"

"Every time she's tried, I've escaped."

Kyleer sneered, "Fitting for her to send her best killer and manipulator."

"You flatter me, commander."

"Yet I'm guessing they don't know of your weakness in letting me live."

The dark fae's expression darkened on him, and her hand dropped. "A mistake on my part, I'll admit. One I won't make again."

Faythe shivered at the promise in her monotone voice. She was about to brace against Zaiana when a new awareness crept across her nape.

She spun right as arms reached to grab her, but thrusting a hand to the chest in front of her was a mistake with the surge of power that emerged from that connection, clashing with the magick she summoned from her palm.

One second she was standing; the next she was flying. Then what stopped her projection was a solid, unforgiving force.

Faythe wheezed for breath, scrambling to collect herself while magick seized her entire body like currents of lightning. So much so the initial impact of the wall hadn't hurt her, but now the power was subsiding, a throbbing ache spread across her head and her back, and warmth pooled at the base of her skull.

What in the Nether was that?

Now her consciousness was coming back, she picked apart the familiar dark essence.

She'd felt a touch of that power within the tent her target general had been in. Faythe forced her head up, needing to blink few times to gain focus, but there he was...the dark-haired general with deep blue eyes.

Faythe pushed through the pain threatening to shackle her down, peeling herself up just as he did. At least she wasn't the only one to have suffered in that unexpected collision, but what had happened?

His chest...she'd only pushed a hand to his chest for that dark power to detonate.

"You don't want to try that again," he growled.

Faythe could hardly organize her thoughts and tame her wild heart. She didn't have time to do either when he surged toward her, and Faythe pulled Lumarias free just in time to cross blades with him.

She'd known exactly how he'd do it. Exactly how he'd move. Staring into those blue irises, though filled with loathing, Faythe was certain, so sure in her soul…

"I found you," she said through a breath, trembling with the strength it took to hold their locked blades.

His eyes flared, and her brow furrowed deeper before he pushed, and Faythe stumbled, immediately on the defensive. She stepped to dodge most of his swings, watching his every flicker of movement that had become memory to her. There were dozens of patterns he could take, but there was always a style she would never mistake.

"Reylan, stop!" she yelled—not a plea but a command.

He did, perhaps only to decide whether to maintain the façade he wore.

"Why is she making you hide?" Faythe asked, softer now.

Marvellas had to have known Faythe would figure it out easily— she just had to be close enough. Then Faythe realized that was the Spirit's plan, because once she found him, Faythe wouldn't let him slip away again.

It tore her apart to stare into her anchor to this world in those sapphire irises that were placed on the face of a stranger. She wanted him to shift back, but he didn't. The color was him, but the unfeeling, harsh stare he held with was not Reylan at all.

"What did she do to you?" she tried again when he stood there like cold steel.

He stalked to her slowly, like a predator confidently approaching its prey. "You made this as easy as she said you would," he said, but these words weren't his either.

Marvellas had succeeded in breaking his mind, and Faythe crumbled at the mere thought of what it took.

She paid the error for her pining stupor when she allowed him to get close enough to wrap his powerful hand around her throat.

There it was again. Ripples of dark, sinister energy emanating from him. In his sapphire eyes, she thought shadows flickered through them occasionally. He wasn't completely restricting her airway, and Faythe's attention was drawn to his chest. Right where she'd touched him before.

It was a reckless move to press her palm to it again, this time without summoning her own magick in defense, but the moment she felt something solid there Faythe gasped, and Reylan's grip turned deadly around her neck.

With little time to think, Faythe wrapped one of her hands around his, summoning magick to burn him, and he let her go with a hiss. At the same time, she'd retrieved a small dagger from her side, slashing at his chest deeply enough to only cut his leather armor.

When a glow broke through the black material, Faythe stumbled back until she hit the wall.

"How did she…?" Faythe couldn't believe what she was seeing. *Feeling.*

She wanted to deny what was damagingly obvious.

Reylan had a ruin embedded in his chest.

Faythe didn't know the full gravity of what it meant, but one thing was certain: it was powerful enough to have split his mind for Marvellas's influence, and it had granted him unparalleled power.

At the same time, Faythe could still feel its pull, wanting to merge with her and amplify her power too if she dared to reach back.

She was too untrained to give in to the tempting lethal advantage. It would risk killing her or Reylan if she didn't resist its dark chants.

"Let me help you," Faythe said desperately.

Reylan's smile was scarily sinister. "Help me? I have more power than you right now. The more you resist me, the more it will hurt, but it makes no difference to me."

Faythe hadn't felt him take any of her power, but her eyes flew wide when he cast his palm toward her and a gold flare surged at her. She clashed her own lazy attack against it, but that was the wrong response since it vibrated through her as if she were a struck gong.

Her head slammed against stone again, and more warmth leaked down her scalp and her nape.

"Giving up yet?" he taunted.

Never. She would never give up on him.

Reylan gripped fistfuls of her jacket and her cloak, hauling her up to stand on weak knees.

"You can't contend with me, Faythe. I can take everything you have."

Staring into his deep blue irises that were her home and her orbit tore her apart.

"You're still in there," she whispered. "You have to be."

Reylan let her go, only to grip her jaw, and she whimpered at the vise grip.

It's not him. It's not him.

She'd wanted him to shapeshift back, but now she was glad for the disguise that soothed her heart. *This is not Reylan.*

Yet every time he searched her eyes, a glimmer of hope sparked that he would push through the poisonous influence of the ruin and Marvellas.

"Your lack of self-preservation is astounding."

He pushed her head against the wall again, and her vision blackened around the edges with the sharp pain that ricocheted through her skull.

"In every realm and in every time," she breathed. A promise he'd once made to her.

His grip on her jaw slackened, and Faythe would have crumpled to the ground were it not for his arm that snaked around her. Reylan's cold stare never changed, but his head canted thoughtfully. Curiously. As if she were a puzzle he was trying to figure out.

Faythe hissed when his fingers slipped through her hair and touched the gash at the back of her head. His brow flinched, and he pulled his hand back, examining her blood coating his fingers. His nostrils flared, and his breathing deepened.

Her mate, her Reylan, would never harm her. She thought, just for a second, that realizing the injuries he'd caused her would snap him back.

It didn't.

His tongue touched a sharp fang in his mouth, and his chest heaved. He'd never drunk from her before, but the wildness in his look told her he didn't have the restraint or the consideration not to right now.

"If injury won't make you come easily, this will," he said.

"Reylan, wait—"

She got no other words out before his head angled to her throat and his teeth pierced her flesh. The initial burst of pain seized her body tightly against him. The shock made her frozen prey in his arms.

Faythe had imagined this moment many times. She'd long craved it. But not like this.

Though the pain subsided, there was no pleasure to follow, only numbness, as he took her blood against her will. She didn't fight him. He drank and drank and wouldn't stop until she fell unconscious.

There were worse ways to greet the inevitable darkness, she supposed. He groaned against her throat, pulling her to him tighter, and she let her mind pretend this was happening under other circumstances. Being held in Reylan's arms this way was a cruel, deceptive safety, but she was so tired of yearning for him that she didn't care.

She'd found him.

Faythe stared up at the midnight sky, so beautiful and full of stars. She'd always thought his irises captured them so she could bathe in the glittering beauty even in the daylight.

He took more and more and more of her blood, until she let herself sleep in his arms.

CHAPTER TWENTY-TWO

Zaiana

Zaiana couldn't shield herself from Faythe's blast. Helplessness tightened her chest, and her arms rose feebly to brace herself.

Light magick didn't hit her because shadows stole her.

She was saved from the brutal strike, but the moment her feet felt ground again, she was slammed against a wall. Her eyes flew open, met with equal fury in moss-green irises that lashed her with punishment.

He was a weed of weakness she should have exterminated the last time she had the chance.

With his body caging her to the wall, her survival instinct kicked in. When she twisted her wrist, held by him, Kyleer hissed before loosening his grip on her other hand, enough that her elbow angled toward him, jabbing into his chest. Ducking, she pulled her blade free, turning on her knee. The swipe of Nilhlir only cut through starry shadow.

Kyleer reappeared behind her, and though his ability made it a challenge to track him, she focused on the drum of his heart. She rolled to avoid his attempt to grab her again, kicking out her foot, but he took her ankle. She used him as an aid to twist onto her hands, reaching for another small dagger in her belt and throwing it in her handstand. It struck his thigh, and he cried out, releasing her again, and she cartwheeled back to standing.

The most intoxicating scent filled her nostrils enough to slip her focus. *Blood.* It wasn't like the craving she'd battled all her life from humans. This was sweet and metallic, with just a hint of bitterness. It made her *salivate*, so she had to swallow hard. His blood was...

She stilled in the warmth that wrapped around her from behind. In her moment of distraction, he'd used his Shadowporting to once again compromise her, pressing her back to his front. Her eyes fluttered closed only for a second before she snapped them open in bewilderment at herself.

His scent encased her, starting to drown her senses and subdue her fight.

Foolish, childish, weak. Her cruel mind tore her apart.

"I should kill you," he said, a warm whisper across her ear. It was twistedly seductive.

"Then what are you waiting for?" she breathed.

"For you to fight back. You've allowed me ten seconds longer than I expected before you use that stunning lightning." His hand around her middle tightened a fraction. "Where's your storm, Zai?"

Her storm. It was gone. Even Kyleer knew it to be an integral part of her, and now it was gone.

"I don't need it to fight you."

"Hmm..." His low murmur skittered along her jaw.

The warmth of him contrasted with a cold breath of metal against her throat.

"What did you do to my brother?" he asked.

Zaiana laughed bitterly. "That fool orchestrated everything himself."

"Is he working for Marvellas and Dakodas?"

"The fact you have to ask that really shows how little you trust your kin. It's no wonder you're all flailing in this war."

She hissed at the sharp sting of the blade almost cutting her flesh with his added pressure.

"As if you aren't the one with no allies—not true ones. You don't even know where you stand anymore."

"Don't I?"

Her teeth slammed together against the slice at her throat she had to take from his blade, but with her spin, one hand lashed around the commander's wrist, twisting, and his cry was music to the cold being she became. In her second breath, she freed her own dagger at her waist and hooked a kick around the commander's knee, aided by the slip of frost. It brought him down. The sharp point of Magestone pinched into the bulge of his neck as she stared down at him with a promise of death.

"Impressive," he said though a clouded exhale. "But more effort than you should have needed to use."

His prod at her methods flashed a white anger that made her angle the length of the blade to his skin, and Zaiana leaned in closer, leveling their eyes.

"There are over a hundred ways I can kill you. I would never be so predictable, so you may never know which one will finally come to claim you."

"You can't follow through," he taunted. The note of hurt in his tone wouldn't be heard by anyone else. And she felt it like the hot brand against her frozen heart.

She said, "There is still fun to be had. You haven't seen the best of them yet."

Kyleer's eyes narrowed, and he was admirably fast to grip her wrist, hissing at the piercing of his skin as he stood. But it was his Shadow-porting she was too slow to detect before it engulfed them both.

She gripped his hand around her throat. Not because it choked her, but because it was the only purchase she had, save for her toes on the edge of the rooftop she leaned off. The wind whipped annoying strands of her unbound hair over her vision. They were very high.

"I'm tiring of this dance," she said.

"Show me," he said.

Her brow furrowed in annoyance. "What?"

"The best of your ways to kill me."

Zaiana chuckled darkly. "You're a twisted bastard."

Kyleer pulled her to him by her throat until she was balancing straight on the ledge, their bodies flush. His breath trickled along her lips.

"Still my most recurring, tormenting, beautiful nightmare," he said, a husky murmur near lost in the whistle of winter air.

For a second, she thought he would kiss her, and she would let him, knowing the poison but consuming it anyway. His lips brushed hers. Then he pushed her of the roof, letting go completely.

Zaiana growled, releasing her wings to catch her, before landing in a crouch on the ground. Kyleer was already there, watching her with an amused, unbothered smile. Her anger was rising, having let this go on for too long.

"You've lost your lightning, haven't you?"

Of course it would be obvious to him, to anyone, when she engaged in combat. It made her realize how much she'd leaned on her magick, but she would make him and everyone see she didn't need human blood to be stronger, and she didn't need magick to win.

Zaiana straightened, tunnelling herself deep into a focused battle calm. Kyleer was certainly an opponent she couldn't underestimate even if he didn't use his Shadowporting. She assessed they were matched in battle knowledge and experience; it was just a matter of outwitting him in skill.

With Nilhlir gripped in one fist, she adjusted her stance and answered, "I don't need it."

Then she moved, as quick and silent as wind. Her advantages lay in her size and her speed, opposing his strength and broad stature.

Their steel clashed against each other, and she couldn't explain the hypnotism that overcame her listening to the song of their blades. It was a battle melody unlike any other she'd engaged in before, and she began to *enjoy* their dance.

He wasn't going easy, but his attacks responded with a magnetism to hers. He swiped high; she bent low. She twisted around him; he spun to find her path effortlessly. The exertion began to ache through her bones, but she didn't want it to end so quickly. Fighting Kyleer…she wasn't thinking about striking him down. Not yet. She wanted to keep expending her bottled-up emotions because he could take it, let her cry and yell and release everything that killed inside, all of it pouring out through her blade, not her mouth.

"Be done with this."

A loud voice broke through her trance, but she didn't lose focus on Kyleer. She caught a glimpse of the Rhyenelle general carrying Faythe in his arms.

Kyleer must have too, because he faltered. Absolute dread then fury contorted his face, and that was his last mistake.

Zaiana knocked his sword from his right hand with a slam of hers. In the same breath, her left foot shifted for her middle to pivot, and her right foot kicked his chest hard enough to send him sprawling back. The impact might have even broken a rib or two.

Before he could even try to peel himself up, Zaiana straddled him and sent the pommel of her dagger into his temple to knock him unconscious.

When all had turned cold and still, Zaiana couldn't move for a moment while the adrenaline dwindled. She was transported back to the cells in Rhyenelle with how similar this moment felt to the first time she'd bested him.

It hadn't been as easy this time, but still…she expected more from him. Wished he hadn't toyed with her and instead had poured his wrath and loathing over her.

Several sets of footsteps approached, and Zaiana suppressed her urge to snarl at the dark fae who'd come to take Kyleer. She could move him herself.

"Let's go," Reylan said from behind her. "You did well."

Zaiana blinked at that. She'd never heard the small praise before, and it came from the most unlikely source. She forced herself to stand, not watching as the dark fae took Kyleer.

The general was so different from when she'd seen him all the times before. She scented Faythe's blood before her eyes found the bruising puncture wound on her neck in shock.

What was more shocking was the ugly, horrible essence of the ruin she could feel from him. Faythe had managed to score his chest, and Zaiana shuddered to see the glow of it peeking through his black clothing.

It was absolutely astounding he still lived with it embedded into his chest. An extreme measure Zaiana never could have predicted by Marvellas, but it had worked for her. She didn't doubt his mind would have been near impossible to warp to her mercy without it. But though she knew the general was powerful like Faythe, he shouldn't still be alive.

"Where are we going?" she asked.

Reylan walked as he answered. "Back to Marvellas, of course."

"Where is that?"

"Across the sea."

He was being cryptic with his answers, but she couldn't figure out if it was because he'd become a mindless soldier or if he lost his own capacity to engage normally.

"Your interference was unexpected but welcome," he went on.

It was jarring to be walking and speaking with someone who, not so long ago, had harbored a strong will to kill her. He still did, but having to see him as an ally right now was strange, and she didn't like him this way.

Reylan placed Faythe into the back of a wagon, being careful with her despite the injuries he'd inflicted to capture her. He lifted himself in too, pulling the heir to lay her head in his lap. He did so as if it were a habit, not conscious thought. Tragic, really.

Kyleer was already in the back, and she wished to claw the itch from her skin to check on him.

Reylan looked to her expectantly, but Zaiana considered taking to the skies and following. When she thought of being seen by Dakodas or Maverick, she decided to smother her discomfort and climb in, sitting on the edge to dangle a leg off the open back.

She didn't look at Kyleer when it took off, jostling them.

"Do you feel anything for the harm you caused your mate?" Zaiana asked curiously.

"I did what I had to."

"What does Marvellas plan to do with her?"

His brow furrowed. Zaiana could see how mindless he was. He wasn't acting with any given reason, only following what was asked of him.

"She wants Faythe's fealty."

It would be hopeless to keep testing him for any true information when he likely couldn't give a good explanation as to what the Spirit wanted with *him*.

Zaiana planned to find that out herself. She would go to the Spirit of Souls, Goddess of the Stars. She would promise her allegiance to her and hope the desertion from Dakodas wasn't unforgivable when she came to serve her instead.

Her sights found Kyleer when she didn't mean to. Part of her wanted to lay his head on something soft to keep it from knocking off the wooden wagon with every movement. She didn't. Zaiana tried to erase him from her thoughts as she watched the streets they left behind.

She understood what Dakodas meant now. Reylan had been undercover as the leading general here, but now he had retrieved Faythe, Zaiana was to take over. She was supposed to stay and lead this legion in Fenher.

Zaiana smiled with defiance as she rode away from the insulting position she'd been given.

She didn't have a plan, really. Didn't know how outraged Dakodas would be to find her missing, or how annoyed Maverick would be. Honestly, for once in her life, she didn't care at all.

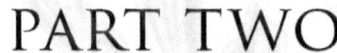

PART TWO

THE PHOENIX AND THE ICE QUEEN

CHAPTER TWENTY-THREE

Faythe

Faythe had never traveled by boat, and it was a shame she was hardly awake for the first time she ever crossed the sea. The blindfold hadn't helped the dizziness and the nausea, but luckily, she managed to avoid being sick, though her stomach couldn't handle the peculiar motion of the boat against the waves.

The cold became sharper, with her breaths gathering ice chips in her throat.

"As if this is going to stop us knowing we've crossed to Lakelaria," Kyleer grumbled.

All she could be grateful for after their capture was that they hadn't separated her from Kyleer yet.

"It's to stop you being noticed or doing something foolish," Zaiana answered from somewhere nearby.

"Considerate of you," Kyleer said with more chill than the frozen island.

Faythe was yearning to know where Reylan was. He'd remained elsewhere, letting others handle her, in the long journey Kyleer had been tracking better than her. He estimated around three weeks had passed.

She was tired of the darkness now, but she feared the lashing contrast of light when they would finally take off the damn wrap from around her head.

When they were taken off the ship, Faythe trekked through more inches of snow than there had been on the mainland. Water flowed beside them, and from what she recalled about the great western island, river paths stemmed through the kingdom like roads.

They were pulled to a stop, and Faythe's chest raced with anticipation. A presence crept closer to her. Unmistakable. Reylan reached to the back of her head, pulling the tie of her blindfold under her hood.

Her eyes immediately watered and slammed shut at the first attack of daylight. She bowed her head, blinking to adjust and subdue the dull ache it pulsed in her head. The crystal stone beneath her feet was mesmerizing. This path had been flattened of snow for people to walk safely.

Faythe was roughly pulled from her moment of admiration by a firm grip on her chin, yanking her head up. Reylan maintained his guise of brown hair and different angles to his face, but those irises were the same, and every time she was forced to meet the vacant loathing in them, a piece of her heart cracked deeper.

"We'll stop here for the night. Getting to the castle by foot will take a day in itself, and it's nearly nightfall."

Faythe's gaze tracked over his shoulder, and she was taken by the sculpture of the buildings she could only glimpse the peaks of. It was like she was standing in a city of glass and white stone. It reminded her of High Farrow—Caius City, specifically—in some ways, but far colder, and with more ice. The other detail that set apart this kingdom was the accents of gold—Lakelaria's sigil color. It adorned parts of the stone in elegant filigree, or was stamped on shop signs, or on the white fur cloaks of the few fae she caught passing distantly.

"Go inside. Try anything, and I won't hesitate to do this again," he said, sweeping his fingers across the bruised bite wound on her neck.

Faythe shivered with a break of pleasure at the contact. Despite everything, he was still her mate, and her body gave away her yearning for him.

The bruising was almost gone, but thanks to her Magestone shackles, it took longer to heal. She wondered if the small puncture wounds would stay, however. Even though he'd bit her in malice, she didn't want it gone.

"I doubt the Lakelarian citizens would run to my aid if I called," she grumbled, heading inside the inn they'd stopped at.

"You'd be surprised how far word of you has spread," he said low from behind her.

That was genuinely surprising, but whether they'd heard of her or not, she wouldn't expect them to care about her captivity in their kingdom. A Phoenix Queen without wings or a crown—pitiful, really.

Faythe skulked down the narrow corridor, her nose stinging at the notes of alcohol and wafts of musk. Before she could veer into the main room, Reylan's firm hand pushed her the opposite way. She muttered her curses, but they fell on uncaring ears.

"You watch over him," Reylan instructed. She cast a wary look at Kyleer, whose face fell in discontent. "But don't kill him."

Zaiana smiled with pretend sweetness, opening the door in front of Kyleer before pushing him inside. "If he doesn't give me cause to," she sang, following him in.

Faythe genuinely feared for her friend, doubting he'd see the dawn without injury at least.

It was her turn to be roughly handled, thrust into a room with one bed occupying the center. There wasn't much else. Her craving for heat had her staring into the dark fireplace, but her stubbornness didn't want to ask him for anything.

"You should rest. I reckon it will be the best you'll achieve for a while."

Faythe found him by the corner of the room, leaning into the shadows like he didn't plan to move from them anytime soon.

"I didn't think you'd care."

"I don't. Stand there all night if you wish—I will not interfere."

Faythe sighed dramatically. If he wasn't going to light the fire, the blankets alone would have to do. She sat on the bed, too tired to even take off her boots. Grabbing the covers, she awkwardly slung them around her shoulders, gritting her teeth with the burning against her wrists, then she sat against the headboard.

"You'll regret the stiff neck if you fall asleep in that position."

She ignored him. "Why didn't you change your eyes with the rest of you?"

"Shapeshifting always leaves a trace. Trying to imitate another fae or human has the most noticeable distinction like a scar or eye color."

Faythe wanted to believe that even if she didn't recognize his eyes, she would have still known it was him as soon as she was close enough.

"Why the guise at all if she wanted me to find you?"

"You're not the only recognizable face. The Valgard armies wouldn't have trusted Rhyenelle's leading general even less than they did this newly appointed façade."

"It's just us now. You can let it go. It must be tiring you to hold the ability for so long."

"Nothing tires me now. Not with this," he said, tapping his chest.

Faythe swallowed hard. She was trying to push aside the whispers of darkness that came from it.

A strip of moonlight pouring in from the single window kept the bottom half of his face in view.

"Go to sleep," he ordered.

"Aren't you going to?"

"I'm not risking you attempting something foolish."

"I'm certain you'd wake up before I could try."

He huffed, pushing off the wall and coming closer. Conflict raged in her. The trick of this mask while knowing it was Reylan inside wrecked her.

Reylan sank a knee onto the bed, watching her with those icy sapphire eyes. Their stare grew with tension, as if he anticipated she'd break, to provoke him into something that would be catastrophic in here.

"Release the mask," she said.

"Why? Do you want to pretend?"

"You're the one pretending."

He eased more pressure onto the bed, leaning closer. Then, to her surprise, he did as she asked. Faythe's ribs rattled watching the strands of his dark brown hair spill with silver, as if ice had formed along each strand. His eyes shifted shape, and she realized it had been a mistake to provoke him when she was overwhelmed with delusion now. Her mind had fooled itself into believing she could break through Marvellas's influence on him with the yearnings of her heart alone.

By the time the last of his features had turned back, he'd eased all the way over, and Faythe couldn't resist the hand she slipped across his face.

"Come back to me. Please."

Reylan's body hovered just shy of pressing into her. His face came down inches from hers, and for a second, she thought...

"You're so pitiful it's no wonder she will win without resistance."

Faythe went to snatch her hand back, but his lashed around her wrist, and before she could struggle, she was on her back. Fire and ice blazed against each other in their battling stare, passing the same breath of anguish back and forth.

Her impulse and defiance won. Faythe lifted her head, pressing her lips to his. She didn't know what she was doing, only that desperation and heartbreak were responsible for all that followed.

He answered with equal anguish, deepening the kiss in an instant, and Faythe almost lost herself to the passionate wrap of him. He let go of her bound wrists, and she gripped the front of his jacket, needing him closer in any way she could muster. The taste of him, the scent of him, it wanted to draw her into the clutches of a painful delusion. All that kept her from falling for it completely were the dark whispers that amplified in the heat of their anger and their hopeless need for each other. The shadows of the ruin circled them with glee, wanting Faythe to give in to its power as it held Reylan.

Their kiss was a clash of tongues and teeth, feverish grasping of hair and clothing. The cold was now forgotten with the heat of his body pressing her into the mattress.

She didn't want to stop. Her resolve was slipping away under the familiar weight of him, and she wanted to pretend a little longer. Faythe didn't know when he retrieved the key to her shackles—she was too focused on him and what to do next—so when they came free, she moaned into his mouth with the relief, giving over for a few more seconds. He hooked a hand under her knee, drawing her leg around his hips to push against her tighter.

So familiar. So much lust and yearning. So much pain and longing.

She drove her hands into his soft silver locks as his groan vibrated along her neck, scattering pleasure across her body. Faythe had allowed her desire to cloud too much. The pinch of his teeth against her neck shocked her back with a gasp.

Before he could fully bite her, Faythe's hand slipped up his chest, and she wasn't thinking straight when she forced her palm to encase the ruin embedded in his flesh beneath his leathers.

When she did, the world around her ceased to exist, and all she explored beyond was death and darkness. The dark at the end of everything.

Faythe grappled control within herself, remembering who she was. Threads of the real world started to weave her surroundings back. Shadowy power engulfed the room, hissing and flowing like she'd opened a world of dark beasts clawing to be free.

Reylan's hand gripped her throat, and that dragged forth her instinct to survive. She had no discipline nor experience to wield a ruin and could feel it threatening to claim her instead.

She had to break it.

With both of them attached to the ruin, Faythe was more powerful than Reylan. They'd both always known this. She was a descendant of Marvellas, with Aurialis merged within the core of her magick, and with this amplifier, she could destroy the world in a few heartless thoughts.

And *Gods*, did this dark power whisper such temptation for it.

Faythe cried out, hooking her leg around his waist and managing to flip them. She pressed both palms to the ruin now, trembling with the fragile grasp she kept on her humanity.

"Do it," he growled through the chaos battering the room. This establishment was close to collapsing if even a fraction more power was released from the ruin.

His blue eyes glowed, swimming with ethereal power.

"Break the ruin, Faythe. It's what she wants, and it's inevitable."

The ruin attacked that thought, slicing and clawing deeply into her mind and her flesh with no physical trace. She whimpered, feeling herself set alight.

Deep within the essence of the ruin, Faythe found a faint crack. All she would have to do was hook her magick into the thin crevice and *push*. It would take every ounce of her being, and it could wipe out a devastating radius of innocent civilians. But she didn't know what it made her when that wasn't the thought that stopped her.

Reylan was so hauntingly beautiful. The malice was gone, and instead he almost *pleaded* with her fiery gaze as it pierced his. Was he in pain? When he'd watched her all these weeks, so steely and pretending not to care, was he writhing inside to an unimaginable, unseen agony?

The door behind them slammed open, but Faythe couldn't lose focus, or she risked letting go and causing a blast far worse than the first time she'd touched this ruin in the alley of Rhyenelle.

"What are you doing?" Zaiana yelled over the shadowy hurricane destroying the room. Faythe was surprised the walls still held up when the desk and the chest of drawers had become deadly splinters carried in the storm.

"Get out!" Faythe shouted back.

"You can't harness the ruin! Stop her!" That was Kyleer.

"I can't. Not this time."

The flicker of hope that Zaiana could help her release this magick died out with those words.

"Then tell her how, dammit!"

"It's not that easy!"

Reylan reached a hand up, so jarringly tender it widened her eyes when his fingers brushed soothingly over her cheek.

"Break it."

"I don't know if it'll hurt you. Or…or kill you."

He appeared the most convincing, as the Reylan she loved, but she couldn't figure out if it was just a trick. That was what Marvellas wanted, but was it also the only way to get him back?

She'd put his life in danger, and Faythe was about to let go—

"Don't!" Zaiana yelled, far closer to her now.

"I have to let go."

"You'll collapse this place and several others like a house of cards if you do that so recklessly," she hissed. "Untrained fool. What were you thinking?"

She hadn't been thinking. All she wanted was to know if she could reach Reylan. All she believed was that if he was with her, maybe they could break it together, and he would be okay. They would win this twisted game before Marvellas got a hold of them both.

Now she could *feel* this kind of magick was so uncertain and out of her depth, and she wouldn't gamble his life before knowing more.

"I can't hold on much longer," she panted. Her gold tattoos torched like lines of fire over her arms and her spine, her skin slicked with sweat.

Zaiana said, "You're fighting it, and let me tell you, it will always win. You have to be in control to lock the power back inside."

"How do I do that?" Her words came sharp in her panic.

"Trick it into believing you are the dominant force."

"That makes no sense."

"Maybe not to your simple mind," she snapped.

"Zai…" Kyleer warned.

Zaiana tsked her irritation. She tried to explain again. "A lion will always have more power than a man, but it can be tricked, taught, into submission. Magick is just a beast. You are the guidance, the smarter entity. Don't let it devour you—figure out what makes it yield."

Faythe leaned into Zaiana's words as they became clearer, but she feared she was too far gone.

"A man wouldn't jump headfirst into a lion's den without experience," Faythe said in daunting realization at what she'd done.

"No. That was your fatal error, so now you have to adapt to survive, I suppose."

"What does that mean?"

"It's going to hurt all of us and cause a lot of wreckage, but I don't think you have a choice but to sever the tie. Without a willing vessel, it will snap back into its containment, but not without rage in its defiance."

"Break it. You're right here and have the strength to do it," Reylan coaxed again.

Faythe shook her head. "We need it intact to use it against Marvellas, and I will find a way to release you from it without breaking it."

"There is no way. It's either me or the world, Faythe Ashfyre."

"Then I choose you!" she cried.

The words came out of her so quick and sure. Even when she repeated them, she did not reconsider. It was in that moment Faythe realized power didn't make villains; love did.

One of the walls of the inn caved in, and so did part of the roof. Faythe recoiled, hands still braced on Reylan's chest. His palm cupped her nape, their faces so close.

"Then choose me, my Phoenix. Break it."

Reylan would never ask that of her. He was loyal and brave and would sacrifice himself if it meant the survival of his kingdom, his people.

This was not his right mind beneath her.

It was Marvellas.

Faythe let go.

All she knew next was endless chaos and weightless projection. Until she slammed into something solid in a punishing claim of gravity. It would have been worse were it not for Reylan, who held her tightly to him, shielding her with his whole body and taking the worst of the impact from the explosion.

The magick that had explored every internal piece of her was gone, and she breathed easier, peeling her eyes open to survey the destruction she'd caused. Yet in her selfishness she couldn't even look around to face the consequences of her actions—all her attention fell on Reylan beside her, his arms limp around her.

"Reylan," she choked. His eyes fluttered open to her relief, and she cupped a hand to his face. "I'm so sorry."

"Faythe," he whispered back.

"I'm right here."

"We can't let her win."

"We won't," she promised. "I'm going to find a way to get this out of you and kill her with it."

Reylan's lips parted again, but he was too injured to release his next words.

Faythe forced herself up to face what she'd done. They lay amid the splinters of pain and tragedy. She hadn't just collapsed this establishment—several surrounding buildings were caved in at various impact points because of her.

She didn't know who she was anymore. Choosing violence for her own cause. She expected to see more casualties, and while there were bodies being pulled out of the icy wreckages, many more were cowering in fear. Had most managed to evacuate?

It didn't matter. Lives were lost, and Faythe had claimed them with her newly tarnished soul.

Reylan was unconscious. His forehead bled, and dust coated his tanned skin. Faythe could run. It would be logical since he only had a mind to capture her and hurt her for Marvellas. Yet she shuffled closer, debris cutting her flesh and digging into her skin, until she was tucked into his body.

"I'm going to get you back," she whispered into his chest. "I promise."

CHAPTER TWENTY-FOUR

Zaiana

Kyleer, the fool that he was, hooked his bound wrists over her head right before the impact of the ruin's power sent them—and the whole establishment—flying in pieces. His body easily encased hers, and she couldn't be separated from him because of the chains locking them together. She wasn't spared from the impact—his body was hardly a cushion as they hit whatever it was that stopped them from being projected further—but he did save her from worse pain.

When they lay against each other in a heap of wreckage, Zaiana couldn't even lift herself immediately.

"You're a damned idiot," she seethed. Wiggling her body, she managed to duck under and out of his chains.

"Yeah, I think I am," he groaned in pain.

Zaiana scrambled up, fully aware and searching through the debris and panicked civilians. She hadn't expected Faythe to be so naïve as to try wielding the ruin. *What an insufferable, overpowered fool.* It was incredulous the heir had refused to die until now.

She had to brace on her knees to catch her breath from the surge of adrenaline. Zaiana had never felt so useless. The power of the ruin had vibrated and taunted her core of magick, caressing her skin in dark strokes. Mocking her. She should have been able to silence it safely herself, yet her magick only battered the seal on the vault she could not open.

What was it all for?

Her suffering, her training, all the times she'd conquered death to defy the claim of a ruin and become its master. Now she was nothing.

It was all for nothing.

"Zai—"

She spun, dagger drawn in a flash of rage, and he was the closest thing to unleash it upon. Her steel screeched against metal, wedged between a link on his Magestone chains, which he raised to protect his face.

"What happened to your magick?" he asked—not with any teasing or mocking but *concern.*

"Nothing."

"You've demonstrated how well you can use a ruin's power, so you can drop the bullshit."

She pushed him with a hand to his chest. "I just can't reach it right now," she said defensively.

He frowned, assessing her in a way that made her itch at the attention. At the thought, Zaiana surveyed the room for Faythe. Perhaps she would engage in combat with her instead to release her sour resentment that the heir wasn't suffering any loses since their battle like she was.

At first glance over the wreckage and commotion, she couldn't see her or Reylan. Kyleer's chains rattled in her pursuit as she searched for them. The town was in a state of upset with what Faythe had done, the scent of human blood lingering with an icy note through the air, and Zaiana's tongue traced her sharp fangs.

She stopped her search when a compulsion pulled her attention. Zaiana found a man on the ground, clutching his leg while the snow drank his blood. She swallowed dryly, unable to tear her sight from the waste. When human blood was spilled warm and fresh in front of her, it tested all the restraint she'd spent centuries mastering.

"You spent months in our cells and didn't crave it," Kyleer said carefully. His large form blocked her view of the man, and her lethal stare latched to him instead.

"He's going to die anyway," she snapped.

I don't need to drink. I don't need to drink.

Zaiana scrunched her eyes and swallowed again, but each time only reminded her how damned *thirsty* she was right now. She wanted to kill that man himself for tempting her this way.

"Drink from me," Kyleer said.

What an outrageous suggestion.

At least, that was her immediate thought, until she found the pulsing vein in his neck by instinct. She'd never craved blood from a fae before. Never considered it.

"You don't mean that," she said a little breathily.

All she could smell was *blood*. She needed to get out of here.

"I do."

Zaiana's violence was growing under her skin.

"I'm fine. Let's just get away from this," she said, already marching away.

If he wasn't hers to guard and escort right now, she would have taken to the skies. Instead she gripped Kyleer's chain and dragged him along with her marching pace. Her mouth wouldn't stop salivating. Her breathing came in harsh drags, but not even the icy air could numb the itching thirst in her throat.

Finally, the scent of blood drifted away, faint enough for her to start composing herself. Letting go of Kyleer, she cast her sights skyward and counted the stars to distract herself.

"Your control is admirable. That didn't look easy to resist."

She didn't want to talk. Too bad that was Kyleer's favorite pastime.

He said, "My offer still stands, by the way—"

Zaiana was still volatile, and the reminder of blood pushed her violence through her hands on Kyleer's chest. Caught unawares, Kyleer grunted when his back slammed into the closet building.

"Don't tempt me again. If I sink my teeth into your throat, I won't stop until there's nothing left," she snarled.

"Understood," he said, but there was still a hint of deviance in his eyes.

As they kept walking, Zaiana admired the beauty of a kingdom bathed in glittering snow, but the temperature left little to be desired. She was accustomed to cold climates and had faced training and trials in the thickest of winters, but she always preferred the heat of bright summer days or the warmth of a fire outdoors where it became a shield, battling the bitter temperature and wrapping her in protective arms.

Childish thoughts. Her mind cast them away.

Icicles hung as if the buildings had wept and their tears had frozen before they could melt against the snow. For the main streets, two narrow stone paths were separated by a river big enough for small boats to pass through. Occasionally, Zaiana lost herself to the rippling water, feeling a certain pull to search deeper, as if creatures beyond her knowledge might lurk below.

"Can you swim?" Kyleer asked after their long walk of silence.

"Yes."

She didn't know when it had begun to happen, but she could feel certain emotions from him, and when she stole a glance, she confirmed his hardly suppressed smile.

"Did you know, your jaw tenses and you let one heartbeat pass before you tell a lie?"

"You can't possibly have picked up on that."

"I had enough time to think over everything from those months you were my captive."

"I haven't thought about you at all."

There it was again—that smile of infuriating callout.

"I can swim."

"But if I pushed you into that river, you might not make it to the side?"

She dared him in her cold stare.

"The river isn't that wide."

"Ah, so you can swim well enough, but you fear unknown waters with depths that could host—"

"Stop that."

"What?"

"Trying to read me as if I'm some damned book."

"You're not a book. They're peaceful and quiet, with words of wonder and wisdom," he said.

She didn't want to know what that made her in contrast.

"You said you didn't enjoy reading unless it was battle strategies," she said.

"I'm touched you remember that."

He was riling her up on purpose.

"I make it a habit to retain intel on all my enemies."

"Even such trivial things?"

"Has it ever bothered you"—Zaiana decided to switch topic before she reached for his throat—"to always be second to Reylan Arrowood? To be known as such in title and to everyone around you."

"No. Not at all," he answered easily.

"So your ambition has a limit?"

"Just because I don't seek to gain Reylan's place or more doesn't mean I don't strive every day to better myself in my current role."

She tried to understand.

"You don't want to be a general? You're content to never rise to anything more?"

"I wouldn't say never, but it would mean leaving Reylan's side, and

I don't want to do that. I fight side by side with both my brothers and serve my kingdom to the best of my ability—why would I want more than that?"

All Zaiana knew was the pursuit of greatness. To be better than everyone around her: faster, stronger, smarter. To rely on no one and care for nothing but her own rise and survival.

But there was a certain contentment in Kyleer's experience that felt worlds apart from hers.

"What are you thinking about?" he asked thoughtfully.

She stared through the snow-darkened clouds with her thoughts, but her face firmed to steel when she looked at him. "That your ideals are pathetic."

He took no offense. "Where is your next ambition, Zai? Who stands above you that you clearly want to overtake?"

"Everyone" was too arrogant and broad of an answer, but it was what swam in her mind.

"Anyone who stands in my way," she settled on.

"Right now, who is most imminent? You're a higher rank than your lover—that seemed clear enough."

"Maverick isn't that," she defended too quickly.

"Then what is he?"

"Like you, a pretty distraction I wouldn't hesitate to turn my dagger toward."

"That's what I can't understand. Your tastes. I'm nothing like him."

He was right but also wrong. There was one thing, a certain kind of darkness, that Maverick wore on his sleeve but Kyleer harbored deep within. The kind of darkness that touched hers. But otherwise, they couldn't be more different. Where Maverick was cold, Kyleer was warm. Where Maverick was cruel, Kyleer was kind. Zaiana related to Maverick, and there was no denying the tragic bond between them from their wicked past, but she couldn't shake being drawn toward someone who offered new perspectives on life.

She'd stopped walking, overwhelmed by her own thoughts, and she despised the commander for making her consider either of them in any regard.

"Are you all right?" he asked tentatively, having walked a few paces without her.

The snow began to fall, and she hated it, wanting to stop and attempt rest but in another establishment Faythe wouldn't blast apart. Zaiana had also discovered as of late that she hated being at sea. She'd flown as much as she could, but the vessel was too slow compared to her flight speed, and she was tasked with keeping close watch on the irksome commander.

"We should find a new place to rest for the night," she advised.

She couldn't keep walking with him. It seemed to make him too talkative, and she needed him to stop with his words that felt like a trick to draw things out of her she didn't want to expose.

"You do look tired," he commented.

That only made her expression sour more, but his expressions were becoming weighted too. The long weeks at sea had been grueling, and this was their first day on land.

They approached the next inn they found—a slender building wedged down a narrow street, with little to offer inside.

"Are you hungry?" Kyleer asked.

Zaiana swore before admitting, "I don't have any coin." Then she regarded his chains. "And Reylan has the key to those."

"I doubt you planned to release me from them."

Zaiana didn't know what compelled her to stop in the hall and reach for one of his wrists, holding the Magestone. She stared at the thick abrasions burning his skin from the material, and yet she was unharmed by it. This was what separated what they were. Fae and dark fae. He was of the weaker species—it was what she was always told and had observed, and yet it was hers that was driven to the brink of extinction. Her kind that was forced into hiding for centuries. Her people who cowered high in the mountains.

So if the wicked could be afraid, and the good could be ruthless, why was there such divide at all?

"Do you need a room?" an elderly voice croaked like nails across wood, jolting her to release Kyleer.

Her sight didn't turn to the human but rather flicked up to find Kyleer's moss-green eyes watching her with a frown of confusion and question.

"I'm going to kill her," Zaiana informed him.

"You don't have to do that," he protested firmly.

"We have no coin, and she's not just going to let us pass."

"Just let me try before you result to murder," he grumbled under his breath, stalking away from her, hiding his bonds under his cloak.

It didn't take long before he was returning, grinning like an idiot.

"How did you manage it?"

"My irresistible charm, as you're familiar with."

She pushed him and followed his lead, resisting the urge to take a blade to his back to stop his gloating.

They didn't head upstairs—they came to the top of a set that headed down, and she didn't follow when he descended a few steps.

"She wasn't going to give us a cozy room she could get coin for," he explained when he noticed she'd stopped. "She took pity on my story of us being a couple running from our betrothed, having no time to gather previsions and coin in our desperate pursuit of true love together."

Zaiana's stare on him widened to disbelief at the outlandish lie, and he broke into deep laughter.

His voice grew more distant as he headed down. "It might be a little colder in the cellar, but it'll be better than being exposed to Lakelaria's lethal temperatures. She said there's blankets."

Kyleer was swallowed by the dark abyss that set everything in her on edge. Her breathing hardened as she took her first step down. She couldn't show her weakness here. Yet her hand lashed tight to the railing as she forced her next step. Fear was a terrible, hideous beast.

She heard his chains before his head came back into the light. He looked up at her, about to ask, but he read her exterior instead, so easily it was like she'd become clear words on a blank page to him.

"You have a fear of the dark?"

"No," she bit out.

He reconsidered with a glance behind himself. "Underground?"

The confirmation was in her glare. Instead of mocking her about it, his expression relaxed.

"I'm not fond of it either. I can't Shadowport underground."

"You can't do that at all right now."

"True. But I've always been uneasy underground."

It was far more than a dislike for her, but she reinforced the vault of her mind that threatened to blast open every time she was forced to face this weakness they'd created in her.

Kyleer's chains rattled as he held out his hand. She wouldn't accept it.

Zaiana mentally chastised herself for being so pitiful, and with a deep breath, she forced herself down the remaining steps without him.

The cellar was still really cold but admittedly better than the icy breeze outside. A spark of light made her whirl around to find Kyleer with a lantern. There wasn't much down here, just some supplies like alcohol kegs, blankets, pillows, and other materials.

Zaiana watched Kyleer stick his head over various shelves,

collecting things and investigating despite his pain and restriction with the Magestone shackles. He acted as if they didn't bother him at all, and for a moment she stilled, wondering if it were possible he wasn't as affected by it as she believed. That he could be fooling her just as she had him when she was bound in Niltain steel shackles, a material that was incapacitating to her kind—but she'd mastered those effects long ago, and that was how she'd escaped her Rhyenelle cell when it was time.

No. The fae had long forgotten the existence of Magestone until recently. Kyleer was just very resilient to physical pain, and that she could relate to.

Kyleer threw blankets and anything cushioned he could find onto the ground before settling himself down on it, placing the lantern next to himself.

"You're going to have to tolerate the closeness, I'm afraid. There aren't enough supplies to make two makeshift beds far apart. Besides, it makes sense to share body warmth. Purely survival instinct, of course."

Zaiana's reluctance held her still. The last time she'd lain with him...

Her body grew warmer of its own accord at recalling the pleasure he'd given her. And Dark Spirits be damned, he was good with his hands. Too good.

"Don't get any ideas," she warned.

She lowered next to him and almost raised her unsheathed dagger to his throat when he slung a blanket over her shoulders unexpectedly. The extra barrier against the cold was enough for her to yield her defense a little and hug it around herself tighter.

Kyleer shuffled to a lying position, and Zaiana had the right mind to stay sitting. She couldn't truly sleep, but the relaxation would be enough to replenish some of her energy.

"You can sleep," he mumbled, already sounding like he was on the cusp of it.

She didn't answer, only tipped her head back against the stone and closed her eyes for a moment of peace.

It didn't last long before he said, "Why do you fear being underground?"

He was really Nether-bent on testing the limits of her tolerance with him.

"I was born with wings. Underground is the opposite of what I desire."

"It's more than just unfavorable or inconvenient to you. And you lived under mountains."

Curse her for being unable to hide her childish terror on those damned steps.

"The masters would use it as a form of punishment," she confessed, if only to sate his curiosity and shut him up.

She should have known it would only open the door for him to barge in with his questions. Kyleer shifted onto his side to face her.

"By locking you underground?"

"In far less space than this."

It was like she could feel his growing tension. Dangerous and angry.

"A cage?"

"A stone cage," she said. He wasn't going to stop. "Barely big enough to turn around in, and no space to sit, only stand. Sometimes the insides would be made of a thin layer of Niltain steel, so you couldn't even lean against them. No sound or light could penetrate. In that kind of isolation, a minute quickly feels like an hour. Then hours become days, and days weeks. It turned many dark fae mad, and I almost lost myself a couple of times."

"They put you in there more than once?" he asked.

She shivered at the gravel of rage in his voice.

"I might have a lot of discipline and ambition, but my drawback was often being rebellious to authority. There were many times any other fae would have died by their hand for the things I did."

"But they kept you alive."

"I'm an asset with my ability. They're not wasteful. Abilities are coveted among the dark fae as it's not as common as in the fae—not even close. They think royal blood is key. Some dark fae have weak abilities, likely from long diluted royal lineage somewhere. But Maverick—*Callen Osirion*—was the first Transitioned to keep his full power."

"What about you?"

"Me?"

"You're exceptionally powerful."

"I'm born dark fae."

"Are there others born with great power?"

Her brow knitted. "Not that I know of."

She couldn't stand his silence and glanced at him to decipher his thoughts, but he gave away nothing in his faraway stare.

"Who were your parents?"

"I don't know."

"How?"

"Darklings are given to the masters when they're young. To train as soldiers."

"That's...absolutely terrible."

"Is it more terrible than knowing the parents who harm or abandon you?"

She regretted those words as soon as she spoke them. Zaiana could hardly stand how much it unsettled her to witness his emotional pain, however fleeting.

"That's a fair point. I guess we all become soldiers one way or another."

Kyleer turned silent for a moment, and she hoped it would stay that way.

"It's not normal, what you went through," he said quietly. "These masters...why do they still hide?"

"They're our teachers. The oldest of our kind. I wouldn't expect them to leave their safe confines."

"They're cowards."

She almost smiled at that.

"That much we can agree on."

His hand slipped over her thigh, and Zaiana tensed.

"If you don't kill them, I will."

Her sharp stare angled down to him. "Don't act heroic for me, Ky. I could watch them kill you and not feel anything for it."

Lies. Such terrible, haunting lies.

At that, Kyleer barely smiled. He squeezed her thigh before releasing her, and he turned the opposite way.

Zaiana relaxed when she was released from his attention, but his words were going to replay in her mind for some time. When her head grew too heavy and Kyleer's breathing deepened, she risked shuffling to lie down, facing his broad back.

The impulse to feel the wavy locks of brown hair spilling behind him itched her skin so much that she turned around. The warmth of him behind her became a craving she was restless to resist. The slither of cold space between their backs sent a chill rippling down her spine.

At the first chime of his shackles, Zaiana rolled as he did, purely out of a triggered instinct since he could easily wrap his chain around her neck with her back to him.

When they both stilled, they shared a breath, and his heartbeat echoed into her vacant chest. The only barrier between them now: the tip of her blade under his chin. His large hands wrapped around her wrists, but she was confident she could end him swifter than he could stop her.

"This is better," he said, the gravelly lilt in his voice crawling over her skin. "That breeze between us was terrible."

To her utter dismay, he closed his eyes again, peaceful despite the threat of her blade. In her annoyance, she scratched the tip under his jaw, and his lids flew open with a frown of annoyance.

"Let me go," she hissed.

"My hands can't really go anywhere else. Besides, maybe you'll actually sleep knowing your blade can take my life at any second and you'll wake up if I release you or move."

He had a point. But how was she to sleep when his face was so close to hers? His mouth was a temptation she shouldn't think about, but her traitorous eyes explored every part of him.

"Sleep, Zai," he said, as much to himself as her.

The warmth was nice. His body shielded her from more cold than the blankets could, and she fought her body's desire to bathe in it.

Just one night. Just for warmth.

She let her eyes close but kept her hearing sharp. Soon she found herself only focused on two things: his breathing in tempo with his precious heartbeat. Sounds that, against her better judgment, she found peace, maybe even safety, in the cadence of.

CHAPTER TWENTY-FIVE

Faythe

Reylan put her back in the Magestone shackles. They'd walked in silence for a measure of time lost to Faythe. Though she could have been free, she didn't regret not leaving him when she had the chance.

"We'll get rest here," he said at last.

Faythe looked up from watching her feet sink into the snow. Across a short, undisturbed blanket of snow stood what looked to be a temple long in ruins. The roof was partially caved in at the front, but it expanded farther back and might provide more cover.

"Why here?" she asked. He'd taken them far away from any life or buildings.

"You can't destroy anything of value if you decide to be foolish again."

Faythe internally winced. She'd been battling gut-wrenching guilt ever since he'd woken quickly from where they'd lain in the wreckage and immediately restrained her, then he'd marched her away from the pain and destruction she'd caused.

"I didn't mean to," she whispered, more to herself.

Reylan answered anyway. "Exactly. It's a miracle you're still alive with your unpredictable, impulsive nature."

Honestly, Faythe had to agree with that statement. He guided her with a hand on her arm toward the temple.

White trees surrounded them, and Faythe's face was numb from the bitter temperature. Lakelaria was a kingdom of ice and beauty, a land that appeared too pure and peaceful for this world, but Faythe decided she preferred a warmer climate. Her chest beat with the pride of the Firebird.

While the ruins wasn't much of a barrier against the cold, Reylan led her over to a corner that still had a roof.

"Why don't we venture in further, to a room that isn't half-exposed to the elements?" Faythe asked, surveying the beautiful decay of the space.

"This temple has a rather cursed history. Most believe it's superstition."

"Cursed?"

"It's one of four cursed temples throughout Ungardia. They were all infiltrated and destroyed, the worshippers all killed."

Faythe became eager for more of the story. Reylan let her go, beginning to collect any stick and branch he could through the snow for a fire.

"What did they worship?" Faythe edged for more as she helped him sift through the snow for tinder.

"Death," Reylan said. That single word shadowed over them.

"Like Dakodas?"

"She's but a whisper of the true primordial."

Faythe shuddered. "Why would people who want to live pray to the God of Death?"

"Death can take away what life gives. But it's more than that. The primordials as old as time have the power to snap worlds in two should they wish. There are those who believe Death is the strongest and fairest of them all."

Dropping her sticks on top of Reylan's pile, Faythe sat with her thoughts. The wind whistled an eerie song through the gaps in the stone and down the pitch-black passages. She fixed her eyes down one, chilled by the illusion of the dark reaching out a hand. Faythe jumped, snapped from the hallucination, when Reylan threw more sticks down.

He crouched on his haunches, staring at her with their pile between them.

"If you let me out of these, I can light that in a heartbeat," Faythe said.

Reylan almost smiled. He raised a hand, snapped his fingers, and Faythe's mouth parted at the blue fire that sparked in his palm.

"You can't reach your magick, but I can."

It was becoming clearer how powerful he was with the ruin in him.

Faythe's look soured, but her irritation was quickly forgotten when the fire grew and the heat enveloped her. She sighed, hugging her knees to her chest. The sticks snapped and popped, and the air howled. Her lids grew heavy.

"Why didn't you run?" Reylan asked, so soft against the warring elements.

"You would have found me."

"You doubt yourself that much?"

Faythe shook her head, not looking up from the flames. "It's just what we do. We find each other."

Reylan didn't respond. Instead he said, "You should get sleep."

"So should you."

"Are you always this stubborn?"

Her eyes pricked. How much of his memory about her had Marvellas buried in her cruel scheme? Faythe couldn't allow herself to panic. Once she got that ruin out of him, he would remember. She would *make* him remember everything.

Faythe lay down in silence. She didn't think she would get any decent rest with only her hands to cushion her head and her cloak as a blanket. When she couldn't stand the impression of his eyes on her above the flames, she turned her back on him.

The distance of strangers, of *enemies*, ached in her soul. Faythe untucked one hand from under her head to glance at her golden butterfly ring. A reminder of time defied and distance erased between them once, and they would do it again.

"There's a stream nearby. I'm going to collect water for our travels tomorrow," he said.

Faythe listened to the shuffle of his movements without a word.

"You're right. I will find you no matter how far or fast you try to run. Don't waste your energy."

With that, he left her, and Faythe closed her eyes, knowing it didn't matter the circumstance or peril…she wasn't capable of running away from him.

Faythe was woken by a whisper—one that caressed her ear like a stroke of darkness, snapping open her eyes but holding her still in the mercy of unknown terror.

When it subsided, she released her breath and willed her heart to calm. She peeled herself up, daring to sit and discover the origin of the cold, eerie presence.

She found nothing.

Reylan was sleeping, which surprised her. She didn't expect him to take the chance of a potential ambush or her fleeing. He didn't stir at the ominous echo she'd felt creeping over her skin.

It came again, a tickle of air with notes of dark beckoning. This time Faythe was more captivated than alarmed, though her body still locked with tension. She got up slowly, wincing at the chime of her shackles and slicing a glance at Reylan. Still, he slept soundly. So peacefully her heart savored the sight for a few seconds.

Until the whispering call wrapped her again.

Faythe followed it despite it leading through one of the depthless halls. The darkness claimed her all at once.

Moonlight spilled into a room ahead, and when she emerged, it took a moment to survey the hall in her awe.

A huge statue loomed in front of her—a cloaked figure with no face, only a void as depthless as the passage she'd emerged from. It held a scythe taller than itself, and the only sign of imperfection was the missing chip on the underside of the figure's blade. Around it, hundreds of black ravens were frozen in flight.

It was a mortal depiction of Death itself. The primordial the worshippers at this temple prayed to. Did they pray for a kind death? For this entity to spare them pain and misery in the end? Or was it far more than that? Possibly more than she could comprehend.

Faythe's pulse skipped when she thought she caught movement. Her eyes darted over the birds, which remained stationary, frozen in the air by nothing at all. They began to *twitch*, coming alive right before her eyes, and Faythe stumbled back. She couldn't have darted out of there before their feathers puffed in the wind and their wings cracked out of their frozen state until they could fly.

In a few heartbeats, Faythe was surrounded, holding her bound hands up to shield her face. They didn't attack, but they swarmed her instead of fleeing now that they could.

"What do you want?" Faythe begged, terrified by the pounding of wings filling her ears, the brush of feathers like icy grazes.

"I need him to return to you for a while," a deep, otherworldly voice said. "I need you to help him, and in turn, he will help you."

Faythe squinted through the slash of black birds. She found the hooded form, shrunken to mortal size. She tracked its looming scythe —an instrument to reap souls, and she was perfect prey.

"Who?" she dared to ask.

"The first and only son."

Faythe lowered her arms, overcome with dread.

"What happened to him?"

"He is a son of war. Between mortals and Gods. He is a binding tether between more than you can imagine. You are the heirs who, once united…will decide whether this world ends from the wrath of broken hearts or finds peace after all it will take to win."

She had to be dreaming. Faythe sank to her knees, trying to grapple something that would expose this as nothing more than a horrifying nightmare.

"What will it take?" Faythe broke a sob with her question. Her mind spun with the faces of everyone she held dear. Her threads to each of them strained so threateningly she couldn't know which would be in danger of breaking until it was too late.

She was haunted, completely awash with the worst dread of her existence, while this moment felt so familiar to when the Dresair had cursed her with the knowledge one close to her would die. The primordial didn't say such words, but it was only now she was being crushed with the gravity of the war, realizing she must harbor a fool's heart to believe the battles to come would spare those she loved.

Faythe took a breath. One long, sure breath to fill her lungs. She couldn't predict or prevent or control the uncertainty of war. But she was Faythe Ashfyre. She would not be weak, she would not cower, and she would fight with her last breath for everyone.

Hands touched her upper arms, and Faythe gasped, her eyes flying open. She gripped the assailant back, about to fight them off, when their hood slipped down.

Not an angel of death, but one of light.

Beautiful lengths of silver hair spilled against her brown complexion.

"Nerida?" Faythe breathed in disbelief. Now she really wondered if she was dreaming.

Glancing over Nerida's shoulder, she found the statue of Death was real, but all the birds weren't. Not even a part of the sculpture. A violent shiver wracked her body.

"Are you hurt anywhere else?" the healer asked.

Faythe could only look at her in her stupor. Nerida was crouched in front of her and scanning Faythe with careful attention.

"How did you find me?" Faythe asked.

"I heard what happened at the inn. People are whispering about the Phoenix Queen. Then I tracked you."

Her guilt surged once again. "I didn't mean to do that."

"I know."

"How could you?"

Nerida's smile always inspired a warmth like no one else's. One that freed souls from burden just for a moment.

"It's not your heart," Nerida said.

Faythe's head bowed. Then she had to ask, "Have you found anything for Tarly since you've been here?"

The sorrow that dropped on the fae's face was answer enough.

"I haven't been here much longer than you, and a lot has happened since we parted."

Nerida rolled open her pouch of herbs and medicines.

"What's happened?" Faythe pressed.

Finding what she was looking for, Nerida uncorked a small vial and handed it to Faythe. "This will help with the pain of the Magestone."

She didn't really care about that, but Faythe accepted the kindness.

When she swallowed the sour liquid, Faythe's head snapped around. "Reylan…"

"He'll be out for at least another couple of hours. The tonic I slipped into his water at the stream should hold someone unconscious until morning, but I would anticipate the ruin's magick will burn it off far faster."

Faythe's helpless look swung back to the healer.

"I don't know what to do," Faythe confessed.

"Luckily for you, I have some theories and options. But I need you to listen carefully, and none of this is without risk. There's something I need to tell you first, and I hope you'll still see me the same."

"Of course I will," Faythe said with absolute certainty.

Nerida remained uncertain. She broke Faythe's stare to pack away her pouch with a new edge of nerves.

Faythe took her hand and held her beautiful hazel eyes. "None of us are just friends anymore, Nerida. We're family. Whatever you have to say, that never changes, and how we fight this…is together."

"Family," Nerida whispered, lost in her own thoughts at the word, until an endearing smile twitched at her lips.

Unexpectedly, she leaned in and embraced Faythe tightly. When she relaxed, Faythe treasured the blessing of Nerida's comfort.

"I can't stay with you, and what I'm going to propose will be dangerous, but I don't know if there's any other way."

Faythe's arms tightened a fraction—from fear, from anticipation—but when she let Nerida go…she was ready for whatever had to come next.

CHAPTER TWENTY-SIX

Tarly

"It's your lucky day," a male voice sang into his cell.

Tarly turned taut. He'd been wondering when he'd hear it again.

The dark fae came into view, shadowed mostly right outside his cell. *Maverick*, Zaiana had called him. But Tarly knew him by a different name.

"You're a traitor," Tarly said. It had been burning in his throat ever since he laid eyes on the presumed dead Prince of Dalrune.

The only reaction he gave was a mild flex around his cold, black eyes. Once a vibrant cobalt blue like his lightning, now they were completely soulless. But it was enough to wipe the small kernel of hope Tarly harbored that he didn't remember who he was. Only then could Tarly understand his aid of the enemy.

"You don't know a thing," Callen said resentfully.

"By all means, explain to me how you've been killing innocents and siding with the ones who collapsed your kingdom all this time you were *dead*," Tarly hissed.

He couldn't help it—part of him was reeling with betrayal. They weren't all that close personally, but their families had hosted one another, their parents been friends, respected and loved by each other. To see what had become of Callen washed him with horror.

"Now you've come to do the same?"

"Your family were *slaughtered by them*!"

Tarly's rage kept building, yet Callen remained so emotionless, and it only riled him more.

Dakodas's proposition of Transitioning Tarly to dark fae recoiled in him even more now. Would he become just as heartless? Would he look at Nerida and forget all the dead pieces of himself she'd brought back to life? Would it all be for nothing?

He couldn't let that happen. He would *never* choose that.

"You think I don't know that?" Callen seethed.

"It's been over a hundred years, and you've been helping your family's killers. Your mate's killer—"

Callen's hand slammed the bars, silencing Tarly's reel of outrage. The stare he locked on him was nothing short of a deadly warning. Callen took a few calming breaths before he spoke.

"Like I said, you don't know a thing. So before you go pointing traitorous fingers, why have *you* betrayed them all to come here? Like father like son?"

Tarly would have lunged to strangle him were those bars not there. Though he knew he wouldn't stand a chance. Callen was stronger as dark fae now, and Tarly hadn't forgotten he was powerful in his Firewielding ability. Tarly was once again reminded how weak of an heir he was compared to the rest of them. Shit, even a *human* had risen from the ashes to become something capable of taking kingdoms if she wished.

Tarly chastised his mind for the pitying comparisons now. This wasn't the time for reflecting on himself.

"As if I would tell you anything," Tarly grumbled.

"Then let me tell you, if you've come as some spy or on some heroic endeavor, you'll be snuffed out before you can get close."

"By you? Is that why Dakodas sent you—to keep an eye on me?"

"Yes."

"What a good lapdog you are."

"Careful, Wolverlon."

"Nik would kill you without a thought if he saw you now."

In their younger years, Tarly had been jealous of the quick bond between the two other princes. Any parties or meetings, the princes of High Farrow and Dalrune found enjoyable company in each other.

"Probably," Callen agreed.

"I want to speak to Jakon and Marlowe," Tarly said.

Callen scoffed. "Could you make your false allegiance here any more obvious?"

"They're making Phoenix Blood. I can help. My mother was a healer, and I know how to make the potions for Marlowe to spell."

"Is that so? Well, in that case, let me set up three of Faythe Ashfyre's closest allies in a fucking tea party."

Tarly glowered. "Then what have you come to do with me? I'm hardly of use elsewhere."

"That much we can agree on."

"You'll be watching us the whole time," Tarly reasoned.

Callen considered. When next a key twisted in the lock of his cell, Tarly sagged with relief. He thought he might go insane, gaining hardly any sleep against the hard floor, without anything other than his cloak against the bitter night air.

"As you might have heard, I don't spare a second for mercy. That's your only warning," Callen said, his smile jarring at these words.

Before he Transitioned, Callen had always carried an edge of playfulness and cunning, but he was also considerate and utterly enamored with his mate. Thinking of that, Tarly looked over the fallen prince with his first slice of deep sympathy for him. Perhaps losing her had been the thing to give his soul over to the unfeeling dark completely.

As he left his cell, Tarly couldn't help but think of Nerida. *Gods*, all he did was think of her, both in torment and as the only thing that kept him wanting to wake up every day. She probably despised him for leaving, but she never would have let him go. He might have hurt her, but it would spare her from worse pain later.

Every movement had begun to ache in his poisoned side. He was rapidly running out of time.

Tarly followed Callen up the winding steps, back into the main body of the castle. He'd only been here once in his life. Rhyenelle was mostly unfamiliar to him, but he'd always admired the tales of the legendary kingdom that had birthed the Phoenix riders.

"Were you the only one to make it out when Dalrune was invaded?" Tarly couldn't stop the curiosity that spilled out in their silence.

"No one made it out."

"Your parents, your brother—"

Being shoved against the wall shouldn't have hurt as much as it did. The impact against his bad shoulder, even though not that hard, blackened the edges of his vision.

"I am *not* that prince. My name is Maverick Blackfair, and if you want to live, you'll remember that."

Tarly's thoughts swam with the jolts of pain that were seizing through his chest, so he couldn't respond, but he heard.

"What's wrong with you?" Callen asked irritably.

Pushing off him, Tarly had to brace his hands on his thighs until he could breathe right again.

"A bite by your kind, *Maverick*," he said resentfully. If that was who he wanted to be, Tarly had no problem with that.

When he found the strength to straighten against the wall, he found the dark fae studying him.

"When?"

"A few months ago. I've been told I shouldn't really still be alive, but death is catching up."

"How did it happen?"

"In Olmstone—from someone who was posing as a friend to Tauria."

"Tauria." Callen said her name as if he'd forgotten her after all this time. "When her kingdom fell, at least she had the sense to run to Nik—her mate, am I right? Or is that still a secret to no one but themselves?"

"I thought you weren't Callen."

He shrugged. "I can still be curious."

"Yes, they mated. Until Marvellas broke their bond. Tauria's in Valgard."

He kept insisting he was Maverick, an uncaring dark fae, yet Tarly swore that news disturbed his expression.

"I guess they don't tell you everything," Tarly said.

"And where, dare I ask, is Nikalias?"

Tarly sealed his lips against that. He wouldn't divulge any of their whereabouts to this traitor.

Callen huffed with a cruel smile. "Not doing a very great job of convincing me you're actually here to join our cause. They should have sent a better liar."

"I don't know where any of them are," Tarly snapped.

"Then how do you know about Tauria?"

Shit, maybe he was terrible at this.

"She was taken to Fenstead before that. The word of a returning princess is bound to spread fast. My guess? Nik has gone after her, but I wouldn't know where he's been all this time."

Callen hummed. "Good attempt. Now let's go."

He was brought to a room in the far west side of the castle. Guards became less, which was surprising if he was being led to Jakon and Marlowe. He'd have thought Faythe's allies, as Callen still called them, would be under closer supervision. It made him think they didn't want the knowledge of the Phoenix Blood to be made public yet.

Callen welcomed himself through a door, and Tarly found a man with dark brown hair and a blonde woman. He'd never really met them before, only seen them briefly when they'd infiltrated the Olmstone castle with Nik to help stop Tauria and Mordecai's wedding. He'd thought that incredibly courageous of two humans.

They were in one of the kitchens, with the room entirely to themselves for this task. Many vials of clear and red liquids were scattered across the table, along with various herbs, containers, and equipment.

The blonde woman sat at the bench, her eyes lifting at their intrusion, and they were so hollow and tired that he pitied the human, who was clearly being forced to work beyond her magickal capabilities. Her skin was pale and sickly, and the human man didn't seem much better. Only, his deterioration was purely out of concern for her.

"This is how two people working to grant your side an astronomical upper hand are treated?" Tarly said in distain. He had no emotional attachment to the humans, but their neglect stirred his anger.

"She is the one pushing herself," Callen countered.

There was broken glass and spilled glittering crimson against the walls and over various counters, as if every attempt she'd failed had ended in a slip of violent frustration. It seemed so unlike the gentle nature he'd heard of, but this was war, and war broke even the calmest of souls.

"What are you doing here?" Jakon directed this at him.

Callen clapped a hand to his—mercifully—good shoulder. "You have yourselves a new eager helper."

Jakon didn't shed a fraction of his distaste or hostility. It was no matter—Tarly was well-acquainted with needing to be in places where he wasn't wanted.

"How are the potions coming along?" Callen asked, weirdly cheerful. He strolled into the room, one hand in his pocket, while the other swiped one of a dozen vials of crimson liquid. When he shook the contents, it swirled like liquid stardust.

"She's doing all she can," Jakon said through his teeth.

Callen tutted. "Not good enough, I'm afraid. There's only so much patience Malin has, and let me tell you, it really isn't a lot."

"It doesn't help that he's taking vials for himself so often. She can hardly keep up," Jakon snapped.

Callen shrugged. "This is his operation."

"How many is he expecting?" Tarly asked.

"Enough to heighten an army of magick wielders."

Tarly surveyed the amount created—a few dozen. It seemed a ludicrous expectation.

"Aren't there others with the same magick to help her?"

"We've been scouting, but the human mages are a long dead breed. Most never even know what they're capable of, so they're impossible to pick up on. Others are very well adept at keeping hidden."

Tarly couldn't understand why the human would accept this task alone. Faythe was adamant Jakon and Marlowe hadn't truly betrayed her; that Marlowe—an *oracle*—had a greater plan she had no choice but to trust in. Yet at this display, Tarly was beginning to wonder if that had been a lie and their betrayal was true.

"This one is active?" Callen asked, still admiring the bottle.

"Yes," Marlowe said, her voice barely a broken whisper.

Tarly thought Callen would take it; try the effects for himself. He set the bottle down.

"Seems like the new king will have to rethink his grand plan if you die before you produce an amount of substantial impact."

Callen headed for the door.

"You're leaving?" Tarly said.

"I have better things to do with my time than babysit this poor show."

"What happened to keeping a close eye on me?"

"I have my ways, but by all means, do something foolish if you think you're safe. It makes it more entertaining for me."

Callen didn't glance back again before he disappeared.

The tension in the room grew awkward. He didn't know how to place himself around the two humans who continued to study him with bemusement and distrust.

"I can make the potions," he said. "Then you just have to focus on spelling them."

"Tauria believed in you," Jakon threw at him with accusation.

Callen's threat lingered in his absence. Tarly scanned the corners of the room for eyes.

"Faythe believed in you. I guess we're all disappointments."

Marlowe pushed something across the table to him. "We're glad you're here," she said, so kind he didn't expect it when her husband looked about ready to lunge for his throat.

What lay on the piece of fabric was small cuts of a Phoenix feather. A real one. He could hardly believe it and actually started to build excitement to work with it.

Jakon caressed Marlowe's shoulder and neck, peering down at her with pain and concern, but she smiled up at him in an attempt at reassurance. That unspoken exchange relaxed Jakon, and Tarly had to admire their close bond.

He took up a seat on the bench, leaning into Marlowe's warmth. Tarly's heart ached worse than it ever had before. It reached and strained toward ripping in two from being apart from Nerida. He hadn't meant to let her burrow inside him so deeply, but now there was no prying her out of his chest. So Tarly began his task, hoping it would distract him from the heavy parting he felt in his soul.

CHAPTER TWENTY-SEVEN

Tauria

Tauria had fallen asleep in Edith's room for three nights now. She would retire right after supper with Mordecai, who mercifully didn't subject her to any horrors. He didn't ask her to sleep with him, but she didn't want to take the chance of sleeping in her own room since he could infiltrate it at any time he liked.

Mordecai was occupied a lot, and she'd been rallying the courage to try to discover what kept him so busy here, but she was still shaken after his brutal display at their first supper, fearing his strength and unpredictability.

They would be returning to Fenstead soon, and she had to take every chance she had while in enemy territory.

So that night, Tauria dressed in all-black, her lower face covered and her hood tight, to become a wraith of the night. Edith insisted on coming with her, and though Tauria protested out of concern for her safety, she couldn't deny the asset of having someone who knew the layout of this kingdom and castle.

"We should leave by the balcony," Edith suggested.

Tauria agreed, as the risk of being seen dressed like this would alarm Mordecai.

"He should be leaving now," Tauria said with a glance at the clock above the fireplace. Routinely, for the past two nights, she'd watched him from her window exiting the castle and disappearing after taking to the skies.

"Let's go!" Edith chirped, far too eager for this dangerous venture, while Tauria was sharply on the edge of caution.

Edith had her wings, Tauria had her ability of wind, so neither feared the height nor the precarious climb across the frozen stone and slate roofs. As soon as Mordecai took flight, they would have to race to follow him. If Tauria couldn't keep up, Edith would fly a little ahead just to keep track of him and act as a marker for Tauria to track.

Though the winter made the task more of an obstacle, scaling and racing across rooftops was a pastime of hers she was excited to test now.

The dark silhouette of the high lord made her tense. Edith was so giddy beside her it was almost concerning.

"Don't get too close if you need to fly," Tauria reminded her, slightly doubting the dark fae's ability to stick to instruction.

"Of course. I'm small—he won't see me."

They watched him take flight as usual, and as soon as Tauria deemed it safe, she took off.

Adrenaline pushed through her limbs and honed her focus. From the castle walls, she had to make her way down, sprinting when she met land. Her natural agility was aided by her wind at all times. She became the element, flipping forward and leaping up walls with ease as though they exposed personal ladders just for her. Tauria could run and climb and jump as easy as breathing when she gave over to her magick and instinct completely. It was in these times she felt weightless and unstoppable.

Her focus on the course ahead only broke with frequent glances up. Mordecai was a particularity fast flyer, and as she anticipated, the distant silhouette of him blended too much into the dark night for her to keep track.

Edith noticed too, flying ahead, and Tauria's anxiety built watching the dark fae get closer without her. She was going too far. Tauria gritted her teeth, pushing her body harder. She soared as though she were flying too, but it would never be enough to match the perfect clear path of flight in the sky.

Edith stopped, to her relief, and Tauria slowed as the dark fae backtracked and swooped down to the roof Tauria was climbing onto. She doubled over, bracing her hands on her thighs to catch her burning breath. Pulling down her face covering, she couldn't gulp the icy air fast enough.

Edith had caught up to her, but the dark fae didn't speak. Tauria glanced up, reading her ghostly expression with a sense of foreboding straightening her stance.

"You have to see," Edith said.

That was enough to inspire Tauria's dread.

She trod more carefully as they got closer to where Mordecai was. Buildings became less frequent, and Tauria ended up on the ground, treading carefully through a thick, dark woodland. These trees…it was like they were frozen in time. Tauria paused to hold a hand to one, feeling only a distant beat of life, which should be full and strong. She didn't think they'd shed and grown new leaves and timber in a very long time.

"Just over here. You'll want to climb to get the best view," Edith said.

Tauria took her advice, scaling the tallest tree she came across.

What expanded before her eyes… Tauria had to clamp a tighter purchase around the tree with the horror that slammed into her.

Warriors. So. Many. Warriors.

Torches blazed up and down the formation lines, and Tauria tried to count how many to a column…how many to a row…then the countless blocks of them.

"I'd wager over a hundred thousand soldiers," Edith whispered close by her ear.

Tauria knew High Farrow's army consisted of around three thousand, maybe an additional five thousand with the armada. She didn't know what was left of Fenstead's armies, and though Rhyenelle was guaranteed to have a significantly higher number…they still weren't enough to stand against this.

"Transitioned?" Tauria breathed, trying to figure out how Mordecai could have amassed such numbers.

"And many born. I'd say the numbers are almost half. He's been very forward in encouraging his people to conceive all these years. The children are regimented by the masters in the Mortus Mountains to be soldiers as soon as they can hold a sword. This isn't just a force of numbers—these soldiers have only known one purpose all their lives and have no love to balance that harsh upbringing. All they have is rage and vengeance. Nothing to lose."

And they were stronger, faster, than the fae on their diet of human blood.

Tauria could have collapsed to her knees on the ground staring at the war already lost, tipped too greatly against them by sheer numbers and ferocity.

"I need to find out when they might start moving to the mainland," Tauria said, already trying to calculate how she might escape. She needed to warn the others, and they all needed to prepare for an age about to descend far darker and far bloodier than the Dark Age of legend.

If Mordecai had this scale of an army, why hadn't they attacked yet?

Tauria's answer might lie in the Spirit of Death, who glided like their reaper down the center of the uniformed blocks. She headed to meet Mordecai returning from the back, and when they reached each other... Tauria was shocked when they didn't hesitate to reach for each other intimately. Then they *kissed*.

Though she hadn't expected these kinds of relations between them, if Mordecai had genuine feelings for Dakodas, it made sense why he hadn't insisted Tauria sleep with him or even made persistent moves on her despite their potential marriage ruse.

Tauria was growing with dread... Had Mordecai been tricking her all along for some other reason? If not to have her kingdom, which was already his in Mordecai's eyes, what did he plan for her, other than keeping her close and content...

For Transition.

Her eyes cast up to the near full moon and saw nothing but a timer toward her death. Her change. The next full moon was days away.

CHAPTER TWENTY-EIGHT

Zaiana

They made it to Lakelaria's castle the evening after they woke up in the cellar. Zaiana had rested far better than she had on the ship, but part of her was dealing with turmoil over why that was.

Kyleer hadn't talked much during their long hours walking. She was grateful for it. When they came to the center of Alandra, the castle was a magnificent spectacle. Sharp fangs of glass that appeared like ice made up many tall peaks of the architecture. Surrounding the castle was a wide lake—a good measure of defense considering the Waterweilders no doubt posted in the guard surrounding it.

At the bridge to take them over, she was surprised to find Reylan Arrowood waiting, standing cross-armed, with a pissed-off look of loathing.

"What took you this long?" he snapped.

She gave no reaction to that. "We took our much needed rest bite after your volatile mate nearly killed us all."

Reylan led them over the bridge as if he were the general of this kingdom, not Rhyenelle. It was tragic really, and if he ever broke free of Marvellas's influence, he was sure to despise himself for all he'd betrayed.

Kyleer's expression remained torn with anger and pain when he stared at his friend, but he stayed obedient, having not fought in the slightest.

The interior of the glass palace gave a conflicting warmth she enjoyed. They could watch the snowstorms rage and ice form around them through the many clear walls while held in the confines of their protection. Zaiana marveled over the white stone that complemented the halls, and the gold filigree that decorated pillars and stone walls. Everything was so pure and delicate she couldn't help but feel like a dark stain on its crystal elegance.

They were led into a hall lined with pillars, with a heightened dais at the far end. The throne appeared as if the heavens had rained tears that had speared into the ground to form a chair of icicles, pointing in many directions but still forming an oval back and short sides. Upon it sat the depiction of an angel, if she were ever to imagine the mythical creature, though without wings. The Queen of Lakelaria, Zaiana deduced.

Her hair was as white as snow, as were her eyebrows and lashes, Zaiana saw the closer they got. Her dress was white and silver, making her blend in with her surroundings, and there was a certain haunting aura about that. As if she were a ghost bound to this hall.

Though nothing stunned her as much as seeing Faythe Ashfyre at the bottom of the dais.

"Welcome." The queen's voice was like a breath of frozen wind: gentle but not kind. The monarch stood. The flowing fabric of her white gown moved like the sea as she descended the wide white stone steps. "I was just inviting my first guests to dine with me this evening. Now I'm glad there will be more to share the spoils."

Zaiana hoped that wouldn't include her. She would stand by and guard if requested, but she hadn't expected the Queen of Lakelaria. She'd hoped Marvellas would be here, but the Spirit was absent.

"You're kind to host us," Faythe said tightly.

Reylan had been the one to lead them all here, and Zaiana had followed, under the impression it was to deliver Faythe and Kyleer to the Spirit Marvellas. She slipped Reylan an accusatory look he met with vacancy, once again a shell of the great general of Rhyenelle.

"Where's Marvellas?" Zaiana blurted.

The tension in the room thickened at the mention.

"You come into my castle and request to see someone else?"

The question froze like a sheet of ice beneath her feet: one wrong step, and she would fall right through.

"Forgive me." Zaiana forced the words with no sincerity. "It's just that she sent for us to retrieve these two and bring them here, it seems."

"As I hear, you were never part of that request."

"If I hadn't interfered, she wouldn't have two prizes instead of one."

The queen's hazel eyes flicked over Kyleer, but her expression didn't shift in the slightest. "I suppose not. The Spirit is out of sight for now. It's hard to know who you can truly trust."

She bit her tongue against speaking out of line, but this was ridiculous.

"All this time, Lakelaria has pretended to be peaceful and uninvolved in this war. The truth is, you've been harboring Marvellas all along, I assume?"

"You would be wise to keep assumptions to yourself."

Zaiana decided she didn't like this queen in the slightest. Something wasn't right.

"What do you want us to do with the prisoners?" she asked reluctantly.

"Don't let them escape. I will see you all at supper."

With that, the queen made to leave, and Zaiana was left bemused and beyond frustrated.

"What is the meaning of all of this?" she hissed to Reylan, since it was his instruction to cross the sea with Faythe and Kyleer.

"We got them to our destination," he said simply.

"And now what? We let them roam free?"

"No. Keep him in chains. I've got an eye on Faythe until the queen requests our presence later. Keep yours on him."

Zaiana was itching to sink her claws into his eyes so he couldn't keep them on anything. She observed how Faythe wasn't chained anymore, nor did it look like he was going to replace the chains. Zaiana took it as an insult, implying she couldn't handle Kyleer without incapacitating him.

Reylan steered a sour-looking Faythe Ashfyre toward the side exit, and Zaiana was at a complete loss over what in the Nether was happening. She'd never been in the middle of such confusing, disorganized mess.

"Disappointed they're not ordering you to string me up and torment me?" Kyleer said in question as they stared after Reylan and Faythe. "Me too. I think we both could have enjoyed it."

That snapped her glower to him. What was she supposed to do with him until their damned dinner party?

"Let's go," she said, shoving him toward the same door.

"I've never been to this castle. Have you?"

"No."

"You don't like the cold—that's clear enough."

"Who does?"

"Lakelarians, probably."

Something had been bothering her that she hadn't been able to place. Nothing about this situation felt right, and she was beginning to suspect she was the only clueless fool among several with a hidden agenda.

They curved down a hall that was deserted, and Zaiana pushed Kyleer against the wall.

"You didn't appear the least bit concerned nor surprised to see Faythe just now, considering you had no idea what happened to her after the blast."

"She's powerful and smart—my concern isn't needed."

"You just hoped she would show up eventually? Bullshit."

"What exactly is your accusation?"

There was an edge of amusement to his tone, twitching on his face too, which was boiling her anger. She was used to being a step ahead, knowing what others didn't, and it was infuriating her to no end to feel two steps behind here.

"It's not too late for you," he said, barely a whispered breath, but it slammed into her with the weight of a rock.

"Are you really that pathetic?" she hissed. "Will it only take a dagger through your chest for you to accept I'm not on your side and never will be?"

"Why? What have they ever done for you?"

"No one has ever done anything for me."

"Then why are you helping them?"

Maybe she didn't even know that herself anymore.

"Stop trying to see if there's redemption in me—there isn't."

"There's a lot in you, Zai. There's a soul you want to deny exists and a heart you want to forget could feel."

Kyleer choked. Zaiana hadn't realized what she'd done until trickles of his blood spilled over the hilt of the blade she'd lodged into his side. Pain twitched his expression, and surprise filled his eyes.

"That look right there…that's why you're a delusional fool."

Yanking the blade free, Kyleer's bound hands put pressure on the wound. The blade was small, but his fae healing was nullified with the Magestone around his wrists. His groans of pain disturbed her, but her resentment was stronger, and she tunneled away to feel nothing at all.

She would not be dining with them all tonight, and no one had given her instruction over the state he was to arrive in either.

"I've been waiting for that," he said, strained.

"That's just a scratch compared to what I'll do if you keep pushing, Ky."

His green eyes found her, and there was a glimmer in them as he said, "I like it when you call me that."

He was impossible.

Zaiana snatched ahold of the chain between his hands and yanked him without care down the hall.

"Where are we going?" Kyleer asked. She felt nothing for the faint labor in his voice, forcing him to move with his wound.

"I'm hungry."

"Good call. Me too."

They hadn't eaten in days, and it was the only thing on her mind right now, turning her mood even more volatile.

Kyleer said, "Wouldn't it be quicker for you to feed on human blood?"

"Have you ever tried it yourself?"

"Absolutely not."

"You might enjoy it."

"It's barbaric."

Zaiana huffed a laugh. "Some of *them* enjoy it."

"I'd much rather sample yours."

She didn't allow the temptation of a shiver to break at that suggestion. "Keep that fantasy to yourself."

The kitchens were bustling, with bodies at work, preparing many dishes she assumed were for the queen's ridiculous welcome feast. They regarded her intrusion with wariness, but she marched past them all, scanning for something that looked appealing.

"That meat looked nice," Kyleer commented.

She let go of his chains. "Take what you like. Might be the last good meal you get for a while."

He didn't hesitate, but he didn't take without asking the staff, and it was annoying how easily people warmed to him. A few of the fae even began to help him, holding his plate and filling it with anything he asked for. She watched all of them with bitterness growing in her chest. They were *flirting* with him.

Zaiana had picked up a piece of bread and dipped it into some sweet but spicy oil that danced over her taste buds. It was delicious, and somehow that annoyed her more. Her sight could hardly be torn from the commander. He was smiling with them. They examined his chains with sympathy. Occasionally, one of the fae around him would cast a look in her direction but quickly averted their gaze the second her dark stare was met.

She found a perch on a counter at the far end that wasn't being used. After a few minutes, Kyleer headed toward her. She didn't fail to notice how his bright grin for the others fell the moment he gave them his back. Not because his infectious brightness wasn't genuine toward them—it just wasn't within him. Zaiana also noticed the discomfort in his walk. He needed to use both his bound hands to carry the plate, and his clothing had to be grazing angrily against his stab wound.

Now she was feeling mildly guilty for that impulsive trigger.

"They said the tiny fish pie things are the best you'll eat across the seven kingdoms," Kyleer informed her, setting the plate beside Zaiana. "Something about wine and goats milk and the best fish you could ever hope to sample."

She surveyed the mountain of different foods he'd gathered.

"How would they know? Valgard might have them beat, and it remains a mystery."

Kyleer huffed, finding a bucket of water to wash the blood off his hands as best he could.

"You're dark fae—an esteemed one at that, unless that was a lie—and you've never been east across the sea where your people came from?"

"I've never had reason to."

He hummed curiously, drying his hands and returning. He picked up the bite-sized aforementioned irresistible fish pie and threw it into his mouth.

"Still, I would have thought you curious."

"My curiosity doesn't matter. I was a soldier—you know how it is. We go where we are stationed."

His eyes lit up as he chewed, and he immediately retrieved another pie. Two of them, in fact. One he offered to Zaiana. She wanted to refuse out of nothing more than pettiness, but since she'd stabbed him, she supposed she could be a little nicer.

"You have wings. Surely you could have flown over at least once in your lifetime."

In truth, she'd never really desired to. Zaiana ate the fish pie in one mouthful, and the flavor explosion on her tongue surprised her. She'd never been one to admire food—it was just sustenance and often short in supply for most of her years under the mountain. But for the minute it took her to chew, she thought of nothing but this simple pleasure, wondering if there would ever come days to enjoy such trivial things for longer.

She found Kyleer watching her, with a pleased smile at the corner of his mouth.

"Your face told me all," he said.

Zaiana hopped off the counter. "You should get that wound dressed while you have the chance. I'm sure your fae admirers would gladly aid you."

"Not one to clean up your own mess?"

"You are not my mess. You're nothing to me."

Those words were icy, and it wiped any kindness from his expression. Every time she was the cause of his upset, it twisted within her. Infuriating.

Zaiana made to leave. "If you're not here when I get back in ten minutes, that wound will be the least mess I make of you."

"I could take that in far more enticing ways."

He didn't see her glower since he invested his efforts into inhaling the plate of food. Zaiana left him, passing the kitchen staff and lingering her warning on them too.

Zaiana just needed a moment to breathe away from the commander. After weeks forced to be close to him, she felt his presence like a layer of skin. He was all over her even when he'd hardly touched her. The worst thing about it was, she was beginning to grow antsy that he wouldn't be her problem anymore soon. Even though all they did was argue, she had to sever the threads of attachment that were linking between them again.

CHAPTER TWENTY-NINE

Faythe

Faythe couldn't reach the last of her dress ties on her back. She arched and struggled, growing frustrated and ultimately letting go. Her head bowed, hardly able to stand the unnecessary spectacle she was being made to wear.

The gown was ruby-red, with crystals that glinted like spilled fresh blood down her bodice. She couldn't shake the ominous thought. Her hair had been pinned back with dozens of red-jeweled hairpins too.

She let her sight drift over the bright, snowy mountain and cityscape through the single wall of glass in this room. Her breath was stolen every time she glimpsed such purity and innocence—a vision of peace or a tragedy of obliviousness, Faythe couldn't decide.

Faythe's sight snapped back to the mirror when fingers brushed her back. She found Reylan in the reflection, resuming the ties she'd abandoned. He didn't hide his appearance anymore, and while she was glad, her heart permanently ached to watch him so emotionless.

"Why hasn't Marvellas greeted me yet? I thought she'd be most eager."

"*You* shouldn't be," he said, his voice stripped of any feeling.

Faythe swallowed down her grief. "She's masterful at hiding," she said, watching his face to catch any hint.

"She has to be."

"Marvellas has many talents, doesn't she? The abilities may be Spirit-blessed, but they can borrow each other's," Faythe tested.

He tugged the strings a final time, meeting her gaze in the reflection. "Many skills, many faces."

Faythe's heart skipped. Reylan finished tying the back of her dress, and her stomach sank with the absence of his warmth when he stepped away. She turned around, debating in her mind how to gain any small insights she could before this dinner with the queen.

"You retrieved her ruin from the Sky Caves, didn't you?"

Reylan folded his arms, taking up a lean against the bedpost. "Yes."

"You couldn't break it, so she planted it in you, knowing I would break it to save you."

"I believe so."

"But you feel nothing for me. So maybe I won't bother."

"If I had the choice, I wouldn't want you to."

It would have hurt less for him to have carved a blade into her chest.

"You do have a choice," she ground out. "You have the power of a ruin in you—enough to contend with her. Why not take over?"

"She is my queen."

Faythe resisted the urge to double over with the tightening in her gut. The betrayal those four words winded her with.

They're not his words.

She approached him, a careful doe toward the lion. He didn't move, but his eyes tracked her every step, debating whether to strike before she could get too close. Faythe dared to reach up a hand, slipping high up his jaw, until her fingers brushed his temple.

Faythe tried to enter his mind, but immediately she was slammed with so much dark resistance she almost buckled.

"Stop," he warned, but he didn't pull away.

Faythe searched deeper through his sapphire eyes and touched their bond to aid her. All she wanted was to show him one thing. One reminder. The shadows invading his mind hissed and wailed, and misery spilled across Faythe's features. So much pain and darkness and *death*.

"Oh, Reylan," she whispered.

She found a space to throw a light. A memory.

"My Phoenix. My Queen."

Reylan's touch brushed her cheek, and Faythe thought for a second that tenderness flickered in his eyes. Until ice froze over his irises the same second his hand wrapped around her throat.

"They're hollow words to me now. Those of a past fool I am no longer. You mean nothing to me, Faythe."

The loathing poured into her name sounded so torturously wrong from him. She stumbled back when he pushed her. Faythe's eyes burned. She bowed her head to the ground and collected herself while heat flushed her skin.

It was no use. She wasn't enough to reach him. Worst of all, Faythe drowned in the misery of failing him, but she wouldn't give up. That was why she was here.

"Let's go," he said flatly.

All Faythe could do was follow with her hollow heart.

Despite everything, Faythe was glad he was here with her. Even if only to hurt her, she didn't want him to slip from her sights again.

The banquet hall of Lakelaria's castle was a picture of vulnerable beauty. Faythe's shoes clicked across glittering white floor—a flat, smooth imitation of the snow that encompassed them from the walls on either side and in front of her, made of glass. The pillars in the room dominated like proud icicles thrown down from the Gods in the heavens. Guards in black littered down each side stood out starkly. Faythe briefly met one set of hazel eyes, while the rest of them were clad in a hood and a face covering, hiding their identity from the sins that might be asked of them at any moment.

The air hummed with a fragile peace as Faythe slipped her sight to Iana, who was already seated at the head of the banquet table. Faythe accepted the chair at the opposite end that was pulled out for her.

The table, a proud slate of white marble, was filled with a feast far too much for just two of them, and Faythe had no appetite with her storm of emotions. At the side of the hall, Faythe almost lost her composure to see Kyleer as the first break in the tranquil illusion, a roughed-up sight. Unlike Faythe, who had been bathed and presented, he was still in his Rhyenelle attire, but what quickly threatened her volatility was the scent of his blood. Faythe glanced at his crimson-stained hands clutching a wound on his side, then she targeted an accusatory glare on Zaiana that was met with cool disinterest.

She was already struggling to contain herself, but the queen merely kept eating. It was almost as if Faythe had disturbed her feast and she was used to dining alone.

"Lakelaria is more magnificent than we're told," Faythe said, testing the conversation.

Those hazel irises slipped to her, lingering long enough to weigh every word Faythe spoke as if searching for tricks in them.

"This is what peace looks like," Iana said with pride.

"There are no humans," Faythe observed calmly. "I didn't see any on our short venture around the city."

A flex of the porcelain skin around her eyes spoke of suspicion. "There are some, but you are right. Lakelaria is mostly populated by fae."

Some. Yet Faythe hadn't seen a single one.

"I am new to my position. Court and politics. History." Faythe picked up her drink, needing to soothe her drying throat. "But I had a friend tell me some things about your kingdom once. I am sorry to hear of the passing of your daughter."

The queen's chin rose a fraction. "It was a long time ago," she said coldly.

Everything about her repelled company and conversation.

Faythe pushed a little more. "Around two hundred years ago. She would have only been past her first century. She was to be married right before it happened."

The pauses between the queen's engagement raced in Faythe's chest.

"Yes. There's not a day that goes by that I don't think of her."

Lies. All Faythe could hear was deception, and her composure was shaking.

The queen wore sleeves that extended over her hands, and her neckline was always high on her throat. Faythe watched her hand reach for her goblet.

"The food will be getting cold," Iana said.

Faythe didn't respond to that. Instead she had to take a risk.

"Nikalias met you when he was young." Her nerves were betraying her now.

Iana set her cup down, and there was a hint of suspicion in her pause. "Yes. I believe I visited his kingdom."

"He seems to recall you had blue eyes. I guess, being in his youth, he might not have recounted the details so well."

They were hazel, and as Faythe stared right into them, she thought they flicked a brighter hue.

"The young prince was hardly present during my visit."

Faythe hummed, but her skin prickled. Then she had no patience left and threw all caution to the wind.

The knife in her hand spun through the air for a mere heartbeat, heading straight for the queen...

Thump.

The queen moved her head just in time. The blade pierced the back of her chair, inches from her eyeline.

Faythe couldn't stop now.

The guards in black advanced, but Faythe yanked the tablecloth, sending everything sprawling from it, before her palm slammed to the table and a flare of her gold magick cracked across the surface, breaking the table apart.

Iana never summoned her legendary Waterwielding abilities.

Shapeshifting always leaves a trace.

Reylan had told her that. Then today, before leaving her rooms:

Many skills, many faces.

Faythe didn't know if he'd helped seal her thoughts intentionally, but she couldn't back down now as she ran across the wreckage she'd made of the table, having only done so to slow the guards from reaching her before she could reach the queen.

Command of a creature is more akin to your ability. Nik had told her that when he spoke of the legends he'd heard of the Queen of Lakelaria; that she could command the creatures of the sea.

The queen raised a hand...and that was when Faythe saw the final confirmation to her daunting theory.

The symbol within her palm glowed gold. So familiar. Faythe wore one just like it in hers.

A circle, with three lines scoring past the circumference.

Faythe's steps slammed to a stop. Her chest heaved. No guards moved anymore—the hand Faythe couldn't tear her sight from was her signal to stop them.

"Aurialis once said she lost track of Marvellas two hundred years ago," Faythe said, her heart thundering. "It also happened to be when the Queen of Lakelaria lost her child. The queen might not have been the most loving parent, but losing her daughter left her alone and vulnerable. The perfect target."

Adrenaline pumped her blood, threatening to sway her balance in this confrontation.

"So you can come out now." Faythe took three terrifying breaths before she summoned the name of her terrors. "Marvellas."

The silence that settled was so cold and deadly. She wore Iana's face, debating if it was possible to grapple with the lie Faythe had torn open.

Then, there it was. The smile that chilled her blood every time she saw it. One of triumph and wicked glee, so not even another face could hide the intent behind it.

"You are still every part *my* daughter, Aesira," Marvellas said in her own voice.

The heat blazing her skin cooled at the fear that crept in with the changes in her appearance that followed.

"Maybe even more cunning in this second life of yours."

Flame engulfed the lengths of white hair, starting at the root and devouring, until the brilliant red returned. Shapes of her face morphed so slowly Faythe had to blink consciously, struggling to believe she wasn't asleep in some terrible nightmare.

Marvellas shed the skin she'd worn on these lands, hiding, for hundreds of years. Biding her time. Masterfully puppeteering a war from this one safe place no one thought to go looking.

Face-to-face with Marvellas at last, the purpose for her existence had never sung so clearly. She was created to be the end. To kill Marvellas once and for all. Her will to live beyond that goal lingered behind her.

Reylan had remained so still despite Faythe's outburst.

Kill Marvellas. Free Reylan.

Faythe was willing to contend with how villainous Marvellas could be to achieve both.

"Dine with me—"

Faythe's magick reacted before Marvellas could finish. The Spirit defused her flare easily, but Faythe tried again, and again, until Marvellas attacked back and Faythe was slammed into by a force of magick like her own.

It sent her sprawling across the broken stone, cutting her flesh where it was exposed in this gown. The wind was knocked from her lungs, and Faythe struggled to roll off her back and gather breath. Kyleer yelled her name, but she listened to his struggle as he was detained from reaching her.

All Faythe could do was grant him a weak look, hoping he read that she was okay. Zaiana stood by him, with purple eyes that darted from Faythe to Marvellas, but what it showed was the dark fae had no knowledge of Marvellas's guise until now.

Marvellas's face finally lined with harsh anger, but it was nothing compared to what Faythe was burning with.

Faythe peeled herself from the rubble. "I could burn this castle to sand, and your soldiers to ash."

"You wouldn't kill innocents."

"There are none if their allegiance is to you."

Perhaps she'd lost her sanity. Morality. Maybe she wouldn't be able to live with herself after what it took to win. But he would be safe, her friends would be safe, and that was worth condemning her soul.

"You always did have a temper, Aesira."

"Aesira died trying to escape you," Faythe said coldly. "All of this, bringing back my soul—why? What was so special about me?"

"Everything." There was an ache in that whisper of a word from the Spirit.

All Faythe saw were markers to hit to make her bleed as much as Faythe had over two lifetimes. Each time Marvellas had come between Faythe and the only thing she wanted in the world.

"You could have taken the realm without me."

Marvellas stepped over plates of food without even looking. Faythe wanted to retreat, but she stood firm against the instinct.

"This war began because I had someone who meant the world to me stolen from me."

"Me?"

"No."

Faythe didn't want to see the humanity that was surfacing in the Spirit, but it felt important to understand.

"Your son," Faythe said in realization.

At the thought, a new set of bright gold eyes flashed to the forefront of her thoughts. She'd dreamt of him before, and it had been the reason she'd snuck out to meet Gus in Rhyenelle—the last time she saw him. She'd needed answers, and it was then he'd told her Aesira had discovered Marvellas had a son. A male with dark hair and eyes like hers. But something had happened long ago…something that had taken him out of this realm, beyond where Marvellas could ever go looking.

"How do you know of him?"

"I don't know how…but Aesira found out about him."

"I never told you about him in the past," Marvellas said, turning to suspicion. "Oh, my dear, perhaps I didn't get to find out all of what you discovered back then before you foolishly got yourself killed."

"How-how did she die?"

"Misplaced bravery. A mere mortal wound, of all things, on a battlefield you should never have been on." Marvellas stopped, glancing over the ruins Faythe had made of the table. "We could change the world together. This doesn't have to be a fight."

Faythe shook her head, unable to fathom this ages-long delusion of partnership Marvellas still clung to.

"You want to eradicate an entire species," she said. It was the first conclusion Faythe could make of Marvellas's driving motives for this war. "Starting with the humans. Why?"

"They're too weak to survive in this world. And if left unchecked, they will try to take a power that was never meant to be theirs. Time that was never theirs."

This vengeance was personal to the Spirit. After all this time, Faythe had to learn the story of Marvellas, as far back as the beginning of her fall to land, or she would never have closure.

"What happened to you?"

Marvellas held her with a deep look, so cold and detached as she said, "Love." Then her gaze dropped, one note of sorrow, before her guard firmed and she walked away from Faythe. Casting her sight out the glass wall, she added, "It will always find a way to destroy you."

Faythe's throat turned dry, her next words an attempted plea. "Just release him from your ruin and compulsion, and we'll leave."

"I thought all this time, Reylan would only get in the way as he tried to tear us apart in the past. But now there is a way for you to stay together. We can finally start to bring this world to its full potential."

Her head was already shaking, making the slight flicker of hope turn ugly on the Spirit's face.

"Then you leave me no choice—"

"You leave *me* no choice," Faythe cut in. Slipping into the minds of the two guards who moved in behind her, Faythe had to set aside her morality to snap their necks. It wasn't without consequence. Each life, even those of the vicious dark fae who were loyal to Marvellas's cause, tainted black spots on her soul. "I never knew I could contend with you in villainy until you gave me the right motivation."

To win, to get Reylan back, she was prepared to give in to the darkness completely.

More guards flooded into the room, and she braced to kill again.

Until Kyleer's groan of pain stopped her, and she found him on his knees, Zaiana poised over him with a hand fisted in his hair, the other holding a blade to his throat. Marvellas smiled, pleased with the dark fae's initiative.

Faythe was seeing murderous red toward Zaiana. She remembered her greatest fear of having her mind infiltrated, and Faythe was tempted to shatter it right now.

"Don't," Kyleer rasped, reading her intent.

She couldn't understand why he would object after what Zaiana had done to him. How even now, she was proving Faythe's hope of redemption in the dark fae was a childish fantasy. She would always be their enemy.

"You only prove my point, time and time again. Love is a weakness that will always be exploited against you," Marvellas said calmly.

Too calm. It grated against Faythe's trigger to erupt.

"Kyleer Galentithe," she drawled. "As I hear, your brother is adjusting quite well to Malin Ashfyre's new rule. Perhaps I may have use for you too."

"It's only me you want," Faythe hissed. "I am your heir, Marvellas. I despised that for a long time, but now, seeing the fear that crosses your face when you try to hide it, you're beginning to realize what you have created in me is the end you cannot escape. A weapon crafted so perfectly to bring about your own downfall."

"You always have been ungrateful. Selfish. It is because of you every one of them will die."

Her blood raced with the challenge. Heat flooded her palms with a dare she could hardly contain. If she clashed powers with Marvellas here…Faythe knew no one in this castle would be spared.

Faythe said, her voice as calm as death, "Release Kyleer. Release Reylan. You have me now."

"In truth, I thought the ruin would kill him. It was to my great surprise that he not only lived but also *became* my ruin. His magick is unparalleled now. How can I not see this as fate meddling in my favor? For now I have a bargain for you," Marvellas said.

A cold shiver of dread broke over her skin at Marvellas's cruel smile.

Marvellas continued. "I quite like the weapon he is, but as I'm sure you're starting to figure out, the only way to free him is to break the ruin."

The gravity of what that would mean for the world wasn't lost on her.

Faythe's gaze shifted to Zaiana, who retained her steely exterior. "You could be lying. Breaking it could kill him as well," Faythe said.

"How might I convince you of my truth?"

"A blood bargain."

Marvellas's eyes narrowed in consideration. "Very well."

Faythe's pulse skipped as she watched her glide across the chaos toward her. A small pocket knife slipped out of somewhere in her ruby dress, which flooded around her like blood and water.

Marvellas held it out to her. "You first."

Faythe took the knife, with her wary sight fixed on Marvellas, anticipating some kind of trick. She sliced a small cut in her palm and then handed it back. When Marvellas cut her own flesh, Faythe almost expected her blood to be a different color, or that she wouldn't bleed at all, but crimson beaded across her wound.

Marvellas reached for her suddenly, clasping their bleeding palms together, and Faythe gasped at the pulse of energy that exploded through her body.

Then...a reel of moving images. As if she were watching forgotten memories through the eyes of Marvellas. She saw Aesira. Faythe looked like her, with the same color of hair and eyes, but the younger fae had shorter hair, and some of her features were different shapes or angles.

The Spirit seemed distracted by the unexpected connection too, and Faythe used that opportunity to draw a dagger from her side and slice it across her cheek. The blade flew out of her hand when next she lunged for Marvellas, and they both crashed down among the stone and spoiled food.

Faythe was quickly grabbed from behind and restrained by two dark fae. She was forced to her knees as Marvellas rose, the heat of a God's rage in her amber eyes.

"If you're going to behave like a beast, then you leave me no choice but to treat you like one," she hissed venomously.

Faythe knew her attack wouldn't go unpunished, but it had felt damn good.

"You are nothing without me. Nothing more than the peasant your birth mother made of you. I gave up my pretense—now it's your turn."

The guards let her go, and she caught herself on her hands.

"Take it all off."

It took a second for Faythe to understand, until she glanced at the beautiful ruined material pooling around her. The jewels she wore on her body and her hair. She'd been dressed up for Marvellas's show.

"Or he suffers until you do," she warned.

Tight sounds of pain echoed from Kyleer, and Faythe became horror-struck. Zaiana still held him, but it wasn't her inflicting the pain. Marvellas was in his mind.

"Stop!" Faythe yelled.

Marvellas did, turning her attention back to Faythe, coldly impatient.

She forced back the humiliation she felt at this display. In front of Kyleer...Reylan...and...*Nerida*. The fae healer stood in perfect disguise among the guards. Faythe had met her eyes on the way in but couldn't bear to see the disturbance that would be filled in them now to witness Faythe's defeat.

Faythe started with her hairpins, plucking them one by one, and the only sounds to echo in the room were the chimes of her dignity hitting the ground piece by piece.

Red crystals fell around her like tears of blood, but she would not feed the Spirit's sick pleasure with her emotions. Faythe kept calm, pulling the ties of her corset bodice. The front came loose, and Faythe let it fall. Then she kneeled there in nothing more than a white camisole, her hair unbound.

Marvellas approached with the intent of a serpent, and she struck just as fast, taking a tight grip of the back of Faythe's hair. She pinched her lips to smother her whimper from the torn roots. She took hold of Faythe's hand, slipping off her golden butterfly ring before Faythe could fight it, and she gasped.

"No—!"

Faythe's plea was too late as the ring turned to gold dust between the Spirit's fingers.

"It was a wretched thing then, and now," she said spitefully.

Faythe's heart withered watching the gold particles float away until they were nothing.

It wasn't just a ring.

It was a thread of time that kept Reylan on the path to finding her soul again. It was their love in all its defiance. That ring was a bond, a promise, between them.

Faythe glanced over her shoulder to where Reylan stood in the shadows. He held her with an intense stare but gave no indication he felt anything at watching the ring get destroyed.

Her head bowed in sorrow.

"Finally...if you loved your poor and powerless life in High Farrow so much, then you don't need your magick."

Marvellas released her with a shove, but Faythe was caught by guards again.

Kyleer struggled, shouting profanities and pleading for her. Faythe couldn't bear to look at him.

One guard pulled her arm, and before she could register what was happening, a blade sliced deeply along her forearm. She was wrong to think that score of fire was pain when what followed was enough to make a person beg for death.

She only caught a glimpse of the dark iridescent stone, and when it was pushed into her wound, Faythe couldn't scream. An agony so consuming stole her will to do anything at all.

"Faythe!" Kyleer yelled her name, but he sounded so distant now.

Faythe's consciousness brushed darkness, but it wouldn't fall under completely. She wished it would give in and let her go. The blood boiling in her veins tested the very limits of her physical endurance.

"I could ease your pain, but you deserve to feel it all for your rebellion," Marvellas said close to her ear. "But I'll ease you into the next."

Faythe was floating in a dark oblivion. She felt a new sharpness scoring her other arm. Her throat burned, but she couldn't hear the screams clawing from it.

Her veins were torched, and she was burning from the inside out.

Days, weeks, years she was set ablaze, and didn't know when the flames began to dwindle. She lay now, her cheek cutting into broken marble, with her vision coming in and out of focus. All she wanted was to drift away. Why wouldn't her mind let her leave this state of torture?

She thought she saw Kyleer. On his knees, still being restrained from reaching her. But it was someone else's struggle that broke sobs from her when she realized...saw a glimpse of silver hair...and became desperate to break from this poisonous hold to crawl to him too.

Reylan was fighting for her. To reach her.

Multiple guards restrained him, now on his knees, so close she wanted to reach out an arm but couldn't move her body.

It was too late.

He couldn't save her.

Faythe's mind flooded—not with picture but color. Swirls of sapphire and silver. She would never forget, for it was a sea that didn't drown, nor could she ever be lost in it as she let go and floated deeper, and deeper, and deeper...

CHAPTER THIRTY

Reylan

She was most perfect thing he'd ever laid eyes on. He hadn't been able to stop thinking it since he'd apprehended her in the Rhyenelle town. How beautiful she was, and how he'd never seen her before then—or at least he couldn't remember if he had, because in his chest…something familiar awoke.

Marvellas wanted her, and he was her servant.

Now he'd brought her to the Spirit he'd begun to grow anxious. Angrily, confusingly so. He'd done what was asked of him, and it had been easy. Too easy. Why hadn't Faythe fought him harder?

She shouldn't be here. No—she was something to be protected and loved. A soul worth waiting lifetimes for. Worth trekking across realms for.

Her blood…he couldn't be sorry for taking it when it was the single most divine thing he'd ever tasted in his life. He wanted her to give it to him willingly, anticipating it would be even more incredible if she did.

Conflict grew in his mind. A frustrating influence tried to banish his desire for Faythe's touch, taste, and mere presence.

All he did was stand and watch as Faythe faced off with the Spirit. When she pulled a dagger and went crashing down on top of Marvellas, Reylan could hardly stand his ground. He didn't want to pull Faythe off to save Marvellas; he wanted to save *her* from the Spirit's wrath that came next.

She undressed the finery she wore, but it couldn't diminish how she shone more brilliant than a pure diamond in nothing but her own flesh.

His chest was pounding, and an itch to do something, *anything*, had his fists clamping tight when they began to tremble.

They sliced her wrists, and Reylan almost broke to snap their necks for it.

He shook his head that battered with confusing, conflicting emotions. He had to leave this room, but he only twisted a fraction before…

Her *scream*—

It obliterated the world around him.

Her agony shattered a hold on his mind he wasn't aware of.

Reylan blinked, and what he saw, what he realized was happening, snapped a rage so volatile he lunged.

Fae tried to restrain him, but at Faythe's scream he'd snapped two necks that had attempted to stop him.

He'd let them take her. Restrain her.

His Faythe. His Phoenix.

"I'm going to tear the head from your fucking neck," he snarled, snapping feral eyes up to the wicked Spirit who watched his mate writhe in agony as if it were all a spectacle.

"You're stronger than I thought," Marvellas said. No emotion. Nothing. "To resist my influence with the ruin inside you. I have to admit, you continue to exceed my expectations."

He would kill her. No—that was no longer enough for all she'd done to Faythe.

Reylan was helpless to watch, but he kept trying to fight off the fae to reach her.

The battle of fire and ice from the Magestone being clamped around his wrists, then his neck, was nothing compared to the ear-splitting cries from Faythe that brought him to his knees. Reylan wept, utterly broken at that sound, this sight, he would let haunt him for the rest of his days.

"Reylan." Kyleer was here. His rage targeted his friend, his brother in everything but blood, and though part of him wanted to feel sympathy for his capture, all he harbored was resentment. Ugly, perhaps unfair resentment that Kyleer had failed Faythe just as much as he had by being caught here with her.

Kyleer's face was desolate. Pleading and straining to say something else.

Marvellas approached, and he snarled, animalistic at the sight of the flaming beauty that torched a rage so scorching he thought it could set fire to the world to watch her burn within it.

"Come back to me, Rey," she cooed. As if she couldn't hear Faythe's torture. The scent of her blood tainted the air, and Reylan wished it were his. Would bleed every drop to this floor now if it would spare her.

Marvellas's touch hovered over the dark thing she'd sunk into his flesh, and the world turned absolutely silent. Every sense was stolen by the power that consumed him. Every scream, every image, every memory. Reylan was nothing.

Nothing but her servant.

When he blinked and found the world around him again, he didn't know why he was here. Only that he belonged to her. This creature of triumph and conquer.

"There you are," she said, pleased.

Reylan bowed his head. His ears rang with a high pitch though everything was soundless. He got to his feet, not remembering when the manacles around him had been placed there.

"Take her to the tower," Marvellas instructed him, walking away as if boredom became her. She added to other guards, "And take him to the cells far below."

Two dark fae began to drag away a fae male. "I'm sorry," he said in Reylan's direction over his shoulder.

Two words that meant absolutely nothing.

Reylan found a beautiful fae on the ground, so still and quiet. Peaceful, were she not bleeding so much, lying on crimson-painted stone that made the sight of her devastating. Reylan took her into his arms, not knowing why there was a nagging within him at the harm done to her.

Reylan walked and walked; he didn't want to reach the tower cells. He didn't want to let her go. But he had a duty, and his Goddess wanted this.

He set her on the small bed. It wasn't enough. Her form was so vulnerable in the bloodstained, thin white undergarment. He unfolded the feeble blanket and laid it over her. It still wasn't enough. So he unclipped his cloak and draped that over her delicate body too.

"You're not to give her anything," a guard outside the cell warned.

Reylan didn't think twice—the power that was too much within him rejoiced at any flicker of emotion it could strike out to. He wasn't sure what the entity was, only that it was an ending to everything it touched. A silent delivery of death, though not a painless one. All it took was a look from Reylan, a thought, and the guard barely made a sound as the life drained from him. Hollowing his cheeks, turning his skin to paper, revealing his veins that dried out slowly. Then he fell as nothing more than a skeleton barely given flesh.

He turned back to the sleeping fae, reaching to brush the hair from her face.

"Faythe," he whispered. The name came to him as a distant star in the darkness of his mind. He decided to keep the small flicker of light alive.

Reylan left, closing her cell, but the twist of the key was like a knife in his chest for a reason lost to him. He pulled up his hood, grabbing the back collar of the dead dark fae to drag him out.

Every step away strained something within him—a tether he should sever to be rid of the madness it grew in his mind. But for some reason, he didn't want it gone. He wanted to protect it.

CHAPTER THIRTY-ONE

Izaiah

I zaiah thought this might be it. The end of him.

He lay on his back, hanging onto his consciousness by a final thread. The roof of the catacomb flickered with the amber from the torches he'd lit, but it was his own skin that felt set aflame. He'd even taken his jacket and shirt off after the fourth attempt at merging with the ruin's power—the most he'd tried in a single session, because he was running out of damned time.

Izaiah was about to give in to the pull of darkness. Maybe some rest would replenish him enough to try again. A hand slipped around his nape and yanked him up, making his eyes fly back open. He was met with a frightening intensity in the familiar brown eyes of Tynan.

"What in the Nether do you think you're doing?" the dark fae snarled.

Izaiah was too shocked to speak, and still held in the soft clutches of death.

Tynan growled, setting him back down, and Izaiah felt no more useful than a sodden stick. Next thing he knew, ice shocked his system, animating his body against his previous thought of incapacity. Now sitting upright, with both hands against the floor, Izaiah blinked, some clarity returning as he watched the droplets from his hair gather in a puddle.

"Did you just throw ice-cold water over me?"

"I'm surprised it didn't turn to steam hitting your scorching flesh. Do you have a damned suicide wish?"

Izaiah rubbed his eyes, shifting with a groan to his knees. His muscles barked in agony.

"I don't expect you to understand. How did you follow me? Dammit, I was careful."

"Zaiana told me before she left."

His eyes scrunched shut, internally cursing her for divulging this when he'd explicitly conditioned her not to. Then the second part of his answer registered, and Izaiah slid a look at Tynan.

"Left? Where has Dakodas sent her?"

Why hadn't she told him? He wasn't done learning from her, even though their sessions had started to consist of her merely watching his failures, claiming she'd provided all the information she could.

"Zaiana left on her own to track down answers about our still hearts since Malin planted the idea of a curse, not a birth defect."

Izaiah leaned back on his knees, his breaths finally starting to feel normal again. "Did she? Good for her." He meant it, glad the dark fae was taking her own initiative for once.

"Before she did, she told me of your own plan of stupidity. Honestly, it's like running a daycare here sometimes."

"I told her not to tell you."

"And why not?"

Tynan stood cross-armed, staring him down. Izaiah pitied the emotion that slipped through the dark fae's anger toward him.

"For the reason you're looking at me now. I told you not to care about me."

"Too late," he snapped.

Izaiah knew he'd done wrong by Tynan in letting him attach feelings to their moments of lust. In his defense, he hadn't expected Tynan to be capable of caring. Everything they thought about the dark fae, all the sinister tales of their history, it was not a linear truth. It seemed so ignorant and desperate upon reflection, an easy way out, to pin blame out of fear and condemn an entire group of people by letting the heinous acts of a few be loud enough to define them all. Perhaps the good in their history was merely hidden in the shadows.

"I didn't know Zaiana cared so much about me to send a watcher."

With unstable balance, Izaiah rose to his feet, taking a moment to brace on his thighs. "She doesn't. But what she won't admit is that she cares for me, and she foolishly cares for your brother. So by association, you have more care than you damn deserve."

There was no arguing with that.

Tynan said, exasperated, "What are you hoping to achieve here anyway? What could you possibly want with more power?"

"The power of a crown is just an illusion. True power is worth everything."

"You've never struck me as one to desire a throne."

"I don't. But the ability to take one for someone else, to stop tyranny before it can warm another seat of influence—that's worth everything."

Tynan took a pause for thought. "You're doing this for her? For Faythe Ashfyre?"

"She's my queen."

"The second she gained that title, her kingdom was stolen right in front of her. That's who you're giving your life for?"

Izaiah straightened, challenging Tynan with a dark stare-off. "The first half of my life I was a coward. I let my father tell me who I had to be. He didn't like my preference for males, and I wasn't a fighter—not back then. I didn't want to be. I let him take his anger toward me, the world, and himself out on Kyleer," he confessed. There was no reason to hide his failings. "Agalhor was the best ruler of our time, and he saved me from the mines my father sent me to. But Faythe has it in her not only to make a change for Rhyenelle but also the world. She falls, she gets back up, and she fights. But it's more than that. She sees, she hears, and she understands. In her, I see a world where fewer of those like me have to fear being themselves, because she will lead by example, as human, as fae, as a commoner, and as a royal. And I'm going to do my part to see her rise."

Tynan's harsh expression had relaxed while Izaiah talked. "Believe it or not, I actually understand. For I see the same in Zaiana."

That set them on a road of mutual perception.

"Then don't try to stop me."

"What will the ruin help you achieve?"

Izaiah smiled, musing to himself, "A greater form than a mouse, I assure you."

Tynan circled around the box, coming closer. "No one but Zaiana has been able to wield that thing. I've watched many die trying, and I can't—" Tynan stopped himself, both in speech and in his steps, less than an arm's reach away.

Izaiah said carefully, "Only you can stop your feelings. It's only going to hurt you in the end."

"Then don't let there be an end."

"I know the risk I'm taking."

Izaiah's jaw tightened when Tynan reached for his nape, drawing them closer but keeping their stares tangled.

"Then I'm taking it with you."

"I don't need you here."

"I don't care."

"I don't *want* you—"

Tynan crushed his lips to his, and Izaiah became torn by anger over the dark fae's stubbornness and a passion that had begun to grow deeper roots beyond thoughts of lust. He had to stop them, but it felt as futile as commanding the darkest clouds not to break their rain or the brightest sun not to cast its rays. Izaiah's resistance now was only in an attempt to spare Tynan. To keep his feelings whole and wrapped precious for someone more deserving when he was gone. After the life the dark fae had lived—believing, like Zaiana, they had no hearts to give feelings to—at least Izaiah could leave this world with the fulfillment to have proven that wrong.

So fast, they became a furious collision of shattered resistance. Izaiah didn't know when they'd moved, but pinning Tynan to the wall allowed his body to press into his, reliving some of the tension to be impossibly closer. Before he knew what he was doing, he was helping Tynan out of his jacket, pulling his shirt over his head, not knowing how since they barely paused for breath.

To the Nether with it all. If that was to be his destination, by the ruin or in some other scar of this war, then why not give in to lustful—maybe even romantic—notions for a while?

CHAPTER THIRTY-TWO

Faythe

Faythe awoke with ice growing under her skin, slicked as though she'd walked through fire. Her body felt ripped apart by two contrasting forces.

Opening her eyes, her vision came and went in blurry images. Her head pounded, and when she cracked her lips apart, her mouth was bone-dry.

Against all that wanted to remain drowning with her sinking anchor of pain, Faythe found the will to angle her arms and push herself up. A weight slipped off her shoulders as she did, and with it, the scent of her true home hit her all at once.

Reylan.

Faythe's eyes filled as she sat back and pulled the cloak over herself again. Burying her nose into the fabric, a sharp sob escaped her.

For a moment, he'd broken through Marvellas's influence. He'd tried to reach her…hadn't he? She couldn't be sure if she'd imagined that in the delusion of her agony.

Faythe shivered violently and couldn't steady her breathing. There wasn't enough air. Her hand caught her against the cot when a sway of dizziness washed over her. Pain exploded up her arm with the slightest pressure, and she fell, hitting her head against the wooden edge.

There was no end to her misery.

She couldn't move for what dragged like hours. Recalling the

Magestone forced into her body, Faythe couldn't control the tremors racking through her. When she found the will to move, she dragged fearful eyes to the nasty wounds slashed down her forearms. Her skin had blackened around where the Magestone was submerged under her skin.

"Looks like you're in a serious predicament."

She wasn't aware of company until a silvery male voice jolted through her.

Faythe pushed up on her cot, finding a fae sitting on one across from her in the cell attached to hers, separated by thick iron bars. What stopped time for a beat and washed her skin cold...were the familiar golden eyes piercing into her own.

"Who are you?"

"I've been waiting to ask you the same thing."

She'd never seen eyes like hers before. Faythe blinked as if he might be a figment of her imagination and would disappear. He sat lazily against the wall, one knee bent on his cot, with his arm wrapped lazily over it. In that molten stare was patient darkness and a mystery she couldn't decipher.

"You're an heir of hers too," Faythe said in barely a whisper.

That caused him to peel away from the wall. His legs fell over the cot that was far too small for him, and he leaned his forearms on his thighs. His golden irises were alive, shining brighter than her own.

"An heir of what?" he asked. His voice slithered over her skin like a compelling trap.

He had to be toying with her.

Faythe humored him. "Marvellas, of course."

His face blanked at the name, as if he didn't expect to hear it. Had someone else thrown him in here? Was it really possible he didn't know what his gold eyes meant? Faythe decided it was very possible, for had she lived out her human life as Faythe Aklin in High Farrow, she would have been none the wiser too.

So how had he been captured, and why now?

"Where are we?" he asked.

That question stirred more confusion in Faythe. Maybe he'd been drugged and unconscious when they brought him here. He didn't appear disheveled or roughly handled. In fact, he was dressed elegantly, too well-kept to be a prisoner. A scar ran from his temple over his left cheek, but it was an old wound. His hair, as black as ink, was straight, with some strands falling into his eyes. His attire reminded Faythe of starlight and midnight with its navy colors and gold accents. Unlike anything she'd seen before. Almost otherworldly. He was mesmerizing in a way that made her start to doubt if he was real.

Or if she was truly awake herself.

Faythe answered his question. "Lakelaria."

The furrow between his brow deepened. "A kingdom?"

"Yes. One of seven in Ungardia. Are you missing your memory?" It was all Faythe could think of to explain his complete confusion.

"Ungardia," he repeated. Then he laughed—a breathy sound of disbelief and irony.

He stood, slipping a hand into his pocket as he paced, processing that information. Faythe noticed he wasn't shackled, but she couldn't see if he had Magestone embedded in his flesh like she did from his long sleeves.

Faythe knew she should be wary of him, but he was like her. He had to be. One of the gold-eyed children of Marvellas.

She gasped to herself. An Heir of Marvellas…but he wasn't just any, was he?

The lost first son.

He gave her his attention from her quiet alarm, but Faythe couldn't speak. She stared at him, unable to erase the obvious conclusion her mind fitted together.

"I know who you are," she said, blanching at the fact.

Question was, did *he* know who he was? He seemed completely clueless as to why he was here in a castle usurped by Marvellas.

His head canted, a few locks of black hair tipping over his forehead. "Do you now? That doesn't seem fair."

Faythe pushed herself tighter to the wall as if it could give way and grant an escape from him. "You're her son."

His gold eyes turned a shade darker. Another attribute that sealed the fact. She'd seen the way Marvellas's irises could shift tone, as if the language of her feelings spoke from them.

"Yes, I am. Son of Marvellas, the great Spirit of Souls and Goddess of the Stars."

Hearing him speak it with sarcasm wasn't what Faythe expected, but at least he knew who he was.

"Did she think I wouldn't figure it out? Did she put you here to see if you could break me by gaining my trust?"

"I don't know who you are or why you're here. I don't really care. What I desire is to get back to where I need to be."

Faythe's mind pulsed with a new ache. He wasn't making any

sense. She scrambled to recall the very little knowledge she had about the Spirit's son.

"You're not supposed to be in this realm," she said, though it felt foolish to say when he was undeniably right here.

"Exactly."

Her heart skipped a beat.

"So how are you here?" she dared to ask.

Unfathomable, maybe. But Nik had been right when he'd said they couldn't throw anything out of the realm of possibility anymore. Her denial only worked against her, so Faythe would play along.

He pinched the bridge of his nose as if it pained and frustrated him to recall the events that had led him here. "I fell under a curse in my realm," he admitted. "I suppose by some trick of fate, my mind crossed here to protect itself."

His mind. Faythe didn't understand what that meant. He was physical, right in front of her.

"When your curse breaks, you'll be gone again?"

"I hope so."

"How long do you have?"

That turned his expression dark, and he was quite frightening. There was an edge of unpredictable volatility about him that kept her on edge.

"For the sake of both realms, I hope not long. I have someone I need to get back to, and I will find a way to tear the fabric of the universe if I'm kept away from her for too long."

Faythe shuddered involuntarily at the promise. She didn't know how he would achieve it, but she believed he could.

She tucked her knees to her chest, contemplating. If she chose to believe his incredible story of crossing realms, she had to figure out if he could be of help against his mother. It may be selfish thinking, but she had to consider he could be leverage or an advantage somehow.

He withdrew something from his pocket and began to flip it absentmindedly in his palm. When Faythe caught a glimpse of the brass, it was her turn to wear the shock.

"Where did you get that?" she demanded.

The fae looked at her and then down at the item she stared at. "I think someone sent it to me. There was a note inside telling me I would need it to get home someday." He frowned at it, flipping it over, and Faythe caught a glimpse of the unmistakable symbol of Marvellas on the back. "It was in my pocket when I fell into the death sleep curse. At the time, I had the delusional thought it might prevent the curse."

Faythe was shivering, but not from the cold. "Do you know who sent the note?"

"It was signed by someone of the name Aesira. That doesn't happen to be you, does it?"

Her palm cupped her forehead. She didn't have Aesira's memory of that note, but the compass...she'd found that within an abandoned store in Rhyenelle. The Dresair had asked for it, and Faythe had thrown it into the mirror before she'd shattered them all, freeing the Dresair, who'd adopted the life of Presilla. For now.

Sneaky, meddling creature.

But how had he found it?

"Your reaction is telling me yes, and now I'm very intrigued," he said.

"Not exactly," she murmured.

"I've never been fond of riddles."

"My soul was once Aesira. Now I'm Faythe Ashfyre."

Those two words may as well have been a blade since his pacing stopped abruptly, as if she'd plunged one into his chest. His amber eyes sliced into her.

"Your father...?"

Of course, if he were telling the truth, this fae had no knowledge of the kingdoms here, or their rulers. Though she didn't know why the name of her father was important to him now.

"Agalhor Ashfyre."

The tension in his locked shoulders diffused like relief. Not the name he thought she might speak.

"Your turn to give a name," Faythe said.

The fae's unnerving gaze roved over her as if he was still trying to process something, and Faythe grew more anxious by the second. She never could have predicted his identity would collide with her own in a truly incredulous, unfathomable way.

"My name is Nyte," he said, holding her with golden eyes of kin. "Rainyte Ashfyre."

CHAPTER THIRTY-THREE

Faythe

R *ainyte Ashfyre.*
It didn't make sense. The name. His existence. Faythe was certain she was hallucinating or conjuring an outlandish dream after she'd succumbed to her agony at the banquet with Marvellas.

"It's been a *very* long time since I've used my family name. I like to forget it exists, but the Gods seem to be having a wicked time with me," Nyte said, running a hand through his inky hair as he paced around the cell, lost in deep thought with this unbelievable revelation.

Faythe couldn't wrap her head around it, slammed dizzy and confused.

"Agalhor never would have…*been* with her," Faythe said in horror. Her stomach churned, and she slipped off the cot. She ached and shivered, but she couldn't sit still with this world-shifting information.

"He's not my father, I assure you," Nyte offered. He appeared far too composed, whereas Faythe was on the brink of insanity.

"His brother…" Faythe recalled the memory of the family painting Agalhor had shown her in Rhyenelle. "But he died in battle centuries ago?"

"He is very much alive, and someone I'm really itching to return to so I can kill."

"Where?"

All Faythe knew was Ungardia, but could it be true the Prince of Rhyenelle, Agalhor's brother, had crossed realms?

Did anyone know of his relationship to Marvellas and the son she had of his?

"She put you here to mess with my head," Faythe said, reverting back to her original assumption. It was far more logical to believe. She took her head in her hands and rocked on her cot, feeling a madness creeping into her mind. "You're not real," she whispered.

"Faythe—"

She clamped her hands over her ears, wishing she could take back the token of her name.

He's not real.

Faythe couldn't stop whispering that to herself as she lay down with her back to him. She blocked him out of sight and sound, willing the torment of his appearance to disappear.

Yet the Dresair's riddle in the abandoned Rhyenelle shop repeated through her desperate denial.

Come the return of the lost first son.

What did it mean?

Faythe curled into herself. So much pain ran through her body, her mind, her soul... Marvellas would be able to break her easily if she didn't pull herself together.

"Death said you would come," Faythe whispered, recalling the haunting vision in the ruined temple.

Nyte's curious hum focused her to release her hands from her ears, but she couldn't turn around and meet those golden eyes again.

"That primordial seems to have made a sport out of meddling with my fate," Nyte grumbled, displeased.

"Did they send you here to help us against Marvellas?" Faythe hugged herself, staring at the gravelly stone wall.

"No. I'm rather hoping I'm here because you'll help me."

"If it isn't obvious, I'm not much help to anyone here."

He left a pause of silence. "So what are you going to do about it?"

Faythe didn't expect that to strike a chord in her.

What was she doing? Lying here in a pitiful heap of agony, defeat, and denial. She had promised her friends and herself she would fight, and already, she was allowing pieces of herself to crumble.

With a deep breath, Faythe pushed herself up. "I'm going to win."

"You have a plan?" he asked.

"Not exactly. I can't predict what Marvellas will do—each day is uncertain. But she can't predict what *I* might do."

"Sounds like a very dangerous game."

Faythe finally looked at him. Not a detail had changed. She almost wanted to touch him, convinced he was just an illusion. He was too perfect, even with his facial scar. Too frightening…too much like his mother.

What would Marvellas do when she discovered him here?

It could change everything.

Nyte looked past her, down the hall. "Someone's coming."

A head of dark blond disheveled hair came out of the shadows to stand in front of her cell. She'd seen this guard before and had only remembered him as he was one of the few who didn't hide under a mask and hood. There was something sadistically gleeful in his dark eyes every time he stood by Marvellas's side, even as the Lakelarian queen.

"Are you going to be nice?" he taunted.

Faythe's body tensed against giving him the satisfaction of seeing the shiver it broke over her skin. She had dealt with fae males like him before, and it had been a long time since she'd remembered Captain Varis in High Farrow at all.

"Are you her pretty pet playing fetch?"

It may not be wise to provoke someone in a position to hurt her, but she couldn't help the natural loathing that surfaced as if she were right back in those cells in High Farrow.

He jammed the key into her cell and swung open the only barrier of protection she had against him. Faythe despised that a cage was her idea of safety in the domain of Marvellas and her band of volatile fae and dark fae allies.

"My name is Captain Daegal. I want you to remember who conquered the continent as the Goddess's right hand." He stalked into her cell with the slow anticipation of a predator.

"You're of no more value than a footstool to her."

The captain reached for her, but Faythe anticipated it. Though she had no magick and was still regaining her strength, she wasn't completely useless. All it took was predicting his brutality and a carefully timed step, twist, and a marginal duck out of his path. He tripped over his footing when he didn't grab her for purchase, but he caught himself, palms slapping the wall.

"That was embarrassing," Nyte commented from behind her.

The captain snarled his outrage, head snapping to her with fury sparking in his eyes.

Faythe realized the position she was in, and her impulse took three backward strides just as he pushed off the wall. Her fingers gripped iron, and then…

Slam.

The captain reached the cell door just as she closed it. She blinked in bewilderment, having not predicted how easy that would be.

Nyte's smooth chuckle broke through her stupor. "Aren't you going to run?"

"You insufferable *child*," the captain seethed. The clang of keys rang through her senses as he scrambled to find the right one to free himself.

Faythe couldn't move. Her sight slipped to Nyte, and she realized the captain hadn't once acknowledged him or reacted to his commentary. She had no intention of running—her actions just now had merely been on impulse for her own amusement.

She floated over to stand in front of Nyte's cell while the captain hissed profanities and tried to find his key out of there. Faythe couldn't care about him anymore.

Standing right in front of Nyte, with his ethereal gold eyes bearing down on her, she couldn't be sure what was happening—or, more dauntingly, if he was a blessing or a curse.

"You're not trapped in there, are you?" she said.

The captain couldn't see him.

Nyte's jaw worked. "I think I'm trapped with you. Wherever you are, or wherever you've put me. I'm beginning to believe you harbor my consciousness with your gift."

"I manifested you as a cell mate?"

"Could have been worse, I imagine."

"Can you hear my thoughts?"

"No, but I have a sense of your emotions."

That was a relief at least. She didn't know what having Nyte here meant—if he would be any use to her at all in her fight against Marvellas.

Rainyte Ashfyre had become a piece in their war that no one could have predicted.

Faythe was too distracted in her thoughts to have heard the captain's escape. She winced at his iron grip on her arm and bit her tongue against a whimper when she was roughly pulled away.

She lingered a final look on Nyte over her shoulder. He remained right where he was. She was both fascinated and terrified to figure out more about him. Her secret weapon, if she could find a way to leverage him against Marvellas somehow.

The captain had been muttering loathing words as he marched, tugging her along in his bruising grip.

Zaiana appearing around the end corner was a surprising sight even though the dark fae had been in their traveling company here. Faythe's mood darkened as she remembered Zaiana's harm to Kyleer.

"Let her go," Zaiana ordered.

"You don't command me," Daegal snapped. His insecurity was showing.

Zaiana didn't have to do much to clearly pose as the higher authority. She didn't even speak again, standing with hands clasped behind her, but the impatient warning was in her piercing amethyst eyes

With a disgruntled huff and a shove, Daegal released her.

"Come," Zaiana said, turning back the way she came, expecting Faythe to follow.

Faythe did, only because she had questions and a wrath to settle.

"Did you have to hurt him?" Faythe asked inn resentment.

"He gave me good reason, and I gave him fair warning," she answered coolly.

Faythe gritted her teeth, realizing that was probably the truth. There was something about Zaiana that sparked a light in her friend she'd never seen before. Every time Zaiana fought him, defied him, it was like he enjoyed it.

"How is he now?" Faythe asked, reluctantly setting aside her grudge.

"I don't know."

"You haven't seen him?"

"Not since they locked him below, no."

"You have to make sure he stays alive."

"His life isn't my concern."

Faythe was exasperated within herself. That wasn't true, and Zaiana knew it too. Her detachment was convincing to the world, but Faythe didn't believe it. She'd been face-to-face with Zaiana at the peak of their rawest emotions. She'd seen the fear and pain on the dark fae's face when Zaiana had truly believed she might die. She'd heard the break in Zaiana's voice as she admitted her regret for what she'd done to Kyleer in Rhyenelle. Faythe had glimpsed inside a vault of emotions that was sealed tight from a world that had taught Zaiana she couldn't have them.

"Where are you taking me?" Faythe tried instead.

"To look more presentable."

Faythe had expected a torture chamber at the top of her list, so it was a surprise to be led to a ladies' powder room.

A couple of timid younger fae approached in servants' uniforms. "We're to bathe you and present you for Her Grace," one said.

Faythe didn't know why she looked at Zaiana. The dark fae merely rolled her eyes and leaned against a far wall to wait.

A bath did sound glorious, considering she was still wearing her bloodstained camisole after days, and the nights had been so cold. Her only hesitation came when they removed Reylan's cloak. But at her reaction, one red-haired fae smiled reassuringly, taking it with care.

The sunken pool of water steamed while the moonlight glittered outside the glass walls. She sighed pleasantly, the hot water caressing her skin while the picturesque view of ice and snow surrounded her. It let her forget war and bloodshed in this tranquil contrasting embrace.

She didn't mind the sting of the soapy water against her Magestone wounds as she basked in the beauty for a while. Faythe found Lakelaria to be the most beautiful kingdom, second only to her own. She thought about how she could make her own mark on the castle by taking inspiration from here, imagining bathing with a full open view of the sun splitting over crimson-peaked mountains. It brought a joyful sting to her eyes to think of what could be if they won the war and earned their peace.

Being scrubbed of the dirt and blood cleared a fog in her mind. Every time the Magestone in her wrists was even slightly knocked, it seized Faythe with pain, but she was learning to grit her teeth and bear it without a sound by now.

"You're very brave," one fae whispered, cleaning over her shoulder. She had pale red hair and beautifully freckled cheeks.

Faythe felt compelled to take the young fae's hand at the timid fear in her eyes. "Bravery isn't in what we can endure, but in the way we keep fighting even when we're terrified. And often the bravest fighters are the most silent."

Her smile lit up in her beautiful brown eyes. Faythe caught Zaiana watching her by a slip of her gaze, seeming to have manifested a sense for when the dark fae's attention was on her.

"Hurry up," Zaiana said coldly, pushing off the wall and stalking out of the room.

"She's terrifying," the red-haired fae whispered, helping Faythe dry off.

"And she hasn't even done anything," another added.

Faythe actually smiled. "She's not that bad."

"Is it true you won in a fight against her?"

"No. I don't think I could have. Some powers can't win against each other—they can only destroy each other."

They watched her in awe but didn't falter in their routine of tending to her before leading her toward an ornate, silver-rimmed vanity.

Faythe's hair was styled, and she was dressed in a white-and-blue gown. This was a far cry from the torture chamber she'd first presumed the Spirit would summon her to. While Faythe was immeasurably glad to feel her skin refreshed, she couldn't settle her stomach that the price was about to be revealed to her.

Just as the fae around her began to relax and Faythe was starting to enjoy their kind company, the air in the room shifted. It was subtle at first, like the brief silence before a storm. Then she saw it—just a flicker in the mirror's reflection: the fiery glow of Marvellas. Faythe's stomach dropped, and icy fingers of dread crawled up her spine, freezing her in place. Marvellas's presence swallowed the room, and the fragile moment of comfort shattered, leaving only the pounding of her pulse in the stillness.

The servants bowed to the Spirit, and their gentle presence escaped through the door, replaced by the suffocating air of battle and dominance.

Marvellas didn't speak, and Faythe had no words either. She watched Marvellas approach with hateful eyes, but the Spirit's neutral expression didn't shift. Marvellas moved with the grace of water, keeping her anticipation sharp. The last thing Faythe expected was for the Spirit to pick up the servant's abandoned hairbrush.

So it had all come down to this. Not a rage-filled power struggle, nor hateful words, but finally being alone with the Spirit of her nightmares after all this time. Marvellas began combing her long chestnut tresses with the convincing tenderness of a mother.

"You used to love it when I brushed your hair," she said, her voice so peaceful she hardly recognized Marvellas right now. "It was our favorite way of bonding."

"I'm not her."

Faythe wondered if she should stay silent and let Marvellas play out her delusion, but her resentment prevailed over her self-preservation. She would rather her wrath than this sick pretense.

The Spirit's irises flashed to hers in the mirror at last, their core like liquid metal. They always moved in the heat of her anger. Her hand had stalled, but with a breath of composure, Marvellas continued her ministrations.

Faythe had so much she wanted to ask, and none of it had a gain in the war. Everything that wrecked her on a deeper, more personal level now flooded her mind with a sea of vulnerability.

"Why them?" Faythe let her first burning question slip. "Liliana and Agalhor. Why their child?"

Marvellas thought on her ask, head tilting while hypnotized by the brushing of Faythe's hair. "It was both a personal and a practical choice."

"You were involved with Agalhor's brother."

Marvellas's gaze snapped to hers in the reflection. Faythe's chest struggled against the beat that surged within it, because her reaction was confirmation.

"There is no one left alive who knows that," she said, her voice edging onto a warning.

"Are you sure?"

"Who told you?"

"He betrayed you, didn't he? By taking your son from you."

"My…"

The brush in her hand became nothing more than gold dust leaking out of Marvellas's clenched fist. Faythe swallowed dryly.

"Who told you that?" she demanded again.

"No one—"

Marvellas took a fistful of Faythe's hair, yanking her up from the stool. Faythe's body jerked painfully, the sharp tug wrenching a strangled cry from her throat as her scalp throbbed under the Spirit's ruthless grip.

"Anything you try to keep from me," Marvellas hissed, her breath hot against Faythe's face, "I will break your mind to discover."

The threat hung heavy in the air, suffocating. But despite the ache blooming at the roots of her hair, Faythe refused to yield. She steeled herself, her heart pounding as defiance flickered in her chest. But then Marvellas's hand lashed out, gripping Faythe's wrist. A searing, immobilizing pain shot up her arm, and Faythe's back arched involuntarily as the agony soared. Marvellas's nails raked at her skin, splitting open the scabbed wound with the pressure, and the Magestone embedded within it roared to life.

The Magestone's toxic power surged through her veins, its energy screaming in her ears. Faythe's vision blurred, the world spinning as Marvellas pressed deeper into her mind, her mental dominance tightening like a vise. The Spirit's presence slithered through Faythe's thoughts, wrapping around her memories and emotions with chilling precision.

"Stop," Faythe gasped, her breath ragged.

"It will all be over soon," Marvellas purred, her voice soft, almost soothing, as her grip on Faythe's mind tightened further.

That was when the memories surfaced—the ones Faythe had fought so hard to protect. Those of Reylan. His face, his smile, their moments of shared laughter and stolen glances. Faythe whimpered, feeling the weight of Marvellas's intrusion threaten to tear through those precious fragments. Reylan was the brightest light she had clung to in the endless darkness.

Not him. Faythe couldn't allow her to take him.

Her heart hammered as Marvellas pressed harder, forcing images of Reylan into sharper focus, threatening to strip them away. The thought of losing him, of having his memory erased or tainted, sent a wave of fierce resolve surging through Faythe's battered mind.

"If you take him from me…" Faythe's voice cracked, her chest heaving with deep, painful breaths. She was weak, teetering on the edge of collapse, but she couldn't let go. "It won't matter. I'll find him again and again."

Marvellas's eyes glowed with amusement, as if the very idea entertained her.

"Each time…" Faythe's voice strengthened, her determination burning through the fog of pain and the Magestone's grip. "Each time, we'll come back stronger…until we finally win. And we will destroy you."

The defiance that laced her words was the last shred of strength she had left, but it was enough to cause Marvellas to pause. Faythe dragged the only thing she could think of to the surface, causing Marvellas to release her in shock.

She showed her Nyte.

Marvellas stared at Faythe wide-eyed while she clutched her bleeding wound and caught her breath. "You can't possibly know his appearance in adulthood," she whispered in disbelief.

Faythe had never seen the Spirit appear so…*human*. As vulnerable and desperate as any mortal at the quick vision of her son Faythe supplied.

"Rainyte Ashfyre," Faythe dared to say.

It became a weapon that backed the Spirit a ghostly step away and severed the final threads of denial Faythe had been holding onto. Nyte was real. Faythe would never have known his name otherwise.

"He's here?" Marvellas asked, hopeful and broken. "Tell me where."

"He's not," Faythe said quickly. "I have visions, that's all."

It was like she could see the wheels turning in Marvellas's mind. The Spirit was used to having control of everything, but she couldn't comprehend this. Faythe didn't know if she'd sabotaged her chances by using the knowledge of her son so soon.

"Can you show me again?"

That request didn't come as a demand—nothing vicious. It was a quiet plea from a mother.

Faythe had to block her empathy that threatened to open. She firmed her face. "Take me to Reylan," she demanded.

That returned the icy demeanor to the Goddess.

"I was going to remove the Magestone for you to try reach him, but now all you've done is weaken yourself beyond being able to. You'll go back to your cell to recover."

"Take it out now," Faythe said, even though it nauseated her to think of the agony it would put her through.

"I won't ever underestimate you again. Chains alone aren't enough to combat your will. The stone stays in your flesh and will only be removed for each attempt at breaking the ruin."

Each attempt.

Faythe had to spin, barely making it to a bucket before she retched. Not much came up, and hunger pains clenched her stomach when she finished dry-heaving at the thought of the repeated torture like what she'd endured in the banquet hall the first time the Magestone was embedded in her.

"I've had enough of you," Marvellas said.

Faythe detected a note of defeat and distance in her tone. When she lifted herself off the floor, she found Marvellas standing with her back to Faythe, staring out the long window. She didn't insist Faythe show her the vision of Nyte again, but she didn't think it was needed while Marvellas hugged herself, lost in thought.

She didn't know how Captain Daegal had known to come, but leaving with him wasn't much more pleasant than staying with Marvellas.

Back at her cell, Nyte was sitting in the same position she'd first seen him in when she awoke.

Before the captain would let her go, he pulled Faythe tightly to him, and she resisted the urge to spit in his menacing face.

"You try something like that stunt earlier again, I don't have instructions not to hurt you," he seethed.

He pushed her so hard she almost didn't catch herself quickly enough before her face hit the wall. The cell door slamming shut was distant to the pain roaring in her ears from the disrupted Magestone in her arms.

She stayed in that position, hands plastered to the cold stone wall, until the stone stopped pulsing through her.

"I might have an idea," Nyte said after a stretch of silence.

"Tell me." She peeled herself away from the wall and slumped onto her cot.

Nyte was staring down the hall, his expression dark as if he were thinking of the departed captain. "I don't know if it's possible, and I'm not the most thrilled about it if it is."

"Then why share it?"

"Because it might be the only way for me to have a temporary presence beyond your mind in this world."

CHAPTER THIRTY-FOUR

Tauria

Tauria missed Nik with a soul-deep ache everyday. The fact she had no certain countdown as to when she would be reunited with him made the pain unbearable. She thought of him now, as she stared over the lands of Fenstead from one of the highest balconies of her castle. They'd returned from Valgard days ago, and Tauria was antsy more than ever to return to Nik so they could start preparing for the colossal army preparing to descend upon them.

She thought about leaving, but she was so close to achieving a victory on her homeland that she couldn't abandon that now.

Tallia arrived at her rooms. Tauria had employed her before she'd left for Valgard under the guise of being in charge of hiring staff to run the castle. Mordecai had barely reacted to Tauria's proposal, allowing her to begin restoring the castle to some sense of structure.

The Fenstead rebel had been less than enthused about her new position, but no one could deny it was a perfect plan to slowly grow allies within the castle walls. Tallia reported the number of staff she'd managed to recruit so far as soon as Tauria was back from Valgard. It wasn't as many as they would need to attack from the inside without being immediately overwhelmed, but they couldn't bring too many new faces in too soon without arousing suspicion.

Tauria paced her room, growing antsy and impatient. "The full moon is tomorrow," she said, chewing at her fingernail as she stared up at the glow in the sky. So beautiful yet sinister.

"You really think he plans to use it to change you? Wouldn't he have detained you by now?"

"He's been allowing me freedom to roam the castle and recruit staff. I can't be sure what his motives are."

"Exactly. Something doesn't add up."

Tauria thought so too. She'd barely achieved any rest trying to figure out what Mordecai's plan was.

She stopped pacing, coming to a conclusion that punched her in the gut.

"What if he's waiting for Nik to come?" she whispered to herself.

"Who?" Tallia asked.

"Nikalias, the King of High Farrow."

Tallia slumped down onto the edge of her bed. "Are you sure he's coming to your rescue?"

"He's my mate. Nik might already be close. I hoped to have some information, or Dakoda's ruin if it was still here, and to have been able to escape before he made it this far."

"Ah, I didn't realize the mate part. I'm guessing Mordecai knows."

Tauria nodded. This was like their close call in Olmstone all over again.

"Then we need to get you out. Losing our queen and the King of High Farrow would be detrimental for both kingdoms."

"It can't have been for nothing." Tauria was exasperated, running a hand down her face.

Breaking their bond. Leaving Nik when he was gravely injured. Getting here.

Tauria refused to believe it had all been for *nothing*.

She raised a hand to her chest, feeling the thump quickening under her palm with growing fear as though it could be stolen come tomorrow night.

Tauria said, "We need to act tonight."

"Tonight? Are you insane? We don't even have two dozen of our people in this castle as *staff* yet."

"But they're assassins, are they not?"

"Fighters. We've been training to fight in battle."

"Then I hope you've picked the stealthiest so far."

"Tauria...what can this possibly achieve? Even if we somehow managed to eliminate the few dozen dark fae in the castle, all we'll have done is locked ourselves in a grand cage that will not hold when Mordecai summons the armies to take it back. Have you seen our fields? Fenstead has been used as army holding grounds for decades. There are endless tents over the valleys."

"You will manage to eliminate the dark fae within our walls. Because I'm going to make sure Mordecai is occupied for you to do it. Silent and careful. Then you'll alert Berron, and the rest of the rebellion will come."

"Then what?"

Tauria might have lost her mind. Her plan was reckless, uncertain, but she was running out of time.

"With the rebellion flooding these halls…you declare me your enemy right in front of him. I'll flee with him."

"No," Tallia said immediately, launching to her feet. Anger firmed her face. "What was any of it for if you just *run* again?"

Tauria winced at that blow. "You have to trust I have a plan that benefits Fenstead after that point."

Tallia huffed a humorless laugh. "You think I'd agree to let our greatest asset, our *queen*, sacrifice herself on a whim?"

All Tauria could see was a giant chessboard. Yes, she was the queen, and she was damned good at chess.

"You have to trust me. As your queen, this is my order."

She called for Edith to help her change, and while she distracted the serpent in this castle, her people would cut off the heads that lurked in the corners.

Tauria stood outside Mordecai's chosen room in her castle. It was a grand guest room in the east quarter, while he'd assigned her to the west quarter. She began to doubt her plan to keep him interested in her tonight when she realized he'd hardly shown an interest in her company at all.

Since seeing him with Dakodas, she had her suspicions that his ambitions were set far higher than just becoming the King of Fenstead.

Tauria straightened her poise and knocked gently.

Every footstep approaching from the other side of the door thumped her heart higher up her throat. When the door swung open and Mordecai stood in front of her, she resisted an instant urge to bolt away at the sight.

He was far less put together than she'd ever seen him. No jacket, just a plain shirt with open ties at the top to expose the top contours of his chest. No neatly combed hair—it was messy, as though he'd run his hands through the shoulder-length tresses many times tonight. She'd disturbed him in a rare moment of relaxation. It painted him in a light she wanted to snuff out. So…ordinarily dark fae. Though his wings were glamoured.

"I wasn't informed you were planning to visit me tonight," he said.

The awareness of his current vulnerable state seemed to register in him. He stood straighter, his face firmed harshly, as if to compensate for the roguish appearance.

"I didn't know I would come myself," she said, having to take a moment to swallow against her drying throat. "Until I found myself lonely tonight."

Tauria put all her effort into taming her heartbeat.

His expression relaxed in surprise. "I see. Well, I am glad you came to me. Would you like to join me?"

Mordecai stepped aside, inviting her into his most private space. Tauria smiled, gliding in easily, even though everything in her rebelled at the mere thought of being sealed in intimate quarters with the ruthless, unpredictable high lord.

When the door clicked shut, the game began.

Inside his rooms, she didn't expect the calmness the space invoked. She thought it was the familiar layout she knew—most guest rooms were the same. He'd even kept the accents of green, and the room was perfectly preserved in Fenstead style. She'd half-expected he would destroy the decor and make his living space match the vicious turmoil that lived within him.

She discovered she must have interrupted some kind of study, as there were papers and charcoal strewn around the small table in front of the fire between two low-set armchairs. Tauria gravitated in that direction, trying to catch a glimpse inconspicuously.

Tauria stiffened when Mordecai brushed by her. At the table, he shuffled a few papers, which piqued Tauria's curiosity. She looked away as though disinterested, however. Giving her attention to the balcony, her nerves bubbled as she stared at the moon that was just a fraction off being full tomorrow night.

"Does something trouble you to inspire a restless night?" Mordecai asked, more gently than she was accustomed to.

"Our nation lingers on the cusp of war—it makes all nights restless, anticipating when battle might break."

She trod carefully but tried to coax some intel from him.

"I'm sorry that troubles you. But rest assured, the war is not your burden."

Tauria gritted her teeth, insulted by that.

"It is," she said. "What are your burdens? I wish to share."

Mordecai gravitated closer, not breaking their stare. Tauria had come prepared, though it twisted her gut with guilt and betrayal to Nik to be luring Mordecai into her web by subtle seduction.

"You need not concern yourself. Everything is going to plan."

He loomed over her, and she felt frighteningly trapped in his shadow.

"You don't trust me," she accused bluntly.

Mordecai's half-smile was amused. "What is it you wish to know? How our numbers are so great that even if Rhyenelle, High Farrow, and Olmstone stood strong with their forces, they would still not be enough to contend with us? Do you wish to know that this continent is all but ours?"

"Then what are you waiting for?"

"Timing is everything, my dear."

"Like the full moon for Transitions."

His eyes narrowed a fraction. "Yes."

"I want to be changed." That request slammed between them like a gauntlet thrown. "Tomorrow night."

Mordecai contemplated her request with suspicious eyes. His pause for answer tingled over her body with growing suspense.

"What changed your mind? The last we spoke of it, you were adamant it would not be necessary for your allegiance."

"Because I realize you can't trust me unless I do this. Maybe I can't even trust myself. Nikalias will always come for me, and this will get him to see there is no getting me back. For my people, for yours, it is the ultimate declaration of unity and loyalty."

He closed the distance but hovered behind her as Tauria turned to stare back at the haunting moon. Mordecai's fingers brushed her bare shoulder, and she stifled a shiver.

"Are you truly ready to be mine?" the huskiness in his tone wasn't lust—it was a taste of triumph.

"Yes," she whispered. Tauria played the doe, but she was ready to strike as the stag with sharpened antlers. "I want it to be public."

"That would bring me great pride."

"Tomorrow night then?"

"As you wish." Mordecai's mouth leaned to her ear, and she stifled a shiver when his warm breath fanned across her skin. "We can make it quite the spectacle, as I received word today about an underground rebel force that has been building against me in this kingdom for some time."

Tauria's spine locked in horror.

"What's left of the survivors after the dozens of savage dark fae have taken their fill to flush them out of their sewers…it will be most ceremonial to have the kingdom bear witness as you end the rest of them in your glorious new dark fae body. It will set the precedent for Fenstead's new beginning."

Just like that, everything she'd planned required sudden reassessment.

How had he found out about the rebels who had remained hidden for decades? Tauria could only conclude she had to be the cause somehow despite believing she'd been careful.

Her vision swayed, but she kept her footing steady. She couldn't lose her composure or give the high lord the impression she cared. This was a test.

"I'm surprised it took you this long to discover them. I imagine they've been gathering for some time," Tauria said coolly.

Inside, her mind raced in turmoil. Was she too late to warn the rebels underground of a possible attack?

Mordecai turned her to face him, and her chest constricted. His fingers grazed her chin, tipping her head back a fraction. The look he held her with was part-desire, part-fascination.

"I'll admit, I haven't trusted you. But once you are dark fae, things will change for the better here. You will rule as you always should have."

Yes, she would.

The door to Mordecai's room burst open, and he pushed her behind him. Tauria's fear sharpened to see Tallia and the half-dozen other fae behind her. The rebel's stance was braced to fight, her expression absolutely lethal, cutting into Tauria as much as the high lord.

"What is this?" Mordecai seethed.

He advanced a step, but Tauria hooked her hand around his elbow.

Tallia said viciously, "We've slaughtered every one of your serpents in this castle."

With that news, Mordecai reconsidered his next move. Instead of bracing against them, he moved so fast Tauria's gasp choked in her throat as his hand wrapped around it from behind her.

His mouth leaned to her ear. "If I discover you had anything to do with this before tomorrow night, I'll kill you and replace this throne with someone *loyal*." The last word was a hiss, and she whimpered in true fear when he dragged her back.

The balcony doors slammed open from the force of his body as he used her as a shield against the rebels attempting to throw a dagger or arrow. Next thing she knew, they were standing on the stone railing. Mordecai lifted her into his arms, and his wings shot them high.

"Where are we going?" she asked.

"To the war camp. Those pests won't have long enough to warm a single seat before I slaughter them all."

CHAPTER THIRTY-FIVE

Zaiana

Z aiana needed the air no matter that the wind cut ice chips across her cheeks. Atop the Lakelarian castle, she could admire the beauty of the kingdom. Though the temperature left her with little desire to fantasize about a life here. Her eyes cast over the snow-thick mountain peaks, envisioning a world with no end beyond Ungardia.

After they'd locked up Kyleer, she'd resisted the impulse to check on him.

Zaiana shook her head, hissing under the mask she wore over her mouth and her nose to ward off the lashing, bitter air. Her resentment toward herself clawed at every crevice of her thoughts, and she could hardly bear it. She needed out. Free of her own mind, and as she balanced on the pointed crest of the highest part of the castle, she did not unglamour her wings.

She didn't know what she was doing here. What she hoped to achieve.

She scrunched her eyes shut and stood from her crouch. Her boots maintained their grip on the snowy slope of the roof. Her single hand wrapped around the spire was all that kept her from falling the fatal height.

"What are you doing?"

That voice was the last she wanted to hear. She snapped her lids open and looked down to where the bastard stood across another part of the roof.

Maverick watched her, arms folded, with his wings towering over his shoulders. His brows bore the weight of his disappointment and anger.

"Has she sent you to kill me for leaving without order?" Zaiana asked.

"No. I'm wondering who she'll send to kill both of us for it."

Zaiana's jaw tightened. "Why would you follow me, if not by her command?"

"Boredom, I suppose. It was getting rather dull in that awful castle."

"Dakodas favors you. She won't be pleased."

"I don't really care."

Her response was nullified at that, because she didn't care about the Spirit's retribution either.

"Now, want to tell me why we're freezing our asses off for no good reason?"

"Go inside."

He asked, "Did Marvellas reprimand you for being here?"

"No. I brought her a prize. So I hope you have one."

"You're hoping for my safety? Now I'm even more concerned."

His assessment of her footing and his tracking over her shoulder gave away his thoughts.

"I'm not going to throw myself off this roof."

"Then I inquire again, what are we doing?"

"*We* are doing nothing. I'm scouting, and it was rather peaceful, if you don't mind."

It was a quick and obvious lie. Truthfully, Zaiana didn't know why she'd come here specifically, only that her wrath had festered to her bones inside the castle, and she'd feared it might snap to recklessness if she exchanged paths with Marvellas right now. She had to pull herself together and figure out what she was going to do to find out the truth about the dark fae curse.

"In fact, I do mind." His stare cut into her, as sharp as the wind.

"What do you want?"

"I'd rather not chat in the freezing rooftop air."

"I'd rather not chat at all."

"What do you know of the curse of our still hearts?"

Zaiana sliced him with a look. "You've been spying on me?"

"You don't make it difficult."

She considered what to share with him. It had been part of the reason Zaiana needed to come here. She just didn't know how to begin finding answers about the curse with the Spirit of Souls who may have cast it.

"How do I know you won't just run to them with anything I say?"

"Zaiana," Maverick said with a hook of sincerity unlike him. He reevaluated what he was going to say in that pause. "This affects me too. It affects all the dark fae, and I want to know what else the curse could mean. You know who I was before they turned me. I've resented them all this time, and now I discover there's even more to their manipulation."

She considered him for a moment, and she believed him.

"Now, will you please come down from there?"

Zaiana was about to slide down the dome toward the flat part of the roof, but the sound of moving water caught her attention. The guards had left their posts to rotate positions, and there was a moment of vulnerability. To her fascination, the river surrounding the castle *parted*, and from its depths emerged a hooded figure who quickly ran into the surrounding woodland.

Zaiana locked everything on that small target.

"Don't follow me, or I won't tell you a thing when I'm back," Zaiana warned, then she unglamoured her wings and swooped down from the roof.

They took a deserted path in the night. It was too easy to trap this prey. She trailed them until she found the right moment, and in the space of a breath, Zaiana pushed them to the wall under the threat of her dagger.

But she was on *their* land, with no ability, and they were surrounded by ammunition as theirs.

Before Zaiana could react to what was happening, snow came down from the roof in a force too strong to have been unfortunate natural timing. It wasn't enough to bury her, but Zaiana was knocked to the ground.

With a growl of annoyance from the wet seeping into her and turning her even more freezing, she shoveled out of the heap. Her chase turned more deadly, with a laser focus. She tracked them by the footfall they tried to hide by manipulating the snow, but that was a sure path in itself. Minutes dragged, and Zaiana was fearing she'd lost them. When she came to a dead end, she hissed with frustration.

"Why are you following me?"

Zaiana stilled at the threatening voice at her back. Not because she was trapped, but...

When she turned, the fae was still concealed, much like Zaiana with only her eyes on show, shadowed by her hood. But it was that *voice*.

It might have been foolish to expose herself, but Zaiana pulled down her mask with the confidence she was right. Then she drew back her hood.

The fae straightened, her poised hands making the snow vibrate, and she copied Zaiana's movements to expose herself.

"Nerida?" Zaiana blinked at the fae. Though she knew this to be her homeland, the fact she was here right now stunned her.

"I had more faith in you," Nerida said, her voice colder than Zaiana had ever heard. "I know I shouldn't have. You tried to warn me many times, but still, I couldn't stop myself thinking you were different."

Zaiana was already sharp with anger. "It's not my fault you see monsters and believe you can help them," she said. Nerida didn't deserve her tone, but Zaiana's claws were already out.

"I have never tried to help you, nor would I. The only person who could is yourself."

Zaiana's gloved fists tightened. "Why are you here?" she asked.

"It's a long story. But yours seems clear. Are you going to capture me and take me to Marvellas?"

"If I wanted you, I would have taken you by now. You may be powerful in your ability, but you are no fighter."

"I may not wish to fight, but I haven't survived this long alone without needing to."

Zaiana had so many questions about her that for once had no gain. She wasn't sure what it was about Nerida, but she didn't truly want her to leave like everyone else.

"If you're not going to stop me, I'm leaving—"

"Wait," Zaiana said, scrambling for a reason for her to stay. "My magick is gone. Or, it's still there, I just can't reach it, and, well, you're a healer—maybe you could feel if there's…" Zaiana trailed off, gritting her teeth from how pitiful she sounded.

Then, when Nerida's face released the tension to display her usual care, she hated herself for using the healer's nature for her own gain this time. No matter who asked, Nerida wouldn't refuse help with the ability she had.

"Since when?"

"Since I battled Faythe. I was unconscious for weeks, then when I woke, and it's been silent since."

Her brow furrowed in assessment. "Faythe's abilities are fine."

Yes, much to Zaiana's burning annoyance.

"I shouldn't have mentioned it," Zaiana grumbled, making to leave.

"Wait." Nerida stopped her this time. "Maybe we could help each other."

Zaiana turned back with curiosity. "What can I do for you?"

Nerida debated a second longer. "Come with me."

She followed the healer, having nothing to lose anyway. Nerida brought her to a tall home wedged between many others.

"Are you sure you don't have your lightning? Would make this a lot easier," Nerida said, stripping out of her cloak and kneeling by the fire. Zaiana watched her begin with the tools to light it.

"No," Zaiana barely whispered. "Sorry."

Though Nerida had meant it lightly, every time she acknowledged her missing ability, it grew on the hollowness inside her. She could be strong without it. Still fight and fly, but she would never be whole again without it.

When flame caught across the debris, Zaiana gravitated toward the heat, crouching with a contented sigh when the warmth caught her skin and began to spread over her.

"Let me see if there's something I can feel," Nerida said, shifting closer.

Zaiana jerked away by habit but forced herself back at the healer's soft, patient look.

Nerida approached again tentatively, taking Zaiana's hands. Her hazel eyes slipped shut, and Zaiana could do nothing but sit there with a growing anticipation in her stomach.

"I met...*someone*. They thought it might be tied to my heartbeat," she offered.

Nerida peeled one eye open curiously. "You heart is still."

"I don't think it always was."

"Fascinating," Nerida said, closing her eyes again to concentrate. "I have always theorized myself that it's not a born cause."

The silence turned painful, grating over her skin, while she gradually felt exposed at the thought of Nerida searching within her.

"Your magick is still there, but yes...something is blocking it."

Zaiana was always cautious of hope, but a wick caught flame inside her before she could stop it. "How do I get it back?"

The shake of Nerida's head sank in her gut. "I'm not entirely sure. It's all you."

"What is?"

"The resistance."

Zaiana closed her eyes as if it she could search within herself with the healer's help, perhaps draw out what was stifling it. Her throat began to tighten with the memories that flashed to the surface. Tight walls. No light. No air. She was helpless.

Nerida ripped her hands from Zaiana's with a gasp, which made her eyes fly open too. The healer's expression became ghostly, searching Zaiana's face as if someone else was sitting there instead.

"You can't...*see* things?" Zaiana asked, horrified.

Nerida shook her head. "I'm not Faythe. But I can *feel*...what—what happened to you, Zaiana?"

Her shoulders deflated. Once, she would have raised a shield against such a question. To speak of it was to acknowledge how damaged she was.

"Many things," she whispered, sitting to hug her knees.

Nerida picked up a small kettle, filling it up in the dainty kitchen before returning and setting it over the fire.

"It's possible the suppression you've built all these years is causing it," Nerida said gently. "Something terrible happened to you. Not just once—you have centuries of trauma you've hidden from all this time."

"Why would it be an issue now?" she snapped, only in frustration at her own self.

"I think it's what happens when the body and mind go through drastic change."

"What do you mean?"

The healer's look was thoughtful, and Zaiana resisted the urge to shrink away from it.

"There's something different about you," she said. "I think the only way you're going to find your lightning...is if you find yourself first. What you want to be. *Who* you want to be. That choice has never really been yours."

"That doesn't make any sense." It came out like a plea. How was she supposed to do that?

"It might not right now, but you're not alone to face it. Not if you don't want to be."

Zaiana was tired of being alone. Tired of only depending on herself. Trusting herself. Her walls were crumbling, and she was being buried in the debris. Maybe she would find her lightning when the final wall tumbled, and then she would die under the rubble of her past life.

"I know you can't trust me," Zaiana said. "But Marvellas cursed me, and I want retribution for that."

Nerida squeezed her hands before letting them go.

"I did trust you. I wouldn't have stayed with you on that quest if I didn't."

"We would have had to kill you if you didn't."

Nerida only smiled at that, and Zaiana was beginning to wonder if she'd severely underestimated the gentle healer.

"If you want my trust now, you'll tell me why you're still helping people who have done nothing for you."

"I'm not," Zaiana said, but she realized how weak that sounded. "At least…I don't know what I'm doing anymore."

The healer reached with a cloth to pull the whistling pot from the hook. "If you want revenge, one thing that would infuriate Marvellas most is having someone she thought she'd conquered side with her enemy instead."

That word was a blow to her existence: *conquered*. Zaiana had been in denial to believe it, but now, spoken so easily, she was beginning to realize how much of a fool she had looked all this time as Marvellas's puppet.

"I wouldn't go as far as that. I doubt Faythe, Kyleer, or any of them would ever trust me as an ally anyway. But I need answers, and I will make her pay."

"You might not have a lot of time left."

"What are you planning with Faythe on the inside?" Zaiana asked. Trickles of foreboding slithered through her.

Nerida retrieved two teacups, but the fact she didn't answer confirmed something to Zaiana anyway. Faythe knew Nerida was here. Had the healer been tracking them since Rhyenelle?

She accepted the steaming cup of tea Nerida offered. The scent relaxed her, with notes of jasmine and honey. The cup warmed her palms while she gave a soft sigh at the gentle caress of the first sip.

Zaiana said, "I get it. You can't trust me, and I can't really trust you. But let me tell you, Maverick is here, and he is not one to hesitate with mercy."

"Callen Osirion," Nerida said. The alternative name was still jarring to Zaiana, but she nodded. "I can't believe I didn't realize sooner."

"How could you have?"

Nerida dropped her sight into her cup. She changed the topic.

"I've only been able to get to the cells. I didn't expect Marvellas would use the tower. Kyleer told me what she did to Faythe. It's barbaric."

Even Zaiana agreed. She'd built a tolerance to Niltain steel, but if someone embedded it in her flesh like Marvellas did with Faythe and the Magestone, Zaiana didn't know if she'd be so resilient then.

Nerida's gaze turned hopeful when it flicked back up to Zaiana. "If you want to help, you could make sure she doesn't break Faythe's spirit. You're the only one who can check on her for us."

"I can't offer anything to keep Faythe from breaking. In fact, my recurring presence might have the opposite effect."

"You're wrong."

"You can't say that. You don't know all I've done. There is no forgiveness for me."

"You can't trust. I understand why, but you underestimate compassion."

"No one has any reason to offer me that."

"Compassion doesn't form from reason but from understanding. Don't think about them forgiving you—think about how everyone harbors demons and has committed actions they're not proud of. There are parts of you in them, just as much as there's part of them in you."

She didn't know who they were speaking of anymore. No one at all, actually. Only the good versus the bad, how nothing was wholly either.

"I don't know how to…help." Zaiana tasted that word with bitter hope.

"It's a scale. It balances trust and requires you reach out a hand, or to take the one that's offered to you."

Zaiana thought of Kyleer, and for once she didn't hate herself for it. Even though she'd betrayed him, even in all her attempts to make him see her as a monster, his hand had never fully retreated from her.

Then she also thought of Maverick. He'd killed Faythe in her place, then he'd killed the King of Rhyenelle instead of her. Had she fulfilled her roles, she would be condemned in the eyes of Faythe, Kyleer, and all of them. Instead it was Maverick who'd taken the target of their wrath, and how could she pretend she was any better?

No—Zaiana couldn't side with them. She couldn't hide in the shadow of Maverick's acts.

"A Transitioned dark fae bite on a fae…" Nerida began, her voice reducing with pain. "Do you know of its effects? If there's a cure?"

Zaiana didn't expect the question. "I've never seen it before, but

I've heard of Transitioned dark fae killing fae with their bite. There's a certain poison in it—a lethal consequence of defying the laws nature set, I suppose."

"What about a cure?" Nerida prompted again. Her hazel eyes were so sad Zaiana pitied her.

"Who was bitten?"

She studied her fingers fiddling with the loose threads of her skirt.

"Tarly Wolverlon."

Well, that name had unexpectedly slammed her with confusion twice now. She hadn't cared to get close enough to him to detect anything wrong.

"He's your friend?"

"Yes."

"What's he hoping to achieve in Rhyenelle's castle?"

The healer's eyes snapped up to Zaiana with shock. When she processed what Zaiana said, it filtered from confusion to concern then *anger*. She'd never seen so many emotions flick across a person's face so fast.

"That damn sullen bastard," she muttered under her breath.

Again, Zaiana thought she was in the company of an entirely different fae for a second, but she quite enjoyed Nerida's spirited side.

Nerida ran an exasperated hand over her forehead. "I didn't know that was where he'd run off to. He was supposed to come with me, but the stubborn prince is determined to accept his fate."

"He's dying," Zaiana concluded.

The heartbreak that fell over Nerida as she looked away tensed Zaiana still. She cared for the prince. More than just as a friend.

"He's not, he's just…he's going to be fine." She sniffed, squaring her shoulders to suppress her grief.

Zaiana felt for her. The worst pain always came from harm to loved ones, not to ourselves. It was once again a reminder of how vulnerable and exhausting love was.

"You won't like my only suggestion," Zaiana said, as gentle as she could.

Nerida glanced at her with misplaced hope.

"Have you considered attempting to Transition him to dark fae?"

Her shock and denial were immediate. "No. He would never want that."

"Want isn't his luxury anymore."

Nerida's eyes glistened, and Zaiana had an unexplainable urge to make them stop filling with sorrow.

"He would rather die. He would rather leave me than become that."

Zaiana was torn between pity and envy to watch how affected Nerida was by another person.

"Then he's no survivor, and this world isn't built for people like that."

Her words were harsh, but they were the truth. Nerida stood, pacing away.

"He's survived a lot," she argued.

"I don't doubt it. Many have, and they become too tired to keep fighting."

"What about me?" Her voice cracked, and Zaiana was beginning to despise the prince for upsetting her. "I'm tired too, but I'm *here*."

"If he cared as much for you as you clearly do for him, he would want to keep fighting regardless of the pain." Zaiana pushed herself up, turning to the fae. "Spare your heart, Nerida. The kind you harbor is rare in this world of spoiled and tainted love."

Nerida's face turned determined. "I can't," she said firmly. "I *won't* give up on him."

"Some people don't want to be saved, and there is nothing we can do."

"We can keep reaching out a hand," she snapped. It wasn't just in regard to Tarly now. Zaiana felt the accusation in that statement.

Zaiana let ice form over the warmth that had started to flutter around Nerida. She couldn't pretend to be good, to decide today that she could forget all she'd done and aid the tragic heroes.

"Then don't be surprised when the hand that reaches back drags you down instead."

CHAPTER THIRTY-SIX

Faythe

"This plan of yours sounds impossible," Faythe said, pacing her cell.

"So does my being here at all," Nyte countered.

That was a good point.

Faythe considered it again. His theory suggested Faythe might be capable of transferring the thread of his consciousness, which had latched itself to her, into someone else's mind instead. Therefore, he might be able to control their mind and have a physical body.

"The mind is far more complex than we can ever imagine. An ability like ours to tap into conscious and unconscious brains is unparalleled and full of unexplored potential. Reading thoughts, compulsion...that's all at the most basic level."

"That's easy, and fascinating to talk about in theory, but in practice, it's never been done."

"Yet," Nyte added with a small, wicked smile. "Everything is unexplored until the first curious person ventures beyond what's already known. I have no doubt in my ability once I have a host, so I need you to believe you can give me one."

"And Captain Daegal is who you're choosing to become?"

"Unless you have a host of others to choose from that you're keeping to yourself."

Faythe pursed her lips then groaned in defeat, running a hand down her face. "If this doesn't work, all I'll receive is a brutal beating from him."

Nyte shrugged. "It's a risk."

He didn't care at all. As he'd reiterated many times, even this plan to gain him a host was his attempt to aid himself. Nyte had no intention of helping them in this war against his mother—he had a far more important person he needed to get back to.

"The one who's waiting for you…she's your mate?"

Faythe lingered it like a question, but she felt his sharp edge was made of the deepest concern and distress to be parted from her. Just as hers was for Reylan.

"Yes," he said.

Reylan was still close by. She couldn't imagine the tear her soul would feel if she woke up in a new realm away from him.

"I'll help you," Faythe agreed. "But while we're figuring out how to get you back, you have to help us in any way you can in return."

The gold in Nyte's eyes darkened a shade before it subdued. He didn't like negotiation—that was clear.

"How exactly do you plan to stop my mother?" Nyte asked.

Faythe debated what to share with him. If she could grant him a temporary mortal form, how could she be sure he wouldn't turn against them and side with Marvellas? Anything she told him would be compromised.

"We're still figuring that out," she said.

Nyte's eyes narrowed, knowing she was withholding information. "I can feel your emotions, remember? I thought we were beginning to trust each other. I'm wounded."

"You're her son. Her blood. How can I be certain that won't change your allegiance when you have the ability to speak to her?"

Impatience fell on his face. "There's only one way to kill a God, so what is it you have of hers that can kill her?"

It wasn't surprising he would know that.

"Maybe nothing, but if we lose the weapon to kill her, we know of something that can at least silence the power of a God."

"Do you also know who will forfeit their life to use either weapon to bring her down?"

That slammed into Faythe. "Forfeit their life?"

Nyte gave a breathy laugh without humor and pushed himself up off the cot.

"You didn't research too far into this, did you? Yes, Faythe. To either kill her or silence her power will kill the person who achieves it.

You're dealing with *very* powerful magick. It always demands a high price."

Nerida hadn't mentioned that about the Aetherbonds. Though that news was devastating, it changed nothing.

"I'll do what I have to."

"Then what was all of this for? Saving your mate, who will follow right after you if you die."

Faythe swore inwardly, knowing he was right. She was willing to do what it took to save her friends and their world, but Reylan wouldn't stay here without her. Not unless she took his memory like Aesira had done…

She fell onto her cot with the dark weight of that option. The mere thought tasted like bitter betrayal to his devotion, but it would save him.

Faythe's head fell between her hands, and her fingers threaded through her hair. Her mind began to spiral.

"I can do it."

Her head snapped up to lock his gaze. Nyte's expression stayed passive.

He said, "In Daegal's body, I can use the weapon against my mother, and you can pull my consciousness back in time."

Faythe turned the proposition over and over in her mind. It was a brilliant loophole, and hope sparked in her chest. She rose from the cot, standing face-to-face with Rainyte Ashfyre, son of Marvellas… Was it possible fate had finally fallen in their favor to grant this solution?

She didn't want to die. There was still so much she hadn't had the chance to experience.

"Are you sure you'll be able to go through with it?" she asked. Her pulse raced to place the most trust she ever had in an uncertain alliance.

"Your only option is to find out." His eyes flicked over her shoulder. "And your time to do so is now."

Faythe's heart skipped, and she turned, anticipating the vile image of Captain Daegal to appear. The footing sounded too light, however, and the scent she captured next exposed Zaiana before she slipped out of the darkness.

"Who is that?" Nyte asked. There was something in his tone that felt like shock.

"Zaiana," Faythe said aloud, as it wouldn't seem odd to answer with her name.

Faythe didn't move, tracking the dark fae with slight curiosity to see if she might acknowledge Nyte behind her. She didn't.

"She's sent me for you," Zaiana informed her.

"No Captain Daegal this time?" Faythe asked, keeping her tone disinterested.

"Marvellas wants me to supervise your attempts to break the ruin. She thinks I might be able to *teach you*."

"Why doesn't she make you break it?" Faythe grumbled.

"It would be a waste of my talents to die that way when you have it in you to break it and live."

Nyte said, more as a thought to himself, "She's fascinating, and I'm assuming quite powerful."

He had no idea.

Faythe followed Zaiana out of the cell, leaving Nyte behind and focusing to rally her composure if she was to make her first attempt with the ruin. Above that, Faythe was yearning to see Reylan again. Even if he still looked at her like the enemy.

"How is Kyleer?" Faythe tried to inquire with the dark fae again. She'd been in turmoil over her captive friend.

"I took the task of watching you instead. You should be glad—the alternative would have been Maverick, no doubt."

Faythe's spine locked.

"He's here?"

"Yes."

"He'll torture Kyleer."

"Probably."

Faythe stopped walking. Zaiana turned back lazily, doing a commendable job of appearing like she didn't care what happened to Kyleer. Was she bluffing? Faythe didn't know why she kept believing Zaiana harbored a shred of feeling toward her friend, if no one else. She felt in her gut that Zaiana wouldn't let him be tortured or killed.

"Are Jakon and Marlowe—"

"I don't care about you or any of your friends. It's been mildly entertaining watching your circle break apart while everyone tries to be the hero. One way or another, you'll all get yourselves killed, and you should focus on yourself, like they are." Zaiana stopped, and Faythe flinched, backing against the wall when she. swallowed the distance between them. "I've always thought you reckless and weak and in over your head. Too many times you've proven me right. She's going to try to break you. Both of you. I can't say I'm confident you're strong enough not to let her. But if there's ever a time to put everything you have into proving me wrong, it's *now.* They call you the Phoenix Queen? Then set your heart ablaze for those you swear to protect."

The second half of Zaiana's speech was contrary to the first. She *did* care—about more people than she could admit even to herself. Faythe didn't display her empathy—Zaiana would despise it—but all she saw when she looked at the dark fae was a softening heart at war with a steel mind.

Faythe gave one nod of affirmation. That was enough for Zaiana to back away and lead again.

Her skin chilled with every step. Her cage had become safer than wandering the wild in Marvellas's domain.

Two fae in all-black uniform waited ahead. Before they reached them, Zaiana came close, hovering behind them. Her voice whispered across her ear.

"Do not break."

Zaiana shoved Faythe, who almost lost her footing. The fae in front caught her, and the next second she felt the familiar pull of Shadowporting.

When the darkness cleared and the temperature dropped, she immediately saw why she'd needed that reminder from Zaiana.

Reylan was here. Faythe's horror kept climbing the more she took in of the scene. The dried blood around where he kneeled in this small cabin. His bound wrists splaying his arms, and his bare chest. His bowed head that didn't look up.

Marvellas stood like a beacon of blood and fire. Faythe couldn't even spare her a kernel of her attention beyond a glance—it was all fixed on her mate as fingers jabbed into her spine, forcing her further across the space.

While Reylan's skin was free of fresh marks or blood, Faythe began to tremble, knowing that wouldn't last long.

"You don't have to hurt him." She whispered her weak words, knowing they were futile.

"I wish that were true," the Spirit said, so calm and uncaring.

Do not break.

Faythe thought she could find the strength of mind, the physical resistance to pain, against what Marvellas might do to her, but this... Reylan was her biggest weakness.

Marvellas glided like a poisonous red snake around Reylan, and Faythe jerked at her proximity. She was stopped from taking her first step by a rough grip on her arm from the fae who'd brought her here.

"I really hope you both make it," Marvellas said, tipping her head with an admiring look at Reylan as if he were her prized pet. Faythe's rage boiled under her skin. "Zaiana will stop you if you get too close to your limit."

She'd agreed to do his. Condemn the world by breaking the ruin —the only thing that could send the Spirits back to their realm or kill Marvellas herself. Faythe approached Reylan even though he paid her no mind. She crouched in front of him…and knew in her heart her choice to save him was absolute, no matter the cost.

"What do I need to do?" Faythe asked quietly.

"That is what you must figure out. I cannot touch it. Zaiana is the only one in our history who has been able to wield the colossal power they contain. She will guide you."

Zaiana stood poised, as straight as a soldier, by the small fireplace in the room.

Marvellas had sworn a blood oath it wouldn't kill him, but what if Marvellas knew a broken magickal bond couldn't kill her anyway, and Faythe had been a fool to stake her belief in it?

There was no more time for questioning, no time to reconsider her choice, but still, her mind spun and spun on an endless loop of doubt, terror, and dread.

"I'm not very patient, my dear," Marvellas said calmly.

She gave Faythe no second to respond before she intervened. Reylan's body tensed, and a pain sound escaped his gritted teeth.

"Stop hurting him!" Faythe yelled, taking his head in her hands, wild panic in her eyes.

His body relaxed, heaving deep breaths, and Faythe could hardly stop shaking from the pure bottled rage within her.

"We're going to get through this," she whispered to him. "I'm going to get you back."

"I'll need time to explain how she can open herself to the power without letting it dominate," Zaiana interjected.

Marvellas's attention swung to the dark fae. Impatience flexed in the Spirit's jaw.

"If she dies on your watch, your life will be next, and it will not leave this world painlessly," Marvellas warned.

Faythe didn't expect such a lethal threat. As she passed Faythe like a red river, her knuckles reached down to brush Faythe's cheek with a stinging tenderness.

"I'll see you for supper."

Then she was stolen by darkness, leaving Faythe alone with Reylan and Zaiana.

"I've faced many challenges in my grueling upbringing, but keeping you alive is by far the most infuriating," Zaiana grumbled.

The dark fae relaxed from her strict stance, slackening her hands from their clasp behind her back. Faythe watched her, wondering if it was nerves she saw spilling over Zaiana now the Spirit was gone.

"This should be easy for you. It sure seemed that way on the Fire Mountains when you showed off your ability to wield the ruin."

Zaiana's purple eyes sliced into her with accusation. "I can't do that right now," she said, low and dark.

Faythe's brow furrowed. "What do you mean?"

"I mean it's your fault I have no magick!"

Zaiana spun away from Faythe with that, pinching the bridge of her nose as if she hadn't wanted to admit it. Faythe was stunned. She never would have guessed since Zaiana had seemed as frightening as ever.

"How is that possible?" Faythe asked, genuinely curious.

It should be a win for Faythe, shouldn't it? But all it inspired was concern.

"If I knew, I would have recovered it by now," she answered bitterly.

"So you can get it back?"

"I think so, I just…don't know how yet. Which means I can't contain the power of the ruin if you lose control again, just like I couldn't when you recklessly exposed yourself to it at the inn."

Faythe should have realized sooner.

Her sight fell back to Reylan, who remained utterly unmoving. She had to track his shoulders to soothe her panic that he was still breathing.

"What do I do?" she whispered in horror.

Zaiana gave a groan, pacing the small cabin behind Reylan. She appeared deep in thought, trying to figure out how to explain the complexities of where to begin with wielding a ruin.

"I really hoped I would never have to do this again," Zaiana muttered under her breath.

"You were made to teach others?"

"No. Kyleer's foolish younger brother was Nether-bent on attempting it. I wouldn't be surprised if it's killed him since I left."

Faythe gasped, covering her mouth and standing. "The Light Temple Ruin," she whispered.

Oh Gods. She'd entrusted its location to Izaiah and didn't want to believe he would betray that. Now she couldn't be sure. What possible reason would Izaiah have for wanting to learn to wield it?

"Did he say why?" Faythe asked.

"He wouldn't tell me."

"Then why would you help him?" It slipped out of Faythe like an accusation. She didn't know Izaiah's intentions, but she cared for him as deeply as she always did, hoping in her heart he would never truly turn against them.

"I owed him a favor. He kept Amaya and Tynan alive when your father betrayed our agreement, and he captured them again the moment they were out of my sight."

Faythe blinked, steadying her thoughts that were battered with this new information. She'd been an oblivious fool to Agalhor's plans, and she couldn't decide what emotion was dominating her now at discovering this.

She wanted to believe in Agalhor's actions. He'd only done what he'd had to do in the interest of his kingdom, even if it was dishonorable to betray Zaiana's deal in offering herself as a captive in place of her friends. But the dark fae had been cunning—she'd already known Agalhor wouldn't honor it.

Zaiana was incredibly preceptive and cunning.

"Why did Izaiah come to you in the first place?" Faythe asked, needing all the pieces she could get of this picture before the Battle of Ellium unfolded.

"He wanted to know about the ruin, and he taunted me with Tynan as if I didn't know he'd grown feelings for him and wouldn't have let him die anyway. Amaya was my concern, and she wouldn't have survived without him."

Izaiah had feelings for Tynan. Unexpectedly, Faythe found a sense of hope in that. The fae and the dark fae weren't born enemies. They just had to make the world see that.

Her thoughts reeled back to Izaiah's motives with the ruins, running over why he could possibly need to be more powerful... Or, the question was, what could he become with his Shapeshifting ability if it was amplified by the ruin?

"You're wasting time," Reylan said, cutting through their building tension. "I'm rather hoping it kills you before you can break it."

Faythe's heart squeezed. Even Zaiana gave a flicker of disturbance at the cold statement.

"Too bad. I'm not dying, and neither are you," Faythe said,

kneeling back down in front of him. She glanced up at Zaiana. "Tell me what to do."

"It's not as simple as that," she said bitterly. Zaiana cast her sight to the heavens as if a God might hear the plea for sanity in her thoughts. "I guess we'll see if your stubbornness against dying can hold out with this too."

Faythe listened to Zaiana with all her attention. Nothing that left her as instruction or personal experience sounded remotely appealing. The more the dark fae went on, the more Faythe grew riddled with terror, disbelief, and anxiety to achieve the impossible.

"You're not trying to wield it, however. My guess is that you have to trick it. Open yourself just enough for the beginning of an alliance, feel for a crack of weakness, and throw everything you harbor in your own well into the ruin."

In conversation it sounded plausible; in practice, Faythe knew it wouldn't be so easy.

"And you can't take over if I lose control," Faythe said in a fearful breath.

"I might be able to sever your connection, but it will hurt both of you. A lot. I can't be certain it won't leave permanent effects."

"Like what?" Faythe dreaded to ask.

"Madness."

She swallowed hard against her dry throat.

Faythe slipped her hands over Reylan's cheeks, coaxing his face up until she met his sapphire irises. They were so cold and lost it ached in her soul.

Her trembling fingers slipped down his chest. Threads of the ruin's power wound around her fingertips, quickly spreading a vibration up her arm. It slowly raked over her body and latched onto her well of magick.

Faythe held her panicked eyes on those of the other half of her soul. "Just please stay with me, no matter how much it hurts. I hurt with you," she croaked, absolutely terrified for them both.

She didn't know what she was doing. The power began to flood her veins and crash like a shadowy storm through her mind. In her panic, Faythe struggled to keep the magick from overwhelming her in an instant. This terrible, ferocious, *starving* power that clawed and shrieked and wanted to claim her, mind, body, and soul.

She couldn't let it, but already, it was winning. Faythe tried to search for Reylan in the chaos of dark power—the only anchor that could keep her from drowning in the shadows.

"Please stop." Reylan's voice of pure agony echoed through this void of ending they were lost in together.

"I have to do this," Faythe said. Her soul tore to hurt him.

She hugged his physical body tighter. At least, she thought she did, but her tether to the real world was slipping fast. Faythe might have the power to break the ruin, but she had no skill to navigate this fight for dominance. The ruin was a force that could not be defied or controlled easily. It was fighting to take over, and if that happened... Faythe would be no more than a vessel for the deadly power.

It wasn't something whole she could target. It circled her, evading her, mocking her. Faythe was too overwhelmed and frightened, and she didn't know how to stand against it for a chance.

An arm of smoke grew around her, growing in size, until she knelt helplessly in a raging tempest of wailing souls and furious darkness. The sound...the beating wind, it was familiar.

Like hundreds of crows.

Faythe gasped when a thick tendril of smoke surged down from the eye of the tempest, ready to devour her—

Faythe's eyes flew open though she didn't remember closing them. An eruption of pain in her shoulder tore a scream from her throat. When she found Zaiana straddling her, a Magestone blade dripping crimson in her hand, she understood it had been the dark fae's last resort to snap Faythe's attachment to the ruin.

She slumped against the floor, panting and sweat-slicked.

"How long did I try for?" Faythe asked, trying to get her vision to stay focused on the brown roof flickering with firelight.

"Two minutes."

Horror doused her. Two minutes had felt like hours on her body.

Zaiana got off her as she said, "We knew you weren't going to achieve it on the first try."

"That almost sounds like you have faith in me."

Faythe had never heard the particular huff of light amusement from Zaiana. "Your name is ironic."

Her head lolled to find Reylan, head bowed again, but he was breathing with more exertion now. His skin was paler, with a sheen the flames glowed over.

"Are you okay?" she barely whispered.

Reylan's head lifted a fraction. He took a pause of silence before he spoke. "So long as you remain afraid of the dark, it will always hold power over you."

CHAPTER THIRTY-SEVEN

Zaiana

She didn't want to be here, cramped in a dark servant's supply room with Maverick Blackfair. They leaned against opposite walls, mirroring each other, with crossed arms and a foul stare, but the space between them was barely a wide step.

"The easiest way to test this theory is to kill you," he said plainly.

Zaiana's mood soured. She'd told him everything she suspected about the curse on dark fae hearts, and how she believed herself to be the anchor for it somehow.

"I'll give you one attempt to try," she answered flatly.

Maverick almost yielded a half-smile.

"It makes you wonder, doesn't it…? In history and now, the fae and the dark fae have been at war with each other. Marvellas merely took advantage of what was already a simmering conflict. But no one wants to admit evil isn't born, it's made. And the fae are just as suscep-tible to it."

"It doesn't matter."

"It does. This changes everything. *You* can change everything."

"I may be powerful, but I'm not enough to take down Marvellas. Nothing but her ruin can do that, and it's embedded in Reylan Arrowood's chest."

"Then we retrieve it. We have the one weapon that can kill her, and I'll rip it right out of him for you to wield."

She didn't doubt he would hold true to that.

"I think it would kill him to remove it intact. That's why she did it —she wants Faythe to break it to save him," she said.

Maverick didn't flinch at that. Of course he wouldn't.

Zaiana calculated. She actually thought of the general's death if it meant stopping the evil even Faythe and her company wanted to end. But at the thought of Reylan dying, Zaiana actually *shuddered* with a cold lick of dread at Faythe Ashfyre's wrath toward the world.

"No. That can't happen. Reylan needs to stay alive."

"I didn't know you'd grown to care so much for him. Did he treat you kindly in Rhyenelle?"

She shot him a look of daggers. "Faythe is just as powerful as Marvellas, and she wouldn't stop with the death of us if her mate died."

"She's too *good* for that."

"Love and grief make a deadly weapon, and Faythe is not immune to wielding it for those she loves."

Maverick hummed, considering her opinions. "I suppose those months in Rhyenelle served you well. You're particularly observant. I trust your intuition."

To have Maverick admit he believed in anything she would say came as a jarring surprise.

He said, "So what is your plan then?"

She hated to admit it. "I don't have one...yet."

"Maybe not something certain, given the gravity of what you hope to achieve, but you must have thought of some options."

"The dark fae aren't going to believe the curse by word of gossip. Even if some did, the moment the masters hear of it, they'll just start killing anyone who speaks of it. But if I can't reach Marvellas directly, she's nothing without the forces she's gained over centuries. All the dark fae, the masters, Mordecai."

"Then why don't we start with them?" he said. "The masters are ancient, but they bleed silver like you. They can be killed."

"I've considered that. But if I kill them without the sway of the dark fae led by them, I'll only be branded a traitor to my kind. They'll believe I've sided with Faythe against them, and I will not allow everything I've built to be thrown into the shadow of an insufferable, overpowered heir."

"We kill Mordecai then."

Zaiana ran an exasperated hand down her face. "Do all your suggestions begin and end with killing and no thought or strategy beyond?"

He shrugged. "I like to kill and deal with the consequences as they come."

"Mordecai is another unknown," she argued. "We don't know enough about his resurrection to be certain he can be killed by mortal means."

"Someone might be on the path to finding that out," he enlightened her.

Zaiana's interest piqued.

"It seems he's taken a liking to Tauria Stagknight. She's with him now, and he's taken her to Valgard."

Zaiana became puzzled at that. "He's trusting her in his kingdom after what she did in Olmstone?"

"It seems so. Unless he has another motive and the Fenstead queen is naïve prey in his trap."

That seemed more logical, but though Zaiana had never really met Tauria Stagknight, all she'd heard had made her believe she was more silently cunning than people gave her credit for.

"Do you know when they'll return? She must be planning to escape him, or...where's Nikalias? Her mate, is he not?"

Maverick's expression shifted with the mention of the High Farrow king. "I assume he's gone after her, but I don't have intel on his movements."

Zaiana's mind was reeling with what to do. Where to go next. She didn't feel like she could leave yet, and infuriatingly, there was only one thing that made her reluctant to any plan that involved leaving Lakelaria.

What were Marvellas's plans with Kyleer?

She shouldn't care. Her mind tore itself apart over that question that only served to distract and delay her from advancing her own goals.

"How can we get your magick back?"

Maverick's tone turned softer, and she despised it. The topic made her fists clench, with her now useless iron guard cutting into her palms. Even though she couldn't conjure her lightning, she couldn't leave them off.

"Stop using the term *we*," she hissed. "I'm only telling you this since you already know half of it. Our plans aren't the same."

"I want Marvellas dead as much as you do."

"Then why have you been her willing soldier all this time?" Zaiana snapped, her voice rising. She straightened off the wall, which brought them closer. "All this time you've been aware of the life she stole from you, yet still you did her most heinous bidding. You killed Faythe and Agalhor when you could have *joined* them to stop Marvellas. They were your people long before I was."

Maverick didn't speak right away. He watched her with a deep, studying frown, and she could hardly stand to be caught in it. She couldn't understand him, and something told her she never would.

"Someone had to."

That stung the wound of her failures. He'd done what she'd failed to.

"It didn't have to be you," she said.

"Yes, it did."

Maverick pushed off the wall, pausing with only a slither of space between them. He wore nothing on his face as he stared down at her. His black eyes were so vacant, so...*dead*.

"This was a very insightful chat," he said calmly. "I think we both need time to figure out the best move forward with what we know."

He brushed by her, and light spilled into the small room when he opened the door.

"What are you going to do?" she asked.

"Play my part in this show, as always."

He left without another word, leaving her in this cramped space where her thoughts began to suffocate her. There were too many wheels turning in the war that was heading to a climax. She could feel it. The familiar aura of death hung in every new dawn. The building crescendo of battle hummed in every twilight. Only, this time, there was no telling when each battle would come.

Zaiana walked the foreign halls of Lakelaria's castle, and if it weren't for how cold the island was, she would have said the kingdom was the greatest in the continent. After being suffocated under so much rock all her life, there was no other place indoors like this, with so much glass, that invoked a similar sense of freedom to what she felt standing atop open mountains.

"Zaiana, my child."

Her next step paused at the unexpected caress of her name from within the room she was about to pass. The door was slightly ajar, and Zaiana had no choice but to answer the Goddess's call.

Slipping inside, for a second it was jarring to watch Marvellas so... *peaceful*. She sat in a large reading room, a book splayed between her palms, but she wasn't reading. She stared intently into the fire blazing in the pit beside her, so lost in thought or something else that she didn't react to Zaiana's presence.

"Join me," the Spirit said, gesturing with a graceful hand to the gold velvet chair opposite her.

Zaiana really didn't want to, but she obliged. Refusing would only rouse suspicion or anger.

When her sight fell to the book in Marvellas's lap, Zaiana read the title: *An Immortal Heart of Vengeance.*

"Everyone wants to be remembered, but history seldom tells the right story," Marvellas said, catching her observation before swinging her golden eyes toward the marching flames in the fireplace.

She propped one of her elbows on the arm of the chair to rest her chin against her knuckles. Right now, the Spirit who'd started a war and become the greatest villain in centuries appeared so soft, with the gentle glow of the fire over her features, and so *tired.*

"You've been alive all this time—why let them tell your story any differently from the truth?"

Marvellas's head tipped back against the tall seat. "Because it wouldn't make a difference. There's no amount of truth or sympathy that could atone for all I've done now."

Marvellas didn't talk with regret for what she'd done, but there was something displaying right now that Zaiana didn't think the Spirit harbored anymore: humanity.

Zaiana asked carefully, "Why do you want all the royals as dark fae? Why not just kill them and replace them?"

Marvellas's delicate brow pulled together, and her sight tore from the flames to Zaiana. "That is not part of my plan. The only time the dark fae are more powerful than the fae is when they consume human blood. That's too volatile and uncertain for my world."

Zaiana was slammed with confusion, trying to recall where the rumor about her plan for the royals began if it wasn't true. Then the question arose: Why would she curse her kind to be unfeeling soldiers without hearts?

"Then what is your endgame?"

"The humans are greedy and weak—I plan to annihilate them all. Then I will replace every royal except Faythe Ashfyre. She is too powerful and will bend for me. The others...they may have strong abilities too, but if they get in my way, I won't hesitate to cut them down. I have plenty of very powerful fae loyal to me that could bring a new reigning name for all the kingdoms in my empire."

Marvellas told her this with such confidence, as if that future was already set.

"What about the dark fae?"

"They will still serve a purpose. Once all the humans are gone, I will have to put down those who become too savage from the overindulgence. The rest will find use in other ways."

Use. Zaiana's bones began to shake. Her very core repelled everything Marvellas spoke of.

The Spirit added, "You have nothing to worry about. Your future is very triumphant—we've made sure of it."

"We?"

Marvellas cocked her head, a hint of a smile at the corner of her red mouth. "Sometimes I look at you and think I made a mistake in letting the masters raise you. There was a moment of weakness where I..." She stalled, considering her next words.

Zaiana's skin grew too hot. "What do you mean?" she asked desperately.

"I thought you could replace what I lost with Aesira. But it was too soon, so I gave you to them."

"You're not my mother."

Marvellas chuckled lightly. "No. Your mother is dead, and your father would have killed you too...until he saw your eyes. The purple color that foretold the power you would come into. His legacy would live on."

"My father..." Zaiana choked on the word. "Who?"

"I think a part of you has always known, child."

Zaiana stood abruptly. Her breathing heaved out of her, but she didn't know what she wanted to say.

"I have no parents."

"Good. You have become stronger than anyone could have predicted just on your own. We are creatures of darkness, Zaiana. We were born to be alone."

She couldn't stop the rush behind her eyes, and that infuriated her. Zaiana's blood trickled in her palms, but the pain wasn't enough to stop the emotions battering the vault within her.

"May I leave?" she ground out.

Marvellas gave a single nod, and Zaiana turned, marching for the door.

She wanted to claw free from her own mind, but there was no escape. She needed something to overpower the weak feelings flooding through her body.

Zaiana didn't acknowledge the destination her storm was marching her to until it was too late.

She didn't let herself get closer to the cell that held Kyleer. Zaiana had avoided coming down here for days, even though her nights kept her restless with the itch to just *look*. To see where he was being kept and what provisions he had.

He sat alone in this cellblock, and Zaiana stayed in the shadows down the hall. He gave no reaction, so she believed she remained hidden. Spying was one of her greatest talents. She couldn't understand why looking at him calmed her. Knowing he was breathing and within reach allowed her mind to stop raging for a moment.

Making herself known to him might break that peace she was desperate to hold onto just for a while longer. So she breathed the faint scent of him from where she stood. Once, twice, three times. Then she left.

CHAPTER THIRTY-EIGHT

Faythe

Faythe didn't know how many more times she could withstand the ruin's furious power tearing through her body. This was her eleventh—or twelfth?—attempt.

She came around, cheek pressed to a cold, unforgiving surface, after having no choice but to reach back to the grip of darkness that offered reprieve. Just for a moment. Faythe knew Reylan would be feeling everything she was. His own pain collided with hers, and the agony was like nothing she'd endured before.

Her gaze took a minute to gain clarity when she managed to peel her lids open. She wasn't where she expected to be. Usually, she would see blurred colors of amber and brown from the blazing fire in the quiet hut Marvellas had chained Reylan in, high in the sky caves. Then, when she found the will, Faythe would see Reylan, bare torso and sweat-slicked, but utterly silent despite his agony at her attempts to break the ruin embedded in his flesh.

This time, everything was dark. Peaceful. Faythe's breath rippled over a shallow sheet of water, but she wasn't cold. In fact, her body felt weightless and free.

"You can't give up, Faythe."

Her eyes peeled open fully at the echo of that voice.

Her shock clashed with horror.

Had she failed? Was she dead to be hearing the voice of a dear lost friend?

Faythe found the will to drag her arms and push herself up. Watching the droplets fall off her hair and distort her reflection, her eyes flooded with the emotion that slammed into her chest at seeing another's face in the water, standing beside her.

"Caius?" she croaked, finally turning her head.

When she found him, a whole and clear picture of him, Faythe sobbed as he smiled in greeting. That warm, boyish smile that had always made her feel comforted, which she'd missed so much.

"Did I die?" she said, voice hoarse.

Faythe couldn't take her eyes from him, afraid he would disappear in a blink, as she pushed herself up slowly to stand. The pain of challenging the ruin was just a memory in here.

"No. But you could. You have it in you to achieve what she wants, but you're resisting."

"I'm not," Faythe defended, but even though she believed herself, there was a note of a lie settling in her gut.

"Your resistance isn't conscious, but there's a part of you still hoping there's another way. To keep the ruin intact and save Reylan."

Faythe swallowed painfully against the marble forming in her throat. "Is there a way?"

"I wish there was."

Faythe's head bowed in defeat. "If I do it, how am I any better than Marvellas if it condemns the world?"

"The choice you have is a heavy burden, but it is yours to make."

"What should I do, Caius?" Faythe wept.

He came a step closer. Every piece of him was exactly like she remembered, and it tore her with gratitude and agony to see him here, in this void she could only think was a careful warning before death's true claim.

"You heart hasn't led you astray yet. Don't doubt it now," he said warmly.

Faythe dared to reach out a hand, and when she didn't pass through his form, a whimper escaped her, and she fell into him with an embrace.

"I'm so sorry for what happened to you," she whispered.

"You should know I was prepared for the fate that befell me," he said. "I knew the chances of walking away from it weren't high. But it's different...knowing you're going to die and being in the moment of dying. I don't think any amount of time can truly prepare you for that fear."

Faythe pulled back, a crushing weight of grief threatening to buckle her knees. "You should be here, Caius, not me."

He huffed a laugh. "I don't think I could have survived half the things you have since. I'm at peace, Faythe. I knew what I had to do then, and I have no regrets. You didn't let me be forgotten."

"Never." She sniffed.

Caius reached his hand up to swipe away her falling tear. "Nik named an entire city after me. I didn't know I meant that much to him."

Though he said it in humor, Faythe was fierce as she said, "You meant more to all of us than you know."

Bittersweet joy pulled at his expression. His eyes glistened, but before tears could form, he straightened his posture.

"You can't linger here, and we have to make sure you don't return. I'm so glad I got to see you again, but you can't join me. Do what you have to do, Faythe. Follow your heart and trust you can rise from the ashes you will burn. Nothing is without sacrifice."

Faythe pulled Caius to her again. Her arms tightened when her body began to feel too light to stay grounded, and she wasn't ready to let him go. To lose him all over again.

"I'm still with you. In here, remember," he said, reaching between them and tapping her heart.

Faythe cried freely, grieving for him all over again and filled with terror to return to her world with the choice she had to make.

"Thank you for being my friend," Faythe choked.

Caius turned to sand in her arms, and a breeze swept in to take him away from her. She didn't get to drown in her sorrow when a sudden wave of dizziness slammed into her, sending her crashing to the ground. The sheet of water had turned into a deep lake, which she plummeted into.

He eyes flew open, and her body jerked up in the opposite direction to the one she was being pulled in. Faythe panted hard, shivering violently.

She was soaked in ice water, but drowning she was not. The shock of the frozen water lashed her consciousness to clear faster, and she found Zaiana staring down at her, an empty bucket in her hands. They met wide-eyed stares, and Faythe had never seen such *panic* within the purple depths.

Her expression quickly shifted to absolute rage, and Faythe jerked when she dropped the bucket and crouched, seething at Faythe.

"You are *not* allowed to die," she snapped.

Faythe blinked, not expecting that to be her reprimand.

"After all this, you don't get to leave this gods-forsaken world so pitifully, so get up and get yourself together."

Her teeth bashed together as Faythe rolled onto her hands and knees. She almost left her dignity behind to crawl toward the blazing fire across the cabin, but Zaiana was right. She was being pitiful. So Faythe forced herself to stand, limping over to it.

She cast her sight over her shoulder to Reylan while she warmed her body.

"Did I come close?" Faythe asked Zaiana.

"I think so," Zaiana grumbled, watching her with a sour glare. "When I can hardly stand the sound of it, the feeling of it clawing at my skin, that's when you must be close to splitting it apart. Your heart stopped before you could push your magick a final time and win."

She'd come so close. Faythe recalled her vision of Caius with a heavy heart. Was what he'd said true? Had Faythe yielded right at the last moment before it broke without realizing? A piece of her subconscious hesitating out of morality.

Zaiana studied her intently, and it was like she could read Faythe's thoughts. "You're two halves of a whole—that's always been insufferably clear," she said. "Save him and damn what comes after. You can figure out the rest together."

Faythe's burden lifted off her shoulders a fraction as she slipped her attention back to Reylan, who kneeled with his back to her. She watched the fire glisten off his map of scars, aching to have him back so much her soul had been slowly dying ever since they were parted in Rhyenelle.

"I'll try again," she said.

"Not today." Marvellas's voice came from the shadows. When the darkness cleared to reveal the Spirit, Faythe didn't think her body would ever stop seizing with dread. "Look at you, my dear. You need to replenish your strength. It's no matter. It gives us more time together before the next part begins when the ruin is broken."

Her teeth gritted when Marvellas extended a palm toward her, wanting to steal her away from Reylan again. Faythe's heart cried at having to move toward the Spirit and leave him here bound and alone until she could return.

"Can't I stay with him? I'll rest here and try again."

Marvellas's darkening gaze spoke of her impatience, Faythe reluctantly crossed, and Magestone was clamped around her wrists—a measure to contain her magick enough until she was taken to have it embedded into her flesh again. Sparing a last look at Reylan, she was taken away in a plume of smoke.

Back in the castle, they didn't get far before Captain Daegal fell back a step from Marvellas, following like an obedient dog. He cast Faythe a disdainful sidelong glance, but she didn't react to it. His presence reminded Faythe of her theory with Nyte—their agreement for Faythe to try to plant the thread of his consciousness into Daegal instead.

Her pulse skipped at the thought. If she waited for the right moment when they removed her Magestone chains, she would have a chance to try. Hopefully, she had enough strength to attempt it.

They brought her to a chamber, where a stone chair appeared to be crafted from the ground. Marvellas usually took away her pain, but still, they strapped her down in case the Spirit wasn't feeling merciful or Faythe rebelled.

She held out her wrists to Captain Daegal, who held the key to her shackles. He glared at her with the desire to hurt her swirling in his brown eyes. Faythe couldn't muster her usual glower back.

Was she really about to attempt this plan in front of Marvellas?

Faythe decided she might not get another chance like this, and somehow, she believed Nyte having the ability to roam their world was important in their war against Marvellas.

She flicked a look toward the Spirit, who was oblivious that the child she'd started this war for, because he was taken from her, would get to witness all she'd done.

"Your Grace, you're needed in the drawing room. The scouts of Rhyenelle are back," a masked soldier informed her.

Faythe's interest was grabbed, but Marvellas's eyes flexed in ire to be pulled away. Would they be reporting news about her friends there? She felt sick not knowing if they were safe or if they'd been taken captive despite professing their alliance to Marvellas.

"Take her back to her cell when you're finished," Marvellas instructed Daegal, then her fiery sight shifted to Faythe. "I'll come for you soon. Rest your body and heal your power. We're so close to breaking that wretched ruin I can feel it, and then our real work begins."

With that, Marvellas slipped away like a snake on fire.

Faythe barely processed what Marvellas said. Her own spur-of-the-moment planning was swirling her mind now she was alone with the captain. Aside from Zaiana, who stayed.

Daegal was never gentle, pulling her toward him by the chain between her wrists and making her hiss at the chafing stone.

"Maybe I'll have fun with you before I take you back," he said, disgustingly low in her ear. "Payback for that little stunt you pulled in the cells before."

His hand slipped around her waist, and Faythe's whole body surged with repulsion. Instinct took over as her bound hands reached over his head, then she crossed her wrists, strangling him with the chain.

Daegal choked and hissed, grappling the chain, which burned his skin with the Magestone.

"Help me," he spluttered to Zaiana.

"I don't think so."

Zaiana took up a casual lean against the wall, but Faythe needed the shackles off to reach enough of her power to attempt to infiltrate his mind. Daegal pushed her, sending them crashing into the wall. A jolt of pain lanced up her spine, slackening her grip, which was enough for him to drive his knee into her gut, causing her to let him go.

Faythe fell to her knees, winded and gasping for breath. He kicked her again, and Faythe slumped in a pitiful heap. Her sight focused across the dark stone she lay on, catching on a glint of metal. The key for her shackles.

She couldn't give up.

Faythe crawled for it, but Daegal dragged her back by her ankle, flipping her onto her back and straddling her. His eyes were wild are terrifying as he gripped her wrists and yanked her hands above her head.

"I actually quite like your fight," he said gutturally.

Nausea roiled in her stomach and burned in her throat.

She *couldn't* give up.

Faythe clamped her knees onto his hips, and with a battle cry, she threw every ounce of her rage and adrenaline into her core. The momentum flipped them, sending Daegal slamming onto his back. In Faythe's next breath, her fist flew into his temple once, twice, and by the time she pulled back for a third, she noticed his head rolling back limply.

She panted above him, and when the adrenaline to survive started to cool, tremors racked her body. Tears stung the backs of her eyes, but she would not cry.

"Impressive," Zaiana commented.

A rattle skidded against stone until it hit her knee. Zaiana had kicked the key to her.

Faythe's glare couldn't be more hateful slipping up to the dark fae.

Zaiana rolled her eyes at it. "He wouldn't have gotten much further than pinning you had you not fought back."

Her anger tried to cool, but it was difficult around Zaiana's unpredictability. Did Faythe really believe Zaiana would have intervened before Daegal could violate her?

"You could have helped sooner," Faythe grumbled, swiping up the key.

"All I've seen is your fight for others. I wanted to see how determined you could become to fight for yourself. For once, you didn't disappoint."

That almost sounded like a compliment.

Faythe fiddled with the key, gritting her teeth against the stinging and burning that grew worse from the Magestone with every slight movement.

Again, Zaiana let her struggle, not offering to help remove her shackles. When they finally clanged to the ground, Faythe sighed in relief, examining the thick red torn skin.

"You could try to run now there's no Magestone stopping you. Though I'd recommend waiting at least a few minutes for your magick to stir."

"You wouldn't stop me?"

Zaiana shrugged. "I think it would be more entertaining to watch the chaos that would ensue before you were inevitably caught and brought back."

Faythe couldn't figure Zaiana out. What she wanted or sought to gain from being here.

She banished the thoughts from her mind, Zaiana was not her concern. Instead Faythe's attention fell back to the captain, remembering what she needed to attempt to do. Now he was unconscious, would Nightwalking achieve the task better?

Falling asleep on command would be impossible, and she didn't have much time before someone noticed she hadn't been returned to her cell and came looking.

Internally, she groaned that she had to ask the dark fae for help without arousing suspicion.

"I don't suppose you have mercy enough to get me a sleep tonic?"

Zaiana lifted a brow, but she seemed to find her own conclusion without asking. "Who do you want to Nightwalk to?"

She was too damned perceptive for her own good.

"I want to see if my friends are safe while I have this chance," she lied easily, but once again, Zaiana wasn't even remotely convinced.

"You're a fool by many accounts, but you wouldn't waste such an opportunity for a wellness check."

"Does it really matter to you?"

"You're asking the enemy to aid you with the greatest ability you have." Zaiana crouched on her haunches to level with her.

"You're not my enemy," Faythe dared to declare. Zaiana's cruel smile should have proved her wrong, but Faythe didn't balk. She added, "You're no one's enemy but your own. You're here, but you're not wholly working for Marvellas. I don't know what your agenda is, but it's not in full allegiance to Marvellas or Dakodas like you want them, maybe even yourself, to believe."

Zaiana's smile faltered slowly like a withering black rose. Her eyes tilted down, looking through her with a piercing warning.

The dark fae rose then stalked the few steps to Faythe. What she didn't anticipate was the quick strike of her hand lashing around her throat, pulling her up. Faythe was pressed against the wall, while the metal guards on Zaiana's middle and pointer fingers dug into her flesh like the fangs of a serpent.

"This is far quicker than fetching a tonic," Zaiana said, her voice like sin-filled shadow. Pressure was added through two of Zaiana's fingers and her thumb at a precise pressure point.

The twin cores of Zaiana's amethyst eyes were captured in her mind before darkness swallowed her.

CHAPTER THIRTY-NINE

Faythe

A gloomy gray had begun to darken the white whorls of her subconscious essence, and it started to chase more of the gold away.

Faythe didn't feel comfort here anymore. She wanted to escape the creeping burden her own mind was becoming. Heavier by the day.

At least she had awoken here and not fallen into some torturous nightmare when Zaiana knocked her unconscious. Faythe was sour about her methods, but she couldn't be mad when it was exactly what she needed.

"Mine used to look like this too," Nyte said, his voice a gentle silver disturbance in her quiet void.

She found him standing a few paces away, lifting a hand to swirl it though the gray and gold clouds.

Seeing him here and knowing what she was about to attempt, her nerves began to doubt this plan. Granting the son of her greatest enemy the ability to walk her world as Marvellas did. It could be a trick. Rainyte Ashfyre could instead become a weapon with his mother, and they wouldn't stand a chance against them both being reunited.

"You doubt me," he said, feeling her emotions more acutely in here.

"I don't have much to trust you with. This is all a leap of…faith," she said.

"Then all you can do is trust you'll fly this time."

Faythe had taken a life-risking leap before. Literally. Off the side of the Fire Mountains, with nothing but pure belief that Atherius would catch her. Deep down, Faythe could feel a similar inkling toward Nyte, but it didn't make the decision to trust him any less terrifying.

"Do you really think you can kill your mother?"

"I don't know," he said honestly, and she believed him. "I haven't met her, and all I know are stories of her from her enemies."

"Every villain has their own story that justifies their evil actions."

"I agree. But does that mean they shouldn't be heard?"

"So, what if you hear her side and decide to turn on us?"

Nyte took a few steps closer. "My war isn't with you. All I want is to get back to my Starlight. I need this body you will give me to start looking for a way back. Whatever I learn of my mother and my origins here in the meantime matters naught to all I have waiting for me. So you see, you could never be an enemy worth my efforts even if I come to sympathize with Marvellas."

That consoled some of her terrible anxiety to give power to one who could drastically shift the scales of her war against the Goddess of Stars for better or worse.

"Then let's give this a try," Faythe said, taking a deep breath and squaring her shoulders.

Focusing on the viscous Captain Daegal, Faythe gripped the thread to his mind, which was exposed to her through a web of endless subconscious roads she could follow. With all her focus, Faythe hoisted the anchor keeping her there and let go to project into Daegal's subconscious instead.

She landed with a familiar weightless grace, immediately wrapped in the presence of Daegal's thoughts and feelings. His subconscious was dark, with streaks of bloodred—a sinister contrast befitting of his personality.

"Do you ever wonder which minds are born so vicious and which turn this way?" Faythe asked Nyte, scanning the void that brought on a chill.

"I don't think any are born this way," Nyte said. "Whether things happen to people to give them a thirst for violence and a scarred moral compass or they simply build a desire out of sampling such things, I don't believe a cruel mind like this was always inevitable from birth."

Faythe agreed with him.

In a mind that didn't harbor the Nightwalking ability, Faythe would usually have to be vigilant. Any wrong move in their subconscious could cause irreversible damage to their brain when they awoke. This time it was Faythe's objective to drag Daegal's awareness here with her. She'd schemed various methods to achieve their task with Nyte while they were in the cells; his skill and knowledge of the Nightwalking ability surpassed even what Nik knew and had experimented with. The ability could be conveyed simply as an invasion of a person's sleeping mind, but there were far more layers and chilling possibilities no one could imagine the extent of.

Like the concept of what Faythe was about to attempt. Killing a person's consciousness and implanting another's.

"You'll only get one precarious chance at this, which could end badly for us if you make a wrong move," Nyte rehashed.

Faythe shivered. "A boost of confidence would be better right now."

"You don't need that. You *know* you can do this. You're just as much her heir as I am—the origin of this ability. You are strong enough, and your potential is limitless."

I am strong enough, and my potential is limitless.

Faythe repeated those words to herself over and over, gathering the strength she needed to put her plan into practice.

She dissolved the rampant thoughts of her mind one by one, steadily falling into a collected calm that focused on nothing but her magick, channeling it all through her Nightwalking. Reaching through Daegal's mind wasn't without pain and resistance. His confusion slashed into her, recognizing an invading force and trying to cast her out. She battled him for dominance only for a few seconds. It was too easy to take control. Faythe reached out a physical hand, grabbing his consciousness and dragging it to join her in this space.

She looked down at him, his brown eyes wide, terrified, and helpless. He couldn't utter a sound. She only had seconds before his brain would shut down completely, killing him.

"Do it now!" Nyte yelled through the storm that raged. It was Daegal's mind, fighting with all it had against her.

Her head throbbed with the countdown.

Faythe closed her eyes, straining to reach for the quickly fraying thread of Daegal's mental being. She grabbed it in one hand, then she felt for the end of Nyte's, which lived in her own mind. The pounding in her head amplified, slipping her control.

"You're almost there," Nyte said, but his voice was so distant now.

The danger of what she was doing wasn't lost on her. Night-walking was not without severe risk, and what she was attempting was against all moral code of the Spirit-given ability. Her magick rebelled in her veins, a scream tore from her throat, but Faythe pulled the threads together. Their frayed edges sparked against each other, each finite strand fusing together.

When it was about to finish, Faythe was slammed into by a force so great she propelled back endlessly. She gasped and flailed to catch herself from drifting into oblivion. The moment she saw her way back —a prominent gold fiber in the web of infinite mental connections— Faythe reached desperately for it.

As soon as she touched her mind link, Faythe was pulled back into her own subconscious, falling to her hands and knees and blinking down at the gold-and-gray mists weaving through her splayed fingers.

Had she done it?

Faythe couldn't be sure. She had to wake up, but she was so tired, giving in to the weakness of her body as it crumpled in a heap.

Something was tugging her consciousness. The familiar pull of someone trying to wake her up. Faythe resisted for as long as she could, but they weren't giving in.

With a deep inhale, when Faythe opened her eyes, she was back in her physical body, fully awake. Faythe heard a voice across the room, and her head lolled. She didn't find the source of the conversation; instead her body stiffened when her eyes fell upon Captain Daegal, whose eyes fluttered open.

Faythe couldn't move when their eyes met. She waited in antic-ipation.

He *winked* at her.

It had worked. Nyte now had full control of the captain's body, and once he left it...Daegal would be dead.

Faythe couldn't say she felt an ounce of regret for killing him.

Nyte pushed himself up, his expression turning frightening. He lunged for Faythe, yanking her up by the scruff of her clothing and slamming her to the wall. He was only upon her for a few seconds before he was ripped away. Nyte grunted when Zaiana instead pushed him against the wall, angling a blade to his neck.

Was his violence for show as the captain, or had she been a fool and Nyte's aggression toward was genuine?

Her mind spun, and her heart raced, staring at the stand-off between Nyte and Zaiana.

They stared deeply into each other's eyes. Zaiana's brow twitched, and she scanned his face. Faythe's pulse was erratic—it had to be her own paranoia that detected the confusion and suspicion Zaiana wore. One second she was ready to slice his throat; the next she'd pushed off him, backing a long step up as if he would burst into flame.

"You're ruining the fun."

That voice.

A searing white rage overcame Faythe in an instant, and the moment she saw Maverick Blackfair...all she knew was vengeance. All she saw was him standing behind her father, his sword plunged straight through him.

He took her father from her.

Faythe's magick left her palms before any rational thought could intervene. Maverick's blue fire exploded into it, but her light was stronger, blasting him right through the stone wall.

She lost herself to a state of mind she'd only felt once before. The moment Maverick had killed her father. This place sharpened every emotion to a weapon that made her feel unstoppable.

Faythe found Maverick retreating over a pile of rocks, and she didn't think twice before sending another attack. Over the pulse in her ears and the electric blast of power, she thought someone might have called her name. That wasn't enough to take even a fraction of her attention off her target. She destroyed another wall, taking them into the body of the castle, where ruins were made of glass and white marble.

She didn't know how she was moving so fast to keep up with Maverick, who was still *alive*.

"You're a coward," she roared in anguish to him.

He ran like one. Killed like one. Faythe didn't care about his life as the Prince of Dalrune, nor that Nik wanted to see him one last time. Faythe *had* to kill him.

She didn't expect the dark fae who'd killed her, then her father, to be so bold as to show his face to her again, so closely within reach. What enraged her more was how casual he appeared. His days went on with nothing changed, while her father would never see another. Would never get to spend another with *her*, rebuilding all they'd lost over their estranged years.

Faythe's grief was the only thing to dampen the urgency of her pursuit. She lost sight of Maverick, but her power was screaming inside her to find him and make him feel what she was.

"You have to stop!" Zaiana called.

The darkest side of Faythe perked up at her voice. She turned, realizing she didn't need to find Maverick—the greatest way to hurt him was by hurting Zaiana. When she met those purple eyes watching her with wary disbelief, the first sensation of doubt crept through her.

Faythe needed Zaiana. She didn't know exactly why—maybe she would never figure that out—but even back when they had the dark fae captive in Rhyenelle cells, Faythe had never celebrated that fact as capturing the enemy but capturing the most unexpected kernel of *hope*.

"Why?" Faythe asked. "Why do you care for him?"

Zaiana's mouth opened, but her words faltered. She didn't know herself.

At the sound of a crack behind her, Faythe spun, catching a flicker of cobalt hurtling toward her. She managed to defend herself, her gold magick swallowing his fire. In the same breath she sent a spear of his own fire power back to him, striking his chest. Faythe used Shadowporting next. He was not getting away from her.

Appearing at his feet while he used the wall to push himself back to standing, Faythe swiped a shard of glass from the ground and lunged, cutting her palm, which bled crimson while the edge she pressed into his throat started dripping black.

"We have to stop meeting like this," he groaned in pain.

"Do you regret anything you've done?" Faythe snarled.

Maverick was far too composed. Accepting. He didn't stare at her with loathing or anger. There was nothing. Absolutely *nothing* in those onyx eyes.

"No," he said calmly.

Faythe's teeth gritted harder, the glass cutting them both deeper.

"Why did you do it? All of it? Marvellas and the masters took everything from you, and yet you did their bidding."

"You wouldn't understand."

Gods, she wanted to kill him so badly her whole body vibrated with violence. But something was making her hesitate. Perhaps a desperate need to know *why*. Staring into his eyes was like staring into the dead. Yet she refused to believe his actions were mindlessly evil. There *had* to be a reason, and if she killed him without knowing, she wondered if she would ever find closure over why her father had to die.

"I told you to stay away from her," Marvellas's sharp voice bellowed from behind.

Maverick's jaw twitched in reaction, slipping his sight over Faythe's head.

"It was an unfortunate crossing of paths," he lied.

"I'll take her back."

Faythe stiffened at the sound of Captain Daegal approaching. Of Rainyte Ashfyre coming to retrieve her.

Faythe sliced Maverick's neck before she felt the clamp of Magestone around her wrist, causing her to drop the shard of glass. Maverick clutched his neck, which spilled with black blood—not deep enough to kill, but she hoped it would scar.

"I hope you never rest a day knowing I'm going to kill you. Doing so now would be too damn merciful for all you've done," she said venomously.

"I look forward to it," was all he said.

Faythe couldn't hate someone more than she did Maverick, but for now, she let Nyte restrain her other wrist and lead her away.

They stopped before Marvellas, and the Spirit looked down at Faythe's hand bleeding onto the floor. Reaching for her, Marvellas examined her deep cut thoughtfully.

"Your anger is understandable," she said calmly. Then her blazing gold eyes flicked up to Nyte wearing Daegal's face. "Dress this properly and leave the Magestone out of her flesh. It seems she might be ready to try to break the ruin again sooner than I thought."

Faythe's heart was in her throat for the seconds Marvellas stared at her son, but not even a flicker of recognition disturbed her placid face. It was pure tragedy but a relief.

She couldn't fathom what Nyte would be feeling.

He pushed her, keeping in character as Captain Daegal. They passed Zaiana, and once again Faythe couldn't relax with the look she pinned on Nyte, as if he were a puzzle she couldn't figure out.

Back at the cells, Nyte led her inside then locked the door, with himself outside it.

"What now?" Faythe asked him.

She was aware there was no telling what Nyte would or could do now. She'd made the choice to give him the power of a physical body, and what he did with it was entirely his own control.

"Now, you're still trapped, and I'm free."

CHAPTER FORTY

Tarly

They weren't allowed to leave this room. Tarly couldn't really complain—his makeshift bed of a sack of flour and an empty burlap sack was far more tolerable than the icy stone and prickly dead hay of his previous cell.

Jakon and Marlowe had each other and seemed to have made the best of what they had over the many weeks they'd been here. Tarly massaged his stiff good shoulder as he sat up, finding the humans already awake and chatting quietly to each other. He could eavesdrop, but he decided against it.

Then there was Reuben…a man who'd lost his sanity to Marvellas, cowering to himself in the corner, often muttering nonsense as if his thoughts were of a different person. His brown eyes darted all over the room, with no attention on his true surroundings, as if he were in a darker place none of them could comprehend.

Some of the things Tarly caught from his incoherent ramblings were mentions of the ruin and Faythe and how terrified he was—for himself, for her, for the world. Little made sense. Reuben often asked Jakon and Marlowe about Aurialis's ruin, convinced they knew where it was. While Jakon was growing frustrated with him, Marlowe kept so patient and kind, making sure he ate from their small rations and kept warm. Unlike them, Reuben wasn't made to stay in this room under watch—he just chose to some days and nights.

Tarly's bad arm was numb. It had frightened him the first time it had happened, and he hadn't alarmed Nerida at the time. Throughout the morning, feeling returned to it, but he wondered if there would be a time it would stay lame, and he would no longer be able to even use his bow.

He was becoming more useless by the day.

With that thought he stood, righting his clothing and slipping back into his position on the bench. He'd been here a week at least. Callen hadn't come back. They were given food and water and escorted to relieve themselves or bathe under watch, but otherwise, they were locked in here. Tarly glanced over the table and the counters filling up with red vials of Phoenix Blood, but to his other side, Marlowe had only achieved another dozen, spelled for its intended use: to amplify the magickal abilities some fae already possessed.

"Does it hurt?" Marlowe asked gently. "It's not until long past afternoon you start using that arm."

The numb hand rested over his lap, while his other worked more intensely to compensate, grinding the herbs he needed, mixing the liquids, chopping other things. It had become routine now, and he didn't mind it.

"There's a dull ache. I have a pain-relieving tonic."

From Nerida, and it was running low. He'd watched her make it and knew how to replicate it, but he didn't have her magick to add to it, which he feared was the only thing strong enough to relieve his pain.

"I'm still trying to understand you," Jakon said, less hostile than the beginning of the week but still holding his suspicion of him.

"You don't have to understand. Come on—we have work to do."

He watched them exchange a wary look.

Over the week, he done a lot of observing them, trying to understand *their* motives here. One thing he couldn't shake was how well Marlowe appeared at times. Jakon would make her laugh, or she'd wander around the room in a picture of health. Then, other times, especially when the guards would bring food or escort her out, anyone would think she couldn't keep this task going for long before it killed her.

Tarly's next move was a risk, but he scribbled on a piece of parchment, leaving it under a bottle he handed across to her. He didn't make eye contact, keeping as disinterested in them and as focused on his task as possible.

They were always alone in this room, but maybe that was the security Callen wanted them to believe they had to watch them slip up and reveal an ulterior motive. He kept vigilant.

Tarly waited all day for her to respond, but a message never returned to him.

At night, when they retired from the duty, Tarly spent his last hours crafting arrows. It was more for distraction than enjoyment. His bad arm gave him enough functionality to whittle the scraps of wood he found, and he had a pouch of arrowheads. He didn't tell anyone he'd taken negligible pieces of the Phoenix feather, only wanting to add something special to the fletching of his next craft.

A soft knock sounded on the door, and he exchanged a puzzled look with Jakon and Marlowe across the room in their sleeping corner. No one ever bothered to announce themselves. After a pause, when no one answered, a head shorter than he expected slipped around the door as it creaked open.

"Oh, sorry. I didn't realize how late it was."

She was a younger dark fae with long black hair, and for a second, he thought of Zaiana in her youth.

"You're Amaya," Marlowe said warmly.

The dark fae nodded. "Maverick said I'm to keep an eye on you. He's left."

Of course the dark fae who were born had once been young, children with the same complete innocence as anyone else. Amaya was at least seventeen in human appearance, but there was something about her that had retained a harmless nature.

When Amaya's eyes slipped to him, her brows lifted, and excitement sparked in her eyes. "You're an archer?" She crossed to him without hesitation. He didn't answer, but when she spied his bow behind him she gasped softly. "Your bow is incredible."

Tarly didn't see the harm in showing her. In fact, it was unexpected to have such enthusiastic company for the skill.

"It's made from silver oak," he said, passing it to her. It was too big for her to use, but her entire expression lit up tracing the craftsmanship.

"From Fenstead?"

"Yes. It was a gift from my father long ago."

He didn't know why he'd added that second part. The memory lashed him—a time when his mother was alive and his father had loved him. Now, after the passing of his mate, Tarly had become nothing more than an object of his sorrowful resentment for resembling her so much.

"That's pretty," Amaya said, her dark eyes fixed on the arrow he'd finished in his hands.

Tarly smiled, considering the arrow, which had red woven into the regular pheasant feathers he'd stored.

"I've been saving this one," he said, holding it out to her. "Use it when your fear is strongest and your aim threatens to waver. Even the greatest archers will face those uncertain moments. This arrow won't miss."

A tale crafted of hope was not a lie, and watching the darkling's eyes widen with wonder over the ordinary arrow he'd crafted, it was worth it.

"Why are you giving it to me?"

Tarly shrugged. "I have a feeling you'll make better use of it than I will."

He didn't know why his attention drifted to Marlowe across the room. She watched them with an endearing smile. In her eyes was something that broke a shiver over Tarly, as if she saw something in the exchange he couldn't begin to comprehend.

Amaya started talking about her archery, and Tarly was glad for the distraction of a topic he was well experienced with—more than anyone he knew for once. It wasn't an uncommon skill, but there was a specific mastery, so many tricks and styles that very few took care to learn beyond the primary purpose of aim and hit.

The dark fae wasn't the only intruder that night.

"I heard there was a party in here."

Tarly didn't immediately recognize the brown-haired fae, but when he turned to look down at him, the facial resemblance to Kyleer Galentithe and matching eye color quickly gave him away. Izaiah, he recalled his younger brother's name. Who was followed in by a blond dark fae male.

Izaiah whistled low, swiping up one of the Phoenix Blood potions. "You've been busy. How many of these are spelled?"

"Around five dozen," Marlowe said.

Izaiah set the bottle down with a click of his tongue. "That can't be satisfactory for Dakodas."

The room was littered with hundreds of unspelled potions.

"She's starting to pick up speed," Jakon added.

"The war is all but won in their favor with these," the blond dark fae said. Though it should be a triumph for his side, Tarly detected a hint of fear. "The dark fae with human blood were already a force Faythe would struggle to contend with, but now…if all the fae with abilities have amplified magick, she doesn't stand a chance."

A dark, sinister tension settled throughout the room. As if they should all celebrate the fact, considering right now they were on the side with the most power, and they could keep it that way if they wished.

"Why are you here?" Tarly asked Izaiah.

"Curiosity and boredom. This calm before the break of either side has me jittery in no pleasant way," Izaiah said, taking up a lean against one of the counters.

"What is Dakodas doing?" Jakon asked.

"Who knows? I rarely see her, in fact. Perhaps she's exploring our lands, seeing what she'll lay claim to when Marvellas conquers it all."

"So Zaiana, Maverick, and Dakodas are gone from the castle?" Tarly concluded.

"Seems so, but I wouldn't get comfortable with the fact. They have many spies, and Malin is losing his sanity by the minute. I can't tell what he'll do next," Izaiah said.

"It's the Phoenix Blood. He's taking too much to keep his mind ability," Marlowe said.

"Didn't you say Nikalias has kept the effects of a potion for months? Why can Malin only use it for a day?" Izaiah wondered.

Marlowe shrugged. "Nik is more powerful."

Tarly knew Nik's ability was strong, but still he wondered if Marlowe had imbued more magick into the potions she'd made for Nik, unwittingly or not.

"Why is he taking it so often?" Tarly asked.

"It's helping him twist the minds of suspicious council members or reluctant generals. He's slipping his control. He's been taking these potions almost daily," Izaiah answered.

Jakon said, "So our only concern is Malin right now. None of us have access to his council to know what he's been planning throughout Rhyenelle, and to gauge the extent of his tarnishing of Faythe's name with them."

"You're speaking as if we're all on the same side here," Tarly said apprehensively, with a deliberate glance at the two dark fae in the room.

It was Marlowe who said, "We can stop pretending we aren't. I've seen it—that's all I can say. We don't need to know the specifics of why, but none of us have switched allegiance."

"You're bold to admit that with us here," Tynan said.

"No, I'm still right. Your allegiance has always been to Zaiana, and you know there's been a shift coming with her, even if it hasn't fully locked in her mind yet."

No one objected to that statement. Everything he'd heard about the notorious dark fae, including his short encounter with her, told him the opposite of Marlowe's judgment. But what did he know?

"Where has she scuttled off to?" Izaiah asked Tynan curiously.

The dark fae pursed his lips, clearly in turmoil if trusting the people in this room was disobeying an order from Zaiana—or helping her.

"All I know is that she discovered our still hearts are a curse, and she wants answers."

It wasn't the whole truth, and everyone knew it. Tynan knew *exactly* where Zaiana had gone to start looking. No one pressed further on the answer that was satisfactory enough.

"The threads of Marvellas's lies and manipulation are starting to unravel, it seems," Izaiah said.

"Once you achieve what you need here, you need to go to High Farrow," Marlowe said.

"What does High Farrow have to do with any of this?" Izaiah asked.

"Everything. It's where it all began, and it's where it has to end."

Her words lingered an ominous foreboding between them all.

Izaiah said, "Can we get a when, all-knowing oracle?"

"Don't mock her," Jakon warned.

"For all we know, she's standing there with the answers to all our problems."

"It doesn't work like that."

"It's fine, Jak," Marlowe said.

"It's not," Jakon snapped, silencing the room with his anger. "None of you have a damn clue what her ability even means or how it works, so instead of pointing accusations, work on your own plots to get out of here alive."

"You can achieve it," Marlowe said, her sight fixed on Izaiah. The fae's jaw shifted to an answer no one else knew the question to. "But even if you conquer power, the bigger challenge will be not to lose yourself."

Izaiah pushed off the bench. "Thanks for the advice," he grumbled, nearly setting Jakon off again.

Tarly stiffened when Marlowe's gaze shifted to him. "You've been deceived as meticulously as the dark fae have about their hearts. I think you know it too. You just have to figure out how."

Tarly's chest thumped wildly. She couldn't mean... No. His mind scrambled, not fully present for her next words.

"There are infinite ends to this war, and few of them are triumphant in Faythe's favor. She is the one, and if she falls, we all fall. But she cannot rise without us."

The tale of Faythe Ashfyre was certainly one to rival fiction, but he was somewhat honored to be written into the story, however small. It was why he had to leave Nerida, but also why he was determined to return to her for however many days he had left by the time he reached her. All he could hope for now was to make it to the end, just to see a glimpse of the better world promised by the most unlikely of people.

It had been some hours since the dark fae and Izaiah had left, but Tarly couldn't sleep. He tossed against his awkward arrangement on the sacks for some time before he sensed he wasn't the only restless mind tonight.

"Are you awake?" Marlowe whispered softly. She'd crossed to him with careful silence.

"Yes."

She didn't say anything else before she came all the way over, and when she sat against the wall next to him, Tarly got up too. They sat side by side in a strange silence for moment. He couldn't place what was wrong, only that his gut was unsettled as if he were bracing in the calm before a storm.

"It's terrible, isn't it, feeling death's touch grow warmer but never knowing when it'll claim?"

Tarly's chest sped a little. He couldn't fathom her gift of being an oracle. In fact, he didn't think "gift" was an appropriate term for the burden of knowledge she carried.

"Do you speak of yourself?" he asked carefully.

"What I see is not always so clear."

"You knew I'd come here." He'd suspected it. At first, he'd thought her kind reception was just her nature, but over the week, he'd caught glimpses of her that had felt more accurate than that.

Marlowe didn't answer. Tarly stiffened when she took his hand, only briefly, to place something cool into his palm. He knew what it was before he looked down at the bottle.

"I have no use for this," he said.

"You'll know what to do with it," Marlowe said, her voice so soothing he didn't know why it inspired sympathy for her.

"If you're planning something—"

"I'm not." She cut him off.

Tarly pursed his lips, fiddling with the vial of Phoenix Blood.

"You must have a plan to get out of here, but what are you waiting for?" Tarly asked.

"I don't have any plan, but I wondered if I could ask something of you."

"If I can grant it, I will."

"Make sure Jakon gets out when the time comes."

His head turned to her, and an urge to protect her filled his chest. "You're getting out together."

"But if something goes wrong, he'll need someone to force him to leave even if I have to stay."

"Marlowe…you have to tell him this—"

"I can't. You've seen how he is, fiercely loyal and so brave. He'll fight no matter what, but I fear it might get him killed."

She choked on the last word, and Tarly's whole body flushed cold. Had she seen a vision of her husband's death? Tarly couldn't fathom such a burden; was sure he would go insane if he harbored a possible fate to pass where Nerida could die.

"Please," she whispered at his silence.

"I promise," he said. He had to. "I'll look out for both of you."

She smiled, her shoulders relaxing a fraction. "The most silent warriors can make the greatest impact, Tarly Wolverlon. I hope you never forget that."

Tarly mustered a small smile, but his gut was unsettled with a need to protect the gentle human. He just didn't know what from.

"You've had the ability to make these potions far faster all this time," Tarly said, not leaving it to question.

"Yes. I've been buying time."

"They'll punish you when they find out."

Marlowe said nothing at that. Instead she shifted to her knees, facing him fully. She was so delicate in her human beauty it was hard to imagine the depth of her troubles. How someone so kind and hopeful could be tormented with such vicious visions.

"It was Faythe who suggested you come here, wasn't it?"

Tarly nodded. Faythe hadn't asked him to, but she'd placed the option into his hands to abandon course with Nerida and seek his own salvation, to offer what he could to the war efforts instead.

"She told me where the Light Temple Ruin is—I just need to find a moment to try to retrieve it."

"Izaiah knows too."

That sparked hope in his mind. If the Galentithe brother was still on Faythe's side, all he had to do was get him to retrieve it while he had free rein of the castle. Then Tarly could make his escape. Until Tarly realized, with a drop of uncertainty about Izaiah's loyalty…

"Why hasn't he fled with it himself?"

Marlowe's face pinched. "He's trying to use the power within for himself."

Now he really was concerned about Izaiah's allegiance. He was already relaying all they'd spoken of earlier, which would be condemning if he took it to Dakodas.

"I don't trust him," Tarly said.

"Marlowe?" Jakon interrupted them, pushing himself up. Tarly could see his accusing frown through the dark at finding his wife all the way over here.

"We couldn't sleep, and you were out cold," Marlowe teased.

She went to him, and they talked quietly to themselves. Jakon draped their blanket around her and hugged her to him. Tarly had to look away, settling back down.

He couldn't shake the tension Marlowe had left in her wake.

Tarly stayed awake, reeling over how they would all escape. Faythe was right—they were all threads of fate, and somehow, he knew they were important.

He wouldn't be of any use if he wasn't well and rested, so he forced his eyes to close. In the confines of his mind, he found peace, pretending for a while that no matter where he went, it would lead him back to Nerida one way or another, and he couldn't wait for her to reprimand him for leaving.

CHAPTER FORTY-ONE

Izaiah

Izaiah's whole body ached from the many practices with the ruin so far, but he'd be damned if he let it affect how good he looked sauntering down a hall. Especially when he felt a particular presence nearby.

Tynan appeared around the bend ahead, walking toward him. Izaiah wore his usual devious side-smile, which triggered Tynan's familiar glower. He was beginning to enjoy the natural harmony of this tense greeting.

"Another suicide attempt today?" Tynan muttered under his breath when they stopped beside each other.

Izaiah hummed, mirroring Tynan's cross-armed stance. "It's likely, yes."

Tynan cast his eyes up as if in a plea for sanity. "At least let me have breakfast first."

"Meet me in the study in an hour. We can fit in some literacy lessons too."

Izaiah made to leave, but Tynan caught his wrist. It was bold when accompanied with the heated stare that drifted to his lips.

When he heard shuffling and thumping down the hall, Izaiah retrieved a dagger, pushing Tynan to the wall. The dark fae was caught unawares, slamming into it with a grunt and staring with wide, pissed-off eyes.

"Can't give anyone the wrong impression," Izaiah said, scratching the point of the dagger under his chin while delighting in Tynan's vulnerability under his blade.

When the person arrived within view, Izaiah stole a glance. Who he saw slackened his pressure against Tynan immediately. The dark fae pushed him off, and Izaiah caught his own stumble, too stunned and confused to care as he righted himself and faced down the hall.

"I can't come up with a single good reason as to why you might be here," Izaiah said.

Augustine, despite Izaiah's accusing reception, smiled brightly, tipping his tricorn to reveal more of his blue eyes. His wooden leg tapped in a steady rhythm toward them. He'd long mastered his balance with it.

"Ah, my boy, pondering reason for other people's motives is a sure spiral to madness."

Izaiah's expression flattened. "I've never been a boy."

Gus came right up to him, patting a large hand to his shoulder as if they were old friends. No—in fact, Gus looked at him like he did see a child, though not in any condescending manner. He couldn't figure out what had the pirate so high-spirited considering what he'd walked into.

"Who are you?" Tynan asked with an edge of hostility.

"Augustine. And you are Tynan Silverfair, Zaiana's second-in-command."

That only added to Tynan's growing tension.

"You should really let people introduce themselves. It's creepy when you do it," Izaiah said. He added to Tynan, "Gus here is a pirate, and despite appearing human, he's a centuries-old Oracle. Marlowe's biological father."

Augustine's smile fell, and his blue gaze flicked over his shoulder. Izaiah realized too late he'd blurted too much, having not felt the quiet presence behind him.

Izaiah turned, finding Marlowe at the end of the hall, staring at them all with wide doe eyes as if she'd been caught somewhere wrong.

"Shit," Izaiah muttered. "Marlowe—"

She turned away, disappearing around the corner swiftly, without another word.

"Marlowe," Augustine echoed as he stared after the ghost of her.

"You didn't know she was here?" Izaiah asked.

Augustine drew in a long breath. He didn't answer.

Tynan asked instead, "Does Malin know of your arrival?"

"I don't think I would've made it past his threshold if he didn't."

"This castle isn't *his*," Izaiah muttered under his breath.

"The pretense keeps you alive. Let me warn you, he's hanging onto his sanity by a thread, and none of you are safe in his volatile proximity."

Izaiah wasn't afraid of Malin Ashfyre, but he couldn't deny Gus's warning shivered down his spine. He had noticed something different about the prince who was growing worse each day. He'd always managed to carry himself so composed and arrogant...but he was slipping. Izaiah couldn't be sure if it was the Phoenix Blood he kept consuming when he couldn't hold the conscious mind ability for more than a day, or if it was the weight of his stolen crown that was spiraling him to paranoia and madness.

"Why have you come?" Izaiah asked.

"To offer my ships and allegiance. Malin was most forthcoming to it, as he needs all the allies he can get with the resistance to his claim on the throne."

He soured at that, slowly shedding his warmth toward the pirate that had barely been a trickle to begin with. Augustine was a fickle bastard. He played with his gift.

"He has all the nobles backing his claim," Tynan pointed out.

"I know. Quite cunning, he was, to achieve that and pin Faythe as an outsider responsible for her father's downfall. But the people are not led by politics and scheming but with their hearts and beliefs. They still spread the tales of Faythe Ashfyre, the human turned fae, Agalhor's declared heir, the Phoenix Queen. They have not given up on their belief in her, and that is a power greater than nobility Malin is fighting against."

That was a statement of inspiration at least.

Izaiah glanced down the deserted hall even though he couldn't sense anyone nearby. He was beginning to grow uneasy talking about such things in the open.

"Where are you going now?" Izaiah asked.

"Well, it seems I have a daughter to meet."

Izaiah winced, apologetic for that sensitive knowledge he'd let slip unknowingly when she was near. However, Gus didn't seem fazed by it, as if he knew she would be there. Nothing was out of the realm of suspicion with this man.

Gus smiled pleasantly before shifting past him and making off in the direction Marlowe had gone, back to her area for making the potions, he suspected. Then he tensed, wondering if he should follow when he realized...did Gus have the same magick to spell the potions too? Had his offering of allegiance with his ship and crew been of the least interest to Malin compared to this skill that would rapidly advance the production of Phoenix Blood?

Izaiah didn't know what to do if it were true. How to stop him without suspicion. He couldn't kill Gus, though the thought crossed his mind.

"Change of plan for today?" Tynan pondered as if reading Izaiah's contemplation.

"For now, no," he said, still mulling over the possibilities—everything Gus could potentially do here that could truly work against them. "But we could use that little darkling of yours to keep an eye on him."

"Since when did we turn into a team?"

Izaiah ignored that, clapping a hand to his back before walking off. "Study in an hour," he reminded him over his shoulder.

CHAPTER FORTY-TWO

Nikalias

Nik kept his back pressed to a wall in the shadows, only curving his head around the corner to scout the street in Fenstead. It was thanks to Lycus they'd made it this far so efficiently despite the dark fae that crawled through the kingdom. The Fenstead general navigated them through inconspicuous routes to get them to the heart of the kingdom.

He could see the castle from here. Its tall spires still stood as a proud beacon of grace despite the darkness that smothered these once prosperous and peaceful lands.

Nik's soul yearned to get there, and he hoped with every fiber of his being that Tauria was within her castle, waiting for him.

"Is that…?" Lycus let his thought trail off, then the general slipped out of hiding, darting across the wide street and into a narrow alley.

Nik swore, having no choice but to follow him.

He had to jog after Lycus, whose attention had latched onto something. No—*someone*, considering their chase. Nik only wished he would confer his motives. When Nik heard signs of a struggle, he picked up pace, skidding around the next corner of the back-alley paths he'd lost sight of Lycus in.

Nik drew his sword, but his mind prepared to breach the assailant Lycus was engaged in a struggle with. It took him a second to distinguish the general from the other male clad fully in black, hidden by mask and hood, like them. The pair were of similar build and fought with hands alone.

Before Nik had to intervene, Lycus's hood slipped down as he threw the assailant over his shoulder, ending the fight. Nik advanced, pointing his sword at the assailant's chest for extra measure.

"Old age is getting to you, Lord Berron," Lycus commented in far too friendly a manner, and Nik suffered emotional whiplash.

Lycus pushed up from pinning the male down with a knee on his chest, then his hand reached down in offering.

Lord Berron's dark brown eyes shifted warily to the tip of Nik's sword.

"He's a friend. A trusted adviser of Tauria's father," Lycus explained.

Nik wasn't so quick to trust. "And where does his loyalty lie now, after all this time?"

"With my queen," Berron answered with a hint of irritation that his allegiance was being questioned.

Nik reluctantly sheathed his sword, and Berron was helped up by Lycus.

"You look like you're in hiding," Lycus commented.

"I have been since the kingdom fell. It's been a long century, but by Gods, is it a relief to see a familiar face. Another strong pillar in Fenstead's primary defense."

Lycus and Berron's hands clapped together before they pulled each other into an embrace. Nik began to relax. He trusted the general would know if Berron was being untruthful.

"You could have fled to Rhyenelle with us. There we rebuilt a strong army. Not the numbers we once had, but our soldiers have been training tirelessly, knowing their objective would be to reclaim this kingdom someday."

"Yet you come alone," Berron said, careful with his bitterness. The lord's eyes skimmed over Nik. "And so does the King of High Farrow. So I assume you have not come to aid us but to take our queen, who has only just returned."

Nik said, "Tauria is here?"

Berron nodded, and all the tension that had been growing in Nik the whole journey to Fenstead didn't deflate—it sharpened into determination as he cast his sight up in the direction of the castle. He couldn't see it from the high walls of this alley, but Tauria was so close it took everything in him not to abandon all strategy and reason to march right through the front door to get to her.

"You've made contact with her?" Lycus asked.

"She made contact with us," Berron said.

Nik's attention was gripped wholly. "Tell us everything."

"Best if I show you first," he said.

Berron led them carefully, and Nik put his complete faith in Lycus that they weren't letting this fae lead them into a trap for Mordecai.

They headed underground through a drain. Nik was familiar with this type of labyrinth, considering he'd used such passages to leave his own city in High Farrow many times while his father was king.

At the end of a wide cylindrical tunnel, Nik could see the column that expanded vertically. They stepped onto a metal balcony and stared over the expanse. It was a hideout. Many fae were littered around the stacked balconies, and on the floor below.

"There's been a rebel movement all this time?" Nik concluded.

"We've been growing our numbers slowly since the monarchy fell," Berron informed him.

Nik's chest swelled with pride for the resilient people of Fenstead. He knew Tauria would have been awestruck to have seen this, and that only inspired his need to see her more.

"What is Tauria's plan?" Nik asked. Because there was no chance she'd seen this beacon of hope and hadn't started conspiring.

They'd come to get Tauria away from Mordecai's clutches, but Nik knew Tauria would not leave now without gaining back Fenstead.

"She's been getting as many of the rebels into the castle walls as possible, posing as staff. Once we have enough allies within, we stand a chance of taking back the castle at least. Had you come with our army, we might just have stood a chance at pushing the dark fae out of the kingdom town by town."

Nik exchanged a look with Lycus. The general said, "We didn't just bring Fenstead's army. We have legions of High Farrow and Rhyenelle forces too."

Berron's eyes bulged. "Then what are we waiting for? We need to set positions, alert Tauria, and…"

Everyone stilled, hearing the disruption at the same time. It was a noise that stood every hair on Nik's body. The snarls were distantly familiar. Then the scent…

"Dark fae," Nik said in horror. "The most vicious and beyond humanity of them."

As he said it, the rumbling snarls grew from the passages, and the first cries came from a few levels above them as they infiltrated the space.

"Did you lead them here?" A woman came rushing toward them, accusation outlined harshly on her face.

"Of course not," Lycus snapped.

When her eyes fell on him, recognition relaxed her expression.

They didn't get a moment to converse further as dark fae dropped from the balconies and spilled in from the tunnels at all angles. The force of them was terrifying. Nik had only seen one this savage under his library in High Farrow. It had bitten Faythe and nearly killed her.

Nik's sword sliced through the onslaught of them, but there were many. Too many. They were completely overwhelmed and wouldn't hold out long. It was hard to believe these creatures were once ordinary fae. The attempt to Transition them must have gone horribly wrong to have stripped them of sanity and morality.

He needed a plan. These were all Tauria's people, which meant they were *his*, and they'd remained hidden and ready to fight for decades. To see them all be slaughtered now so quickly and brutally would be a tragedy that would break Tauria.

"Where is the main water system?" Nik yelled over the chaos.

Berron answered, his voice distorted from the fighting, "Two floors up, in the east vault."

"Everyone needs to prepare for an evacuation. Keep fighting, but get close to an exit."

Nik's blade drowned in black blood to get to a tunnel opening. He took a slash of claws to his arm and narrowly avoided fangs that snapped close to his thigh. Nik raced through the passage and climbed up the ladders that took him two levels up. He would have to flood the tunnel system and hope most of the rebels could make it out before the thrashing of water.

He found the giant wheel that would release a catastrophic amount of water, but there was no other way to wipe out so many dark fae. Nik heaved, but the metal, so long dormant, barely turned an inch. He kept trying, aware of the hisses and snarls growing louder, heading toward him.

Come on. He chanted for momentum, but it wasn't turning fast enough. He would have to leave it and fight soon, and with the velocity that carried through the passage, he didn't know if he would get another free moment to try again.

Nik strained and groaned, pushing the wheel with everything he had. A small stream of water trickled from the circular opening, but there was a long way to go. He focused everything on it, growing that stream that began to spray his face. Shadows grew down the tunnel ahead. He wasn't going to make it.

Then the resistance lessened, and Nik's determination surged. Because Lycus had joined him, and together, the opening crawled open faster. Water sloshed under their feet, and then…

"Hold on tight!" Nik yelled. Lycus lunged for the nearby ladder to hold onto it as Nik's next push unleashed the force of the trapped water.

The dark fae who raced savagely for him were all swept away in the brutal current. Nik's body was dragged, but his hands held desperately to the wheel.

Lycus reached an arm toward him while keeping purchase on the ladder. The water level was rising up to his knees. Nik reached back, only skimming his fingers, but on his next try he threw more momentum out. Lycus gripped his arm, pulling him toward the ladder. As soon as Nik could grab it, they scrambled up it.

Nik followed Lycus's lead until they found a way out. The roaring of water still echoed in his ears as Nik leaned his hands on his thighs, catching his breath.

"Do we need to shut off the water?" Nik asked.

To his relief, Lycus shook his head. "It will lead back into the rivers around the valleys. These tunnels were designed to help with flood control, but there hasn't been a river break in centuries."

Nik straightened, scanning the eerily quiet streets with dread.

"Did any make it out?" he dreaded to ask.

Had he just drowned dozens of his own people?

It was Berron who answered, hobbling over to them. "As luck would have it, most of the rebels had already left the underground. Tauria called action tonight. Tallia, one of our leaders, managed to swiftly eliminate the dark fae within the castle, and the instruction was for the rest of the rebellion to be let inside to strengthen the force for when the retaliation would come, but…" Berron paused to skim a look toward Nik.

"Where's Tauria?" Nik asked immediately.

"Mordecai took her. She's been spotted in the middle of their war camp, which has expanded to stretch across the entire valley over the decades."

Nik's rage boiled. He turned to Lycus. "Ready our forces."

"We are a little over half the number that sits on the valley hills," he argued.

Lycus was thinking logistically, strategically. Nik only knew his mate, the queen of this damned kingdom, was behind, held in the midst of the enemy camping on their doorstep. The mockery was enough to drive him mad, and the thought of anyone hurting her threw his caution to the flames.

"It'll create enough of a distraction for me to slip in and get her out. Then you call a retreat," Nik reasoned.

Lycus's expression firmed. He exchanged a look with Berron to mull it over. "That could work, but I need you to understand you're all but asking our soldiers to walk into slaughter."

"For their queen and kingdom, that is their pledge. As their king, I will be the one to ask it of them."

Lycus didn't disagree nor argue.

Nik looked up at the moon and felt Tauria within it. He always did. He just needed her to hold on a little longer before he came for her.

CHAPTER FORTY-THREE

Zaiana

When she reached the cells, Zaiana knew she shouldn't have come. Everything in her was at a painful tug-of-war, wanting to retreat and desperate to get closer to him.

She'd lost her fight to stay away from engaging with him and saw him through the bars of the many empty cells before she reached his. Kyleer was leaning against the back wall, one knee bent for his elbow to be propped up on, and his hand shielded his eyes.

"I guess it was only a matter of time before they called you in to enjoy this," he said. His voice was stripped of any emotion.

"Why would I enjoy it?" she asked.

Kyleer let his hand fall to look at her, and when she met those moss-green irises she wasn't prepared for the yearning that pulled in her. Especially when they speared nothing but ice in her direction.

"Our positions have switched. Don't tell me you don't find a certain ironic amusement to it."

Zaiana curled her fingers around one of the bars. "I enjoy flying. I often enjoy killing. Watching you sit in a pitiful heap…I'm not finding much of a thrill, no."

Kyleer's smile was a blade, and his laughter pointed the knife.

"What have they sent you here for? To see if my weakness for you is still there? Tell them to skip straight to the physical stuff."

Her jaw worked. He assumed she was here by Marvellas's order. Zaiana didn't correct him. The Spirit was so concerned with Faythe right now that Zaiana wondered if she'd forgotten the leverage she had with him against the heir.

"I warned you not to fall for me," she said.

"I didn't. Not really. I fell for your performance."

Zaiana tried to ignore the tightening in her stomach with that. "Why are you such a fool to have gotten yourself captured?"

"Don't waste your breath, Zai. You're far too smart to believe I'll tell you anything after what you did."

"I thought you were smarter than this," she said.

"The truth is something incomprehensible to you." He stood, and the resounding clank of his Magestone chains rattled a fury in her. "Imagine a loyalty where someone would damn themselves for their friend. Faythe is far more than my queen. Reylan is far more than my general."

Zaiana didn't believe that was the sole reason he was here. They were planning something from within, just as Zaiana had in Rhyenelle. She was patient enough to figure it out sooner or later.

"She is alone. Your plan was never going to place you two cozy in a cell together."

His smile showed teeth, but there was nothing friendly in it. "If you're to inflict my physical punishment, get on with it."

Kyleer approached the bars. Zaiana didn't move, though his proximity flipped her stomach.

"I might even enjoy it, coming from you."

His large hand lashed around hers, tightening against her instinct to retreat. All he did was hold her with eyes of hypnotizing, deadly beauty.

"Maybe you haven't been provoked enough to strike your lightning back into your palms," he challenged.

She ripped her hand from under his. "Is that what you're trying to do?"

Kyleer's mouth quirked a fraction. "I'm just bored, I guess." He took up a side-lean against the wall.

Zaiana could hardly breathe right from the lingering scent of his blood. "Did you get that dressed?" she asked, indicating the stab wound she'd inflicted in his side.

"There was hardly time."

"If it gets infected from your mortal pace of healing in those shackles, don't count on the same treatment you offered me."

"No bath?"

She gave him her deepest scowl.

He paced to the back of the cell. "Terrible hospitality. Anything I can do to get an upgrade?"

"What are you doing, Kyleer?"

"This method of interrogation doesn't suit you. Try again."

He was the last nerve of her already thin patience.

"You're going to get yourself killed."

"Does that concern you?"

"No."

"Good. Then leave. Tell them I want Maverick to inflict any torture."

"Why him?"

Kyleer didn't answer. He didn't need to since the dark vengeance that firmed on his features told her he believed he could stand a chance against Maverick. Even in those bonds.

Zaiana admired his determination, even if emotional for his queen and misplaced. But she knew how vicious Maverick could be, and how merciless he could become.

Then again, there were times when Kyleer had this gleam in his eye that made her wonder what he was truly capable of. Especially for those he loved.

Perhaps love wasn't a weakness. Perhaps it could fuel a wrath so dangerous it could triumph over anything.

"If you're not here on their order, I'd rather you weren't here at all," he said.

The comment stung. Like a prick in her chest that spread the more she dwelled on it, trying to figure out if he truly meant it.

When she couldn't stand the hurt, she chose to leave in silence.

"Before you left, you said there would be no place for a hero with a villain," Kyleer said to her back.

Zaiana stopped walking.

"You're not a villain, Zai. You're not a hero or a victim either. You're a survivor."

Words shouldn't lasso around her as strongly as these ones did. Repeating. Tightening. Tormenting. Remembering his scars. His hand over hers with different lines, different stories, but embedded with cruelty all the same. She didn't want those words to place them on the same desolate ground, because that would mean he was within reach. That would split a seam on a void of emotions she was constantly adding stitches to.

No. It didn't matter what he saw her as.

There was no place for *him* with *her*. Not before what she had done to him, and certainly not now he despised her.

Zaiana came back to him. "I killed the last male who loved me," she said.

Kyleer's heart didn't even waver at her confession. "I didn't take you as one to enjoy tragic poetry," he said.

"It's not a damned poem," she snapped.

His mouth twitched.

"Are you hoping to exchange tragic love tales? I'll tell you how I killed my mate if you tell me how you killed yours."

"He wasn't my *mate*."

That seemed to disturb something in his chest, but Zaiana was coming to find the rhythm of his heart the most challenging to decipher. It was never so whole and steady. It always beat with fractures— too many for her to know what could cause them in someone so strong and resilient on the exterior.

Kyleer took a long, lazy inhale. "I think you should skip the bullshit, open that door, and test your many ways that you could kill me without your lightning."

"Trust I'd enjoy nothing more."

"Neither would I."

He met her dark look with a slow, enticing smile. Her skin prickled with it. What should have been ire and anger was somehow tuned to sinful desire with this stare.

"You said she died, not that you killed her."

Kyleer shrugged, tipping his head back against the stone. "The one who killed her did so because of me."

"You take fault by association?"

"Wouldn't you?"

"Unless I took their life, no."

"Ah, so the blood on your hands is a little thicker."

Her fingers clenched as if they would drip with Finnian's silver blood just to show him the truth.

"Why are you telling me this?" Kyleer asked, bored.

Zaiana resisted the impulse to hurt him and then leave him to bleed out. "For you to drop that insufferable wounded look you have as if you expect *better* of me."

Kyleer laughed bitterly. "I'm not wounded, Zai. It's going to take a lot more than luring me to you only to stab me in the back. Believe it or not, I've been through it before. You're still not that special."

She could credit him for his resilience, yet all it did was emit a sharpness in her chest that threatened to cut.

She would not bleed for him.

Kyleer said, "Go on then—tell me how you did it. It's rather tedious in here day by day, so I could use a good horror story featuring my favorite beautiful nightmare."

He riled her like no one else ever had. Not even Maverick. This was a different kind of irritation that wasn't about winning but figuring him out, maybe even *protecting* him.

Zaiana paced in front of his cell. "The Blood Trials had three stages. The first was a game. We were set at the foot of a mountain and had one week to reach the top. Many were eliminated, being killed by their competitors. I didn't spill a drop of blood to get to the top first. The second trial, we faced each other in combat. The winners would go on to compete against each other until there were only three. The final trial, we were told we would face our greatest enemy."

Kyleer had fixed his attention her without any taunt or teasing. It made her skin crawl worse than when he was getting on her nerves.

"You faced your lover," Kyleer concluded.

Zaiana glanced at her hip, at the strip of Finnian's shirt tied there on the hilt of her sword, and the memory rammed into her. "Love is always a delusion. This ideal that a single person would truly put you above anything and everything. There will always be a temptation that overpowers it."

"What was his?"

Kyleer voiced her eternal torment. She would never know. Heartache consumed her so wholly that when he'd attacked without mercy or hesitation, she'd had no choice but to fight back. Then rage embraced her for the betrayal as he tried to cut her down and she *had* to end him.

"Power. Status. Do one person's reasons really matter?"

"Was he in the running for Delegate?"

"No. He claimed he didn't want that. But perhaps that was the exchange for killing me."

Kyleer's frown deepened. "Why would they grant one person the chance to win without needing to complete the other trials?"

"You don't know their ways," she snapped. "They don't need reason to bend the rules. No one needs logic to do as they damned well please, and they're always starving for cruel entertainment at our expense."

Kyleer groaned against the ache of his wound and shackles as he straightened. "All I'm saying is, even the wicked have a motive. Surely you've found out what that had to be for him to betray you like that. It's a rather extreme way of trying to win a—no offense—hollow title, when he could have just competed himself."

She did take offense to the gibe at her title. It infuriated her, because she knew it to be true now. Her whole life she'd trained for it, thinking it would prove something, but it didn't matter; she would always remain the masters' foot soldier.

"Zai," he said. The jarring softness snapped her sight to him from her tunneling thoughts. He'd come close, right to the bars, and his moss-green eyes were searching. "Have you ever considered his will wasn't his own?"

"What?" she snapped. It was a ridiculous notion. She had been there. Felt the ferocity of his attacks. Listened to the taunts he'd goaded her with.

I never loved you.

It was all a trick.

You are weak.

Zaiana shook her head, having nothing but anger to torch those taunts she'd buried with his corpse.

"Think about it. They wanted you to be unfeeling. Their perfect, ruthless leader. They never would have accepted you falling for someone, because they've made you believe that is the ultimate weakness. That you're incapable of love."

"You don't know anything," she hissed. "You don't know what it was like down there."

"You're right. I don't. But I know you...I've *felt* you. Your biggest war will always be within yourself, because you want something you've been told your whole life you can't have. That it will always betray you, and so you try to get there first."

"I didn't want anything from you, Ky. Not then, and not now."

The skin around his eyes flexed. Zaiana was held by him. She didn't want to be, and there was a threat in her that was screaming to turn away. Because when Kyleer looked at her, he didn't see what everyone else did. Somehow, he had the ability to dive deeper, as if the vault of depravity and sin and heartbreak didn't exist to him. He saw everything and never balked.

"When are you going to break free of their manipulation to think for your damned self?"

He might as well have struck her since those words held the impact of a blow to her gut.

"I should have killed you."

"Probably. Because Gods forbid I actually shine a light on your delusions."

The key to his cell was thrust into the lock before she even knew what she was doing. His irises flashed with wicked delight when the barrier between them swung open and she marched to him.

Kyleer's back met the wall, and Zaiana braced her hands against his abdomen, leaning in close.

"I bet you're running through the many ways you think you could overpower me and escape right now," she said in a low, seductive murmur.

To her delight, Kyleer's pulse picked up in speed, not expecting this reaction from her.

"I also bet there's another voice that wants to stay," she said, pushing up on her toes, but it wasn't enough to reach his mouth unless he inched his face closer to meet her. Slowly, his head did angle down, enough that they shared breath.

Zaiana couldn't deny the closeness affected her. That she too had to silence voices in her mind that wanted to surrender to the enemy.

Just as his irises began to cloud with the same alignment of thought, it winked out with a hiss when her metal guards pressed into the wound on his side. Zaiana pushed off him, slicing into it as she did.

The scent of his blood flooded the air stronger. Zaiana was transfixed by the crimson over the metal on her middle and pointer fingers. The thirst in her throat tightened to pain. So fast she'd never experienced this rage of desire for it before. Especially not from a fae.

"Do it," he said thickly.

She hadn't heard him approach, so temptingly close. Zaiana should have gained distance, but she didn't. Not even when his hand reached around the wrist she held up.

Their stares locked with a heat that battled fire with fire.

Zaiana lost herself, letting him guide her hand to her mouth. Her breathing quickened.

This is so wrong.

Yet the craving roared over all her senses.

The moment the blood touched her tongue, Zaiana exploded with euphoria. Her lips closed around the metal tip of the talon adorning her finger, and she was hardly aware of the arm that wound around her waist, pulling her against a solid warmth that entangled with the taste of him.

"You are a stunning little monster," Kyleer said as a quiet gravel. His pupils were so large they'd swallowed most of the green. His thumb traced over her bottom lip, and her hand dropped.

"There are at least seven ways I could kill you right now," he said.

"Only seven?"

"How many do you have?"

"At least nine, but I can get creative in the moment."

"I don't doubt that for a second."

Zaiana slipped out of his hold. "You're lucky Marvellas is too focused on bending Faythe's mind. She doesn't care what happens to you. You're nothing to her."

"I'm not offended by that. What is she doing to Faythe?"

"I don't owe you anything."

"Then why are you here?"

Once again, Zaiana didn't know why she'd come. She wanted to blame boredom when it was only the partial truth. As in Rhyenelle, she was left to wander with no purpose during the days, while Marvellas was occupied with her plans for Faythe. Her nights were also getting restless. She'd awaited her sleep demon, but he hadn't come back yet.

"How many Nightwalkers do you know?" she blurted.

Kyleer frowned. "A few. Not many that personally though. Why do you ask?"

Her insecurity came rushing to seal her lips. "Never mind."

"Zai," he said as she tried to walk away. "Ask something more specific. Your company is mildly better than the delirious silence."

She didn't have anything more specific.

"It doesn't matter," she mumbled.

"Clearly, it does."

Zaiana ran a hand over her face, debating whether she should abandon him.

"Is it possible for someone to have more than one ability?"

"Of course. It's very rare though. Most who have two are Water-wielders with healing as a second stem."

"What about two that have nothing to do with each other?"

Kyleer's brow hooked as he looked her over. "Now I'm intrigued. Is this about you?"

"No."

Her quick reaction exposed the lie.

"You think you can Nightwalk?"

"No. I mean…I don't know. I guess not," she rambled. It wasn't often she was so flustered.

This new uncertainty about herself had been slowly eating away at everything she thought she'd mastered in herself. She didn't want to discover that was what it was. Rather, she hoped it was simply the fae who visited her dreams who was responsible for her being able to meet him there.

"Who else have you told about it?"

"No one. Forget I said anything—no one will believe you."

"Damn, I was itching to tell the nighttime rats."

She glowered at him. Kyleer huffed a laugh before sliding himself down the wall to sit. Zaiana harbored a note of guilt for his wince of pain as he did.

"When did it start?" he coaxed.

She pinched her lips. There was some lift of liberation in getting to speak of it. She couldn't tell Tynan or Amaya. Certainly not Maverick. With Kyleer, she could pretend it would be forgotten. Irrelevant.

"When your king infiltrated my mind, I woke with him in there," she began, pacing with her reeling mind. "He seemed surprised by it. I didn't know it was something I shouldn't be able to do. I think it's the only way I survived it. Or he would have taken what he wanted without my knowing and killed me."

Kyleer was silent, and she found him with a tense, distant expression.

"I assumed Faythe managed to wake you before that," he said, devoid of emotion.

"She arrived too late."

"Faythe was against what he did to you. As was I."

Zaiana didn't want to hear it. The damage was done.

"It doesn't matter. I was going to kill the king for what he did. I would have, if Maverick didn't get to him first. If I didn't *hesitate*."

"Don't hate yourself for your hesitations," Kyleer said. "If anything, it may be the last thing you have to remember you can feel anything at all."

"I don't want to feel." It slipped from her mouth like a plea.

Around him, she was always *slipping*.

"Why?"

Because it hurt too much. No matter what she did or who she tried to be. It always cut and tore, and she bled.

When she didn't answer, Kyleer said, "If you don't feel, they win.

It's what they've always wanted. An army fighting to a vicious degree because they have nothing to lose. They made you kill your past love to claim back your full attention. They're afraid of you, Zai. Of what you could become in the name of something you love, rather than on their side by hate and vengeance. They could have just killed him themselves, but in having you do it, believing as strongly as you do now that he betrayed you, they win again. I've seen it—there is not a piece of you that will ever fully trust again."

"Finnian made his choice to betray me," she seethed.

"It's not a choice if it's forced."

He was wrong. So, so wrong.

"You weren't there."

"Zai...the dark fae have been under the command of a Spirit with the power to command *minds*."

That slammed into her worse than anything physical. So hard she didn't feel anchored to this gravity anymore.

Marvellas had never visited her under the mountain. To her kind, she'd been all but a fable growing up.

Then she remembered the dream, a memory, that had been plucked from her subconsciousness by the male who'd visited her. Had that been real?

Zaiana couldn't be sure.

She was spiraling.

Through time, space. She didn't know where she was anymore.

"Zai."

She only heard his voice when it was accompanied by a touch on her hand. Zaiana glanced at his fingers against hers, and she ripped them free.

"I know it must be difficult to believe—"

"Difficult?" She mocked the word. What a silly, insulting word for the weight of the world that was crushing her.

Your love is deadly.

Agalhor had been right. And staring into those moss-green eyes that had shifted to sympathy, she couldn't bear it.

"I won't come back here again," she said.

"What if I want you to?"

"Then you're already falling for the easiest way I could kill you."

CHAPTER FORTY-FOUR

Faythe

Faythe couldn't stare at her hollow reflection. Instead she picked at the pearls of her skirts while Marvellas combed her hair. The nausea turning within her hadn't stopped since she'd been brought to this room, the same as before, when the young servants had bathed and dressed her before Marvellas arrived.

It was the act she was forced to endure that troubled her. Because every tender touch was like poison, every comb though her hair like betrayal, every sweet smile the Spirit gave her like pure manipulation, trying to convince Faythe that Marvellas could replace her mother and should not be her enemy.

She might have pitied Marvellas for the tale she tried to spin around them. An alternate reality she tried to force. It was tragic, and Faythe was nothing more than a trapped doll in her delusion.

Faythe's sight kept catching on Nyte in the corner of the room, standing poised and quiet while he posed as Captain Daegal. He'd been the one to bring her here, and now he was forced to be in close proximity with his mother and couldn't do a thing.

"You used to enjoy your hair in braids," Marvellas said. "You would sit for hours and let me decorate your beautiful locks. They were lighter and shorter back then. Would you like me to cut it?"

The fact Marvellas was giving her the choice was jarring but just another seed of delusion, trying to convince herself Faythe would surrender in her fight to stop her.

I'm not her, Faythe wanted to say. *I am not Aesira.*

How she kept referring to Faythe as Aesira was starting to confuse her mind. Every time Faythe was weakened enough, Marvellas had been planting fond memories of herself and Aesira, which was starting to break apart Faythe's right to retain her own identity. At the same time, she'd started to pluck Faythe's most treasured parts about Reylan out.

Faythe couldn't remember

She couldn't rebel against Marvellas's attempts to slip Faythe into the role of Aesira in the past. She had to learn more about Marvellas's true history.

"Agalhor never mentioned his brother's name before," Faythe said.

Marvellas drew in a long breath, so lost in her task. "That's because I wiped it from existence when he left me and took my son."

"Not even I know my father's name, because he doesn't know it himself," Nyte said—a loud thought projection meant for Faythe to catch.

Faythe blanched at the power that would take. To erase his name from the minds of everyone who knew him as the Prince of Rhyenelle.

"You forsook your duty as a Spirit for him?" Faythe posed it as a question.

"No. It was for a human."

Faythe was slammed by that admission, realizing she was about to understand Marvellas's hatred toward humans. It began with the reason she'd bound herself to a mortal form on their lands…for *love*.

"He visited my temple as nothing more than a wandering traveler with a thirst for knowledge on the three Spirits that balanced your world. There was something charming about him—blond with brown eyes and a kind face. He kept coming back, and I grew to enjoy his company. The way he talked, complimented me—I grew feelings I'd never had in all my eternity of watching over your lands. We both wanted more. I'd never known what it was to want something for myself—it is not what we Spirits are supposed to be capable of. But I did…and my want grew into an obsession. I confided in Dakodas to help me find a way to bind myself into a mortal body."

Faythe swallowed hard, watching Marvellas lose herself in her own tale as she absentmindedly tended to Faythe.

"We lived nearly a decade together, and I had a human daughter. Then everything changed shortly after. I was ambushed by a dozen men who bound shackles on me that stole my power."

Faythe's heart skipped. *The Aetherbonds*, she thought.

"I waited for my human lover to come for me, and he did…

CHLOE C. PEÑARANDA

because he was the one who'd orchestrated my capture. I couldn't understand. I thought someone had gotten to him, a Nightwalker must have warped his thoughts...but it didn't take long for the reality to shatter my delusional hope. He told me it was all a lie...his love for me was a lie. He knew all about the Spirits, every legend, every God. He knew my blood could be used to turn humans into fae. That was always his goal, and all he had to do was bide his time until the manacles were forged."

Faythe couldn't believe the story, but with the melancholy that kept Marvellas using the same lost tone, she did.

Nyte came a little closer, watching Marvellas with deeper attention as she told her tale.

"So you see, your books tell some truths, but they are never the whole and only truths. My love for a fae warrior came after my human lover's betrayal."

"How did you escape?"

Though her irises moved like the sun, she met Faythe's stare in the mirror for a single pause that was so cold Faythe almost felt *pity* for what was to come.

"I was rescued from him—and from all those who'd worked with him and held me captive for centuries—by the Prince of Rhyenelle. I was still bound in the manacles, and we were searching for a way to release me. But they were forged in dark magick. I met an Oracle, who foretold that to be free of them I had to lose that which was most precious to me. Then I found out I was pregnant, and for a while I didn't care how mortally bound I was in those manacles. I gave birth to a son—a fae this time. I loved my daughter for the decade he allowed me to keep her. Then she was taken from me, and two centuries passed. I only knew she'd gotten to live a full life and had her own daughters. I became aware of rumors of the gold-eyed children once I was freed. I was glad for that at least, but I couldn't bear to seek any of them out, for they were only a reminder of the motherhood I'd lost. Then my fae son...the moment he was born, I could feel how powerful he would become. I loved him more than I thought myself capable of loving anything."

Faythe dropped her eyes with the weight of the story. How a terrible, terrible turn was about to happen. Her sight flicked sideways to where Nyte had turned his back to them, his fists clenched tightly by his sides.

"I remember..." Faythe shook her head with the threads of

memory she didn't think she would ever fully grasp from her soul's past. "I think Aesira knew where he was. Not in this realm."

The comb paused in Faythe's hair, and her heart skipped a beat.

"No, he is not," Marvellas confirmed, starting a new braid. "The prince took the only thing I ever treasured truly in this world, assuming I would kill my son to break the manacles, since he was most precious to me. Do you believe me when I say that I would never have been capable of it?"

Faythe's heart squeezed. "You killed me—or at least you planned to."

"I don't know if I would have gone through with it," she confessed. Marvellas stood, wandering over to a jewelry box. "In taking my son beyond where I could search five hundred years ago, I did lose him. The prophesy was fulfilled. When my manacles released and my power was freed, all I had left was vengeance. My downfall started with human greed—when one who claimed to love me had tricked me and used my blood to make himself and others fae—so it was there I would begin. I visited the same Oracle as before. He told me I would need the help of another powerful entity like myself, but he warned such an alliance could turn to betrayal just as fast. So I planned to Ascend my sister, Dakodas, who was the only one who understood my choices. I needed Dakodas's help to assume a mortal form, but Aurialis would never help in the same way as Dakodas. She always has been insufferably obsessed with her duty. But there was another way for Dakodas to gain a mortal form, which the Oracle showed me."

Marvellas returned, holding up one red earring, then a sparkling blue sapphire, reminding Faythe of Reylan with a painful stab in her chest. The Spirit chose the red, fitting them on Faythe's ears.

"To sacrifice one of your bloodline?" Faythe guessed to continue the tale.

"Not just any. My bloodline had long since been diluted from the human girl I gave birth to. So for the Ascension, it would take one who would come close to that purity. The offspring of a bloodline-blessed paired with a direct descendant."

"Aesira," Faythe concluded.

"Yes. Your soul is just as fierce as it was in that life. I captured Aesira's mother and kept her under the mountain, and I killed her father, but I did not intend to form the attachment I did to Aesira. To you. You were so bright, joyous. You loved me back in the way I'd always dreamed of, but you were human, with such a fragile amount of time. When you came into adulthood at sixteen, I Transitioned you with my blood to keep you alive long enough to ascend Dakodas as I'd planned. But you became everything I hoped I would have found in my son. Light in my days when I was still making movements for the war I had started, using Valgard as the driving force. We were happy, and for a while, I thought we would conquer together, and I wouldn't need Dakodas."

The cool metal of the necklace she adorned Faythe with next was sharp compared to the heat of her skin from the adrenaline. The story of Marvellas was unfolding in Faythe's mind with terrifying clarity. Images that should have been monochrome were given color, perhaps from some influence in her soul. Never full memories, but she could imagine it all so vividly as Marvellas spoke of their history.

"You said she died from a battle," Faythe prompted.

"Yes, and I mourned deeply. I found you dying from three arrow wounds next to Reylan. The two of you looked a perfect picture of tragedy on that battlefield. I tried to warn you he would only bring you pain, but you would not listen. I knew of another use for your life when it was far too late to save you, and I was so angry, so impatient, that I used the last of your life to raise Mordecai Vesaria, the dark fae king who led the Dark Age. He might have failed in that conquest all that time ago, but I was hopeful he could amass and lead a great dark fae army for me. Your life force was a sacrifice to raise the dead, and I held onto your soul."

Faythe watched her own lost and broken expression in the mirror. None of what Marvellas said felt real, but she couldn't deny it touched her deep inside.

"Why did you bring me back?" she asked quietly.

"Your soul was fading in me. I was running out of time. So I planted the essence of a mating bond within your mother—a descendant of mine—for Agalhor to become compelled to her. Perhaps it was petty of me to wish pain upon him for what his brother had done, but aside from that, he was known as one of the most powerful Nightwalkers to have ever lived, and I needed you as strong as possible for Dakodas's Ascension on the millennium eclipse. I vowed this time I would not fall for you. When I first sensed Lilianna had finally conceived, all that was left to do was plant your soul before another could manifest. At first I thought I would leave Lilianna and Agalhor to raise their child until the time would come for me to take her. Until Lilianna Aklinsera stole you away. She went to High Farrow, because it's where Aurialis's temple is, and with her help, you remained masterfully untraceable to me."

Wetness trailed down Faythe's cheeks, but she made no sound. It was twisted, what Marvellas had done, but all her actions were crafted in heartbreak. Faythe was merely the unfortunate soul to have been caught in it all.

"I'm sorry all of that happened to you," she said, and she meant it.

Marvellas gave Faythe's arms a gentle squeeze as she leaned in, her smile warm and motherly, and it was jarring to *feel* it in her chest.

"I didn't expect you come back after you were killed for Dakodas. So how can I not see this as destiny finally leaning in my favor? All that came before can be forgotten, because we will rule together, *be together*, for eternity."

Despite knowing the truth, Faythe would never lose sight of the end that had to come. Marvellas had to die, and Faythe despised her for all she'd done. That would never change.

Faythe met her eye in the mirror and immediately wished she hadn't.

Marvellas seized the connection to unfold images in Faythe's mind. Old, old memories that Faythe knew didn't belong to her. This wasn't her life.

Aesira's joy was so genuine with Marvellas. They laughed, enjoying the simple pastime of brushing her hair, just as she was doing with Faythe now.

Faythe's hands slammed to the dresser as she stood, her breathing heavy as she tried to expel those memories.

It was not her. *It is not me.*

Even with that settling in her heart again, Faythe was overcome with sadness for young Aesira, who'd had no knowledge she was in the arms of her captor.

"You murdered her parents to take her," Faythe said. "That is not love."

"I spared her from a life of poverty."

"I had a life of poverty," Faythe said, her fire rising, "and I was happier than I ever will be with you, no matter how you try to twist my mind."

The Spirit's hand connected with her cheek with great impact when Faythe stood and whirled around. Nyte shifted in the corner, but he couldn't intervene without arousing suspicion.

Marvellas's beloved *son* was right there, and yet Faythe was at the mercy of her cursed love, not him. She bit her lip against the cry that wanted to escape, holding her throbbing cheek, with a few breaths to calm herself. When she did, she spared a look of sympathy for him.

"I will never be yours, Marvellas. Even if there are times you manage to twist my mind enough to hold this fantasy of yours, I will always break free, and I will never stop despising everything you are."

Faythe whimpered at the sensation of sharp talons sinking into her mind. They kept tightening, and Faythe's legs became weak, sinking her to the ground slowly.

"I've been too merciful with you thus far," Marvellas hissed. Her mental claws sank deeper, and Faythe's head exploded at the pain as if her brain were bleeding. "I will break you, Faythe. Then you will be mine willingly."

Her knees met the ground, and Faythe stared up at the smooth white roof. Her eyes traced the filigree medallion around the chandelier.

All she could do in her helpless state was recite to herself the things she guarded with iron will from Marvellas's vile intrusions in her mind. To remember who and what she was and would always be.

My name is Faythe Ashfyre.

She paused, and with a rush of determination to survive this with her mate in her heart, she amended, starting again:

My name is Faythe Arrowood Ashfyre, soul-bonded to Reylan Arrowood Ashfyre. Daughter of Agalhor and Lilianna. Rightful Queen of Rhyenelle. I am Reylan's strength, Nik's wisdom, and Tauria's resilience. Jakon's courage, and Marlowe's knowledge. I am not alone, and I will not die today.

CHAPTER FORTY-FIVE

Tauria

Mordecai didn't trust Tauria. He never had. As soon as they'd reached the war camp in Fenstead's valleys last night, he'd bound her wrists in Magestone and chained her to the middle of a large tent, where she'd sat vulnerable to the jeers and mockery of the dark fae soldiers who used it for mealtimes.

She hadn't been able to sleep from the noise and the loss of her dignity, but her spirit remained strong. Tauria tuned them out under the constant reel of her own planning. She hadn't expected Mordecai to treat her this way, though that was her error in judgment. Night was falling, and the full moon would rise to its peak. The Transition was still scheduled—it was all the soldiers could talk about.

None of them touched her. They were strictly prohibited. But they did approach, crouching around her and inspecting her as if she were some wild beast. She gave them no show. Nothing but her face of pure resentment that promised their death.

Mordecai would have to remove her shackles for the Transition. That window of opportunity with her magick was all she would have to stop the sinister fate from befalling her.

Despite all of this…Tauria knew she was exactly where she needed to be.

A dark fae came over with an arrogant, sloppy swagger. He crouched like the others, canting his head curiously as though he'd never encountered a being like her before. He was handsome, she supposed. But his beauty masked the cruelty that was evident in the gleam of his onyx eyes. A Transitioned dark fae.

"You are far too beautiful to be chained like a pet," he said smoothly.

"Come any closer, you'll find out why."

His smile took that as a challenge. The dark fae dared to shuffle closer on his haunches. Their faces came intimately close, and she could scent the old blood from his breath, which churned her stomach. Tauria gritted her teeth at the thought of her human people being the prey he fed on.

Her leg kicked out, tripping him off-balance. He slammed to the ground, and she twisted over him, jamming one knee into his chest and the other into his neck. Her wrists twisted awkwardly, still tied to the thick pole, and the Magestone burned her flesh, but she didn't care.

Tauria was close to crushing his throat when someone brutally intervened, slamming her head against the wooden pole she was tied to. Her vision blacked out for a moment, and warmth flooded down the side of her temple. Tauria breathed steadily on her knees, willing herself not to fall unconscious to be left vulnerable to these vultures.

"I said no one was to hurt her."

The dark, menacing voice of Mordecai rumbled through the tent, silencing their laughter and her shouting from the altercation with the dark fae. Despite her misery right now, it had been worth it.

"She attacked me!" the dark fae cried. Those were the last words he spoke before Mordecai's large hand lashed around his throat and crushed it.

Mordecai dropped to her level, taking her chin and examining her wound. His dark eyes were tender for a second, until fingers slid down the trail of her blood from her temple to her jawline, then he *licked* the crimson from them.

Tauria looked away in complete repulsion.

"It is time," he said. Three words that struck through her like a gong.

She was led out by the chain connecting her shackles by a dark fae in front of her. The field glowed with torches and was packed full with bodies. They parted to let them through, and Tauria was pulled like a dog through the thick of her enemies who'd emerged from their tents to bear witness to the Queen of Fenstead becoming *one of them*.

Something of a stage was fashioned, and she was led up onto it. A fae was already kneeling as a spectacle. His head was bowed, but his shoulders shook with sobs of terror. She wanted to console him, but Tauria wasn't pushed to her knees beside him.

She stood overlooking the endless blots of bodies blending into the dark horizon, broken only by the occasional flickering amber torch. Tauria Silverknight held her chin high. She would not let them see her fear.

Her chain was released which silenced the murmurs around the field.

These valleys had always been so tranquil. Now they were defiled, and Tauria's soul cried at the invaders who took no care in the land they trampled and the rivers they polluted.

There had to be at least ten thousand soldiers here. There was only one of her. But they stood in *her* element. The air that wrapped around her skin, caressing her cheek now, waiting for her call.

"The full moon is upon us," Mordecai's voice bellowed through the still night. "And tonight it shall bear witness to one of the greatest Transitions of our time. As Queen Tauria Stagknight joins us as dark fae. For in darkness, we shall triumph."

In the eerie silence that followed, Tauria said, "Silverknight." Taking a long breath, she squared her shoulders, and more striking than the power of Mordecai's voice was the sound of her shackles slipping off her wrists and clanging to the ground. "My name is Tauria Silverknight, and this is my home."

Mordecai's eyes widened with rage and mockery, glancing from her shackles to her face. "Who released you?"

"I did," she said.

The first dark fae to move—the one who had been holding her chain—choked as she stole all the air from his lungs with a twist of her wrist.

"You made the mistake of underestimating what I can do. You are always at my mercy. Always surrounded by not just one of my powers, but two."

As a demonstration, Tauria touched the life essence of a root under the ground at the dark fae's feet as he struggled for his stolen air. The root launched out of the soil, piercing through his back. He fell, suspended on the root like a spike. It took a lot more effort to use her Florakinetic ability, but her determination knew no bounds to do what she'd come here for.

"Why wait until now?" Mordecai asked, simmering with loathing.

"To make a spectacle out of *you*. To show you are nothing more than a powerless dark fae reliant on a history that painted your reputation. Now…you are nothing to contend with on your own."

Tauria reached under her skirts, retrieving her staff, which she extended to full size in a breath. Then, in her next, she conjured a sharp gale of wind and sent it slamming into Mordecai.

Then she became spellbound to the wind and nature around her. Tauria was a hurricane sweeping through the field that erupted into chaos. She was just one person, but none of these dark fae had abilities, and she would fight for as long as she could, eliminating the enemy force that had plagued her land for too long.

She hoped she'd also damaged Mordecai's reputation. That word would spread of how easily he was fooled and overpowered, and how he'd allowed Tauria to wipe out an entire legion.

At least, that was her ambition. It would sound incredulous, laughable, to most. But Tauria's wind wrapped around necks and stole air as she danced through the crowd, cutting down everyone who advanced for her. She blasted others back from reaching her while she commanded the roots in the ground to kill others instantly. Her body quickly ached, and her skin slicked with sweat from using more magick than she ever had before, but she pushed past the warnings. She fought *harder*.

Maybe she was a fool, about to be overwhelmed and cut down at any moment, but the purpose in her heart thought it was worth it. She'd run from her enemy once, leaving them to overthrow her kingdom. She owed them this for her failure all that time ago.

"You can't fight forever, Tauria," Mordecai yelled at her from above.

The advance of soldiers was endless, but she tuned out the high lord's taunt.

One body at a time, she told herself calmly. Thinking of the masses would only waver her will.

Her staff twisted and spun and cut between her hands, and slowly she pushed forward. She was surrounded but not alone. So long as she had the pairing of the wind and the anguish of the nature, Tauria kept going.

She didn't know how much time had passed, but her lungs had passed the point of burning, and she knew the moment she stopped she would collapse. At some point, she thought the push of enemies became less, but the sounds of battle grew. Some of the dark fae shifted their target, and it was then she saw…

Something rammed through the throng in front of her. It made the dark fae scramble to fly to get out of the way, but many were thrown unnaturally into the air before slamming down. Even Tauria balked at the massive thing that charged right in her direction. The dark fae stopped attacking her, and Tauria's vision peppered as she struggled to catch her breath.

Then the beast burst through the mob, causing her to stumble back, but what she saw struck her powerfully.

Tauria gasped, in complete awe as the giant white stag reared up, mighty and triumphant, declaring itself with a loud call like a horse. Its antlers shimmered silver, and Tauria knew there was something sacred about this stag. Something of myth and legend come to life. She blinked consciously, wondering if she'd fallen in battle and this was some beautiful vision.

She couldn't explain the pull she felt when its silver eyes met hers. *Ride with me*, it seemed to say.

Tauria wasn't thinking about the impossible—she raced forward, lunging up onto the beast that lowered enough for her to use the wind for aid onto its back.

The vantage point flooded her with a sense of pride and power. The dark fae balked, but some began to resume their stances and brace for flight.

With another powerful rear, the stag launched forward, and Tauria's legs clamped tighter around its body. It charged through the dark fae as though they were mere twigs under its giant hooves.

Ahead, Tauria couldn't believe what she saw billowing over the heads of a force that headed over the hills toward them. When the moonlight caught the stag crest and revealed the vibrant green of the material, pride thundered in her chest like the stag's hooves.

If Fenstead forces were here…had Nik brought them?

Tauria was so distracted she missed the dark fae that swooped down, knocking into her and sending her flying off the height. She slammed into the ground and screamed from the impact that dislocated her shoulder. Her will to survive numbed the agony, giving her enough adrenaline to swipe up her staff in her right hand and stand.

She faced off with Mordecai.

"It's not too late for this Transition," he seethed.

"Yes, it is."

Tauria's cry shook through the soils beneath her as she plunged deeper into her well of magick than she ever had before. She focused all her energy on the nature deep underground. The endless roots that connected far and wide. Tauria crouched, slamming her good hand to the trampled ground. The web of roots awoke, trembling as she asked them to grow; asked them to fight with her.

Then, shooting up from the soil, nature's spears took their vengeance. One plunged through Mordecai's chest, and he grunted, back arching over the root. Another speared his abdomen. Then a final one shot through his throat, killing him. Though he wasn't truly dead.

Across the field, many cries rang out as the root continued to launch out violently and unexpectedly, spearing the enemy that couldn't outrun it. She kept pushing her magick into the soil until her whole body tingled and the heat smothered her. Tauria had pushed beyond her limits, but she thought it was worth it.

When she channeled every last drop she had…Tauria fell onto her dislocated shoulder.

The pain made her black out, but the nauseating sound and feel made her believe the fall might have pushed her bone back into place. The stars came in and out of focus, and the sounds of fear and pain drifted away. For a moment, Tauria felt at peace.

Someone found her.

They kneeled, speaking to her, but their words were above water she didn't know she was drowning in. She couldn't breathe. Her eyes slipped shut.

"NIK!" the person yelled.

Nik… His name jolted through her like a demand to stay awake.

"Stay with me, Tauria." She recognized this voice.

Lycus.

Tauria blinked a couple of times, but her heavy lids wanted to stay closed. She swallowed, but her throat was as dry as sand. She was outdoors…it was winter…but she was on fire.

The soil under her turned colder, as if answering her needs, and she moaned.

When she next opened her eyes, she was staring into the most beautiful set of emeralds.

"Nik," she breathed.

Was this real?

"Oh, my love," Nik said, panicked. He lifted her into his arms. "I've got you. At last I've got you back, and you're not allowed to leave me again."

Tauria burrowed into his chest more. She inhaled his scent, which brought her back to full clarity.

"Never," she croaked.

"You're hurt," he said darkly. "We need to get you inside."

"I'm okay. More than okay, now you're with me." She ran her hand down his abdomen, haunted by the last time she'd seen him with a sword through him. "I'm so sorry I left you when you needed me."

Nik forced her to look at him with fingers around her chin. His expression was firm. "You did what you had to, and you've done a brilliant job here."

She didn't know if that was true. They may have wiped out a few legions of Mordecai and Dakodas's army, but it was just a fraction of their numbers.

Tauria patted her bodice, pulling out scrunched parchments she'd managed to swipe from Mordecai's room before he brought her here after the rebel ambush.

"We might have more insight into their planned movements," she said, examining the contents.

Nik's lips pressed to her head. "Absolutely brilliant," he muttered softly.

When they retreated to the castle, Tauria didn't know how she felt. It was like the darkness still clung to the corners of the walls. They'd won the battle and reclaimed Fenstead's fortitude, but the war to come still lingered heavily.

Tauria sat, letting Edith fashion a sling for her arm, though she felt it unnecessary. Nik filled her in on all that had happened since they'd parted. Her eyes welled at hearing about his short reunion with Faythe. She pined after her friend so deeply. While they were fighting to get Reylan back, and they would all reunite in High Farrow, Nik said they had one more mission before they headed there.

Lycus approached to inform them, "It's going to take time to push the dark fae out of the kingdom completely, but we have a great stronghold now."

That was a relief to hear. She had enemy plans to take back to the others, and her people had a beacon of hope for their kingdom to be purged of the evil that had grown for too long.

"What happened to Mordecai?"

"We didn't see him on the field."

Tauria sighed. She hoped she'd made an impact on his reputation by humiliating him and wiping out his legions in Fenstead, but clearly, he still had allies when she'd left him perfectly skewered on roots.

"I trust you'll lead our forces well to continue our efforts," Tauria said.

Lycus nodded fiercely.

Her gaze slipped to Nik. "What is next for us? Dakodas's ruin isn't here."

Nik pursed his lips, and she detected a shift of nerves in him. "Did your father ever mention another lover? Another...child, perhaps?"

Tauria stood when Edith was finished. She frowned at the odd question. "No. Of course not. He was a great father and a loyal partner to my mother."

"I have no doubt," Nik said. His tension grew uncomfortable. He led her into a walk down the hallway for a little more privacy. "This would have been before you arrived. Before he became devoted to your mother and you."

"What are you trying to say, Nik?"

Tauria had to lean back against the wall as he explained.

A half-sister.

The fae that had been with Tarly...

Tauria was haunted by the truth. She didn't know what it meant... what it might change. Would Nerida want to stake a claim on the Fenstead throne? Nik spoke of her fondly, which gave Tauria some comfort. The fae healer and Waterwielder didn't even want her own Lakelarian throne, it seemed.

"You really think our abilities together can get into Hilia's Cave?" Tauria asked. The task sounded monumental, but the reward if there was a dagger—the *Spellthief*—inside meant it was certainly worth trying.

Nik took her hands, looking at her fondly. "I believe you can do anything, Tauria Silverknight."

He slipped a ring onto her finger. No—he'd returned her marital band, his mother's ring, but now it held stronger meaning than their engagement. Tauria slipped a look across, but Lycus and the others were occupied in conversation. Nik kissed her.

"No one knows yet," she whispered against his lips.

Nik smiled, caressing his knuckles down her cheek. "I want everyone to know you are my wife, Tauria."

Tauria and Nik had wed in private before they'd conspired to fool Mordecai and left High Farrow. If one of them fell, the other would have rightful claim over both High Farrow and Fenstead thrones. They'd wanted that security. For themselves... Tauria couldn't wait to truly have their wedding celebration with all their friends.

She was admiring her ring when Edith bounded over.

"Oh, that's pretty!"

Tauria dropped her hand to release the attention from it. "Thanks for being my friend, Edith. I hope you know you'll be safe here."

The dark fae frowned. "Are you going somewhere?"

"I have to leave for a while. Lycus will be in charge in my stead, but no one will harm you."

"Please let me come with you." Edith tugged at her good arm like a child.

Tauria exchanged a reluctant look with Nik. He said, "It's not safe where we're going. We can't afford to have more people in danger for no reason."

"But I'm excellent at finding things. And building fires! And I can look out for myself! Oh, please? I've been locked away in this castle all my life."

Tauria's mind spun with her frantic pleas. She shrugged at Nik and could practically hear his internal groan.

"If that's what you wish," Tauria agreed.

Though she didn't feel right about it, she couldn't be another person in power shackling her to servitude where she didn't want to be.

"We'll leave at first light," Nik said, taking her hand.

"Where are we going?" Tauria asked as he led her away.

"I've been separated from my wife far too long," he said, his voice dropping to a seductive murmur. "We're going to find a room where I can exhaust you until dawn."

CHAPTER FORTY-SIX

Tarly

When Tarly retuned from relieving himself, he didn't expect to find another tall, broad human in the room. The man wore a pirate tricorn, with lengths of dirty blond hair poking out the bottom. When he turned at Tarly's intrusion, the *thud* as he stepped in drew Tarly's attention to one leg made of wood.

"Who are you?" Tarly inquired. Scanning Jakon and Marlowe only firmed his defenses when he detected some kind of upset in them at this man's presence.

"Augustine," he answered easily. "It's an honor to meet you, Tarly Wolverlon."

He was taken aback to be addressed by his full name.

"Is everything okay?" Tarly asked Marlowe, who seemed the most uncomfortable.

"He's my father," she informed him.

Once again, Tarly was slapped with surprise. "This is opening more questions than answers," he said.

He was prevented from gaining any more information when someone burst into the room right behind him.

Tarly spun to find Izaiah, who scanned the room, glossing over them all like he expected to find someone else.

"What's wrong?" Jakon demanded.

Izaiah was panting as if he'd sprinted around the whole castle in his search. Tynan was right behind him.

"The Light Temple Ruin is gone," he said though gritted teeth, seeming to conclude something else as he followed with, "and so is Reuben."

Jakon swore, and Tarly's stomach plummeted.

"He must have followed me to know where it was, the little rat," Izaiah seethed. Bottles and instruments clanged when his fist slammed the nearest counter.

"It couldn't have been long ago. Maybe this is your sign to leave and track him," Tynan said in a tone that was sensitive to how volatile Izaiah was acting right now.

Izaiah pinched the bridge of his nose, considering. "If I'm going, so are you two," he said, directed at Jakon and Marlowe. "You can head to High Farrow. Gather what you need—we leave in an hour."

"How do you plan to escape?" Augustine asked.

"I'm sure you've seen it in some way or another," Izaiah said flatly, then he left without another word.

Though Tarly wasn't regarded in Izaiah's plan, if he didn't tack himself onto it, he didn't know how else he would get out with his life. Besides, now the Light Temple Ruin was missing and Marlowe wasn't going to craft more Phoenix Blood, he had no further purpose here.

Once out of Rhyenelle, he could escort the two humans as far as Stenna's fall, where he would wait, for if all went to plan, Nik, Tauria, and Nerida should be meeting there sooner or later.

Tarly could hardly last the next hour. He didn't feel grounded with the dark sense of foreboding choking the air. Augustine had left, and Tarly hadn't asked what he was here for.

"We're sitting ducks here," Tarly said—the first any of them had spoken since Izaiah left. The tension had grown too thick to breathe right.

"Izaiah is the only one who knows this castle blindfolded and can walk around without suspicion. We have to wait for his lead," Jakon said.

"Isn't that strange to you? Why is he so freely roaming when you two were just as close to Faythe and you're under close watch?"

Maybe it was irrational—he didn't know Izaiah, and they did—but he couldn't shake his nerves since nothing felt right here.

"He has his own tasks," Marlowe said in his defense.

Tarly let it go.

He was equipped with his bow, just waiting with his senses sharpened for the next person to come through that door. Marlowe continued to spell potions far faster than she'd pretended to be capable of before, easily making a dozen in the hour they waited.

Izaiah stayed true to his word, but when he returned, it was not with the kind of demeanor that was planning a risky escape. He stepped in calmly, with an immediate aura that hit Tarly with dread. Izaiah kept his sights on Marlowe and gave a barely-there shake of his head.

Then the guards flooded in.

Tarly didn't have time to react. The proximity was too short in this room to nock an arrow, and he was apprehended before he could try. They disarmed him, and in his shock at trying to process what was happening, he didn't resist their handling.

Jakon did, however. He was the only struggle in the room, because the guards pulled Marlowe away from him. She didn't fight. Marlowe Kilnight held her chin high, and Tarly's heart might have stopped beating. Because that wasn't the face of someone who feared for their life—it was the courage of one who had already made peace with death.

Tarly broke through his stupor then. He couldn't let that happen.

"Where are you taking her?" Tarly snarled, pulling against the hold two dark fae guards had on him.

"To the king," one said plainly.

"Take us too," Tarly demanded.

The guard who spoke looked to Izaiah for permission. How could the humans trust him when it was clear he held authority among the enemy? Tarly didn't want to know what he'd done to gain it.

"It makes no difference to Malin," Izaiah answered.

They were taken to the throne room, and when Tarly was close enough, the madness he'd heard about claiming the new king from his consumption of Phoenix Blood was nothing compared to seeing it clearly over every inch of him.

Malin Ashfyre sat on the throne, leaning with one arm on the metal side, with no grace. His slouch was tired, his hazel eyes were concerningly bloodshot, and the angle of his dark stare watching them get escorted in sent a chill over his whole body.

Tarly and Jakon were forced to their knees before the dais, but Marlowe remained standing. Izaiah stood close by, and Tarly noticed Tynan and Amaya were not present.

"We have done everything you've asked." Jakon was the first to speak boldly.

Malin's head moved like a serpent, studying Marlowe with a

chilling silence. There was a level of unhinged in his expression that kept Tarly on a razor's edge.

"You've done what I asked, yes," he agreed, his voice a dark lick of warning. "But not to your full capabilities, have you?"

"I've been working tirelessly," Marlowe said calmly.

She didn't allow him to feed on her fear, and Tarly found her bravery both admirable and tragic.

Malin lifted himself from the throne as if his own weight were a burden. There was a madness about the way he moved. Slow, assessing, one wrong trigger away from doing something irreversible.

Tarly didn't know what to do. He couldn't fight this many fae and dark fae—they lined the entire hall. He didn't have his bow. But watching Malin approach Marlowe, a venomous snake primed for a gentle doe, Tarly could hardly stand the sickness tightening in his stomach at being so helpless.

"The potions," Malin said, low with an ominous chill, "are useless!" His voice was elevated, and a small bottle he'd been carrying shattered to the ground, spilling the crimson liquid at Marlowe's feet.

"They affect everyone differently—"

Marlowe choked with the hand Malin wrapped around her throat. Jakon turned savage, but he was no match for even one fae, never mind the three that surrounded him.

"I'll fucking kill you!" Jakon snarled—a sound so unlike his usual nature.

"Tell me, *Oracle*—in fact, *show me* my reign at the end of this war."

His pressure around her neck wasn't enough to keep her from talking.

"It doesn't—" She struggled for breath. "It doesn't exist."

Malin pushed her with a growl of outrage, and Marlowe sprawled on the floor. Tarly jerked again. His teeth hadn't unclenched since he'd entered the room, and his anger was growing palpable.

"You either show it to me, or I have no more use for you."

"Please!" Jakon yelled. "She's done everything you ask. She can't write the future!"

Gods, it was agony to hear his desperate pleas for his wife.

"You can kill me," Marlowe said—a cold, hushed breath of acceptance. "It won't change a thing. It will not stop the wrath of the Phoenix that's coming for you."

Malin's eyes flared wide, crazed. He dipped into his pocket and produced another vial of Phoenix Blood, downing the contents in a single swallow.

"So I kill her first," Malin pondered, trying desperately, though he stayed chillingly calm, to calculate a way out of the inevitable future Marlowe foretold.

"You are nothing compared to her," Marlowe said.

Then she cried out from no physical interference. Malin was attacking her mind.

"Stop!" Jakon cried—a broken sound.

"She's telling you everything—you don't need to do that!" Tarly growled.

He shot a look at Izaiah as if he might be able to intervene, but while his expression was masterfully composed in steel, his eyes blazed at the display, and Tarly thought he might break.

"You'll only seal the future she taunts you with if you kill her," Izaiah warned.

Marlowe hardly made a sound, but her body was tense with invisible pain, and her glass eyes were fixed on the celling.

Tarly's chest was pounding. Every movement in this room balanced on a ledge of no return.

Malin contemplated with a furious stare on Marlowe, then he let her go. Tarly's breath fell out of him when Marlowe's body slumped, released from the torture and mercifully still alive.

Marlowe slowly peeled herself up, braced on her hands as she caught her breath. The human shifted her head back, locking eyes with Jakon, and it was then Tarly felt the world stand still. He'd never seen such ghostly, helpless horror overcome a person as he did now as he followed her line of sight to Jakon. He'd gone so pale with the declaration that appeared on Marlowe's lips.

Malin crouched before her. "Your mind is filled with too many reels for me to know what is true, so show me the path I win."

Marlowe *laughed*. A few breathy sounds of mockery as she shook her head and then turned it to the king.

"Step into my mind, and I'll show you," she said in a voice so unwavering despite the monster she started into the face of. "Here— you win. The kingdom is yours."

Malin's eyes darted between hers, widening with hunger at whatever he was shown.

"How do I achieve it?"

"You must lose everything you've ever held dear."

"I have nothing."

"Your father never died—he left you. He had another son with a powerful Goddess, and you were nothing to him compared to that son. He will return. An ember of the Phoenix is always destined to return."

"My father?" Malin repeated—the first slither of humanity he'd yielded in the voice of a child.

Marlow shook her head. "Your half-brother. Only for a little while. Only enough for you to see what he chose over you."

The king's knees met the marble, and Tarly's heart leaped with every inch closer he got to Marlowe. He was a bomb on the brink of detonating, and she was too close...they had to get her away from him.

"You're lying," Malin seethed in a low rattle that Tarly felt in his core.

Closer...a fraction closer. Tarly watched Malin's hands tremble as if they were knives about to be thrown.

"Remember this in all I've told you..." Marlowe spoke—words that struck the world and snapped the beast inside Malin Ashfyre. "My truth is just as powerful as my lie."

The wildness that flared in Malin's eyes was a sentencing.

Izaiah yelled, "DON'T DO IT—"

Jakon screamed, "NO!"

Tarly shouted Malin's name.

But they were all words against a blade. Futile.

The hands of the king moved too fast. The calls of protest, Jakon's cry of anguish, Malin's roar of outrage, the drum of Tarly's pulse—everything clashed, but still he heard the second when Marlowe's neck...*snapped.*

Chaos erupted, but Tarly couldn't move. He kneeled, staring at the precious form of Marlowe so still against the marble floor. A life that deserved so much longer to prosper, stolen by an evil that would get to keep breathing.

Jakon's heart-wrenching cries split through him, and he knew without looking the human was frantic in his struggle to reach his wife. He was owed that at least. So that was where Tarly targeted his wrath over the utter outrage of this tragedy.

Izaiah had the same idea, and Tarly forgot his own pain. It was all numb under his rage and disbelief as he fought off guard after guard. He managed to steal a dagger, then a sword, cutting through bodies in a way he didn't know he was capable of with this course of adrenaline pumping through him. When no one could hold Jakon back anymore, the human slammed to his knees, cradling his wife's body, and it was an image that would haunt Tarly for the rest of his days.

"What have you done!" A new roar of soul-tearing anguish boomed through the room.

Malin had retreated up the dais, surrounded by dark fae guards.

The person who stormed in was Augustine, Marlowe's father.

Augustine's horror-filled sight slipped from Jakon and Marlowe to the king.

"We had a deal!" he bellowed, torn between wrath and heartbreak. "She was to be spared to take me instead!"

Malin didn't answer. His eyes were fixed on Marlowe, shed of all malice now. His chest heaved as if he couldn't believe his own actions, maybe even regretted that split second he'd lost his mind without considering the gravity of what he was doing.

Tarly didn't care. There was no regret or remorse in the world that could redeem this despicable piece of shit.

Malin said, his words vacant, "Your deal was not with me. And they still expect you to fulfill your role for them."

Augustine was surrounded then. They were completely outnumbered, and Tarly saw no escape for any of them.

Tarly caught a flicker of Izaiah's movement as he uncorked a small vial.

Phoenix Blood.

Izaiah quickly downed the contents. Then as light grew around him, he looked to Tarly who braced.

"Get Jakon and Marlowe out with you."

The next second, Tarly was shielding his eyes against a bright flare of light that engulfed Izaiah and a burst of heat that had him scrambling back. The brightness didn't ease, but the hue changed, and when Tarly looked to where Izaiah last stood, he couldn't believe the sight of the Firebird he'd transformed into.

The bird gave an earsplitting screech, and Tarly winced, but as it was directed toward Malin and his swarm of guards, Tarly realized the opportunity Izaiah was granting.

Tarly's instinct raced for Jakon and Marlowe as Izaiah, who dominated the room Tarly feared he might set ablaze, used flame and claws to keep the enemy from him.

"We need to go!" Tarly yelled when Jakon remained on his knees, tightly holding Marlowe's body.

Jakon shook his head, utterly distraught.

There was no time to be gentle. Tarly tried to take Marlowe from him, but Jakon's glare was absolutely vicious. It got him to stand with her at least.

"They'll only lock you up and dispose of her in a way that you'll never forgive yourself for if they capture you again," Tarly said—the harsh truth.

This time, when Tarly directed him, Jakon followed his lead.

They raced out of the throne room and down a hall before guards flooded the bottom end. Tarly braced to fight, but he wasn't as adept with the sword he'd taken from one of the fallen.

An arrow whizzed by them, taking out one guard, quickly followed by another, then another. Tarly spun to the skilled archer and found Amaya as she let go of another arrow.

"Here!" she called, swiping up Tarly's bow and throwing it to him. She was quick to sprint toward him, and he slung the quiver of arrows she gave him over his body.

It only took three more arrows from him and one from Amaya to clear the path.

"Thanks," Tarly said, already running again with a gentle push on Jakon.

"This way!" Tynan called from their right at the bottom of the hall.

They'd planned this. An escape. Tarly couldn't stop the tormenting thought of why they couldn't have come just a few minutes earlier; that it might have prevented Marlowe's death. He couldn't afford to think like that. Jakon was still alive, and he was determined to keep it that way for Marlowe.

Tarly and Amaya took care of any fae or dark fae that tried to stop them. Occasionally, the screech of Izaiah as the Firebird rattled through the halls, but they kept pushing toward a way out.

They hit open air, and when they crossed toward a body of trees, Amaya stopped. Tynan approached, and he watched her nock an arrow of lint. Tynan set it ablaze before she took her aim toward one of the throne room windows.

It shattered through, but that was just a signal.

Tarly didn't know what he was expecting—perhaps that Izaiah would shift back and be able to escape with the commotion he'd made. Instead Tarly winced, ducking, as a loud *boom* resounded and the wall collapsed in an explosion of fire and rock.

Izaiah's cry pierced the twilight, and Tarly thought there was something pained in it now.

"Those bastards," Tynan growled.

Tarly saw the arrows then—two in his chest, close to his wing—

and he didn't know how lethal those wounds might be on his fae body when he transformed back.

"Let's go," Tynan instructed.

He ran out of the tree cover toward Izaiah, and Tarly understood the next leg of the plan with hesitation.

"He's wounded," Tarly protested.

"We'll be caught in minutes if we don't fly. Now hurry up!" Tynan snapped.

"If he drops out of the sky with us, we're all dead!" Tarly argued, but he didn't hesitate to follow anyway, making sure Jakon was close with him.

Izaiah lowered enough, and Tynan climbed up first, then he helped Amaya. The dark fae took Marlowe while Jakon mounted. Tarly gripped fistfuls of feathers, and Izaiah shrieked, his giant body shifting dangerously. Tarly was almost thrown off, but he held as tight as he could. Flicking a glance up, he saw Tynan wrapping his hands around a new arrow in Izaiah's back, while Amaya braced her legs and fired at the archers trying to take Izaiah down.

The Firebird began to move, bracing to take flight, and Tarly scrambled up with all his might, barely managing to throw himself onto its back and clamp his whole body against it to avoid being thrown off.

Even tension in his body and concern for the humans stretched endlessly in the bustle and commotion of Izaiah trying to take flight against the onslaught of enemy attacks. Fire blazed brighter from his feathers, and Tarly felt the growing heat. His massive head turned back and Phoenixfyre blasted from his breath into the torn throne room.

His powerful wings cast out, and Tarly managed a maneuver to a better position to help Jakon stay secure while he held on tightly to Marlowe's body.

Those uncertain moments using every ounce of his strength slammed his heart…then they were flying.

It wasn't smooth and without risk, considering Izaiah's injuries, but after a strung-out minute, Tarly managed to loosen his grip and let go of Jakon.

The silence that followed was as icy as the whistling wind that cut his skin.

They escaped as six bodies…but only five lives, and the gravity of that ache shackled him all over again.

"Maybe she'll come back," Jakon said, barely audible with the air whipping by. His stare was a million miles away as he held Marlowe's head to his chest, using his body as if he could warm her from the icy temperature. "We have to go to Faythe. Maybe she can help."

Jakon wasn't thinking right, only in delusion and denial.

"I'm so sorry," Tarly said, knowing the words meant nothing, but he didn't know what else to offer.

"She can come back," was all Jakon repeated.

Tarly didn't have the heart to break him more. Grief worked in terrible ways.

Tarly asked Tynan, "Where are we going?"

"High Farrow. Izaiah insisted it would be the only place safe from the enemy until we can make contact with the others to form a plan, and I guess now to tell them we've lost the Light Temple Ruin."

"The enemy," Tarly muttered. He didn't know what that meant anymore now they were riding with two dark fae.

Before, it had been an easy line to see. Fae against dark fae, and the humans as tragic collateral in their ages-long feud. Yet that was never the whole truth, only what they were led to believe by forces higher than them all. Spirits and kings and meddling Gods.

Amaya wiped her eyes, and Tarly noticed her staring at Jakon and Marlowe. The darkling was spilling her own grief because of another's, and if that wasn't a true heart, he didn't have right to believe he had one.

Marlowe could have been mistaken for sleeping as she appeared so peaceful in Jakon's arms. Tarly hadn't had the privilege of knowing her more, but he wanted to. Now every chance was frozen in time, and as he looked upon the least deserving life to have been taken this night, Tarly felt how cruel and unbiased war was, and he was plagued by the haunting reminder none of them were safe.

CHAPTER FORTY-SEVEN

Zaiana

Nothing about this day felt right. Something dark and chilling tainted the air. As if Death had crept into these walls, waiting. Not Dakodas, but the true and most final entity of the word.

Zaiana decided today she would confront Marvellas—that had to be the cause of the nerves racking her body. She was no stranger to questioning authority, but this was the pinnacle of her rebellion, and she wasn't certain she would walk away.

It didn't matter to her now, so long as Marvellas went down with her.

Her plan was neither for Faythe nor the dark side. It was purely for her own vengeance.

She just needed her confession. To know what Malin claimed and Kyleer suspected was true. Marvellas had tied a curse to her somehow that stilled the hearts of every dark fae, born or Transitioned, making them believe they were unfeeling monsters. Then, when Zaiana herself had started to feel love in her chest for Finnan, Marvellas had stolen that too in the coldest way.

Zaiana was a storm of wrath, but she kept herself collected.

Her path was intercepted, and Zaiana could have taken her blade to Maverick's chest to remove him.

"Whatever you're doing, it can't be today," he said, a rare urgency in his voice.

"Get out of my way before I make you."

"Come with me, please."

It was the plea that dissolved her ire just a little for how out of character it was.

"What's happening?"

"Run away with me."

That statement hit her like a blast of her own lightning, so much so she couldn't respond right away, blinking as if she could still be asleep. Then she laughed—the only logical thing that came to mind, because he had to be joking.

His expression never changed.

"I'm serious. We can leave and never look back. They won't find us, I promise."

"You can't be serious. That…that's ridiculous."

"Why?"

"Because I hate you. And you hate me."

"Hatred is a bright form of passion."

"Tell me what's happening," she demanded.

He'd lost his mind. At that thought, Zaiana blanched, backing away from him.

Could Marvellas be manipulating him right now? Could she have caught on to how much Zaiana had figured out, knowing she was coming for her, and was trying another trick with Maverick like she had with Finnian?

Or worse, had Maverick gone to Marvellas with all Zaiana had told him of her suspicions? She'd been a fool to trust him, but she was not backing away now. Not running away.

"She'll kill you, Zaiana."

"For what?"

"If you go against her now—"

Zaiana pushed past him, but he grabbed her wrist. Hers lashed over his, twisting and crouching, with a cry from the effort. He was thrown over her shoulder, and she seethed down at him.

"Don't try to stop me," she warned.

Zaiana was too far gone in her need for retribution. Even if it killed her.

"It's a full moon. She hasn't been keeping Faythe and her commander for no reason with no action. She's been waiting."

It registered in Zaiana immediately. She was going to Transition Faythe? Of course. A royal. But why would Maverick be so concerned about that?

"She got herself caught knowing that was a risk."

Zaiana pushed off him, and Maverick stood, still blocking her way. Her fists clamped against the tremors of her temper.

"It requires a *fae* sacrifice."

That was when she understood. With a claw of panic in her chest and a siren blaring louder than ever…she understood.

"You're too volatile right now." He tried to grab her again, and they fought, slamming each other into the walls. He tried to restrain her, but she was lost under waves of anxiety that he was preventing her from interfering.

"So help me, Maverick, I will kill you."

He grabbed her arms, pushing her against the wall, and she held him with a death stare.

"Just think for a moment, dammit," he said, heaving breaths like her. "We've both been summoned to the celestial dome, so I'm coming with you. I just thought I'd offer one last out before you set your course for him."

"It's not for him," she hissed. It was a lie, but Kyleer wasn't the sole reason she needed to face Marvellas. "She killed Finnian."

Maverick's face relaxed. Not in surprise at the knowledge, but almost like…

Zaiana became awash with a sickly dread, feeling her world start to spin. "You knew."

He didn't deny it. Zaiana couldn't see; couldn't feel. Her hands planted to his chest, and the next moment Maverick crashed against the wall opposite. She'd pushed hard enough that pieces of the stone crumbled, and he groaned in a hunch to collect himself.

"I never confirmed it, but I suspected," he confessed. "That bastard wasn't capable of harming a damned insect. And it was disgusting how much he loved you."

Zaiana wasn't thinking anymore. Unseeing rage overcame her as she slammed her fist into his jaw. Maverick could have blocked it, but he didn't. He spat black blood onto the ground.

"Be glad you're the least of my problems right now, but I will come for you if you don't stay out of my way," she snarled.

Zaiana stormed toward the place he called the celestial dome, knowing nothing but grief and guilt and sorrow and pain and anguish and…

Her eyes burned, and her hands trembled. Every emotion she was told she could have stirred like a volcanic eruption, on the verge of breaking.

Zaiana still had her wits, however. She concealed the lower half of her face and pulled up her hood. Though she wanted to raze the Nether, she still didn't have her magick. She had to be strategic.

"Dome" was accurate to describe the sphere of glass that encased the large circular room. It was breathtaking. Very little light was needed in here when the moon blessed the space, flooding a beautiful cool glow over the expanse. The stars shone brilliantly, magnified by the glass. Constellations spilled over the floor, and Zaiana felt pulled to chart them, drawn to one in particular that began to glow from the others, but she snapped her focus back down to survey her surroundings.

It was tragic what the stars were about to witness tonight.

Cloaked, masked, and hooded, Zaiana slipped into the space, keeping to the back of the guards and poised as still as them.

Marvellas stood as the brightest thing in the room, surrounded by darkly cloaked guards. Zaiana's wrath toward the Spirit was a fire she kept under conscious control.

Zaiana had nothing to lose in seeking her retribution.

When Zaiana spotted Maverick approaching close to the Spirit, her resentment for him sparked anew. His cheek was bruised, but it would heal fast. She despised him even more...because despite it all, she still felt something else in the pit of her stomach that wanted to tell him to flee. To leave her behind and just *go*.

"Let's not waste a moment, shall we?" Marvellas said, so proud and calm.

They brought in Faythe, and Zaiana internally winced at the sorry state of her. So much power and potential reduced to nothing. But she was still fighting. She had to be, or this Transition wouldn't be necessary.

It was tragic, really, what the Spirit wanted from her. To play house was so twisted and wrong, yet one could sympathize with her craving for the one thing always slipping out of her reach. Love.

Zaiana's resentment twisted like a knife when in turn the Spirit had deprived her people of such an emotion too.

Zaiana had watched this sinister ritual many times. Something wasn't right.

A stunning silver-haired fae was dragged in, with sky-blue eyes that might have once sparkled like the great waters, but now they were lifeless. This fae was brought to her knees in the middle, but she wondered at her purpose.

Had Maverick been wrong? Had he tricked her into believing

Kyleer would be the fae sacrifice so she would leave with him like a coward? She didn't let her relief soothe any of her anxiety just yet.

Next, Zaiana least expected to see this particular familiar face. Faythe's sobs broke with fresh heartbreak at seeing Augustine escorted in, not fighting. The usual spirited, playful Oracle bowed his head, led in like a broken dog. Had he seen this coming? What a terrible burden it would be to know where, maybe even exactly when, death's hand would reach.

"I had sent for Marlowe as it would have been all the more poetic. But her father happened to be there, offering himself up, and I can't deny his blood will be more powerful with how long he's lived," Marvellas said, pleased. "Before Mordecai, I could create dark fae with the spell of Transition using the spiritual blood of an Oracle. But it is not so effective. It would often create those too savage, like a disease rather than a powerful function. It worked to create some fully able dark fae, but it wasn't until I had Mordecai's blood that the odds of it were far greater. I guess we'll see if this one turns out successful."

After all the Spirit had done to get Faythe, it seemed ludicrous she would risk her life on this Transition.

When shuffling sounded, Zaiana expected to find them dragging Faythe forward to kneel with the sacrifices. Instead, it took everything in her—absolutely everything—not to break her position.

It was Kyleer.

Her blood turned cold.

They brought him to the center of the room and pushed him to his knees beside Augustine and the silver-haired fae. Zaiana's vision tilted. There were one too many fae.

Faythe gave the outward reaction Zaiana could hardly tame from within herself.

It became clear to her then...so hauntingly clear.

This night wouldn't be to Transition Faythe.

It was for Kyleer.

She could only conclude it was meant to break Faythe's spirits, which remained strong despite any other efforts. And it was working. Faythe didn't stop struggling against the two guards who held her. Despite the Magestone buried in her flesh and the near-death sight of her pale, slicked flesh, Faythe fought for him.

It was futile, and this Transition...unstoppable.

He won't survive it.

It was all her thoughts roared. A pounding erupted in her head, filling her ears with cotton and blocking out any logical sense to leave, only impulse and desperation threatening to break her.

"Maverick." Marvellas called him over.

Kyleer meant nothing to her. *Should* mean nothing to her.

Yet that statement gave a haughty laugh in the voice of Death that laid a closer claim to him.

Maverick *hesitated*. Near undetectable. No one else would have noticed.

"Please!" Faythe cried, becoming hysterical.

It took three guards to restrain her, and she sympathized with Faythe then, knowing exactly how it felt to harbor magick that could destroy them all and have it silenced when she needed it most.

Zaiana had never wanted anything in her life. Never thought she cared for anything enough to place it above her own survival.

Her fingertips flexed behind her back, feeling a prickling sensation grow. It wasn't enough. Not close to the well she knew could erupt lightning through this room.

"You've defied me for too long, Faythe. I'm hoping this might make you realize how impatient I'm becoming."

"I'll do anything you want—just please don't hurt him!" Faythe sobbed.

Zaiana could hardly hear her. Anything. Her mind was stilling to a calm so cold and lethal as she watched only Kyleer. Seconds turned to a sound in her mind: a loud countdown to the end of the world.

"I've tried to be patient with you—even kind. I'm afraid your chances are gone."

Augustine spoke, spilling a silent tear as he did, only to Faythe. "You were right. She was absolutely wonderful, and a privilege to have met."

Faythe knew what he meant, and it broke down the heir even more.

Then a blade sliced his throat. Zaiana wanted to look away from his final stare of agony held on the stars.

She couldn't move an inch.

A guard came forward, collecting blood that pooled from his neck as he choked on it. Everything about this was a painting of gruesome depravity. A heinous way to have Faythe watch her friends die.

Zaiana's next exhale shuddered from her with a slip of rage when Maverick gripped Kyleer, yanking his head back. Augustine's blood spilled over the sides of his mouth as he was forced to drink it. Murderous rage toward Maverick overcame her far more powerfully than anything she'd felt in the heat of their worst battles. He leaned down subtly, saying something in Kyleer's ear.

A cloaked person on their knees was reciting the forbidden and ancient words of the dark spell, tracing markings on the ground with the spilled spiritual blood.

"Please stop," Faythe sobbed.

Time raced forward so fast. Too fast.

As a guard drew a blade to approach the silver-haired fae, Maverick poised his over Kyleer's throat, and Zaiana's fate became sealed to his knowing what she was about to do.

Zaiana finally broke.

Her first dagger lodged into the throat of the dark fae in front of her. Spinning, the one beside her clutched his hands to his neck with the slice she'd made over it in the same breath. There was nothing but her and those in her way to Kyleer. She fell two more before she caught the flicker of blue she was all too familiar with.

Zaiana moved like the wind to the dart of flame, feeling the hot breath of it pass her before it slammed into two dark fae she'd maneuvered in front of.

"Stop!" Maverick called, but he braced with another attack.

Zaiana pinned him with a promise of death.

The room erupted to chaos, with guards advancing to stop her, and Zaiana gave herself over to the merciless killer she was. Her hand plunged through the chest of a fae, tearing the heart from his ribs, and she kicked his body away only to reach back, hooking arms around the neck of a fae behind her, and his neck snapped as she lunged down, crying out with the force it took to twist his head over her shoulder.

"Enough!" Marvellas bellowed.

Zaiana felt the invasion in her mind. It took hold of her movements, but Zaiana was too far gone in her defiance that she shattered the mental grip. It wasn't without a pain like no other that split her mind, blackening her vision.

Zaiana. Didn't. Stop.

Two guards managed to take hold of her in the moment she was debilitated. As soon as her vision returned enough, her iron guard pierced the flesh of one of them, scoring across his neck, and her other sharp finger guards plunged into the eye of the another. Their shrill cries in her ears were as victorious as they were damning when the weight of her headache to defy Marvellas was becoming too much.

Then a heat scorched her chest, having been too occupied with the guards to keep track of Maverick.

Her back slammed into a wall before she fell to all fours.

She couldn't give up.

It wasn't over.

Zaiana's head snapped up with a frantic fear, locking her sight to the wide, moss-green eyes of Kyleer.

This moment became a cruel mirror copy of the time she'd watched Maverick in the same position.

She never should have cared for that fae. Callen Osirion. Not now he'd become the thing that stood to take everything from her.

When she watched the knife Marvellas held slice over Kyleer's neck and drown in his blood, something more deadly than fury overcame her. More powerful than hate.

Kyleer was her fight.

The first fight she had that wasn't just to survive but to *live*.

She recalled the time she'd had the choice of kill or mercy, confronting him in a meaningless alley in Fenstead. For the first time in her life of emotionless killing...

She'd let Kyleer live.

Only to watch him die now.

The dormant well of magick inside her didn't just awaken.

It exploded.

Her lightning expelled from her in waves so strong she was only the vessel for the storm that snapped around them. As if through all this time of silence it had been building for this moment. Glass shattered, and it rained beautiful weapons. She stopped any of them from hitting Kyleer.

It couldn't be too late.

Zaiana had one target overall, and when she found the flaming beauty, it was a triumph to see the cuts across the Spirit's pale skin from the fallen glass dome.

"You were supposed to be everything, Zaiana. Now look what you've become," Marvellas spat.

Zaiana answered by drawing her hands together, charging a ball of energy within, and sending it hurtling for the Spirit.

She didn't get to witness whether it struck when movement caught in the side of her vision. Zaiana spun low, her knees cut over the glass shards, but it was worth it for the twin blades that sliced through the backs of the guard's knees. He didn't get the chance to fall before she plunged one through his neck.

Then she came face-to-face with Maverick.

"Stop this," he said, far too soft and calm.

The monster in her laughed gleefully.

"Never."

She attacked, seeing nothing but a traitor. This was his fault.

Maverick only deflected, and the lack of strike back only made her push harder.

The next gathering in her palm that prepared to shoot for him never got to release.

Zaiana tensed against moving. An invasion twisted her thoughts, turning her mind against itself, and her head throbbed wildly in resistance.

Zaiana was being pulled under, into a peaceful darkness she didn't want.

She had to know that Kyleer was alive.

In her helplessness, all she could do was search for his heart.

Maverick caught her before she had the chance to fall.

The last of her fight struggled against him. "You're a coward!" she cried. Zaiana hit her weak first against his chest but he held her tightly. "You're a *coward!*"

Gods, she was hurting more than she thought any person could withstand. Not on her flesh, or even her mind. Her chest caved in on itself, and she might have been dying from her tight bottling of emotions she'd guarded for centuries that finally shattered.

"I'm so sorry, Zaiana," Maverick said, so quiet maybe he hadn't spoken at all. "I'm so sorry."

The sounds were canceled out one by one. That control remained hers. She found three heartbeats in the room but kept searching. She would know Kyleer's in a room of a thousand.

It happened so silently and slowly it wasn't something she could stop, this attachment she harbored at the sound of it. Zaiana found herself looking for it even when she knew he was nowhere near. She listened to other beats, finding every one of them was off-key. His was her perfect song.

And it was gone.

It was then she learned still hearts could break. They could shatter. And the pain of that erupted in her chest, so desperate for an outlet she screamed. The world blasted to pieces and reformed at that cry of anguish.

When it did, a drum was racing in her chest.

It battered against her ribs as if a beast had made a home inside her and she had to claw it out. Hands clasped to her chest, she was ready to sink her iron guards into her flesh to be rid of the taunting creature. No one was restraining her anymore.

"Make it stop," she breathed, not familiar with this kind of panic. "Make it stop. *Make it stop.*"

Zaiana crawled to Kyleer.

Make it stop.

Make it stop.

The more she tried to block out the loud drum, the more it pulsed in her ears and sped in her chest, making her skin feel like paper in its efforts to break free.

Make it stop.

Make it stop.

Make it stop.

She slumped over Kyleer's body, head falling to his chest that was so still.

Hers wasn't.

It was...*alive.*

Though she wished it were vacant to match his. She deserved it, not him. But maybe this was her penance with the agony those beats pumped in her blood, faster and warmer than she'd even felt before despite the snowfall lying around them from the ruins of the celestial dome.

If it killed her, if she died here, Zaiana promised to search for Kyleer's heart in the next life.

CHAPTER FORTY-EIGHT

Faythe

W hen Faythe watched Kyleer's life get claimed by the blade across his throat, her mouth opened in horror, but it wasn't her scream of denial that turned every color of blood in the room to ice.

Lightning erupted. Violent strokes sharpened to anguish and rage. Faythe knew in that moment everything about the still organ occupying the dark fae's chest was false, as Zaiana's broke and bled her emotions. All for Kyleer.

Faythe could only brace to absorb the ferocity from her, knowing she wouldn't avoid the outpouring of a storm that had been bottled for so long it had been unleashed now with devastating force.

The impact threw her back. Curving into herself, Faythe couldn't move, immobilized by the soul-obliterating torture shredding her own heart, which clashed with the shock of Zaiana's defiance.

Zaiana had tried to save him.

Faythe couldn't stop replaying that moment that would haunt her for the rest of her days.

Kyleer…he was gone.

She had been helpless to stop the fatal wound.

This wasn't supposed to happen. It was supposed to be *her*. They had gotten it all so horribly wrong. Gus… Faythe mourned for him too.

All Faythe could do was bow her head while chaos ensued around her. Zaiana was still fighting. Faythe clamped her eyes shut and pressed her hands over her ears. Faythe wished only for one person. Over and over. The one she needed to survive the worst nightmare of her existence.

Then everything around her stopped.

The crashing. The voices. The chaos.

Beneath her became so much colder. Then wetter.

Finally, she opened her eyes to the harsh air across her face. By her sheer desperation and heartache alone, she must have Shadowported herself here.

Faythe scrambled to push herself up, gasping at the ice that nipped her palms.

Her vision was restricted by blasts of wind that forced her to squint through the blizzard. The air she breathed was sharp and bitter, bashing her teeth together, but as she looked through the trees and found windows with gentle glows of flame…Faythe knew where she was.

This was the cabin Reylan was tied up within.

By the time she reached the small dwelling, Faythe's wet hair was slicked around her face, and she burst through the door, panting with exertion.

"Reylan," she breathed.

He was still there, still kneeling, with arms splayed and head bowed as if he were a tragic statue of sacrifice. He didn't even look up at her frantic intrusion. Detecting his shallow intakes of breath was the only indicator he was alive.

Faythe fell to her knees with him and took his limp head in her hands.

"Reylan, I need you," she croaked, her tears spilling over.

The ruin still pulsed with deadly power in his chest. Faythe shook her head as if it would expel its calls.

Faythe didn't want to use any more power. She clamped her hands over her ears, willing the dark chants of the ruin to stop calling to her just for a moment. Her grief made it even more difficult, translating to the chaos the ruins fed on. Aurialis had once warned her she needed to better control her negative emotions if she ever hoped to wield a ruin.

So tired.

She was so, so tired.

"Phoenix." That single word. His gentle tone. Faythe cried, wanting to push through her agony to see him.

Her gold eyes peeled open, but she couldn't stop the world from spinning around her to catch a clear picture of Reylan.

"I need you to free me," he said, and his voice was her way back to full awareness.

Faythe reached for his face again, but it didn't take long staring into his beautiful blue eyes to see the shadowy possession still holding him. He was trying to be convincing, but she knew. Faythe smiled at him, playing along.

"I'm going to free you," she said.

"The key is above the fireplace," Reylan informed her.

Faythe could hardly bear to stand, but she made it to the fireplace that scorched her skin too hot. Returning with the key, she hesitated when she took his first wrist. Sapphire melted into gold with their shared look of pain.

"Please."

Her heart *squeezed*.

Faythe freed his first wrist, aching more at the sight of the thick abrasions. She went for the other.

Reylan took a moment, rubbing his wrists. Faythe's heart was erratic watching him, his head bowed. Then, slowly, a cruel, foreign smile crept up the corners of his lips.

"Such a bleeding heart," he growled. "You shouldn't have come."

Then he lunged for her.

Faythe opened her mouth to respond, but her words were choked by Reylan's hands lashing around her neck.

He was far stronger right now. He would be unless she harnessed the power of the ruin. But she would only have one chance if she opened herself to it—one moment to either break it or let it amplify her power to a deadly capacity.

Faythe had fled from one horrifying nightmare into the clutches of another.

"You won't kill me," she wheezed.

He wasn't capable of it. She had to believe that.

"I've been thinking," he said, his voice so sinister it were as if the ruin were speaking through him. "Marvellas doesn't have what it takes to rule this world, but I do. With this power, I can contend with her."

Faythe choked, thrown onto her back. Reylan circled her like a lion while she struggled for stolen air.

"You can't kill her without the ruin," Faythe enlightened him.

Reylan's wicked smile widened. "I have it," he said smugly. Crouching, Reylan's fingers brushed the tangled hair from her face with deceptive tenderness. "I'm surprised you haven't realized yet... *which* ruin I have in me."

Confusion fluttered through her panic. Faythe eyed the distortion on his chest she could see through his thin shirt. It called to her like it always did, but Faythe focused on it—actually listened to the whispers and let her body feel it.

Darkness caressed her skin; shadows leaked through her mind.

Darkness...like *death*.

"Oh Gods," Faythe breathed.

All this time, there hadn't been even another consideration, another reason to believe the ruin embedded in Reylan was any other than Marvellas's.

"Dakodas found me in Rhyenelle," Reylan said. He cupped a large hand around her nape, pulling her up and holding her. "Before we all ended up on that courtyard. She offered me a choice. We were backed into a corner. Marvellas was always going to implant her ruin in one of us, and Dakodas wanted me to swap them before she did. I agreed then to be able to give you Marvellas's ruin to kill her once and for all. I didn't care what happened to me. So when Marvellas took me to retrieve hers, I switched it with Dakodas's before they embedded it in my chest."

How could she not have seen it sooner?

"Now I have Marvellas's ruin to kill her, and as I've come to learn, there are manacles—Aetherbonds—which can seal away the power of the greatest being, and then I can stop Dakodas too. You don't happen to know where they are, do you?"

Faythe's mind was racing too fast for her comprehension right now.

Reylan switched the ruins.

Reylan has the Death Ruin inside him.

"That ruin is corrupting you," Faythe said desperately.

"Do you know why I wanted you to break it? Because if you do, it will split a void for shadow creatures to emerge."

Horror flooded her veins.

"Why would you want that?"

"Because they will purge this world of sinners."

"Everyone is a sinner."

Reylan's smile spread, wickedly triumphant. "Exactly. Death's realm will begin to thrive again."

"No…"

"Yes, Faythe. There are two choices for you. I kill you here, then I kill Marvellas with her ruin she thinks is in me, then I find the Aetherbonds to lock away Dakodas's power. This realm will be mine."

It wasn't him in the slightest. He was a vessel to this ruin that wanted conquest in death and darkness, perhaps a worse fate than Marvellas had planned in her course of genocide.

If Faythe broke the ruin…she was enlightened to the creatures she would unleash that would begin devouring *everyone*.

"The other choice?" Faythe asked, keeping her voice steady as she stared into his beautiful alive eyes.

"You break the ruin. We kill Marvellas together, lock away Dakodas together, and watch the world burn from its sins."

Two choices, both damning to the world. The second would give her Reylan back, but he would be horrified with what she'd done to have him.

Faythe held his eyes with such desperation, as if his true self would surface to tell her what to do.

Unexpectedly, he kissed her, and Faythe gave in to it. Just for a moment.

Then she braced herself…and splayed her palm over the ruin, opening herself to its power.

His fist tightened in her hair, pulling her close as surges of magick tore through them both, raw and electric. The pain that had once racked her body faded. She forgot why she had been crying. Everything dulled to nothing under the overwhelming rush of power now flooding her veins. For the first time she felt unstoppable, a fierce strength blazing within her, hot and boundless.

Faythe seized that newfound power, feeling it pulse under her control, and channeled it through her palm pressed firmly against Reylan's chest. Her hand glowed with intensity as the energy surged forward, flowing into him with a force that made the air crackle around them.

But she couldn't make such a detrimental choice yet.

Reylan flew back from her force of magick, crashing into the wall. Faythe flipped herself onto her hands and knees, but before she could scramble up, Reylan was already upon her again, dragging her back by her ankle.

Flipped onto her back, Faythe kicked his chest, connecting with the ruin again. Every time they physically connected through the ruin, together they skipped through so much color and space. Towns and cities. Paths of endless possibilities.

An entangling inferno of darkness and fire raged through her, and Faythe turned *starving* for it.

There were few times Faythe had felt this alive. Unchallenged. This kind of magick, if not careful, could corrode her soul.

When they plummeted back to their reality, Faythe was breathless but reforged.

"You chose death then," Reylan snarled, furious with her rebellion.

"Not today," she said, right before her hands collected a gale of light that she threw at him.

Reylan broke *through* the wall of the cabin this time.

Faythe didn't waste a precious second—she raced out of the hut.

Reylan or the world. Reylan or the world. Reylan or the world.

How was she to make such an impossible choice? One was selfish. Completely, villainously selfish. But she wanted him so badly, clinging to a thread in her being that screamed at her to never let him go; that once they were together, they could figure out how to right all that Faythe had wronged.

Only the moon illuminated the night enough for her to make it out of the tree line. She didn't have a plan as Reylan's chase stormed over the snow. Her mind whipped between the two choices Reylan left her with. Both were so detrimental Faythe struggled to accept either.

Her time was running out.

Faythe felt him following. Lightning pricked her fingertips, and she turned to send a strike toward Reylan. He took the power from her effortlessly, sending the strokes of amethyst parrying right back. Faythe narrowly avoided their paths by ducking behind trees.

The timber behind her split with the next blast Reylan sent into it, and Faythe shrieked, her heart choking in her throat as the tree began to fall. She had to dive out of the way to avoid being crushed under it.

Faythe had barely managed to scramble back to her feet when a sense raising the hairs on her nape made her whirl around. Light magick surged from her glowing palm as a natural defense. It collided with a stroke of dark power of the likes she'd never seen nor felt before. Faythe's other hand joined the strain to hold steadfast against Reylan when the dark was winning against the light. Their collusion fused, so beautiful yet deadly, and Reylan stood just as mesmerized as the world around them began to gild in her vision.

Pushing harder, the strength of their powers became so much for them that it erupted in a flare that sent Faythe soaring back. She slammed into a tree, and the pain that impacted her head threatened her consciousness. Faythe's senses lapped back slowly to feel the snow melting under her face, turning her skin numb. She was so tired, barely able to angle her arms to lift herself from the freezing ground.

Faythe cried when she was flipped onto her back suddenly, and Reylan straddled her, pinning her hands by her head. Even with the loathing and rage sharpening his features, he was so beautiful against the moonlight, with the snow falling around them.

"It's okay," she breathed. There was nothing left to do but accept peace. This moment she had with him. "I found you. I will always find you. In every realm and in every time, Reylan Arrowood."

Reylan only stared at her, searching her eyes with confusion but struggling against the demand in him against her.

"Why do I feel this way?"

Her heart skipped a beat. "What way?"

Reylan's eyes scrunched shut. He was slipping. There was a glimmer of hope he could come back to her, and it was slipping away.

"Like I have to kill you but I don't know if I have the strength to do it."

Faythe's eyes dropped to the glowing ruin in his chest. "Me neither," she whispered. Tears slipped down past her ears.

Their time was up.

Faythe had to *try*.

A shrill caw broke over the silent night. Faythe had felt Atherius moments ago. The flaming beauty soared up from the edge of the mountain like the sun rising blazing and triumphant against the night. She landed, melting the surrounding snow instantly, and her chest heaved, ready to blast toward them.

It distracted Reylan long enough that Faythe's leg hooked around him, flipping their positions.

Her vision blurred, her heart cleaved in two, and her soul wailed as she said, "Please come back to me," and pressed both her palms to the ruin.

Their souls...*transcende*d.

They touched the beginning of time and the end of it. She saw the birth of stars and the chaos of constellations. The first light and the last darkness.

A voice echoed to her through the void she drifted in.

If you break the ruin, you will damn your world.

It was Aurialis.

Reylan's face came to her in opaque flashes. It had never twisted with so much pain and pleading.

"It's not my world without him," Faythe whispered.

Her soul plummeted back into her body, returning the sensation of the magick that burned through her more powerfully than she'd ever known before. Faythe anchored herself through the feeling of her hands on her mate, and she would *never* let him go. With a battle cry from the Gods, Faythe pushed her magick *harder*. Deep into the crevices, splitting apart the ruin with piercing wails.

Time fractured, and the world erupted.

Faythe was flying, thrown by an impact that separated her mind from the explosion of pain in her body. The bright flare of light stole her away from the consequence of her actions.

She was standing in a dark hall, in front of a massive statue towering high. A cloaked figure with no face, only a depthless hood. It held a scythe, a chip missing from the under curve of the blade.

Around the huge statue, the still black birds began to find movement, twitching until the first broke off to fly. Then another. And another. Terror seized her when hundreds of ravens beat around the space. The towering figure warped and shrank, the illusion weaving a dizzy spell as it became a tall mortal size and glided for her across a shallow, rippling pool of dark water.

"What are you?" Faythe breathed.

"I am the thing every being fears to meet, but their hand in mine is inevitable."

Faythe was chilled to her core. "Death," she uttered.

Oh Gods, had she failed?

"I like to ask, what is it you fear about coming with me?"

Faythe broke inside. "I can't leave my friends. I can't leave him. I'm not done yet."

The primordial hummed. "My children have caused something of a mess in your realm. It is why I had to awaken the essences of the mortal Gods to unite against them. Power, strength, wisdom, resilience, courage, knowledge, light and dark as one."

"Your children?"

"Life, death, and soul. I have many of them, across many ages and realms."

Faythe raised a hand to her heart that didn't beat in here. "Aurialis has been helping us."

"Or is she another power that has managed to manipulate you with gentler means?"

Her instinct was to rebut that accusation. All this time, Aurialis had guided her. She'd been the Spirit on their side, and Faythe wouldn't have gotten this far without her.

"No. You're the one with your own agenda, wanting to unleash the shadow creatures that will feed your realm with the people from mine."

"I will admit, that is a highly advantageous turn of events for me. You see, fate has many paths, and this one leads in my favor. My realm has been starved by meddling Gods in another realm not so different from yours. Reaping all the souls is highly tempting, but against every law of how balance should be achieved."

Faythe couldn't decide if this primordial was against what would unfold with the shadow creatures.

"How do I stop them?" Faythe pleaded.

"You already know there is one weapon that can kill the undead. You also know what was used to forge it."

Faythe racked her brain desperately.

"The Ember Sword," she concluded.

"Phoenixfyre destroys, while Shadowfyre controls."

She didn't know what that meant—*Shadowfyre*. She'd never heard of such a concept.

Death said, "I'm going to show you some memories, Faythe Ashfyre. They don't begin with you, but they have always been destined to end with you."

Faythe fell to her knees, not entirely of her own conscious thought. Her hands fell into the shallow pool around her, and the reflection of her horrified expression changed. The water swirled, filling with color, starlight, and wonder, and she wanted to tear her sight away, but that wasn't within her control anymore. The moving pictures hooked onto her, and she was compelled to watch the past of her world unfold.

Faythe saw the dawning of the world the seven Gods had created. Zaiana had told her their names before: *Demetris, the God of Strength. Erosen, the God of Wisdom. Iyana, the Goddess of Knowledge. Helios, the God of Courage. Fedara, the Goddess of Resilience. Kitana, the Goddess of Darkness and Light. Lasenna, the Goddess of Power.*

She watched the mortals they'd created in their image live their age, bear their children, and see through ages of peace. Faythe saw the age of demons, human-like beings with piercing red eyes, and the annihilation of them. She tumbled through the Dark Age led by Mordecai Vesaria and saw how the mighty continents of Ungardia and Salenhaven came together to stop him. Faythe got to see the fall of Marvellas to land, her tragic captivity, and her freedom.

In the mere blink of her eyes, Faythe had captured the beginning and the end of her world.

She couldn't move. No mind should harbor this much knowledge, and Faythe didn't know how hers would contain it.

"*Fesia omarte, Fesia lasera.*" Death spoke the old language Zaiana once had.

Fall one, fall all.

"You are the One, Faythe Ashfyre. Not just the Heir of Marvellas but the Heir of Lasenna. But without the others fulfilling their destiny, you will fall, and all will be lost for this world."

Faythe's mind began to recite her vow, because a part of her had already figured it out:

My name is Faythe Arrowood Ashfyre, soul-bonded to Reylan Arrowood Ashfyre. Daughter of Agalhor and Lilianna. Rightful Queen of Rhyenelle. I am Reylan's strength. Nik's wisdom, and Tauria's resilience. Jakon's courage, and Marlowe's knowledge. I am not alone, and I will not die today.

Death said calmly, "There are infinite worlds much like yours. It is not personal."

"You mean we're disposable," she snapped.

"All things must die. You are all but a blink of time, a grain of existence, to the expanse of all that is. The universe births new worlds, Gods create new systems, all in a never-ending search for something that cannot and will not ever exist—perfection."

"Then let us be flawed."

"That is not something we can accept. So we try again, and again. That is infinity. But your small world can be saved so life can be lived for many ages to come. A Godless world can survive. It is up to you now."

"What if the Spirits win?"

"Then they win. My final interference was to awaken the mortal essence in the bloodlines of the seven who created it."

"If you don't care what happens to us, then why are you telling me this now? Why bring me here at all?"

"Because Gods are proud and do not like to be bested by each other. The Spirits were bestowed from my realm, and what they have done is an insult. Much as I would have liked for you to send them back to me, that is no longer a possibility now one of the ruins is broken. They are all cunning. I cannot hold you here any longer. You must go back."

Before she could speak again, Faythe's body seized.

With a long draw of breath, the vision around her collapsed. What was endless black above her started to lighten to a hue of navy and flood with glittering stars. For a second, the view brought her complete peace.

Pain started to creep back through her bones, but a wave over her soothed the sharpness. An amber hue danced against midnight, and Faythe remembered Atherius. She was helping her now. Healing her. Faythe's arm reached until she felt something.

Someone.

Her head lolled, finding Reylan, and her whole world turned still.

Because his chest…it wasn't rising.

And as she listened…his heart was silent.

"Reylan," she said, pushing up and swaying with the dizziness, but she shook her head. "Wake up."

Faythe got to her knees. Panic trembled her hands that rose over him, but she didn't know what to do. She tore down the front of his shirt and saw the ghastly sight of the ruin still in him, but she only felt the echoing cries of its fading magic. It was black and crumbling within his flesh.

He needed Nerida. A healer.

But that wouldn't matter if his heart wasn't beating.

He couldn't lie there in the cold, so she maneuvered him around, crying out with the weight of him but managing to hook her hands under his arms. Faythe sobbed trying to hold him off the snow, only lifting his head to her chest.

"I need him!" Faythe cried. She looked around, but no one was coming.

Atherius gave off a sound like a soft cry of pain that she couldn't help.

No one could.

Faythe's forehead leaned to his silver hair as she cried.

She'd failed.

"I can't *lose* him!"

She didn't know if any Gods were listening, but her head straightened with the rage to defy them all.

Slipping a hand over his chest, Faythe reached for her magick. It glowed brightly, and Faythe searched for him. His soul that was *hers*. He wasn't getting to leave this world before they'd gotten to claim their bond.

In her distant senses, Atherius beat her wings. Her cries pierced the air, and Faythe felt threads of Phoenix magick entwining with her. Then a touch so barely-there hovered over her hand, and Faythe gasped—then her face crumpled, and she broke a sob.

"I can't save him," she wept to Caius.

"We're right here with you." Caius crouched with her, his boyish smile so assuring.

Then another hand took hers, adding to the glow of magick that was growing over Reylan.

Faythe was distracted for a moment of shock and joy, but an old wound cleaved open within her.

"Mother?" she breathed.

Lilianna nodded, and Faythe knew this was no dream. It was something precious, and perhaps the last of the Spirit of Life inside her that, despite all Faythe had done in condemning the world, was giving her this one last gift.

Behind Lilianna, Agalhor lowered too, placing his hand with theirs, and Faythe never thought she would get the chance in all her lifetime to see this.

Her parents—together. Fresh tears flooded her eyes.

"I'm so sorry," she said to him.

Agalhor shook his head. "We are so proud of you, my girl."

Faythe didn't think she deserved it, but she was so grateful they were here.

Then two more hands eased over hers, and Faythe's attention was stolen by them.

"Freya," Faythe said. Then her eyes fell to the other, who she only remembered from a flash of vision. "Kerim."

Both of them smiled. "It wasn't your fault back then," Kerim said. "You might never remember, but it was a privilege to be your friend, Aesira."

She remembered him on a battlefield, about to be struck down, and Aesira's arrow could have saved him...but she'd missed.

"He needs you," Freya said. "You need each other."

Faythe smiled her gratitude, returning her focus to Reylan. She couldn't feel his heart when so much life was coursing through the both of them. It was light and binding and promising. Her eyes closed, and Faythe searched through the endless darkness for him. She would keep searching until her last light winked out.

She found him in a dark expanse of time and space. He had his back to her this time, kneeling in a shallow pool of black water while flocks of ravens flew violently around him.

"Reylan." His name escaped her in a breath.

The birds didn't harm him, but it was like they were aware of his presence. Maybe even protective of him.

Faythe approached slowly, cautiously, trying to tune out the pounding of wings to find his heartbeat, but not even her own existed in her chest here.

This Void of Choosing.

Faythe didn't know what was about to come; what had to happen for this second chance. Whatever the price, she was willing to pay it to have him.

Reylan was shirtless, and his back was marked in ink. The closer she got, the air was stolen from her lungs at the beautiful black wings tattooed there, draping over his shoulders and his biceps.

Her hand reached out when he was close enough to touch, and her fingers trailed up his spine. Reylan was so still she didn't know if he could feel her.

Until he spoke.

"Faythe."

"I'm here," she said, emotion tightening her throat.

"I don't know what to do," he said. So lost and broken.

"It has to be his choice," the primordial said. *"To die a hero. Or to be reborn."*

"As what?" Faythe dared to ask.

"My servant."

Of this God as old as time.

Faythe came around to Reylan's front, sinking to her knees, and the icy water lapped around them. She took his face, guiding his bowed head up, but he couldn't see her. His eyes were wholly black, the white and sapphire swallowed by depthless obsidian.

"All I see is darkness," he said.

"I'm with you."

His brow flinched at that, hand rising over hers. "If this is where you are, it's where I want to stay," he said.

"I'm not leaving without you." Tears slipped down her cheeks as her forehead pressed to his. "You don't have to come back. I'll stay right here with you."

Faythe's hand upturned between them. She sobbed when Reylan's slipped into it, and the black branches that crawled across his skin began to reach over hers, entwining with her golden tattoos. She wasn't afraid of the darkness. Not with him here.

"I choose you," Reylan said.

Reylan's sapphire irises started to come back as the black pool dispersed.

Faythe leaned in, and the moment their mouths met, she found a heart. One that beat for both of them.

She wasn't afraid. As long as she had him, she could never be afraid.

The real world came crashing down around her, and Faythe's throat was speared by a deep inhale of winter air.

Faythe kneeled, holding the weight of Reylan's upper body. She was alone. Blinking, she remembered her parents and her friends. Under her palm…

She gasped at Reylan's cold hand that slipped over hers on his chest. Over his heartbeat, which Faythe treasured every beat of with a euphoric, breathy chuckle that was pure exhaustion and relief.

"Faythe," Reylan said, shifting his head to look up at her.

"I'm here," she rasped, delirious and overwhelmed. "It's me."

When Faythe saw sapphire, the world of war and heartache around them ceased to exist.

Reylan pushed up with a groan of pain. They stared at each other as if they were both reflecting on the same dream, trying to puzzle together what was real of it. Until it didn't matter.

Faythe sobbed into his shoulder when his arms encircled her, and their bodies met tightly. He pulled her over him and held her like they were one person.

"You shouldn't have come for me," he mumbled into her hair.

"There's no realm that I wouldn't crack the spaces between to find you."

His arm tightened a fraction before his body tensed with a hiss.

Faythe pulled away, only to examine the ruin that was still embedded in him. The flesh around it was getting worse. They needed to reach Nerida.

His hand cupped her cheek, eyes filling with an ocean of grief. "I'm so sorry. Everything I did—"

Faythe shook her head, bringing her mouth to his. She kissed him, needy and desperate, wanting to treasure every feel of him after clawing them out of their worst nightmare together.

"I'm sorry too," Faythe said against his lips. "But this is the last time we say it."

Reylan kissed her again. Their lips were almost numb with the cold, but she felt it all in her heart.

A loud boom sounded so distantly below. Faythe shuddered at the reminder nothing was won. Not for the world, but now she had Reylan, Faythe had her strength to conquer it.

"What is happening?" Reylan asked, shifting into a battle focus he was too injured to maintain. "Where are we?"

"Lakelaria. We have to get away from here. You can't fight like this."

"Where are the others? Kyleer?"

She helped Reylan stand, but she was close to collapsing again at the devastation his name pummeled into her.

"He…oh, Reylan."

His attention was immediately fixed on her, cupping her cheek and searching her eyes for the answer she couldn't speak. Hadn't accepted was true yet.

"No…" Reylan muttered. She'd never heard such heartbreak in a single word. He looked over at Atherius and started toward the Firebird.

"We have to leave," Faythe sobbed.

"He's not gone," Reylan said firmly.

"He might have survived it."

Reylan's head whipped back, but it gave away how weak he was when the sudden movement stumbled his balance. Faythe circled her arms around him again.

"Survived?"

"The Transition."

His eyes closed, and Faythe bit her lip hard when her own grief threatened to shatter her.

"We have to get you to Nerida or another healer," Faythe pleaded.

"I have to see for myself. I can't leave him here."

"We'll come back."

Reylan leaned his forehead to hers.

"I can still move. I can feel your magick and swing a sword. Until I can't do that, I'll keep fighting."

"You can't swing a sword. And you don't have one *to* swing."

"I'll—*fuck*—" Reylan hissed, a hand rising to his chest.

Faythe began to panic. Her eyes scanned back to the hut. "Atherius can lend some of her magick to help. Let's just rest for a few hours. Please."

He followed her line of sight, jaw working with a desire to protest, but to her relief, he nodded.

Faythe bore a lot of his weight as they trekked back through the treacherous weather. Her teeth bashed together violently with her adrenaline worn off, and her fatigue made every muscle strain.

Inside, she took them right to the fire still blazing. Reylan sat by it while Faythe collected every blanket and cushion she could from around the quaint little home. The hole Reylan's body had made in the side wall was the biggest inconvenience now with the nasty draft of bitter, snowy air. Until a large red, feathery barricade blocked it.

"I didn't think she'd be tolerant of this climate," Reylan remarked.

"She's not, but she knows we need her," Faythe said sadly. She could feel the Firebird's distress, both for the weather and their pain. Faythe echoed her gratitude back.

Tuning back in to Reylan, she threw a blanket over his shoulders, immediately standing again. She had to find something to clean his wound as best she could.

Faythe stalled when her eyes caught on a picture above the fire. She hadn't had the time to notice the painting of Marvellas before... and next to her was a man. Human.

This was her first love. The one who'd betrayed her, held her captive, and stolen her blood. He looked so familiar. With blond hair and brown eyes, tall, with a boyish smile. He looked...like Reuben.

Faythe's fingers touched her mouth with the eerie coincidence. Then she shuddered, realizing this hut must have been their home at some time. Such a humble setting she could never envision the Spirit in.

"Come here," Reylan said gently.

Faythe slid her eyes to him. "I need to find water...a salve, maybe, or—"

"Please."

She couldn't resist the compulsion in that single word.

Faythe sank to her knees in front of him. He didn't waste a second in pulling her close. She turned resistant when he tried to nestle her against him.

"Your wound—"

"Is nothing compared to the ache I have of missing you."

Faythe melted into him with that.

She felt him. His warmth. His scent. His touch.

"I missed you," she said in a whisper. "I missed you so much."

Reylan tipped her chin, coaxing her to look back at him. He was so beautiful, and she was completely taken by him, as if it were the first time. His eyes sparkled now, free from the manipulation of

Marvellas. They held her with such devotion her heart swelled too big for her chest.

He kissed her, deep and promising. "You brave, incredible thing," he muttered against her lips. "I love you with all the defiance in my being against everything that has tried to tear us apart. We may have broken a ruin and condemned the world to the Neither. Now let's set the heavens ablaze, my Phoenix, and walk through the fires hand in hand."

PART THREE

SET THE HEAVENS ABLAZE

CHAPTER FORTY-NINE

Zaiana

Zaiana awoke to a sound that consumed all others. A blast that boomed loud and left an eerie silence in its wake. The ground beneath her rumbled, and Zaiana felt in her core the split of something dark and damning. An imbalance that cracked through their world.

Faythe did it. She broke the ruin.

There were no Gods to save them now.

When the rumbling stopped and her senses returned, Zaiana jolted up at the foreign sensation that slammed within her. She couldn't survey her surroundings while her trembling hands rose to her chest, hoping it was just a taunting illusion. It couldn't be real.

But there it was. A precious life beating too fast under her palms, and she didn't know what to do with it. Her vision blurred. How often had she fantasized about owning this fluttering, uncontrollable beat in her own body? She knew the symphony of a thousand others, what it took to make them speed and slow, but this one would take so much more time and care to figure out. Perhaps she never would and that was the true curse of having a heart—its ever-changing movement and the helplessness to fight against what disrupted it, good or bad.

Zaiana's knees pulled to her chest, and her hands cupped over this new delicate thing as if it were cradled in her palms. It felt so vulnerable. Like her flesh and bone wasn't enough to protect it and she didn't know what else would be.

With the only sound coming from her, she realized she wasn't alone when she took a long inhale and a familiar scent filled her. Snapping her head to the side, she saw a bundle through the thick iron bars beside her. The last memory she had lurched the beat in her chest, and she didn't know it could choke in people's throats like this. Her balance swayed as she crawled across the short space. Zaiana wept silently, completely numb to the Niltain steel around her wrists as she curled her hands around the bars.

Kyleer lay so peaceful. A few locks of brown hair fell over his eyes, and she yearned to be close enough to brush it away. For those moss-green eyes to open and tell her he was going to be okay.

He had no wings. Yet. Maybe not ever.

Zaiana searched for the cadence of his heart.

It was gone.

All she wanted in that moment was to rip out the one she now owned and give it to him. It was an impostor in her chest. Something Kyleer deserved to have, not her.

"Ky," she barely croaked.

No response.

The despair that grew inside her could kill. Zaiana didn't care. Of all her failings in life, she bowed her forehead to the icy metal, accepting this was the worst of them.

"If I hadn't tried to stop you, she would have killed you if she didn't get what she wanted."

A hot rage clenched her fists to a white-knuckle grip at the sound of Maverick's voice.

"I should have known your loyalty would always be with them. Always their precious, obedient pet."

"A thank-you would suffice," Maverick said.

"I'm going to get out of here, and you'd better not be within reach, because I will kill you," Zaiana promised. Words so sharp and lethal.

"At least you're alive to do so."

She glanced at him where he stood with arms crossed, leaning against the wall, cloaked in shadow.

"Did Marvellas call for you to come here for this? You had no hesitation in killing Faythe, nor Agalhor, and she knew it would hurt Faythe more seeing you take her friend too."

"Perhaps. But I had no hesitation in killing Faythe nor Agalhor only because you did."

"You wanted the glory, and you got it."

"Believe what you want," he said coldly. "It makes no difference to me."

"How can you do it…?" Zaiana got to her feet, stalking to the side he faced. "Betray those who were once your friends, like Nikalias?"

"Nik is no one to me."

"Let's not play games, Callen."

He flinched at the name. Barely, but Zaiana had made her mark.

"Congratulations," he said. "You may have brought back the heart of Callen, but it is too tainted by the deeds of Maverick. It means nothing."

She heard it then. His heartbeat. It stunned her completely, making her forget everything for a moment. It knocked around behind his ribs, the song of a broken soul. Zaiana buried the notes of tragedy that fluttered in her own heart for him. She *despised* him.

"How many others have their hearts?" she asked.

"All of them. Somehow, you broke a curse none of them knew they were under. I have a feeling you've caused something, Zaiana. Something that could shift the tide of war."

"How—?" She couldn't process what was happening. How it was possible. All she'd done was try to save Kyleer.

Her magick was back too. Despite the heavy weight of the steel, it was distantly there, and she knew she could drag it forth to strike Maverick now if she so desired. She wouldn't out herself just yet to give away that upper hand.

It didn't matter right now. She wanted to kill Maverick, and she despised that she had to ask him for anything.

"When did you remember your past as Callen?" she ground out.

It had been puzzling her this whole time, how Maverick could have his memories when the Transitioned were said to lose them. But if Kyleer didn't remember anything when he woke…she had to find out how he'd done it.

Maverick came closer, giving no emotion through his steel features. "I remembered…" he said, his tone so detached and icy her skin prickled, "the day I held my mate as she died, and I looked down to see my hand around the hilt of the blade in her heart."

Zaiana held her breath for a second. She didn't want to feel the slither of *remorse* for the wicked fallen prince.

She didn't want to feel at all.

"So this is how villains are made," she said.

Maverick looked down at her from his height, and she saw it: his black irises like a mirror.

One and the same.

They were two sides of the same coin, tainted by irredeemable sin.

"No," he said at last. "You don't get to blame something for that choice. If the villain is what you want to be, then *own it*. Not for some past that has wronged you, even if time and time again. Or you are no better than Marvellas."

"And what are you?"

Maverick leaned away. "Nothing," he said.

She watched his back as he left, raging with so much turmoil she didn't know how to handle it.

So many wounds inside her strained toward bursting, and if she let it all go...Zaiana didn't know who she would be if she bled from all the open scars.

She lay back down, so close to the bars, next to Kyleer. Zaiana reached through, slipping her fingers over his limp hand until her restraints met their end. His skin was as cold as the dead.

Her brow crumpled, and her eyes slipped shut.

Zaiana lay with him, and if he didn't wake in that moment, she didn't think she wanted to either.

But hours passed in torment. Sleep wouldn't find her to offer her some reprieve from the miserable wait of knowing if Kyleer had pulled through his Transition.

"Your lover, I presume?"

The new voice that crept over the cells tightened her body with a mix of anger and irritation. Zaiana sat up, slipping her lazy, dark sight to Captain Daegal.

She didn't like him in the slightest, and she'd grown to hate him even more since the day he assaulted Faythe. Not for what he did—that was pathetic, and she would have cut him down before he got to fulfill any sick fantasy—but after he awoke, Zaiana had been unable to shake a new sensation that crawled over her, *within her*, when he was near. She could hardly stand to look into his brown eyes that she believed had somehow become brighter too, luring her in, and if she dared to get close enough, she was sure to drive a blade through his heart to sever the hypnotism he invoked.

"Has she sent you to see if he's alive?" Zaiana asked bitterly.

"No. Marvellas is more livid about you, in fact. And that Faythe Ashfyre is missing."

The heir had broken the ruin and got away. Zaiana had stopped underestimating Faythe long ago, so anything less than this news would have been disappointing.

"Have you come to take me for punishment?"

The captain smiled with cruel amusement, taking a step closer to the bars of her cell. "I can see why she despises you. Even before your grand rebellion in the dome, you were completely untamable. Something tells me many have tried to tie a leash around you."

"Many things tell me you're a powerless, low-life piece of shit. So get on with what you came here for."

Daegal smirked, then his face turned unnervingly serious. He scanned her from head to toe, and she wanted to claw his eyes out. Then, when he shifted his attention to Kyleer, Zaiana rose to her feet.

The captain lifted a hand, curling his fingers around one of the bars. His eyes pierced into her, gripping her attention. "I need you to listen to me very carefully," he said, hushed, in a tone unlike him. "I am not Captain Daegal. He's dead. Faythe killed him to give me control of his mind."

He carried on explaining an outlandish story of Realm-Walking and his collusion with Faythe. The most incredulous part that made her laugh out loud…

"You expect me to believe you're her long-lost son?"

His eyes narrowed to a warning, casting a brief glance at the exit. "We're alone for now, but you'd be wise to keep silent," he hissed.

"Rainyte."

"Just Nyte."

Zaiana huffed—a humorless sound this time. She paced her cell, spinning his tale around in her mind. It was too outlandish to be believable.

Yet her instinct, which had always served her well, wouldn't dismiss his claim entirely.

Her eyes roved over him again, taking in what seemed to have changed from the vicious captain she'd been in the displeasing company of a few times. His irises were lighter, as if the dark brown they previously were was struggling to contain the ethereal gold they should be if he was Marvellas's son. His demeanor too seemed changed, less rigid and defensive, more lax, borderline arrogant now. The way he talked was smoother and confident.

"Even if I believe you, I want no part in whatever you're up to with Faythe," Zaiana said at last.

"That's too bad. You're very much a part of everything—you have been for some time, I believe."

"Then what is your objective?"

"Getting you out of here seems like a good start."

"I don't need your help. Go find Faythe."

"You're an invaluable ally to her, and you're in a cage."

"I'm not her ally."

His gaze shifted again to Kyleer as if that were proof of the contrary.

Zaiana amended. "I'm not anyone's ally."

"Taking on the world alone isn't as noble as you think it is."

"You don't know anything about me."

"I doubt there are many who know about you truly."

His mere presence crawled her skin, and the way he spoke, like he resonated with her, was growing her intolerance.

"What do you want from me?" she snapped.

"Cooperation," he said flatly. "I have a deal with Faythe Ashfyre to help where I can in exchange for her helping me to discover a way back to my realm. From your epic display to save your lover, her friend, I'd consider you an asset to the cause to stop my mother."

Part of her still held onto reservation. This could be a trick. The tale he spun was elaborate, but what if it was an attempt to get her to lure out Faythe?

"I want you to do something to prove what you say is true—that you're not Daegal, and you're not working for Marvellas."

"I'm all ears. It's been getting dull around here without Faythe, and I don't particularly enjoy the awkward presence of my unsuspecting mother while I'm in this body."

Zaiana's request could work against her if *Nyte* betrayed her. But she had little left to lose anyway.

She said, "You're going to need to find someone with wings who can deliver a fast message."

CHAPTER FIFTY

Faythe

Faythe sat in front of Reylan, wishing she could take some of his pain as she plucked at small pieces of the ruin crumbling in his chest. She winced for him, pulling another sharp serration, but Reylan sat there like steel, his breathing measured and controlled, enduring it.

"We need a healer with magick. It's like it's dissolving." Faythe was panicked but tried to maintain her outward bravery for him.

The tan of Reylan's skin was washed pale and slicked with fever. Atherius's magick wasn't helping with the punishment the ruin had inflicted on him. She'd thought rest might bring back some of his strength, but his condition had worsened overnight.

Faythe gathered the pieces she could retract in a piece of cloth, but what remained now looked like broken coal buried deep in his flesh, turning his skin gray.

"I'm fine," Reylan said.

"You're not fine. Nothing about this is fine."

"I have you back. I'm more than fine."

He absentmindedly stroked her thighs, straddled on either side of him, as if she were the one in need of reassurance. His head tipped back against the wall of the hut. It was their second night here, and Faythe was aware of how much they risked by staying should Marvellas come. But at dawn this morning, Reylan could hardly move, and they wouldn't survive the temperature outside to find another shelter. Faythe's magick constantly hummed in her veins in anticipation, making her jittery and antsy. She could hardly be still for a moment.

The Firebird lay curled in a tight ball, having not moved since she'd blocked the hole in the hut wall to keep them warm within.

Reylan's hand ran up her spine while his lips leaned into her neck, distracting her. Faythe sighed with the bliss of his touches, but her mind remained stern.

"You need to rest," she whispered, willing herself to push him back.

His eyes never left her though they watched her through hooded, tired lids. She wished he would try to sleep, but it was like he was too afraid. As if those hours of vulnerability in his sleep could give his mind back to Marvellas.

Faythe leaned over, cupping his cheek. "Please."

Reylan almost smiled. "I would drop to my knees and tear apart cities if you asked like that. But I'm not letting you out of my sight so soon after getting you back."

"You have to sleep."

He tucked her loose hair behind her ear. "I shouldn't have left you in Rhyenelle when the battle first broke."

That confession slipped out as barely a pained murmur through his lips.

"You had to lead. It was your duty."

"I should have taken you with me."

Faythe shook her head. "Don't do that. Don't try to rewrite the past for an outcome that will never be. This is where we are now. And despite the Nether we had to go through and that is still open around us, we're together now."

He inhaled a long breath, heavy with burden. "You're right."

"I always am."

Reylan gave a light, tired chuckle. The sound spread warmth through her. He drew her close.

"I'm terrified," he whispered against her mouth—a secret passed in a shared breath. "I remember everything from the time she had me at her will, and I'm terrified I don't have the willpower to refuse her influence when we see her again, even without the ruin in me."

"You do," Faythe said fiercely. Her fingers threaded through his silver hair. "She won't get the chance to be close to you anytime soon. We'll train. If what you've been through has weakened your mental barriers, we'll train with me. I'll try to infiltrate your mind, and you'll block me each time. I'm just as strong as her."

At least, she had to become as powerful. *Believe* she could contend with Marvellas when the time came.

Faythe was afraid to ask, "Where did you hide Marvellas's ruin after you switched it with Dakodas's?"

Reylan stiffened under her. "I gave it to Zaiana."

Faythe's eyes widened. "Why in the Nether would you give it to her?"

"She knew. The moment we were alone, she asked why Marvellas would plant Dakodas's ruin and not her own if you were to break it. I had to tell her what I'd done, and then eventually...I don't think I trusted *myself* not to tell Marvellas the ruins were switched. I feared she would figure it out, and something about Zaiana felt *trustworthy*." He said the last word as if, in his right mind, he now refused that idea profusely.

"She fought for him," Faythe said, slashed brutally with flashes of vision from the horrifying night in the dome. "She fought Marvellas and Maverick to try to save Kyleer like I would for you."

Reylan's brow creased. "What happened to her for that betrayal?"

"I don't know."

"I can't say I'd mourn for her."

"She's important. I know she is." Faythe paused, contemplating her thoughts. "Aurialis once said I had to find the teacher who tames the storm. It has to be Zaiana. She's the only one who can wield the ruin safely. She can teach me."

Reylan groaned, pulling her with an arm around her waist, until she was sitting sideways against him and he could rest his head on hers. "I wish that weren't so."

"Well, I wish you would rest and stop worrying about anything else but yourself right now."

His body relaxed, and Faythe thought he might actually be caving in to his fatigue.

"Promise you won't leave for a second without me."

"So clingy."

He squeezed her thigh, and Faythe giggled softly, nestling into him more with a contented sigh.

Reylan said, "I can't tell you how sorry I am. Everything I did to you..."

"It wasn't you."

"It was me. I can't explain how that ruin touched the darkest parts of me and dragged them all to the surface. Marvellas may have commanded me to do things, but in that frame of mind I was willing.

She stole the parts of you I loved, but no one could erase the pull I will always feel toward you. It made going after you something I wanted more than anything. When I found you, I became obsessed. I could hardly stand it. Every time you were near, I wanted to claim you. I bit you…"

Faythe angled her head back, brushing her lips against the edge of his jaw. "I've asked you to do that before."

"It's not the same thing, and you know it."

"I don't care. I plan for you do it again—on our terms. I'm rather looking forward to it." She kissed below his ear, delighting in the low sound of desire in his throat.

"You don't need to bury all that happened. You're allowed to be angry with me."

"With you? Never. I'm furious with Malin. I'm livid with Marvellas. I'm going to tear them both from their positions of borrowed power, along with Dakodas and Mordecai." Faythe shifted up to straddle him again. "And in fact, the way you kissed me with all your darkness hasn't left my thoughts for a moment."

Passion swam in the pools of his sapphire irises. "Is that so?"

She spread her thighs wider to feel him beneath her. Reylan made a pained sound, curving his palms over her ass and gripping tight.

"How I wish I could devour you right now," he said huskily.

Faythe ground her hips against him slowly. "If I can't convince you to sleep, there are other methods to tire you."

"This is completely unfair."

His hard length beneath her sparked pleasure through her core with every pass, but this was about him. With her eyes locked passionately on his, she began to unfasten the ties and button of his pants.

His face twitched in protest and pleasure, but he didn't stop her. Faythe reached for the length of him, stroking tightly and watching a sleepy lust overcome him as his eyes slipped closed and his head tipped back against the wall.

"You don't have to," he groaned.

"I want to," she said, shifting down before adding playfully, "It's a thoroughly proven method to aid rest."

Faythe woke to an alarm piercing her within. She shot up, haven fallen asleep against Reylan. Just as he sat up too, the early warning she felt from Atherius turned to a piercing wail.

They both scrambled to their feet, but Faythe was aware they had no weapons, only her magick, and if Reylan was strong enough, he could use it too.

"Do you feel anything?" Reylan asked.

"Something's here, but I don't know what."

"Marvellas?"

"I don't think so."

Atherius moved, and the harsh air whipped into them from the gap in the wall. It was the thick of night, and Faythe couldn't see anything beyond the radius of the Firebird's glow, which traveled away from them. Reylan curved an arm around her, and she felt him touch the well of magick inside her, preparing to use it with her.

"Do you sense anything?" Faythe asked.

The wind howled through the deep, ominous dark of the surrounding forest, rattling the bare branches like bones.

"Yes," he said, turning more rigid.

Every hair on her body stood on end.

"What is it?"

"The shadows," Reylan said with a chilling realization. "They're alive."

Just then, Atherius shrieked, a sound of distress, and Faythe launched into action, jumping through the broken wall and out into the night. She could hardly see through the depthless black between the scattered timber bodies. She followed the direction of Atherius's glow and darted toward it.

Faythe found the Firebird in the clearing where she and Reylan had battled. Atherius was *afraid*, backing away from creatures that only vaguely had a form resembling an unnaturally tall, slender human made of pure shadow that rolled off them in sinister waves, blending into the dark.

Reylan took steps away from her, and she followed where his attention led him.

A rift crackled violently, the sound a mix of roaring flames and grinding metal, muffled by the oppressive night. It hovered in the darkness like a wound torn into the fabric of reality itself, a thin vertical slit that pulsed and shimmered faintly. It resembled an eye, its jagged edges glowing faintly with a strange, unearthly light that flickered erratically, as if alive and struggling against its own existence. Despite its faint glow, it was barely visible in the black void surrounding it, but Reylan appeared compelled to it.

Faythe reached out a hand, which snapped him out of a trance.

"That has to be what's conjuring them," he said. "A rift opened by the breaking of the Death Ruin."

Oh Gods. These new foes unleashed into their world were her fault.

"How do we close it?" Faythe asked.

"I have a feeling…it requires a life sacrifice."

Faythe looked at him, stunned and terrified, but for some reason, she knew to trust his intuition on this.

"We don't need to think about that right now. Let's just get rid of these creatures before more emerge."

Faythe nodded vacantly. All she had was her magick, and with Atherius retreating, fear pounded in her chest that it wouldn't be enough.

Reylan's hand grazed hers, and she felt his gentle touch within, reaching into her magick with her. "You try lightning, I'll try fire," he said, tracking the half-dozen foes that were fixated on Atherius as if she were food, not a threat.

Atherius puffed her chest, splaying her wings, then heaved a blast of Phoenixfyre toward the creatures. Faythe had believed the fire of a Phoenix was the most potent form of the ability, but these shadow beings mocked it, dissipating as the fire surged, only for their shadows to crawl through the air like a deep inhale to resume their animated shapes.

"I don't think either is going to work," Faythe said in horror.

Reylan sensed the attack behind them before Faythe did. She jumped in fright at his sudden movement, watching a dart of blue flame expel from his palm, casting up into the tree canopy. The piercing cry from the shadow creature he'd struck made Faythe wince with the pain in her ears.

The being dissipated, and it didn't reform.

"If they anticipate the strike, they can easily avoid it," Reylan concluded. "But fire will always consume the dark if you can make the hit while their shadows are gathered. If one person distracts, the other can attack."

"How did you know that one was up there?" Faythe hadn't felt anything.

Reylan didn't get to answer before hisses caught on the wind. The wail of the one he'd killed summoned the attention of the half-dozen others.

"We just lost that element of surprise," Faythe said, bracing for their advance.

They raced toward her. All toward *her*.

Faythe threw out lightning, then blue fire, then she even tried to stop or slow them by manipulating the snow with the small grasp of Waterwielding she'd acquired from Nerida. Though it was the wrong time to discover she could no long feel that particular ability.

Nothing worked since their shapes expanded before impact, only to rapidly reform while advancing closer.

She gasped when the first reached her, circling a shadowy hand around her throat, strong enough to choke her. It had bloodred eyes that captured her like stunned prey the moment she met them. Faythe couldn't fight...then she began to forget why she was fighting in the first place. Her soul had been touched by this creature—that was what it fed on. Part of her mind was screaming to protect herself, but it was distant compared to the serene calm that overcame her in the shadow's trap.

That calm illusion was severed like a broken limb, and Faythe stumbled back, gripping her throat with pure terror when she realized what had happened. The creature that had held her died in a plume of black smoke with a piercing wail from Reylan's fire.

Faythe sparked blue flame to her palms in a panic when more shadow bodies raced for her, passing Reylan, with their full focus on her. Reylan struck them through the back one by one as they passed him, and Faythe couldn't understand how it was as if they couldn't even see him in their path to her.

When he destroyed the last, Faythe blinked into the still night in confusion while her adrenaline calmed. Reylan's moan of pain snapped her out of her thoughts. She moved toward him quickly as he hunched, bracing a hand on his thigh.

"How did you do that?" Faythe asked, puzzled.

"I'm not sure..." he said through a labored breath. Even that small round of attack was too much for him right now. "When I was... dead, I think I went somewhere. Ever since waking I've felt strange. I can't explain it."

"So they can't see you?"

"Or they recognize me as one of their own."

A chill slithered down Faythe's spine. She recalled the faceless, cloaked depiction of Death itself, chipped scythe in hand. Had that primordial bestowed a gift or a curse on Reylan? A final meddling before sending him back to her?

It had helped them this time, but a sense of worry crept over her that they could discover more repercussions.

A caw broke the eerie silence, and Reylan straightened immediately, folding an arm back around her and scanning the area. But Faythe looked up, finding an eagle flying overhead before it swooped low.

Her stomach flipped, and she gasped.

"Izaiah," she said, right as she had to shield her eyes against his burst of light as he transformed back into fae and landed on his feet.

Faythe's brightening expression faltered completely when she beheld the desolation in his. A look of pure ghostly shock she'd never seen on his usually bright face.

The most stomach-churning dread of her existence punched at her core.

"What happened?" she asked, already struggling to breathe with how fast her heart had picked up.

"Faythe..." He said her name like an apology, and Reylan's arm tightened around her.

Faythe shook her head, denial building, though she didn't even know what for yet.

Izaiah swallowed hard, straining to find his words. His skin was pale and clammy, as if he were recovering from some kind of wound too, but he'd had to make it to her regardless.

"I wanted to come sooner, but I was injured badly, and..."

"What happened?" Faythe snapped this time, dizzy from the anticipation.

"Marlowe, she...she's—"

"No." That single word of refusal cut deep within her. "No, she's not."

A high-pitched ringing filled her ears as if protecting her from hearing the truth that would shatter her into a million pieces. Faythe couldn't breathe right. Her heart couldn't move right. The world...it no longer spun right.

There was only one reason Izaiah would have come to her this speechless. Neither his words nor his expression held any reassurance, not a flicker of hope, which couldn't mean anything else but the worst of her spinning conclusions.

"Where's Jak?" Faythe whispered.

A numb sensation spread over her body. A stilling calm waved over her mind.

"High Farrow."

She didn't register anything but her need to get to him. Faythe was running toward Atherius, her steps battling the snow. The Firebird rattled her cry through the night, mirroring Faythe's charge of anguish. Reylan called her name and tried to follow, but he was too injured. She had to leave him behind right now for her friend.

Atherius took flight, soaring over the mountain edge and dipping just as Faythe leaped off it and was caught on the Firebird's back.

Just before she'd left, she'd stolen images from Izaiah's mind. Faythe had never felt such a concoction of rage and heartbreak turn her so icily cold, so calm, collecting her storm.

Her grief crystalized to shards of glass she would aim at the world to make them feel her pain. Her fury burned deep and sinister. This time, when Faythe Ashfyre let out her rage, there was no telling what would be spared from the ashes in her reckoning.

CHAPTER FIFTY-ONE

Zaiana

Zaiana startled at the awareness of a nearby presence. She winced, retracting her arm, which was caught awkwardly between the bars with her chains.

When her heavy lids peeled open, her eyes widened, and she pushed up to her knees.

"Ky," she breathed.

A stiff tremble that had nothing to do with the cold shook over her body.

He was examining his hands, face drawn in confusion as he huddled in the corner, and towering behind him…

Wings like none she'd ever seen before.

Zaiana stared unblinking. They were the most beautiful things she'd ever laid eyes on. Dark with feathers, giving a moon-spilled gleam. How could it be possible?

"What happened to me?" he mumbled, so terrified and detached it cleaved her.

"You're going to be okay." The words ached up her dry, tight throat. She didn't have the right to tell him that.

"I'm a monster," he said in disgust.

Zaiana winced. She'd never heard him use the term so truly. He teased her with it, but this was something he believed about himself with the wings he had now.

"You're not," she tried to say, but she didn't know how to make it convincing. Didn't know what sequence of words could possibly get him to believe nothing had to change.

Kyleer reached behind himself, but he stopped shy of touching his wings, as if it repulsed him to acknowledge they were real.

"What do you call this?" he snapped.

"I have them too."

He finally looked at her, and the fear she knew she would confront stole the air from her all the same.

No recognition. He didn't know who she was.

"Where?"

"They're glamoured. Hidden."

"Why?"

"Because they could take them from me, and that would be as good as death for me."

He contemplated her words. "Did they do this to you too?"

"No," she whispered. "I was born this way."

"Then why do they imprison you?"

Zaiana didn't know what to do. How to begin to explain everything. He had to remember.

Maverick remembered.

Though finding out what it took for him to remember filled her with hopeless despair.

She neglected his question. "I'm sorry they did this to you."

He weighed her sympathy, and she watched his guard rise against it. It was the wrong thing to say.

She wasn't the person he needed right now, but *Gods*, that hurt. Not caring was easier to live with. Zaiana wanted to be the right person for him, but she was already failing.

"I don't remember anything," he said.

"You were Transitioned to dark fae. Not many survive it, but you did. You have people counting on you. Those who love you."

She couldn't bear the distance in his moss-green irises. Then, realizing the color of them…

"Your eyes aren't black," she said, more to herself as she puzzled over his unique Transition. All the fae who had become dark fae by the same ritual had lost the color of their eyes. Maverick's had been a brilliant cobalt blue the first day she'd seen him.

Kyleer frowned. "Should they be?"

Zaiana looked around her cell. Finding a rock, she swiped it up. "Come here," she said, holding out a hand.

He hesitated before obliging, glancing between her and the rock warily.

"This will just be a sting," she warned before cutting his skin.

Kyleer hissed, yanking his hand back and staring at her incredulously. Zaiana was too distracted by the crimson that beaded from the shallow cut, sliding over his tanned skin.

Not black blood either.

She didn't know what it meant. What he was, if not dark fae. Then why had his memories been stolen? That reminder brought back her despair, but she wouldn't stop trying to help him gain them back.

Zaiana said, "It's not going to be easy, figuring this new life out, but you're alive."

"I don't know if I want to be," he confessed.

"I do." It slipped from her mouth before she could stop it. "I want you to be."

Zaiana was riddled with nerves and vulnerability. All her life spent shunning such emotions was now her ultimate downfall as she became as fragile as glass.

"Did I…care for you?" he asked.

"Maybe. I think you might have been starting to."

"What happened?"

"I betrayed you. I hurt you."

His eyes flexed at that. "Why would you do that?"

"Because I am a monster. Not you. No matter what, that is not you."

Every word she spoke he calculated as if deciding what to harbor as truth, but he hardly showed emotion.

"My name…?"

"Kyleer."

"Yours?"

"Zaiana."

Kyleer shuffled after a moment of observation. She thought he was about to turn from her, but he came closer, until they sat face-to-face with only bars to separate them. His green eyes and his heartbeat… In all the tragedy, Zaiana found peace that those precious parts of him remained.

"Zaiana," he repeated, as if he were *feeling* that single word, and she braced for it to be met with rejection. Instead he watched her thoughtfully. "Why are you sad?"

The sob that escaped her came so suddenly she couldn't hold it

back. As if he'd released the bubble she didn't know she was choking on.

"It hurts," she whispered.

"You're wounded?"

"Yes."

Zaiana collected wounds like armor. So many of them hidden
inside her she was a map of scars, torn and broken, and she didn't
know how to fix it. Fix herself.

"Is there...anything I can do?" he asked carefully.

She sniffed away her pitiful spilling emotions. "Try to remember,"
she said. That was all she wanted.

His brow twitched at that. "You said you betrayed me—then why
do you want to help me?"

Zaiana had nothing left to lose. Kyleer would live, and she didn't
plan to be around much longer to face all that was threatening to kill
her before she could have her revenge.

"I regret it," she confessed. "I don't regret much in my life, but I
regret hurting you."

"Then why did you?"

"I thought I had to, and I guess I thought you would be better off
for it. Without me."

"Was I?"

"I don't know."

Kyleer took a long breath, shifting to lean against the wall, but he
struggled with his wings to find a comfortable position.

"It's best if you splay them a little. Just relax them," she offered.

Kyleer tried to do as she suggested. It slipped his feathered wing
through the bars of her cell, and she fought the urge to reach out and
find out if they felt as soft as they looked. The puzzle of them not
being membranous like every dark fae she'd ever seen still swam in her
mind.

"So what are they going to do with me?"

"Nothing," she said. "She's not going to get a chance to do
anything else to you."

"Are we allies then?"

Zaiana shook her head, and her gut twisted with his flinch of
disappointment. "I'm only going to make sure you get out of here and
back to them. Then I'll go my own way."

"Who is 'them'?"

"Your brothers," she said. "One just looks far more like you."

Zaiana's nose stung to pass back the same words he'd used to describe them to her once in his room.

"Brothers," he repeated, staring distantly as if he were trying to find their faces. He shook his head in frustration when they didn't surface. "How am I supposed to remember?"

"I'm going to help you," she said, shuffling closer. "I don't know if it will work, but if you want to try, I'll tell you everything I know. It might not be enough, because there were so many things I wanted to learn about you."

"Thank you," he said.

"What for?"

"Wanting to know." He paused, his face turning thoughtful. "I don't think many would."

She didn't answer. A long stretch of silence fell between them.

"You're freezing," he said.

Zaiana thought she was doing a good job of stifling her trembling. She glimpsed the snowfall out the high box window.

"I'm fine," she answered.

"Come here."

Her sight snapped to him with the bold request.

"What's the point in any of it if we both freeze to death?" he added at her hesitation.

Zaiana shuffled over to the wall, moving tentatively, as if one wrong move would retract the wing she leaned into carefully. It curved around her, and the radiating warmth of his body edged her in closer.

She didn't deserve this comfort, but it might be the only thing she had to remind herself she couldn't die yet. She had to plan their way out of here.

Her fingers rose as if in their own trance, and she inhaled delightfully at the first contact with the black feathers. When they shuddered, she snatched her hand back, cheeks heating at the impulsive touch.

"So, how are we going to break out of here?" he mumbled, as if it were only a fantasy and they could conjure the wildest escape since none of it would come to pass.

"I have a feeling it'll take spilling a lot of blood," she said.

Kyleer swallowed at the mention. Then it dawned on her.

Blood.

Did he need human blood to survive like a Blackfair?

No—that wasn't the name he would carry.

It sounded so wrong.

"Your name is Kyleer Galentithe," Zaiana blurted with an urge. "Don't forget that."

"You already told me."

Zaiana shuffled closer, tucking up against the bars. She extended her senses, head throbbing with the extra effort considering her bindings. "I'm sorry I couldn't stop them. But I have a second chance while they think I'm powerless here in Niltain Steel."

"You've said you're sorry twice now."

She had no energy to form the defense she usually would. He could expose every vulnerable part of her, every weakness, and she was too broken right now to fight it.

"I know. It can't fix anything."

"I only mean…why do you care so much?"

Zaiana didn't want to deny anymore. "I think I gave you my heart," she whispered, clutching the bars and leaning her forehead to the cool metal. She couldn't look at him with the confession—it was taunting her to take it back. "Before it had a beat, it was yours. Even now, it's cold and not worth much. Should you not have woken up… you would have taken it with you, and I don't know what I would have become in my vengeance. Should she have killed you for good, I might have caved in the world just to take her down with me."

For the first time in her life, she felt at peace giving him possession of what was left of her while she still could. She didn't have the courage to look up, nor the strength to pull away when he reached closer.

"Then I promise to protect it with everything I am. Beyond this life, I'll use it to find you again. That's what it's worth."

A tear gathered, falling before she could stop it, but it felt *freeing*. Ironically liberating to be this breakable in front of him and not care about hiding it.

Zaiana nodded though it scraped the metal over her skin. "Maybe in another life, things would be different. A few days ago…you died in front of my eyes, and all I could think of was that you were gone and you would never know that I might have hurt you, but in doing so, I'd have hurt myself more. You're not done breaking me, Ky, but I don't fear it anymore since you've never let the pieces shatter. Despite the sharp edges, you still held them."

His warmth slipped over her cheek, shivering her body stiffly at the treasured contrast to the bitter-cold air wrapping the cells.

"In truth, I don't think I know myself anymore either," she said in defeat.

"I want to remember," he said.

All Zaiana knew was to how be strong, and that meant building wall after wall against anything that threatened to *feel*. To feel was weakness. Emotions clouded judgment and exhausted the body. She faced it now with crushing punishment as all her walls tumbled down and she became buried under their weight.

Kyleer said, "Maybe we can find ourselves with each other."

Zaiana enjoyed the notion. To be found with him...or *within* him.

CHAPTER FIFTY-TWO

Faythe

Atherius landed on the hills in Farrowhold that held so many of her childhood memories with Jakon. Humans nearby ran from the flaming bird and screamed as if they were under threat. Faythe couldn't pay them any mind.

She sprinted through the Eternal Woods, knowing from Izaiah's thoughts this was where Jakon would be. The familiar sight of the waterfall clearing burst within her for a second before she was darting past trees again, letting the branches cut at her hands and cheeks.

Stumbling past the tree line into the temple clearing, Faythe's world stopped for a beat of broken time.

Jakon was down on one knee before a simple gravestone. He didn't look back to see her, continuing to twirl a bluedrop by the stem between his fingers as she approached. Faythe's tears fell uncontrollably, but she couldn't sob.

This image felt so morbidly wrong.

So untrue. A dark, hideous lie.

They were supposed to be together. All three of them. An unbreakable bond until the very end.

"These are her favorite. Did you know that?" Jak said.

Faythe could hardly recognize his voice. It belonged to a shell of her best friend, who'd been hollowed out by the deepest grief.

"No," Faythe confessed.

That realization cut her deeper. One of many things Faythe had neglected to find out about Marlowe, and now she would never get the chance. The thought was inconceivable, and now so many small pieces she wanted to know about her friend skipped through her mind. So many things she'd wanted to do with Marlowe screamed with severed endings.

Faythe's eyes fixed on the dull gray headstone, and the monotone started to steal all the color from her world.

"I brought the first bunch here. Then they started to bloom themselves," Jak said.

The area around the headstone was covered in the delicate bluedrops.

Sorrow plummeted Faythe to her knees short of reaching Jakon.

He went on, "I couldn't bury her for days…thinking if you just came back in time…maybe it wasn't too late to bring her back."

The broken pieces of Faythe's heart turned to ash in her chest.

"I don't have that power," she choked.

Finally, Jakon turned his head to look at her, and his cold brown eyes were as painful as a knife to her flesh. They were rimmed red and hung with dark circles. In all their twelve years as friends, Faythe had never seen him come close to this absolute devastation.

"You came back," he said, harsh with resentment. "You died, and you came back *stronger*. How is that fair?"

"It isn't."

Jakon's jaw tightened. He wanted to lash out at her, and part of Faythe wanted him to. She would let him weigh the blame for Marlowe's death on her shoulders if it could relieve his pain even a fraction.

Instead he was so calmly cold, and that was worse than anything.

"I don't want to see you right now. Because I don't want to blame you, but I can't help it. Looking at you…it's like I don't know who you are anymore."

"You don't mean that." Faythe broke her first sob. "I can't lose you too."

Jakon stood, turning fully and looking down on her with the intensity of his grief.

"I remember your mother saved me from the illness that took my parents. The memories started coming back after you died, and I think…I think I died for a moment with you that day."

The revelation stunned Faythe, confused her, but she listened.

"Your mother brought me here, but the yucolites always demand a price. Mine was to protect you. It's all I can think about now—how our friendship was always a duty. How I was always destined to you from that day, maybe even before then. Your mother took my memories of that day. I can only think it was so I wouldn't try to rebel against the idea. It made our friendship seem like a choice, not fate."

Faythe felt herself crumbling where she knelt. The ground softened beneath her, and she wished it were her buried six feet under. Not Marlowe. Not the kindest, most gentle friend Faythe had ever been granted the privilege of having in her life.

Jakon's unfeeling stare became too much. In her cowardice, Faythe bowed her head.

"It was a choice. I love you, Jak. You're my best friend—nothing changes that."

"The worst part is…I love you too. For some reason, it feels like a betrayal to Marlowe's sacrifice, but I can't sever the love I have for you, and she wouldn't want me to. I can only bury what I don't want to feel for you under my grief."

"Please don't leave me."

"I can't. Even if I wanted to. Duty…fate…choice…I don't know what it is. I don't really care. But I need you to promise me something."

"Anything."

"I'm coming with you when you go to kill Malin."

Faythe forced her eyes up. Jakon's expression hadn't shifted a fraction. Then he reached down a hand, and Faythe didn't know how many pieces she could break into before she would fall apart beyond being able to mend herself back together and keep marching on.

"Tonight," Jakon added.

The determination in that word crafted her grief into rage. Faythe wouldn't be able to do anything else knowing Malin still lived after taking Marlowe's life.

Accepting Jakon's hand, she rose carefully, as if every movement were fragile around him and she'd become utterly terrified to lose him too.

"Tonight," she agreed.

Faythe wanted to embrace him, but as they stood there, his tension alone pushed her away.

"I'm so sorry I wasn't with you," she whispered.

Jakon's jaw tightened, and Faythe braced for the resentment that flashed in his eyes.

"No. You weren't there as she stared bravely into the face of her death and did not waver. You weren't there as your cousin snapped her neck in the heat of his rage, as if she meant nothing. My wife, your *friend*, was murdered, and you weren't there."

Faythe whimpered sharply. "We're going to make him pay."

"Death and more death. Yes, I want him to pay, but in the end, it doesn't change nor heal anything. She's gone... Marlowe is gone, and she's never coming back."

What broke her more was how emotionless Jakon stayed as he spoke. How alone and in agony he'd been in the thick of his grief to have not shed a single tear now.

He broke her stare. "You need stop by the Greens' mill. Then I'll meet you back on these hills to go to Rhyenelle."

With that, he slipped by her, heading through the trees and leaving Faythe in the heart-wrenching silence this place now held.

Faythe turned back to Marlowe's grave.

Marlowe's grave.

The sight, the reality she stared at... Now she was alone, Faythe let herself drown. Unrelenting agony surged up—a tide that dragged her under. Despair gathered in her knees, buckling them again, sinking her into the scattered bluedrops as tears blurred her vision, spilling unchecked.

A hollow ache clawed at her chest as if her heart were tearing itself open piece by piece. She gripped the edge of the gravestone, fingers pressing into the cold stone as if it might anchor her, keep her from slipping away entirely. But the sorrow was relentless, pouring through her, filling every empty space, until she was nothing but pain —a vessel for all the words left unsaid; all the moments they would never share.

Faythe couldn't stop wondering if Marlowe knew she was going to die. If she'd been burdened with that possibility through her ability as an Oracle.

"Oh, Marlowe," Faythe choked. "We need you."

Faythe had seen the spirit of Freya, Reylan's lost love, at her grave before. Yet now, Faythe wanted to see Marlowe so desperately, but her friend didn't come. A scream tore from Faythe's throat in place of her friend's greeting, which she tried so hopelessly to summon.

Was it because of what Faythe had done in breaking the Death Ruin? She'd seen Aurialis briefly...had watched the Spirit of Life dissolve and leave her.

What had she done?

"I'm sorry I wasn't there to protect you." Faythe could hardly squeeze out words from her tightening throat. They were all meaningless anyway.

Faythe would carry this failure as the greatest of her existence for the rest of her days.

When her tears ran dry, Faythe's sight cast toward the temple as she rose slowly. A clam started to take over her. One of icy detachment, which she would need to move a step beyond the gravesite of her dearest friend.

She couldn't get inside without her sword, Lumarias, needing the Riscillius stone in the pommel to see the hidden symbols on the doors. Her fists clenched at the absent weight at her side. She wondered if she'd even be able to retrieve her sword, which had been taken from her in Lakelaria, with Marvellas still dominating the island.

She *would* retrieve it. Lumarias was more than her sword—more than the key to enter the Spirit temples. Now, above all, it was a token of Marlowe, who'd crafted the blade with her brilliant blacksmiths' hands. Faythe had to carry her friend to the end of this war.

Marching up the steps to the temple doors, Faythe didn't know why she wanted to get inside. Why she jammed her fingers into the crack where the doors met, straining to pull them apart until her brow beaded with perspiration and her muscles tightened in protest, her scream tearing free as her magick surged to the surface. Gold essence blasted from her palms and splayed over the stone, rebounding off the structure in powerful waves.

Her efforts weren't futile. She felt the web of thin cracks splitting at the velocity of her magick. Faythe attacked, with the magick of Aurialis still left within her.

With one final push, the stone gave way. The resistance against her faltered, but she caught her balance before she tumbled in like the wall.

Panting, Faythe's boots crunched over the debris, entering the temple now in ruins at the front, with only the back wall and partial sides still intact. She wandered in until she stood over the symbol of Aurialis on the floor, staring down at it with such anguish and resentment she could hardly contain it.

Faythe thought of what the primordial of Death had said. How he'd made her question whether Aurialis was ever on their side at all, or if she was just another self serving entity who wanted to win against her sister Spirits and was using Faythe as her pawn.

Using all of them.

"Haven't I given enough?" Faythe's question wouldn't receive an answer, but her mind was spiraling with her own conclusions. Those words repeated in a scream of anguish as she kneeled, slamming her palm, charged with the Spirit of Life's power, to the symbol that matched her palm. Both glowed brightly, connecting like a fuse that exploded the world around her.

Faythe was no stranger to these experiences that took her mind from her body and transcended her soul. They reminded her how fragile her world and existence were. How inconsequential everything was in the vast expanse of the infinite web of universes.

Though not to her. This world was hers, and she was not giving up on it while she had her friends to protect.

"Fall one, fall all," Faythe choked, returning to her own time and body with every inhale that defused the currents of power she'd connected to within Aurialis's symbol. "Did I fail?"

More answerless questions. No one was coming to liberate her torment.

All she could do was remember her destiny. Something Marlowe believed in so powerfully she'd let it guide them all. The vicious hands of war spared no pure heart, and when it came to eradicating her enemies, all who stood in her way, Faythe gave hers over to the unfeeling dark.

CHAPTER FIFTY-THREE

Faythe

Leaving the Eternal Woods, it took everything in her not to mount Atherius, whom she passed while heading into town. Jakon said she needed to go to the mill, and though she couldn't fathom why, she would do anything he asked without question.

She had to pause for a moment before the building she hardly recognized anymore. The structure was a corpse of the joyous place she'd known in childhood. The mill didn't turn anymore—the gathered green algae indicated it hadn't in a long time. Nature had staked its claim on the abandoned home. Vines gripped the mortar like a hand ready to drag it under the soil for burial.

Faythe had come here so many times with her mother, then continued to visit and deliver pastries to Mrs. Green while visiting her friend Reuben. She'd first crossed paths with Nik right in this spot, not knowing then, on that seemingly ordinary day, her life would change forever.

The door was already open, and the floorboard groaned louder than ever with her intrusion into the eerie space. Faythe wanted to retreat the moment she took her first steps inside, but she had to discover what Jakon wanted her to see.

Making her way through the familiar hall, she rounded into the long-abandoned kitchen, stripped of all color and joy, but still she could hear the ghost of Mrs. Green's cheerful greeting. Could scent from memory the glorious warm pies Faythe would bring, and how the mill owner wouldn't waste a moment to open them and invite Faythe in for a slice. She never refused.

Magick pricked her skin and brought heat to her palms when she first detected she wasn't alone. Following the first shuffle that gave them away, Faythe tentatively rounded the table, spying the edge of a body huddled behind the tall cabinet.

"Reuben?" Faythe didn't expect to see him despite this being his former home.

So many conflicted emotions battered her.

The last she'd encountered him, he'd driven a Magestone blade into her shoulder to weaken her before an ambush from the enemy. Reuben's mind had been torn and tortured so much by Marvellas that his objective of collecting the Light Temple Ruin Faythe possessed had become his sole purpose.

The worst part was…Faythe blamed herself for the fate that had befallen him. It had been her idea to send him across the sea to Lakelaria as the only hope of escape from his crime of spying for Valgard. Even that had been a lie. Reuben was nothing more than a victim of powerful people.

Right now, he appeared no more than a terrified, quivering dog. Faythe couldn't surface an inkling of anger for what he'd done. Instead she pitied the broken sight of him.

"What are you doing here?" Faythe asked, gentle but not kind.

His tired, frightened gaze slipped up to her. Reuben sat with his knees and arms tucked up to his chest, shaking violently. Faythe sighed, marching into the adjoining living area and swiping a dusty blanket from the sofa. She crouched, slinging it around him. It did nothing to stop his tremors. She didn't think were only from the cold.

"I-I'm so-so sorry-sorry, Fay-faythe."

His stammer was so bad he could hardly form words.

Faythe cupped his cheek. "I am too, Reuben. You didn't deserve this." She swiped the tear that fell down his cheek.

"C-can you make-make it st-stop? Pl-please."

She leaned back with the gravity of what he was asking. "This doesn't have to be the end for you," she said.

All Reuben had done had been orchestrated by Marvellas. She harbored no true resentment toward Reuben and certainly didn't want him dead. She'd lost too many people already.

"The claw-claws and the voi-voices, they don't-don't stop," he croaked.

Faythe sat beside him. Tentatively, she slipped her arm behind him and coaxed his head onto her shoulder, where she held it. Carefully, Faythe entered his mind, and she began to shake too. Her eyes flooded from so much torment and shredded thoughts that it was all she could see. There was no light; nothing of hope to search for. Marvellas had stripped away anything warm or joyous to keep him afraid.

Reuben whispered, "I don't want to-to live like this."

Tears fell from her eyes as Faythe tried desperately to find a way to heal all that was torn apart in his mind. She didn't know how to begin repairing the damage that had been done. She tried to sew the tears and tame the shadows. Faythe tried to hush some of the vicious whispers plaguing him and relieve some of the poison running through his thoughts, but it was too much, the damage too permanent.

He was suffering so miserably and painfully every second that Faythe understood his request now.

Reuben said, "I'll only hurt-hurt you again. She can use me anytime, and when she hears of my running away...she'll find me and know-know where you are. She'll know about the ruin if you keep me alive."

"The ruin?" Faythe asked.

Something tumbled out of a cloth Reuben was holding, and when it did, Faythe grasped, slackening her hold on him not on purpose as a wave of immense power slammed into her.

Familiar, daunting, delicious power.

Faythe's sight fixed on the ruin. Its markings glowed, and the symbol of Aurialis shone proudly at the peak of the serrated arrow shape.

Her trance was snapped when Reuben quickly threw the rag over it. Whatever it was made of must have powerful suppressing properties like the Blood Box for her not to feel even a hum of its call now.

"I brought it for you," Reuben said, scooping it up and cradling it.

Relief washed over her. They still had Aurialis's ruin she'd had to leave behind in Rhyenelle, hoping it would remain hidden where she'd stored it in the catacombs Agalhor had once shown her.

"I followed Izaiah and stole it when I had the chance." He answered the question blazing in her eyes when they met his.

"What was he doing with it?" Faythe asked.

She'd only told him in case someone needed to retrieve it if she couldn't.

"He's been trying to master it."

That stirred something ugly and suspicious in her. Izaiah had never disclosed his plans. All this time, she'd chosen to have faith in him to believe he wasn't truly up to anything nefarious. But where was he when Malin murdered Marlowe? Why was he trying to master the ruin? What did he mean when he'd told her he was one step ahead?

Faythe held her hand out for the ruin, their first test of alliance. Reuben hesitated, and Faythe's heart skipped. She didn't want to harm him anymore than he'd already suffered. To her relief, he handed it over.

Even concealed, she felt its power caress her skin and stroke her senses. She believed she had enough wrath and power to kill Malin without it. He was nothing compared to her. But with the ruin in her possession, Faythe wouldn't stop with him—it wouldn't be enough. She needed the world to feel a fraction of her loss...and Marvellas's ruin would be her weapon to unleash it.

"We need to go," Faythe said, making as if to stand.

Reuben gripped her arm to keep her down. His wide eyes turned desperate. "Please, Faythe," he said in a broken tone. "You're the only one who can make it painless. Maybe even pleasant. I can't... Please don't make me live like this."

Her heart slammed in her chest. Faythe had never killed to *help* someone before. The concept felt so twisted. How could it be help if she ended his life? She knew without a doubt he'd suffered incredible pain and torment, but what if he could be saved if he just held on and wanted to fight?

"You have to want to live, Reuben. If you fight back against the shadows and claws, I might be able to help you."

Reuben shook his head and broke into heart-wrenching sobs. He let her go and began to crawl across the floor. Faythe watched in agony as muttered incoherent thoughts. When he next stopped, hitting his head with his clenched fists, Faythe grabbed his wrists and pulled him into her. He just cried as she held him tight, rocking with him, while he kept mumbling fractured sentences.

"I'm so sorry, Reuben," she whispered, stroking his hair.

Faythe severed the pain receptor in his mind, and Reuben's body relaxed a little. They rocked, and she painted bright colors into their surroundings, breathing life back into this mill. She showed him a vision of their past. Faythe chased Reuben around the dining table with a wooden makeshift sword, while Mrs. Green called after them to be careful.

Reuben chuckled faintly. His mumbling began to cease. "I miss my mother," he said sleepily. "I think I'll go see her now."

"She misses you too," Faythe said with a tight chest. "Rest now, Reuben. No one can hurt you anymore."

His mind started slipping away gently. "I'll see you again, won't I? You're my...my best friend."

"I'll see you again, I promise."

She pressed her lips to his head as she took the final step to end his pain once and for all. In the silence of death and the grief that followed, holding Reuben's still body, Faythe became numb. Saying goodbye to another dear friend so soon who had also suffered too much in this war...Faythe became fast-burning fuse.

When she detonated, her enemies would know the true meaning of *ruin*.

CHAPTER FIFTY-FOUR

Zaiana

"I need your help," Zaiana called into the void of her subconsciousness. The male wasn't here, but she couldn't stop imagining him, as if she could will him here by her desperation alone.

She didn't know how to Nightwalk when their lessons so far had all been in aid of taming her storm and finding her magick.

"Please!" she cried out of frustration.

Her mind was starting to collect its anger again. While it was still bleak colors of black and gray, at least it had calmed its fury. Until now. The clouds gathered, and electricity hummed over her skin in anticipation for the thunder and lightning to break.

"I didn't know you missed me so much." The male voice eased into her mind.

A weight of relief lifted.

"Where have you been?" she ground out irritably.

"I have things I'm dealing with too, you know. I don't exist at your beck and call."

"I need you to teach me Nightwalking."

"It's not something you'll learn in a day. It's very volatile, and you can end up hurting someone. Besides, we don't even know if you're fully capable of it yet."

"I don't have *time*," she pleaded.

That shifted the energy around them.

"What happened? Are you in danger?"

"It's nothing I can't handle."

He seemed to read her bravery was bullshit. Gods, she was slipping her steel composure so easily it was becoming to exhausting to even try to convince anyone she could still lift it.

"You don't have to do everything alone."

Zaiana pressed her lips together. A natural defense rose against admitting she was out of her depth.

"Have you ever Nightwalked through someone with lost memories?"

"In all my centuries, not that I was aware of, actually."

"Do you think you could find their memories, help them remember, if you tried?"

"I wouldn't know."

"If I can't Nightwalk to them, could you try?"

The male deliberated for a moment. "I can't Nightwalk through someone I haven't seen before."

For a second, she questioned her trust in him again.

"Search my memory for him," she blurted.

She could practically feel his surprise.

"He must be important."

"Just...do it," she grumbled. "His name his Kyleer Galentithe."

That seemed to invoke a reaction.

"You know him?" Zaiana concluded with disbelief.

"The name is familiar," he said quickly. "Show me, just to be sure."

Zaiana let the image of him surface, but it wasn't without the male's help that it unfolded for both of them to see.

"Shit," he said, stepping forward, and Zaiana shivered at the panic slipping through the shadows. She was becoming accustomed to untangling what feelings triggered him or herself in here. "What in the Nether happened? Who else was turned?"

She eyed him carefully, not expecting the rush of urgency.

"How do you know him?" It came out as an accusation. Suddenly, she was overcome with the sense she couldn't trust him.

"Was this your fault? Did you hand him over to them?" he snapped.

Zaiana flinched. "No."

The smoke shifted at their conflict, circling them. This was the first time she'd truly feared he might turn on her when something dangerous rang through her. Though this was her mind, he was far more powerful here.

"Tell me who else, or I'll look for my damned self."

"You swore you would never do that."

"This is the exception."

There it was. Everyone was capable of betrayal when their end justified their means.

"I shouldn't have asked for your help," she said coldly. "I'll figure it out myself."

"To cause more harm than you already have? I don't think so."

A weight pressed down around her like a phantom cage. The pressure in her chest expanded.

"Get out of my head," she warned.

He said nothing, and the anticipation was a helpless sickness as he prevented her from doing anything. She couldn't push him out—she wouldn't be able to overpower him.

"You called for *me*."

"I won't forgive you," she said, slipping her panic. "If you take a single thought without my permission, I will never forgive you. And I will come for you. Don't doubt I will figure out who you are just to kill you."

Their stand-off intensified. She had his memory of a particular woodland she could scout for across the kingdoms if she had to figure out his identity. Now she had something else, as he'd let slip that Kyleer was someone known enough to him to invoke such an angry reaction to what had happened to him.

Her thoughts were already trying to piece together more of him, but she needed him right now.

"No one else went through what he did," Zaiana said. "I'm locked up just like him. You can see that for yourself if you must."

"Your heart," he said.

Zaiana's hand naturally rose to her chest. The feel of it was becoming more tolerable, so she was beginning to forget the new beat she carried.

"I have my lightning again too," she confessed.

The male was silent. Considering.

"You broke your own chains. Well done."

She didn't feel deserving of congratulations when, despite it all, Kyleer had lost.

"Actually, I was put in them for my defiance."

Zaiana might have mistook the faint smirk from the shadows of his hood.

"I'm sure you'll figure those out far easier."

"Will you help Kyleer?"

"I'll Nightwalk to him. Don't bother waiting here—it will take some time."

Zaiana wanted to argue, too on edge for answers with this budding seed of hope he could unlock Kyleer's memories.

"You won't harm him?" she added like a question.

How could she be certain he didn't know Kyleer as an enemy instead?

Though she couldn't see his eyes, she felt them upon her.

"No, I won't."

She knew he could be lying; could tell her whatever she wanted to hear and betray her. But somewhere along this unexpected path they'd joined, she'd given her trust to him, the kind that formed without effort—and that was most frightening.

Zaiana woke peacefully, but her head ached with her first movement from leaning against the iron bars. A warmth circled her, and she drew a shallow gasp, remembering Kyleer.

She didn't have to look far.

Kyleer was already awake, but he'd stayed still and close, not waking her to take back the wing that had curved around her through the bars separating them. Her fingers curled around the iron.

"Do you remember anything?" she asked, assessing him for the answer in recognition.

Her small flicker of hope died out with the shake of his head.

She leaned back against the wall with him again, their heads turned to each other, and part of her was glad for the bars separating them that prevented her from doing something pitiful.

"Can I be honest with you?" he asked.

"Yes."

"I don't remember what you did to me to make me hate you. Nor I to make you hate me." Kyleer looked off for a second as if he wondered whether his words were worth saying.

"I hated you…only for making me want you so much," Zaiana said. This tentative way of conversation was foreign to her and itched with vulnerability.

This had to be trust. Trading truths one by one like shards of a soul.

She didn't know how, but the distance continued to erase fractions between them where they sat side by side.

"With you…" he said, "it's like the pictures are gone but the feelings are left behind. Minute by minute they're coming back. I don't remember what we had before. What we've done to each other. But I don't harbor resentment or fear or anger toward you. Truthfully, I'm confused by just how much I'm glad you're here. I'm terrified, but it's not for myself. And I know that if they came and tried to take you, I would fight with everything I had left."

Zaiana fought against the defense inside her that was brewing a storm to snuff out any candle he could light, the voices that wanted to twist the words and find the trick.

She was too tired, and that wickedness couldn't thrive as harsh as it once did.

Not toward him.

"You didn't deserve to fall for a monster," she said.

Kyleer reached a hand through the bars, and though her body tensed with the siren to reject it, she couldn't. When Kyleer's palm slipped over her cheek, Zaiana wanted to bow in defeat. Lay down her weapons against fighting what he invoked in her.

"Can I try something?"

Kyleer inched forward, and it was like her body had already responded. She wasn't used to this tenderness between them, but it was necessary for what he'd lost.

Zaiana knew the patience of a precise kill. The patience of revenge. This… She didn't know this kind of patience that was not to harm but to cherish. It terrified her. She couldn't see an end to how long she was willing to wait for him.

"You shouldn't," she said, a note of panic slipping through when their lips came shy of meeting.

"Do you want to?"

"Yes."

He needed nothing more.

Kyleer kissed her, and it was like the world didn't exist anymore. Not her revenge. Not this cell. Just them in a slow, searching connection like nothing she'd known before. Didn't know it was something she would crave for him, yet she wanted him to take his time with every piece of her. To see things she couldn't show, and she would do the same for him. As long as it took, she wanted to give him the time.

Her mouth opened for him, and he kissed her deeper, gripped her tighter, like he was trying to find himself in her, and when that didn't come, passion took over.

Zaiana cursed the awkward position of the cell bars that refused the demand her body craved to be so much closer. His hand trailed up her thigh, but he couldn't pull her to him. Her hands threaded and tightened in his hair, but it wasn't enough.

They seemed to realize they wouldn't get what they wanted. Kyleer pulled away first, staying close, and she delighted in his rugged breathing. Her leg had slipped through, and he didn't let her go, keeping it hooked over his and beginning an idle caress of her thigh.

"Any luck?" she asked.

"Still no pictures," he said. Kyleer took her hand in his scarred one, mapping the lines that marred them both. "But I feel…alive with you. Something tells me my past made that difficult."

"I never got the chance to find out every name that stood by and watched as that happened to you," she said, resting her head to the stone, perfectly content in their tangled closeness. "But if I don't die taking down Marvellas, I will find them all."

"You can't defeat her yourself."

Zaiana huffed a laugh. "You really don't remember anything."

"I don't mean you're not capable," he said, turning more serious than she was in the mood for.

What they'd created felt like a sphere of shelter from the cruel world she was to face. She wasn't ready for it to shatter so soon.

"Don't concern for me," she said.

"I can't do that. With or without memories, I know I can't."

"Listen to me, Ky." She tried to maintain the composure that threatened to waver to get him to listen. "They're going to come for us, and the only way either of us survives is to not think of the other. If there's a moment for you to kill them and flee, you take it, and you don't think of me. Past this cell, I won't think of you."

She was a lie with skin and darkness with bones.

Kyleer drew a long breath. "Good."

Still, he didn't take the hand from her thigh or gain a fraction of distance from her. They had to live in each moment, not thinking of the next minute or hour that could turn them to enemies once more. He had to remember everything for his friends, but once he did, he wouldn't want her the way he did now.

So Zaiana joined him in this moment, letting the silence welcome the fantasy that this was it. Him and her. This moment was a glimpse of belonging that could never be.

CHAPTER FIFTY-FIVE

Zaiana

They came for Zaiana.

Nyte wandered ahead of the three guards who trailed behind him. They obeyed his command to stay back while he approached her gate, unlocking the door to her cell.

Zaiana studied him closely, recalling what she'd requested of him the last time he was here.

Nyte grabbed her, causing Kyleer to shift closer to the bars that joined their cells. He did so for show, as he was playing the role of the vicious Captain Daegal. Too well. She hissed to his fingers digging into her biceps as he leaned in close.

"You're not going to like the answers sending that message brought back."

Zaiana's newfound heart skipped a beat of trepidation. "What have they done to Acelin, Kellias, Drya, and Selain?" she dared to ask.

Nyte's caramel eyes flexed around the edges. "I hope they weren't dear to you. They were executed by people called the masters."

The weight of that knowledge slammed into her, and she ripped out of Nyte's hold.

"What's wrong?" Kyleer asked, worried.

Those four dark fae had been Zaiana's trusted team of the best. She'd selected them herself, watching each of them for many months before she'd brought them into her close circle. Their bond had forged over centuries, and they were the only people she knew with absolute certainty their loyalty to her was true. That they would lay down their lives for her.

The masters had killed them. Killed them simply for what they meant to her.

"Did you find out when?" Zaiana asked, hardly present when the reel of the masters' faces turning in her mind grew her need for bloody retribution. She could hardly think straight.

"Many months ago. They weren't exact."

That meant they'd killed them not long after Zaiana left the mountain on her first endeavor to capture Faythe Ashfyre—a quest given by Mordecai. Was he behind their murders too? Was it another cruel lesson for her to receive when they believed she would return?

Zaiana had to turn away, tipping her head back in horror over the wetness that pooled in her eyes and threatened to spill. She willed them to turn to glass and cut, to add to the scars she carried within, because this was her failure. Their deaths were on her conscience.

Though one thing became absolute in the cold darkness Zaiana paced within in her mind: the masters would pay, and it would not be quick nor merciful.

She had nothing to lose anymore, and the more she pictured her spree of blood and vengeance against them, the more determination trembled in her bones to get out of here.

"Marvellas sent me for you," Nyte informed her. "Do you have a plan to get out of this? I need to know, because I'd like to be escaping with you and could prove useful if you tell me."

Zaiana didn't have a plan. She'd asked Nyte to get a message to the inner circle she'd left behind in the Mortus Mountains, hoping they'd make it here to assist when she inevitably made a lot of commotion to escape. All she had now was her intuition she hoped would collide with her drive for violence when a moment to escape presented itself.

Had she known the information about her inner circle before now, she might have considered a more stealthy plan of escape before Marvellas decided to summon her, if only to exact her revenge on the masters first, in case she never made it out of here alive after facing the Spirit for punishment.

"If you have any ideas, I'm all ears," she said under her breath as Nyte began leading her out.

"Take me as well!" Kyleer yelled.

Nyte slipped a look to her in question.

"Please?" she asked him, not accustomed to the sour taste of begging, but she had little advantage here.

If Zaiana managed to create a moment for escape, even if she couldn't make it out herself, she hoped Kyleer would.

Nyte obliged.

He led with her, escorting them to the glass throne room, where the flaming red hair of Marvellas stood out starkly, surrounded by snow beyond the transparent walls.

This castle was beautiful. A true observational masterpiece.

But entirely fragile.

Maverick was here, observing silently by the throne Marvellas spilled herself over. She couldn't read him. His expression remained more cold and distant than ever. They had been rival allies before Zaiana's traitorous actions. Now they really were enemies.

The hall was weighted with judgment, and Zaiana didn't know what to anticipate. One thing remained certain in her chest: she would not submit. She would fight with her last breath for herself, and for Kyleer.

Right now, she had to forget the commander shackled beside her and hope he'd remain compliant until Zaiana achieved what she needed.

They were pushed down roughly, and she gave no sound, though her knees felt close to shattering against the marble floor.

Then, silence. Chilling, tense silence fell in the stare-down between Zaiana and Marvellas.

There was something more savage in those glowing amber eyes—something out of place about her usual impeccable composure.

Despite the lethal edge to the Goddess's eyes, Zaiana dared to edge a smile on her mouth.

Marvellas surged up from the throne, her irises flaring a darker shade. "You made the greatest mistake of your life," she spat. "You threw away everything you worked to build, for what?"

She'd never heard Marvellas sound this unhinged. She was faltering. Slipping the reins on her own internal control.

"I threw away everything *you* built of me. The anchor of your manipulative curse. I will commend you for it. Preying on my people who were desperate, hunted to the brink of extinction, using a history that painted them as nothing more than ruthless villains anyway. The curse of a still heart solidified the belief they were immune to any feelings of care or love like the humans and fae. Making them your unfeeling, merciless soldiers."

Marvellas stalked down the long glass steps, challenging Zaiana with those molten eyes. The beat in her chest sped up, which tightened her throat. Zaiana had played with the rhythm of other people's heartbeats many times, but for some cursed reason, she couldn't control her own.

"Your people?" Marvellas said in a dead calm. "You have nothing, Zaiana. No people. No dignity. No power."

The Spirit loomed over her, and Zaiana's teeth gritted painfully when her cruel hand curled around her chin.

"You gave it all up." Her blazing sight flicked to her left. To Kyleer. "For a fae who will always have a loyalty above you. Who, if his *Phoenix Queen* demanded it, would betray you."

"I would never betray her," Kyleer snarled.

Marvellas let go of Zaiana roughly, shifting her focus to Kyleer, which turned Zaiana more furious than if she were the target of the unpredictable Spirit.

"Your wings are like those of a fable. They are not meant for this world," she said. It was then Zaiana realized Marvellas knew more about their origin. *Not meant for this world.* What had touched Kyleer when he Transitioned? "Tell me, can you still Shadowport?"

"I wouldn't know in these Magestone shackles."

The Spirit hummed. "And your memory?"

Kyleer stayed silent, and Marvellas's cold smile returned.

"You place your loyalty with a dark fae who will never choose you," Marvellas said, slipping a knowing look to Zaiana before she paced away from them both.

That wasn't true. Not anymore.

"The Blood Trails," Zaiana said thought a tight breath. "You manipulated Finnian."

Marvellas had to take a moment to recall what she spoke of. *Who* she mentioned. That the Spirit had forgotten his name, or perhaps had never cared to know of it in the first place, boiled her blood.

"Ah, the young dark fae you cared for. Yes. He was becoming a problem."

Zaiana knew the Spirit was behind Finnian's death, but hearing it so effortlessly confirmed by the culprit flashed her vision. She had to breathe and reel back her impulse to explode in a chaos of lightning like she'd done in the celestial dome.

"He would have broken the curse—is that why?"

"No. In fact, it was a risk that could have broken the curse had you chosen differently."

"What do you mean?"

Zaiana was growing dreadfully wary. She wasn't accustomed to this fragility, feeling like glass in the palms of this wicked Spirit.

"The curse couldn't be broken just by love. You had to be willing to sacrifice yourself for it. Had you let that dark fae truly attempt to kill you, or succeed, the curse would have broken. Instead, you did what I hoped. You saw his betrayal and chose yourself."

"It was *your* betrayal! It was—"

Zaiana stopped short because her voice *broke*. It had never done that before, and when a wet trail made its way down her cheek before she could prevent it, she was horrified.

She was *crumbling*.

Zaiana swallowed, but there wasn't enough air getting past the marble growing in her throat. Her vision started to pepper around the edges, and her ribs became too big for her chest. She didn't know what was happening to her, but she couldn't get the images of Finnian to stop flooding her mind. Couldn't subside the guilt over her choice. Couldn't erase the battering possibilities of all that could have been if she'd *trusted* her love for him and believed his was true for her.

One choice…and she'd picked wrong.

A hand lashed around her throat, and Zaiana choked, caught completely off-guard in her vulnerable spiral. Harsh brown eyes came into focus. Nyte.

He kept a vicious front but spoke to her mind with a sense of calm.

"Keep yourself together."

She thought she was a master of composure, but her steel walls were softening. She'd come here fueled with anger and scorching resentment, believing she could end Marvellas.

But she was nothing.

The clanging of chains wasn't from her. She couldn't move. Kyleer was struggling against two guards to reach her.

"What do you want me to do with her?" Nyte asked in a cold tone, not looking at Marvellas. *His mother.*

Yet the Spirit was still completely oblivious to her son wearing the skin of her trusted captain of the guard.

Zaiana focused on her breaths.

Her son.

Her mind started to spin with that fact all over again. Marvellas could only be killed by something she was made of... Nyte didn't have his true form in this realm, but could he still be valuable?

"I haven't decided what to do with her yet," Marvellas said, bitterness coating her words. She looked at Zaiana like a festering plague.

The feeling was more than mutual.

"What else do you know?" Marvellas asked her.

Nyte let go of her throat, and Zaiana rubbed the tenderness growing there. She gave nothing away on her face, but her curiosity was grabbed. What else *was* there to know about the curse? She was reminded of the male in her subconsciousness. The memories he'd dragged forth, which had been blocked somehow.

Marvellas had been there. So had Mordecai.

"What do you know of my parents?" Zaiana blurted.

She'd never cared to know before. They'd given her over to the masters, and she'd suffered an upbringing in their merciless custody. The dark fae didn't hold sentiment to their offspring, so why would she care about her parents?

"I don't know why I'm wasting my time on this exchange," Marvellas said.

Zaiana's skin crawled as she came closer, and Nyte was forced to back away from her. She didn't trust him, but regardless of what she thought of him, she couldn't deny an unexplainable feeling that he was safe at least. He wouldn't truly hurt her.

"I can find out everything I need from you," Marvellas taunted wickedly.

Her gold eyes pierced into Zaiana's, and she gasped, slamming her lids shut, but it wouldn't help. Zaiana was powerless to stop Marvellas from infiltrating her mind, and the invasion was vile.

"Stop," she breathed, but her plea was like a rock thrown to stop a broken dam.

"It's been a long time since I've been in your mind. How quiet and innocent it was back then compared to the storm of darkness that rages now."

"Show her me." Nyte's voice filtered through the wild pounding in her head.

Zaiana doubled over, fighting the forces in her mind.

"My real face. It will distract her enough to stop," he added.

An image of an ethereally beautiful dark-haired fae passed through her mind. His eyes were as striking as the sun. His tall, broad build made him a statue of powerful authority. A scar ran from his right temple to his cheekbone, giving him an edge of danger. She could even hear the smooth, silvery tone of his real voice, with an accent not of this world.

Rainyte Ashfyre had been so criminally downgraded in the body of Captain Daegal compared to his real self that he almost didn't seem real.

Marvellas retreated all at once. Zaiana's palms flattened against the cool marble, and she panted, relieved of the swarming presence combing her mind.

"I'm here," Kyleer said, beside her now.

His touch on her skin was a lifeline, and she let him peel her upright, leaning into him while she trembled. She caught her breath and braved a look up at the Goddess.

Marvellas held eyes on her, but there was no malice. No rage. Nothing. She looked at Zaiana, but that wasn't what the Goddess saw.

"Rainyte," Marvellas said in a ghostly tone. Zaiana glanced sideways only briefly, so as not to give up his cover. "How…where did you see him? What is this trick?"

"You won't find that answer in my thoughts," she said. This was her upper hand.

"I will find everything, even if it shatters your mind."

That threat was so doused in savage desperation that Zaiana shivered, bracing and clutching Kyleer tighter. He shifted as if he would lunge between them. The spirit took one single step—

Guards came rushing into the room, their urgent steps vibrating under her.

"There's been an infiltration," one said hurriedly.

"Who?" Marvellas snarled, slipping farther away from her usual elegance.

"We're not sure, but she's a powerful Waterwielder."

"One fae?"

"Y-yes." His voice quivered to admit this.

A single person. Powerful enough to make her way across the bridge alone.

Zaiana pictured the brown-skinned, white-haired beauty before cries echoed in the halls outside the throne room. Then a sudden flood rushed past the doors. Zaiana and Kyleer gripped each other, bracing to be swept away in the violent current.

Sharp slices of ice came next, and Zaiana followed the flow of the water in awe as it parted, shooting high in twin waves before freezing in time.

Who stood between them…?

Nerida.

Though her entrance could not be as stunning as the words she followed with.

"You've sat for too long on my throne, Marvellas."

CHAPTER FIFTY-SIX

Zaiana

Nerida Da'Naid.

The lost heir to the Lakelarian throne. No—not lost. Nerida had always known who she was and where she wanted to be. Or rather, where she didn't want to be.

It was so clear now. The fae's elegance, her calm but firm charge when needed: leadership was in her blood, and the way she stood now, facing Marvellas, with defiance in her stance, proved exactly who she was.

Marvellas didn't answer right away, and the hall fell into a fragile, deadly silence. If Zaiana didn't know any better…the Spirit appeared confused over the declaration.

"There is no heir for this throne. Iana had one child, and she is dead."

"As you can see, I'm very much alive. And this kingdom remembers their heir."

"I saw it in her mind," Marvellas snapped, clearly despising the mockery she thought this to be.

"You saw her grief and my funeral—that was all true. She didn't want anyone to know her only heir had run away. My death was an easier acceptance for her."

"I'll see your lies for myself," she snarled.

Zaiana feared for Nerida. Her friend. In this moment when their lives all hung in the balance, Zaiana allowed the term of endearment to attach itself to the one fae she couldn't stand by and watch being harmed.

When they'd locked her up, they'd taken her weapons. All but one. The most deadly, and the only one she needed.

Zaiana had Marvellas's ruin tucked within her layers. Unbeknown to the Spirit, who'd believed all this time hers was embedded in Reylan Arrowood and Faythe would break it to save him.

It was covered in a suppressant material—all she had to do was reach it.

"I infiltrated the castle alone because I knew I could, but I have this place surrounded. You didn't fool everyone in this kingdom when you took my mother's place. There's been a movement against you for centuries. You know that."

The Spirit's eyes flared in confirmation.

"No reign is without needing to weed out conspiracy and resistance," Marvellas seethed. "I have just as many allies as you here, Nerida Da'Naid."

"You underestimate the loyalty and intelligence of this kingdom. As if the people of Lakelaria wouldn't notice or care that the gentle humans who once coexisted with them have slowly vanished. How our island has filled with outsiders that bring more coldness to the land than the weather."

"This island would have crumbled under the weak reign of Iana Da'Naid. I saved your people and made the population of Lakelaria the strongest it has ever been. Over time, more abilities will flourish. Waterwielding will grow as a powerful force to be reckoned with in the new generations."

"So that is your goal then? You start with eradicating the humans for having no power, then you shift your target to fae with no magick?"

"In a world as cruel as this one, only the strong survive."

"It is vultures as power-hungry and bloodthirsty as you who make it so cruel. "

Zaiana admired Nerida's confidence and spirit in the face of her mother's killer, the usurper of her throne, the continent's greatest villain. She'd always thought there was more than met the eye with the gentle healer, but this was beyond her expectation.

Marvellas declared, "I am not the poison. I am the antidote."

Zaiana caught the flicker of movement from outside—only a split second—before the arrow shattered the glass wall, heading with incredible speed toward Marvellas.

It was Maverick who stepped into the path of the arrow, which speared through his shoulder instead of the Spirit's.

Then chaos erupted as the walls of the room came crashing down, inviting the rage of the winter weather outside to join the battle that ensued inside. At least Marvellas's soldiers fought back against the Lakelarians who had come to avenge their nation, believing in their fight now more than ever with their lost queen returned.

This was not Zaiana's fight. Not her battle. She had one objective, and that was to make Marvellas pay for all she'd done to her. And Zaiana had the one weapon that could end her once and for all.

She didn't know why Reylan Arrowood had entrusted her with the Soul Ruin. He wasn't in his right mind, but still, he'd harbored a secret rebellion against the Goddess who'd tried to manipulate him against his mate.

Zaiana pulled the serrated slate out from inside her leathers. It's power hummed faintly. As soon as she removed the suppressant cloth, it would become a calamity to the chaos Zaiana charged within herself.

The room cried with soldiers' final breaths. Steel sang around her. Magick coursed from different angles.

Zaiana only acknowledged one person. Her lightning raked hot over her skin, and her steps moved, urgent but slowed, in time with her sight as it locked onto the unsuspecting Goddess of Stars. Marvellas's attention was on the charge of adversaries.

Maverick noticed her advancing as he clutched his bleeding shoulder, now freed from the arrow. He turned to her fully, and Zaiana's retribution was ready to cut him down if he tried to stop her. His sight dropped to her hands as she pulled her wrists apart with gritted teeth, breaking the chain of her shackles.

It wasn't Maverick who stopped her.

A firm grip on her wrist holding the ruin spun her around, and her lethal stare pierced into the caramel of Nyte's.

"You played the part well," Zaiana hissed, trying to yank her arm free, but he was stronger than her with the Niltain steel manacles still around her wrists. "Let me go before I kill you too."

"Using that on her will kill *you*," he growled, as if he thought he were doing her a favor.

Zaiana could have laughed. "I don't care," she snapped.

"I do." Kyleer stood close behind.

Those two words conflicted her, but her resolve hardened.

"If you had your memories, you wouldn't. Trust me."

This time, when she pulled her arm, Nyte let her go. Zaiana spun, intending to head straight to Marvellas again, but the sight of Kyleer distracted her. He was her greatest weakness.

"I would advise we get out of here!" That voice, strained in the midst of fighting, made Zaiana's spine lock, and her eyes sought out Tynan.

He fought with a sword, and Amaya with a bow. Both of them moved in tandem, watching each other's backs.

How had they known to come here?

A Phoenix cry rattled through the night. Zaiana believed it was Faythe with her Firebird, Atherius. But this one was different…and on its back was Reylan, without his mate. She couldn't figure out what their objective was in being here, but right now, all that mattered was making sure they all made it out alive.

Zaiana might not get her chance to end Marvellas today, but whether by her hand or another's, she pledged her life toward ending the Spirit.

Nyte reached for her wrist again, but she snatched it away. She beheld the key in his hand, intending to free her from the manacles. His impatient ire wasn't subtle, but with a flat look, Zaiana clenched her jaw, hooked her fingers under the stinging metal of one of them, and broke the binding, letting the wretched Niltain steel clatter to the ground.

"I could have made that far easier and far less painful," Nyte grumbled.

"Remove Kyleer's instead," she said, not paying him much attention as she surveyed the chaos, slipping into a battle focus as she charged her lightning.

Tucking away the ruin, she decided to keep that element of advantage secret. Marvellas truly believed it was broken and that she was untouchable by death now.

Tynan and Amaya were keeping the fighting back from them. Their skills in tune with each other were admirably effective. Nerida was a force to be reckoned with on her own, using powerful currents of water to strike and manipulating the snow to bring the storm indoors.

A flicker of silver caught her eye, and she didn't know how to react to Reylan running through the broken wall and into the chaos. He didn't come to join the fight or confront Marvellas. Instead Reylan Arrowood slipped through the bodies masterfully before disappearing through a door, venturing deeper into the castle they should all be escaping from before their opportunity closed.

He was unnoticed by all but one other person.

Marvellas took a step in his direction, and Zaiana didn't know when the line between enemies had blurred, but instinct drove her to act, running again toward the Spirit to stop her from following the general.

Her lightning charged to her fingertips, and without a second thought, she braced her stance, casting her fingers out to throw the might of her lightning toward the Spirit. Marvellas sensed it just in time to spin. Waving her hand expelled a flare of gold that clashed with the purple bolt.

"Go after him," Marvellas snarled to her captain. *To Nyte.*

He watched his oblivious mother as she didn't even spare a glance his way. Zaiana couldn't imagine the turmoil he must feel.

But she couldn't consider him right now. Her need for violence coursed so strong while she held the Spirit's attention that her magick came out in a lethal dance of storms. Instinctual, precise, and deadly. Lightning so vicious and dominating exploded from her, so she could hardly see Marvellas through the jagged strokes of purple.

The Spirit didn't attack, only defended, with bright flares of gold. Then, when Zaiana caught her attention subtly shifting sideward, she realized Marvellas wouldn't make a target out of her—wouldn't risk accidentally killing her—but she could harm Zaiana far worse by taking Tynan or Amaya from her.

Zaiana wouldn't make it to them in time. She threw out more darts of lightning in a frantic attempt to stop Marvellas, until the Spirit invaded her mind. Zaiana cried out, having her movements halted, but she'd broken Marvellas's influence before in her desperation.

This time she was too late.

Zaiana's eyes flew wide, and a scream was all she had left to warn Tynan and Amaya, who were so focused on the relentless surge of Marvellas's soldiers

The powerful flare of the Goddess's power slammed against a wall of rippling darkness. She'd seen those starry shadows before, but never like this. When the barrier that saved Tynan and Amaya came drifting down, Kyleer stood there, tall and vengeful, staring off with Marvellas.

Discovering that Kyleer had not only kept his Shadowporting but that it had somehow advanced to *more*, she couldn't be anything but immensely relieved.

"Enough!" Marvellas's declaration was accompanied by the strangled sounds of everyone in the room.

Every mind on both sides of the fight was seized by the Goddess, who panted, hunched, with a manic expression, as she blazed over the scene she'd lost control of.

Zaiana turned nauseous with the invasion in her mind. It held her still like everyone else, and she could break free, but there were too many others to consider. Tynan, Amaya, Nerida, and Kyleer. She had to figure out how to get them all out safely.

"Is this one not worth more than all of them?"

Marvellas heard the voice of her loyal Captain Daegal; Zaiana saw Nyte entering.

He escorted Reylan—or rather, threatened the general with a blade to his back into the ruined throne room.

Zaiana glanced down at what Reylan gripped tightly. He'd risked himself to retrieve Faythe's sword, Lumarias. It held the Riscillius stone they required to access the Spirit temples in its pommel, but Zaiana knew that wasn't why he'd recklessly gone to claim it for his mate.

Her hip felt suddenly too light, and she wondered with a pang in her chest if she would ever get her own back, *Nilhlir*, which was taken from her when she was locked away.

Marvellas blazed at the sight of him, shocked and suspicious. "Faythe Ashfyre?"

"She's not here," Nyte informed her.

Marvellas took that information as a trick, eyes darting around as if her heir was lingering in the shadows waiting to strike.

"I wanted to spare you, Reylan Arrowood. Now I'm forced to make such a tragic waste of power," Marvellas seethed.

Nyte pushed Reylan to his knees, and Zaiana should have been tense, concerned, but Reylan was too calm as Zaiana studied him... bracing for something she didn't know what yet.

"Kill him," Marvellas ordered.

Nyte's eyes shifted to his mother, contemplating. The tension of the room thickened with a battle frozen in time.

"You don't want the satisfaction of doing this yourself?" he asked chillingly. Nyte lifted the common blade to Reylan's throat, and the Firebird outside gave a piercing wail.

Izaiah, Zaiana realized. It had to be.

Marvellas schooled her expression. "I will reunite him with Faythe Ashfyre piece by piece."

Nyte stalked around Reylan with the blade resting on the general's shoulder. A mere second of movement could take his life, and Zaiana didn't know if she should act to prevent it...or trust Nyte.

His chilling, tilted-down gaze never left the Goddess of Stars. "No, you won't," he said. His blade slipped from Reylan before he dropped it lazily. The clang rebounding around the deadly silent hall was like a declaration, and it was then Zaiana didn't know who she was more fearful of. Nyte embodied more sinister energy than she'd felt even from Marvellas herself.

"What are you doing?" Marvellas hissed.

Nyte slipped a hand into his pocket, so calm and composed it was frightening. How he moved like a predator and looked with *peace* at the death and bloodshed he walked around.

"The Oracle you killed showed me what would have been my alternate path of fate in this realm. Should I have never been taken, had I been raised here with you, *I* would have become the villain of this realm."

Zaiana couldn't believe he was exposing himself now. She whipped her gaze to the Spirit, who blazed at who she believed was her captain, but the confusion of his words began to settle in the deep fold of her brow.

Nyte continued before she could interject. "You had to lose that which was most precious to you, your son, to break the Aetherbonds and regain your power all that time ago, and you would have done it. Even if I had always been here. The greatest irony is, you would have killed me to stop me. A heroic act, but in your grief, you would have carried on down the path you're taking now, believing your plan of genocide is liberation. With all the power I was born into, with the drive for supremacy you and my father harbor, my path would have been inevitable. I would have conquered this continent far easier than you."

Nyte paced the hall, gripping everyone's attention.

"In all the endless loops my fate travels on, there is only one that shows me a path beyond villainy. A path with a chance to be *good*. I had to follow the brightest star. Only Astraea could find the light in all my darkness. Only she could love a monster and show me freedom isn't in conquer or power—it is in loving and being loved in return. So, you see, though I will kill him, my father saved me by taking me away from here. Or I would have ended up just like you now. A tyrant on the brink of true madness."

He poured that world-shifting revelation at the Spirit's feet with the confidence and ease of any weapon. Zaiana's heart thumped hard, waiting for the tension to break. She didn't know if what Nyte had done in revealing all to his mother now could trigger something even more unhinged and volatile in the Spirit.

Marvellas didn't speak right away, but her expression contorted, slipping that hint of madness Nyte probed at through the cracks of her mastered composure. "You don't know a thing about my son."

"I *am* your son." Nyte's voice rose to declare it. "You know all about Gods and curses, *Mother*. This isn't exactly my vessel of choice to possess, but it has served me well."

"Impossible."

Just like that, it were as if Marvellas forgot who she was. The battle, the *world*, around her. Zaiana didn't think the Spirit was capable of wearing the kind of terror she inflicted on others, but there it was.

"Rainyte." Marvellas took three steps toward him before she cried out.

Zaiana stepped back out of nothing more than shock at what she was witnessing. Nyte had infiltrated her mind, stopping her from getting closer. Zaiana was sure Marvellas could easily break past his influence, but she didn't. Pure heartbreak split her features, slowly absorbing all Nyte claimed as truth. This was the desperate yearnings of a mother forgetting everything else she was in the presence of her child.

Kyleer's fingers grazed hers, and she didn't tear her eyes away from the scene as she embraced his closeness, linking their hands. She wasn't leaving here without him anyway.

"I really hoped they were all wrong about you," Nyte said. His face bore no emotion at all as Marvellas sank to her knees into a pool of blood, almost close enough to reach for him. "I hoped I would discover your motives were justified, considering the scale of the massacre you see fit—or at the very least, that your plan had some merit, even if it meant sacrificing so many lives for a greater good. But there is nothing but vengeance in your broken heart, which has built this ideal where only the powerful deserve to live."

"Please…" Marvellas let go of that word in a breath. As if her reaper were standing over her, not her son. "Stay with me."

"If I stayed here…I would become the war. No side could stop me. I would rip apart this world and every other I fell into until I made it back to my true home. To Astraea."

"This is your home. With me."

"Never."

Zaiana flinched at the sudden flare of light that erupted from behind Nyte. She was pulled into Kyleer's firm body when a roar shook the room. Reylan Arrowood, in his legendary white lion form, lunged for Marvellas. A giant paw pinned her to the ground, while his powerful jaw snapped at her face.

Marvellas must have infiltrated his mind, as the lion roared and wailed, fighting an invisible force. Then his lethal talons swiped at the Spirit's face, slashing deep across her porcelain cheek.

Zaiana was snapped from her stupor in observing the fight by a tug on her hand.

"We need to go!" Kyleer yelled over the commotion that began.

Before she left, Zaiana's eyes found Maverick, as if there was a magnet within her that would always find him no matter how much she despised him. He clutched his bleeding shoulder, standing by the side of the hall like a shadow. He was already watching her. For just a second, his eyes dipped to her hand joined in Kyleer's. Then, without a flicker of expression, he sank deeper into the shadows, disappearing around the bend of an arch and out of the throne room.

Zaiana tried to cast him out of her mind. He was not her problem right now. She ran with Kyleer, accounting for Tynan, Amaya, and Nerida, who followed.

While they had wings to flee with, Nerida made steps of ice, which she climbed up to mount the Phoenix. The way the Firebird examined her and Kyleer confirmed her suspicion: it was Izaiah in shapeshifted form.

"After my brilliant intervention to grant this escape, you're not leaving without me," Nyte called, following after Nerida.

Zaiana spared a glance back, with adrenaline tight in her chest. The white lion tore through soldiers in black before Reylan charged out of the castle.

There were too many of the enemy on both sides of the wide river that wrapped around the castle. Arrows cut through the air, aimed for them, and they were all wide-open targets. Izaiah, being the largest, took two arrows to his wing.

"Go!" Zaiana yelled.

Izaiah splayed his wings, and right before he used them to shoot to the sky, Nyte leaped off Nerida's ice steps, grabbing onto his feathers, and Nerida helped him find a stable position.

Amaya covered him, taking out the archers aiming for Izaiah, until he cleared range.

Her fingers tightened, and her heart skipped a beat, realizing

Kyleer should have left on Izaiah as well since he'd never used his wings before. Flying took practice, and those with wings were trained from young.

"We need a running start," Zaiana said, glancing over his shoulders at his stunning black feathered wings. She said to Tynan and Amaya, "Follow Izaiah—now."

Hand in hand with Kyleer, Zaiana sprinted toward the bridge that would take them across the river. As they reached it, Reylan transformed from a lion into a white eagle, but he didn't fly high to join the others; he stayed with them, tracking from the skies.

"What are we doing?" Kyleer asked.

"We need to get to a cliff edge—it'll give you some momentum for your best chance of flying. I'll warn you, no darkling I've taught has ever flown well on their first try."

"I'm not a child."

"Exactly. You're worse, since your size will make it significantly more difficult."

Zaiana had though Marvellas was incapacitated enough for them to have time to flee, but the Spirit's voice struck their backs as though it were one of the arrows they dodged.

"You will not win against me!"

The bridge beneath them shook violently, breaking apart as a gold flare cracked in various vines across the frozen structure. Before they were swallowed by the icy river, Kyleer wrapped her tight, and familiar starry shadows pulled them both.

They landed in a rolling heap through the snow at the other side of the bridge. Voices shouting toward them had them both scrambling up. Zaiana threw darts of lightning, and Kyleer attacked with shadow, but they couldn't stay stationary with Marvellas still at their backs.

Kyleer took her hand, pulling her through his shadows again, and this time they landed on their feet, breaking into a run the moment the darkness cleared to reveal a high ledge. Zaiana released the glamor on her wings, her fingers tightening in Kyleer's. Then, together…they took the leap.

She knew it wouldn't be easy.

Kyleer's wings were as good as deadweight, dragging him down fast and clumsily. Zaiana cried out, pulling him toward her and wrapping her legs around his waist, using her own wings to steady and slow them. But agony strained between her shoulders from the weight, and she risked breaking her wings. She didn't care. She couldn't let him go.

"You can do this," she said—a strangled note of encouragement. "It's just like breathing. In and out. A steady pulse between your shoulders to keep you soaring."

Kyleer listened, and some of the weight she carried lifted as he pulsed his wings. Off-beat and crooked at first, but he kept trying until he started to find rhythm. Zaiana could let him go a little more. He was flying.

As Kyleer held a steady flight in the air, he drew her closer, slipping his hands under her thighs.

"You're incredible," he said, holding her with an adoring stare that should belong to treasure, not her.

Then his lips were on hers, and Zaiana's soul, as dark and ugly as it was, flew higher than her body. She had to remember Kyleer didn't have all his memories; she couldn't take advantage of his lust and attraction for her. But Zaiana wanted this more than anything. She didn't know when it had happened, but slowly, unsuspectingly, Zaiana had decided she would leave it all behind for him. The war, her vengeance, her status—none of it mattered more than this.

They continued to fly for a measure of time lost to her. Sometimes Kyleer drifted closer, and she couldn't help the natural way her body wrapped around his. Occasionally, his flight would stumble, and Zaiana despised the beat in her chest every time it was tested by fear, slamming hard against her ribs and lodging up her throat.

Zaiana cast a look over her shoulder as she held onto Kyleer to see the white eagle flying higher and farther away. Through the clouds below, Zaiana frowned, registering the territory Reylan had taken them to after they'd crossed the Black Sea. She'd noticed they'd picked up pace a short while ago but hadn't thought much of it until now.

They were flying over Rhyenelle.

Zaiana had overheard the rendezvous point was High Farrow, which should be where Izaiah was taking Nerida and Nyte, with Tynan and Amaya following.

She realized why they'd come here the moment the clouds broke and Ellium expanded below. The inner-city wall she'd collapsed still lay in rubble and ruins. That had been Malin's request of her in their bargain when she was captive.

But it was beyond that, in the courtyard of Rhyenelle's colossal fortitude, that Zaiana understood Reylan's urgency.

Atherius circled above, carrying Faythe's human friend, Jakon.

There were at least a hundred guards protecting the castle.

Then there was Faythe Ashfyre, her wrath and power tangible even from the skies, already in the thick of fighting them all alone on the ground.

And she was winning.

CHAPTER FIFTY-SEVEN

Faythe

Faythe Ashfyre descended from the skies like a wrathful strike of the Gods. Her impact cracked the ground over the Firebird emblem in the courtyard of Rhyenelle's castle.

He had been anticipating her. Lines of soldiers stood in her way to getting inside the castle—far more than would be expected to guard the fortress.

She didn't try to count. It didn't matter how many bodies Malin Ashfyre hid behind—she'd paint the streets red, black, and silver to get to him.

As the Phoenix Queen straightened, the world held its breath. So much heartbreak and fury hung in the silence that followed.

She roared one word. A name.

"MALIN!"

Her anguish trembled through even the most unfeeling of souls who bore witness to the brewing storm about to be unleashed. No solider moved, waiting steadfast for her to act first.

Gripped in her hand was the Soul Ruin, uncovered and vibrating with power that was already creeping through her, threading into her well of magick, wrapping around her soul. This time Faythe welcomed the dangerous alliance. It gave her the strength to tap into the minds of every person around her, ready to strike them down at the mere thought of their attack.

Faythe's voice elevated, carried across the courtyard by the influence of the ruin. "You know who I am, and you can stand down or be cut down."

Every beat of silence held judgment.

"Stand and protect your rightful king!" a general yelled.

These were not her allies. They were Malin's. They'd chosen their side, and Faythe had discarded her mercy.

"Then let me show you how a king slayer earns their name with purpose, not cowardice."

Faythe's grip on the Soul Ruin sliced into her palm. Her blood trickled down the jagged slate, which roared with renewed life at the taste of her spilled life force. The power surging through her became too restless and furious, and Faythe charged forward to hunt for her enemy instead.

Bodies moved to stop her, but they were only animated shades of gold to her now, one touch away from becoming dust by her hand.

Faythe would gild the whole world if she had to.

Phoenixfyre blasted through a band of fae soldiers in black. Jakon rode Atherius above, making sure she would make it inside. For Marlowe, their vengeance and grief came together.

She didn't know who she was under this surge of raw anguish and action. Every slash of magick that cut down a person barely released the agonizing web of suffering that spread within her.

Faythe used her magick like a lasso, decapitating one adversary while another gold whip spun around the feet of a foe on her right. He crashed to the ground before the rope of magick animated into a golden snake that lunged for his throat. Faythe's magick was no one thing; it became a whip, a snake, a blade, an arrow. She knew nothing but the obstacle of never-ending bodies she had to eliminate to breach the walls of *her* castle and slay the false king within it.

The first to clash steel with one of her attackers spiked hot determination through her. Until she made out the face through the gold mists storming around her. She met the one set of deep blue eyes that were striking enough to reach her through the fire that raged within.

"Reylan," she breathed.

His eyes softened in acknowledgment, but they had no time to pause in the thick of their enemies.

Reylan used fire to strike the foes behind her, and Faythe dove back into her focused calm to fight in harmony with him. They moved like magnets, covering each other, getting closer to their destination.

Faythe would have gotten there alone, and she wasn't afraid of the immense power she harnessed, but she was so grateful to have the other half of her soul fighting by her side.

"That ruin is as much a danger as it is an asset to you," he warned through their mental link as they fought unfalteringly.

"I can handle it."

They both knew that was uncertain.

When Faythe next turned, by chance her eyes caught on the hilt of another sword tucked into Reylan's belt. She gasped, twisting around him, pulling Lumarias free and slicing the sharp blade across the neck of her next target in the same breath.

The weight of her sword between her palms was like the first time —when Jakon presented it to her in their humble hut. She held the blade aloft, inspired, with an unexplainable charge of energy running through her chest as if Marlowe had forged the steel with a piece of her spirit.

"You're always with me," Faythe whispered.

Reylan fought around her, but the soldiers had started to ease off, frightened of the tempest of light spinning around her. Phoenixfyre blasted in front of her, and a wave of searing heat slicked her skin, flaring the ruby on her amulet. When the flames died out, leaving only charred ashes, Jakon and Atherius had cleared the rest of the path into the castle.

She exchanged one affirming look with Reylan, and they ran up the steps.

They fought any guard within the walls who wouldn't back down at the warning Reylan tried to give each one. Some people they came across made him hesitate more than others, and Faythe realized some of them who'd chosen to be loyal to Malin were those Reylan had once fought with side by side. Lived in and protected this kingdom as allies.

Reylan slammed a fae male to the wall. He was frightening in his battle focus.

"Where is Malin?" he snarled.

"You're just as much of a traitor to this kingdom as she is," the fae spat back.

Reylan snapped his neck in a split second of rage. "He'll be protecting himself in the throne room," Reylan said coldly, not looking at her as he stormed past.

The doors were sealed shut, guarded by a dozen fae, which told Faythe he was right.

Before Reylan could advance, seeing the painful recognition on his face again, Faythe stepped in first to eliminate them. She coated her soul in ice, tapped into the power of the ruin tucked in her coat, and reached into the minds of them all, shattering them with a thought.

They all collapsed into a heap, and Faythe couldn't bear to meet Reylan's stare that branded her. She marched forward, stepping over the bodies and bracing a hand on each of the doors. With all her strength, they pushed open, announcing her arrival in a groaning whoosh of air. The moment she saw her wretched cousin high up the dais atop the Phoenix throne, she almost lost her complete composure and sanity.

The only thing that reeled her back from becoming a force that could collapse this castle with one wrong thought was Reylan's influence within her. The ice to her fire, taming the inferno. She had done reprehensible things to get here, but she didn't want to destroy her kingdom.

The winter air blew across them and Faythe discovered the right wall was almost completely crumbled. She stared at the wreckage caused by Izaiah's escape in Phoenix form and her chest tightened with heart-obliterating grief, tormented that Marlowe hadn't made it out of this room alive with them.

She turned her lethal edges to her cousin in a stare that sentenced his death.

He hid behind more guards arranged in an open triangle, which left a path to him. More of her people he was using as pawns. More of her people he was forcing her to kill.

Faythe's resentment grew more dangerous with every calculated step she took toward him. She hung the silence deliberately, letting the growing suffocation of it declare her arrival as his reaper.

"You expect this kingdom to bow to you when you demonstrate how coldly you would kill your own people to get what you want?" he said bitterly.

Faythe laughed, the sound bordering villainous. "How bold of you, to condemn me with breath still warm from your own traitorous lies."

There was something unhinged about Malin Ashfyre. The angle at which he sat, the crookedness of his crown, the bloodshot eyes lined with dark circles. He'd been consuming Phoenix Blood so much it had become a detrimental addiction, spinning his madness faster.

She said, "My people wouldn't protect their king's killer."

Malin's wild eyes twitched and darted around in a way that wasn't natural. "You are the reason Agalhor Ashfyre is dead," he seethed, pushing up from the throne with an unsteady balance that kept him leaning on the wide stone edge.

"Tell them how it was you who let the enemy inside our walls," Faythe yelled.

She wanted to kill him so badly, but he'd turned this kingdom against her, and she would be damned if he died a hero in their eyes.

"Tell them," Faythe said icily, "how Agalhor raised you like a son —the bastard of his brother—keeping your illegitimacy a secret. Tell them how he loved you, *trusted you*, and you betrayed him!"

Faythe slipped the tether of her control, casting out a hand that sent a flare of light pummeling into his chest, sitting him back on the throne.

She advanced through the lines of soldiers. At the first flinch to stop her, their movements were seized. Not by her. Reylan took a kernel of her ability to make sure no one could stop her while she kept focused on the only target she'd come for.

Someone entered through the back. A lord she recognized. Seeing her, he stumbled to a halt, ready to turn and race out of here.

"Wait," Faythe said, straightening as she reached the top of the dais. "Gather the council. Now."

The fae glanced at the back of the throne, then back at her.

"You have ten minutes," Reylan announced.

He nodded, scrambling from the room, and Faythe gave her attention back to Malin. When she did, he finished tipping back a vial of Phoenix Blood. Then Faythe felt his attempt of infiltration in her mind. She saw white.

Her hand wrapped around his throat, pinning him to the back of the throne.

"You think you can contend with me?" she said daringly. "You are nothing but a poor imitation of what I am."

Faythe shattered through his mind barrier easily despite the Phoenix Blood. She let him go physically, but mentally he was hers to command. Faythe made him remove his crown, and only then did fear begin to widen his eyes.

She commanded him to stand while Faythe lowered on one knee. Malin resisted her influence, trembling violently, with his face contorting furiously as he reached out with the crown between his hands. He placed her father's crown on her head, then Faythe rose slowly, unblinking, as they stared off with powerful hatred.

"I told you that you would yield all to me."

Malin had never looked so deranged. His desperation for power, to prove himself, had driven out such a corrupt pursuit she didn't think he even recognized himself anymore.

"This is him?" The voice that echoed through their tense stand-off made Faythe turn around.

She didn't know how Nyte was here, but he'd come to see the half-brother he never knew he had before Faythe killed him.

"Unfortunately so," Faythe said. "I wish I could say there was a better version of your half-brother that once existed, but he has always been spineless."

"I have no brother. No family," Malin snapped.

"You have me," Faythe said to provoke him further. "Dear *cousin*."

"Everything would have been better if you'd just stayed away," he spat.

Faythe couldn't deny she'd thought that often herself, but those were the weak and cowardly sentiments of the woman she killed long ago.

Nyte approached, and Reylan intercepted him.

"After all my help in your escape from Lakelaria, you still don't trust me?"

"One act doesn't make you an ally. You're her son."

"I'm as much her son as your mate is her daughter."

There was a twisted truth in that. Much as Nyte was her direct blood, Faythe was more kin by unfortunate experience.

Faythe said, "If you came to stand in my way, I'll kill you before I do him."

Nyte's attention fell on Malin behind her. Reylan glanced over his shoulder, and Faythe gave a nod for him to let Nyte approach.

She kept her laser focus on him. So far, Nyte had acted in their favor, but she couldn't let go of her doubt that he could turn on them all if he saw a benefit for himself.

Nyte silently assessed Malin in every step, and Faythe backed away a few steps to let the estranged brothers meet before they were parted permanently.

"He was never worth this," Nyte said, his voice reducing to a personal level. "Our father is no one worth proving yourself to. That's why you sought power, status, isn't it? He abandoned you, and what else were you to believe other than that he saw you as weak and unworthy of his attention?"

"My father is dead," Malin growled, but Nyte's words were making their mark.

"No. He left you for the pursuit of something greater. To *create* something greater. And he did... He created me."

Malin's hands lashed out, and Nyte could have maneuvered out the way, but he let Malin push him. Faythe had watched the Prince of Rhyenelle crumble more every second since she'd arrived.

"Who are you?" Malin seethed.

"Doesn't matter," Nyte said, barely audible, as if he were reflecting on something or someone else in this moment. "There is only one way for you to find peace. You know this too. You've fought for too long and never truly for yourself, brother. I hope you find solace in the next life."

"NO—" Faythe's magick slammed into Nyte at the first glint of steel that caught her eye.

Nyte thought to take his life swiftly. To grant Malin *mercy*. Faythe wasn't ready for him to die so quickly.

Nyte was thrown back, but Faythe spun to Malin, finding him on his knees clutching the deep wound on his throat, which poured crimson over his pale complexion.

"You do not get to die yet," Faythe growled, kneeling and pressing her hands over his wound. She pushed her magick into it, which wasn't as effective as a healer's ability, but she chanted in her mind for it to sustain him.

Malin wasn't Nyte's kill. He wasn't even Faythe's, much as she itched for it. This kill was Jakon's to avenge his wife.

He should have joined them soon after with the courtyard clear, and Faythe grew concerned for him.

"The council is gathered, you-your High-Majesty," the fae lord from before informed them in a nervous stumble.

Faythe glanced up at Reylan, who knew without speaking what she needed. She straightened as Reylan gripped the back of Malin's collar, dragging him choking on his blood out the back entrance. Faythe spared one lethal warning glare for Nyte, who was still peeling himself off the ground. The impact she'd thrown at him had slammed his body to the stone hard enough to form a deep dent of crumbling stone.

She would have to deal with him later.

In the council room, the deep mahogany table was full of familiar judgmental faces. As Reylan dragged in Malin, Faythe pulled out the head seat, but she didn't take it. Instead, Reylan hauled Malin up onto it.

Faythe slipped the crown off her head, placing it in front of him on the table, while she took in the horrified faces of every council member who'd turned their backs on her.

"Since the beginning, most of you have resisted my being here. You've questioned me, tested me, despite your king's faith in me. Now you've been loyal to his killer, and I can't have traitors on my council when I take this kingdom back."

She stalked down the length of the table, and the only sound to echo though the hall was her steps and the wet chokes of Malin.

"Twice a king slayer," one voice uttered. She found the old fae staring at her as if she were death incarnate. She quite liked that look.

Faythe ignored him, slipping her attention to Malin. "I'm hoping you can still speak to tell them all you conspired. How you let the Spirits of death and souls walk right into this kingdom, leading the slaughter of innocents and the death of your king."

When he didn't answer, Faythe took matters into her own hands. Reaching into his mind, she tried to force the confessions out of his mouth, but Nyte had cut too deep. All that left him with were barely coherent gurgles.

"As if we would believe his words when you puppet his mind," another of the council said, more boldly than the last.

"Then believe mine."

All heads snapped to unexpected intrusion.

Zaiana strolled in as though she were late to a social gathering. She looked over the table of seated lords with insulting disinterest, then her purple irises took in Malin on the brink of death as if he were a mere insect.

Zaiana followed with, "I'm sure you all remember me. I like to think I made quite the impression when I infiltrated this place."

"Before you were captured," a lord countered bitterly.

Zaiana gave him a wicked side smile, not bothering to argue her surrender was intentional.

Faythe was distracted by the person who entered through the same door Zaiana did. Everything froze in time as she beheld Kyleer. Her anger. Her grief. Faythe was numbed by shock followed by a crushing weight of relief.

He'd survived.

"Ky…" His name slipped from her in disbelief.

Kyleer's eyes flicked to her then, but he gave her no warm reception.

"He doesn't remember us," Reylan informed her.

Faythe's heart withered.

Her friend had towering wings that were magnificent on him. *Feathered wings*, she noticed. All Faythe wanted to do was embrace him, overwhelmed with joy that she hadn't lost another dear friend. It soothed some of the aching rage in her bones, helping her regain the control she was silently slipping to the ruin. Her chaos calmed.

Zaiana explained her role in tearing down the wall by the order of Malin Ashfyre, and the council looked between each other, not knowing what to believe. But coming from the mouth of the enemy, there would be no viable reason for Zaiana to lie.

One chair groaned against the marble floor as the lord stood. Faythe recognized him with a touch more fondness than anyone else. He'd been one to stand up for her before.

"There are many of us who have been waiting for your return, Faythe Ashfyre. You are the Phoenix Queen we chose, whom our late King Agalhor believed in, and we have not faltered in that loyalty. Forgive us if it has seemed that way."

Pride swelled in her chest. She was home. As war-stricken and terrorized as her lands had become, but this was the first torch of hope for the end to bring new peace under her reign.

Another stood, with outrage contorting his face. He blazed at her, casting a hand toward Zaiana.

"She stands here with the enemy who killed our king! She is a masterful manipulator, and we cannot let her take over this court. Someone fetch a damned healer for our king."

No one moved. Malin was counting down his breaths. *Where is Jakon?* He was owed this closure, and if Malin died so pitifully, she would aim her retribution at Nyte instead.

"Is there anyone else who agrees with him?" Reylan addressed the table with a hint of dark warning.

Another stood. "I never would have thought our most legendary protector would betray his king by falling for his pretty daughter."

Reylan didn't react. Neither did she.

In the tense silence, another four had risen to side against her.

"Take them to the cells under the castle," Faythe ordered the guards littered around the room.

For a few heartbeats, Faythe thought she would have to swallow her ego if they wouldn't answer to her, but then they did. The lords who were removed from the hall called out their disagreement and profanities. All Faythe heard was the fading echoes of corruption leaving her hall.

Faythe opened her mouth to address the rest of her loyal council, but a piercing cry of beast not man, followed by a sharp pain within, made her gasp, whirling toward the long windows.

She couldn't see Atherius, but the Firebird was in immense distress and pain. What alarmed her even more...was that Jakon was with her.

Faythe spun on her heel, sprinting without a second thought.

Bursting back out into the courtyard, Faythe was awash with horror. So much darkness battled flame. Atherius wailed and tried to shake off the shadow bodies that climbed over her in frightening masses.

"JAK!" Faythe yelled.

She couldn't see him. He'd been riding Atherius, and now he wasn't.

"Faythe!"

Relief threatened her balance as she spun to his answering voice drawing closer. He was out of breath, as panicked as she felt.

"They swarmed as soon as she landed. I tried to get her to fly again, but she wouldn't go. She made sure I got away from them. Somehow, she's attracting them to herself."

"Like moths to a flame," Reylan muttered, assessing the situation with his battle consideration.

Atherius cried out, and her pain slashed through Faythe again and again. She couldn't lose her.

A battle yell tore from Faythe as she didn't think, just acted on instinct, connecting to the ruin more deeply than before to summon light as blinding as the sun itself. Her palms pushed out, sending a flare of potent magick around the Firebird to engulf the shadow creatures that continued to race for her.

She managed to kill some, but it was hardly a dent in the shadows that seemed to keep manifesting. None of them charged for Faythe despite her attack. Somehow, Atherius made her fire the most desirable thing for them, but Atherius's flames weren't harming them. Screams echoed in the distance, alerting her that the army of shadows had infiltrated the whole city.

"What do we do?" Faythe asked, at a complete loss, turning to Reylan as her general for this.

"The shadows can only be killed if they don't see the attack coming." Reylan spoke to everyone as more Rhyenelle warriors began to gather to hear the instruction. "You need to work in teams. Pairs at the least. One has to attract, while the other attacks."

Attract and attack. Bait and kill.

Their soldiers nodded, not missing a beat to spread the instruction and begin protecting the city.

Faythe threw out her magick again and again, trying with all her might to help Atherius, but there were too many.

"Teams," Reylan said, pulling her arm back from releasing her next desperate flare. "You and me, Phoenix."

She nodded but didn't tell him how hot she felt. How sick and dizzy she'd become inside. It wasn't the nerves or fear—it was the ruin weakening her mind and body, and the moment Faythe couldn't sustain herself, it would take over completely to push her past her mortal limits.

Faythe had no choice but to be the bait since it seemed the shadow creatures still couldn't see Reylan or thought he was one of them. She didn't enjoy having to grab their attention and run around like a fool, throwing pointless attacks with her magick. Reylan was efficient, and they couldn't dispose of more shadow creatures even if they tried.

They couldn't grab the attention of those that covered Atherius's body, climbing all over her. Faythe's soul cried watching the brilliant embers of the Firebird become slowly smothered by complete darkness. She blinked back her tears, running around until she was staring into one of her brilliant amber eyes.

It was then, in the connection of their eyes, that Faythe understood.

This wasn't a fight; it was a sacrifice.

Denial torched every fiber of her being. Reylan figured out the Firebird's intention too as his strong arm hooked around her middle, pulling her back, just as she lunged forward.

Because Atherius spoke her goodbye in that pained stare she held on Faythe. Her goodbye...and her gratitude. To have found a bond again after so many centuries alone. To have gotten the chance to fly free and protect the kingdom of Rhyenelle once more before the end.

This end.

Faythe voice cracked and splintered. She fought against Reylan, who pulled her away as Atherius pushed herself up. Shadow bodies clung and climbed over her viciously, feeding on her magick and blood and feathers.

She didn't shake a single one off, deliberately enticing as many as she could to her. Then she splayed her wings, launching herself into the darkening sky.

Faythe wasn't ready to say goodbye. They hadn't had enough time together. The bond that ran through them strained, and Faythe's hand reached up—reached as though their bond were a physical string she could grip as it tugged painfully toward breaking.

She choked on her next sob when their bond *snapped*.

The world silenced at the ringing that filled her ears, only allowing Atherius's final cry to filter through.

Her knees gave out, but Reylan didn't let her fall. He lowered with her until they were kneeling, watching the brave and brilliant bird soar higher and higher, almost lost to darkness completely.

Then she erupted.

Atherius became the brightest, most breathtaking star to ever grace the sky, exploding into embers that rained down. Even if some of the shadow creatures anticipated it, she burned for long enough that they would be caught in her dying flames the moment they tried to reform.

The end of Atherius was as legendary as her beginning.

Faythe's head bowed, and Reylan held her tight. But not even he could stop the dark grip that had begun to take hold of her.

Too much loss. Too much bloodshed. Too much sacrifice.

The ruin answered to the eruption of her chaos, and the ruin she became.

CHAPTER FIFTY-EIGHT

Reylan

Faythe's tense body slackened against him. Her quiet, deep sobs eased away. Reylan felt the shift in her with a spike of dread in his chest.

"Faythe." He tested her name, not certain it was one he could reach her through anymore.

She'd taken the ruin's power. All of it. He'd watched her harness it inside the castle with careful caution, hoping it wouldn't come to this, but her grief had slipped her past the point of caring. And the most heartbreaking part was, he understood.

He repeated her name again but was met with the silence of her building wrath. If he was smart, he would gain distance before she erupted, but Reylan's promise to stand by her if she destroyed herself remained absolute.

Within, he carefully tried to reach her through the burning core of magick inside her. Reylan tried her name one last time, but before it was finished leaving his lips, Faythe's palm pushed back, pressing to his wounded chest and projecting him away from her.

The pain spotted his vision. Her attack to his chest was so prominent he didn't feel the impact of the ground at all.

Blinking furiously, he focused on his breathing, subconsciously pushing up to quickly regain focus. He'd been detrimentally wounded in battle many times. He could push past this. He *had* to, for her.

When Reylan found enough consciousness and breath, he searched for her.

He didn't find Faythe, but her magick…it was everywhere.

Everything was gilded in shimmering gold. It burned and danced, swallowing darkness and catching on perishable things as collateral. Faythe was purging the city. Of shadow creatures, of dark fae, of anyone and anything with an opposing heart against her or this kingdom.

The city burned in the wrath of Faythe Ashfyre. The line between hero and villain became smoke in the flames of the Phoenix Queen. For the act may hold true to malice, but the intent was a furious will to purge evil. Even if it meant sacrificing the beauty and mortar of own kingdom, and the fragile morality within her soul.

"She's gone," Zaiana said.

Reylan stood, unable to regard the dark fae and Kyleer.

All they could do was watch, and Reylan didn't know what he felt. Shock and horror over this unleashing of pure anguish from Faythe, but also pride. So much damn pride for his mate, who had the strength to fight back with everything she had.

For the brutal and senseless killing of her friend. For the loss of her brave Firebird.

To end a war of greed and power she'd been twice born into.

Faythe appeared, shooting above the highest building in the city. Wings of Phoenixfyre carried her, and she was absolutely magnificent.

"She's never gone," Reylan said, staring at his Phoenix on fire. "Not while I'm here."

"You're not enough to stop her now. The ruin is in complete power. Even if you try to take some of it, you only risk dying, and she'll never come back if that happens."

"I'm not going to take it—I'm going to become it with her."

"You're a damned fool to think that's any better than what's happening now. You'll only be two mindless beings of rage and magick rather than one."

"Then help me," Reylan snapped, turning his gaze to let her know he was serious. "You want us to trust you? Help me seal that power back into the ruin. You're the only one who knows how to wield it safely."

Her jaw worked, and those purple eyes flared against the fire raging from nearby wreckage. She gave a disgruntled sound, barely audible through the roaring flames and wails of burning enemies.

"The ruin will always pick the strongest vessel. Faythe has the essence of two Spirits within her. It won't answer to me so easily when it has her."

Reylan's jaw worked as that sounded like refusal.

Zaiana went on. "If it's forced to split between two cores, I might have a chance at sealing half the power when it's in you. Then it's up to you to reach Faythe and convince her to *let go* of the other half so I can seal that too."

Reylan knew it wasn't going to be easy. His Phoenix was ablaze with a torn heart, and he had to hope her soul tethered to his was enough to pull her back to him.

He nodded, and his sight slipped to Kyleer for a second. The blankness on his face every time he looked at Reylan was a punch to his gut. If he remembered how much Faythe meant to him, Kyleer would be just as concerned and desperate to save Faythe as he was.

That was a problem to fix later, so for now, as everyone ran from the raging power, Reylan plunged himself deep into the waves of it. He would always, in every darkness and danger, in every realm and every time, run toward Faythe.

Reylan scaled the buildings he could, knowing the labyrinth of this city so acutely he could navigate it blindfolded. Faythe's golden essence spilling through the streets didn't burn him, and from the few glimpses through the wreckage he spared, he was relieved to find many citizens, weary and fearful but alive and unharmed by the living magick.

Racing across rooftops, he didn't have to fight—Faythe was eradicating every darkness in the city. He focused solely on reaching her. He did not falter in pace, climbing higher and scaling closer to where Faythe hovered in the air like a Goddess of light and fire. Her eyes glowed with her tattoos, the light bright enough to break through the seams of her clothing.

When he got as close as he could, he had to shield his eyes against the tempest around her. He yelled her name, but already knew it would be futile. Reylan didn't have wings to match her in the sky, but if he jumped…

Reylan didn't have time to deliberate—the ruin was burning past Faythe's reserves, and she would die.

He backed up, he ran, then he leaped.

Faythe's head turned right before he slammed into her, twisting them to take the impact when they hit the roof opposite. They skidded with force against the unforgiving slate before rolling and tumbling. He tried to keep hold of her, but Faythe regained her orientation quicker than him, pushing off him with a surge of magick.

Her wings caught her, and as Reylan stopped rolling, she floated down, her feet touching down gracefully on the flat stone of the street they'd fallen onto.

No—not a street. They were in one of the market squares. The one where Agalhor had visited many times, as it was where Liliana had sold flowers at her stall.

"What are you trying to do?" Faythe said, her voice not entirely her own when another echoed over it. She stalked toward him as he rose. So hauntingly beautiful.

"You have to come back to me," he said, taking steps to meet her.

"I am with you. So long as you don't try to stop me."

"The ruin is killing you. Soon you will only be a vessel to it."

Faythe smiled, but it didn't truly belong to her. It was like the ruin was a living entity, wearing her face.

She raised her hands to his cheeks. "I have never felt more alive."

He reached for her too, using the physical connection to strengthen his will to reach past the raging core of magick that blocked him from their bond.

"With you, I am alive," he said. "Let me join you."

Reylan touched the core. Immediately, his own well of magick roared in protest, recognizing the danger of wanting to harness such velocity in even *half* of what Faythe harbored.

She was remarkable. Even as a human she defied every odd, proving time and time again she was more powerful and capable than anyone believed. Even herself.

"I see you, my Phoenix. I see you, I hear you. I wouldn't blame you if you didn't want to come back when this world has hurt you so truly. But you've always known you could numb the pain by giving in to your power even without the ruin. You've known all this time what you're capable of, and you've been careful, gentle, in learning your power instead of raging against the world when you had every reason to. You're the strongest, most resilient person to have lived when after all you've been though you keep *fighting*. That is your heart, Faythe Ashfyre. That is the heart I have the most incredible privilege of loving. So if you won't come back, then take me with you."

That softened her molten eyes, swirling like the surface of the sun.

"All I feel is pain," she whispered. Her eyes glistened, and liquid gold spilled over them.

"I know," he said, resting his forehead on hers.

"All I know is *pain*, and it never ends. I've been a coward all this time. Now I'm free."

"Now you're free," he echoed. "Take me with you. You promised."

The mass of power within her started to ease in his presence, allowing his ability to begin absorbing some of it. He'd barely taken any before his skin began to slick with sweat and his veins heated in warning. Reylan ignored it, taking more.

"It's hurting you," she said, studying his pinching expression.

"Nothing can hurt me more than your pain."

Magick like he'd never felt before flowed through his body, as transcendent as it was punishing. Reylan focused on the physical touch of Faythe to bear it. He cupped her nape, her skin burning against his so hot they could fuse into one person.

Then his lips slanted against hers. The moment they kissed, he lost all sense of time, gravity, and being. All he knew was power beyond what should exist in this world, and his love for Faythe, which was beyond any test of distance or time.

If the ruin killed them here, he no longer cared. The power was as addictive as the taste of Faythe. He gripped her tight, crushing their bodies together. He would recognize her soul wherever they might be reborn next. With Faythe, he believed in true immortality. The kind that defied knowledge, logic, or reason.

"Don't give in!"

That feminine yell frustrated him. It tried to pull him away from the power and Faythe, but he wanted more of both.

He couldn't breathe when the air was too hot. His passionate kiss with Faythe faltered when he didn't want to stop for a moment.

"You can do it," Faythe soothed, holding his head, which fell to rest against her chest. "Stay with me, and we can make everything right."

He lifted his arm to grip hers, but his body became lead.

What were they doing?

So much power and heat and…

"REYLAN!" Zaiana's yell jerked through him this time.

He remembered what he needed to do and became horrified he'd almost lost himself to the overwhelming magick with Faythe instead of helping her release it.

Reaching into her jacket, Reylan straightened, tugging her closer against resistance when he felt the icy stone of the ruin. A bitter contrast to the fire it invoked.

Faythe felt him pull it free as she tried to push him away, but Reylan threw it before she could, sensing Zaiana across the square.

"You're a liar!" Faythe cried, pushing harder with her magick this time. It wasn't enough for him to lose his footing, but the look of betrayal she pinned him with tore his soul.

Every breath he drew released the power of the ruin he'd taken from Faythe slowly, and Zaiana harnessed it back into its stone prison.

"I have never lied to you," Reylan breathed. He was close to passing out, having to brace his hands on his thighs.

Faythe approached him, gripping his hair and yanking his head back to look at her. Even in all her anger and loathing, she was the most beautiful thing he'd ever laid eyes on. He collapsed to one knee.

"Your mother sold flowers right here," he said. Reylan pictured the beautiful stall, flooding Faythe's mind with the image. Her grip in his hair loosened, and her face let go of some of her anguish.

"My mother," she echoed.

"Agalhor became utterly smitten with her. He would visit this market more times than any king should desire, and it quickly became known why he came. The last time he did, he asked her to marry him, unknown to anyone. He kept it private by her request."

More golden tears streamed down her cheeks, and he could feel the split in the core of her magick. Reylan reached for her. With everything he was, he reached for their bond to pull her out of the misery she was drowning in.

"I am with you. If you burn this world to ash, I'm burning with you. I'm on my knees for you, begging for you to hold on, to want this life. Bond with me, marry me, allow me the honor of ruling by your side. Because we will win. Together, and with our friends both standing and fallen, we cannot lose."

Faythe sobbed, a sound that tore his heart to shreds. But it was an immense relief to see her emotions. She broke softly, and he broke with her. His sight slipped briefly to Zaiana, who gave an affirming nod. Faythe was letting go, and Zaiana was masterfully drawing the ruin's power back into the stone slate.

"I want to live, Reylan. But I don't know if I have the strength to see the end anymore," she croaked.

"You do. But in times you think you don't then lean on me. You're not alone. Never."

Faythe kneeled slowly, so calm it broke a terrifying chill over his skin. Before she let go of the ruin's power completely, Reylan felt the tap into his mind, a gentle brush, like an omniscient presence that spread beyond this kingdom. He couldn't believe it was possible, as Faythe spoke far and wide to the people of Ungardia.

"My name is Faythe Ashfyre, Queen of Rhyenelle and the last true Heir of Marvellas. I have touched death and seen worlds beyond ours. I have fallen, but I have never known defeat. From the ashes our world may burn to, I will always rise. And with me, so will all who stand with me. In this war we are not kingdoms—we are one people. Let your tears for the fallen water the ground we march on, for we, the living, are the soldiers who will grow peace from ashen soil. Never fear, never surrender, and always be ready. The beginning of the end is upon us."

CHAPTER FIFTY-NINE

Jakon

Jakon Kilnight harbored vengeance like wildfire through his veins in every marching step he took through Rhyenelle's castle. For his wife, for Marlowe Kilnight, for the most caring, intelligent, and gentle soul to have ever lived, he would not stop until this world felt his grief.

With all the chaos, Jakon slipped past every guard. They all fought shadow creatures or raced through the halls to gather formation against the new foes. He'd left Faythe—there was nothing he could do against the darkness to save the Firebird anyway. He had no magick, no fae strength or speed. But he had a dagger in his hand and pain sharp enough to kill with it.

In the council room, only one person remained seated at the head. For a second, Jakon stopped still just past the threshold since Malin Ashfyre was so still. He clutched one hand covered fully in crimson to his neck, slumped into the tall red velvet seat, with his head hanging to the side.

No. He couldn't be dead. His life was *his* to claim. For Marlow, his life was his!

Malin coughed—a tight, wheezing sound that flew his bloodshot eyes open, barely any white around his caramel irises anymore.

Jakon's shoulders relaxed in relief, then they squared again with renewed retribution at the sight of his wife's killer.

He couldn't see straight; couldn't think straight. Jakon stormed across the hall with reaping intent. Gripping the arm of the chair, the wooden legs screeched across the marble floor as Jakon turned Malin out to face him. Rage shook his whole body so violently he didn't know where to begin unleashing it.

Malin's eyes bulged from lack of air and bleeding out. Had Faythe slashed his throat enough to incapacitate him? Jakon had come prepared to face Malin in his full strength—maybe he would die tonight trying to kill him—but the prince was so weak, already dying. There was no satisfaction to watch him suffer when it was not by Jakon's hand. That only enraged him more.

His hand lashed around Malin's on his throat, rocking the chair back with the force. Malin choked, struggling against his hold. Malin was still fae, still stronger, but Jakon's adrenaline-fueled wrath didn't feel afraid.

"Why did she have to die!" Jakon yelled, accentuating his pain with another push, digging deeper into his neck wound.

Malin's mouth floundered, and Jakon knew he couldn't get answers unless he let go. Jakon's anguish echoed through the hall, releasing his neck, but his other hand rose, and his dagger plunged into Malin's thigh. Malin's scream was a gurgle in his own blood. A wicked torture for a wicked soul.

Jakon stared down at the prince with his shoulders rising and falling to the beats of his impatient retribution. Malin's pain subsided enough that he shuffled, trying to sit up more in the chair, but his purchase slipped on the side of the seat, slumping him down again.

This was hardly a victory when Malin's life was already hanging on by a thread.

"She..." Malin choked again, and Jakon trembled with restraint. "She knew...too much."

Jakon saw white. He pulled the dagger from Malin's thigh, plunging it down into his other leg. Malin could hardly outwardly react to the pain, but his strangled cries were horrifying.

"She was far more than her power!" Jakon yelled. "She was everything good in this world. She was mine!" He pulled the dragger our again, aiming for his gut. "And you took her from me!" The blade lodged to the hilt.

Still, Malin held on.

Agony swam in his blood-filled eyes. "She saw...the end of the world."

Jakon's teeth clenched so tight.

"Her lie is as powerful as her truth," Jakon muttered. Those were

Marlowe's last words, which had reeled in his mind as he'd wondered if there was something hidden in her meaning. He growled in frustration, turning his loathsome stare back to Malin. "Was it all worth it? Everything you've done to end here?"

"Jakon..." Malin coughed and choked. His eyes rolled to the back of his head before snapping back to him. He was borrowing minutes, perhaps seconds, now. "It's all on you now."

Malin's body began to fall limp. Jakon removed the blade from his gut, making his eyes fly wide and lock onto his for his last breaths as he plunged the blade a final time into his heart.

Jakon wished he felt even a *fraction* of relief to watch his wife's killer die under his hand. He felt nothing. So cold and numb as he released the handle, leaving the blade Marlowe had crafted lodged in, as if they'd done this together.

But he was alone. So terribly alone he couldn't bear it.

Jakon fell to his knees, aware of a presence watching him from the shadows, but he didn't care. He wept. With nothing left to work toward, no one else to kill or blame to unleash all that was killing him inside without her.

How could she leave him here? Oh, how he wished he'd died right next to her.

She saw the end of the world.

This world had been so cruel to Marlowe that maybe he wished for it to end. Maybe he was rooting for Faythe to burn it all to the ground if that was what Marlowe had seen.

"At least it can't hurt you anymore, my love," he whispered to the ghost of her spirit that lived within him.

Jakon lifted himself off the ground. His frayed and heavy soul wanted to keep him down, but he wasn't finished. Not yet. For Marlowe, he wasn't finished.

CHAPTER SIXTY

Tarly

Tarly had fallen unconscious when he hadn't meant to. He came around groggily, registering the lightly snowed-on grass under his glove. Dusty snowfall fell on his face as water ran above his head. He was beside a small stream.

A loud huff jerked his stiff body in fright. Until he remembered his horse. He'd dismounted to refill his water skin and tend to the beast, but he must have passed out. His fatigue and pain were becoming intolerable.

Tarly pushed himself up on his one good arm. He'd had to fashion a sling for the other that had become useless. He wasn't fighting the tiredness with hope anymore. He could no longer wield his bow, so he was of little use to anyone.

All that kept him moving was the persistent image of an angel in his mind—with beautiful golden-brown skin and the most stunning curly silver hair. He recalled Nerida's firm encouragement to push forward, her laughs to wake up, the ways in which she looked at him like no one else to brave the wretched days.

He'd traveled for more than two weeks from High Farrow, where Izaiah had taken them after they'd fled Rhyenelle. Tarly harbored guilt for leaving so soon, when Jakon was grieving deeply and Izaiah was wounded badly. Selfishly, the dire events they'd escaped from made him even more desperate to reach Stenna's fall—the meeting place Tauria, Nik, and Nerida planned to head to as well.

Tarly didn't know if Nik would have gotten Tauria out of the high lord's clutches yet. Or if Nerida had made it back from Lakelaria to be there by now. With Tauria and Nerida's magick combined, they hoped to reach Hilia's Cave and discover if it safeguarded the Aetherbonds that could silence a person's magick no matter how powerful. Or the Spellthief, a dagger that could *steal* a person's magick.

Though he yearned to see Nerida, he didn't know how she would receive him after he'd abandoned her. He'd gone to Rhyenelle to serve a better purpose in this war rather than accompany her to Lakelaria on a selfish quest to find a cure for his dark fae bite.

He felt awful for it now, but his time was rapidly running out, and he wanted to try to make something of an impact.

His teeth bashed together as he trekked through the forest despite his feverish skin. Tarly believed his life hung in mere days, or less.

It took everything he had to mount the brown stallion. Barely able to sit straight, he edged the horse forward, using all his focus not to lose balance in his hunch and fall off.

Tarly found his fate both cruel and amusing. The moment he found the will to live, life was no longer his to plan for. If he hadn't met Nerida, perhaps this ending would even be welcome.

The deep echo of crashing water told him he was near his destination. Peeling his sight up, through the tree line ahead he saw the rocky shore of Stenna's fall. He'd only been here once: on the day he met Nerida.

She'd told him the stories of the fall and the nymphs that had once ruled the lakes and oceans—or still did but remained secluded from land beings now.

He never wanted Nerida to stop telling him the wonders she'd gathered in all her travels. He wanted to follow her, even when she didn't want him, to the ends of the world.

Tarly had learned that love was the most vulnerable emotion a person could expose themselves to, but the reward, should that love be true, was worth the risk of a shattered heart.

The great lake expanded far and wide through the end of the trees he passed through.

His heart pounded in his chest, tight and protesting, warning it didn't have many beats left. Tarly dismounted clumsily, barely finding steady feet. Urgency gave him a false sense of stability as he stumbled out through the trees, catching himself on one at the edge to scan down the rocky bank.

He was alone.

The next breath that left him deflated his whole body, which sank down. He rested his head back against the tree, looking over the peaceful sight.

Oh well, he thought. *At least this is a calm place to die.*

He hadn't feared death for a long time, so it was quite irritating for sorrow and disappointment to fill his chest now.

I'm not done here.

Was it the curse of all dying souls, no matter how prepared for death, to find unfulfilled desires they never strived for when their days were vast and uncertain? When time was their gift with no knowable countdown?

Wicked, tormenting thoughts.

Tarly might be losing his mind in his final hours. Believing he'd have days left broke a breathy chuckle from him now.

"You look like shit."

His eyes, which had begun to close, flew open at that irritating, infuriating, but damn relieving voice.

He looked up as Nik's footsteps left the soft grass and crunched over the rocks. But it was Tauria, her steps hurried after whacking Nik's chest, who lit up his world.

They'd left each other after the horrific events of the near wedding in Olmstone. He'd betrayed her, giving up her escape location thinking it would save his sister, Opal, but he'd been double-crossed by his father and Mordecai, who planned to Transition her to dark fae anyway. His sister was now safe in a human's farm home with her mother, far from here, but he'd never gotten the chance to explain this to Tauria and beg for her forgiveness.

So to his surprise, when she dropped down in front of him with nothing but concern over her delicate features, he didn't know why she wasn't upset with him.

Along with Tauria, Asari came bounding toward him. The white wolf sniffed him furiously and licked his face in greeting.

"You didn't find any cure for this yet?" Tauria asked, assessing his graying skin, which had spread up his neck, touching his jaw now.

A feminine gasp drew his attention to a small dark fae who stood a little behind Nik.

"What type of creature caused that?" she asked.

"This is Edith. She's a friend," Tauria explained. She must have felt his tension and seen the weariness in his stare. He'd never encountered a dark fae on good terms before, and he didn't let go of his reservation around Edith either.

"There is no cure," he answered. Tarly's hand cupped Tauria's at his face. "I'm so glad you're here. I can't tell you how sorry I am."

"I know why you did it. There's no need for apologies now. We need to get you help, because we have so much work still to do, Tarly Wolverton. You're not allowed to die."

"It's over for me, Tauria. But I need to ask for something…for you to carry a message to someone for me—"

"You're going to tell her yourself," Nik cut in. He stood tall, cross-armed, with a deep frown, as if disappointed in him.

"I piss you off even by dying," Tarly sulked.

"It's you giving up that's pissing me off. It's pathetic."

"Stop being mean to him." Tauria reprimanded Nik.

"I'd be worried if he was anything else," Tarly said. He was so tired, letting his eyes slip closed.

He only got a second of dark peace when a sharp slap across his cheek snapped him wide-awake. Tarly stared at Tauria in bemusement.

"You can't sleep," she said firmly.

Tarly tipped his head back again with a groan. The clouds were thick, debating a storm, but the sun glowed behind them, fighting to break through.

"Nerida should be here," he said quietly.

Tarly assumed Nik would have told Tauria everything. Her features twitched, and she scanned along the bank.

"We hoped she would be, but we may need to make camp for a few days and hope she still makes it," Tauria said.

"I don't have days," he said. He knew that in his core.

Her eyes turned desolate, accepting no amount of denial nor words of determination could slow or stop the inevitable claim death had on him.

Tarly coughed, turning violent, and he reached into his jacket for a cloth when the tang of blood filled his mouth. What he felt instead made him pause…

Blood.

He pulled out the vial he felt, having forgotten his possession of the Phoenix Blood potion. Tarly stared at the liquid, swirling as if alive in the bottle.

"Ooh, that's pretty. What is it?" Edith asked.

"Where did you get that?" Nik inquired.

Tarly froze.

They didn't know about Marlowe's death yet.

He looked up at Nik, unable to suppress his horror with the news he had to deliver.

Nik's stance slackened. "What?" he demanded.

"Marlowe gave it to me," he rushed out, scrambling to find the right sequence of words to tell them how their friend had been killed.

No arrangement would lessen the devastating blow, and so he relayed the horrifying events to them as quickly as he could.

Tauria broke into cries, and Nik held her, his face completely blank and wide. He'd never seen him so ghostly, angry, and grief-stricken all at once—all of that displayed in Nik's utter stillness.

"Are you sure?" Nik asked vacantly.

"I'm so sorry. I wish there was something I could have done to save her, but…" He trailed off.

Tarly had reeled over that grim day many times, tormented by all the ways he could have seen Malin's snap of madness just a moment sooner. Could have provided a distraction. Intervened somehow. Yet in all his reorganizing of events, he could hear the human's gentle voice carried in his mind. As an Oracle, she would tell him the future could not be known by those involved in it.

"We need to get back to High Farrow," Nik said tightly, no doubt thinking of Faythe's reaction to the news.

They needed to grieve together, and Marlowe deserved to have her friends together to mourn and celebrate her life.

"What about the Spellthief dagger?" Edith said timidly.

Tarly didn't know why he felt distrusting of this dark fae. She seemed shy and innocent, and maybe it was his own prejudice instilled in him against her kind that he had to work on.

"If you want to go back to High Farrow first, I understand—"

"No—she's right," Tauria croaked, sniffing hard and wiping her tears with the back of her gloved hand. "If the dagger or bonds are in that cave, we have to find out."

That was the heart-wrenching side of war still in motion—it granted no time to grieve the fallen properly. Healing was its own battle that awaited the living when it was over.

Tarly gritted his teeth, using his back against the tree for purchase to stand. He didn't want to, but he had to use every last hour he had. He stared at the Phoenix Blood as if it were a riddle.

"What if she gave this to me to give to someone else?" he asked aloud, mulling over other possibilities in his mind.

"If it could give you more time, you have to take it," Nik said coldly.

Tarly didn't take his tone personally. Nik was dealing with his loss.

He looked at Tauria. "Nerida consumed the potion Nik gave her. We hoped it would advance her healing for me, but it didn't. What if it amplified her water ability instead? For this task. Maybe Marlowe gave me this for you, to make your wind stronger to reach the cave."

Tauria immediately shook her head. "I don't need it. You're taking that potion."

His grip tightened around it. Why was he always the one with only selfish options?

"Marlowe believed with all her heart in an order. She gave me this for a reason, and if it was to prolong my time, she would have told me to consume it right there and then," he snapped.

Tauria's lips pursed, and their disagreement sparked in their stare-down.

All Marlowe had said when she gave the potion to him was that he would know what to do with it. This felt right. He pushed it into Tauria's hand, and she didn't reject it, though her face fell sadly. He didn't know what he'd done to deserve her care and friendship, but he was so damn grateful for it in his darkest hours.

"We should find the best tree cover to rest in case the rain breaks," Nik said.

"I'm staying on the bank in case Nerida comes," Tarly said, already resisting the urge to sink back down. "I'll take first watch. You two need rest. I'm banned from sleeping anyway."

Tauria met his humor with a flat look. "You will need to sleep, but not unless I'm watching you. I'll push the air in and out of your lungs myself if I need to."

"You both need to come to terms with the fact I might just drop dead any hour," he said, growing exasperated.

"Not on our watch," Nik muttered, staring off into the trees.

By nightfall, Tauria and Edith were the only ones resting after Nik built a small fire for them. Luckily, the rain had spared them so far.

Nik sat against the tree next to his, angled to not quite face each other but close. Tauria's head lay over his lap, and he absentmindedly brushed her hair or cheek.

"I haven't forgotten you almost followed through and married my mate," Nik said.

It wasn't what Tarly expected, but he supposed it was coming sooner or later. And he might not have much later.

"Had to get that grudge off your chest before I died, did you?"

"No. I guess I've been wondering if you're just a mindless follower of your father or if you had some other motive."

"Why don't you just ask me outright, did I fall in love with Tauria?"

Nik's eyes flared, and Tarly acknowledged the dangerous territory he walked with a mated male.

Tarly said, "I care for her deeply. I always have. Don't forget she came to Olmstone with the *intention* of marrying me. I don't care for your reasons—you hurt her more than I ever did by making her believe you didn't want her. So I was prepared to love her, but it never would have been the same as how you feel for each other."

Nik didn't take Tarly's enlightenment well, but it was nothing but the truth. "So now you can't have her, you fall for her sister instead."

Tarly's surge of anger was far beyond what his body could release. "If I wasn't dying, I would beat the shit out of you right now."

"You would try and fail."

"Arrogant as ever. You've never even fought me."

"I know you favor the bow as a weapon. Hand-to-hand combat would be child's play against you. Stick to shooting bunnies."

"You don't deserve her," Tarly said sourly. "You never have and never will."

"We might actually agree for once."

Tarly looked away, his jaw working in his vexation, so easily and quickly inspired in Nik's company.

Nik's implication for why he he'd fallen for Nerida riled him far more than it should. Dominantly, possessively so. Tarly stood, needing to walk off his anger if he couldn't swing it at Nik.

He got two steps before Nik drawled, "Where are you going?"

Tarly spun back. "Don't ever taint my affection for her like that again," he seethed under his breath, mindful of Tauria and Edith sleeping. "Nerida is not Tauria. Your mate has nothing to do with what I feel for her. All Tauria and I had was a desperate attempt to try to find joy in something that was forced upon us. But Nerida is *mine*. Do you get that? My person for all *her* reasons."

Tarly's chest heaved, hating that he had to spill this all to Nik. That he'd confessed something he hadn't even dared to think fully in his own mind.

Nerida is mine.

At least, with all he was, that was what he wanted more than anything.

He couldn't stand to have it linger anywhere that Nerida was a second choice. She wasn't. He felt more intensely for Nerida than he'd felt for Isabel, the one he'd believed was his mate and who had rejected him. Nerida wasn't just his first choice—she was the only damned choice he'd ever wanted with every fiber of his being. At times it was tormenting.

Nik sighed. "I do get that," he said, looking down at Tauria's peaceful face. "Shit, that was wrong for me to say. I don't know what came over me."

"Your territorial bullshit with the three of us finally getting to address the awkward *near* arrangement last summer, and your usual insufferable arrogance," Tarly ranted.

Nik smiled, actually huffing a laugh. It defused some of their tension, but Tarly didn't want to sit back down. The more he looked upon Nik and Tauria's peaceful closeness, the more his dire situation became despairing.

"You can't go walking on your own—you might pass out and die. Between you and me, I might not shed a tear, but Tauria would kill me."

It was Tarly's turn to let go of a partial laugh. He looked at Nik, and perhaps it was his draining time that opened alternate scenarios in his mind. The wonders of what could have been.

"Why did you always hate me so much?"

To his surprise, Nik frowned as though confused. "Hate you?"

"You weren't exactly welcoming to me. You or Callen."

The mention of the Prince of Dalrune struck a chord in them both.

"And here all this time I thought you detested me."

Tarly scoffed. "I tried to be your friend."

"When? In any formal gathering you would stand awkwardly by yourself, throwing daggers at me."

"Because every chance you got, you would either insult or humiliate me!"

Nik *grinned*. Tarly's fists balled.

"I've never hated you, Tarly. I've always thought you were stuck-up and gloomy company in our youth, but I guess I misread your loneliness, and for that, I'm sorry."

Tarly felt hit by a wave. Did Nik really just apologize?

He shook his head, questioning for a moment if he was awake. Asari stood, coming over to his side and brushing along his leg. Reaching down to the soft fur confirmed his reality a little more. Tarly looked down at the wolf with a twinge of yearning in his chest for

Katori, his own companion wolf. Though he hoped she was keeping Nerida safe instead.

Tarly said, "I'm not going far, and I risk falling asleep if I stay down."

He was so tired, but he feared closing his eyes in case he could never open them again. He just had to hold on until Nerida got here as the last thing he wanted to see in this world if he was to leave it.

"Fine. I have a feeling Asari is smart enough to call for us on your behalf."

Tarly turned away, heading along the shore.

Every step became heavier, and it wasn't long before he was regretting the idea to walk. He just wanted to lie down, rest his aching body for a few minutes. His bad arm still hung in a sling.

When Tarly cast his sight up, he stumbled to a halt.

Smoke billowed from the small home atop the hill. The one that had belonged to Nerida's friend. A gentle glow filled one window, and Tarly's heart skipped a beat.

"Nerida," he breathed.

Was it her inside? Who else would occupy such a home in seclusion not long abandoned?

Tarly forgot his fatigue. He didn't feel the aches of his body pressing forward with more determination than it had in days. He climbed the hill, reaching the home completely breathless while dark spots crept into his vision.

He just had to reach her. Just see her one last time and tell her how sorry he was for leaving, but that he'd done so for her.

His hand slammed down on the handle, and he tumbled inside with her name on his lips.

Yet Tarly wasn't welcomed by a warm embrace of fire and the bright smile of his angel.

Instead he stumbled over debris, unable to catch himself before tripping, crumbling to his knees. Tarly's head bowed, staring down at the splinters of charred wood that surrounded him.

His confusion started to clear, recalling the day they'd come across this home and found Nerida's friend murdered inside by the hands of thugs who'd wanted to capture Nerida for her Waterwielding ability.

Before they'd left, Tarly had set fire to the home rather than leave the body to rot.

Tarly couldn't even hold the weight of his upper body anymore as he fell over the burned wreckage. Asari whined but didn't howl to summon Nik for help. He was glad to be spared of that humiliation.

That is until the wolf took off, perhaps going to retrieve him instead.

Then he didn't know what the wolf was thinking when it returned within a minute, more boisterous than before. Tarly was about to yell at it for nudging his side and face and sniffing his body.

Until the most exquisite voice called his name.

"Oh, Tarly, what have you done to yourself?" Nerida said.

He must have fallen unconscious after his delirious vision, but he didn't care. This was the most beautiful dream he could have fallen into. Two wolves circled him now. Katori had come back.

"I was ready to be very mad at you, and yet I have to find you like this." Her tone was irritated, and he loved that. Loved her voice in every emotion. "It's hardly fair."

She was right beside him now, lifting his head and slipping her knees under him. *Gods*, her scent was bliss in his misery. He reached his good hand up, and before he could touch her thigh, her hand slipped into his.

Their eyes met, and he was home. He'd never known what that truly felt like until right now.

"I'll...I'll make it up to you," he answered. His words were slipping away from him, but he grappled at them desperately, wanting her to keep talking to him.

"Yes, you will. The more extravagant the better. Drink this," she instructed, bringing a small bottle to his lips.

The liquid eased down his throat, but he was only focused on her. Next, the gentle blue glow of her magick over his chest lifted a crushing weight he hadn't been fully aware of. He was so immeasurably beholden to her in this moment.

"Nerida..." he said, letting go of her hand to attempt to reach her face.

"Yes?"

Her brow was tightly pinched in worry, and he wished he could take it away. Her gentle fingers brushed the loose locks of his dark blond hair from his eyes. The full clarity of her attacked his soul. So powerfully that he had to say his next words, as mad as they seemed.

"I think you're my mate."

She drew a shallow gasp before her brow deepened more. Her eyes glistened. "I think so too," she whispered.

Tarly stiffened, not expecting the agreement. He blinked, slowly realizing this was no dream. Nerida was really here. She'd found him.

"I don't know how it's possible," he confessed. "Maybe I just feel for you that strongly it's like a mating bond, but…I haven't felt this way before, and I'm confused. So painfully happy but confused."

His thumb brushed her tear before it fell.

"I don't know either. But in a life as fragile and uncertain as this one, I don't really care how."

He swallowed hard. "Do you…do you want it to be true?"

A smile broke wide across her face, and she laughed through another falling tear. "Yes, Tarly Wolverlon. I want to be yours. So long as you stay alive for me."

His eyes closed with the warmest, brightest wave of reprieve he'd ever felt in his existence.

"I really, *really* want to stay alive for you."

"Good. Because I've said it from the start, you're not going to die." She sniffed, adjusting her position and assessing his wound. "It's spread a lot more since you left me. Why did you leave me?"

"I wanted to use what time I had left to make some kind of impact in the war, not search for a fantasy of a cure. And I…I tried to make you hate me so you wouldn't hurt so much when I'm gone." His hand slipped down over her collar as he listened to the song in her chest. "Your heart is so full and beautiful, and I wanted you to keep it whole for when you finally give it to someone."

"It's yours. You took it long ago, and I took yours in return. That was an exchange our souls made before our minds could find a hundred reasons why we shouldn't."

She was so precious it hurt. So *his* that he couldn't believe it.

"I love you, Amelie Valaria Nerida Da'Naid. I have for some time."

Her eyes widened, and he knew it wasn't his declaration of love for her.

"How did you know?"

"Your father was the King of Fenstead. I came across a book once in the Livre des Verres. It documented frequent and consistent travels to Lakelaria taken by the King before Tauria was born. When I found you, you were a traveler of many centuries, wanting to stay hidden. So I knew you had to have a mother wealthy enough to potentially have spies. You were afraid when you learned who I was, because a link to another royal could get you found out quicker." Tarly felt so much more alive from her presence and her magick that he sat up with more ease than he'd felt in weeks. He cupped her cheek then ran his fingers through her hair. His eyes marveled over every perfect inch of her. "It makes so much sense. You'll make a spectacular queen, Nerida. If that's what you still want to be called."

She nodded, tearing up more. "To the people I'm Amelie, but I want to always be Nerida with you."

"My Nerida," he said tenderly.

He kissed her. Deeply and only once.

"My Sully," she murmured against his lips.

That pulled a genuine chuckle from him, and he circled an arm around her, tucking her against him, never feeling so light from any burden than while she was in his reach.

"I want to hear everything that happened in Lakelaria," he said.

"Then you have to tell me where you went. If you've been wandering around in self-pity all this time, I'm going to be very mad again."

Tarly smiled though she couldn't see it. He kissed her neck, running a hand up her spine. "I'm so relieved you're here. I promise to stay by your side from now on. I promise to *fight* to stay here against the odds. For you."

CHAPTER SIXTY-ONE

Nikalias

When Tarly returned, Nik was both surprised and unsurprised Nerida had found him first. They'd let Nik get a few hours of sleep alongside Tauria, but he'd expended it on an urgent call he'd felt from Zaiana through Nightwalking.

He was still dealing with the devastation of Marlowe's death, now discovering Kyleer had almost met his end too. It was another blow to those he considered dear and friends. Nik didn't know if becoming dark fae was a fate much better, and he was dangerously antsy to be reunited with Faythe and the others.

Faythe. He couldn't begin to fathom how she was coping with her grief. She'd suffered and lost more than any of them, and he feared deeply for her well-being with these catastrophic events.

He felt deeply for Jakon too, haven grown somewhat close to him and Marlowe after Faythe first left High Farrow. Nik trusted Jakon as a close friend.

Tauria's presence wrapped around him from behind, soothing some of his sharpness. Her delicate hands massaged his shoulders before slipping around his chest. Her soft lips pressed to his jaw, and he drowned in the bliss of her touch and scent for a moment.

"Did you get any sleep at all?" she asked, already knowing he hadn't.

He really needed it, but the never-ending movements of war made such a thing scarce.

"I'll be fine. It's you who needs the strength for today. How are you feeling?"

Tauria shuffled around on her knees until she was in front of him. Her face of sorrow spoke all. "I know war is unbiased to pure hearts, but Marlowe...how is that fair in any sense?"

"It's not. Her death was senseless and brutal, but it won't be in vain nor forgotten. Faythe will exact her vengeance on Malin, and we'll help her take on the world that has turned too cruel."

Tauria sighed, and he shared her burden of tiredness and fading hope. She sat back, fiddling with the loose ends of her wild, unbound tresses. "Can you braid my hair?" she asked.

Nik smiled. "The last time I did, you took it out immediately and called for a handmaiden."

"They might have better skill, but I much prefer your hands."

Her quick wink at him before she turned around made his length jerk in his pants. Nik gripped her hips, yanking her back against him as she squealed.

"My hands are itching to feel you in ways you can't imagine."

"We've explored quite a lot—my imagination knows no limits."

He groaned, burying his forehead into the back of her neck, and the devious thing rubbed her ass against him. Nik turned his head just enough to be sure Tarly, Nerida and Edith were still out of earshot by the lake, watching the wolves catch fish for breakfast.

"Do you want a braid, or do you want me buried where you're teasing me?" That made her stop her ministrations, and he could practically *taste* her uncertainty and curiosity with the suggestion. "I know you, Tauria. Your imagination has been there before, hasn't it?"

Her desire ruined his senses, and before she could answer he'd clamped an arm around her middle, pulling her up with him as he stood. Nik spared another look across at Tarly and Nerida, still laughing and engrossed in the wolves' attempts.

Nik ran two fingers down the base of her spine. Tauria gasped, pushing into him as he curved down the seam of her pants, right to the front.

"Breakfast is going to be a while anyway, it seems," he said huskily. "So what do you say we backtrack to that small cave we passed on the way here for a while?"

Tauria nodded, and Nik dragged his teeth along her collar.

"Lost your words, love?"

"Yes—I mean, no—I want...I need you now."

He bit down shy of breaking skin, and she choked on her moan.

"My favorite words."

When they returned to the shore of Stenna's fall, the scent of freshly cooked fish was a blissful welcome.

"You must be famished," Nik said, pulling Tauria to him as they walked, with a teasing squeeze of her waist. "With the amount of noise you made—"

He adored her shyness, playfully whacking his chest.

"Where have you two been?" Tarly inquired, finishing half his fish before throwing the rest to Katori.

"Scouting," Nik said at the same time as Tauria answered, "Training."

He slipped her a devious look, saying to her thoughts, *"We'll definitely be working on that particular training again."*

Tauria smiled innocently at Tarly, pretending she hadn't heard him.

Nik didn't fail to notice how Tauria quickly looked away from Nerida. She tried a smile, but it was as if nerves took over. The two estranged half-sisters hadn't had any time to talk, and Nik thought about diverting away from them with Tarly for a while before they would attempt to reach Hilia's Cave far below the lake.

"Your braid," Nerida said timidly. "I could fix it if you'd like."

"She's very good at it," Edith said, admiring her perfectly woven twin braids.

Nik had tried his best with the attempt he'd made after making more of a tangled mess of Tauria's hair. In his defense, with no comb, he'd found it twice as difficult.

Tauria ran her hand over her head, slipping him an accusing glare. "Thank you," she said warmly.

Nerida's body loosened at the acceptance. She handed the rest of her skewered fish to Tarly and got up.

Nik plucked a whole one off the fire and stood. "We should scout the area for bandits who know about the cave before we try to enter. We don't want any altercations."

He said it to Tarly, who didn't immediately catch his hint to leave the sisters alone for a while.

Tarly frowned. "I thought you said you scouted already?"

Nerida giggled, and Tauria fought a sheepish smile.

Nik refrained from rolling his eyes before hooking Tarly's good arm and hauling him up. "We'll be close enough to hear if you call," he said over his shoulder as he walked Tarly away.

The wolves stayed with Nerida, Tauria, and Edith.

Nik chewed at his breakfast, enjoying the peaceful walk with the crashing waves of Stenna's waterfall. Tarly wasn't always terrible company, he supposed. In fact, since he'd returned last night with Nerida, he'd noticed a change in the Olmstone prince—one Nik thought he could relate to.

"You had a mate who rejected you?" Nik said, realizing how insensitive it came out.

"Thanks for the reminder," Tarly grumbled.

"I only meant... Shit, sorry. I guess I'm trying to say I'm glad you found a bond just as strong elsewhere."

Tarly curved an apprehensive brow at him.

"Is this your attempt at atoning for centuries' worth of being an ass to me now I'm dying?"

Nik's mouth quirked. "Maybe."

"It's unnerving."

He chuckled, tossing the stick after finishing his breakfast.

Tarly spoke again. "Do you think it's possible for someone to have two mates? A second chance?"

Nik contemplated. "I don't think anything is impossible, but I've never heard of such a thing. But people can find feelings for another as strong as a mating bond can inspire. That's not uncommon."

That didn't seem to satisfy Tarly.

Nik added, "Is a mating bond really that important to you?"

"It's not that," Tarly defended. "It just...I can't explain how I never felt this pull to Isabel. It was different, like I recognized her as mine instinctively, but the feelings took time. With Nerida, there's a different kind of instinct. It's like I'm in tune with her emotions, her actions...with her, it's sometimes like we're one person."

Nik mulled over Tarly's explanation. "Have you tried mating with her?"

Tarly's cheeks flushed. "No."

"That's one sure way to know."

"And what if it's true and she is my mate?"

"What if she isn't? Would it change your feelings at all for her?"

"No," Tarly said immediately.

"Then just enjoy what you have. If you discover she is your mate, you can search for answers then, or embrace the blessing and forget about the tricks of fate."

Tarly looked at him again like he didn't know who was really walking beside him. "Who knew you could be kind of wise?"

"A lot of people know. My wisdom is a privilege."

"Arrogant, as always."

Nik didn't see this coming, but Tarly had other sides to him he kept guarded from the world. Tauria had once said if he opened himself to see it, Nik would find he had more in common with Tarly than either of them wanted to admit. What he knew with absolute certainty: Tauria was always right.

Nik felt the tug of distress within him before any sound. His body whirled back, but they'd traveled through the trees and couldn't see Nerida or Tauria anymore.

"They're in trouble," Nik informed him, already sprinting back with Tarly close behind.

"You can still feel Tauria without your bond?"

"Echoes of it are still there. I don't think we can share power anymore, and our mental connection is weaker, but there will always be a part of her living within me."

Nik missed their full mating bond terribly since it had been broken by Marvellas. It would always be like a severed limb, but it didn't change a thing about their feelings.

Making it back to Nerida and Tauria, Nik had never seen creatures like the three that surrounded them and the wolves.

"What depths of the Nether did they crawl from?" Tarly said, as horrified as he was at the wraithlike beings.

Tauria attacked one with her wind at the same time as Nerida animated a stream of water to drown another. He thought they'd succeeded in killing them, but as powerful as Tauria and Nerida were, he should have anticipated by their appearance it wouldn't be that easy to eliminate shadow.

Katori lunged for one, but a shadowy arm slammed her to the side as though *she* were as light as shadow. The wolf wailed, careening into the nearest tree and whimpering as she tried to stand again. Asari growled deeper, lowering her stance as if to try next. Nik might joke and pretend he didn't want the wolf's companionship, but the truth of his feelings was exposed right there in his surge of fear for Asari.

Nik didn't know what to do, quickly discovering these creatures didn't have minds for him to tap into. He freed his blade just as a rock went flying by him.

Nik was about to throw sarcasm at Tarly for the pathetic attempt of an attack, but the rock actually proved useful. It *hit* one of them, knocking their head to the side and proving they could be struck. Then how had they dissipated and reformed at Nerida and Tauria's attacks?

The one Tarly hit emitted an eerie hiss before spinning its attention to him.

"Do that again," Nik said, swiping up a rock too and aiming it for the one closest to Tauria.

The rocks hit the other two, who targeted Tarly and Nik now.

"Strike them now!" Nik called to Tauria and Nerida.

They didn't miss a beat. Nerida's strong tide slashed through one, while Tauria's cutting wind sliced through another, both forces of nature colliding in a breathtaking spectacle to blast the middle one apart.

When the water crashed to the ground and the wind stopped howling, the four of them stared at the air, dumbfounded and catching their breath. No trace was left of the shadow beings.

"What were they?" Edith squealed, appearing from her cover behind Tauria and Nerida.

Nik pressed forward, reaching Tauria to scan her from head to toe for injury. Finding her unharmed, he began to relax from the adrenaline, kissing her forehead.

Katori whined, and Nik watched Nerida and Tarly kneeling by her. Nerida's hands glowed blue, and Nik marveled at her wonderful ability.

"We were practicing to try the passage to the cave when they came out of nowhere," Tauria explained.

Nerida said grimly as she worked, "I have a theory it has something to do with the quake we all felt when Faythe broke the ruin. I think it's opened a passage into our world for the shadows lost from their bodies to crawl out."

"How do we close it?" Nik asked, horrified by the concept.

Nerida's wince confirmed she didn't have that solution.

"We need to get to the cave," Tauria said. Her exasperation made him tense, and he tried to soothe her with a touch around her waist.

"We will," he said.

"Now. We keep losing, keep having odds stacked against us and people dying. We need this upper hand. We need to *win*."

When her voice cracked on the last word, Nik pulled her into an embrace. She let him hold her while Nerida finished tending to Katori, who jumped back onto her feet in perfect health.

"We can wait another night to try to reach the cave if either of you need more rest. We couldn't have predicted that ambush," Tarly said, concern written all over him.

Nerida smiled, placing a hand on his good arm. "I'm perfectly well. My Waterwielding is much stronger than usual. I think it was the Phoenix Blood I drank." Her expression fell as she looked over his sling and the graying skin of his neck and jaw. "But I really do wish it had amplified my healing instead."

Tarly pulled her to him, and Nik looked away.

He said to her thoughts, *"You're going to reach that cave, love. I know you're strong enough to work with Nerida and make it."*

Tauria peeled herself off him, speaking her gratitude in her hazel eyes.

Nik and Tarly had no choice but to follow and believe in them. He felt utterly hopeless, unable to help even through their bond now.

They followed Nerida along the bank for a few minutes until she stopped.

"I've studied maps of Stenna's fall before. There are multiple of them, so it's hard to know which tell the truth of the exact location of the cave. If I'm wrong, we'll have exhausted ourselves to the bottom for nothing, and I don't know how long it will take to recover for a second try."

Tarly said, "I trust your intuition."

"As do I," Tauria added.

Nerida gave a nervous laugh. "You hardly know me."

Tauria reached for her hand, surprising the healer.

"I have good intuition too. It must be a Stagknight trait," Tauria mused.

The casual statement expressed so much on Nerida's face, and Nik's chest burst with pride to witness their blossoming bond.

"Definitely," Nik added.

Nerida squeezed Tauria's hand before letting go, and her shoulders squared with confidence.

"Do you still trust me when I say I believe it's right here, but this point has never been on any of the maps I saw?"

Nik tensed at that and sensed he wasn't alone with an inkling of doubt in Tauria's shift too.

"Yes," Tarly said with absolute certainty.

She was the Queen of Lakelaria. A Waterwielder. Nik had to believe she had a connection to the lakes and oceans of their world that none of them could understand.

"You should wait here," Tauria said to Edith.

"No way! An adventure to under the lake—I can't miss out!" She skipped up close to Tauria.

Nik didn't like the idea of another body to account for in this risky task. A quick exchange with Tarly told him he wasn't alone.

Tauria stirred the air first, creating a sphere of wind around them all. Then Nerida disrupted the edge of the expansive lake, separating the water from the floor it guarded.

"It goes very deep, and we'll be passing under the waterfall, which will be the biggest test of our strength," Nerida informed them.

Tauria nodded with determination, and the five of them began to walk through the break Nerida made in the dominating lake.

Every minute was precious, every second uncertain. Tauria and Nerida moved their arms, channeling their magick with such elegant precision and grace. Nik hovered close to Tauria, occasionally reminding her of his presence to do whatever she needed with a touch to her waist.

"You're both doing amazing," he said, gentle in their focused silence.

They were deep under the lake now, within the eye of a tempest of air and water. Tauria kept their sphere of air strong, while Nerida controlled the water so it eased off Tauria's current. They worked together flawlessly, and neither could have made it this far without the other.

Nik had felt Tauria's growing strain for the past minute. Her forehead beaded with perspiration, and Nik wiped her skin carefully, slipping a hand around her to guide her steps while she focused on maintaining her magick.

Nerida wasn't struggling as much, but Tarly kept close watch with her too.

"Are we close?" Tauria asked, her breath short.

Nik tamed his panic in concern for her.

"We're about to go under the waterfall. It will fight against our magick more than the body of water."

Tauria swore under her breath.

"You can do this, love. I know you can," Nik said into her ear. He yearned achingly for their mating bond to soothe her senses within. There was nothing more he could do for her, and there was no feeling more tormenting.

Glancing up, Nik's hold tightened around Tauria at seeing the thrashing water rejoining the lake they were about to pass under. The moment they did, their air bubble shrank, and Tauria faltered her walking, trembling to hold their pocket of air.

"We have to keep moving!" Nerida called.

"It's too much," Tauria wheezed. Their air pocket shrank again, shuffling them all closer.

"You're stronger than you think, Tauria Silverknight. Push *harder*," he said firmly.

It killed him to encourage her to dip dangerously into her magick, but if they faltered here...the surface was too far for any of them to make it up by swimming.

Tauria cried out, her arms shaking, but her wind strengthened again, and Nik guided her walk with more urgency.

"That's it. You're incredible," Nik murmured in her ear, continuing his words of adoration and encouragement as all he could offer.

"I see the entrance ahead!" Edith exclaimed.

Nik did too. A single circular stone door with a carving of a trident on its center. Around the trident was an ancient script he didn't recognize. He didn't breathe his relief yet when Nerida parted the water away from the seal as they reached it. Nik let Tauria go to approach the door, digging his fingers into the side and attempting to pull it open. It didn't budge, not even when Tarly joined his efforts with his one good arm.

"None of your reading of the cave mentioned how to open it?" Nik asked Nerida, trying to keep his irritation dulled, but his concern for Tauria made him sharp.

"You need the blood of a descendant of Hilia," Edith said.

Nik found her studying the circle of script.

"You can read that?" Tarly asked.

"It's the old language. I know enough of it to read this."

Nik's eyes closed to collect himself. This had been a waste of Tauria and Nerida's energy. Without the break they planned for inside for them to regain enough strength back, he didn't think Tauria could last the trip back.

His mate wasn't present in their conversation and dilemma. She trembled, struggling to hold her magick, and her skin was slicked with sweat.

"We need to retreat then—now," Nik growled, returning to her.

"Wait," Nerida said.

To everyone's horror, Nerida let go of her magick. Tauria cried as the full force of the deep water compressed against her air. Nik caught her when her knees buckled, but she held onto her magick.

"Nerida!" Nik barked, whipping his head around to find her slicing Tarly's palm before she pulled him, slapping his hand to the stone.

Nothing happened.

Tauria was faltering.

Then the trident…*glowed.*

To everyone's shock, the trident began to flood with light before the door groaned, released of its tight seal.

"Hurry!" Nerida said, ushering them inside before taking stance and pushing the water off Tauria's air again.

"I can hold the water if you can seal the door," she said to Tauria as she slipped by and inside.

Tauria's feet shifted back, and her arms moved, gathering a tight tornado before pulling her arms into her body, slamming the air she conjured into the stone from the outside. Then Nerida let go of her magick, and Nik tensed at the booming crash of water into the closed door. It didn't flood past the seal.

Nik's tension released all at once. He needed to pull Tauria into him, embrace her tightly and smooth down her hair.

"I knew you could do it," he muttered.

"Thank you," she said, gathering her breath.

"How in the Nether did my blood open it?" Tarly stared at his hand, which Nerida was healing. The blue glow of her magick provided the only source of light in the tunnel.

"I hope you don't mind, but I was curious about your lineage when I sensed the essence of healing magick within you that you didn't even know about yourself. Your mother had it too—you knew that. I didn't know for sure, as it wasn't directly documented back in your family tree in any books I found, but through several links and guesses, I began to believe your mother's line came from Hilia herself."

The claim was bemusing.

"Wasn't Hilia a nymph?" Tauria asked.

"Yes. But one of her children gave up her life in sea to walk on land—a Transition achieved by the Trident of Everseas that was lost a very long time ago. So her bloodline spread throughout land and sea from then on."

"I know how it feels to have a secret lingering in a distant heritage," Nik said.

Like the revelation of Tarly, Nik didn't think his connection to the

Vesaria bloodline meant anything more than finally having a trace to his Nightwalking.

"Do you think I could ever...*use* the healing magick?" Tarly asked Nerida. "I mean, wouldn't I have been able to by now?"

"I think it's possible to tap into it, yes. After losing your mother and your...*mate*...it likely suppressed it deeper."

Nik wasn't eager to stay down here longer than necessary. He scanned down the dark passage, realizing they were a body short.

"Where's Edith?" Nik questioned.

They all looked around, their fae sight adjusting to the pitch-darkness they were enclosed in.

"She has a habit of letting her excitement stray her away," Tauria said, but even her tone turned wary at the dark fae's absence.

"Let's just hope the damned dagger is down here," Nik grumbled.

CHAPTER SIXTY-TWO

Tarly

Discovering his bloodline could be traced to Hilia herself had Tarly's mind wandering. He supposed it didn't have much relevance beyond helping them into this cave, but if he lived through his dark fae bite by some miracle, the new fact inspired him to learn more about this essence of healing magick that was buried inside him. Tarly's hand brushed Nerida's as they walked through the darkness, the thought of it bringing them closer.

She smiled up at him, and it slammed in his chest every time. *My mate.* He couldn't stop repeating it in his mind when they were close. Nik was right…there was only one way to be certain if the bond was real, and Tarly's whole body was riled with carnal need at the thought of tasting her in more ways than one.

They came to the end of the passage, which opened up, illuminated by a source he couldn't find. It was as if the very walls themselves glowed, and the air hummed with a warning energy that tightened his hand in Nerida's.

There was a statue carved out of stone and claimed by sea moss, depicting a nymph with a long, curling tail, long hair covering her bare chest, and a circlet over her head. It had to be a memorial of Hilia, who held the legendary trident in her hand. A curved masterpiece of three lethal teeth turning to arrow points.

Droplets of water hitting stone was all that disturbed the silence through their collective breathing. Tarly surveyed the walls and the low-set roof with growing unease at the moisture that leaked through. As if the cave might collapse under the weight of the fall crashing all around this carved-out pocket of air. Off to the side was a second passage, but they'd already found what they were looking for.

Edith stood before a narrow altar, where a sparkling jeweled chest sat. Her hands reached up to open it—

"Wait," Tarly said. "We don't know if it's safe."

"How else are we meant to find out?" Edith snapped, but her sweet smile flashed over her shoulder.

Tarly didn't trust her. He didn't know why, since Tauria seemed taken with the dark fae, but something about her unnerved him.

"I'll do it," Nik said.

He took one step, and Edith swiped up the box. They all jerked at her sudden brazen movement, tensing with eyes darting around as though the walls would cave in.

Tarly was about to relax until Edith flicked open the box, and only when she pulled the dagger within free did the cave groan.

Then all the light snuffed out.

Nerida pressed into him, and he circled his good arm around her. Nik and Tauria came closer until their backs touched, keeping sights on all angles.

"Edith, what are you doing?" Tauria asked, dread filling her voice.

They could see enough to navigate out, but the pure darkness would slow their reaction time drastically.

An eerie chuckle echoed through the cave. When Edith next spoke, her voice was different. Not as high-pitched an innocent as it once was. Now she spoke with the smooth grace of confidence.

"Oh, Tauria, I knew it would be too easy to play to your kind heart. Seeing a poor little tortured dark fae, you couldn't help but want to be my savior."

Tarly's teeth ground, seething with anger over the exploitation of Tauria's fair heart.

"Why?" Tauria whispered.

"Because *I* should be his heir, not her," she snapped.

Tarly tried to track the dark fae's silhouette as her voice moved, taunting them.

"Who are you talking about?" Tarly snapped.

"Zaiana," Nik muttered.

Tarly wasn't familiar with the name. "Who?"

Nik spoke to Edith. "She's Mordecai's daughter, isn't she? But she doesn't know. Tauria discovered Mordecai was a Stormcaster."

"I was the one who showed her that," Edith hissed. "I hoped she would figure it out and want to kill Zaiana with me. This mission for the dagger could have been a genuine alliance. Until I realized you didn't know who Zaiana was, and so I have to take this for myself. I do hope you understand."

"You plan to take her power with it," Nik concluded.

"Yes. Then he'll value me, not her."

"You're her sister."

"I don't care for such terms. I am Mordecai's daughter—that is all that matters—and I doubt I'm the only other he has. After Zaiana was born a Stormcaster, he tried to conceive another, but she was the only one. She's always been the only child he values and will give his kingdom to. I trained as hard as she did under the mountain. I am as good as her in every way, and Mordecai saw that enough to appoint me as commander of a legion in his army, but it's an insult compared to the privileges and value he grants Zaiana."

"Why has he never told her?" Nik asked, keeping calm.

Tarly was reeling with the revelation of the high lord's heir. Nik spoke as if he knew Zaiana. Tarly just didn't know if it was as an enemy or an ally.

"He almost raised her, but Marvellas convinced him she would become better, stronger, more ruthless, without any attachments like everyone else. So Marvellas wiped her memories young, and she grew up like the rest of us. I only found out because my mother told me. She has a position of power. Mordecai listens to her. When she promised him I would rise to the Vesaria name no matter what it took, he let me live. Only if I found this dagger one day to claim Zaiana's power and her life. That is ruthlessness. That is a worthy heir of Valgard."

"You have what you want then," Nik said bitterly. "So let's all get the Nether out of here."

"You must think me a fool to risk the tedious journey back to the surface with the four of you ready to turn on me. Besides, I need to discover if this works. If it truly is the Spellthief. I think with either of your abilities, I could get myself to the surface in time."

Her steps shuffled fast, heading for Tauria first, but water from Nerida's pouch at her hip slashed through the air. Edith was fast—*very* fast. And she was small, darting expertly out the way, twisting around Nik's attempt to swipe her with his sword. Tarly didn't have any weapon or finesse, only a dominant will to protect Nerida, which had him tackling Edith while she was preoccupied dancing around the other's attacks.

They went tumbling, and every knock against his bad side threatened his consciousness with the explosions of pain.

Edith growled, pushing off him, and he tried to reach after her, but his movements turned sluggish, and she was too quick to adapt, a masterfully, brutally trained soldier since birth.

None of them were prepared, and all of them were outmatched.

Especially in this darkness, where the cave's trembles intensified in warning.

He was utterly helpless to stop what came next.

Nerida's cry shattered his world.

The cave shook violently as if it too outraged at the power stolen. Nerida's magick transferred into Edith through the plunge of a blade. He *felt* it. An echo of her pain both physical and within as the threads of her magick were ripped out by vicious phantom claws.

Tarly crawled with his remaining strength to reach where she kneeled, clutching her shoulder.

"Angel," he said in a panic, pushing himself up on his good arm and pulling her to him as she wept.

"I can collect more than one ability," Edith marveled, raising her hand and admiring the sense of magick none of them could see.

"Nerida." Tarly cupped her cheek, forcing her to meet his eyes. They poured with tears, and it wasn't for her bleeding wound.

"She took it all. Both abilities," Nerida confirmed.

His eyes snapped up to Edith with a rage more potent than he'd ever felt before. The dark fae smiled, wicked and cruel, the dagger in her hand still dripping with Nerida's blood as her dark eyes targeted Tauria next. Nik pushed her behind him.

"Nightwalking would be fun, but water and air go so well together."

"You're not getting any closer to her," Nik snarled.

Edith's smile only grew wider.

Though just as she stepped in challenge, the sound of rushing water rumbled through the cave.

"Looks like you're all out of luck. Drowning really is a terrible way to die," Edith said before sprinting toward the exit, which had opened.

They were seconds from being slammed by the violent current.

"We need to go," Nik barked.

Tarly didn't miss a beat, grabbing Nerida's hand and sprinting through the second passage as Nik and Tauria did.

Nerida's cries tore him apart, but he wouldn't let her die down here.

The water chased them, catching up so fast every breath became precious.

They came to a ladder, scrambling up it. The water crashed into the dead-end wall before surging up past Tarly's middle. Only having one arm made it more of a struggle to climb, and the rapidly rising water slammed his heart.

At the top, Nik came back to haul him over.

Their rapid steps splashed through the sheet of water growing past their ankles.

They'd made it to another room, but no one took off running again.

Because they were trapped.

Tauria acted fast, creating a wind barrier against the break in the stone. The water level rose quickly against it. Her footing stumbled with the growing pressure, and Nik steadied her.

"I won't be able to hold this long," Tauria panted.

"Search for something—anything!" Nik barked the command to Tarly.

He assessed Nerida first, overcome with panic. "You're losing a lot of blood," he said.

Nerida sniffed, clutching her wound and pushing past him. "It's nothing."

Tarly ran his hand along the walls like she did, searching desperately for some miracle there would be another concealed door.

"It's hopeless," Nerida sobbed, giving up her search.

She was never one to give up, and he knew her spirit had withered with the loss of her magick, but he would not let her die.

Tauria faltered for moment, but it was enough for a strong current to rush in, building to their knees. They were rapidly running out of time.

"I'm scared, Nik," he overhead Tauria say.

Tarly refused to give up. After all the shit they'd been through, this couldn't be how they all died.

The force of water was winning against Tauria's reserves of wind magick. The ice climbed to his chest. Nerida was on the tips of her toes, her chin pointing to the roof as she took terrified, calculated breaths.

Tarly growled, searching the unforgiving, merciless walls more frantically.

His hand sliced against a sharp piece of stone, and he hissed, pulling away, but he became distracted by the color of his blood that changed from crimson to silver.

Even more perplexing was when the trace of his blood *moved*.

He followed the snaking line as it traveled across the wall before dipping under the water that had reached his shoulders now. Tarly took a deep breath, diving under, needing to ignore the shouts of his name.

The silver line drew an arch, and Tarly swam for it, pushing as hard as he could, but all it needed was more blood from his cut palm and the small stone door *disappeared*, suctioning the water down a passage that was just big enough for them to swim through.

He pushed up for air, finding the water had risen too far for Tauria to keep using her magick, and their heads had to angle against the roof for the last fraction of air.

"There's a passage just big enough to swim through. I don't know if it'll lead us out, but either way, we'll drown if we stay," Tarly rushed out, making it over to Nerida and pulling her toward it.

"There was no passage," she said, terrified.

"There is now—trust me. I'm right behind you."

He stared into her hazel eyes rimmed red with tears. He loved her. With all his heart, he loved her until the end of the stars.

Tarly had to kiss her. Desperate and short.

"Deep breath for me," he said calmly.

Nerida sucked in deeply then dove under, and he followed in the same beat.

Squeezing into a passage of the unknown, with his last breath held in his lungs, invoked an acute terror the likes of which he'd never felt before. Swimming was also difficult with one arm, but his will to survive almost kept pace with Nerida, who pushed through brilliantly. The suction helped pull them, and Tarly couldn't be sure if it was his desperation or real that the current had gotten stronger, drawing them through the passage faster and faster, until...

Tarly flailed when his body was projected hard, fast, and without method to catch himself. As if the tunnel had spat them out. He plunged back into water, and instinct had him franticly kicking for the surface.

His lungs burned with the first breath he drew too fast and sharp. He choked, becoming weaker, but he had to make it. He *promised* to live for her.

He bobbed back underwater a couple of times, catching a steadier breath each time, until he managed to tread on the surface.

"Nerida!" he called, searching desperately.

"Tarly!" Her echo back to him was the greatest blessing. When he spied her silver hair, they swam to meet each other, and Nerida clamped around him when they did. Their heartbeats slammed against each other.

"I knew how special you are before anyone else saw it," she said quietly to him.

Tarly's chest could burst with how much that meant to him.

He saw flickers of movement across the lower waterfall they'd been thrown through, and by the Gods, was he overjoyed to see Nik and Tauria had made it.

They all began swimming for shore, which became an immense test of his strength with the distance. He wasn't the only one, as when they reached it, they all crawled over the rocky bank, breathless and utterly spent.

The silence that hung while they caught enough breath became dark and desolate.

"We need to dress your wound," Tarly said, assessing where Edith had stabbed Nerida's shoulder.

Nerida sat so still as he peeled back the material at her shoulder. She stared vacantly into the lake with her head bowed, the strands of her white hair turned gray and dripping into her lap.

"It's all gone," she whispered, the gravity of what the Spellthief had done hitting her anew.

"We'll get it back," he said.

Nerida looked at him with such darkness he flinched. "Get it back?" she said, her tone colder than their frozen bodies. "How can you tell me that? There is no getting it back—it's *gone*. I feel *nothing*. I am not a Waterwielder anymore, and worst of all…I'm not a healer either." Her anger faded, and a plea filled her eyes, reducing her voice to a whisper. "I don't know who I am if I'm not that."

Tarly pulled her to him. Her knees tucked tight to her chest, and he held her between his legs. "I know who you are. You're the best damned healer without ever touching your magick. I've seen it time and time again. The way you make medicines and tonics. How you experiment with care in pursuit of advancing medical knowledge. If there's a way to get your magick back, I will find it, I promise you. But you are so much more than your magick. Your mind is brilliant. You will *always* be a healer. No one can take that from you."

"I'm sorry," Tauria croaked, coming over to them.

Tarly caught sight of Nik gathering firewood with the wolves through the trees. They were all at risk of falling miserably ill with the icy weather against their wet bodies.

"It's not your fault," Nerida said.

"She came for me first, and I....I don't know what happened."

"I'm glad she didn't get to you too."

Tauria harbored guilt for escaping Edith's wicked scheme. So did Tarly. If Nerida never got her magick back...he would never forgive himself for failing her.

Nik dropped the wood in front of them with a growl of frustration. The wolves kept adding logs to it as Nik tried to light the flame unsuccessfully. He threw the sticks with exasperation, running his hands through his hair. Tauria approached, giving him an affirming touch before resuming his work. His hand ran along her back while he lost himself to his thoughts.

"What's our plan now?" Tarly asked, trying to warm Nerida absentmindedly with his hand and his body.

"Go back to High Farrow with nothing," Nik said bitterly. He swore, pinching the bridge of his nose.

"Maybe the others have something of triumph," Tarly suggested.

Nik looked up with the darkest glare. "Are you kidding? Faythe's best friend was *murdered*. Another good friend is Transitioned into dark fae and likely doesn't even remember any of them. We are all *losing* this war."

"Nik," Tauria said—a gentle warning at his rising temper.

It worked to ground him, and he bowed his head in defeat.

But Nik was right.

Tarly looked up at that bleak night sky, thick with clouds smothering the stars. It became difficult to retain their hope against all that was beating them down.

"We're alive," Tarly said after a long stretch of silence. Tauria got the fire going, and they all huddled close to it. "There's been many, *many* times we shouldn't be, but we're still here. That has to count for something. Nothing is over yet. We can't let out setbacks make it the end because we lost our hope and fight. That is the only way they win before they've even killed us."

"Tarly's right," Tauria agreed. "We have their numbers, and we know where they plan to deploy their legions. The best we can do right now is get back to High Farrow and prepare for the battles that are about to be upon us."

They settled, getting warmer, and luckily, Edith hadn't made off with their things. Tarly retrieved Nerida's satchel, opening her pouch of herbs and medicines. Nerida removed her top layers, and Tarly adjusted his position, keeping his dry cloak he'd left behind partially covering her, but the proximity of another male riled an irrational irritation in him.

"You haven't asked me for instruction once," Nerida mused, drinking the pain-relieving tonic he offered. There was a brokenness in her voice that she hid under a smile, so damn resilient despite the monumental loss she'd suffered today.

"I learned from the best," he said, kissing her cheek before applying a salve he'd mixed together. Tarly paused with his fingers on her skin. "I want to learn more about the healing magick I have... when you're ready, of course. I shouldn't have mentioned it now—"

Her hand closed over his, and he believed her genuine smile. "I'm glad. It might actually help me deal with the absence of mine if I can help you reach yours."

"Are you sure? It can wait—"

Nerida leaned in to press her lips to his. "You're not so sullen anymore, Sully."

He shuffled closer, tucking them together, and pressed his lips to her shoulder. "I was only so because I was waiting for you. You saved me, Nerida."

"I haven't yet," she said quietly, skimming her fingers over his graying skin.

Tarly shook his head. "I've lived countless days, but they're worth nothing compared to the fraction filled with the feelings only you gave me."

Their futures were shrouded in the uncertainty of war, which left only the present to march on for. They were alive, and what they had, which Marvella nor Mordecai nor Dakodas ever would...was the true and unbreakable strength of blood and chosen family.

PART FOUR

THE BEGINNING OF THE END

CHAPTER SIXTY-THREE

Faythe

Faythe sat by the fires in her old rooms, feeling like her spirit was detached from her body. She wouldn't stay this still and useless for long—she just needed to recover her strength and magick before she could act again.

She gripped the handle of the jeweled dagger Marlowe had gifted her before her first fight with a fae in the cave. A part of her past that felt in another lifetime. She supposed it was, when day by day she drifted further away from her life as a human.

Unsheathing the blade, Faythe thought it was her sorrow for Marlowe giving off an energy. As if her friend's spirit were embedded within the steel she'd forged. A vibration hummed along her fingertip as it traced the edge, and Faythe's pain grew in her chest the longer she marveled over the craftsmanship. Something about it was ancient and timeless. The jewels of the hilt were an array of colors the likes of which she'd never seen before.

Her skin was a fraction of pressure away from being cut by the blade, but Faythe was transfixed, wondering if it could relieve some of the ache growing unbearable within her if her flesh was inflicted instead.

Faythe had lost herself so completely to a strange hypnotism invoked by the dagger that she didn't hear Reylan return. His hand wrapped around her wrist, preventing her from applying more pressure with her finger against the blade's sharp edge.

Her eyes slipped up to find deep concern swirling in his sapphire eyes.

"Marlowe gave this to me," she explained, but that didn't ease his worry.

He let her go tentatively. Then, instead of taking up the armchair opposite, he lowered to sit on the ground, knee bent, touching her legs. His hand carefully slipped over her thigh while his eyes scrutinized her every reaction, waiting to see if she would break in rage or tears. Amid her cold detachment, the only feeling she could spare was for him. Guilt that her emotions would always be his burdens too, as his would always be hers.

"How are you feeling?" he asked, not truly expecting an answer.

But Faythe's lips cracked open for the first time since returning from Rhyenelle. "Do you remember the last time we sat here and you asked me that?"

Reylan's brow flinched, and he nodded.

Faythe said, "You convinced me to go to Rhyenelle with you, but you couldn't have known the curse you'd invited into your homeland."

His jaw worked, and she knew the tells of his anger. "You're not the curse, Faythe. You're the liberation these lands have been waiting for."

"The kingdom is in ashes because of me. I am pure destruction and will tear everything else down if you don't stop me."

"Then burn it to the ground. All of it. I will be right beside you as you do. From the ashes we will always rise. Agalhor knew this. We all know this, and we stand with you."

Faythe's eyes scrunched shut. It was the reassurance she needed to hear that Reylan and her friends weren't horrified by what she'd done and could do. But even so, Faythe could hardly look in the mirror without seeing the monster she tried so hard not to become.

"We're near the end, my Phoenix," Reylan said, his voice a low, gravelly murmur. He shifted to kneel between her legs, sliding his hands over both her thighs and holding her with a claiming stare that promised every universe together beyond this one. "I have never once doubted you. Never underestimated you. And I take great offense at your negative thoughts about the one I love more than any creature could hope to love anything."

Reylan was her home. Her anchor to her own humanity. Her guiding light in every darkness.

He stood, unstrapping his sword belt, from which hung the Ember Sword. Then he presented it to her on one knee.

"It may take practice to wield its size, or it can be used ceremoniously. But this is yours."

Faythe smiled fondly, cupping his cheek. "It was never intended to be mine."

"You're the Queen of Rhyenelle—it belongs to the Ashfyre name."

"Then carry it with me."

Reylan's hands dropped the sword to his lap. "Do you mean—?"

"I need you by my side."

"And I don't ever plan to leave it, but Faythe..." Reylan swore, then he chuckled breathily, running a hand down his face. "I'm supposed to ask you to marry me, not the other way around."

Faythe shrugged. "I don't think anything about us has been conventional."

He shook his head, with adoration and amusement sparkling in his eyes. "Regardless, Agalhor would want you to have this sword."

"No. Before he died next to me, he told me I would know what to do with it. He thought of you as a son. You will carry the Ashfyre name as my consort. This sword belongs in the hands of Rhyenelle's greatest protector, who will wield it toward our victory in the war to come."

Reylan held silent for a moment, but everything spoke in his eyes. This moment, this passing of the sword from Agalhor's possession to his, meant everything to him.

Faythe leaned forward, bringing their faces close. For him, there would always be a part of her that wanted to live through the horrors and losses of this war.

"Bond with me," she said, slipping a hand over his cheek.

Reylan kissed her with a pained groan. Just once.

"You know I want that more than anything, but only if your full heart chooses it, not your grief in distraction."

Faythe shook her head. "You're not a distraction, Reylan. You are everything."

He remembered those beautiful words he'd given her the first time he'd kissed her, and the emotion that creased between his brow unleashed in the slamming of his lips to hers. A kiss that claimed and transcended her soul.

She had no control of destiny and couldn't promise the life of anyone with what was coming. This...she *needed* this. The thought of either of them dying without getting to claim their bond invoked such tragic fear she couldn't wait a moment longer. If she had to sacrifice herself to win, she wanted to be fully, devotedly *his*.

Reylan lifted her from the chair to join him on the floor, slipping the Ember Sword aside.

"I missed you," he said, kissing along her jaw. "I love you. *Gods*, I love you in every universe."

"I love you," she echoed. "More than anything."

Reylan laid her down on the rug before the fire. He kissed her chest before easing off her. Faythe watched him collect the cushions and throw them from the bed, returning and beginning to arrange them.

"If we can't be in our own kingdom for this, then we can be by our element. You are the flame of a Phoenix, Faythe Ashfyre, and it's my life's privilege to always be burning with you."

Faythe lifted her hips by his silent prompt, and he slipped a pillow under her lower back. He leaned in, running his fingers up her curved spine while his mouth leaned in, blowing warm breath across her collar. His lips pressed to her throat, and Faythe pushed into him more with a soft moan. Her blood roared, heating for him to claim. To claim her. Wholly and completely.

"Please, Reylan," she mewled at his slow, sensual movements.

"I've waited lifetimes for you. I'm going to take my time. You're going to feel me claim every inch of your flesh before I take your blood. Then you'll take mine. Take me inside you in two ways at the same time. You're going to scream my name as you're filled with me, and I won't stop until you rock into your next finish knowing only this, only us, in all of existence."

Between her legs rushed with heat, and her hips rose, thighs clamping around him, needy for any friction, but it wasn't nearly enough.

His hands undid the fastens of her pants. Reylan kissed her lips once before pulling back, peeling her legs from the leather material. Faythe reached for her shirt, but Reylan caught her wrists, pinning them by her head.

"Keep your hands here. If you can't follow instruction, I'll have to use rope."

Faythe's shiver broke from the tips of her toes to her scalp. The thought of being bound completely at his mercy turned her on more than she expected.

Reylan smiled wickedly as though he'd read her curiosity and scented her surge of desire.

"My Phoenix," he drawled—a low, sinful taunt. His fingers hooked around the seam of her shirt, pulling it over her head and leaving her only in her tight cropped undergarment. "I think I could do a lot with you and a piece of rope."

"Then do it," she challenged.

Reylan tore her undergarment as his mouth leaned to hers. "I was counting on you saying that. First, I'm going to devour you right here. Then I'm going to take you to that bed and make sure these legs can't close until I'm done with you."

He sucked her breast, and Faythe pushed into his assault with a moan. Something about his fully clothed body raking against her skin while she lay completely naked and vulnerable turned her on more. His lips trailed down to her navel. Then his arms hooked around her thighs, and she peered down to catch his devious smile between her legs before he kissed the inside of her thigh.

She was close to begging for his mouth on her apex, becoming so wet she was turning into a puddle. He took his time like he promised, licking and kissing her so slowly and teasingly she couldn't help the undulation of her hips that silently begged him to devour her.

He groaned, licking from her sensitive bud and down, tongue curving inside her. In and out. In and out. She needed deeper. Fuller. Reached to slip her fingers through his hair. He chuckled darkly, then he obliged her body's demands. Faythe cried out, back arching off the ground, as Reylan sucked and explored her with his mouth and tongue. His two fingers joined, sending her into a sprint toward her first finish line. She leaned into it eagerly, knowing it would be the first of many he would give her tonight.

"That's it—take it how you need it," he said, quickening his pace in time with her hips as they bucked, needy for release.

Faythe clamped down on his fingers, but he didn't falter. He sucked harder, pushed in deeper, and Faythe's moan choked in her throat while her legs trembled around his shoulders.

She was only just coming back down from her first high when Reylan hovered over her and his mouth claimed hers deeply. He'd removed his shirt, and Faythe's fingers traced over the hard contours of him. Over his sides, over his scarred back. When she broke the kiss, she stared down at where the ruin had left an arrow-shaped scarring like a brand. The blackness had faded but still lingered around the edges like the vines of a petal. Many of them. Like a black rose.

Reylan's arm curved around her back, lifting her into his lap. He stood effortlessly with her, carrying her to the bed. Being swept away from the caress of the fire made her shiver, but she knew the chill wouldn't last long.

He laid her down, and she didn't know when he'd thought to be prepared with rope, which he retrieved from a drawer.

"You've thought about this for a while," she noted.

Pure lust glazed his eyes as he returned, looking over her naked body before taking hold of one of her ankles.

"You have no idea." Reylan pulled her down the bed, and desire sparked through her core. With her knee bent, he tied her ankle before securing the other end to the bedpost.

His stare tightened her skin, and she wiggled with renewed need.

Reylan tied her other ankle in the same manner before crawling over the bed and straddling her waist. He took both her hands, tying her wrists together before leaning in, holding them above her head.

"Don't move them from here," he said—a deliciously tempting warning.

"Yes, general," she said in a low lilt that flared his eyes.

Reylan's hand wrapped around her throat before he kissed her with abandon. Devoured her like he'd done between her legs. Stealing her breath until she became lightheaded.

He pulled back abruptly, only to descend on her neck, which made her moan loudly, surging toward another climax already with the strong desire for him to bite her; claim her.

"Make me yours, Reylan," she begged.

"I will, but I plan to be inside you in two ways as I do."

His hand slipped down her body before two fingers plunged inside her without warning. The rope burned slightly against Faythe's ankles as she strained, back arching from the sparks of pleasure. She needed more. More fullness; more of him inside her. He was driving her to the brink of pleasure-hazed madness.

Faythe tried to reject another orgasm, but Reylan demanded it from her. His fingers hooked inside her, dragging her toward that edge as if it had become a game between them and he was winning. Reylan chuckled, the low vibration teased over her nipple as he felt her resistance. He sucked her breast, throwing her over the cliff of another climax that burst warmth over her body, tingling from her core, up her spine, and pooling out from between her legs.

Her back flattened on the matures as she caught her breath, so spent but eager for more of his delicious torture.

She didn't know when he'd removed his pants, but the feel of his length sliding over her wet core caused her brow to pinch tightly with the shoots of sensitivity after her climax. Faythe defied his order, bringing her bound hands down to slip between them and grip hold of him. Reylan hissed. His hips jerked into her palms. He glanced between them, watching her pump him over her slickness. His gaze of pure lust turned her on so much she was melting for him.

Faythe lined him up to sink inside her, and he obliged. Slowly. He lifted her hands away by the rope that bound them, and he kept hold of her wrists above her head this time as he watched himself inch inside her.

"This will never not be a sight to fucking worship," he rasped. Reylan groaned when he was fully seated. His eyes met hers with such intense passion she lost herself in his gaze for a moment.

Reylan retrieved a pillow from behind her, and she already knew what he wanted. She lifted her hips for him to slide it under her lower back. Then Reylan let go.

He slammed into her with a pace that claimed her to her bones. Reylan made sure every inch of her would feel his claim on her tonight. She let him have his way with her, bound and vulnerable to his mercy, and she'd never felt so wholly worshipped and pleasured. Much as she wanted to wrap her legs around his hips and take him deeper, there was something so seductive about being under his control that pushed her toward yet another climax so fast.

"I'm going to…" Faythe swore, trying to hold some of herself together, but she was clay under his demanding grip.

Reylan leaned into her, his pants close to her ear surging her lust. "Come for me, Phoenix. You're mine. I claim you under every God that bears witness, and against every objection the stars might have. I claim you in every realm and in every time, eternally."

She'd tried to be prepared for the moment Reylan sank his teeth into her neck, but expectation was nothing close to the real moment. The sting of his fangs piercing her skin subsided under a fast tidal wave of euphoric pleasure like nothing she'd experienced before.

Within her, something snapped sharply, and she gasped. It tugged, finding another severed thread to join with. Her soul transcended with Reylan's, forging through time and space and everything that existed beyond. Her body trembled but soared. Completely weightless, she was a shooting star.

All that was left was for her to claim him back.

Reylan undid her bonds after he let go of her neck. His pupils were blown wide and feral. He released her ankles, and Faythe couldn't wait another moment.

She pushed him onto his back, straddling him and taking him inside her again. Faythe rocked her hips slowly, gathering herself back together from the climax and claiming he'd given her. She wanted to be fully present for this.

"I claim you, Reylan Arrowood. I have always been yours, and you will always be mine. No matter what forces try to come between us. It's you and me."

"Always," he promised.

Faythe leaned in, closing her mouth around his neck near his collar. Her teeth pierced his flesh, an odd sensation, but the moment his blood trickled onto her tongue she was lost in him. She moaned at the divine taste—the single most delectable thing she would ever sample in her life.

Reylan thrust up into her, nearing his climax, and Faythe's hand wrapped around his throat, needing it inside her the way his blood flowed down her throat.

With one final thrust he stilled, spilling himself, and she pulled out of his neck. Her thoughts spun. This kind of delirious high wobbled her balance, but Reylan caught her, lowering her beside him.

Her whole body tingled warmly, and within…a bright new thread pulsed.

Reylan idly traced her golden tattoos, which she'd only just noticed were glowing. "You are absolutely remarkable," he said absent-mindedly.

Faythe rolled onto her stomach, clasping her hands over his chest. "You're quite remarkable yourself, general."

A low groan vibrated in his throat. "I quite like it when you call me that."

Faythe smiled coyly. "I know."

Reylan pulled her up, hooking her leg over his hips. Her lust stirred again.

"Greedy," she said, feeling him needy between her legs.

"You might want to cancel your plans for tomorrow."

"We can't," she moaned as he kissed her neck. Though she really, *really* wanted to.

"You might be pretty sore by the time I'm done with you tonight," he said with gravel in his voice. Reylan's tongue flicked over his fresh bite wound, and Faythe cried out at the sensitive sparks shooting precisely between her legs.

"Do your worst, general."

"Oh, I plan to."

CHAPTER SIXTY-FOUR

Faythe

Faythe was walking through the familiar halls of High Farrow's castle, finding it strange to reflect on memories of a human who'd walked these steps adorned in the royal blue guard's uniform. She felt so far detached from that life as the fae queen of Rhyenelle who was only a visitor in dire times now.

She'd been told Reylan had sent for her to join him in the throne room. An odd request. Until she rounded the corner past the doors and her walk slowed. Taking in the first face she saw, her steps quickened to a run, until she collided with Nik in the middle, swept off her feet in his arms.

"Thank Gods you're alive," Faythe whispered, so choked with emotion that came flooding out of her now.

"Oh Faythe…I'm so sorry—"

She squeezed him tighter. "Not now," she begged quietly.

If they talked about Marlowe now, she would break into more pieces than she had the strength to collect afterward.

Faythe embraced Tauria and Nerida, and even Tarly. With so much loss and damage to their morale, she was overwhelmed with this gift to have them all back.

Reylan stood near the dais with Kyleer, Izaiah, and Zaiana.

Nik curved an arm around Tauria. "I know you've all welcomed yourselves to our kingdom by now, but our home is yours. We have much to exchange and little time to rest, I'm afraid."

"Did you retrieve the dagger?" Faythe asked, hope sparking in her eyes.

Nik's solemn face spoke all, and her body deflated. The four of them exchanged glances, and Nerida's head bowed.

"What happened?" Faythe asked, dread-filled.

Reylan had drifted toward her, feeling the spike of her anxiety.

"We should take this to the drawing room. On top of our losses, we have information that requires we make immediate battle movements. Shifting all the forces we have into place."

Nik glanced between Reylan, Kyleer, and Izaiah at that. The best general and commanders they had. Reylan's expression firmed, and the weight of impending battle hung heavy in the air.

"This won't be like the Great Battles," Nik went on. "This won't stretch over decades. It won't be a series of battles to claim land and soldiers piece by piece. This will be Ungardia's darkest hour, a scale of fighting and bloodshed our lands have never faced before. It will decide the fate of the world."

They spent hours in the drawing room, watching day turn to night as they all exchanged their losses, information, and small triumphs.

Faythe was livid over the story of Edith, Mordecai's daughter, for what she'd stolen from Nerida. Vengeance was becoming a familiar pattern thrumming through her blood.

"Where would she be now?" Faythe snapped at no one in this room.

"Valgard or the Mortus Mountains, I'd wager," Nik said.

Faythe's gaze slipped to Zaiana. The dark fae's stare fixed on Nerida, who wouldn't meet it. She was glad not to be the only one with wrath boiling beneath her surface, though Zaiana masked hers better.

"So we hunt her down," Zaiana said, her voice like a slither of shadow through the room.

"It doesn't work like that," Nerida said sadly. "In the Book of Enoch, it says only the sister dagger can return what was lost. One to take, one to give. She has to be killed with that, or any abilities she takes will just die with her."

"There's *another* dagger to find?" Tarly said, leaning back in defeat.

"I wouldn't know where to start looking this time. It's not as coveted as the dagger that takes. The Spellthief," Nerida said.

Faythe didn't fail to notice how Nik hadn't stopped staring at Zaiana. The dark fae was beginning to notice too.

"Do you have problem?" Zaiana finally addressed him, cutting off the low conversation of others in the room.

"Are you going to tell them, or will I?" Nik said.

"If you give me a hint, maybe I can decide."

"Did you know about Edith?"

Her purple eyes flexed. "No."

"Why would she?" Faythe dreaded to ask.

"Because Nerida and Tauria aren't the only ones with an estranged sister they were unaware of."

Faythe's mind puzzled over what he was implying, but when it slipped together, Faythe's eyes widened in disbelief.

Tauria said, "I discovered that when Mordecai was first alive, he was the most powerful Stormcaster to have lived. Edith wanted the dagger to take Zaiana's power and be Mordecai's chosen child."

Zaiana's laughter was eerie at the thick tension in the room. Reylan's hand hovered over the Ember Sword at his hip.

"I would gladly hand her that title," Zaiana said.

"You've known Mordecai was your father all this time?" Faythe said, surprised by the pinch of betrayal she felt in her chest.

"I only recently suspected it. It didn't seem of particular relevance to share."

She spoke of it like it was nothing. As though she wasn't the heir to the Valgard throne and Mordecai's most prized daughter—his *weapon*.

"You're the heir to Valgard." Tarly spoke the realization on everyone's mind.

"I am *not* that," Zaiana protested, eyeing everyone with a warning. "Whether you think that's a good or bad thing, I will never be that."

"Why would you resist what places you above everyone else? Haven't you fought all your life to be the best?" Izaiah countered.

"You all may wear your crowns and think them pretty, powerful. I see nothing but a fanciful shackle to a land and a body of people for the rest of your days. I've been fighting for my freedom, not to be bound to another construct. That is not my choice."

Faythe understood her reasoning and sympathized with her passion. Though she couldn't deny Zaiana would make a brilliant monarch, and they had her on their side. For now.

Izaiah said, "If this is all true…Zaiana is more valuable to them than we thought. Mordecai will want you back, and now we have your insane sister to track down."

"She's mine," Zaiana said darkly. "If there's a dagger to return Nerida's power, I will find it, and I will kill her."

Zaiana had grown protective of the healer, and Faythe was too. The dark fae's purple eyes slipped to Faythe, aligning their will to restore what Nerida had lost.

"We have bigger battles to fight. Don't divert for me," Nerida pleaded.

Tarly sat beside her, a clear comfort and source of strength.

Faythe said, "I wouldn't consider it a diversion. All our enemies are circling, and we need to be as strong as we can be for when they strike."

"The shadow creatures," Nik interjected. "Any knowledge on how we get rid of those?"

Faythe winced. "They arrived after I broke the Death Ruin. There has to be a place they're entering our world from. Though I don't know what it will take to seal it."

"A life, probably," Nerida offered. "Or several. Maybe the Book of Enoch will have more answers on such ancient, lost creatures. It's in my rooms."

She stood, and Faythe read that her retirement from this meeting was more to do with her sadness and fading hope at discussing her lost power.

Tarly left with her. Faythe's frustration and anger pricked her skin at seeing her bright, joyous friend so heartbroken.

"The Mortus Mountains," Reylan said. Faythe slipped her eyes to him. "Also translated as *the Death Mountains*. It's a guess, but we don't have much time for research. That might be where the split veil is that the shadows are emerging from."

"It's worth a shot," Izaiah agreed.

"I'll go. None of you know that place," Zaiana said, pushing off the wall she was leaning her back against.

"I'll go with you," Kyleer offered.

While he had no memory of any of them, Faythe noticed how Kyleer was most at ease around Zaiana, often looking to her for assurance or guidance.

"You won't be able to Shadowport within those mountains. I'll be quicker on my own."

A protest firmed on Kyleer's face, but he didn't voice it.

"I need your help to wield the ruin," Faythe said to Zaiana.

"I think you need another plan. There's hardly time enough for that."

"No offense, but I don't need as much time as you did to master it. I have the essence of two Spirits within me. I've wielded it's power before. I just need enough guidance to be able to remain in control with the full connection and let it go afterward."

Reylan added, "I can take some of the ruin's influence from her, as we've tested already—likely more now we're mated. We can do this."

Faythe's cheeks flushed at his mention of their mating. His bite wound on her neck pulsed, inspiring inappropriate thoughts. They were pulled away too soon after, and she was dealing with a new primal urge for him to take her for days on end.

"We'll start when I'm back. I won't take long to confirm or deny if the veil is there," Zaiana said.

"And if it is?" Izaiah supplied.

"If it wants life, I can think of five masters I'm itching to throw through it," Zaiana said.

"Don't act on your own—we can't risk losing you," Nik said.

Zaiana scoffed. "I don't need permission from any of you. And to be clear, just because you discovered who my father is doesn't change a thing about my value. He made nothing of me. Everything I am and that you feared now and before is what *I* made."

Faythe had grown to admire and respect Zaiana. Their relationship might always be prickly and tense from their past—Faythe couldn't forget the many times Zaiana had harbored the intent to kill her—and she would be a fool to believe that objective would ever fully fade. Despite this, she was glad the dark fae was here as their ally for now.

Just as the room settled, the door burst open, and everyone stood, shifting into defense at the sudden intrusion when the guards were instructed to grant them complete undisrupted privacy.

Those guards now lay on the ground behind the intruders feet.

Nyte's feet.

"Do you know how long it took me to find where you'd run off to after you destructive display in Rhyenelle?" he said, sounding like the Nether.

Though she was growing accustomed to his dark blond hair and bright hazel eyes, she still saw flickers of his true appearance of midnight hair and eyes of a brighter gold than hers when he embodied the dark side of himself.

"Who are you?" Nik asked, his tone threatening while his hand hovered on his sword.

Nyte canted his head at Faythe, gliding into the room with perfect confidence despite everyone's brace of hostility. "Do you want to explain, or will I?"

Faythe's head throbbed by the time she and Nyte had explained all to the others. About him being Marvellas's son, and his quest to return to his own realm.

"The mirrors," Faythe breathed when they got to that.

She should have thought of it before, and now they were right above the mirrors below the castle Faythe had once stumbled upon, looking for Aurialis's ruin. She'd found it. And she recalled the Dresair's claim of being able to take her through *worlds* if she so desired.

"Say that again," Nyte said, as if he knew what she spoke of.

"There's a creature that lives in the mirrors below this castle. They might be able to help you make it home."

Nyte stood. "Take me."

"Hold on," Nik said, standing too and pinning Nyte with distrust. "You don't get to waltz into our world that *your* mother is terrorizing then *leave* just like that."

"It wasn't a waltz, I assure you," Nyte muttered. "More like a drag through hell before being dropped in the worst possible place."

"Hell?" Izaiah inquired.

Nyte didn't bother to amend his strange terminology from another land.

Faythe didn't forget the stunt Nyte had tried to pull in Rhyenelle. She pinned him as she circled the table until she stood opposite him.

"You had no right to attempt to kill Malin," she said resentfully.

Nyte's stare darkened on her. "I don't expect you to understand why I did it."

"I don't care. He was *not* yours to kill."

"I didn't kill him—you made sure of that."

"Why did you do it?"

"Because I have another brother," he confessed. "In my own realm. And I saw everything he could have become in Malin Ashfyre. I guess you could say grim sentiment to end his misery got the better of me. A surprise to both of us."

"Is he dead?" Izaiah asked darkly.

"Jakon killed him," Faythe said quietly.

Thinking of that had her reflecting painfully on another loss from that venture.

"Atherius was long past her time," Reylan said through their bond, trying to soothe her guilt.

Faythe knew that too. The Firebird deserved her peace after thousands of years, many in solitude and suffering. Reylan's hand slipped over her shoulder, and she relaxed under his touch, but the thoughts of Atherius had her mind turning.

With a careful glance behind him toward Nyte, she said, *"We need to be vigilant with him. He can't be trusted, but he's valuable."*

"If he tries to leave through the mirrors, do you want him stopped?"

Faythe contemplated. *"No. We can't afford another enemy, and we'll win without another ally we didn't hope for anyway."*

Reylan gave a firm nod, pressing his lips to her head before they rejoined the others in discussion.

Faythe slipped out of the room when they'd discussed enough for one night. Everything they had to prepare for and set in place would take many of those long sessions of planning. For now, she trusted Reylan, who was already leading charge to position their armies according to the information Tauria had gathered in Valgard.

Izaiah called her name before she could escape anywhere. She didn't forget what Reuben had told her about his attempts to wield the Light Temple Ruin. That was his reason for staying behind when Rhyenelle fell, and he was the only one she'd entrusted with its safekeeping. Now she was stung with betrayal, but his dropped look of sorrow kept her lips tight if he came to explain.

"Can we talk?"

"I think that would be wise, yes."

They occupied a small study, and Faythe waited patiently as he paced the floor.

When he didn't start, she did.

"Why did Malin trust you?" Faythe tried, as gentle as she could.

Izaiah left a pause of heavy silence. "Malin trusted my allegiance to him because Marlowe showed him it. What he didn't know was that it was an alternate fate where my allegiance *was* true to him. She never told me what events would have turned my heart—she said knowing would only cause an echo of the damage the real fate would have brought. She was so brilliant, so considerate, and kind, and—" Izaiah paused, pressing the heel of his palms into his eyes with gritted teeth. Faythe didn't try to fight her tears that fell freely. "I should have protected her better, and I'm so fucking sorry, Faythe."

"Could you have stopped it?" Faythe barely choked out the words.

"Maybe…if I'd acted sooner. It was my error that I didn't think he would go as far as to kill her and risk your wrath for it. But also… Marlowe told me I would need the Phoenix Blood at the darkest hour.

I thought she meant in battle when she knew I would never be able to wield the ruin, and this was at least a smaller advantage to transform into something bigger. But I was wrong, wasn't I? Did Marlowe ask me to save her, and I...I failed her?" Izaiah's voice cracked at the end, and Faythe couldn't resist the need to embrace him.

He'd come to care for Marlowe dearly, and despite the answers she still needed from him, his genuine loss and heartbreak over their mutual friend was genuine. Izaiah clung to her desperately.

"It wasn't your fault," Faythe said. "Marlowe's knowledge has many interpretations, but only the person her riddle was meant for could truly know, *feel*, when they have the right meaning at the right time."

They let each other go and fell into a sorrowful reflection.

Faythe said, "I need you tell me why you wanted to wield the ruin."

Izaiah slumped onto the arm of the chair by the dull fireplace. "It feels completely foolish to admit. I hoped I wouldn't have to explain— I would just *show* you when I achieved it." He huffed a resentful laugh at himself. "Could you imagine me of all people swooping in as the savior? It was a stupid fantasy."

"You can transform into many incredible things that can tear through masses. And as I hear, you can achieve a Phoenix form with the blood potion. What else could you have hoped for?"

Izaiah's eyes slipped up to her. "Have you ever heard of the Black Phoenix?"

Her mouth fell open. "Of it, yes. Nerida once mentioned it, but... what can it do?"

"It's a Phoenix that was never meant to exist. It came to being when a fae with a morbid curiosity discovered how to resurrect a Phoenix that was slain, right before it would die permanently. It created a breed of Phoenix that was touched by Death itself. They say its flame can resurrect the dead temporarily. It can raise an army of the undead."

It was a concept so morbid and inconceivable she couldn't believe what Izaiah wanted to become.

"Death-touched," she breathed.

Then her fear for him triggered an impulse to push him for his recklessness. Izaiah lost his balance perched on the arm of the chair, falling back into the seat and staring at her like she'd lost her mind.

"The ruin could have killed you! Did you ever consider that's what it might take, but there would be no one to bring you back!"

The thought of losing him was too much in the wake of Marlowe's death. Everyone around her was risking their lives, and she knew they all had a part to play in this war, but the fragility of all her bonds spun her mind with helpless terror.

Izaiah lost himself in thought. "You think I need to die and be brought back?"

Faythe jabbed a finger at him. "Don't you even think about attempting that, or so help me, I *will* find a way to resurrect you just so I can kill you myself!"

Izaiah pulled himself off the chair the same way he slumped onto it. He stood, wrapping his arms around her, before she could reprimand him more.

"I love you too, Faythe."

CHAPTER SIXTY-FIVE

Zaiana

Zaiana followed the King of High Farrow, who walked alone after his mate had excused herself elsewhere. Nikalias surely knew she was following him, but he kept a casual pace, with one hand in his pocket.

When they were away from lingering ears, Zaiana called, "It was you in my mind all that time."

He stopped, turning to her with strange amusement. "When did you figure it out?"

"Just now. Your mannerisms are subtle but quite particular."

"You're very perceptive."

"Why have you been Nightwalking to me?"

"Like I've always said, I find you curious, and I like a challenge."

"I was a game to you."

"No. Games are fun. Trying to train your mind left a headache in mine."

"Then why keep coming back?"

"The truth? Faythe believed you were important. When she spoke of you, I became fascinated and planned to only Nightwalk to you once. Discovering you were also a Nightwalker—a very weak one, but it's there—had me *very* intrigued."

Zaiana's teeth ground together, not liking how it felt like she were his subject to scrutinize. "Did you sate your *curiosity?*"

"Not nearly. You should know Tauria discovered something while she was in Valgard. Mordecai's sister was a powerful Nightwalker—explains your weak essence since Stormcasting took a far more prominent root in you. Tauria also learned that through a long-diluted bloodline, my mother also can be traced back to Mordecai's sister. Magick is its own meddling force, awakening her power as strongly in me all this time later."

Zaiana's thoughts spun with the new information. It didn't mean much other than a sense of closure and clarity. She'd always convinced herself she didn't need to know anything about her bloodline or heritage, but she couldn't deny it settled something in her to discover more of her roots.

"If you think this somehow makes us *related*, you're very wrong," she said.

Nikalias huffed a laugh. "Would that really be so terrible to embrace?"

"It means nothing."

If she didn't know any better, she'd think his eyes drifting away for a split second was a wince of rejection.

"I don't have any blood family left. I've never had a sibling." He looked her over from head to toe and smiled. Genuine, warm, and jarring. "You wouldn't have made such a bad one, I suppose."

Nik turned on his heel, leaving her in the hallway.

She was rooted, replaying his last words, trying to figure out if he was being sarcastic. Why would he say such an outlandish thing?

Zaiana decided she wasn't done with him and stormed the same way when he disappeared around a bend.

"In my experience, siblings only inspire jealousy and want you dead."

Nik turned back with a grin. "Your experience is very limited, having only just discovered you have a viciously jealous sister out for your power."

The reminder itched her skin to seek out Edith.

"I got my power back without you," Zaiana said.

Nik canted his head slightly. "Things can catalyst into others in the most subtle ways."

"Don't visit me in my dreams again."

"I might have made the first contact, but it was often you who called me back, even when you didn't realize it."

Zaiana's mouth opened to counter, but Nik went on before she could.

"Seeking help isn't a weakness. In fact, it's quite the opposite."

"Why did you help me?" she asked. "At that time, I was still the enemy."

"If I'd thought you the enemy, I would have shattered your mind that first night. It would have been so easy—you were completely at my mercy."

The tip of Zaiana's spine tingled. Even though it was a while ago, the realization of how silently and dishonorably she could have been killed that night racked her.

"I managed to throw Agalhor out of my mind before he killed me," she said.

"I can't speak for what happened between you. But I have no doubt you could have tried to throw me out and would have lost."

She wanted to shatter his confidence. Prove him wrong. But she stared into those unblinking emerald eyes and believed him.

"Can you teach me how to strengthen my mind? Against conscious and unconscious infiltration?"

Nik's cold eyes filled with warmth. "Look at you, reaching out a hand. It would be my pleasure, Zaiana. If you ask Faythe, she should tell you how excellent of a mentor I am."

She was already beginning to regret her request with his devious aura.

"Speaking of, good luck training her with the ruin. Faythe is very persistent but often gets ahead of herself with impatience."

Just great, Zaiana thought. She'd trained many darklings in her life —she was a master of patience—but Zaiana was prepared for Faythe to test her worse that any child.

Nik turned away, and she thought he was about to abandon her until he called over his shoulder, "I find it best to train the mind while the body is at work."

She quite admired High Farrow's training arena under the castle. It had every weapon she could hope to find, several raised platforms for combat, and space enough to train a whole squad at once. It was far more fanciful than the pit or mountain fringe she'd had to train in growing up.

"This was a terrible idea. You're hardly in league with me," Zaiana said, holding her sword with little enthusiasm.

Nik leaned on the Farrow Sword—an impressive blade indeed. "You haven't even seen me fight."

"I don't need to. Trained in combat since birth, maybe, but against palace guards who couldn't really give their all against their precious princeling. Probably let you win to spare your feelings too. You don't know what it's like to truly fear for your life even in a friendly competition."

"I'll admit there might be some truth there, but still, you might be surprised."

Zaiana smirked. If anything, this would provide some amusing distraction for a while.

"No lightning," he warned.

"That would be no fun. You'd be on your ass in a second."

His green sparkled with the challenge. It wasn't often Zaiana sparred for entertainment. She had to remember this was just a game, but that didn't mean she would go easy on him.

Nik took stance: a dip to his knees, shoulder-width apart. His wrist twisted with his blade, warming up to the weight of it. His eyes homed in on her.

Zaiana shifted one leg back a fraction and folded one arm behind her back.

Nik's smile stretched at her arrogant position.

"If you think I won't scratch your pretty face, you're mistaken," he said.

"You can try."

He moved first, and she waited for it. Zaiana sidestepped with practiced ease and swung her blade in a low arc toward his ribs. Nik pivoted sharply, avoiding her strike by mere inches. He retaliated with a feign to her left, which she played into, knowing he would take the opening of her right. As his sword hand swung, her body bent, right leg kicking high and slamming into his wrist.

The Farrow Sword clanged loudly across the platform.

"Your footwork tricks are amateur," she said lazily.

Nik rubbed his wrist with a contorted expression of pain and surprise. He retrieved his sword, rolling that wrist a couple of times. He angled his blade toward her with more reverence this time.

"Now it's my time to have fun."

She didn't get to respond to that when he darted for her in his next breath.

Zaiana twisted, kissing their steel for a long note that sang through the motion of her arm.

"Predictable," she said, bored.

This time, Zaiana charged, her blade moving in quick, precise patterns. Nik had a great focus, countering every attack, but she was relentless. Zaiana fell into a familiar acute and lethal calm that had her moving faster and faster on instinct. The room didn't exist—Nik himself barely existed—when all she knew was one long blade to avoid and a body to cut down.

Zaiana saw her opening to end it with a kick to his torso. She should have landed the kick, but Nik avoided it a split second before, catching her ankle before her foot would have knocked the wind out of him hard enough to fell him to his knees.

Her eyes snapped to his with incredulity. Nik yanked her ankle, believing it would crash her to the ground, but Zaiana wasn't giving up that easily.

She caught herself on her hands and turned her body in a back flip. She landed on one foot, immediately swiping her sword horizontal, but he jumped over it. She growled in annoyance. He shouldn't have avoided that either.

Then it hit her—Nik was reading her thoughts. Seeing her next move a second before she made it. Though she'd asked him to train her to block it, the cheat still riled her.

Knowing what he was doing, Zaiana tried to trick him with her intention, but he read her real one right after it, parrying against her attacks no matter how many times she changed her mind. That wouldn't work. She had to block him.

"It can work." Nik answered her unspoken thoughts.

Her teeth ground.

"You can work out how to send a trick thought then block me from seeing your next."

"You're not showing me *how*," she grunted, hitting his blade again and again in their dance around the ring.

"It's mostly going to happen in practice. You learned how to master a *ruin*—you have great control of your own mind already."

Nik stopped the fight by taking two long strides backward.

"Again," Zaiana demanded.

Nik huffed. "I'm afraid my teaching hour is over, and yours has just begun."

Zaiana frowned in confusion. Then she felt the new presence enter the training hall.

Faythe Ashfyre strolled in, dressed in Rhyenelle fighting attire and carrying one of the wretched ruins in a box.

Nik sheathed his sword, stepping down from the platform.

"I thought you'd insist on chaperoning," Faythe mused as he passed.

"Do try not to kill each other. I would stay, but I have far better things I could be doing. Precious time, impending war and all that."

Zaiana assumed that meant going to see his mate.

"I'm going to supervise." Nerida's gentle voice echoed behind Faythe.

She was one of the very few people Zaiana actually enjoyed seeing. Except finding out what had happened to the healer, her wrath swirled like priming shadows. Being blood-related to the one who'd stripped her of her power made her anger boil more. Nerida's power was *good*; she was *good*. It was so wretched to be stolen into a wicked vessel.

"We're going to be fine," Faythe said, but their eyes caught on each other, knowing that couldn't be promised since they would be unleashing a colossal power and had a natural ability to provoke each other.

"This might be better tested outside," Zaiana warned.

Nerida came up with Faythe. She said, "You're not going to tap into the full power anytime soon. Faythe has a lot to learn about breathing, patience, and control. I'm here to help with that too. Water-wielding is the core element for it, opposite to all that comes naturally to Faythe."

"So we're schooling a hotheaded child," Zaiana gibed.

Faythe glowered at her. "I haven't had centuries to master all things," she said flatly.

Zaiana often forgot about Faythe's mere fraction of years in comparison. Faythe had much to learn, but in truth, Zaiana was in awe over the control the heir *did* have in such short time.

"The ruin is going to convince you you're dying over and over again. It doesn't want a master—it wants to master *you*. You let it in Rhyenelle, and if it weren't for Reylan—his Mindseer ability and your bond—you likely would have been lost as a vessel to it forever."

Faythe visibly paled and shifted her weight between her feet. "I didn't mean to. Until that point, I was able to open myself to small doses of the power, then Atherius died...there were so many shadow creatures killing through the city, and I...*gave in*."

"You gave *up*," Zaiana said. Harsh, maybe, but in her experience, it was the only way to drill the lesson deeply. She crossed her arms, pacing around Faythe. "Letting anger consume you, being reckless—

that's easy. Control, remembering you have people counting on you to make it out *alive* despite your grief—that's what takes strength."

Faythe nodded, attentive to her words. Zaiana thought maybe this wouldn't be so tedious after all. Maybe their lessons would be amicable.

CHAPTER SIXTY-SIX

Reylan

"They're going to kill each other!"

Reylan's head whipped to Nerida, who burst into the drawing room. It had been a week since Faythe started training with Zaiana and the ruin.

He ran from the room, with Kyleer, Izaiah, Nik, Tarly, and Tauria in tow. They'd been discussing various enemy sightings and repositioning of certain squads. While the bigger battles that would see great numbers fighting had not broken out yet, smaller fights were happening throughout the kingdoms.

It was how war always went. They were testing each other. Trying to figure out strategy and numbers and coordination in preparation for a bigger attack.

Reylan felt for Faythe, who closed herself off to him when she trained with magick. It distracted him, worried him, and to keep his own mind sharp for his role as leading general, he had to agree it was best for both of them. So when he reached through their bond, beyond the block, all he felt was a rage of power.

He'd been uneasy about Zaiana training her from the start, and if the dark fae harmed her...

Following Nerida and his own direction to Faythe through their bond, they burst out into the thick snowfall of the back courtyard.

Sure enough, the source of the blasts and currents of energy drew their eyes up to where two forms could be spied through the bursts of colliding light. With the velocity of power they threw at each other, amplified by the ruin, it was just as well they'd taken to the skies.

Reylan assessed their battle, and it did seem vicious. They attacked each other unfalteringly and with full force. He tried to reach Faythe's mind for an answer to whether he should intervene, but her block on their bond was solid.

"They do seem a little intense," Izaiah commented. "But Faythe always did respond better to force. She's a ball of chaos."

Reylan was trying to decide if Zaiana was using harsh methods to train Faythe, or if they truly had hit heads and their violence had turned genuine.

They were shooting stars of gold and purple. Putting his concern aside, it was a stunning spectacle to watch the pair fully unleashed.

Nerida said, "They've never attacked this hard at each other before. Zaiana was frustrated and started goading Faythe, mentioning her failures and how more people will die if she doesn't train harder, and Faythe…well, she just *erupted!*"

Reylan's chest beat with pride beside his worry for Faythe. She was a fierce protector, and he adored that about her. It somewhat pissed him off to hear what Zaiana had provoked her with, but his Phoenix needed this. Needed to let her wings out and trust herself to harness the power she was capable of if she found the will to control it.

Zaiana was the only one who was unbiased toward Faythe's feelings, able to pull things out of her they couldn't bear to. And she had the skill to contain the ruin if things got out of control.

"This is quite fascinating," Nik commented, watching them intently, with his arms crossed.

"Are you mad?!" Nerida screeched, clearly in distress with how the duo above were unrelenting on each other.

Reylan said, "With the ruin, I can seize both their power if I think they're going to seriously hurt each other."

At least, he thought he could.

"Just to remind you, I don't have my healing ability anymore if you let this go on until one is falling from the sky," Nerida grumbled.

Reylan dropped his attention to her with a wince, realizing now why Nerida was so upset. She was used to being able to help people and could immediately step in if something went wrong. Tarly slipped an arm around her in comfort.

"I'll put an end to this," Kyleer said, bracing with his wings to take flight. Reylan eyed them with awe and incredulity every time. Still not used to seeing them towering over his shoulders.

"Wait," Tauria said. "You only risk getting hurt going up there. I can interfere from here."

Everyone watched as Tauria retrieved her short staff strapped to her thigh, intrigued about what she was going to do from the ground. Her staff was unique, and Reylan watched in admiration as she kept her eyes on Faythe and Zaiana above while skillfully twisting the baton in a two-step sequence that expanded it to full length.

He felt the gentle interference of her wind ability. She twisted her staff and began to shift her feet in a graceful, focused dance. The wind grew stronger around them, starting to form a small hurricane, and Reylan matched the others, who had begun to step back, shielding their eyes.

Tauria was impressive with the force of the wind she could conjure. He was outside the wall of her hurricane, but still, he had to shift his stance to keep from losing balance. After she'd gathered enough, her hurricane started to tighten, drawing closer to where she still danced in the eye of the storm. Reylan had only seen small usage of the Windbreaker ability before, but this was a stunning demonstration of how lethal it could become, and how powerful Tauria Stagknight was.

When she was satisfied, Tauria shifted her leg back into a lunge, her staff angled skyward in both hands. The full force of wind she'd conjured shot up, blasting between Faythe and Zaiana. The gale was strong enough to knock both of them out of flight. Reylan's heart leaped up his throat watching Faythe tumble down rapidly.

He walked toward her, tracking her while she flailed, trying to regain her balance, but her Phoenix wings had burned out. Reylan was running now, with fear marching in his chest that she wouldn't conjure them back in time.

She did, but the distance she had left to find balance and fly wasn't enough, so all she could do was slow her descent. Reylan caught her, and both almost went crashing to the ground, but he found his footing after the impact.

He cradled her, and their bewildered eyes met.

"Thanks," she panted.

Reylan huffed with a smile, setting her down. "Want to tell me what that was all about?"

Faythe blew a lock of loose hair in her huff. "She's the worst teacher."

"My teaching is *not* the problem." Zaiana glowered as she approached.

"You're right, because this is torture, not teaching."

"I knew you weren't cut out for the discipline this would take."

"We don't have *time*."

"Then here's to the end of the world, all because Faythe Ashfyre isn't as special as she thinks she is," Zaiana said bitterly. Reylan's brows shot up when Zaiana's purple eyes shifted to him. "Good luck with her."

The dark fae began to storm off. Kyleer winced at the rest of them before he followed after her. Izaiah approached, studying Faythe.

"She's actually quite patient and articulate at explaining the ruin's power. You have a particular talent to enrage her."

"Don't you side with her," Faythe mumbled.

Reylan couldn't fight his smile of amusement. He knew Faythe's impatience all too well.

The back of Faythe's hand whacked to his abdomen when she sensed his amusement. He caught her wrist, pulling her flush against him. The fiery irritation in her eyes, along with her pout, was wildly attractive.

"Maybe you need a break." He leaned down close to her ear. "A little stress relief, perhaps?"

Faythe tried to push him away, but he circled an arm around her.

"You're not helping," she grumbled.

"I could be. The choice is yours."

He caught a flicker of her desire for the temptation.

Faythe let go of her tension, slumping into him instead. "Zaiana is right. I don't have the patience to do what she's telling me. Every time I try to tap into the ruin, I just want to take it all and rage across cities. It heightens my anger too fast for me to control it."

"You have a lot to be angry about. More than most."

"Zaiana does too."

"Yes, but her mastering the ruin was a matter of survival. Something she's very good at. Yours... All you have is vengeance to be had, and the ruin is taking advantage of that."

Nik said, "So maybe the key to keeping your control is having something to counter the rage. Remembering you don't want to destroy the world when there's still plenty of people you love here."

It made sense. Faythe had lost and suffered so much in her short life, and it was easy to let the pain take over when the means to make the world hurt with her was right there.

Nik continued, "I'd like to try to guide you as you attempt to merge with the ruin. I do have the most experience in the training of Faythe Ashfyre."

Faythe smiled at that, pushing Nik by his shoulder, which was a relief to see.

Reylan pulled her away from the others. Having claimed their bond just days ago and being separated so much for duty, he'd been riled to the brink of madness every moment she was out of his reach.

"That can wait for a few hours," he said, subtly kissing her neck. Faythe's desire filled his senses with a primal urge, so the mere thought of how close other males were made him highly irritable.

"What do you have in mind until then?" Faythe asked, her breathing delightfully short.

He took her hand, leading her across the field and into the castle.

Reylan thought he could wait until they'd made it to a room—any damned room—but the moment they rounded a corner and he sensed no one nearby, Reylan pushed Faythe into a shadowed alcove, hiding behind a statue within in.

"We can't—"

His mouth crashed to hers, and Faythe lost her protest, moaning into their feverish kiss as he pressed her into the wall.

"This can't wait," he growled, untying the fastens of her pants. He swallowed her moan in a kiss when his fingers dipped past her waistline and over her apex, already slick for him.

They'd been denied the days following their mating to just *be* together, when he would have taken her again and again, until both their bodies were sore and spent but completely entwined with each other.

So it left him feral for any moment they could steal to make up for it, no matter how deplorable their location.

Faythe peeled one leg out of her leather pants as Reylan pulled himself free. He lifted her, legs wrapping around his waist, and the next second he was deep inside her.

It was an immense effort to be quiet. They were alone for now, but anyone could pass, and fae hearing range was sharp.

"Best be quick before someone comes," he taunted in her ear.

Reylan knew it was a risk to surge Faythe's pleasure with where they were, but when his eyes fell on his mark on her neck, a primal need overcame him quicker than reasoning could stop him. His teeth sank into his previous bite mark, and he cupped a hand over Faythe's mouth to smother her cry. Faythe bit his hand, drawing blood, and that only turned him more delirious.

He pounded into her, hard and fast. This was just a quick release to curb their edges for now, even though he wanted to prolong it. Wanted to lock her in a room and not let her leave until he was finished with her. No one would see her for days.

Reylan pulled his teeth out of her and stilled inside her. He rested his forehead to hers as awareness prickled over his sweat-slicked skin. Someone was approaching. He could hardly catch his breath. Buried in Faythe and on the cusp of release, the thought of someone passing turned him irrationally murderous.

He pulled back, dropping his hand from her mouth and pressing a finger to his lips. Faythe's eyes widened as she sensed the person too— a castle guard, Reylan assumed. He gave a wicked side smile as he continued to pleasure her in slow strokes. Her head fell back against the wall, biting her bottom lip into her mouth to keep from making a noise.

Reylan was so close he would erupt inside her any moment. The shadow of the guard passed over them. He thought they'd go right by, but their steps faltered, likely scenting the depravity right beside them.

He thought they would be caught for sure, but after a few seconds of pause, the guard kept walking.

Reylan knew then Faythe had intervened in his thoughts.

"We could do this more often," he purred.

Faythe smiled, devious. Reylan groaned, licking her mating mark, which surged Faythe over the edge, and he went crashing with her.

They rearranged themselves to appear as presentable as they could, but Faythe scowled at him with the annoyance as she had to quickly bathe and change before she could resume her training. Reylan merely smiled, leading her out with the full intention of joining her in every second before he had to let her go again.

CHAPTER SIXTY-SEVEN

Tarly

Tarly had offered to take another room in the castle, but Nerida had asked him to stay with her, and he couldn't be more glad for it.

Nerida wasn't her usual self. He didn't expect her to be. Her smiles were hollow compared to their usual brightness. Her eyes had lost their sparkle. She was still so selfless though, not voicing her upset and even trying to be cheerful, but it was all an act.

He could hardly bear it.

He'd requested the bath be filled, and Nerida sat at the vanity, removing pins from her hair. Tarly reached for the brush before she did, straddling the bench sideways beside her and silently coaxing her to turn. He found such solace even in their shared silence. Every touch and look spoke more between them than words could sometimes.

Tarly began brushing through the tangled locks of her freed braids with gentle precision. Her thick, curly silver tresses were one of his most favorite things in the world. They were both in need of a hot bath, and he was eager at the mere thought.

"You don't have to be so brave. You're allowed to be angry," he said carefully.

"Anger is an emotion that will only exhaust me and push away those around me. And I need you."

Tarly sighed in such contentment at those last words. His new favorite sentence in every language.

He swept her loose hair to the side, planting a kiss to her neck. Then he set down the brush, boldly reaching for the ties at the back of her tunic. Her head inclined to the side more, prompting him to trail his lips from the shell of her ear back down to the base of her throat, and Nerida gave a soft sigh of pleasure. He was aching for her.

"We don't have to do anything tonight," he said huskily.

"I want a distraction. I want something…*good*."

He was conflicted to hear that, wanting to oblige and help her in any way he could. But this was far more to him than a distraction, and he wanted to be far more to her.

With her tunic loose, Nerida stood, slipping the sleeves off her shoulders and letting it drop. He'd seen her in undergarments long before now, but there was a new spark of intimacy between them that painted this picture in a new ravenous light.

Nerida peeled out of her leather pants, keeping her eyes on him, and a twinkle of desire danced across the hazel.

"Are you going to join me in the bath?"

His heart slammed. "Is that what you want?"

Nerida turned, heading for the washroom. She pulled her top undergarment off as she did, dropping it to the floor. Then her lower half followed. He was utterly, foolishly transfixed by the sight of her naked flesh, the firelight casting a soft glow over her beautiful brown skin.

"I wouldn't have asked if I didn't want it," she said—a soft whisper of seduction as she disappeared into the washroom.

Tarly had to take a moment to believe this was real.

He removed his jacket before he reached the open door and watched her climb into the steaming, deep oval tub as he pulled his shirt over his head. His hands undid his pants button and pulled the laces as Nerida drifted around the bath to face him. Their eyes held on each other, and he'd never experienced this intensity of desire building without a single touch before.

"You are so beautiful," he whispered like a slipped thought. Though it didn't feel like even close to an adequate description of the Goddess he stared at.

Tarly removed his pants, and Nerida's eyes wandered over him. Her full lips parted, and he was growing lightheaded with the lust she was inspiring with no words at all.

The hot, milky water lapped around his waist, and he closed his eyes with the bliss of it, wondering when the last time was he'd bathed in warm waters was, never mind this heat.

"Much better than the lake," he commented.

Nerida's precious giggle slipped his eyes open, and he couldn't believe the angel in his bath. Tarly took her hand, coaxing her to turn and relax her back against him. Taking a bowl from the side, he began to pour water over her scalp as she tipped her had back for him.

"When you said you wanted to be mine...did you mean it in the sense of the bond being real?" he asked gently.

Nerida danced her fingertips along the water's surface. "That's likely not going to happen," she said with quiet reservation.

"Would you want to try?"

Nerida turned around, her wet lashes glistening, making her irises sparkle. "Yes," she said, her whispering voice needy.

Tarly's length became so hard it was painful.

He claimed her mouth, and she deepened the kiss immediately. Much as he wanted her with a feverish need, it was Nerida who demanded more, all at once. Straddling him, moving her hips against him. The water sloshed over the sides of the tub, but he didn't care. If she needed this for her pain, he would let her have whatever she wanted of him. As much as she wanted. For however long she would yearn for him.

Tarly lifted her out of the bath, turning and setting her on the edge of it, with her feet touching the ground for balance. He lowered between her legs, and Nerida's breaths sharpened in anticipation.

Tasting her brought out the most beautiful noise. He would never tire of discovering all the sounds she would make and how her body demanded his touch.

"Tarly..."

His name in her breathy tone of pure lust tightened in his core. He wanted her so desperately he devoured her mercilessly to compensate for not being inside her yet. Nerida's fingers threaded through his hair, and he turned wild at the movement of her hips that demanded even more from him. She was close to finishing, but he worried about the slipperiness of the tub and her wet skin if she did so here.

With great restraint, Tarly stopped his assault, and Nerida whimpered, shuddering from the cool air against her skin and the denial of finishing. He kissed the inside of her thigh and rose, hooking an arm around her and lifting her to wrap her legs around him.

Nerida kissed him deeply as he carried her into the bedroom. She was utterly *his*. No matter what the outcome of trying to bond with her might be, she was undeniably made for him. The way she kissed him with a passion he'd never felt before, touching far deeper than the surface of lust and pleasure. She'd burrowed into his soul.

He laid her down, the sheets sticking to their skin, but he was too lost in her to care. Within seconds Nerida's leg had hooked around him, flipping them for her to be on top. He loved this wild, dominant side that came out of her in lust. In front of everyone else, she was so gentle, almost shy, and presented as so innocent. Alone, only Tarly got to see the unleashing of all her passion, and she gave it all to *him*. Only him.

Nerida took what she needed, grinding along his length that was almost as glorious as he imagined being fully inside her. He let her take lead, chasing her pleasure against him as he watched in complete awe. She was a Goddess. All beautiful wet silver hair against glistening brown skin, face painted in pure pleasure. She sat up, not stopping her movements, but she touched her body. Groping her breasts, eyes closed and head tipped back, with breathy moans caressing her throat.

Tarly was utterly entranced by her—he could hardly move. His hands on her hips pressed her down harder, and she cried out beauti- fully. His thrusts were shallow, but mostly, it was all her, claiming her pleasure.

Gods above. What had he done so right in his life to have this? Every trial and torment was worth reliving over and over to get to have her.

"Tarly, I'm going to…" She lost her words, but they were pinched on her face. Her hands planted on his chest, and he helped her rock harder toward that finish line.

Watching Nerida climax was an otherworldly experience. She quivered against him, crying out his name and blessing it with new meaning. He would crawl on broken bones to the call of his name from her.

Nerida panted, shivering in the aftermath of her climax. Tarly tucked the wet hair from her face. Her eyes were fixed on his neck, and her fingers traced along his collarbone.

"Can I try first?" she asked breathlessly.

Tarly's length jutted against her at the mere thought of her biting him.

"Yes," he said thickly.

Nerida leaned down, and his chest constricted so tightly in antici- pation he thought he might stop breathing. She seduced him with so little effort. Nerida's soft lips pressed to his chest, slowly climbing higher, while he lost his damned mind.

His hands ran up her spine and over her sides, basking in every naked feel of her.

Nerida kissed his throat right where she would puncture it—then, to his surprise, she reached between their bodies, lifted her hips, and gripped his length to sink down onto it.

Tarly swore, seeing stars as her heat wrapped around him inch by torturous inch.

"Wait," he rasped before she could bite. Embarrassment flushed him. "If you do that right this second, I won't be able to last."

Nerida smiled coyly. She began to move her hips but held off biting him.

Tarly couldn't take it anymore. He sat up, then he stood with her. All he knew was that he wanted the control now, and so he pressed her back to the wall and set a pace that had their moans of pleasure mixing between their breaths. Nothing had ever felt this raw and real. So damn perfect and right he claimed her in every sense, even if the bond wasn't to be.

"I really want to," she rasped, clutching a tight fist of his hair while her lips hovered at his neck.

"Do it," he said, not slowing his pace that rocked the pictures on the wall and likely announced to anyone passing in the hall what they were doing.

Nerida needed nothing more. "I claim you, Tarly Wolverlon. Here, now, and always, I claim you with the Gods as my witness and with this by my will."

Her teeth punctured his flesh, and Tarly slammed into her, stilling with the shockwave that ripped him apart only to sew the ribbons of him back together, forged into something united and unbreakable.

Was this the mating bond? He didn't want to believe it so surely. Perhaps it was only his desperation for it. Exchanging blood was a powerful connection in itself.

Nerida's teeth slipped out of him, and she shuddered. Tarly let go of her thighs for her to stand, but he kept a firm hold of her. She didn't speak—he couldn't either. He was wrestling a carnal need for her that could only act. Tarly kissed her feverishly and then spun her around.

"Keep your hands firm on the wall, angel," he said huskily.

Tarly spread her legs a little further before he was back inside her. Leaning over her back, he took her in slow, full strokes that pulled the most beautiful sounds from her. His hand massaged her breast before slipping up and around her throat for purchase.

He kissed her shoulder and swept back her hair.

"My turn," he muttered, then he sank his teeth into her.

Nerida's blood on his tongue erupted his world, flowing down his throat and severing who he was before her. Nerida's blood within him bound his soul and swore a promise of who he would become for her. Only her.

His released surged through every fiber and cell of his body. Nerida came with him. Their bodies melted into each other from the heat and sweat and water. Their souls entwined with each other, and when Tarly stopped drinking from her...he couldn't believe it.

"You're mine," he said to her thoughts. Because now he could. "The bond is real," he said aloud.

Before, he'd thought it was just their time spent together that had kept her in tune with her emotions, but now he could feel them more intensely. She was completely open to him.

Nerida didn't speak, and her silence began to gather dread. He pulled out of her, turning her around, and found her crying. Tarly panicked, taking her face in her hands.

"You said—"

"I'm happy," she said, barely a whisper, as if emotion had filled her throat. "I'm the happiest I've been in a long time."

Tarly deflated with relief. He kissed her. Kissed his mate. This angel who wanted him as much as he wanted her, and now their souls were written in the stars.

He walked backward with her by the hand until he sat on the bed, and she straddled him. Tarly brushed her tears and kissed her. He would never get enough of kissing her.

"I love you so much that those words are pitiful to express it," he said.

That pulled a soft chuckle from her, and she sniffed. "This is the first time I've belonged anywhere, Tarly. I love you endlessly."

"You belong with me," he declared. "In every universe, you belong with me."

CHAPTER SIXTY-EIGHT

Faythe

J akon had been the only person missing from every meeting they'd
called. He never came. Instead he'd hardly left the blacksmith
compound in the outer town. Even though he cast her away
immediately every day she ventured out to check up on him, she
wouldn't stop reaching out.

A hollow spot in her grew daily. It would never be filled from the
loss of Marlowe, but now she felt her friendship with Jakon dying too
and she couldn't let that happen.

The citizens of High Farrow latched their attention onto her as
she marched with purpose through the outer town. She didn't wear
any color, but her Phoenix emblem was displayed proudly on her belt.
It set her apart from the woman they knew, the human who'd left this
place and never come back. But still, she would always harbor deep
sentiments and protectiveness for the Kingdom of High Farrow, and
in particular this town.

Approaching the blacksmith compound, her steps slowed to the
vacant drift of a ghost. The spaced carved out seemed so lost and
forgotten, an abandoned shell of the place that used to spark such joy
in Faythe right before the braided blonde hair of her best friend would
swish out in greeting.

Clanging echoed from within, less precise than she'd grown accustomed to expect from Marlowe. Her heart prepared for the uncertainty of how Jakon might receive her today.

She pulled back the curtain, and Jakon spotted her immediately before his next slam of the hammer came down. Faythe breathed, distracted by the rush of energy she didn't expect from this place, as Jakon threw a rag over his work and set aside his tool.

"What do you want?" he asked flatly.

She'd come prepared to be shut out by him, but she would never abandon him, no matter how my slices he made on her heart.

Faythe observed the many attempts and full daggers that littered the workbench. "You've been missing from the castle a lot."

"Forgive me if I don't want to sit around idle and useless in your fae battle plans."

She was always saying all the wrong things. Failing him time and time again. He was her best and longest friend, and yet she couldn't be what he needed.

"Can I help—?"

"You can help by not coming back here," he snapped, leaning both hands on the workbench, wanting to resume his distracted work, but he wouldn't while she was present. "I need someone to blame, and you're making yourself too damn easy of a target."

She'd never seen this side to him—a side so sharp in grief even a glance at him made her bleed.

"What can I do?" she whispered. "I can't just leave you. Please. I need you."

"I don't need you, and if you were honest, Faythe, you have never needed me. Look at you—fae, a queen, one of the most powerful people alive. Our worlds don't *fit* together anymore."

"Why are you saying this?" She was falling apart. Jakon was carving himself out of her life, and she couldn't let him stray from her. "In the woods, you said—"

"I said what I had to because I needed you to take me to Rhyenelle."

He slammed the door on their friendship, and she was the desperate fool banging her fists on the wood, begging for his acquittal for an unforgivable crime. She couldn't push herself on him—all she could do was keep trying and hope that time could heal them both enough to find each other again.

Faythe left without parting words, dragging her feet that became leaden the longer she walked. Her mind viciously replayed every one of Jakon's icy glares; every one of his harsh words. She deserved them all, but that didn't make it any more tolerable to bear.

She passed her old hut. Already in the pits of despair, she fed it more by heading toward it.

The door wouldn't last much longer on the hinges that were close to breaking in their decay. No one had claimed her humble dwelling since she and Jakon left it behind, and she wasn't surprised. It was a drafty, dreary confinement, but still, they'd warmed it as their home.

Faythe couldn't place her feelings at seeing the place now. She couldn't force a smile or reflect on any fond memories. Pushing the door to the back room, her first thought was to wonder how Jakon ever tolerated the feeble, small cot opposite hers. On the nightstand, Faythe couldn't bite back her whimper at seeing the book title *The Forgotten Goddess*.

Marlowe had let her borrow it when Faythe lost herself to the wonders of the Spirit legends within. Legends she had come to learn were only half-truths and fantasies.

Sitting on her cot, Faythe flipped through the pages. She never did get to finish the stories. One page came loose, and Faythe caught it, going to jam it back in, but the paper didn't match in size nor color.

Frowning, she read the page, her heart slowing as she took in what it contained. Then her pulse picked up, and she flipped the page over, surging to her feet.

It was a picture. A familiar, beautiful dagger.

The page crumpled in her grip as Faythe raced out the hut. She didn't stop running—straight through the city gates and all the way back to the castle. Her sight blurred with tears, but she could run this route blindfolded.

Oh, Marlowe. You brilliant, remarkable, selfless soul.

Faythe sprinted up the steps, passing Izaiah and Tynan, who called after her, but she didn't falter. Tauria came onto her path too, but Faythe could only call over her shoulder that she would explain later. They all had to be accustomed to her franticness, because no one followed her.

She burst into her rooms, swiping up the jeweled dagger Marlowe had gifted her so long ago and running back out.

She'd known this day would come.

She'd known they would need it.

Marlowe hadn't crafted the dagger she'd given to Faythe for her first fight in the Cave against a fae as a human—she'd only been the one to find it.

Of all people, Faythe found herself barging into Zaiana's room without consideration of a knock in her high of adrenaline.

Faythe was staring down the point of a blade in the same breath. The dark fae was incredibly fast.

"You really better have a good reason for that, or this goes in your neck," Zaiana said coldly.

Faythe flipped the dagger in her hand before holding it up.

She said, "We have the means to go hunting."

CHAPTER SIXTY-NINE

Reylan

When everyone left the drawing room, Reylan stayed. So did Izaiah, who leaned one hand on the mantle of the fireplace, watching the flames ripple, and Kyleer, who sat at the edge of the table.

The gravity of Kyleer's lost memories weight heavy on them all.

"Nik and Faythe are going to try their best through Nightwalking to try to find my memories." Kyleer broke the silence. "If they can't, at least they can show me things. Memories with them and things they know of me. Though I can't deny, it feels strange to have to trust people I don't even remember at all."

Izaiah straightened, turning to his brother. Reylan watched him warily with the anger he presented.

"I'm your little brother. We went through the Nether with shitty parents and abandonment—the least you could do is remember me."

"I want to."

"Then try harder."

"Take it easy, Izaiah," Reylan warned.

"Can I ask something?" Kyleer hedged.

Reylan perched on the edge of the table. "Of course."

"Zaiana keeps pushing me away, adamant that if I had my memories, I wouldn't want her like I do now. I can't explain it. If you're my brothers, I'm assuming you'd know me and what happened better than anyone. So...would I have forgiven her had I been given the chance? Can I trust her?"

Reylan and Izaiah exchanged a look that spoke of their mutual reluctance over the truth, but they couldn't lie to him.

"You would have forgiven her," Izaiah said. "What she did was wicked, and I don't forgive her myself, but what you had with her was real, and I believe she did regret betraying you eventually."

Reylan said, "I hate to agree. She doesn't make it easy to get along with her, but you understand each other in a way I've never seen in you with anyone."

Kyleer absorbed that information, and it was pain to watch him in so much confusion and turmoil.

"How are the wings?" Izaiah asked, breaking the heaviness.

The feathered wings towering over Kyleer's shoulders were as bewildering as they were fascinating. None of them knew if the obscure manifestation held any significance. Kyleer still bled crimson, and his eyes hadn't lost their moss-green color. It was a relief but an anomaly he hoped wasn't an omen for something bad to come.

"I'm getting used to them," Kyleer said, making them flex subconsciously.

"I'm kind of jealous," Izaiah said.

"You can Shapeshift and fly in any form you want," Reylan pointed out.

"That's not the same. Kyleer gets to look more intimidating than ever."

Making light of the situation helped to ease them into their new reality. They wouldn't stop trying to get Kyleer's memories back, and when they did return, nothing would be changed.

Reylan had another heavy weight of sorrow lingering in his mind. He debating waiting until Kyleer had his memories, but they didn't know when that might be.

"We've not had the chance to grieve for our king," Reylan said quietly. "Agalhor...who was more than that to all of us."

Izaiah swore, turning away and pinching the bridge of his nose. "I need warning before you tear off my shitty bandages on that wound."

Reylan moved toward Izaiah, placing a hand on his shoulder as they reflected on their fallen king and father figure. "I know we still don't have time to honor him properly, but we will. In his name we charge forward in this war. We claim back Rhyenelle with his daughter and heir. He gave us the lives we live today, and I won't ever forget that."

Izaiah dropped his hand, and they embraced, passing their promise and their sorrow. Kyleer stood, uncertain of where to place himself. Izaiah, bold as he was, let go of Reylan and pulled his brother into him anyway. Kyleer's stiffness eased after a moment, and he relaxed.

"We need to get all our messages to the generals out now. Then begin repositioning the armadas," Reylan said, slipping into his general persona.

He didn't like the threat of war and battle—it always meant brave and innocent lives would be lost—but this was what he was good at. Leading, predicting, and strategizing in the face of high threat and pressure.

Faythe had only been gone from him for a little over an hour by the time he'd finished making early plans and sent messengers, but with their newly forged mating bond, every minute away from her unsettled him until he could hardly stand it.

Dusk was falling, and he planned to steal her away for the night regardless of the protest he predicted she'd have, always one to sacrifice her time for others. He had to be her balance. After all she'd been through, and with what was coming, the best he could offer her were moments to forget and feel loved with him.

After trying a few places he believed she might be and turning up lonely, Reylan used their bond, his new favorite link that could reach her no matter how far, so long as she didn't close off on her end.

"I'm all for finding you, but when I do, I'm claiming a prize."

The moment he felt it took more strain than it should to reach her mind, his steps came to a halt mid-hallway.

Before she could respond, he added, voice turning serious, *"Where have you run off to?"*

The moment it took for her to reply flexed his fists at his sides.

"It's probably best you wait until I'm back for that answer."

She was going to be the death of him.

"I would have come with you."

"It can't wait. I'll be back with you soon, and I'll make it up to you."

The devious thing caressed his senses with desire. Though his concern had him on edge, he trusted her, and most of all, he believed in her.

"Then just tell me you're not alone."

"I'm not."

That she didn't inform who her company was made him assume

the worst. Once he decided it had to be Zaiana, he knew then they could have only gone one place.

The Mortus Mountains.

"I'm going to have my way with you the moment you get back," he said, needing to back down from one of many risky tasks they might need to be separated for.

"I'm counting on it, General."

He internally groaned. She knew what that title in her sultry little voice did to him.

Needing to busy himself or he'd risk going after her anyway, Reylan found the one person he distrusted most of all. Rainyte Ashfyre was an incredulous person to have shown up during their moment of peril. Reylan didn't like him regardless of the help he'd offered so far.

"Running home, are you?" Reylan called at his back when he found him wandering the halls.

"Sounds like you care if I stay," Nyte drawled, turning to him smoothly.

Now he knew he was Marvellas's son, Reylan couldn't help but notice the uncanny mannerisms they shared sometimes.

"I would rather you didn't."

"Then have you come to escort me to the mirrors?"

Reylan's jaw heightened. Nyte served no use to them here. If anything, Reylan could only see him as a potential threat if he decided to join his mother's cause. It was clear his allegiance wasn't with them nor anyone. He was a liability.

"Gladly," Reylan said, passing him to lead the way toward the library.

He didn't particularly enjoy venturing back down into the passages under High Farrow's library. Nik had already informed him he'd ordered the Magestone that had once lined the corridor toward the room of mirrors to be carefully mined. He had various blacksmiths working on turning it into as many weapons as possible to be used in their war.

When their reflections were cast back to them from a hundred angles, Reylan sharpened his caution for the trickster of a creature that could taunt them at any moment.

"This is it then?" Nyte asked, standing casually with his hands in his pockets.

"I thought you'd be more enthused."

"I've learned not to get hopeful of the words of others. I'd be none the wiser if you'd led me down here as a trap and these are nothing but ordinary mirrors."

"Then why did you follow so easily if you distrust me so?"

"Because I do not fear you."

Reylan gave nothing away. Reacting in offense served for nothing. It might even prove why he shouldn't be feared. Instead Reylan leveled Nyte with his cool demeanor.

"I'll leave you to it then," he said, beginning to turn.

"Has Faythe told you she'll die too if she kills my mother with her ruin?"

Reylan stiffened, sliding a warning glare at Nyte.

Nyte added, "Well, anyone who does will die, but in the short time I've gotten to know her heroic qualities, I would wager she planned to keep that secret to make the sacrifice herself."

"Why would you tell me this?"

"A parting gift, if you will. Believe it or not, the only reason I won't stay a moment longer than I have to in this realm is because I too have a mate to return to. Had she the same foolish idea, I'd want to know and make sure she was the farthest person away from plunging that ruin into the heart of a Goddess and going down with them."

Reylan might not trust him, but he believed him. As it was exactly the type of thing Faythe would do.

Gods, he loved her. And she drove him to madness. She may not be willing to be selfish, but he could be. He would not lose her, and she would not lose him.

As he left Nyte, not staying to see what taunts and riddles the Dresair would humor him with before taking him through, Reylan was beholden to the insight. For if this war was won at the cost of his Phoenix, Reylan would start a new one in his grief.

CHAPTER SEVENTY

Zaiana

Zaiana hadn't known Faythe's human friend, Marlowe, but in her wake, the human Oracle may have provided more for their gain in this war they were yet to discover. Starting with the dagger to revert Nerida's power back to her. They just had to find the pesky little dark fae, her *half-sister* Edith, before she got killed by her own stupidity and Nerida's magick was lost for good.

The family term didn't settle with an inkling of sentiment. Discovering she was a blood relative might have spurred her violence even more. What she'd done was a coward's way to power.

Edith wanted Zaiana's lightning, and she would make sure the dark fae felt the full force of her storm before they used the dagger.

She crouched with Faythe Ashfyre near the entrance Zaiana used at the edge of the Mortus Mountains. It wasn't used as often, but she didn't want to take any chances of being seen yet. If Edith wasn't here, Zaiana still planned to kill all five masters before she left. She liked to think some part them had always known Zaiana would return as their demise and that they slept with one eye open.

"No one has come in or out in ten minutes," Faythe hissed. Her small, antsy movements were beginning to grate on Zaiana's nerves.

"You shouldn't have come," Zaiana grumbled.

Faythe didn't defend that fact. The human-turned-fae was a like a firecracker and had always been able to unleash that fiery side of herself—had to, or she most certainly would not still be alive. Though it made her insufferable in a task of patience and quiet.

"I have the dagger."

"Which you could just give to me and stay here. You're a liability."

"You just can't stand the thought of help."

Zaiana cut her with a look. It was jarring to meet those gold eyes so close and not be hunting or fighting the heir. The impulse was still there—Faythe didn't make it easy to subdue the itch for her throat.

"Let's go," Zaiana grunted, not waiting or accounting for Faythe as she slipped stealthily down the dark mountain edges.

Within the cavernous labyrinth, Zaiana breathed steady to calm her irritating suffocation at being back here.

To her credit, Faythe kept pace and remained as vigilant as her now they were within tight enemy confines. These jagged stone walls had raised her and sharpened her. This place had been her home for many centuries, but she could watch it crumble to the ground and feel nothing but joy warming her cold, black heart.

"The smell isn't pleasant," Faythe muttered under her breath.

Zaiana had learned to naturally shallow her breaths under here, avoiding the pungent mix of blood and despair as much as possible. The passages were always the worst.

They made it to the open cave where training would usually take place. Zaiana slipped in just to catch a glimpse over the edge, down into the pit. Young dark fae lined uniformly across the whole floor. She'd never seen them gathered like this. These darklings weren't nearly old enough to be considered for army positions, but she spied four of the masters walking up and down the lines, examining them as if they were a legion.

Nephra wasn't one of them. She stood, poised and arrogant, observing from one of the other balconies.

"What are they doing?"

Faythe speaking to her mind shocked her enough to make her spin, gripping her by the throat and curving them out of the balcony. Her gold eyes flew wide with anger, and Zaiana released her immediately.

"Don't do that!" Zaiana hissed under her breath.

"Do what!" Faythe whisper-shouted back.

"Infiltrate my mind!"

"Would you rather I announce our arrival to those very welcoming dark fae down there?"

Though it was a slight overreaction on her part, Zaiana hated her own voice in her head, never mind the sudden intrusion of another's.

"Just stay out of my head," Zaiana grumbled, leading them away from the pit.

She had a few other places to spy for Edith if she scuttled off to these mountains. They checked the dorms and other higher up sleeping quarters. Nikalias had relayed that Edith claimed to have led in Mordecai's armies, and that was a high status to reach for her age description. Zaiana wasn't truly hopeful to find her here. This was where the weak became strong, or they died. She didn't tell that to Faythe when Zaiana had an ulterior motive to come here anyway. The masters would die for killing Acelin, Kellias, Drya, and Selain.

She'd spent all their years together reminding them they were not friends. Not family. They were a duty to each other, and nothing more. Even then, she knew in a buried piece of herself that wasn't true. In their last moments, she hoped they'd known too.

All she had to offer their loyal souls was vengeance, and it would be hers.

"She's not here," Zaiana said, knowing it was pointless to venture anymore even though they'd only checked a small fraction of the labyrinth carved under these barren mountains.

"There has to be more we can check. She could be in a meeting, or terrorizing children, or maybe your dear father is here and they're plotting your demise as we speak."

"Don't call him that," she warned.

"Denying your blood doesn't make you any less a Vesaria."

Everything in Zaiana recoiled at the name. It didn't belong to her. She was Zaiana Silverfair. Even though she despised that name too. When the war was over, she would shed both. What use was a family name to her anyway?

"You really are insufferable company," Zaiana said, brushing past her and leading them down a narrow spiral staircase.

With Faythe's distracting words, her sharp focus had split, and because of that she didn't detect the body ascending the stairs until she had him pinned to the wall, with her dagger drawing a line of black blood on his throat.

"Zai-Zaiana," he stuttered, recognizing her immediately.

She didn't have the time nor the patience to wager on his ability to stay silent. Her blade cut deep and swift before she pushed the body to avoid getting blood on her.

"Was that really necessary?" Faythe said, following hot on her heel again.

"It wouldn't have been if you stopped distracting me and stayed focused."

"I'm following your every movement and trusting you. It's *you* who needs to become accustomed to teamwork," Faythe complained.

"I'm not counting on this *teamwork* happening again. Besides, you give yourself too much credit. You're deadweight to account for more than anything."

When Zaiana picked up more voices over Faythe's grumbling, she pushed a hand to Faythe's chest, pressing them into the wall.

There was a trail of water under their feet. These mountains were always damp, with rainwater seeping through the cracks. Zaiana crouched, conjuring her lightning and dipping the tips of her metal finger guards into the stream. The electricity conducted through the water, gripping those approaching by the soles of their boots before exploding in currents thorough their bodies, sharp enough to drop them unconscious.

"Can I try that next time?" Faythe asked, peeking her head around to see the three fallen dark fae.

The reminder Faythe had stolen her ability roused her.

"Can you give my power back?"

"I didn't *take* any of what's yours. It's more like the fabric of the ability I touch imprints itself in me. If I don't learn to use it, those threads have no substance and fade away. I've learned I don't keep them permanently unless I keep using them to some capacity."

It was fascinating, she supposed.

"So you've kept using my lightning?"

"It's one of my favorites. I might prefer fire though. I don't have Waterwielding from Nerida anymore—it's not typically at the forefront of my mind to use for attack or defense."

"I'm not surprised. Though water is a deceptively lethal element, the flow and practice of it requires patience and calmness. Fire...that makes sense for you."

"How do you know about the practice of Waterwielding?"

"It's useful to learn about skills outside your own. It's how we innovate, by borrowing from other practices and experimenting with techniques that can be useful in our own."

Faythe hummed. "You're more intelligent than I thought."

Zaiana's fist flexed. "I seem dim to you?"

"No. You're terrifying. And hearing of the upbringing in this place…I suppose I was narrow-minded to believe you'd be solely focused on everything physical rather than books."

"I might not have survived this place if it weren't for books."

Zaiana wanted to snatch those words back as though they hung in the air, mocking her for the pitiful confession.

"For what it's worth, I admire you. Even when you were trying to kill me."

Zaiana's mouth quirked up of its own accord. "Who says I've stopped trying?"

The echoes of vicious snarling made the hairs on her nape stand on end. She knew what was down here, but Zaiana hadn't visited this section deep under the mountain since the first day she'd stumbled upon it barely past her first century.

"This is going to be hard for you to see," Zaiana warned.

When they emerged, they kept close to the wall, only peeking their heads around, as this part was patrolled by higher-up dark fae. The bodies that filled the cages stacked high had grown exponentially since she'd last seen it. So many Transitioned dark fae too savage to roam free. Even one of them loose could tear through a village of humans in a single night.

"Oh Gods," Faythe breathed.

It was a barbaric and gruesome sight. These creatures were once ordinary fae, just like Faythe. Now they resembled beast more than person. Torn, decaying flesh; crooked wings; snapping, black-spotted teeth. The scent of death was so potent Zaiana stuffed her nose into her elbow, as did Faythe.

"If they unleashed these creatures on High Farrow, it would be carnage before any army was needed to break your defenses."

Zaiana was thinking aloud, having forgotten this mass weapon lurking in the depths of these mountains. This had to be why they were never ordered killed. They'd been kept down here all this time, fed enough human blood to keep them alive but absolutely ravished, ready to unleash complete savagery on the enemy.

"We have to eliminate this threat," Faythe said.

"Agreed, but short of caving in the entire mountain, it's going to be difficult to kill so many efficiently. This isn't the only room of cages."

Their eyes met, and Zaiana knew what the heir was about to say.

"Do you think you can cave in the mountain?"

Zaiana considered. Though she'd previously thought the idea

pleasurable, the true possibility of watching this place collapse made her doubtful for a moment.

"If I had the ruin to amplify my magick, maybe," she answered.

Zaiana's mind began to flood with memories against her will. They weren't all terrible, living here. There were moments she kept locked and treasured with her friends, Acelin, Kellias, Drya, Selain, Tynan, Amaya…*Finnian*.

This mountain was where she'd met him. The first time she'd fallen in love—her most forbidden secret. This mountain was where she'd killed him.

At that dark memory that slashed through anything warm, Zaiana's resolve hardened. She said, "If we work together, both using lightning, it might be enough to bring this place down."

Faythe's expression firmed to determination with her nod. It was a monumental task—these mountains were huge and ancient. Even together, Zaiana wasn't certain they could achieve the task.

Zaiana began leading them toward the best point of the mountain she believed would be the greatest impact point. The pit.

The lines of darklings were still there, as were all five masters. Zaiana whistled low in a three-beat sequence that echoed gently through the hall. Faythe passed her a questioning look, but it was answered by the stealthy appearance of Tynan and Amaya.

"You've been complaining about my company all this time when you brought your own?" Faythe said sourly.

"Unlike you, Tynan and Amaya know the layout of this place and are far more useful to me." She turned to them. "We're going to bring this place down, but we need to evacuate the darklings first. As many as we can."

Tynan nodded. "We'll start with the dorms and communal spaces."

Amaya's expression had turned ghostly. "Collapse the whole mountain? You can do that?"

"We're going to find out."

"What about the masters?" Tynan asked in concern.

"They're mine."

He looked about to protest, but he thought better than to underestimate her. "Where will the darklings go?"

"High Farrow," Faythe said. "They're innocents. We'll keep them safe."

That surprised Zaiana, and it worried her. She didn't doubt Faythe's word; the heir was a walking bleeding heart. But she did doubt the acceptance of the others, like Nikalias—and he was the king with the overruling authority to order them all dead.

For now, they didn't have an alternative choice.

Zaiana nodded for Tynan to direct the darklings there for now.

They left swiftly, leaving Zaiana to calculate how she was going to get the ones below out of the storm they were about to unleash. The hole at the top of the pit would have to be their escape, and she hoped most, if not all, could actually fly. Sometimes the young were late in gaining the strength in their wings to carry them, or their wings never grew tall and wide enough to support them.

"What are you thinking?" Faythe asked, too close to her for comfort.

Zaiana considered Faythe, deeming she might actually be a great asset after all. "How many minds can you reach at once?" she asked.

"With the ruin, probably all of them. We should have brought one. Without it, maybe a dozen at a time."

"They might not trust an unseen voice in their head, but I'm hoping they will once they see me. Tell the darklings to make their escape above when the fighting starts."

Without another word, Zaiana boldly stepped out onto the balcony, first attracting the attention of Nephra, who blazed at the sight of her from a few balconies to her side. Zaiana smiled arrogantly, released her wings, and swooped down to the ground below.

Gasps and murmurs broke out among the darklings, but she focused solely on the four masters on this level, who targeted her with hateful stares.

"Zaiana Silverfair," one drawled. "We're well aware of all your actions outside. Your failure in capturing the Heir of Marvellas left you at the mercy of the enemy you have sold yourself to," Master Eon said.

"You've hidden yourselves away under this mountain for millennia, too afraid to face the outside world. Who is really a slave and prisoner?"

"Why have you come back?" Master Corrik inquired.

"To kill you all," she answered plainly.

They laughed at her. Mocked her. She'd long since hardened her mind to the grating jeers of their bitter voices.

"You heard about your little companions then? Truthfully, I never understood what you saw in those you chose to defend you. Your judgment has always been weak," said Master Eon.

"Yet you could never kill me," Zaiana taunted back, realizing now why, in all the times she'd thought her rebellion would earn her death, they'd spared her. "You know my true name. You know my father. You know I am Zaiana Vesaria, heir to Valgard."

Every admittance of her heritage burned in her throat, but the masters were bound by the will of Mordecai, and that was what had kept her alive.

Their aged faces contorted in anger and hatred.

"You cannot kill us. He will not allow it," Master Neisah hissed.

"I'm willing to take my chances," Zaiana said. Then she struck.

Lightning shot from her fingers, slamming into Corrik. In the same breath she threw another bolt with her other hand toward Neisah. At the break of chaos, to her relief, the darklings began to scatter, some flying to escape through the opening above, some running through the halls. Zaiana kept focus on the masters as best she could, but when adult dark fae flooded into the pit, beginning to grab the scrambling darklings, Zaiana lost her momentum as they began *killing* the young.

"Kill them all," Nephra ordered, too calm and cold, before she swooped down to the ground.

An amber glow illuminated the dark walls, dropping down. Faythe Ashfyre joined her side, as furious as she over the cowardly bloodshed of those incapable of protecting themselves.

"The blood and brutality of this place ends here," Faythe seethed.

Lightning scattered through Zaiana's body. It had been building like a bated breath since she began combing through these mountains. It vibrated through her like a second force of life. Then...Zaiana never thought she'd be reaching for the hand of Faythe Ashfyre. Lightning sparked between their fingertips, and when their palms clasped, the lightning erupted through both of them. It built to a catastrophic force, and they braced, conjuring as much as they could as two vessels of a deadly storm. It spilled from them in cracks that struck the walls and shook the ground beneath them. Brutal gales of wind brewed around them. When they were at their limit, they kneeled simultaneously, slamming of their free palms to the ground.

The mountain gave a violent roar at the impact as powerful as a God's strike from the heavens. The stone split into a web of small cracks while deadly rocks rained down. Zaiana kept pushing as much magick as she could, and Faythe did not falter either.

Through the wind and rock that crashed and stormed around them, Zaiana caught the five cowardly rodents breaking into a passage, trying to escape. Zaiana's blood boiled.

"Hold it as long as you can," Zaiana yelled to Faythe over the chaos. She severed their connection, racing after the masters. They would not get away.

This passage only led to one place, and Zaiana caught up to the masters just as they were preparing to fly through the opening above their council room. The ground trembled dangerously. If she wasn't quick, she risked being buried alive with them.

"You can't outrun the blade you sharpened," Zaiana said coldly.

Nephra stood closer than the rest, absolutely seething with jealousy and rage. She'd always hated Zaiana most, and she'd always thought it was Mordecai's favor that made her so bitter. Now it made sense.

"You were in love with him," Zaiana said to her.

"He was in love with me too," Nephra bit out. Her dark eyes turned manic with her laughter. "I gave him a daughter just as capable as you."

That came as a shock. If Nephra had been pregnant, she'd hidden it very well. Then again, Zaiana could recall several times months had gone by without her seeing Master Nephra. She'd always noticed since those months went by with the fewest punishments.

Then it slipped into place, so clear she didn't think she could be wrong.

"Edith," she muttered.

Nephra smiled cruelly. Thought it was the flick of her eyes over Zaiana's shoulder that alerted her to the blade she twisted to avoid. Zaiana gripped the wrist by her head, bending and throwing the assailant over her shoulder. Her knee dug into their chest, pushing the blade still gripped in their hand over their neck.

Zaiana stared into dark brown eyes, with inky black hair spilling across the stone, similar to her own.

"Hello, *sister*," Edith hissed.

Stunned, Zaiana was unstable enough that Edith managed to jab her heel into Zaiana's waist, flipping them. Zaiana's hands lashed around Edith's, which was clamped around the blade aimed for her heart.

"I am just as strong as you," Edith said, her voice straining as Zaiana poured all her strength against hers. "I'm just as capable as you." Edith leaned more of her body weight into the blade, and it inched closer to her chest. "And I will be as powerful as you."

Zaiana's arms trembled, but her rage in the face of the one who'd harmed Nerida gave her renewed resistance.

"You're not even close to me," Zaiana said.

Twisting their arms, Edith cried out as Zaiana dislocated her shoulder and threw her off. Before Edith could scramble back up, Zaiana kicked her with such force it sent her careening into the wall.

Faythe had the jeweled dagger. Zaiana had to drag Edith back to the pit. Her step toward the dark fae was intercepted by Nephra.

"You're a spawn of the Nether," she spat.

"Better than being a spawn of you."

Her hand rose to conjure her lightning, but a hand wrapped around it.

Zaiana's lethal glare snapped to them, but her fight faltered at who she saw.

"Maverick," she whispered.

He was always stopping her. Always intercepting her triumphs.

"This mountain will bury us all in minutes," he said calmly. Letting her go, he walked past her, taking in the five masters and Edith on the ground.

Zaiana's emotions clashed from anger to grief. *Why grief?* As though, despite all he'd done, Zaiana still believed Maverick wasn't her enemy.

"You've always been our favored," Corrik said to him. All of the masters seemed to relax, as if their prized and ruthless savior had come.

Maverick turned back to her. She was completely outnumbered. He was the one person she'd fought enough times to know he could contend with her magick.

He said, "Which of them hurt you?"

Zaiana's thrumming heart skipped a beat.

Because he'd asked her that before. In the baths, when he'd first seen the map of scars on her back.

Zaiana's lips parted, and she whispered, "All of them."

Blue flame grew in a blink, and Maverick's twist was so fast no one could have avoided the fire that sliced like a whip in his spin, cutting through the bodies of four of the masters. They fell, torsos splitting from their lower bodies, their last wide-eyed looks of terror glazed on their wicked faces.

When Maverick straightened and turned back, he bore no emotion at all, but Zaiana was stunned, rooted to the spot. He approached her, saying close to her ear, "Snap out of it, Delegate. Last one is yours. Best make it quick. The biggest tragedy would be to see you buried in this wretched place."

The mountain roared, collapsing more rapidly by the minute. The ground shook, and Zaiana had to catch herself on the wall at the same time Maverick hooked her waist. Her eyes snapped up at the strangled sounds, finding Nephra dangling from the opening, one wing limp as if a rock had dislocated it. Edith was safely out, holding onto her mother's arm, but she didn't pull her up.

"Help me!" Nephra cried.

Zaiana snarled. *She was not getting away.* Her lighting charged, and her fingers pointed up.

"Sorry, Mother," Edith said, not in the least bit sentimental, before she let go of her mother's hand, darting out of the way as lightning shot for the opening.

It blasted into the stone, which crumbled and fell, as did Nephra.

Zaiana stumbled over the debris, dodging falling rocks. She *really* had to leave.

Nephra lay under heaps of rocks, her face bloodied, wheezing for her last breaths.

She crouched, not feeling as triumphant as she thought she would. There was no satisfaction in watching her die. Maybe there never would have been.

"Mordecai never loved you. Edith never loved you. You're dying, and there's no one coming. No one to mourn you after your last breath. No legacy left to remember you by, because I will kill Edith if it's the last thing I do."

Nephra tried to speak, but her mouth only floundered. Her chest was crushed, leaving her in an immobile state to suffer a prolonged, painful death. So when Nephra's eyes pleaded for a blade to end it quickly, Zaiana stood. She felt absolutely nothing.

Zaiana was yanked from her state of numbness by a sharp tug. Maverick pulled her out the way of a large, serrated piece of rock, which plummeted, crushing Nephra and nearly Zaiana too.

"We need to get out of here—*now*," Maverick yelled.

Instead of arguing, her hand tightened in his as they raced through the passage that caved in rapidly behind their every step. Adrenaline pumped in her chest and sharpened her senses. The gap above the pit had widened, crumbling in lethal boulders that would make it a perilous flight, but they had no other option.

As they unglamoured their wings, she released his hand and shot skyward, pivoting around the deadly rain of rocks. One slammed into Maverick, and Zaiana's heart lurched. She dropped, lashing out a hand, which caught him before he could fall too far. Luckily, the rock had hit his shoulder, not his wings, and he managed to gain his flight balance again to shoot himself out of the chaos beside her.

A stone slashed through the membrane of Zaiana's right wing, sending her tumbling back down a few beats before she could catch herself. Pain lashed over her right shoulder, spreading down her arm, but she pushed *harder*. Being buried in this mountain was a death that would haunt her soul in every lifetime.

When the icy air wrapped around her, Zaiana could breathe in relief, but she needed to find safe landing before her flight faltered with the pain growing along one side of her body. An injury to dark fae wings affected far more than just that limb.

The mountain continued to cave in, booming so loud it was all that rattled through her. She couldn't see Faythe and could only hope the heir had the sense and agility to have made it out long before now.

She watched the black rock break, the air choked with plumes of smoke and dust. The only home she'd ever known collapsed rock by rock, and she decided to bury Zaiana Silverfair in this dark tomb for eternity.

Zaiana no longer felt attached to the dark fae who'd lived there for three hundred years. She hadn't for some time. There was peace in the destruction she watched, burying the life that was never her choice nor freedom. She didn't know who she was now, nor who she wanted to be, but she turned her sight to the stars, taking her first breath of freedom, with a new will to draw many more.

She landed on a cliffside far enough away from the thundering mountains. Maverick followed her, and they caught their breath in silence for a long moment, letting the action settle.

"You need to see a healer," Maverick said at last.

She turned to find him leaning against a round rock, clutching the bicep on the side of his injured shoulder. "So do you," she said.

"I take it Nerida is with you—"

"Why did you do that?" Zaiana interrupted. "Why kill the masters?"

Maverick let a few beats of silence charge their stare. "You know why."

"No. I don't. I can't figure out what game you're playing. Whose side you're on."

"I already told you, none of this is about sides."

"That's bullshit."

He winced in pain, adjusting his position. Zaiana had drifted closer. Pain throbbed over her entire right side because of the wound to her wing, but she'd be able to fly back to High Farrow. She was glad Faythe wasn't here, for she didn't doubt the heir would attempt to kill Maverick if she saw him, and Zaiana wasn't confident he would escape her this time.

Maverick stood, which brought them near chest-to-chest. Zaiana angled her head back to hold his stare. She wished she could look away, but those onyx eyes were a trap that held her still.

When he leaned down to kiss her, it only lasted a second before she stepped back.

"Maverick—"

"I know." He cut her off. "Everything is about to end in one way or another. I just had to..." He trailed off.

"You just had to take what you wanted one last time," she said, her words intended as humor, but something inside her tugged with an ache. She couldn't stop herself from adding, "I'm going to fight with them to take down the Spirits and Mordecai once and for all. I'm counting on us winning. You can't be here when that happens. Leave, Maverick. I don't know what you've been waiting for, but if you want to live, you have to leave."

He smiled, but it was vacant. She'd never noticed before, but when Maverick wasn't exuding arrogance and hatred and bitterness...he looked *hollow*.

Zaiana's mind started spinning of its own accord, wondering if there was even a slight chance Maverick could be forgiven. But that was a fantasy. In their shared look, they both acknowledged that. He turned to walk away but paused.

"This isn't me trying to atone for what I've done. I have no regrets. Not in killing Faythe nor Agalhor. But give these to the pesky little heir who refuses to die."

Metal clanged over the rock Maverick had leaned against. Before she could see what it was, the tail blast of wind from his wings blew over her as he left. She wasn't satisfied that he was leaving so soon, but as she beheld what he'd left behind...

Zaiana's center of gravity shifted.

CHAPTER SEVENTY-ONE

Faythe

Reylan wasn't best pleased with Faythe when she returned from the Mortus Mountains and explained what they'd done to collapse it.

"I'm not mad you left," he'd said. "I'm disappointed I was left out of some great action."

They reconvened in the drawing room of High Farrow's castle again, which would become a regular routine with all the planning they had to do.

"Now I have over a hundred darklings occupying Galmire during a war when our resources for the people are already spread thin," Nik exasperated.

"They have few survival skills yet," Zaiana defended. "These are children with no parental upbringing."

Faythe added, "We don't close our borders on innocents."

"This isn't your kingdom to decide that," Nik said.

That hurt to hear, though it was the truth.

"Then what you decide to do with them is your choice," Faythe conceded.

Tauria placed a hand on his where they sat side by side. "If they were fae children seeking refuge, what would you say then?"

Nik's lips pursed, realizing his bias. "We wouldn't turn them away."

Tauria said, "How can we expect to achieve peace at the end of this if we don't break the cycle of seeing the dark fae as enemies? They were born into a war not of their choosing."

Reylan stood behind where Faythe sat. He paced and mulled over the map that covered the table, his mind on various battle movements and where to station their legions.

"According to the plans you found in Valgard, they plan to attack High Farrow at four key angles. Through the Stone Passes, the mountain fringe, through Galmire, and our spies have reported their armadas are already moving to close in from the west. Their numbers are beyond us almost four-to-one. With that force, I think they've waited all this time, all but herding us into one kingdom to make it a swift annihilation and conquer. Our numbers are shaken from the Battle of Rhyenelle. We don't have control of Olmstone's armies, which could have granted us more favorable odds."

"Do we know if Chief Zainaid is still in power?" Tarly asked.

"Our scouts say he is. But Marvellas and Dakodas have been sighted there, and they report most of the kingdom's main defenses have been taken over by dark fae leaders," Reylan informed them.

Tarly exchanged a look with Tauria, who must know this chief. He said, "If we can get completely secure information to the chief, I believe he can help us. He's on our side. When I fled Olmstone and my father was captured, the chief stepped in, pretending he wanted the throne all along, and they let him, needing someone to keep the kingdom in order. I've met with him since."

That opened a new advantage that sparked hope through the gloom of the dire odds they faced.

"Our communication into Olmstone must be completely secure then. We might have one opportunity to catch them unawares with forces blocking theirs from the north and south." Reylan leaned over her shoulder, moving various figures with different meanings around the border between High Farrow and Olmstone. He asked, "Do you have an indication of Olmstone army numbers?"

"Before everything happened, around twenty thousand souls. But I fear many might have been taken… If they're looking for fae to Transition to dark fae, best start with those with mastered combat experience."

The grim probability settled an ominous tension.

Faythe said, "We might not have their numbers, but we have me and two ruins."

Reylan's tension built within her. He wouldn't like any suggestion that put her at risk, but this was her purpose.

"We've accounted for that." Izaiah took over with a wary glance at Reylan.

Izaiah pushed a small golden ball across the table, settling it over the castle. Two gray rocks joined it. Faythe leaned in and squinted at them.

"Is that supposed to be me and the ruins?"

Izaiah looked at the markers with amusement. "Your position is uncertain for now. We don't know where Marvellas, Dakodas, or Mordecai will be. They might not be among the battle at all. Some things we can't prepare for. They are our ultimate target. Eliminate them, the battles end."

The pressure weighed on her shoulders, but she would not cower.

"You won't be alone," Reylan said, resting a hand on her shoulder and curving it around her nape. "I'm staying with you."

"You're our leading general—your position is with our soldiers," she protested.

"We're wielding that ruin together, and Zaiana will stay with us as the only other who can wield one of them. If Dakodas and Marvellas arrive together, we'll need all three of us."

Tarly asked, "We have Marvellas's ruin to kill her, but how do you plan to stop Dakodas?"

Izaiah answered. "We're still trying to figure out where the Aetherbonds are. They won't kill her, but they would make her powerless."

"I have them." Everyone's attention snapped to Zaiana who spoke.

"What do you mean you just *have them?*" Izaiah said.

"I don't think the how is as important."

"Of course it is!"

"Then make it unimportant." Her tone warned against arguing, and when she placed the metal manacles on the table, Faythe didn't care about questioning it anyway.

"How can we be sure they're the Aetherbonds?" Reylan asked skeptically.

"You're more than welcome to try them," Zaiana said.

That couldn't happen. For it would silence his magick completely and the only way to release them would be to lose what he values most in the world. *Her.*

Nerida picked one up, studying it. "I have a strong belief they're true. The markings on them are not of any language I've seen before."

They had no choice but to trust they were the real bonds when the time came.

"This is excellent," Izaiah muttered to himself, seeming lost in his own strategies.

Nerida said, "Has anyone actually seen Dakodas and Marvellas together again since they ambushed you in Rhyenelle?"

Most looked to Reylan, who was the point of all spy and scout communications.

"No. Should we be concerned?"

Nerida looked to be puzzling in her mind. "I'm not sure. Don't you find it odd though? Marvellas wanted Dakodas here with her. You'd think they would be planning together a lot. And Marvellas doesn't seem to know that Dakodas switched their ruins and betrayed her."

Tauria said, "I last saw Dakodas with Mordecai in Valgard. They looked…close."

"What if they're conspiring to betray Marvellas again?" Izaiah posed.

Faythe's mind spun with the new possibilities. "Or they already have," she said quietly, turning over the thoughts in her mind. "Marvellas told me a dark fae reign wasn't part of her vision. Think about it… Mordecai was the one who wanted to Transition Tauria, Nik, Tarly, and Opal in Olmstone, because it was he who realized Callen Osirion, a royal, Transitioned as one of the most powerful dark fae. Dakodas is the Goddess who protected the dark fae from extinction millennia ago. She's always favored them. What if she was the one who urged Marvellas to raise Mordecai when that was never part of her plan? For this—for a second Dark Age with more power behind it than ever before. Marvellas wants a world of power and peace for the fae. Dakodas wants a world dominated by dark fae."

Everyone digested Faythe's suggestion in thick silence.

"If that's true, what does that mean for us?" Tarly asked.

Faythe said, "Marvellas is vulnerable. She's not our biggest threat, but she's mine to kill."

Reylan let her go, pacing away. Faythe watched him, feeling his rising distress.

"If we assume Mordecai and Dakodas are together and this army is theirs, not Marvellas's, then we have a chance to draw Marvellas to us before the dark fae battles," Izaiah said.

"How do you plan to do that?" Zaiana asked. She'd sat in quiet observation of their battle movements beside Kyleer thus far.

Nik said, "We have a wedding."

Everyone's gaze snapped to him with the jarring suggestion. Nik grinned wide, taking Tauria's hand in his and kissing the back of it.

Faythe gasped at the sparking emerald that adorned her finger.

"You were *not* wearing that when you arrived—I would have seen it!" she exclaimed.

Tauria giggled. "We married in private before we last left High Farrow. We didn't want Zarrius or anyone who might have intentions for our thrones to find out and risk a double assassination target on us. But if one of us didn't make it with what we set out to do, we wanted to make sure, in law and in bond, our kingdoms belonged to the other."

Faythe teared up. This flutter of joy was such a gift in their dark times.

"Congratulations," Zaiana said, lacking sentiment. "But having a party for you in the middle of a war seems ridiculous."

"I get it," Kyleer said, speaking tentatively. "You want to make it appear like our guard is down and hope Marvellas will exploit our vulnerability."

"She's no fool," Zaiana countered.

"But she's desperate," Faythe said, thinking it over. "I agree it's nothing of a sure plan, but if Marvellas doesn't know Dakodas switched her ruin, then I'll draw her here with it. Use its power enough that she'll feel it."

"Excellent," Nik said, staring adoringly at Tauria, delighting in the idea of a proper ceremony for their union.

Faythe's heart filled watching them.

Even though their day would be used to lure one of their greatest threats, the memories they would capture before the chaos would be worth it. They all needed this. A moment to be with each other. To laugh and enjoy, when they didn't know who would make it to the other side of this war.

Faythe's eyes scanned the room though she knew Jakon wasn't here. She would go to the blacksmiths' again today as she'd been five times now. Her visits never lasted long. Jakon worked tirelessly, throwing his broken heart and soul into craft after craft. She didn't know what to do.

Nik stood, guiding Tauria up with him. "We have preparations to make. We'll have the wedding by week's end."

CHAPTER SEVENTY-TWO

Nikalias

It was the night before the wedding reception, and Nik had been standing by the waterfall in the Eternal Woods for some time. He thought he'd have the strength to wander through it, toward the temple, to visit Marlowe's grave…but he couldn't. Nik was in a state of denial he couldn't confront. To see her tombstone might finally break him.

He was another person who'd failed her. Nik couldn't understand how the quietest, gentlest of them all had to die. He damned fate and destiny and everything Marlowe had been burdened with.

His palms pressed into his eyes with the sting that kept coming back to them as he reflected on her life. She was one of his citizens, and he promised to honor her memory on these lands for eternity.

Sinking down on his haunches, Nik watched the yucolites chase each other. Could they have saved her? So many *what-ifs* and *maybes* plagued his thoughts, feeding the blame he harbored for not being there with her.

"I thought I'd find you here." Faythe's voice held a broken note as she approached behind him.

Nik closed his eyes with the slam of emotion that sank him to his knees in the grass. Faythe's palm slipped over his shoulder. His hand reached back to take hers. He would miss Marlowe, and the utter unfairness of her death would haunt him forever, but he couldn't fathom what Faythe was bottling inside with the loss of her dear friend.

Faythe sat down beside him. They sat with only the familiar crash of the waterfall filling the void of their silence. Then he scented the salt from her tears and heard her quiet sniff.

"How are we supposed to move on after this? We're barely holding ourselves together. We've lost time and time again, and the worst of them…" Faythe buried her face in her hands.

Her grief broke the seal he tried to keep on his. This time he didn't fight the pooling in his eyes, letting it spill freely. Nik put an arm around Faythe, and she leaned into his side.

"I don't know," he confessed.

Faythe straightened, her gold eyes split with misery and desperation. "You can't say that," she croaked. "You're the one who always has the words to pull us through."

He didn't realize his words had meant that much to her at some point or another. Nik swallowed the lump in his throat.

"We're not done facing our losses…but we also haven't experienced the best of our triumphs. We can't have, for the war is still closing in. Marlowe was so brave and resilient in every effort toward winning, so we cannot lose. For every sacrifice toward this better world, we cannot lose."

"We won't," Tauria's voice intruded softly.

Nik's chest eased from the pressure building when he turned his gaze up to her. Tauria sat on his other side. She smiled, lifting some of his burden, and he leaned in to kiss her cheek.

"She deserved so much more than she got," Tauria said, her voice hushed to keep from breaking. "Marlowe believed in me. Believed in the great queen I would become, and I can't accept that she won't be here to see she was right."

"She already did see," Faythe said quietly. "She saw the potential in all of us. Rooted for us and guided us in ways we never appreciated, and I fear…I fear I never told her enough how great *she* was."

The guilt of that speared through him too. He didn't try to recall whether he'd voiced his own appreciation and admiration to Marlowe, because no matter how many small counts he could think of, it would never be enough. Not for all she'd done. That was a tragedy he would live with forever.

"There you are." Reylan entered the clearing next.

Faythe stood as he did, meeting him in a tight, comforting embrace Nik glanced away from, helping Tauria up.

"I wanted to visit Marlowe too," Tauria said sadly. Nik squeezed her hand.

Behind Faythe and Reylan, Nerida and Tarly came through the tree line, perfectly content, and he wondered if there was no trial of fear to enter anymore now the Spirit of Life was not a guardian of their realm.

To his surprise, Kyleer, Izaiah, and Zaiana joined them. Was everyone here to pay their respects to Marlowe Kilnight?

"Thank you for coming," Faythe said, clearly having not expected the support of her friends, even those who didn't know her well.

Nik felt them all like pillars of strength. A unity that would keep fighting, keep marching on, because that was the best way to honor their lost.

Together, they walked quietly through the woodland toward the temple clearing, leaning on each other for support.

It wasn't the sight of the gravestone that weakened his knees and softened the ground he walked on; it was the lonely, lost sight of Jakon, who kneeled before it. Nik hadn't been aware the human was here, or he would have snapped out of his pitiful state to come sooner. To not have left him alone, dammit.

Nik let Tauria go, approaching ahead of the others. He couldn't begin to imagine what Jakon was feeling. Nik visualized that tombstone inscribed with Tauria's name instead, and that was enough for him to know Jakon was holding himself together better than Nik could have. He'd been quiet, keeping to himself. Everyone dealt with grief differently, and he thought silence was the most devastating display.

Nik placed a hand tentatively on Jakon's shoulder. To his relief, he didn't shrug him off. He had no words—they all felt insulting to the gravity of his grief. A condolence; a hollow promise. Nothing would ease a fraction of his pain.

"I can't be there tomorrow," Jakon said, his voice clipped.

"I understand."

"We wanted to celebrate our marriage with everyone when the war was over. At least…I was an unwitting fool in that delusion, since I think Marlowe knew we would never get there."

Marlowe's death had left so many open questions in her wake because of her gift as an Oracle. Nik himself had been reeling over memories as if he could have missed some sign that Marlowe knew her life was in danger. It sickened him to his core to imagine that kind of terror, knowing death lingered like a taunt.

"Jak…if you ever need anything…you have a home in the castle and a friend in me, always." Nik squeezed his shoulder and backed up a step.

His eyes lingered on Marlowe's name, then over the small field of bluedrops spreading around it. Tauria sniffed, hooking her arm through his and leaning her head on his shoulder. Nik cried too. The most silent wounds to cut him a thousand times within.

Faythe lowered near Jakon, not speaking, just joining in mournful silence. Reylan lingered behind her. Tarly held Nerida, who mourned for Marlowe, having gotten the privilege of knowing her for a short time.

It *was* a privilege. Nik would always carry the blessing Marlowe had brought into his life. Offering her knowledge and kindness without hesitation. The kind of soul that was lost in Marlowe…it was rare, and that made her loss all that more tragic.

Zaiana, Kyleer, and Izaiah held back, but their presence helped share the crushing weight of grief in these friends. Family. They were all equal pillars of support, and the only way they would get through what was coming was together.

CHAPTER SEVENTY-THREE

Zaiana

Zaiana couldn't place what she felt staring in the mirror. It was strange how a drastic change of attire could shift the type of person within the silk and lace. She was free to grasp her emotions now, but still they unsettled her. The prickling in her eyes fought against tears, and her mind chastised the pitiful reason she wanted to cry.

Out of joy, perhaps. If that was what the warmth in her was.

Zaiana had never cared for her beauty, but tonight she did. Because this time it was for her, no one else.

She took her time running her fingers along the deep purple accents on the black gown. The bodice hugged her torso securely since the straps offered no support, just a beautiful elegance of draped purple silk falling off her shoulders. The crystals gave her comfort with their illusion of constellations—she was wearing the night sky she loved on her body. The skirts were long and layered, transitioning from black to purple.

Zaiana wondered if she'd made a mistake in refusing any servant help to get ready for this ball. The dress was so perfect, but she didn't know how to style her hair beyond a braid for combat, so it was loose and curly, bound to annoy her throughout the night.

She knew it was past the time she'd agreed to meet the others for this. The ball should have started by now—they wouldn't hold off to wait for her. Zaiana couldn't push down the nerves over her appearance to leave her room.

Everything was foreign to her. The kingdom she was a fugitive in, the dress she wore, the feelings knotting inside her. Zaiana was about to peel herself out the dress and abandon the ball. She could brace herself from the shadows should the enemy strike like they anticipated.

A knock stiffened her spine, and Zaiana spun, taking a step to reach the door and lock it before the intruder could welcome themselves in.

She didn't get beyond that step, and there was only one person who would enter without an invitation.

Kyleer stared at her with just as much shock as she held on him.

He looked... *Spirits be damned,* every word dissipated to describe how beautiful he looked dressed up in finery. There was nothing that seemed fitting enough.

He always carried his marvelous feathered wings rising above his head. There was still time to discover if he could glamour, but so far he'd had no success. She loved his wings, having to resist the urge to run her hand along them every time he was near. He wore all-black, no crimson for his kingdom, and she wondered if he'd avoided it because he didn't know where he belonged with his memories lost.

"Zai..." Kyleer spoke her name in a lost breath.

She picked at her skirts, unfamiliar with these *nerves* coiling like a festering entity within her. Not feeling anything might have been easier, but she didn't want to go back to that cold place.

"The party started nearly an hour ago," he informed her, blinking as if breaking himself from a trance.

"I know."

Kyleer closed the door behind himself. His eyes never left her.

"You didn't have to come for me," she said.

His smile fluttered in her chest. "It's completely dull down there without you."

"It's not like I'm one to offer any life to a party."

He came closer, and her stomach tightened. "Your company is all the life I need."

Kyleer left only a few inches of space between them before brushing light fingers under her chin, forcing her to look up at him. She wasn't accustomed to this kind of tenderness, but she craved it from him.

"It's just as well you haven't come down yet," he said. "It gives the others some time to enjoy the attention before you steal it all."

Zaiana pushed his chest, intended as a nervous gesture from the outlandish compliment, but he caught her wrist, eliminating that slither of cold when he tugged her against him.

"You are the most incredible thing I've ever seen." He stole her breath with mere words. "My beautiful nightmare."

He brought his lips to hers in a single deep kiss that made her forget her tension for a moment.

Kyleer said, "I will stay with you up here if that's what you choose, but I think you'd enjoy the music, perhaps even a dance."

"I don't need you to stay with me anywhere."

Zaiana cursed herself internally. She was *trying* not to push everything away at the slightest hint she wanted it.

Kyleer only smiled again, sweeping the front of her loose hair back from her face. He fixed his arm around her more purposely while his other fingers traced down her arm, breaking a shiver. He took her hand in his, raising them, and she flushed with his intention.

"Will you dance with me, Zai?"

"There's no music here."

Kyleer slackened his hold only to pull her toward the balcony. The winter air was sharp, but she was distracted by the music she heard distantly when he opened the doors. Piano and strings wove a melody through the crisp night, and her senses opened to it, craving more.

"Now there is," he said, resuming their stance.

Zaiana was overcome with emotion, wanting to hold onto him so tightly when anything precious had a habit of slipping away from her. Of dying. She'd watched Kyleer die once, and it had been the worst moment of her existence, and now the price of loving him was to live with this festering, terrible fear that he could leave her in one way or another and rip half her heart away with him.

Her thoughts rewound, replaying one terrifying but exhilarating confession.

She loved him.

Zaiana stopped their gentle swaying, letting him go abruptly.

"Is my dancing really that bad?"

She shook her head, latched onto his moss-green irises and falling through them. "You're perfect," she whispered.

She fell so fast and deeply there was no stopping it now. No amount of denial could spread her wings to stop this plummet. Because *he* became her wings. With the ability to let her go and watch her shatter beyond repair, or hold her tight and fly through eternity with her.

Zaiana believed love truly made fools out of people.

She turned, lifting her skirts and jumping up onto the balcony's stone ledge. Her leather pants in preparation for battle at a moment's notice kept the chill from sweeping under her dress. When she turned back to him, Kyleer jerked forward, his eyes wide with shock and concern.

"What are you doing?"

"Testing whether you'll let me fall."

Zaiana had lost her sanity, casting her arms out and tipping back into gravity's claim.

Her hair and dress billowed around her, and the air wrapped her tightly. Her mind, body, and soul were at complete peace without her wings, anticipating the strong arm that curved around her middle, slowing her descent, before scooping her legs, cradling her body.

Their faces were so close. Kyleer's rugged features softened against the moonlight.

"Never," he said, pressing his lips to hers.

Euphoria beat in her chest as he carried them higher and higher. She didn't want this feeling to end, holding it dear in her chest for times when he wasn't near to breathe life into it.

Zaiana glanced over the landscape that glimmered beneath them. She'd flown countless times, and yet there was something new, magickal, about the sight below her now. It was all because of who she shared it with.

On the outskirts of Farrowhold, fire flew through the air. *What a peculiar type of celebration*, she thought. Were the humans in the outer town juggling torches? Had a small circus come to join the Yulemas and wedding celebration?

It was only a couple at first, but more joined. Then the pattern of flames darting through the air began to make a formation.

Zaiana's body stiffened.

"Are you cold?" Kyleer asked, thinking that was the reason for her tension as she watched the score of amber fire over his shoulder.

"High Farrow has been infiltrated," Zaiana said. Her wings unglamored, and she let go of Kyleer. Now she knew what she was looking at—*fire arrows*—the situation turned worse.

Squinting, she could vaguely make out the bodies moving in the darkness. It was impossible to tell numbers, to see if this was just another test of their defenses, though it was concerning they'd gotten this close, within Farrowhold, without Reylan's scout regimen reporting back.

"We have to alert Reylan," Kyleer said.

Zaiana nodded, falling into a dive toward the castle.

She tore off her skirt in her rooms, though it kind of disappointed her to do so. She hadn't made it to the ball, yet she'd danced with Kyleer in their own bubble away from the world, and that was worth more than any lavish party. She swiped up her sword belt, fixing it to her back as they ran through the halls.

Guards directed them to where Faythe Ashfyre and the others were. In lucky timing, they'd stepped away from the ballroom for a moment.

The reception room they found them in was bright with laughter as the company sat and stood around the fire, clearly lost in the throes of friendship. Reylan was the first to notice their disruption, standing from the arm of the chair Faythe sat on and setting his cup on the mantel.

"We're under attack," Zaiana said, then she explained what she'd seen.

Everyone wore attire quickly changeable for combat, with dress skirts detaching to reveal leather pants, while the males wore more combat-ready formal attire anyway. Their weapons were stashed in this room. They'd been prepared for a potential ambush, only they'd expected Marvellas herself, not an odd attack on the town's outskirts.

Reylan directed several guards, setting certain protocols in motion.

"I'm going to retrieve the ruin," Faythe said.

Zaiana nodded, skimming her eyes to the occupied general while Faythe slipped out.

"Where do you want me?" Zaiana asked Reylan.

It was just as surprising for her to request to be stationed, and even he lifted an eyebrow at her.

"We have a small Rhyenelle legion stationed on the east outskirts. They have a commander, but they could use a general, and you'd get there fastest."

Zaiana had led many legions before in far more ruthless battles, so she didn't know why it felt like *pride* that fluttered in her fragile heart. The world really was ending if she was growing a mutual respect— dare she say, *a potential friendship?*—with Reylan Arrowood.

"Of course." She accepted the position with a nod before heading out.

"Take Kyleer with you," he called.

Kyleer jogged up to her, and she welcomed the experienced company.

She'd trained with him since being here, and they'd discovered that when Kyleer was faced with something he was a natural at, it slowly came back to him in practice, like the many attack and defense sequences he knew.

Before she got to the door, however, the person who sauntered in through it made her halt.

Rainyte Ashfyre.

They thought they'd seen the back of him when Reylan informed them he'd gone to the mirrors below the castle. Yet here he was, to her irritation, still wearing the face of Captain Daegal. What was more concerning was how he pushed Jakon in with him.

"You're still here?" Reylan said, his tone dark with distrust.

"Unfortunately so. I wish you would all at least pretend to be glad to see me."

"Why?" Zaiana asked, just as on edge.

"Well, considering I helped Faythe in her cell, and I'm all but the reason you escaped Lakelaria, a little appreciation would—"

"Why are you still here?" Zaiana bit out.

Nyte sighed, slipping a hand into his pocket. They didn't have time for this distraction.

"The creature in the mirrors—a Dresair?—is a pesky, tormenting thing. It said if I tried to cross while I had unfinished business here, my mind would never return to my body. My passage isn't the same as when I first Realm-Walked since my mind is separated. It was enough doubt that I wouldn't make it back to my realm that I reconsidered my time here."

"Why have you dragged Jakon here?" Izaiah asked, edging closer to the human as if Nyte might lunge to use Jakon as a hostage.

"The Dresair shared an interesting piece of insight. From my observations, I'm assuming he's important to Faythe Ashfyre." He turned his attention to Jakon. "Show them."

Jakon's stare was absolutely lethal on Nyte, and she had to pity the human who knew he was powerless here. Jakon produced something from the inside of his jacket, and when the cloth was removed, Zaiana stared at the blade in shock.

It was made from a ruin, and the longer she listened to its whispers, she felt strongly that it was Marvellas's.

"All of you are so eager to die the hero," Nyte sang.

Jakon had stolen the ruin. *When* he'd done so wasn't important. Did this human really think he could be the one to get close enough to kill Marvellas with it?

"Here we were, planning to run it through her heart blunt," Izaiah said, taking the blade from Jakon. "This is nice work."

"You're a damned fool," Zaiana muttered vacantly. She didn't stare at the ruin crafted into a blade with anything but foreboding. "How long have you been slamming into that ruin to reshape it?"

"Since Faythe got it from Reuben," Jakon said. Everything about him was so cold and detached. There was a part of her that sympathized with his loss, but it had made him thoughtless.

Zaiana cast a glance over the others, who watched her with question. "Marvellas has known since then that her ruin is still intact. She's known since then exactly where it is. I've felt its power in pulses too, though I didn't realize what it was until now."

The silence that fell slammed with realization.

Izaiah said, "Then why hasn't she come for it yet?"

That was the question that raced Zaiana's heart. Why indeed.

"We need to deal with this attack," Reylan said. He looked around the room, realizing Faythe wasn't here.

"She went to retrieve the ruin. She'll panic when she finds Marvellas's missing," Zaiana said.

They'd been training with Aurialis's ruin and had kept both of them separate.

"I'm going to her," Reylan said, leaving the room.

Izaiah asked Jakon, "Why did you do this?"

"Marlowe left the blueprint. I figured it had to be done, though it wasn't easy."

Why would the Oracle leave instruction to turn the ruin into a blade? For ease to plunge it into the Spirit's heart? Their fae strength could have achieved it without the point.

"We don't have time for this right now," Zaiana said. Before she left for her station, she warned the others, "Marvellas doesn't need an army to infiltrate this place. If this attack is part of Dakodas and Mordecai's planning, she might very well use the distraction to slip in and retrieve that ruin dagger."

CHAPTER SEVENTY-FOUR

Faythe

Faythe hurried down the hall, bursting into the library with the intention of heading down into the underground, where she'd given Aurialis and Marvellas's ruin to the Dresair for safeguarding.

She didn't get as far as the passage behind the hidden door.

Shock stumbled her steps to a halt with the bold, lone sight of Marvellas standing in her path. The Spirit didn't wear the same cruel malice on her face. In fact, it was chilling how little she showed at all.

Faythe firmed her stance. Magick pricked her skin in anticipation, and her hand inched toward Lumarias. Marvellas just stood there, no ruby gown. She wore black attire more fit for combat. Her hair wasn't as perfect as usual, with flyaway hairs and a dull flatness to it now. She'd always been as proud and blazing as the sun, but now it was like an eclipse had masked her brilliance.

"Hello, Faythe," she said. Even her tone was jarring, not the song of taunts she was used to. There was a broken note now.

"Have you come to take me?" she asked as the only conclusion she could draw.

"No. I see now there is no world where you and I will be together. Nor me and my son. I see now…there is no world worth saving at all."

They'd spent weeks preparing for the inevitable confrontation with Marvellas. They'd trained their minds and bodies, ready for a catastrophic fight to kill her.

Yet this was far from what Faythe expected.

"What is your plan now?" Faythe asked carefully, not dropping her guard for a second.

Marvellas wasn't armed with any weapon, but she didn't need mortal steel. Still, nothing about her demeanor threatened an attack. Her golden eyes weren't as blazing—they were...sad. So terribly sad.

"I'm going to fix everything," Marvellas said.

"What does that mean?"

"That I failed. As a guardian of your realm. As a mother. Then as a savior. I know what Dakodas has done. I know her ruin is broken, not mine. I should have seen her betrayal coming, even long before she joined me on land. She has been working toward a new Dark Age. That is my failure, and Aurialis was right in trying to stop me...to stop her."

Faythe couldn't believe what she was hearing. It wasn't quite an admittance of wrongdoing, but it felt close to a surrender.

She squared her defense, waiting for the trick. "Why would you say this now?" Faythe accused.

"There is nothing left for me to do. I was wrong in thinking Mordecai's forces are mine. They answer to Dakodas now. My son... he will not see me. He does not want to know me. And you...you despise me, and I can hardly bear to look at you with how much I want to change that. I realize now it will never be."

Faythe wanted to torch the pity that rose in her with the defeated sight of the Spirit of Souls. The Goddess of their stars. All she'd known was Marvellas as her vicious enemy. So she didn't know how to respond to this version who showed vulnerability.

This wasn't her surrender...it couldn't be.

A chill so icy began to creep over her skin. "What are you going to do?"

"End the world's suffering. I will stop this war. None of you will have to lose another loved one again...your souls will fall as one. There is no greater eternity for you all. You won't see right now, but this is my last blessing to you. My atonement for all I've done."

End the world.

That was all Faythe heard.

Her thoughts spun with how such a catastrophe could be achieved. "How?"

"All I need is the Light Temple Ruin. Once I place it into the podium of the Temple of Darkness, the opposite clash will break apart the world enough for me to use myself in my own temple. Placing my power back into the podium in place of the ruin will incite the final collapse."

Horror doused her. They had been fools to think Marvellas hadn't come until now because she was afraid of their defenses. She didn't care about her own ruin anymore. She didn't need it for this new catastrophic course of action.

Faythe pulled Lumarias free with a song of determination. "This is my world. And I won't let you destroy it because you couldn't get what you wanted."

Marvellas's jaw worked, bringing back a flicker of her frightening resolve. "This world is in a state of ruins. I am *liberating* all the souls upon this wretched land. It is a mercy in place of the horrors you will face to no end. You cannot win this war against Dakodas and Morde- cai. And I cannot bear witness to a world shrouded in darkness and blood."

"Then leave," Faythe seethed. "Let us fight. Let us lose, if that is our fate. It is what we *choose*, and I won't let you take that from us."

"Oh, my dear. Your brave, resilient heart will always fight, but it is tired. I didn't expect your acceptance, but it is what I must do. And though you will not thank me, I'm doing it for you."

"No. You're doing this because you *lost*. But I have not. While I still stand, I have not lost."

Faythe threw out a flare of light as a distraction while she lunged with her sword. Marvellas deflected her magick but lost her in the light, which granted Faythe the opening to slice with her blade. Marvellas cried out at the cut along her arm, twisting just in time to avoid Faythe's path to her torso next.

Twisting, she lowered to avoid Marvellas's whip of light that cut deep through a bookcase behind her instead. Faythe winced at the scars she had to make in this library, but Marvellas had to be stopped.

Faythe ran down the aisle of books. As Marvellas followed, Faythe's magick wrapped around the bookcase to her left, and she strained with the force it took to pull it down. The heavy case groaned as it toppled. Marvellas cast her sight up as heavy books rained down on her. Faythe jumped, rolling at the end to avoid being trapped under the mountain of books and the wooden case that slammed into the one beside it with a resounding boom.

More started to topple, and Faythe pained over the destruction of such a gentle and sacred space.

"You always were so ungrateful," Marvellas hissed, so close Faythe didn't expect it.

An impact slammed into her chest, soaring her body through the air before she crashed into something hard.

Faythe felt a sharp, forceful intrusion trying to pierce her mind. She coughed dust from her throat, blinking through the clouds of the wooden wreckage she lay in. Her skin cut on broken pieces, but all her focus rushed to enforce her mental barrier.

"If you won't tell me where the ruin is, I'll find it for myself," Marvellas said, so calm, creeping closer.

Faythe was slow to defend her body while she focused on guarding her mind. Marvellas's magick wrapped around her, lifting her from the rubble and holding her to the wall.

The closer she approached, the more intense her drilling into Faythe's mind became. Pain screamed through her head—she could hardly see straight—but she didn't give up. Marvellas's eyes glowed brighter, piercing into hers so acutely she felt herself close to passing out.

"Join us," Faythe wheezed out. The pressure in her mind eased a fraction. Faythe scrambled to keep her attention. "Help us defeat Dakodas and Mordecai. That is how you atone for what you've done."

"My actions are not forgivable."

"You're wrong. All you've done, all your evils, they're from a place of pain. Something all of us have let consume us before. It doesn't have to be the end for you."

Marvellas eased off her mind a little more, and Faythe thought maybe she was considering Faythe's proposition. Until her eyes hardened, narrowing on Faythe with renewed resentment.

"Lies can be so pretty," she said, then she stabbed into Faythe's mind with more force than before, so her barrier shattered completely, stunning Faythe into a state of complete stillness.

She didn't feel anything. Not Marvellas's intrusion nor the aches of her body. Faythe's mental guard was stronger than anyone's, and having her resistance broken sent her into a place of complete numbness, staring into the molten surface of the sun. She drowned in fire that did not burn.

"Mortal life is but a violent struggle. Generations trapped in this cycle of survival. This is how I will free humanity from the slavery of its own greed. I will break the cycle. I will break the world, and maybe your souls will have a better chance in a new one."

The power holding her body up released, but Faythe didn't feel her body crumple like a piece of the wreckage she lay within. The sun left her behind, leaving her staring into dull nothingness that coaxed her to close her eyes. Just to sleep for a little while. Until the sun might rise again.

CHAPTER SEVENTY-FIVE

Reylan

Reylan marched through the halls, irritated with himself that he'd been so focused on his duty he hadn't noticed Faythe slipping out. The thought of any of them wandering alone right now made him antsy.

A phantom lashing of pain within pushed Reylan into a sprint.

He followed the instinctual trace of her through their bond, entering the library. The destruction he found surged his urgency. He yelled her name, darting frantically through the piles of books and broken cases to find her. She was here—he could feel her.

Reylan became frantic in his search, catching the scent of her blood.

Then he saw her. A beautiful devastation as she lay among wreckage.

He lifted her into his arms, but she was out cold. Still breathing steadily, to his relief. Reylan scanned around for what she could have battled to have caused this destruction, but he sensed nothing else here with them.

As he began to make his way out of the library with her to seek a healer, Faythe stirred.

"It was…" Her words were heavy, with her consciousness returning fleetingly. "We have to stop her."

"Stop who?"

Her golden eyes fluttered open, lost in her recollection of what had happened. Fear struck him to see the emotions play out on her face.

"Marvellas is here," she said with terror.

Reylan stiffened. "She left you?"

They'd believed Marvellas's two main objectives when she came would be to secure Faythe and her ruin. So the fact she'd faced Faythe, fought her, and left her, riddled him with dread.

Faythe's eyes cast up to him, and she tried to move but cried in pain.

"Keep still," he said gently, holding her tighter and leaving the library.

He had to inform the others Marvellas was within their walls.

"She's going for the Light Ruin. Reylan...she knows where it is from my thoughts, but we can't let her get it. She has a plan far more detrimental than any of us thought."

Faythe's breath was labored, and her head fell back. Reylan's concern raced faster. Her body had some cuts and bruises, no broken bones. She shouldn't be in this much pain. Reylan had to stop, setting her down on the floor with her back to the wall. He kneeled, holding her head from falling, and scanned her face. Her eyes drifted to his, lazy and unfocused. A concussion? No—something more serious. Marvellas had broken through Faythe's otherwise impenetrable mental walls, and she was suffering what would be like tenfold of a concussion.

They needed a healer—fast. And she would need rest.

"Stay with me, Phoenix," he said, scooping her up again.

"I have to stop her."

"The others will. You've done your part."

"I let her get away..."

"You bought us time."

Reylan made it back to the reception room the others were last in. Nik, Tauria, Nerida, Jakon, Tarly, and Nyte were still here.

His anger flashed at the sight of Marvellas's son.

"What happened?" Nik demanded.

Reylan lay Faythe gently on the chaise, sweeping back her hair as her eyes struggled to remain open. Nerida immediately assessed Faythe, even though she had no magick, she instructed to be brought her medicines and Nik called for a guard to fetch another healer.

With her in safe hands, his distrust and anger over Faythe's condition got the better of him. Reylan moved fast and sudden, gabbing Nyte by his clothing and slamming him to the wall.

"Marvellas is in the castle. She's heading for the ruin," Reylan informed the others. He kept his eyes piercing into Nyte, his accusation not subtle.

Nyte said, calm but warning, "Remove your hands from me before you find yourself without them."

Reylan held on a little longer, testing their battle of dominance. He'd be a fool to underestimate what Nyte was capable of, even without his own body.

He released him roughly, pacing back to Faythe.

Nyte said bitterly, "Honestly, I couldn't care less about any of you. I would have left if my way home was sure, because frankly, aiding people who continue to doubt me is pissing me off."

"You're the son of the person who began this war. You appeared out of nowhere, only half here at that. You can't expect us to trust you," Reylan seethed.

"The irony is...your distrust is what risks making a greater enemy out of me. So make your choice, because the next one to question me turns my wrath on all of you. Perhaps my *unfinished business* is not to help you but to make sure you fall. And make no mistake, I would have no hesitation in doing so."

"You only prove why we should keep our guards up," Tarly said.

Nyte shrugged, reiterating, "It is your choice."

"I trust you," Tauria said. When she met the wary stare of Nik, she added, "We are not our parents. From what we've heard, what he's done for us so far, we owe him this trust."

"I agree," Nerida said. "I don't think we would have made it out of Lakelaria without his help. I trust him."

"Good," Nyte said. "Be glad you have the sharper sense of your mates to guide you."

He crossed to Jakon in a few quick strides, and everyone tensed. Nyte paused, casting a flat look over them all for the reaction contrary to Tauria and Nerida's words. Nyte swiped the dagger from Jakon, who protested.

Nyte used it as a pointer as he spoke. "Did you plan to pass this around yourselves until the unfortunate soul last holding it in front of Marvellas was the one to sacrifice their life?" No one answered. They hadn't addressed that dire fact. "Luckily for all of you, I'm here. Without a body that's mine, and with someone who can transfer a consciousness." His eyes fell to Faythe with that. She was hardly present in the conversation, but her brow twitched, seeming to understand what Nyte spoke of.

"So you're going to kill your mother?" Nik hedged.

"When Faythe is in full health to make sure my mind doesn't die with this body, yes. Right before the body dies from the power, if we have another vessel, Faythe should be able to transfer me into it."

Maybe Reylan was feeling an inkling of guilt for how he'd treated Nyte, given he might turn out to be their savior, but he wasn't going to give him full merit yet.

"It's brilliant," Nerida said with wonder.

"We need to stop Marvellas retrieving the Light Ruin from the Dresair," Nik urged.

"I'm going with you," Tauria said.

Reylan knew all too well the conflict that passed over Nik's face: knowing she was capable and her magick was invaluable, but fearing to be with her in the face of great danger. The king nodded at his mate.

"I can still wield a blade," Nerida said. "You'll need all the help you can get."

"I'm not much use, but the wolves are," Tarly said.

Just then, the two white beasts entered the room as if they could manifest from Tarly's mere thoughts.

"You don't have time to debate. The more people against her, the better. It's pressure and distraction. Don't let her leave with that ruin," Reylan ordered.

The group didn't falter, and all he could do was pray for their safety. Nyte left with them, though he wouldn't risk trying to kill Marvellas with the ruin while Faythe wasn't there. All they needed was to make sure the Spirit never got her hands on the ruin to be able to take it to Dakodas's temple in the Fire Mountains.

He instructed a guard to seek any healer within the castle while he sat with Faythe. Reylan didn't like being helpless and idle while his comrades were in action, but Faythe was his highest priority while she was vulnerable.

He looked over his mate, and it helped to soothe his sharp emotions punishing him for being too late to help her.

Jakon sat by the wall. Occasionally, his eyes would flick over Faythe, and Reylan wanted to believe her friend still cared deeply for her with his twitches of concern.

"You don't have any idea why Marlowe would leave instruction to craft the ruin into a blade?" Reylan gently tried.

Jakon shrugged. It was clear only the shell of the man sat here without his wife.

"Makes the killing blow easier, I guess."

Reylan stroked Faythe's thigh absentmindedly, selfishly needing to ease his own anxiety at the thought of being here without her. He couldn't fathom Jakon's grief.

"I can't express how sorry I am——"

"Yeah." Jakon cut him off.

Reylan didn't take any offense to the brush-off. His condolence meant nothing.

"She still needs you. You know that, right?" Reylan said.

Jakon's hollow gaze lifted to Faythe again. "'Need' isn't the right word. She thinks she owes me something. I'm her guilty conscience."

"You're wrong."

Jakon's expression turned sour. "You might be her mate and all, but I've known her longer."

Reylan didn't argue that fact. His soul had entwined with Faythe's centuries ago, but Jakon was right. In this life, he did have the blessing of knowing her far longer.

"War is too unpredictable to push away those you love."

"Exactly. Unpredictable. One day you're kissing your wife good night with a promising tomorrow. Then that tomorrow comes to snap her neck right in front of your eyes."

Reylan's jaw clenched to that brutal truth. He hadn't had the time to get to know Faythe's dearest friend well, but for what he meant to her, for all he'd done for her, Reylan harbored pain and grief for Jakon's suffering as though they were good friends themselves. He hoped they would be in time.

"You can't bury Faythe before she's even dead," Reylan said.

"Maybe I'm burying myself." He looked at the ground, the confession leaving him like it hadn't meant to slip out of his thoughts.

Reylan said, "So long as we're around, we're not going to let that happen."

CHAPTER SEVENTY-SIX

Zaiana

Z aiana arrived while the outskirt legion was forming their lines for the impending attack from the east. She surveyed the small field, rearranging the formations in her mind before she swooped down.

A rogue arrow fired in blind fear whizzed for her. Zaiana's body twisted in the air, grabbing the arrow stick before she landed in a graceful crouch. Her eyes flashed up, finding the archer, who quivered with wide eyes on her. He fumbled for another arrow before Kyleer's voice called out with sharp wrath.

"Stand down."

They knew him at least. Though their armies had been informed about her and other potential dark fae allies like Tynan and Amaya, who accompanied her now, this soldier was nothing but an inexperienced, reckless fool.

Zaiana said, loud enough to catch the front lines, "If anyone else is prone to firing so thoughtlessly, lay down your bow now and move to the back of the lines before you get yourself, or a comrade, killed in a heartbeat."

The soldier who tried to strike her was pulled out by a commander, stripped of his bow, and led away. No one else moved.

Folding her arms behind her, Zaiana surveyed the front line. "My name is Zaiana. I am your general, and you will answer to me without question. Once again, if anyone has a problem with that, step out now."

No one moved. In fact, to her satisfaction, most squared their stances. Focused. Determined. Ready to abide by her leadership. This was a Rhyenelle legion, and they had the utmost loyalty and belief in Reylan Arrowood. By his word, they were choosing to stake their belief in her to lead them through this battle. She had expected more resistance and fear, but she was glad to have charge of a predominantly fierce legion. It was a small force compared to what she'd led before for the dark fae, but better than numbers was the strength and skill of these warriors.

Zaiana's advantage in this fight was that she knew the enemy. Had fought among them and knew the ways of every dark fae attack strategy. The commanders listened to her instruction, and with expert swiftness, their lines were reorganized, the arches better instructed, along with spearmen for the likelihood of aerial attacks. She quickly schooled them on the weakest parts of the wings, which would incapacitate dark fae more efficiently.

Though she was leading an attack against her kind, these were not her people. She'd announced herself clearly from her actions under the mountain before she collapsed it. Word would have spread through the dark fae ranks, and it was their choice whether to believe and join her, or brand her a traitor and face her on the field.

This war would bring to light once and for all that it had never been one species against another. It was power against power, a clash of vision and belief, different perceptions of the world they wanted to live in.

Izaiah had come with them, helping pass her orders through the other commanders. He was another highly respected leader these soldiers turned to for guidance.

"You're magnificent," Kyleer commented when she stood alone, assessing the soldiers for the third time. The enemy would be upon them any minute now.

"You don't need to flatter me," she said, strolling down the front line.

"Just admiring."

Kyleer's hand slipped across her lower back, and he stopped her pace by tugging her to him.

"This is distracting and inappropriate for the soldiers to witness," she said, but her tone was enticing of its own accord.

"We're about to face a whole lot of fighting and bloodshed—we're granted a little distraction. As for the soldiers...I don't really care." His lips came down on hers, hard and needy.

The kiss was short, but it stole her breath. She craved him so much it was both annoying and glorious.

"They're here!" a scout called.

Zaiana slipped into her battle calm and focus in an instant. To fight at her best she had to disregard everything around her.

She spoke loud enough for many around to hear, and the rest would carry her words back. "On this field, you do not falter. On this field, you prevail. Your heart knows what it fights for, so listen to it roar, and death will not stop you today."

Tynan stepped up to her side. "Never thought we'd be fighting our kin."

Zaiana raised her chin with a deep, sure breath. "I did."

She pulled her blade free. The cry of it sang to her battle senses before it sliced, sharp and precise, through the neck of the first dark fae to descend for her. Then all she knew was her blade, her lightning, and the field that began to splatter with its first drops of red and black blood.

It was morbid for her to be enjoying herself. Killing was in her nature, and she was not ashamed of it. She darted through the relentless charge of bodies, using only her sword for now. Zaiana had missed the adrenaline that raced in her chest and released through every swing of her arms, twist of her body, and shift of her feet in a dance so exhilarating she was lost to the world beyond.

She felt unstoppable. A stroke of shadow reaping through the masses before they ever saw her coming. Her smaller size was an asset to the brutes who clumsily swung and lunged, allowing her to maneuver around them like the wind, felling them as she passed and did not falter onto the next.

Zaiana liked to count, and by the time she'd reached her twenty-sixth body and his head had rolled from his shoulders, she decided it was time to make it storm.

She'd been charging lightning through her body since she began fighting, and with a battle cry, she released it to surge through her metal-guarded fingertips, which she pressed into the ground. It roared across the ground in a line that broke the land through the enemy hoard, tripping them, seizing them with her bolts, slowing and breaking their formations.

"Impressive," a Rhyenelle commander named Fareman said. He smiled at her, only pausing for a second before he yelled for his comrades to join him, surging forward to push into the weakened enemy.

In all her years of fighting, she'd never experienced such a thing. A moment suspended in the thick of vicious fighting to acknowledge one another. A single boost of encouragement and loyalty.

Zaiana had done enough here, and the commanders were taking over the front lines. She unglamoured her wings, taking to the skies to get a new gauge of the field.

They were winning. The dark fae numbers were dwindling, and what remained became uncertain and frantic. She didn't welcome triumph yet. She knew firsthand how fast the odds could shift by something unexpected.

Amaya was in flight, spinning and twisting through the air while nocking her bow again and again. Zaiana had never seen another use the weapon so expertly while flying. It was admirable. She watched her with pride, and maybe it wasn't the most appropriate time to get distracted, but Zaiana couldn't help but to reflect on how far the darkling had come from the timid, uncertain thing she'd taken into her circle. Zaiana actually welcomed the excitement to see how far Amaya could continue to grow in confidence and skill. She could be a leader herself someday.

Tynan fought in the sky with her. His blade stopped any from getting too close to Amaya, and Zaiana actually *smiled*, recalling how stubborn he'd been to accept her into their group at first, yet over time, he'd protected Amaya more fiercely than even she from the bond that had grown between them.

Zaiana thought she heard water. Like waves gathering, rolling, preparing to crash against rocks. Through the dark night, the moonlight shimmered, and Zaiana realized she wasn't mistaken—only, this was nothing of nature.

She yelled a warning below, but it was futile against the brutal wave of water that came rushing over them all. It hit mostly their side but sacrificed a few lines of the enemy.

An acute rage overcame Zaiana, who knew exactly who the conjurer of that magick-induced water attack would be. Her eyes darted through the sky then the ground, blade poised and magick humming.

But Edith already had her pinned.

An arm of water slammed into her, and Zaiana lost her flight. She tried to reorient, but she cried out when the water that drenched her turned to sharp ice, piercing her skin. Her wings were locked frozen, and she was plummeting in a fatal fall.

Kyleer caught her, but Zaiana couldn't move. They landed away from the thick of the fighting, and Zaiana willed her lightning to the surface of her skin. It thawed the ice slowly, but Edith was already upon them. She watched with fear pounding in her chest as Edith moved fast, striking toward Kyleer, who stood in her way to Zaiana. Kyleer used his shadows to defend, creating plumes and sheets of rolling darkness that stopped the flow of Edith's water attacks.

Zaiana wasn't frozen stiff anymore, but she was so cold it made movement difficult still.

Until a circle of blue flame was cast around her, and Zaiana gasped, caught unawares by the new adversary. She stood, and while she firmed her guard, searching through the tall, flickering tendrils of cobalt, she was glad for the heat. Flexing her fingers and rolling her arms, the fire relaxed her body, though it trapped her in a lethal circle.

Then she saw him.

Maverick Blackfair.

He stared at her through the flames he'd ignited around her. His expression bore nothing at all. No loathing. No taunting. Though one thing was clear in their exchange: they were fighting on opposing sides in this battle.

"You've promised to kill me many times, Zaiana," he called over the chaos of fighting close by and the crackling of his fire. "Maybe this time you'll actually have the guts to follow through."

He was goading her. Zaiana didn't know why she was conflicted facing him now. Her focus was split between the threat of Maverick and concern for Kyleer, who was still battling Edith.

Zaiana had thought over many things since the revelation came about her father. She hadn't cared to mention it before, convinced it didn't matter or perhaps too afraid of how the truth could hurt her, but now she could use it as a distraction. "You've known who I truly am all this time," she accused calmly.

Maverick stalked closer. His cold expression never flickered. "That you are the daughter of Mordecai Vesaria? Not all this time, but I suspected for a while."

"When?"

She recalled the day Mordecai had visited the mountains and Maverick had goaded her into starting a fight.

I knew that if you attacked first, you would be far less likely to be given a death sentence than I.

Because he knew she was too valuable—not out of skill but a heritage she was kept in the dark from.

Her jaw tightened. "Why didn't you tell me?" she asked bitterly. Why did it *hurt* her that he'd kept that suspicion a secret?

"Because he didn't deserve you. He didn't deserve to claim any piece of you. The way he watched you every time he visited was like one would watch while sharpening their prized blade. If you knew who your father was, you might have doubted that all you became was because of yourself."

She didn't understand… How could he talk like he cared for her yet side against her at every turn?

"Why are you still fighting for them?" Her tone quieted as if they might share a secret. "You gave us the Aetherbonds and if they discover that betrayal they'll kill you."

He'd killed most of the masters yet he still fought on their side. He spoke of Mordecai like he didn't hold esteem for him, yet he stood among *his* ranks.

"You have to leave," she whispered, pleading now with how dread for him began to fester inside her the more times she saw him. But somehow she knew he wouldn't flee until this war was over one way or another.

Maverick came to the edge of his ring of fire. The cobalt marched in his irises, bringing back the color they once were as Callen Osirion, the Prince of Dalrune.

He reached a hand through the flames toward her face. Before he could touch her, darkness pummeled into him, and the ring of fire was extinguished around her. Maverick was thrown sideward, and Kyleer was upon him again in seconds.

The two of them clashed fire and darkness, and Zaiana was about to intervene when she remembered Kyleer had taken his sights off his mark. She honed her focus on the loose threat of Edith right before a spear of ice shot for her. Zaiana leaped into the sky with her wings to avoid it, sending a powerful stroke of lightning toward Edith in the same breath. With the water gathered in her palms, Zaiana's lightning hit Edith more powerfully with the added conduction. Her half-sister couldn't catch herself in time before she slammed into a tree, falling to her hands and knees.

Zaiana dropped down in front of her while she panted and trembled with the aftershocks. "You cannot contend with me," Zaiana said icily.

She used her lightning to strike Edith's chest, forcing her into a sitting position against the tree as their eyes blazed into each other. Zaiana retrieved the blade to take back Nerida's power.

"You've stolen something that doesn't belong to you," she said, twirling the small jeweled blade between her fingers.

"Wait," Edith said, fear filling her eyes as she recognized her death approaching. "We're sisters. We're supposed to look out for each other. I have this power now and won't pursue yours. We can make our father proud together."

Zaiana smiled, but there was nothing kind in it. "One of the most important things I've learned is that blood doesn't always make family. And you've stolen from someone in mine."

Edith's expression turned so dark Zaiana realized then her surrender was far from true. She attacked, fast and precise. Lightning crashed into water, and Edith was quick to learn to let go of the water before the lightning could conduct through to her body.

They came into close combat, clashing daggers. One to steal power; one to claim it back. The magickal blades chimed off each other, emitting a screech that made her wince, gritting her teeth with the surges of opposing energy that didn't want to meet.

Edith's sight cast over her head, and a water spear formed in her hand. The distraction gave Zaiana her opening, aiming the dagger for her heart.

Just as the blade plunged through her chest, an arrow sank though the center of her neck. Zaiana's heart slammed.

"No," she breathed, lowering Edith's body as it fell limp in her arms. The jeweled dagger hissed, and a blue essence swirled around it, absorbing Nerida's power, but Edith was dying quickly. "Not yet," Zaiana growled.

The blue light began to slow with Edith's last choked breaths. Then it stopped. Zaiana pulled the dagger free, unsure if all of Nerida's magick had been taken back or if Edith had died too soon.

She let go of Edith's body, taking in her wide, dark eyes held on the tree canopy. She had to pity her at least, knowing the madness of wanting to prove herself, especially to the wicked father they shared. Zaiana closed her lids and stood, feeling nothing for the half-sister she'd lost.

"Zaiana."

The quiet call of her name made every muscle in her body stiffen. Whirling around, her eyes fell on Amaya on her knees.

Amaya's green eyes lifted to her, and it was then she saw the spear of ice protruding from her chest with her small hand around it, drowned in silver blood.

Zaiana collapsed in front of her, assessing the wound and trying to smother her panic.

"You're okay," Zaiana said. *Gods*, how she hated the taste of lies.

The icicle was thick, so close to her heart that it might have pierced it. Amaya's terror-filled eyes pleaded to be saved, but Zaiana didn't have that power.

"Stay with me, Amaya. That's an order."

She still clutched her bow, another arrow resting to be fired. Amaya was so quick, so skilled and brilliant, and she couldn't *die* like this.

"Don't move. If it was in your heart, it would have killed you instantly. If we can get a healer here before the ice melts, you'll be just fine."

Zaiana started to calm, finding her focus to save Amaya's life in time.

"Amaya." Tynan dropped down by her, his face a picture worse than her own fear. "Shit, I got ambushed for a few minutes, and then you were gone. Why did you wander from me? That was *not* our deal."

"Zaiana…was in trouble."

It wasn't the time for scolding as much as Zaiana wanted to rewind time to yell at the darkling not to put her life in danger to intervene.

"You need to stay with her. Keep her as still as you can, or it will kill her." Zaiana stood.

Then everything happened too fast for her to prevent it.

Amaya surged up to one knee, her bow extended in her left arm. Before Zaiana had even blinked, the arrow that had been nocked was gone. She spun, slammed by the sight of Mordecai so close, arm raised with the dagger Edith had, an arrow tipped with Phoenix feathers was lodged in his heart.

Mordecai pulled the arrow free, tossing it aside. He appeared fine until he tried to step toward Zaiana and stumbled, falling to one knee. He still gripped the dagger.

"It was you who sought that dagger all along," Zaiana said, piecing it together. "You've had a bounty out for it, believing it was in Hilia's cave and many humans and fae have captured Waterwielders trying to reach it. If Edith had managed to take my power, you would have killed her with that dagger to have the Stormcasting ability."

"It is mine!" he yelled, coughing at the end and spitting blood. "That power awakened in my weakest and least deserving daughter."

"Weakest? Look behind you, Mordecai. There is no spawn of yours who can defeat me. Send as many as you like."

A plume of shadow appeared behind him, and Zaiana faltered back a step. A firm body stopped her. Kyleer.

Dakodas emerged from her darkness, crouching by Mordecai with the first glimpse of concern Zaiana had seen her display. Then her black eyes snapped viscously to Zaiana.

"You are all going to pay for this," she hissed.

They braced, but Dakodas didn't attack. Instead she took Mordecai away through her Shadowporting, leaving them in a chilling, foreboding silence.

Zaiana spun back to Amaya, who wheezed in Tynan's arms.

"You shouldn't have done that," Zaiana snapped, but her eyes bore only concern and fear, cupping Amaya's cheek. "We need a healer!" she yelled to Kyleer as the only person close who could help.

He nodded, taking off in search of one.

Yet Zaiana knew...listening to the fractured cadence in Amaya's chest...she knew they were counting down too fast.

"Heartbeats are such a precious thing, aren't they?" Amaya said. She kept her eyes on the stars that broke through the swaying trees.

"They really are," Zaiana said, tucking her hair from her face.

She kept her voice steady despite the lump growing in her throat and the scream of grief already bottling in her chest.

"Thank you...thank you for giving me mine."

Zaiana's nose stung, and tears flooded her eyes. She breathed consciously, keeping her smile and bravery for Amaya. "You always had it," Zaiana said. "Your heart showed me the goodness in our kind."

Amaya smiled, but her face twitched with pain. "M-make it sto-storm, Zaiana."

Her first tear spilled as Amaya's face relaxed and the light in her eyes faded. "Always," Zaiana whispered. She leaned in, placing a kiss on Amaya's forehead. "In darkness and in light, you have always triumphed, Amaya Silverfair."

When Zaiana pulled back, she was gone. Zaiana had never appreciated enough how beautiful her eyes were until right now, when she had to close them forever.

It wasn't fair. War never was, but this...losing Amaya was so cruel and cold that despite all the vicious hands this world had dealt her, she could hardly comprehend this fate. Zaiana's head tipped back, watching the stars glimmer while tears slipped silently down her cheeks. She held Amaya's body, but as she searched the constellations she imagined her gentle soul as one of them, at peace in that beautiful palace, and watching over them still.

Tynan mourned. She'd never heard him cry before and it disturbed her greatly.

For his pain, for the loss of another person too good for this world, Zaiana's grief hardened. Justice was in her hands; vengeance beat hard in her chest.

Zaiana stood. Her eyes caught on the red fletching of the arrow that had struck Mordecai with a pang in her chest.

Mordecai Vesaria would die, and there was a certain twisted poetry that he'd created the weapon that would carve out his immortal heart.

She'd shed her Silverfair name when she'd collapsed the mountain that raised her, and she would embrace her new name as Zaiana Vesaria to kill the dark fae king.

CHAPTER SEVENTY-SEVEN

Tarly

Tarly wasn't much help in combat with one arm in a sling, but he could direct the wolves and offer another distraction when they faced Marvellas.

If they weren't too late.

The five of them and the wolves rushed through the castle halls, having to take a more inconspicuous route to avoid the partygoers with the ball still ongoing. Nik had ordered the city to be locked down, and most of their army force had begun to take position around Farrowhold, but they wanted to delay panic spreading through the people for as long as possible.

The passage Nik led them through beneath the library had been mined of Magestone but still hummed with a dark aura that pulsed in his head. Then they held their breath, rounding into the room of mirrors.

They spilled into the small space, and they were alone. Yet the Blood Box lay right there in the middle of the room for the taking. Every hair on Tarly's body pricked, somehow gathering a worse sense of dread than if they'd run right into Marvellas instead.

"Do you think she hasn't found this place yet?" Tauria asked.

She wandered around the room, her reflection casting in a hundred directions.

Until Tarly turned rigid, staring across into Tauria's eyes. The reflection smiled, chilling him to his core.

"Tauria," he whispered.

She turned to him, and he blinked. The reflection was back to following her. He shook his head, wondering if he'd imagined it in his fear.

Nerida picked up the box. "We need to get it to Faythe for her blood to confirm it's inside."

Tarly didn't want to spend a second longer here than necessary. He headed for the break in the wall with her.

"Wait," Nyte said, facing the way out with his back to them. "Did this veil lock you in here the last time you visited?"

He couldn't see it at first glance, but now, enlightened, he detected the faint shimmer over the exit.

"No," Nik answered with a note of dread.

"She promised to free me if I helped her," Tauria said.

They all turned to her, confused. Even more perplexing was Tauria's shocked expression. Her eyes darted over the mirrors.

Tarly saw it again. The single reflection that didn't copy her movement but had stolen her image and voice. The concept was eerily terrifying.

"Take my form instead to speak to us," Nik demanded.

The Dresair laughed haughtily, disappearing from a mirror above to their left and taking on Tauria's image in one closer to their right when it next answered.

"That wouldn't be as fun."

"Marvellas was here," the real Tauria said.

The curve of the Dresair's mouth was so wicked and amused, so wrong to witness on Tauria's gentle face.

"She still is," said the Dresair.

"Rainyte." Marvellas's voice was but a quiet plea.

Nyte hadn't moved. Just beyond the exit now stood Marvellas.

"Mother," he answered, devoid of any sentimental feeling in the word.

The Spirit felt his coldness, yielding a mild wince.

Nyte said, "Stop this senseless war. It is over for you."

There was something different about Marvellas now... His spike of terror at first seeing her dwindled the longer he watched her, seeing nothing but a vulnerable soul so unlike one who had started a great war and harbored so much power.

Marvellas lifted a hand to the veil at the same height as Nyte's face. All Tarly could feel was tragedy for her. He didn't want to, but he did.

"I'm sorry all you saw of me was this. When I wanted to be good...I wanted to be good for you. Then you were taken from me."

Nyte stepped back, and Tarly couldn't see his face to read the emotions that had to be tearing him apart inside even if his composure was steel. Parents were a fragile wound in all. For good, for bad, they were the origins of their existence, and that was an attachment that could never be severed completely.

"You don't have to hurt anymore," Nyte said, "if you just surrender."

"I have a duty I must see through."

"Ending the world isn't your duty—it's a tragic escape from all you failed to achieve. Let it be flawed. Let it be Godless."

"I cannot."

"If you do this...I will never forgive you."

"Forgiveness serves you, not me. It is not an erasure of wrongs. My actions may seem drastic, but I have seen the infinite web of souls and their travel. I am at peace with sending every last one on this land back into that web, knowing they will scatter far and wide, beginning their cycle anew in another place. It is an ending of poetry only I can give."

Nyte lunged forward, slamming his fist to the veil. He tensed with a pained groan as energy rebounded from it, and he sank to one knee.

"Do you even hear yourself? These are *people*, not just souls. These are *lives*, not just pieces of energy."

Marvellas sank down with him, but Nyte didn't look up. "Oh, my son...your compassion is a gift to see, but it will hurt you if you let it."

"You have no idea what I've been through..." Nyte said menacingly, drawing his eyes up with such loathing. "In my childhood I yearned for you. In my adulthood I tried so desperately to refuse the poison Father spun about you. But he was right about you. After all this time, I finally get to look at you and feel *nothing*. You are nothing to me. You are nothing *of* me. Just like my father."

"You found the love I didn't get to give you...didn't you, my son? That is why your heart was salvaged from the villainy of your father, and now from me. Someone protects it."

"Yes," he said coldly. "So how can you continue to say love is weakness?"

"Because it is stopping you from seeing what needs to be done. It will always fool you into believing it is a reward for your suffering when it is the cause."

Nyte shook his head at the ground, emitting a dark, incredulous laugh. "I was born an orphan, and I have long since come to terms with that."

He lunged up, slamming his hand against the veil again, but this time the Ruin Dagger pierced through it like a pin into glass, breaking a web of cracks from the impact that kept spreading. Before the veil could shatter, Nyte was thrown back by an invisible force. He crashed into several mirrors, which obliterated around him.

"In another time...maybe we'll get a chance at the life I wanted for us, Rainyte. Maybe then you won't ever look at me like the monster you see now," Marvellas said vacantly, watching her son lift himself from the broken glass with nothing but hate in his eyes.

He said, "I believe love is embedded in each life cycle of a soul—it's how we recognize our mate in every one. But I also believe our wounds and loathing carry too, so for your sake, I hope we never meet again."

The Spirit's eyes flexed. Tarly was used to seeing her lash out with power and anguish. Used to watching how composed and arrogant she was when she dominated a room. Yet now, even though her plans were still as heinous, Marvellas pushed on to carry it through as a lost and vacant vessel. Her eyes were tired, her skin pale and carrying dark circles. Her vibrant hair was now dull and mildly unkempt.

Rattling surged Tarly's alarm, and the wolves growled louder. The mirrors Nyte had shattered with his body began to reform, and when they did, the Dresair still wearing Tauria's face stood behind him.

To everyone's horror, a hand lashed *out* of the mirror's surface, gripping the back of Nyte's collar and yanking him.

Nik was closest to intervene, ripping the Dresair's hand from Nyte and pushing him away. Then Tarly yelled Nik's name but it did nothing to prevent the Dresair from taking hold of Nik instead, pulling him through the mirror. Tauria gasped, lunging the few steps and taking his hand before he was fully pulled through.

Tarly and Nerida ran for them too, but they couldn't get a hold of Tauria before they were both gone, sucked into the mirrors and leaving only their own horrified expressions to stare into. Still, they reached for large piece of glass that had stolen their friends within, but the surface had turned solid again.

An ear-splitting *boom* caused them to duck and reach for each other instead. Tarly used his body over Nerida's to shield her as best he could from the shower of glass that rained down hard on them. It cut into his skin at all angles as every mirror in the room *shattered*.

"No," Nerida breathed in horror when the chaos stopped.

They looked up, seeing only uneven stone wall. The mirrors lay in pieces around them. What locked Tarly still...was the new terrifying presence that now occupied the room with them.

The creature was unnaturally tall, with limbs too long for its torso. Its skin was like black tree bark, with a featureless face. This was the Dresair's true form, and it was free. It bent to pick up the Blood Box, not giving them any attention as it headed toward Marvellas with it.

"Bring them back!" Nerida cried.

The creature stopped, turning its head around to her, and Tarly shifted, putting himself between them should it decide to attack. It had no mouth, and when it spoke to their minds, he wondered if Marvellas could hear it too.

"Every kingdom on this continent guards a mirror passage through time and space itself. Us creatures within are not merciful to fresh bodies."

With that, it left, following Marvellas with the Light Temple Ruin, and they were powerless to stop them. As they rose, Tarly and Nerida could only stare at the place where the mirror had been in complete shock and helplessness.

"We have to get them back," Nerida said in utter disbelief.

"That went far worse than we thought possible," Nyte commented.

Tarly could hardly pay him any mind. His thoughts were reeling with the Dresair's parting words.

Every kingdom guards a mirror passage.

He scrambled over ever place he'd ever visited in Olmstone. If that were true, there had to be another in which they could attempt to get Nik and Tauria back from the void between all space and time. Though even if they did find another passage, the daunting concept of how vast such a place was to be lost in threatened his seed of hope.

"The Livre des Verres," Tarly said when the spark came to his mind. Nerida looked at him with such desolation and question. "There was a room restricted to the public. I was allowed in once— being the prince had its perks. I recall a mirror there. Not like this place. This mirror had been crafted with an intricate gold border to appear very ordinary. I was young when I saw it, but I remember feeling like something was staring *back* at me through my own eyes. That I smiled even when I didn't think I was."

"It's the best lead we have," Nerida said. Her eyes scrambled with her thoughts. "But the battles...the war...getting to Olmstone will take at least a week."

"We need Nik and Tauria. We don't have a choice."

"The ruin…"

Nyte cut in. "Leave that concern to me and Faythe."

Tarly gave a vacant nod. Their situation had just turned all the more dire at the worst moment, but all they could do was push forward. All they could do was keep fighting.

CHAPTER SEVENTY-EIGHT

Faythe

Faythe jolted awake, believing from the adrenaline coursing through her that she'd fallen asleep in the midst of a battle.

Strong hands took hold of her shoulders, and Faythe's frantic search for danger was quelled by the soothing waves of comfort in Reylan's eyes. She recalled what had happened. Marvellas was here.

Faythe's legs swung over a chaise she lay on. They'd gathered in this reception room during the ball before Zaiana announced a battle threat on the town's outskirts.

"What happened?" she demanded, standing but swaying on her feet.

"Marvellas shattered your mental barrier. You needed to recover."

"How long has it been?"

"Only a few hours."

Reylan filled her in on the rest, and Faythe grew more frustrated and terrified for her friends who were in action while she'd been incapacitated.

When Faythe's eyes fell on Jakon watching her in the corner, her sharpness eased. "Hey, Jak," she said, anticipating that one wrong move would make him shut her out.

He stood, coming a little closer. "I've never seen you out like that. I worried..." He trailed off, but she didn't need him to continue.

Faythe risked closing the distance, and when he didn't reject her embrace, she hugged him tighter. Jakon's face burrowed into her neck, and she almost whimpered.

"Don't scare me like that again. You have to live, Faythe. Promise me."

"I will," she said. "We both will."

Jakon's arms tightened a fraction before he let her go too soon for her heart. But she clung to that returned thread of their friendship with everything she had.

They were snapped from their moment when people rushed into the room. Nerida, Tarly, and...

"Nyte?" Faythe had to blink consciously, believing for a second he was a manifestation of her concussion.

"You haven't filled her in yet?" Nyte asked Reylan.

"She just woke up."

"Nik and Tauria are gone," Nerida cut in loudly.

Faythe's heart skipped a beat.

"What do you mean, 'gone'?" Reylan demanded.

Fear so all-consuming seized Faythe. She stood there vacantly, hand to her mouth, hearing of her friends being pulled into an infinite void with the only way they knew to follow being shattered afterward.

"Tarly and I are going to Olmstone now," Nerida said.

Reylan had gone so silent, pacing and calculating. This was a detrimental blow to all of their plans and strategies without the rulers of High Farrow. All that kept Faythe from crumbling was the small dose of hope there could be another passage to try to get Nik and Tauria back.

"There was a mirror passage in Rhyenelle," Faythe informed them. She told them how she'd shattered it and freed the Dresair there too. It added further merit to the creature's claim there could be one in all kingdoms.

"Go immediately—we need Nik and Tauria back," Reylan instructed them.

Nerida and Tarly nodded, leaving swiftly, with the two wolves following.

Faythe had been concluding her own plan while hearing of all that had happened when she'd allowed Marvellas to slip by her. She couldn't forgive herself.

"I'm going after her," Faythe said.

Reylan stopped his pacing by the fire. "I'm coming with you."

"We need you here. The battle is still moving forward, and we need a leader in High Farrow, as well as one on the mountain fringe, where the biggest mass of their foot soldiers will be in days."

"We have plenty of generals and commanders."

"It's not the same. No one knows the enemy like we do. Nik and Tauria were to be the ones guiding our forces around Farrowhold, but that's not an option anymore."

Reylan crossed to her, pulling her by her waist into him. "We don't separate. Not now. Not when any day might be our last and we stand against our greatest enemy."

Faythe conceded. Selfishly, she wanted him fighting by her side.

Nyte cut in. "I'm the crucial part of killing Marvellas, remember? She's not going alone." He didn't look at either of them, leaning against the far wall while he absentmindedly traced things on the side console, lost to his own thoughts.

Jakon said, "I might not be much help, but I want to fight."

Faythe feared for him greatly, but she nodded. "The forces that broke through the outskirts will just be the beginning. We have to anticipate more will reach even as close to the outer town as they try to divide and conquer."

Jakon understood, standing with a firmed expression. He left, and Faythe fought the urge to go after him for some reason. To not let him out of her sight.

Faythe, Reylan, and Nyte switched to the drawing room, where they pondered over a map for the next hour, reorganizing their plans while waiting on edge for the hopeful triumphant return of Zaiana, Kyleer, and Izaiah from the battle on the outskirts.

One hour turned to two, then three. Faythe bit at her fingernails as she watched the clock, about to suggest she fly out with her wings of Phoenixfyre to see what was happening.

She was saved from doing so by their return, which deflated her sharp tension. Yet the ominous weight they carried into the room between them had Faythe bracing her emotions. Zaiana, Kyleer, and Izaiah were accounted for, but something was wrong.

"Edith was there," Zaiana announced, but her voice was stripped of any emotion. She pulled the jeweled dagger free from her side, the steel now unpolished, with speckles of dried silver blood on the edges. Zaiana had done it: killed Edith and retrieved Nerida's power.

"Nerida just left. Maybe we should catch up—"

"Mordecai was there too." Zaiana cut Faythe off.

Faythe was beginning to suspect they'd won the battle, but the cost...

Her eyes caught on Tynan, who slipped into the room silently, his head bowed. Faythe waited for the dark hair of Amaya, who always followed, but it never came.

Zaiana met her eye, and it was all the confirmation Faythe needed in her cold stare. Amaya was dead. Faythe didn't know the younger dark fae well, but what was clear for all to see was the unfairness of another pure heart and gentle soul lost to the viciousness of war.

Faythe closed her eyes, settling the loss within herself for all it represented. She barely registered the wooden figure in her hand before it went careening into the wall, exploding into splinters with her force.

So much senseless, tragic loss.

Zaiana said, "I don't think the arrow to Mordecai's heart would have killed him, but Amaya saved my life. Or, at the least, she saved my power. It's what Mordecai has been after all this time. Why he kept me alive and prized my Stormcasting ability. He has no sentiment for me—he's been waiting for the day he had that dagger he's been actively seeking, just to take back the ability he was resurrected without."

"Where is the dagger now?" Reylan asked.

"Mordecai has it," Zaiana said.

The gravity of the disadvantage weighed heavy.

Faythe's teeth ground together. "It doesn't matter," she said firmly. "We're in the thick of the war now, and we cannot falter."

"Position me where the worst of the battles will be. I have to keep fighting," Zaiana said.

Faythe understood. If she slowed for a second, her grief would pull her under too.

Reylan said, "We want to intercept them on the mountain fringe. That's where the biggest stand will be. They'll no doubt have forces that make it into High Farrow from the other pressure points, but if the numbers coming from the fringe make it through…High Farrow will be lost."

Zaiana nodded, accepting that she would lead on the front lines there until they could all make it to join her. Faythe didn't doubt the dark fae's ability to hold the lines until then.

"I'll go back to the sky caves," Izaiah said. "In case Marvellas succeeds in putting Aurialis's ruin in Dakodas's podium before you can stop her. Her final step is reaching her temple in the caves to sacrifice herself to end the world, right?

"You need this to stop her," Nyte reminded him, flipping the Ruin Dagger idly.

"Then give it to me."

"Not a chance," Kyleer growled.

Though he didn't have his full memories of his brother, his deep-rooted protection over him could never be erased.

"You'll both go with Zaiana," Reylan interjected firmly. "We need our best on the main battlefield. We'll stop Marvellas."

Izaiah's jaw twitched like he wanted to protest, but he didn't.

Reylan said, "The other generals and commanders have their orders. In Nik and Tauria's stead, we have the lords of High Farrow deploying a steady warning to the people to stay indoors, arm themselves, and stay vigilant. The next few nights are Ungardia's darkest hours. It all ends now."

This moment had been building for some time, but it didn't make confronting it any less of an ominous burden.

Everyone shifted to leave for their station, but Faythe said, "I'm proud to be standing by all of you."

They turned back to her, and though some of her friends were absent right now, she felt their spirits in this room too.

"No matter where we began. As enemies." She glanced at Zaiana. "As friends." She skimmed over Kyleer and Izaiah. "As incredulous long-lost family."

Nyte shifted, not expecting a mention from her.

Faythe took Reylan's hand. "As soul mates," she whispered, meeting his eyes for one brief moment. She drew a long breath. "I would lay down my life for any of you, and I know you would do the same, though some might find it harder to admit than others. I wouldn't be who I am without all of you. And Nik, Tauria, Jakon, Marlowe, Nerida, Tarly. It is my greatest honor to fight by your side. For a better world."

No words were needed in exchange. As she watched her friends leave, Reylan slipped an arm around her waist, pressing his lips to her temple.

"I'm so proud of you," he said, turning her to him. His eyes mapped her face, reminiscing. "From the moment I met you, a human with audacious wit and a steel will, I always knew you were destined for greatness. And it is *my* honor to stand by your side, Faythe Ashfyre. I hope to be here, right here, for many centuries to come." He held her face, and his smile lightened the heaviness on her heart for this fleeting moment. "To watch you reign triumphantly as the Phoenix Queen you were born to be."

Faythe sniffed, forcing back the tears that threatened to spill.

"Thank you for always seeing me, when I couldn't always see my own potential."

His lips pressed to her forehead. "That's why I'm yours."

In her rooms, Faythe equipped herself with more weapons and better attire, preparing to depart. She was lost in a reel of thoughts, pondering over the many situations that could arise in trying to stop Marvellas, so she didn't feel Reylan approach until his large hands took hold of her waist from behind. He kissed down her neck, flicking his tongue over his bite wound, which roused her lust.

"This isn't the time," she said in a partial moan.

"It is. I want to you think of this—coming back to this. You stay alive for me to show you over and over how spectacular you are. How incredible and brave and selfless my mate is." He teased her more with each declaration, running his hands around her body and his mouth over her neck. "You stay alive to take the throne you were destined for."

Faythe turned to face him.

"Promise me one thing," he said. "I don't want to forget. No matter what. I know you're capable of taking my memories—you've done it before, haven't you?"

Faythe's mouth opened, stunned and wondering how long he'd known.

"I...I don't remember the past."

"Neither do I. Nor do I care to. All that matters is that I have you now, but promise me we're doing this together. I don't choose forget. I choose to follow you into the next world if our fate is to leave this one behind."

Faythe's brow drew together. She pushed up on her toes to kiss him deeply in promise.

She said, "Let's give everything we have to this world. One last time."

CHAPTER SEVENTY-NINE

Tarly

B y now, Tarly and Nerida were masterful at stealth and remaining inconspicuous. For the second time, Tarly had infiltrated his own kingdom while it was crawling with dark fae. There'd been a shift in the kingdom since they were last here. Lines of soldiers marched through the streets, preparing to join the forces Reylan predicted would move in great numbers through Olmstone and pressure High Farrow through the mountain fringe that bordered their kingdoms.

Tarly couldn't concern himself with that daunting battle to come. His focus was on retrieving Nik and Tauria.

Nerida led the way as they approached the Livre des Verres, slipping inside. The place was unguarded while the focus was on the war, and the abandoned wreck the library had been left to would never fail to inspire such sorrow in him.

He didn't waste time on reflecting, darting down to the ground level after they climbed in through a window. The room they needed inside was locked, and Tarly used his foot to try to break the door in.

"Waterwielding would be very handy about now," Nerida grumbled, searching for something to help.

She returned with a large rock.

"That's not going to break through—"

With a cry, Nerida's arm pulled back before she slammed the rock against the handle, which broke right off. The door groaned as it casually slipped open.

Nerida smiled at him in satisfaction, and he chuckled as he followed her in. His mate was absolutely stunning in all things she did.

The room was dark, and he coughed on the thick musk of neglect when he inhaled. The only light pooled in from behind them, but it reflected off exactly what they were looking for.

"I really hope I was right," Tarly mumbled, approaching the mirror that already pricked his skin with a sense of peculiar magick.

"Me too, but I'm also frightened."

Nerida was rummaging through things, and he was about to question it when she beamed, producing a lasso of rope.

"What if it doesn't let us inside?"

"The Dresair is a creature of tricks and bargains. We might have some negotiation to do." She slung the rope around her middle, but Tarly took her wrist before she could tie it around herself.

"I'll go inside. Please." He couldn't bear the thought of her facing what was within there alone, and one of them had to stay here to pull the other out.

"You're injured."

"You don't have your magick."

In truth, neither of them stood great odds of fighting in there, but he hoped it wouldn't come to that.

"Like you said, the Dresairs are creatures of tricks and riddles. I don't think they'll attack."

Before Nerida could answer, a new, chilling voice echoed through the room.

"So much debate. So much wasted time while your friends lose their minds day by day within the void."

Tarly curved an arm around Nerida, and when they focused on their reflection, Tarly wasn't holding Nerida like he was now.

"Will you let me pass?" Tarly asked.

The Dresair could wear many faces, but the *smile* of one was always the same. Thrilled and primed with mockery.

"You might lose your mind too. You might never return at all."

"I'll take the chance."

"You are dying, Tarly Wolverlon. You have lived beyond the days that bite should have left you with thanks to the healing magick that lays dormant within you…and because of her." The Dresair crossed to stand in front of Nerida. "The mate who almost never was, because of a meddling Spirit."

Tarly stilled. "What do you know about me having two mates?"

"That it is impossible. Souls have always been two halves searching for each other through eternity. There are many names for the bond when they meet across many universes."

"But I have two... there was another before Nerida," Tarly prompted, getting desperate for the information that he'd thought he was content not to know.

"I will offer you the answer you seek or passage through this mirror. Which will it be?"

His jaw worked. It wasn't even a question of which he would choose. "Let me pass."

The Dresair smiled again. "I want that." It pointed to Nerida's chest. Her hand rose to his mother's pendant there from the Healers Academy on Lakelaria. Nerida cast sad hazel eyes to him.

"We need to find our friends," he said gently, helping her remove the necklace.

The Dresair said, "Every time a healer uses their magick while wearing it, a piece of their magick embeds itself inside. It is how it knows when to change color to determine the strength of the healer."

Tarly paused with it in his grip, uncertain now. "What can someone else do with it?" he asked.

The Dresair tilted a playful downward look at him, declining to answer.

Tarly glanced at Nerida, as it was an essence of her magick they were giving away. She answered with a nod and an assuring smile.

He threw it toward the mirror, which rippled like liquid metal as it passed through. The Dresair caught it, pocketing the necklace.

"Very well, Tarly Wolverlon." It held out a hand, inviting him through.

Tarly turned to Nerida with his back to the mirror. He slipped his palm along her cheek and kissed her deeply.

"I love you. I'll be right back," he said, pressing his lips to her forehead.

Nerida tied the rope around his waist, securing it tightly. "You'd better be," she said, but her playful words were lost to her fearful eyes. "I love you, Sully."

Pushing his hand through the mirror was like dipping into ice water. His skin burned, but the energy within the mirror started pulling him through, and he let it.

Just before he did, the Dresair slithered one last taunt into his ear.

"Though you might just be too late to save them both."

His body jerked as though he'd fallen into a suction void, and his limbs flailed, trying to find something to hold onto before he drifted beyond the rope's limit.

It was the rope that saved him even though it winded him to be yanked to an abrupt halt. Then he was falling, unable to maneuver while there was no wall or celling or floor to brace for in this endless white void.

He slammed into the ground on his bad side, which threatened his consciousness for a minute. Tarly took a moment to breathe through the shooting pain that slowly numbed to a dull throbbing over the right side of his chest.

Damn inconvenient arm.

When he no longer felt at risk of passing out, he stood and wondered how in the Nether he was to find Nik and Tauria when all he saw was white. An endless white void.

But he was determined to find them, so Tarly pressed forward, hoping something would guide him along the way.

CHAPTER EIGHTY

Nikalias

Days, maybe even weeks, had passed. Nik had no way of keeping track in his endless torment. All he did was follow Tauria every time he caught a glimpse of her, but she would laugh, mocking him, as he desperately tried to reach her before she disappeared for a while.

He was going insane. Looping around an infinite white room. Nik occasionally remembered how he'd gotten here. That this was not where he should be. He thought he'd felt Tauria right before the mirror swallowed him fully, but the moment he'd landed here, she was ripped away, only appearing now in taunting images, so he was almost certain she wasn't truly here with him. It was a Dresair playing with him.

He didn't know what it wanted, but every time he saw his mate, he thought she was real and couldn't stop this endless chase.

"Tauria," he croaked, sinking to his knees.

Nik ran his hands through his disheveled hair. He hadn't slept at all, and his fatigue only helped the Dresair play with his delirium. He'd collapsed a few times, closing his eyes with a need to replenish his energy if he had any hope of making it out of here. Then he would wake to the sound of Tauria's voice and begin his chase anew.

"Nik!" Tauria called, her song of a voice echoing around with no direction.

His head whipped up. Her voice sounded more sure this time. Didn't it?

Nik stumbled to his feet, catching a flicker of brown hair and emerald green material drifting around a white wall. The brightness had dried out his eyes and caused a relentless pounding in his head. Nothing cast a shadow, and he'd never craved darkness so badly.

"Wait for me, love," he rasped, catching himself against the wall and following after her.

Tauria walked backward, hands clasped behind her. *Gods, she's so beautiful.* She wore a flowing green dress that wrapped around her torso, accentuating her chest and leaving her brown skin glowing, with no sleeves, only a train of material from her shoulders that started green and ended…blue. A deep sapphire blue that matched the sash around her middle. The colors of both their kingdoms. Her crown was woven gold antlers atop her braided hair.

He wanted to fall to her feet with the powerful, magnificent ruler she was.

This was what awaited them at the end of this war, and he would do anything to see this vision come to pass.

He realized then that was all she was. Much as he wanted to run to her, to chase her into infinity, he knew she wasn't real.

Nik stopped walking. Tauria's smile fell slowly when he did.

He had his sword at his hip, and he thought maybe this was his trial. If he managed to finally reach the Dresair, get close enough to kill it and end the torment, maybe it would open the door home. And it had made it so treacherously difficult by taking on the form of his mate, toying with his mind to be uncertain of whether she was real or not.

"Nik," she said, holding out a hand for him.

He approached, playing along.

For the first time, he managed to slip his hand into hers. He stared into her hazel eyes with such yearning his mind was already slipping, falling for the illusion. Nik blinked consciously. The finery and crown were a prize not yet won, and that was what made him sure enough…

The Dresair hissed, leaping back to avoid the path of his blade. It contorted Tauria's beautiful face into anger and malice, backing away from him until she dipped around another corner.

Nik took off after her again. It had changed clothing, mimicking what she'd been wearing the last time he saw her. A green corset tunic and black leather pants. They were preparing for battle. Her hair was in a single long braid, with her emerald jeweled comb fixed into the back. The one that meant so much to both of them when he'd stolen it from her the day they met in Fenstead, holding onto it for centuries.

He grew tired—not in his body but his soul—and slowed his pace again.

Nik had to make it back to her. He had to catch the Dresair and end this cycle.

"You are so weak," the Dresair taunted in her voice. It was close, but Nik couldn't bring himself to search. "You knew the threat you were to her, and yet you still claimed her."

His spine locked.

"You're the Dresair I met that day...who told me about my prophesy."

"I am."

He found the will to turn around, and it hadn't let go of Tauria's image. His resentment grew fast and ugly, surging the most determination he'd felt in this place.

"That damn prophesy kept me from her for *centuries*. It stole so much time from us I wish I'd never heard it."

"That's the curse of knowing one's fate. Mortals like to think they want to know what lies ahead, that it will grant them a sense of direction, or wisdom of which paths not to take. But the future is not carved in stone. You gain and lose according to which path you take in your own infinite web."

Did that make life a choice, or an inevitable course?

Nik shook his head. He didn't care about fate—not anymore.

"Knowing only made me a slave to fear."

"Exactly. Yet had I told you something of grandeur and triumph, you would have become a slave to greed and impatience. Knowing what is to come serves as a curse either way."

Vexation twitched his jaw. "How do I get out of here?"

"You have already figured that out."

"By killing you?"

"There are many who wander through this void in search of something great. Somewhere new. But to Realm-Walk, you must have something of value to offer a God, and hope they will answer your call and grant you passage."

"I don't want to Realm-Walk. I have to get back to mine."

"Then you must kill me, for I was the one to drag you here."

"Why?"

"Because I once walked into this void willingly, and my call was not answered. It left me trapped here to waste away into this *thing*. There are two ways for a Dresair to be freed. If all the mirrors at the gate of passage are shattered when they're present, that frees them as a faceless creature, cursed to steal others' identities for the rest of their days. This way, by killing one who wanders through whom I have served before, I will have my old form back. The one I do not remember, nor do I remember from which time or realm I came."

Nik's grip tightened on his sword. "Then why haven't you killed me already?"

"I had to make you weak. I have no skills in combat, nor any weapon. This was the only way I could contend with you."

He straightened in defense, blinking the tiredness away. Nik was lethargic and would doubt his skills against most opponents, but not this one. He would fight and he would win to make it back to Tauria.

Nik was prepared to lunge, but his vision swayed suddenly, catching on another image of Tauria. Then another. And another. She surrounded him in dozens of copies, so Nik lost track of which was the Dresair to strike.

One lunged for him, and...he couldn't do it.

All he saw was Tauria's face, and he could not raise his blade to her. They went crashing to the ground, and he held her off by her wrists that aimed to wrap around his throat.

Confusion battered his mind.

Why were they fighting?

What had he done to inspire such loathing in his mate's eyes?

"Please, love," he said through a breath, struggling to hold off her determined strength.

"You should have heeded my warning, *king*," she hissed.

Those words slashed through the illusion, and Nik gripped her throat instead, flipping them and straddling her. He choked tighter.

This is the Dresair. Not Tauria.

Not Tauria.

Yet her eyes filled with so much terror that he let go, stumbling to his feet and backing away in horror over what he was doing.

"Tauria, I'm so sorry—"

She stood, wheezing for breath and pinning him with a look of stunned betrayal. Until she let go of the act and a cruel smile split her lips.

Not Tauria.

Not Tauria.

Nik yelled into the void, his mind splitting apart.

He was grabbed from behind, recognizing her lavender scent as his back was bent back awkwardly by the hook of her elbow around his throat.

"Poor Nikalias," she taunted in his ear. "Pining for years. Missing out on the many joyous centuries you could have had together."

He would never regret anything more in his life. Nik had thought he was saving Tauria by pushing her away; that the wicked prophesy would not come to pass if they never bonded. It had all been lost time, but he swore to make it up to her for the rest of their long lives together.

With a pained cry, he had no choice but to twist, hooking his arm back and ducking to throw the Dresair over his shoulder. When he straightened, he was met with another dozen images of her.

The one in front of him wore amusement that crawled his skin. "It's time for the best part," it taunted.

A new sensation crept along his nape, making him believe the one in front of him was not the one to strike and make it out of here. Nik chose to spin around, driving his blade through the gut of the one behind him.

Tauria's eyes flew wide, and she choked. It felt so *real*. Nik waited for the illusion to break and the Dresair to change into its true faceless form now he'd won.

He'd struck the Dresair true.

Nothing changed.

Every perfect contour of her face remained exactly the same.

"Nik," Tauria choked. Her hand wrapped around his forearm still holding the mighty Farrow Sword, now plunged through her abdomen.

Her heart slammed in his chest, and he shook his head. Sweat beaded down his face.

Not Tauria.

Not Tauria.

This was what he had to do to make it back to her. He had to kill the Dresair.

Her knees buckled, and Nik wrapped an arm around her, lowering them both. She looked down at the wound with pain and terror-stricken eyes.

"I-I found you," she said.

A ringing filled his ears.

I found you.

No. This was another trick. It had to be. Tauria wasn't here.

Her hand rose to his face, and he trembled stiffly.

"It's okay," she whispered. "This wasn't really you."

It was him. Of course it was him.

"Tauria." He said her name in a trance, hoping he wasn't really holding her right now. That in all his days of chase and torment, wishing she were real, that this time she wasn't.

Her eyes flicked over his head, filling with more fear. "Behind you—!"

Nik twisted his head to find another image of Tauria, arm raised to strike him.

A blade flew through the air, lodging into her neck, and she gave a wail unlike any person or creature. The illusion the Dresair wore of Tauria broke off in fragments as its body contorted and writhed, shedding skin to unveil the dark, spindly body beneath.

Nik tore his sight from the gruesome scene to where the path of the blade had come from. He blinked at Tarly, wondering if this was a new vision.

A horrific nightmare.

Something hot trickled over his hand, drawing his attention back to the sword he held. Then reality...bone-trembling, world-shattering clarity started to settle in his mind.

This was no vision.

Tauria's eyes rolled back when he dared to face what he'd done. He caught her head on his shoulder, and the worst panic of his existence tore a scream from his throat.

"Tarly, help me!" he yelled.

Nik didn't know what to do. Tauria's blood stained his hands from a fatal blow he'd been tricked into.

You're so weak, the Dresair had taunted. And it was true, for how could he have mistaken his true mate for that *monster*?

Tarly kneeled by them, and he swore. "We need to get back to Nerida," he said hurriedly.

"The blade..."

"Keep it where it is—she'll only bleed out faster if you remove it."

Oh Gods. Oh Gods. FUCK.

Nik was losing his mind to sleep deprivation now crashing into surges of adrenaline that sped his heart to a dangerous degree.

He couldn't lose Tauria. No, he couldn't *live* without Tauria.

"Stay with me, love, please."

He kept whispering his pleas though her eyes were closed. Nik tried to keep track of her heart, but his was too frantic, slamming in his ears.

Nik followed Tarly vacantly, only registering a change of illumination with how it stung his eyes to be released from the brilliant white surroundings and enter into a dimly lit room. He blinked desperately to keep his sights on measuring Tauria's chest rising.

A loud gasp flicked his attention up to Nerida, who dropped a thick rope to cover her mouth.

"Help her!" Nik yelled.

He lay Tauria down on the ground.

"Nik, I…I don't have my magick," Nerida said quietly.

That realization slammed into him with the force of a warhammer.

Every second counted down to Tauria's last, and without a healer…she didn't stand a chance.

"Tarly," he snapped. "You said you have healing magick in you."

"I haven't even tried to touch it yet!"

"You're trying now." Nik gripped his jacket, pulling him down. He didn't have time to be nice. "Nerida, you must be able to guide him."

"This wound…it's grave. Even I would struggle—"

"Don't say that like she has no hope!"

"Nik…" Tauria's quiet voice dragged his attention to her, and he held her upper body close, careful of the sword as he rocked gently.

"I'm so sorry. I'm so, so fucking sorry. Be strong for me, okay? I'm going to make this right."

"I see the beach," she said.

He pulled back, watching her glazed eyes that held unblinking on the ceiling.

"The one I love…in Fenstead."

"No. No, no, no, you can't see the beach yet. We need to see it together. Look at me instead, Tauria, please."

Nerida and Tarly spoke to each other, but he couldn't hear them. Tarly's hands were on Tauria, and he prayed to every God, any God that might hear him, to spare her and reverse his grave mistake.

Her eyes didn't move, but a tear slipped down the side of her face. Nik kissed her cheek, then her tear, then her mouth.

"You can't leave me," he said in a pained choke.

"My favorite moon…is when it's…"

She didn't finish her sentence, and Nik was desperate to know.

"When it's what? Do you want me to guess? I know you too well, Tauria Silverknight. I know the special smile you wear when you look up at the moon and it's full. Bright in all its glory. You are my full moon, Tauria. I need you."

Tauria's brow pulled together and her mouth moved, trying to speak, but no words came. Then her face relaxed slowly, her eyes dulled, and her heart…stopped.

CHAPTER EIGHTY-ONE

Tarly

"TARLY!"

The pure devastation in Nik's yell severed the focus Tarly was gathering, frantically trying to follow Nerida's guidance to summon the healer's magick within him.

"I can't reach it," he panted, wiping his brow with the back of his sleeve.

"Yes, you can, Tarly! I know you can," Nerida said, but her tone was equally as panicked.

Tauria wasn't breathing.

A clink drew his eyes to Tauria's hand as it fell limp, releasing what she'd held in a tight grip. Tarly's pulse skipped, swiping the vial before it rolled too far.

He held it up. "She didn't drink it," he muttered in disbelief.

The Phoenix Blood swirled with an iridescent sheen within the bottle, and Tarly was transfixed.

You'll know what to do with it.

Oh, Marlowe…oh, brilliant, spectacular, heroic Marlowe.

She hadn't given it to him to heal himself, nor for Tauria to reach the cave, as she'd held onto it instead. It had to be for now—the powerful aid he prayed to the forsaken Gods would work to reach his healing magick.

Tarly uncorked the bottle and threw the contents down his throat.

His heart pounded, too aware of every second that slipped by with Tauria's life hanging in the balance. Nothing felt different...until...

The hand he held on Tauria tingled.

"Tell me again," he demanded of Nerida.

She told him what to reach for it within himself, how healing was like the union of air and water—fluid yet vital. He felt the well within him begin to open, but it wasn't enough. He needed more—so much more—to conquer this impossible task

"I'm going to remove the blade. Keep pushing all you can into that wound to stop the bleeding and start knitting the skin," Nerida said.

She was such a calm and brilliant teacher despite their collective grief and urgency.

"Her heart..." Nik croaked, holding her head to his chest.

Tarly had to shut out Nik's soul-tearing cries.

"There are a few moments in which the body shuts down but a life force can still be felt within. How long varies per person. You have to keep sealing the wound, but I need you to divide your magick and search for the thread of her life," Nerida instructed.

She pulled the blade out slowly, and Tarly gritted his teeth. The flow of her blood broke out again just as he felt like he was getting it under control. It was like holding a sphere of water and trying to seal the cracks that split too fast.

He couldn't let Tauria die.

"I killed her," Nik whispered, absolutely haunted.

"Keep yourself together," Tarly snapped. Nik was threatening his focus.

"You *have* to find her life thread," Nerida urged.

Tarly gritted his teeth. His whole body trembled and slicked. His first test of magick was far beyond what he should be capable of thanks to the Phoenix Blood. If there was consequence...he didn't care. Saving Tauria was worth anything. He pushed into the well of magick *deeper* with a pained cry.

"You're doing incredible," Nerida said, placing her hand over his in comfort.

It helped. Having Nerida there, he could pretend it was both of them working magick within Tauria. He wasn't alone with her life in his hands.

Tarly closed his eyes and focused on finding the thread. He saw darkness and many threads, but they were all gray and snapped, floating within an empty space.

"The life thread is silver," Nerida said gently into his ear. "It will be severed too, but if you can reach it, there's a chance to reattach it, and the rest will follow."

Tarly pushed himself through the decaying web of Tauria's life. When the first flicker of anything bright caught his eye, he surged for it.

"I-I think I found it," he said. Then he frowned when he reached it. "It's gold."

Nerida gasped. "The mating thread."

She stood suddenly, and Tarly gripped hold of the golden thread before he risked slipping his eyes open to see what she was doing. Nerida cut Nik's palm without asking and placed it over the wound.

Tarly jerked at the rush of energy that attacked him.

"Hold on, Tarly," she said, coming back around and dropping beside him. "The mating thread can bring her back if you can join it to Nik's severed thread. It's a miracle it's still there, really. It would have died completely eventually, after being severed by Marvellas, but some bonds are particularly stubborn. But Nik…"

Nik's red, tear-stained eyes met hers.

She said, "By doing this, it might bring her back, but only because it will link your life thread to what's left of hers as the only way to save her. It means if one of you die, both will die. There will be no other loophole, no other possibility to bring one or both back, when you only have half a life thread each."

"Do it," Nik said without hesitation.

Nerida nodded.

"I can't hold it much longer. The resistance is growing."

"We have thirty seconds at most. Find the other half of the gold thread. Nik's half. With his blood in her, Tauria's should help guide you toward it."

Tarly listened. Instead of pulling on the gold thread, desperate for it not to slip out of his grasp, he relaxed and let it guide him.

He tried not to count the seconds, but they drummed in his mind.

Then, there it was: another frayed golden thread floating in this darkening space. Tarly strained, pulling Tauria's thread toward it, but the distance felt too great for the ends to meet.

"Help me," Tarly gritted out, pushing his magick harder, but he needed Nik to reach back.

"I'm trying," Nik said desperately.

His thread inched closer. So close. Tarly panted, giving everything he had, until he could grip onto Nik's thread. Then, with a strained cry, he pushed himself a final time to bring the ends together and fuse their connection.

Energy *erupted*. It cast him out abruptly, which severed his magick output. Tarly was slammed back into his surroundings, caught by Nerida. It was like something physical had pummeled into him.

His right hand pressed to the floor, feeling the cool stone beneath it.

My right hand.

Tarly looked down at the sling he'd pulled his bad arm out of instinctively to catch himself. He lifted that arm that had lost all feeling and mobility, but…not anymore.

He examined his hand and flexed his fingers. The skin was still gray, but he could feel again. Maybe it was only temporary with magick still coursing through him, but Tarly rubbed his chest, feeling lighter than he had since the bite first happened.

"Your arm…" Nerida noticed.

She took his gray hand, running her gentle touch over the skin, and smiled.

"Nik…" Tauria's voice was weak, but at the sound of it…

Tarly and Nerida turned their incredulous attention toward her.

He'd done it. He'd really done it.

Nerida whimpered, leaning into him, as the weight of relief bore down on them all.

"Her wound still needs healing," Tarly said, lifting his hand again even though he felt exerted beyond his limit.

Nerida stopped him and retrieved her pouch. "You need to recover, or you'll harm yourself. You did absolutely phenomenal work, Tarly. I'll give her something for the pain, and I have some medicines that will aid natural healing. We need to get her somewhere warm and comfortable. But the worst is overcome, thanks to you."

Tarly sat back on his knees, in complete disbelief over the power he'd used that had been dormant within him all along. Though he wouldn't have been strong enough to save Tauria on his own, even if he had tapped into his healing before.

His sight fell on the empty Phoenix Blood vial, and he swiped it up. He was so beholden to Marlowe, yet he would never get to thank her. The loss of her struck all over again, and Tarly pocketed the vial as if it were a token of her he would carry.

Nik lifted Tauria carefully, following Nerida and Tarly out of the room.

He was beginning to let go of the adrenaline that had fueled him —until he was stunned to a halt just outside the door.

Fae and dark fae surrounded them, all clad in black uniforms, no sign of Olmstone purple. Leading them…was Chief Zainaid.

"You continue to find yourselves in perilous situations, it seems," he said by way of greeting.

Tarly's spine locked. Last he'd seen the chief, he'd explained his allegiance to Dakodas wasn't true, but a lot could have changed since then, and his appearance now raised his guard.

"Have you come to apprehend us?" Tarly asked.

"I'm afraid so."

There were too many soldiers for them to fight their way out. Especially with Tauria wounded and Nerida without her Water-wielding.

Zainaid noticed Tarly's assessment. "Don't make this a fight. The full moon rises in two weeks—you will not be held in the cells for long before your Transition. Four royals at once… Dakodas and Mordecai will be very pleased indeed."

A shudder racked his body. Zainaid played his role so well Tarly was beginning to doubt his allegiance still held to his Wolverlon name.

They had no choice but to follow.

Tarly took Nerida's hand, interlocking their fingers, as they headed toward the castle of Olmstone.

They were taken to the cells below the castle, and Tarly wondered if it was added punishment that he was pushed into a cell with Nerida, and through the bars in the cell beside them, his father was still fucking alive.

At least, that was what Tarly thought before he stared at Varlas for long enough without detecting movement that he began to suspect it was just a corpse.

Then he took a breath deeper than the shallow pace barely keeping him alive.

Nerida said, "Is that—?"

"My father. The fallen King of Olmstone."

Tarly had been sure his father would be dead by now, yet his torturous slow end had been prolonged far longer than he thought. Tarly even felt bad for leaving him the last time he visited. He'd hoped for closure, but all he'd received was confirmation his father had died along with his mother a long time ago.

The scent was pungent, as if he were a corpse. Tarly directed

Nerida away from watching the grim sight. Nik and Tauria were in the cell next to them.

Tarly unclasped his cloak, offering it through the bars. Nik looked up, taking it when his own around Tauria wasn't enough. There would be a time for the words unspoken in Nik's eyes, but Tarly smiled, knowing what they were anyway.

The cold tensed his body, but it was bearable.

"We need to get out of here," Tarly said, already calculating with all he knew about the castle layout and escape routes.

"I thought you said Zainaid was on our side," Nerida said.

Tarly raised a finger to his lips, mindful of the guards loyal to Dakodas that lingered nearby. "I thought he was, but things could have changed."

"He sure seemed convincing," Nik said. "And look at where we are."

Nerida slipped another vial of pain-reliever through the bars to Nik.

"But we're together, and he didn't order our weapons to be taken," Tarly observed. He wasn't giving up faith in Zainaid just yet.

"Tar-Tarly." The croak of his voice was barely human.

He approached the bars to his father's cell. The last time he'd been here and heard every cruel reality his father had told him, he'd broke. Now, Tarly felt absolutely nothing for the male who had all but disowned him.

"You've outlasted my expectation," Tarly said.

"You-you came back, my-my son."

"I stopped being your son long ago. You don't get to call me that now you think it might save you."

Nerida took his hand. She was the reason he found the strength to climb out of the grave he'd allowed a life of hardship to push him deep into.

Out of the shadows his father sat in, decaying while still alive, his head lolled against the stone, and Tarly met his sunken eyes. They fell briefly to his hand held in Nerida's, which tightened his hold, anticipating something cruel and taunting toward the love he'd found.

"I-I wanted to tell…to tell you some-something." His father could barely push out words. Tarly figured he hadn't spoken in some time. "A con-confession."

"If you think it will atone for all you've done, it won't."

"Isabel was not-not your mate."

Nerida leaned into him more. Shock clashed through them both, but some part of Tarly knew this. He just couldn't figure out how he'd felt so sure, and how the rejected bond had felt so real.

"Marvellas thought it would make you...make you stronger. More compliant. After seeing what losing my...my mate did to me, her plan was that if you thought you lost...lost your mate too, you would be willing...willing to become dark fae to forget it all like me."

The confession drove a spear of betrayal through his heart.

"How could you wish that kind of pain upon your own child?" Nerida said in horror.

Tarly answered, "Because I wasn't his child anymore."

Nerida's grip tightened, then she stepped forward in a rare flash of anger, pointing a finger though the bars at his father. "You never deserved him," she said angrily. "You don't know half the amazing things he's achieved and all the great things he is. You didn't care to discover your son had healing magick within him. Despite everything, he is the most considerate person you had no part or privilege in raising."

Tarly let go of her hand to circle an arm around her waist, drawing her to him. "You saw everything before I could even see it myself," he said, low and close to her ear.

Her anger dissolved, relaxing her body into him.

"Everything was worth it to make it to you. My mate. My one and only remarkable mate."

"You-you have healing magick?" his father croaked. Though it wasn't out of any pride when he followed with, "Will you help me... please?"

His father tried to shift, but it was like his body had decayed into the stone where he sat.

Tarly's jaw locked. "Yes, Father. I will."

He leaned down to Nerida's pouch, retrieving a vial. Nerida exchanged a look of surprise with him, but she didn't object.

The bottle rolled across the stone, hitting his father's leg. He scrambled for it as if it were his first drop of water after days through the desert.

He drank the small potion eagerly, letting the bottle slip from his clumsy grip afterward, and it shattered.

Tarly wandered over to the front of his cell, wrapping a hand around a thick bar and leaning his head to the cold metal. He closed his eyes, tuning in to the shallow beats of his father's heart. Nerida closed in after a few seconds, laying her head against his back in solace.

No one moved. No one spoke.

His father's last breaths where wheezes and chokes. The tonic he'd consumed was an anti-inflammatory, but since that wasn't a correct diagnosis for what his father was going through, it would slowly decrease his heart rate until it stopped.

The silence that settled after the final beat declared Tarly the King of Olmstone, but still, he would not take that crown when the war was over. For now, he would do what he had to do.

Zainaid returned at last just as Tauria woke up, still weak and disorientated, but coming around stronger each hour.

"You shouldn't have come here now," Zainaid said, his tone hushed. The chief's eyes skimmed over to the dead king, and he winced, casting a knowing look at Tarly, who gave no reaction.

"We didn't have a choice. Now tell me what's going on here," Tarly demanded.

"This is one of Dakodas's strongest fortresses. She's stationed much of her army here from Valgard, with more arriving every day. They're planning to move onto the fringe soon."

"We know this," Nik said. "What we're wondering is if you've decided to save yourself and join them truly."

The chief's expression flexed. "They expect me to lead what's left of Olmstone's army into battle with Valgard. I'll admit, I was running out of options until you showed up. Foolish—you were never getting through Olmstone without being detected by the spies that crawl this place—but we need you, Tarly. These soldiers are afraid and will follow me into battle even against what they believe in. Unless they see a Wolverlon still lives—still stands to fight against the enemy and will not yield."

"Why can't you lead them against Valgard?" Tarly asked.

"You royals are a symbol to the people. You have the strength and abilities like many common folk, but it is your legacy they believe in. The name that has led them through every trial and change of history for generations. Not every heir born can live up to the expectation that weighs on a crown… Can you, Tarly Wolverlon?"

He looked to Nerida, his pillar of strength and belief. The Queen of Lakelaria who, against her fears, had declared herself and become the symbol needed for the rebellion on the grand island to act against Marvellas for the first time. Now it was his turn.

Tarly lifted his chin. "What do you need me to do?"

CHAPTER EIGHTY-TWO

Faythe

Faythe flew with her wings of Phoenixfyre while Reylan took the form of an eagle. They landed on in the Fire Mountains for rest before they would press on over to the Niltain Isles.

When her feet touched ground, her wings singed away immediately, and she caught herself on her thighs, exerted from the flat-out day of flying.

Reylan offered her water, and she drank too eagerly.

"We have to rest for at least an hour and find more water," he said.

Faythe nodded even though everything in her wanted to push on despite the fatigue. They walked through the mountain, following a distant sound of running water. Reylan filled the waterskin he'd brought while Faythe's eyes wandered over the chasm between peaks. This was close to where they'd battled Zaiana and Maverick, and she reflected on how much had changed with the dark fae since then.

"Do you think you could ever forgive Maverick?" The question slipped from her thoughts.

Reylan straightened. "No."

Faythe looked at him, seeing no hesitation in that sure answer.

"Even knowing who he really is? Callen Osirion."

"I don't know that fae. I do know Maverick Blackfair, and if I ever get the chance, I will kill him."

She understood and wouldn't persuade him otherwise. Maverick had killed her… He'd killed her father, who was like a father to Reylan too. What he'd done *should* be unforgivable, but…Faythe was tired of carrying vengeful burdens, and she couldn't help but wonder about the tragic Prince of Dalrune, who'd watched his family be slaughtered then been taken prisoner and Transitioned into a dark, bloodthirsty being against his will.

"Is it a betrayal to say I wouldn't actively want him dead anymore? I don't know what I would do if the opportunity was there, but he's been through a trauma unfathomable to all of us. I can't comprehend what it did to him."

"No," he said. "I think it's a testament to your golden heart. I envy it."

She smiled sadly, not receiving it as a compliment. Was it a weakness?

Faythe's sight cast through the red rock, catching on a dark space that appeared like a large cave entrance in the distance.

"Think you'll be able to fly the rest of the distance soon?" Reylan asked.

His question went unanswered when Faythe followed a pull she felt toward the cave mouth. All she knew was that he followed closely.

"We can rest for a few hours if you need," he offered, assuming that was why she sought the shelter.

"You don't feel the energy around this place?" she asked him. Her eyes were fixed on the darkness drawing her closer.

"I don't. And I've come to brace for terror when you get a *feeling*."

They entered the cave mouth, and Faythe summoned a small blue flame in her palm when they ventured beyond the cast of daylight.

Faythe was so focused on the tug of unexplainable energy that when steel pierced the silence, she jerked, spinning to Reylan.

He held the Ember Sword gripped firmly in one hand. "You have a tendency to be attracted to monsters and danger."

Faythe smirked, continuing through the cave. "They're attracted to me."

"I can't blame them."

She pushed him playfully as she spied light spilling in through the end of the cave. Faythe's feet pressed faster, and when she broke through the gap at the end, she was stunned still.

The cave expanded wide, filled with sticks and castaway hair and fur from animals. The mountain opened at the top, spilling the setting sun down over the entire circumference.

"It's a nest," Faythe said in disbelief.

"It must be very old, from the time of the Firebirds in Rhyenelle."

There were none left now. Atherius had been the last to live in these mountains, alone for centuries after her kin were all slaughtered. Faythe harbored hope in her heart that wasn't the whole truth; that some might have fled and lived on somewhere in the world that wouldn't harm them as cruelly as the bloodshed that had happened on these mountains.

Faythe trod carefully as she stepped off the rock into the meticulously crafted nest.

"Are you sure that's a good idea?" Reylan called, staying behind.

"When do I ever lead by good ideas?"

His low chuckle was heard over the cracks beneath her feet.

The nest wasn't even. It had mounds, and Faythe only wanted to glimpse the middle of the incredible structure. Her foot caught the top, and she squealed, tumbling, cutting her skin on the protruding sticks as she rolled into the heart of the nest.

Reylan called her name, and when she stopped tumbling, she was about to answer, but what her eyes met made her words dissolve.

Faythe rose so carefully with the space clearly fragile. A chest holding the greatest treasure. Her wide eyes couldn't tear away from what she'd discovered.

"I can't let you out of my sight for a second," Reylan rambled, much closer now. He climbed over the small mound to find her, and his speech faltered too.

"She didn't stay out of guilt," Faythe whispered. Her heart was so broken and full at the same time. "Atherius stayed to protect her egg."

The shell was the most beautiful thing Faythe had ever laid eyes on. A brilliant red, with gold etchings.

"After all this time…it can't be alive," Reylan said.

"Do you know how Phoenix eggs are hatched?"

Reylan climbed down into the nest with her, crouching to examine it closer too.

"No, actually. Maybe it doesn't hatch from a mere period of gestation like most eggs."

"Then there's a chance it could hatch. Surely Atherius wouldn't have stayed if it were dead?"

"I'm not sure. Best not get our hopes up, but it is a truly remarkable thing to have found regardless."

Faythe splayed her hands above it, carefully approaching.

"Never led by good ideas," Reylan mumbled under his breath, watching her with as much anticipation as she felt. As though touching it could trigger something terrible and ancient.

When she felt the rough surface of the egg, she held her breath for a second, scanning around as if she might find the walls crumbling down at her audacity. Nothing happened, and Faythe lifted the large egg into her lap.

Her eyes watered as she traced the shell, mourning in her heart all over again for Atherius.

"I think she knew you'd find it someday," Reylan said, offering comfort with his hand on her shoulder.

"Me too," Faythe whispered.

The weight of the egg was surprisingly light, which only added to her doubt there was a hatchling inside. Still, she cradled it to her body.

Just as she stood, an ear-splitting *boom* shook through the cave. Reylan grabbed her, steadying them, but Faythe gasped at the large rocks that broke from the mountain, plummeting down around them. She cast her magick out as a shield, nearly buckling at the boulders slamming against it, but Reylan kept her standing.

"We need to get out of here," he urged, guiding her while she kept her focus on shielding them from the crumbing rocks.

They raced out of the cave, emerging onto the mountain fringe, and the waves of power that slammed into her stole her breath. Faythe whirled. What she saw, piercing up into the sky, was a rolling dark beam of power.

"We're too late," Faythe said in horror.

"We would have been even if we'd kept flying," Reylan said.

Marvellas had managed to place the Light Temple Ruin where it should never touch…in the dark temple podium. Marvellas was one giant leap closer to her goal of destroying the entire world.

Faythe gritted her teeth. Her Phoenixfyre wings manifested, about to shoot to the sky in a last attempt to stop Marvellas before she could make it to her own temple in the Sky Caves of Lakelaria and finish her task.

"It's all too late, Faythe."

Marvellas's voice was like a snake coiling around her throat.

Faythe turned, finding the Spirit of Souls with her creature, the Dresair, behind her. It hadn't taken a mortal body yet, still standing unnaturally tall, with spindly black limbs and no face.

Marvellas said, "You should spend the last hours with your friends. The end is coming, and there is nothing you can do to stop it."

"I can stop you," Faythe hissed.

"You have tried many times. When will you give up?"

"Never."

Marvellas barely displayed any emotion. Her gold eyes cast up over the dark beam behind Faythe that stabbed into the sky from Dakodas's temple. Then she turned her head to glance far into the north horizon. Her brow flinched as her eyes searched.

"The Light from Aurialis's temple should have activated too," she muttered absentmindedly. Marvellas turned to her with accusing eyes. "What have you done to interfere?"

Faythe didn't know what could have gone wrong in Marvellas's plan, but by the Gods, was she glad something seemed to be missing from what she expected or needed to carry out the destruction of the world.

When Faythe didn't answer, Marvellas continued to accuse and assess while stalking closer. Her anger returned, and Reylan shifted to place himself between them for first attack if necessary.

"Something is guarding Aurialis's temple, isn't it?"

Faythe was confused, but she didn't let it show. "I won't let you destroy this world just because you couldn't have it."

Her mind was reeling with what could possibly be interfering with the catastrophic connection Marvellas had tried to make between the temples. Marvellas believed it had to be their doing...but Faythe hadn't done anything.

Then she realized.

"Marlowe." Her friend's name slipped from her mouth, and it was like she'd smiled into Faythe's mind.

Jakon had buried her in the Eternal Woods, and Faythe had thought it a beautiful and fitting place. Yet she hadn't considered Marlowe could have made sure somehow that Jakon would know to place her there, where her soul could protect the temple for this moment. To buy them time.

Marvellas's eyes narrowed on her. Then they relaxed, as if the Spirit had figured it out too. "I see..." she said. "I always knew Marlowe Kilnight had such brilliant potential. Such a pity her life was taken so soon. And I truly am sorry that she will die a second time, never to be reborn again, for I have to eradicate her soul that lingers as an interference around that temple."

Marlowe's soul lived in the Eternal Woods. Faythe's eyes watered, but her resolve hardened.

"I'm not letting you get away," Faythe said—a declaration of defiance as she freed her blade.

She used Shadowporting to cross the distance, appearing right in front of Marvellas. Faythe swung Lumarias toward her neck, but her steel slammed into an arm of charcoal that was like hitting thick wood.

The Dresair hissed at her, disarming her since the blade was lodged in its arm. It pulled it free, throwing Lumarias out of reach.

Yet that had only been Faythe's distraction.

Reylan was beside her, the Ember Sword plunged through the gut of the Dresair, and it screeched, piercing Faythe's ears painfully, but she didn't falter.

As the Dresair burst into flames, Faythe reached for Marvellas with her heart in her throat. Marvellas ripped her arm out of Faythe's grip with a fierce cry, but it was too late...

Faythe had managed to secure the manacle. The other was in Faythe's hand.

Just one more.

But magick slammed into her. She hadn't realized Reylan was behind her until his arms encircled her body, and they were both flying back before crashing into hard stone.

Faythe wasn't spared from the impact despite Reylan's protection. They both groaned, peeling themselves off the ground before Marvellas could attack again.

She peered up to find her enemy, but Marvellas didn't advance. The Dresair was nothing more than smoking ash at her feet. Marvellas held up her manacled wrist, staring at it with the most terror she'd ever seen the Spirit display. It clearly hadn't smothered her power completely, with Faythe failing to clamp the second Aetherbond on her other wrist, but it had to have diminished her power by half at least.

"Where did you get these?" Marvellas asked in a ghostly breath. Long ago, she'd been a helpless slave, used for her blood for centuries by being bound in these. "What have you done?" she yelled, looking at Faythe, with the heat of the Nether blazing in her eyes.

Faythe stood with Reylan. She held the other manacle while he braced with the Ember Sword. With gold locked on gold, fire on fire, Faythe dared Marvellas to come closer.

The Spirit yelled in anguish, seeming to decide the fight wasn't worth the risk.

Snarls and hisses divided Faythe's attention from the Spirit to glance in the direction it was coming from.

Reylan swore, announcing, "Skalies."

Her gut plummeted. Faythe caught a plume of smoke around Marvellas and lunged a step.

"No!"

Marvellas escaped through Shadowporting.

Faythe didn't have a second more before the vicious creatures that lived in these mountains came pouring out of various crevices.

Reylan called her name, and Faythe caught her sword as he threw it to her. Before she could summon wings to flee, she was forced to fight back-to-back with Reylan against the foes that snapped jagged teeth at her.

She'd faced skalies before, when she was still human. They'd arrived in a force as overwhelming as this, and they'd only escaped them thanks to Atherius.

"We can't fight this many for long," Reylan said.

Her blade kept severing limbs and cutting down the flesh-rotted bodies, but the pressure of the force didn't ease.

"Marvellas can't get to that temple," Faythe panted.

Her urgency clashed with her frustration that these creatures were stealing precious time she should be using to stop Marvellas. Faythe yelled in anguish, summoning Phoenixfyre in a wheel that cut through the closest skalies. But without Atherius, her Phoenixfyre was becoming weaker by the day, and weaker each time she used it.

Reylan took her hand, tapping into her essence of Shadowporting and using the seconds of reprieve she'd gained them to pull them across the fringe. Again, that power was too weak to get them off this mountain. All they could do was use what they had in small doses.

"I don't know if I have enough Phoenixfyre to fly for long," Faythe said in panic, back to swinging her sword since the skalies were immediately upon them again.

"If I shift into a lion, I can carry you. Our best bet might be to try to outrun them that way."

Faythe didn't like that idea, but she agreed it was their only hope.

Her blue Firewielding wasn't as effective against them, so Faythe conjured another flare of Phoenixfyre to give Reylan the opening to shift. The moment her wheel of searing flame left her, Faythe twisted on her heel, gripping Reylan's fur as he crouched and swinging her body onto his back.

She didn't like this plan, because it left her useless and helpless, having to focus on clamping her body tightly around him to avoid being thrown off. Reylan was more vulnerable to attack from the skalies that pounced on him as he darted through the masses, tearing through them with his giant claws and jaw, but there were too many. They weren't going to make it out of here like this.

They swarmed them until Reylan couldn't run anymore. Faythe tried to let go enough to attack, but she was thrown off him and buried under the stampede. She curled into herself to protect her head while summoning whatever force she could within her. Then…

Heat.

It blasted over her like a blanket of protection, with a familiar essence. Faythe dared to open her eyes and found herself surrounded by the most beautiful red flame. Her hand rose, and it bent around her touch. It morphed from the protection of the Eye of the Phoenix on her amulet.

Then it parted, revealing Reylan, with the twin eye blazing in the pommel of the Ember Sword at his hip, protecting him too. He kneeled, helping her up, and they stood, defiant, in the storm of glorious Phoenixfyre.

Reylan cupped her cheek and kissed her. It were as if this powerful moment demanded it, and her chest burst with euphoria.

But she hadn't summoned this fire…

When it finally stopped blasting around them, the last lick of heat was stolen by the bitter air. Snow had begun to fall, and her body broke with a violent shiver at the sudden contrast.

The plummet in temperature was forgotten completely when she glanced sideward and saw one of the most beautiful creatures in the world.

"Did we die?" Faythe muttered in disbelief.

Reylan released an incredulous, breathy laugh. "I'm debating that myself, because I'm looking at my cousin on the back of a Firebird long believed to be extinct…for a second time."

"Are you waiting for another round?" Livia called from atop the Firebird. Samara had her arms wrapped around her from behind.

Faythe couldn't believe it. Her stupor was broken by Reylan tugging her.

"When you told me Livia went west to try to get help from Salenhaven, you didn't mention *this* kind of help," Reylan said.

"It was a mere gut feeling," Faythe said, recalling her private conversation with the commander before they'd all gone their separate ways months ago. "Well, not entirely. I remembered a book Agalhor gave me to read about Phoenix migration. It was believed that if they felt themselves under threat, they would always travel west. Rhyenelle may not have been the first ever home of the Phoenixes if they sought a new safe haven here from somewhere else farther east a very long time ago."

"Loyal creatures," Livia commented, smoothing a hand down the Firebird's feathers. "There aren't many species that would stick together like that. They all migrate together."

Except for Atherius. Faythe retrieved the egg before they mounted Livia's Firebird.

Reylan sat behind Faythe, holding her tightly. She relaxed into him, letting her body and mind calm just for a moment as they took to the skies.

"I expected to meet you in High Farrow," Reylan said. "When Faythe told me of your venture west, I was worried."

"I knew you would be, which is why I asked her not to tell you," Livia said playfully.

"The months by boat were awful," Samara said, earning a chuckle from Livia, who ran her hand along Samara's arm.

"What happened with Lord Zarrius?" Faythe asked.

Samara answered, "It was easy to get him into bed and kill him."

The way she delivered this news was factual, her features expressionless. But Faythe thought it was only a disguise for how the deed would haunt Samara.

Faythe reached out a hand to squeeze her arm. "You're incredibly brave."

"I wish I could have done it myself ten times over," Livia said, a hateful note to her voice.

Faythe couldn't help but notice their mannerisms. Sure, they were forced to hold onto each other while Livia rode, but there was a new comfort between them, an ease in the way Samara wasn't shy to subtly drift her touch over Livia or lean her cheek to her back. It made Faythe smile.

Reylan told Livia where they needed to go, and Faythe rallied her bravery and resilience to take Marvellas down once and for all to save Marlowe's brave and brilliant soul.

CHAPTER EIGHTY-THREE

Faythe

Faythe was horror-stricken to fly over High Farrow. The enemy had infiltrated right through the outer town, and the screams of the people rang through her senses. Smoke billowed from buildings she'd passed countless times in her youth. Her neighbors fought for their homes and their lives. The only hope to shine through her despair was to notice that High Farrow and Rhyenelle forces were holding strong against the enemy as they tore through the streets. The wall around Caius City hadn't been breached.

They fought several dark fae in the skies to get to the hills of Farrowhold. Landing, war pounded in her chest with a strong urge to join the fighting in the town.

"They've advanced far quicker than we anticipated," Faythe said.

Reylan replied, "The enemy is always uncertain. We can't be sure what went wrong or what intel might have been miscalculated, but what I'm confident of is that our generals know how to adapt. They're leading strong, though it may not look like it."

Faythe nodded, trusting his judgment. She had no choice but to turn away from the cries of battle tearing through her childhood home and face the Eternal Woods. It would all be for nothing if Marvellas succeeded.

They raced through the woodland, passing the waterfall clearing and heading straight to the temple. Breaking past the tree line, Faythe stumbled to a halt.

Jakon stood by Marlowe's headstone, his stance squared and a dagger aimed to protect it with his life.

Because Marvellas was here, standing off with him. A human against a Spirit with immense power even with one Aetherbond. Yet Jakon stood bravely, without a single tremble to his firm stance, and with the determination and rage of an army in his stare.

"If you hurt him…" Faythe had to pause with the dizzying adrenaline and rush of rage that pulsed through her to protect Jakon. "I won't kill you. No. That would be too merciful. I'll bind you in this second Aetherbond and keep you alive for worse torture than your first lover put you through."

Marvellas's golden eyes flashed with that. It was a deplorable thing to use, but Faythe had no kindness left.

"You will all die at the end of this. Who goes a little earlier depends on who is standing in my way."

Her attention slipped back to Jakon defending Marlowe's headstone. Marvellas must need to get to it to drag Marlowe's soul out of the very core of these woods and destroy it.

Faythe would not let that happen.

Out of the corner of her eye she saw Nyte in the tree line. Her heart thundered. He was here with the Ruin Dagger. These next moments would decide the fate of the world.

She exchanged a subtle look of acknowledgment with Nyte, then Faythe struck out at Marvellas with her power in a gold flare.

Marvellas deflected easily, but all Faythe needed was her attention. They erupted into a power battle that clashed gold with gold, shaking the peace and beauty of this sacred woodland.

Faythe felt the humming amplifier of the Ruin Dagger nearby, and she opened herself to it, expanding her magick to contend with the Spirit. Marvellas's magick even in half pushed Faythe to her limits fast. She faltered for a second, and it was enough for Marvellas to land a blow to her shoulder. Faythe cried out, falling to one knee.

Reylan took over, using the power of the ruin too. Through their bond they shared magick, but his well wasn't as deep as Faythe's, limiting him.

Marvellas landed a flare of her magick to project him back too, with more force, slamming him into a tree.

Faythe was aware of Nyte in the shadows. She hoped he remained hidden, only watching, to wait for the right opening. They might only get one chance. Once Marvellas knew the dagger was here, it would be harder to strike.

She remained down, though Faythe fought the urge to lunge up and fight again. Faythe let the Spirit think she was weakened; let Marvellas approach in predatory strides.

When she was close enough, Faythe pulled her blade free, launching up with a quick vertical slice that met the resistance of clothing and flesh.

Marvellas stumbled back, bleeding in a long line from her navel and over her jaw and cheek. While she'd been down and Reylan had attacked, Faythe had been absorbing more of the ruin's power into her body. It raged through her like a storm, and in the casting-out of her palm, the full charge shot toward Marvellas.

The Spirit was blasted back with such force no mortal would have survived it. It threw her into the caved-open Temple of Aurialis, burying her in the stones as she slammed against the back wall.

Faythe pulled out the other Aetherbond, sprinting to take her chance while the Spirit had to at least be disorientated for a moment. She scrambled over loose stone, her heart thrumming in her ears. *Almost there.* Marvellas was already coming around, pushing rocks off herself.

Marvellas freed herself from the rubble enough that when Faythe reached with the Aetherbond, the Spirit grabbed her wrist, throwing her off-balance. They fought in a clumsy struggle. Rocks dug into Faythe's spine as Marvellas managed to crawl out, hovering over Faythe. Her nails slashed across Faythe's face deep enough to bleed, but Faythe didn't stop fighting with everything she had.

A blast of power knocked into Marvellas, throwing her off Faythe. It was Reylan. Faythe hooked her leg, positioning over Marvellas, and then...

The *click* of the Aetherbond locking over the Marvellas's wrist sang to her with victory through the pounding in her ears.

Marvellas cried loudly as the Aetherbond silenced the rest of her magick. Reylan hooked an arm around Faythe's middle, effortlessly lifting her off the Spirit and gaining them distance away.

"Now, Nyte!" Faythe yelled.

When he didn't answer or appear, Faythe whipped her head to where she'd last seen him by the trees. He'd come out of hiding but was standing halfway across the clearing as if an invisible force had stopped his advance.

A daunting dread crept over her as she took in his stunned expression. Faythe walked toward him, scanning every inch of him, but he appeared unharmed.

"Nyte?" she questioned. Something wasn't right.

He drew a shallow gasp, falling to his knees, and Faythe ran to him.

"What's wrong?" she demanded, scanning him again.

"I think...I think I'm going back," he said.

Faythe's panic rose. "No. You can't—not yet."

When his eyes lifted to hers, they were almost gold. His true color infused his irises more, and she clutched his arms desperately, as if it would tether him to the body of Capitan Daegal just a little while longer.

"We need you. Marvellas is right there." Faythe lifted his hand, gripping the dagger, pressing it to his chest with a plea in her eyes.

"I'm sorry... It was a privilege to know you. *Family.* I'll treasure that even across realms, Faythe Ashfyre."

Her eyes welled. "Family," she whispered.

Nyte almost smiled, but his eyes rolled to the back of his head as he threw it back. Only for a few seconds, before the body of Captain Daegal slumped.

Nyte was gone.

Faythe's head bowed, and despite their hope disappearing with him, Faythe hoped he'd made it back to the realm he chose. That the family he'd found there had figured out how to bring him home, and he was safe.

The return of Nyte was a moment of joy in one realm, and a dire consequence in another.

Faythe's eyes fell on the Ruin Dagger. All wasn't lost, and she supposed it was fate to end up here again as the one holding it. As the one who had to end Marvellas's terror once and for all.

"Rainyte..."

Marvellas's heartbroken whisper pushed Faythe to her feet. The Spirit looked down at the body of Daegal with grief falling on her features. Faythe's fist tightened, and she ran the short distance toward the Spirit.

"NO!" Reylan yelled, lunging after her, but she was too fast, and his fingers barely grazed her arm.

Faythe's arm rose, ready to bring down the dagger to strike true in Marvellas's heart.

The Spirit's hand lashed around Faythe's throat in a choking grip, but that wasn't what stopped Faythe's blade. It was the invasion that pierced into her mind so quick and precise she didn't have a second to reform her mental barriers.

Faythe clawed at Marvellas's hand, her wrist, realizing with absolute horror...the Aetherbonds had released.

Marvellas's eyes swirled like the surface of the sun, so ablaze with rage and grief that this was the most frightening depiction she'd seen. The air stirred around them, growing more violent with a charge of powerful energy.

Faythe understood then, even after all this time, Nyte was the one thing most precious to her. And she'd lost him again, releasing her from the Aetherbonds.

"I won't let you get in my way a moment longer," Marvellas said. A chilling, deep voice echoed over hers, making her all the more terrifying. A true Goddess in mortal form.

Marvellas's eyes cast to the side briefly before her hand followed. Faythe yelled and cried, watching a devastating blow of power slam into Reylan, who charged, sword raised, to try to save her.

Oh Gods.

Faythe tried to use her own magick, but Marvellas had a hold of her mind, preventing her from reaching it.

Marvellas's ethereal eyes met hers again, softening just a fraction as she said, voice quiet with sorrow, "Goodbye, Faythe."

Faythe's eyes rolled back at the crushing grip on her throat. She watched the eternal day and thought of all of her friends. Thought of Reylan. She didn't want to leave them...but she'd failed.

In her final moments, it was Marlowe's sweet voice that trickled through her mind, and tears spilled over her face.

"It's not your time yet, Phoenix Queen."

The title changed to a perfect imitation of Marlowe's playful tone. Faythe's whimper turned to another choke. She was going to die in a few more seconds.

At least I'll be with you, Faythe thought in solace as she pictured her beautiful, brilliant lost friend. Marlowe had left behind so much in her wake to aid them in this fight, and it was a tragedy she wouldn't get to receive the credit for all she'd done.

Air rushed down Faythe's throat suddenly, and she was so eager for breath that she couldn't catch herself when her body crumpled to the ground. Her vision came and went with specks of darkness, but she grappled her threads of consciousness, forcing herself to hold on.

Faythe looked up, finding Marvellas unmoving, her hand still raised as if she held the ghost of Faythe still.

The Spirit didn't scream or move. Then, slowly, particles blew from her hand into the gentle wind. Marvellas's skin was *disintegrating*.

Faythe sat back on her knees, watching in utter disbelief as the Spirit of Souls, Goddess of the Stars, turned into stardust. Marvellas looked down as her face half dissolved, and only one golden eye spoke her fear. Even the wicked feared death. Even a God.

"The light cancels out the dark," Marvellas said—final words that stroked Faythe with a shudder.

She watched the Spirit fade away with relief building in her chest. But what was revealed behind Marvellas...

Horror pierced her being deeper than she'd ever experienced before.

"JAK!" she screamed.

Jakon stared at her, wide-eyed and ghostly, gripping the Ruin Dagger that fell from his grip as his hand turned to dust as well.

"Forgive me," he said, fear lacing his distant voice. "I had to...to be with Marlowe again. But I'm always with you, Faythe...always."

He fell to his knees, and Faythe scrambled, reaching for him, but her hand passed through the dust his body became. She fell, palms splayed, to the ground instead. He'd been here...right here just a second ago, and now...

He was gone.

No final seconds to hold him. No body to bury.

Jakon Kilnight had sacrificed himself to save her and the world.

The scream that tore through Faythe Ashfyre could shatter stars and erupt the sun. Her grief was made of the sharpest blade, and when it cut right through her, it fractured the land too.

The ground quaked, but she couldn't stop screaming. Couldn't stop the rage that barreled out of her and attacked the world beyond this woodland. Her body curled into itself, in so much pain she didn't know how to come out of this pit of absolute despair.

She did know how to make the world feel her pain, and so the Phoenix Queen would rage.

CHAPTER EIGHTY-FOUR

Zaiana

Zaiana forgot when she had begun to fight, but she saw no end. The mountain fringe waged with a battle to end all, relentless and bloodthirsty.

Blood of silver, black, and crimson painted the stone, her clothing, and the blade. She led the lines, and they were holding up well. They'd fought for days, managing to push the enemy to fall back and tire enough for them to collect themselves for a few hours through the nights too. But the enemy didn't need as much rest.

By the fifth day Zaiana didn't know how much longer they'd hold out. Something was different in the battle that had resumed today. Something that pushed them harder than ever before, and Zaiana realized what was happening.

They'd been using their weakest soldiers so far. What was most daunting was that the enemy's *weakest* was nearly on par with the strongest among her ranks. They'd always known they were outmatched. The enemy ranks were filled with dark fae enhanced in agility, strength, and speed with human blood. Then they'd discovered Dakodas could command the shadow creatures that still plagued their land, as they never attacked the enemy.

The Spirit of Death lingered somewhere, watching. She knew Mordecai would be too, and that enraged her more. Zaiana wanted to snuff them out, but there'd been no chance to leave the front lines that were relying on her leadership.

They had to find the void that was letting these creatures manifest from shadows. If they closed it, there would be one less ruthless force among the enemy ranks.

Her soldiers were tiring. They were losing hope and strength. Morale was just as important as any skill in combat.

Zaiana realized what else had advanced in the enemy ranks when her boot crunched over something. A vial leaking with a crimson liquid. Their magick wielders had been supplied with the Phoenix Blood potions Marlowe was forced to make in Rhyenelle.

A hum of Firewielding tingled her senses, and with only a split second to react, she threw lightning against the flame that shot for her. Just as she suspected, his magick was too powerful for an ordinary wielder of the ability. As she parried with him for a few seconds, it was clear in the way his fire matched the strength of Maverick's, but this fae had no skill to use it like he did.

Despite the enhancement, Zaiana ended him swiftly. A bolt of lightning to the chest, a slice of her blade across his neck, and because she was growing particularly frustrated and exhausted, she ripped out his heart.

Then she was onto the next, who attacked with wind.

Shapeshifters on the enemy side could take on mammoth forms like oversized bears and lions. The odds grew detrimental against them, and Zaiana tried to calculate a new strategy to adapt while she fought relentlessly.

But then…the Shapeshifters who towered over the bodies began to writhe, and their wails cut over the chaos of steel and the fallen.

The Windbreaker Zaiana battled faltered before she was about to end it. The fae clutched her throat, and the whites of her eyes turned bloodred. Zaiana didn't know what was happening, but she didn't have a breath to spare while the fighting of others still raged on.

She was about to spring back into action when she watched a young female fae take a slash across her abdomen. Zaiana struck a lethal bolt of lightning at the dark fae, who lifted her sword for a killing blow. She caught the younger fae before she fell, and Zaiana shot to the sky.

Landing at one of the healing tents, she ushered her inside, demanding help, but everyone was occupied. Zaiana led the fae over to a bench, grabbing gauze and whatever else she could find to press into the fae's wound.

Her terrified green eyes met Zaiana's, and for a second she was pierced by grief. Her hair was a dark brown, and she was a similar age to Amaya. Their features were nothing alike, but still, the memory of her brave darkling filled her thoughts with sorrow for a distracting second.

Zaiana had to shake off the emotions that only served to distract her. "You're not going to die," she said firmly.

The fae nodded, and Zaiana had to leave her to resume her station.

Kyleer burst into the tent before she could leave it. He came bearing information, and she straightened to hear it.

"They came. Forces from the south, I believe. They're wearing purple."

"Olmstone," Zaiana said. Had Tarly and Nerida managed to rally the soldiers that were close to joining Dakodas's ranks?

Zaiana left the healer's tent, finding her answer as she stared right into the healer's eyes standing next to the Olmstone prince. Nerida smiled, and Zaiana lost her composure, impulsively crossing the distance and pulling Nerida into an embrace. It was odd to instigate a hug, but Zaiana was trying to accept her emotions, especially right now, when all their lives could vanish in a blink.

"You made it," Zaiana said in relief.

When they pulled back, the shock on Nerida's face eased to another kind smile.

"Yes. Nik and Tauria are fighting on the front lines, but we came to aid the wounded."

Zaiana reached to her side, pulling the jeweled dagger free and lifting Nerida's hand to place it within.

Nerida's eyes widened on it, but Zaiana quickly said, "She was dying by another fatal wound at the same time. I can't be certain if it absorbed all your magick back in time. And Nerida..." Zaiana swallowed the lump in her throat. "Amaya didn't make it."

The healer's face fell with grief. She'd helped save Amaya the day they met and since had grown closest to the darkling.

"Then we carry her with us until the end."

Nerida's face firmed, and she hissed, slicing the jeweled dagger across her palm. She gasped, and blue light glowed over the wound. It was such a relief to see, but Zaiana held her breath, waiting to find out how much had been returned to her.

From a nearby bucket, water lifted from it in a thin stroke with Nerida's gentle hand movement.

"My Waterwielding is weaker," she said, but still she smiled, bringing the water closer, and Zaiana drew a breath at the bite of it

674

touching a wound through the leather on her arm. The sting subsided as Nerida healed it fully in seconds. "But my healing feels the same, and that's what matters most to me."

Zaiana's shoulders fell in relief.

A commander came rushing toward her. "General Zaiana, there's been a sudden overwhelming force of shadow creatures coming from the east. We're going to lose that entire legion soon."

Zaiana's battle-focused mind sharpened again. "I want a team of scouts finding where the rift is that is summoning them. Investigate the east mountains—it has to be close to here. Which commanders are east?"

"Commander Izaiah is leading east."

She didn't have to look to feel Kyleer's tension growing beside her. "You should join him," Zaiana said.

So far, Kyleer had been close by her every day, fighting valiantly and leading what he could as more instinctual memory came back to him as the second highest-ranking commander of Rhyenelle's armies.

He hesitated with a pained look. She didn't want to be separated from him either, but his brother needed help, and he was more important to him than she was.

With a nod, Kyleer splayed his beautiful black feathered wings and shot to the sky. She watched him leave with an aching pull in her chest, but her station was in the center point.

An enemy stumbled through their healer tents, having slipped through their lines. Zaiana braced to kill them at seeing the small blue flame in their hand, but it winked out as they clawed at their throat, dropping an empty vial of Phoenix Blood as they collapsed and died.

"What is happening?" she pondered to herself.

"Poison," Tarly said. "All the Phoenix Blood potions in Rhyenelle are poisoned. I wasn't sure if they would detect it or notice people dying before they distributed it all."

Everyone turned to the Olmstone prince, stunned.

He glanced at Nerida. "We found that plant in the woods you deemed nothing but poisonous, remember? When we met with Faythe and Kyleer. The idea came to me when I spoke to Faythe, and she told me what Marlowe was being forced to do in Rhyenelle."

The clang of steel and shouts of battle became louder in their pause of silence.

"You are brilliant, Tarly Wolverlon," Nerida said, pushing up on her toes to kiss his cheek.

Zaiana looked away from them and down at the enemy body. What he'd done *was* brilliant. And a huge relief.

"I'm going back," Zaiana informed them. "They need all the healing help they can get in there."

Nerida and Tarly nodded firmly, and she shot to the sky.

She examined the field, noticing how they'd been pushed back too much, and though Tarly had wounded their magick wielder ranks, it was the bloodthirsty dark fae who attacked brutally that had the fae on her side retreating.

There were barely any dark fae left to help stop those on the enemy side from flying and dropping into the thick of their lines. Zaiana gritted her teeth, disappointed in her kin. They were trying to change the perception of the dark fae, yet the numbers who fought with her were negligible.

Zaiana decided to stay airborne. Instead of two sides of the field, it had turned to four. With Nik and Tauria leading a force in from the south, it helped to trap a large portion of the enemy on two sides. It would be an incredible advantage, were it not for the enemy that kept arriving from the skies and the land, also trapping Nik and Tauria's force on two sides.

The enemy numbers felt endless.

Her heart nearly stopped when she spied the threat racing in from the south.

Skalies.

Zaiana had faced the wretched, mindless creatures in the Fire Mountains before, but why had they come down from there?

She was about to swoop down and warn Nik and Tauria, but to her shock, the skalies started slashing through the enemy side. Did they have no allegiance and simply craved blood? Zaiana didn't have time to deliberate over it. Right now, they were making great impact against the enemy, which would help Nik and Tauria's force.

Zaiana focused on the skies, using her lightning only to strike as many dark fae as she could before they descended into their lines.

It didn't matter how tired she grew. How exhausted her magick was. How overwhelming the numbers were. Zaiana would not falter.

A dark fae approached from behind, and she spun, throwing out a spear of lightning, but they cleared the path of it. She charged again, her two metal-guarded fingers pointing toward the female dark fae.

"Wait, Zaiana!" she yelled, holding her hands up in surrender.

Zaiana held her lightning. She recognized the dark faze as one who had been a year behind her training grade. Giselle, Zaiana recalled.

A blade glinted, and Zaiana thought herself a fool for falling for her distraction, but the small dagger flew by her head, and Zaiana heard a choke before she pivoted, watching a dark fae tumble from the sky with the blade in his neck.

"We've come from the mountain. We've come to help you... Zaiana Vesaria."

Right in front of her, more dark fae flew in from the north where the Mortus Mountains that had once chained them all were destroyed. In their freedom, they'd chosen to join her. Their wings beat fierce and triumphant as they merged into the enemy line and began fighting.

The numbers in the sky started to even out, and Zaiana's body felt the relief that she was no longer at perilous odds in the sky.

"Thank you," Zaiana whispered though they couldn't hear her.

She watched with pride beating in her chest. They'd come at her call. They'd come because they believed in her.

Zaiana noticed the front line faltering and headed back to reform and strengthen where she could. She glamoured her wings, and as a riderless horse charged past, Zaiana ran with it, grabbing hold of the reins and leaping onto its back.

"We can't fall back any farther—hold your lines!" she yelled to the commanders as she rode past.

Just as they were beginning to form a new formation, a loud *boom* trembled the ground. The horse reared back, throwing Zaiana out of the saddle, but she caught herself with her wings, spinning in her lunge toward the source of the impact.

Darkness spilled over the ground, touching them all with chilling welcome of death. Standing in the center of the smoke that began to clear...

Dakodas had finally come.

The fighting eased off with the arrival of Dakodas. The enemy welcomed their leader; the opposition balked at her.

Zaiana would never yield.

She headed toward where Dakodas stood while the warriors behind her braced anew for when the battle would collide viciously again.

"Took you long enough," Zaiana goaded. Her voice cut through the eerie, tension-filled pause of battle.

"I'll admit, your efforts have outlasted our expectation. But you lead everyone behind you to a slow slaughter."

Behind the Spirit, Zaiana's chest tightened to see Maverick. He stood there as cold and expressionless as ever, eyes fixed on Zaiana.

Zaiana said, "What you see is a realm that will always fight back. That does so with purpose in its heart."

"I never expected you to become so weak to the hollow notion of a *heart*. Such sentiment doesn't suit you, Zaiana Vesaria."

"Is my father with you, or does he still cower behind his soldiers?"

Dakodas's smile crawled her skin. "You are merely a carrier of the power that is his, and it will be returned."

Zaiana *laughed*. "Mordecai is nothing but a warm corpse. A failure of plan you had to step in to revive."

"Then you know it is for your kind we march, and you are a traitor to the dark fae. I'm looking forward to the spectacle they'll make of tearing out your wings."

Everything within her recoiled at the horrific notion. She fought a strong urge to glamor her wings at the mere thought. "You want the dark fae to dominate as the bloodthirsty savages history painted of us. We want peace too, and you destroyed that."

"There will be peace when the war is won. Peace and power for the dark fae, never again to be undermined or cast out again."

"You're right," Zaiana said, bracing her stance. She couldn't contend with Dakodas's power for long. Maybe if she had a ruin to amplify hers with. But she would give her all no matter the odds. "The dark fae will prevail alongside the humans and the fae when *we* win."

Zaiana prepared for this to be her final fight, but she was ready.

For Amaya, who was a dreamer. For Acelin, Kellias, Drya, and Selain, who believed in her. For the better world they all wanted.

A golden flare illuminated the night above, so sudden and out of place it demanded everyone's attention. Then, in the blink of an eye, that shooting comet plummeted *down*, slamming into the space between Dakodas and Zaiana with the force of a boulder and the heat of the sun. Within the ripples of bloodred flames...stood Faythe Ashfyre.

The world held its breath at her arrival charged with so much vengeance and rage even Zaiana feared her in that moment.

Something had happened to bring Faythe here in a blazing storm of anguish.

Faythe didn't speak. She barely let the world take in the compelling sight of her before her palm cast out and light erupted against the darkness Dakodas threw out in challenge.

Zaiana ducked like everyone else, shielding her eyes and bracing her legs against the gales of wind that pummeled into them from the catastrophic collision of magick. Many were thrown off their feet; some were struck and killed by tendrils of dark or light that spat out from the beam of their connecting magick.

The kind of power they gave to each other was enough to destroy this entire fringe with one wrong move.

"Fall back but stay in formation!" Zaiana yelled down the line.

The battle would resume, but for now, the field belonged to Faythe and Dakodas, who were ruthless in their attacks.

A white eagle flew overhead, catching her attention for how out of place it was. Until it swooped low, and from a small burst of light, Reylan Arrowood stepped straight into battle, alone on the enemy side.

Along their front line many started to notice him, his white hair stark against the night and his black-clad enemies. Though she thought it reckless, they charged forward, matching the bravery and valiance of their great general.

Zaiana nearly lost him through the throng of bodies, but a blue flare caught her attention, and Zaiana pushed through the soldiers more urgently.

Maverick was attacking him.

Damned fool, she thought with her heart speeding.

Reylan wouldn't have mercy for all Maverick had done, and he was placing himself as the perfect target in front of Reylan, who slaughtered enemies with as much rage as Faythe had.

She followed the flickers of blue that drifted farther away from her. Zaiana would have to fly to keep up, but she realized Maverick's game...

He was goading the general away from Faythe, and Zaiana knew, now he was within reach, Reylan wouldn't give up until Maverick was dead.

CHAPTER EIGHTY-FIVE

Izaiah

He'd fought many battles over many centuries, but none had come close to the endless and relentless fighting that had raged on for days. Izaiah was tiring, switching from fighting with his sword to tearing through the enemy in various large-cat forms. The panther was always most efficient for him. Its dark, sleek coat and agility made it a swift predator.

Once, he'd used the Phoenix form, until the Phoenix Blood potion in his system seemed to have worn off at least. He was too aware of the second vial he had, but he didn't want to get it wrong this time.

Izaiah had been in torment, believing he'd taken the first dose too late to save Marlowe, who'd provided him with the portions. Why had she given him two? Was he supposed to give the other to someone else?

Something scored thorough his side, and Izaiah roared in his black panther form as he leaped. He skidded in his landing, twisting at the threat. Shadow creatures. He was surrounded by five. In all the chaos of fighting, it was hard to maintain an efficient tag team to take out the pesky shadow foes.

They needed to find that damned rift that was letting them into their world.

The number of shadow creatures grew over his east side suddenly. Izaiah wondered…

What if the rift could move location? And now it was close...very close.

Izaiah snarled at the five shadow creatures that made him his target. He needed comrades to notice and kill them while he held their attention.

No one was noticing, and they closed in around Izaiah. In groups, they moved slow, as if knowing they had their prey trapped and they enjoyed the anticipation of the feed.

Izaiah braced to lunge.

Darkness met darkness in a horizontal sheet that cut through all five shadow creatures. When their wails died out and their forms blew away on the wind, Kyleer stood behind them.

Izaiah shifted back into his fae body, catching his breath and examining the slash on his side with a hiss. He said, "Excellent timing, brother."

Just then, Tynan dropped down from above. "I was just about to intervene."

The dark fae had been covering the skies of their east legions.

Kyleer said, "You're wounded. You need to retreat back to the healers' tents before you keep fighting."

Izaiah waved him off, but he knew the wound was particularly nasty and would impair him. He couldn't leave now. Izaiah didn't want to tell them he suspected the rift was nearby. He figured it would be easy to lose them in the thick of the fighting.

He pulled his blade free. "I can go a while longer. I'll retreat if I need to."

Kyleer's brow furrowed in protest, but Izaiah was already darting into the masses of enemies and comrades.

The days of war were tiring; the nights grew long and blood-soaked. Izaiah couldn't be more proud of the resilience of the warriors who kept following him to battle.

He gained distance from Kyleer and Tynan, pushing through the front line and heading to the edge of the mountain. He knew a series of passages ran through the fringe behind this main peak, and that was where he'd drift away to investigate if the rift was here.

When he was out of the thick of the battle, he ran through the narrow passages, killing any stray foe that tried to use the labyrinth to slip by. Many of his soldiers were guarding these hidden passages and didn't stop him as he passed.

Izaiah shifted into a hawk to fly and scout faster. Forms grew out of the shadows cast by rocks. *It has to be close.*

Then, behind the next peak he soared over...there it was.

Wedged into a small open plane between tall peaks. It were as if a scar had torn through the air, rippling with darkness and opening a thin, eye-shaped door into a deathless void.

Izaiah's adrenaline burst. He might have lost his mind, which would cost the ultimate price if his belief was wrong.

That was all he had...a strong desperation and the belief he could do this.

Izaiah flew lower, staring into the mouth between worlds and wondering if he was a complete fool. It was too late to deliberate anymore. The rift was closing, the eye of darkness slowly drawing together, and it would relocate again. He wouldn't get another chance to make a great impact for all his warriors in this fight. For his brothers. For his queen.

He got so close, feeling the gentle, chilling strokes of shadow reaching out as if to greet him. Out of the corner of his eye, he saw the winged figure about to catch him, and Izaiah had to adjust course, tilting his body and descending low enough before shifting back into his fae form.

Tynan landed, facing off with him wearing an absolutely loathing stare.

"Maybe in another life," the dark fae threw those words resentfully.

Izaiah almost flinched. "Your reading is coming along, I see."

That was the note he'd given him, though Izaiah didn't expect him to find the time to figure it out so soon with all the mess they were tied up in.

"I'm not going to let you do this. Sacrifice yourself. Because if that was your cowardly attempt to confess you care about me too, then you're staying the fuck alive to say it better."

Izaiah could have laughed. A delirious grin split his face because it was too late.

"Maybe in another life I'll give you the grandest confession you desire, Tynan Silverfair. In this one, I'm afraid I'm the asshole who let you down. That should make it easier for you."

Tynan's jaw worked and his stance shifted, preparing to fight him to stop him if that's what it took. Izaiah didn't want to hurt him, but he had to... to save him.

The void sounded like trapped roars and strained wails swirling in powerful gales of wind behind him. It tousled Tynan's dirty blond hair, lashing strands across his pleading eyes. *Gods* he was beautiful. In a way so precious Izaiah had never admired a person like it before when it struck him far deeper beyond the surface of natural attraction. Izaiah had come to look at Tynan as though he were *his*.

"What do you think you're doing?" That harsh demand didn't come from the dark fae, and Izaiah's sight slipped to Kyleer as he landed.

"We're not children anymore. I need you to stop acting like a damned suffocating parent for once." His bitter words carved in himself as much as they caused a wince on Kyleer's expression.

Izaiah had thought Kyleer missing his memory might be a temporary blessing. Just for this. Yet his brother was still looking out for him as fiercely as ever.

"We don't know how to close that void," Tynan argued. "I assume that was your objective."

"We do know how," Izaiah argued.

Tynan's eyes narrowed. "You're not walking into that thing. If it wants a life, I'll go."

Izaiah gave a dark chuckle. "Don't act a hero for me. It's pitiful."

"Arrogant of you to think I'd be sacrificing myself for you."

Izaiah took a long backward step closer to the rift behind him, and both Tynan and Kyleer jerked forward as if they could stop him if he twisted and ran. His frustration grew.

In his peripheral, Izaiah caught the moving shadows. They were seconds from being swarmed, and Kyleer's eyes widened on him, terrified.

"You've always looked out for me, brother. Always sacrificed for me and shielded me." Kyleer's eyes widened on his, and the pain slashing through him for this goodbye was immeasurable. "It's my turn for once. Because you deserve to be happy in this life that has made it difficult for you to find those things."

"IZAIAH!"

Kyleer's scream of his name attacked his very core, while Tynan's pierced his heart. Neither could stop him as the shadow creatures reached them first and they were forced to fight, giving Izaiah the opportunity to spin on his heel, sprint toward the rift, and leap through into cold, reaching arms of Death.

CHAPTER EIGHTY-SIX

Kyleer

Kyleer fought harder than he ever had before. He *had* to stop Izaiah from sacrificing himself to close the rift. The drum in his chest amplified. His mind spun too fast as Izaiah ran toward it.

My little brother.

He was supposed to protect him, and yet Kyleer had failed him. He screamed Izaiah's name again as his brother leaped into the rift, and Kyleer's mind…*erupted*.

So many reels of moving images hammered through his head that he lost focus on his fighting and fell to his knees. Shadow creatures lunged for him, but Kyleer didn't really care anymore. He couldn't tear his sight from where Izaiah had been swallowed by the rift.

Tynan defended him, cutting through the shadows that raced for him while he kneeled there helpless and devastated.

He remembered everything. His past with Izaiah were the first memories to tear through him. They weren't all joyous, but the company was. Without Izaiah, Kyleer didn't know who he would have become. Izaiah had given him light in all the darkness. A purpose and a will to fight against anything that tried to hurt them growing up.

And he'd let his little brother die.

A new surge of creatures swarmed in and reached to grab him… then they seized before they could attack, hissing and wailing before, one by one, the shadows lost their animation and blew away as nothing more than smoke on the wind.

To Kyleer's horror, the rift began to close faster.

He scrambled to his feet, racing toward the rift, recalling the horrifying day of his Transition. The new wings he carried now slowed him down. So many memories cut through him, but he didn't stop running.

Zaiana... She'd been there when they killed him. She'd fought for him.

Her stunning face flooded his mind. The biggest regret that filled his chest if he were to meet his end permanently this time...was that he wouldn't get to thank her. To tell her she was wrong. In all the time they'd spent together while his memories were gone, he'd wanted her there. Remembering their rocky past changed nothing. And his only wish...was that they could have had more time together.

Kyleer raced time. Raced the closing door about to seal with his brother inside.

He wasn't going to make it.

A battle cry tore from him as he reached out a hand, thinking if he could just *touch it*, maybe it would suck him inside too.

But it didn't...

Kyleer stumbled with the desperate last push of his body before the rift slammed shut with a violent burst of air.

He stood deathly still, in complete denial over what had just happened. His chest heaved, and the silence that settled turned his heart to glass, one bottled scream away from shattering in his soul-tearing anguish.

"Izaiah..." he breathed. As if he would get a response from his brother and turn around to find out this nightmare wasn't real.

Instead he found Tynan on his knees, staring blankly at the space where the void had been. Izaiah had done it. Freed the world from the shadow creatures and given their forces an immense reprieve.

In his selfishness, Kyleer couldn't accept the price as worth it.

Even though the rift was gone, the whispering presence of it lingered on his skin. Kyleer didn't know all that had changed within him since Transitioning, but he remembered something like a dream during his change. He'd seen a tall, looming hooded figure with no face, holding a scythe. He didn't know why that flash of vision came back to him now, but he wondered if something had interfered with his Transition...and left their mark in his feathered wings.

He heard whispers in his ear that goaded him. Taunted him. Whispers of death that shredded through his mind. When he couldn't stand it a second longer, Kyleer lunged forward with a cry dragged from the Nether itself. Right where the vertical strip of the rift had torn thorough the air, Kyleer plunged his hands between it…and met a resistance.

Maybe it was his own delusion—a frantic force of his imagination —but Kyleer let the vibrations rake over his skin. He gripped the invisible seams of the rift with a God-defying determination to rip it back open himself.

If it returned the shadow creatures…to the Nether with the world if it meant he got his brother back. Kyleer wondered what that made him to be so cold and selfish, but that was a consequence he would harbor later.

"Gods above," Tynan muttered.

Kyleer could hardly hear his voice as dark energy tore through him, resisting his will to split the rift open with his bare hands.

Two dark lines manifested behind his hands that trembled as if trying to split a boulder in two from a mere spiderweb of a crack. A slither of the dark void beyond opened up, and Death chuckled in his ear, delighted.

Fire tore through his muscles that protested to let go. He couldn't. Kyleer stood there like a God, determined to rip open the void that had stolen his brother. If he could just open it large enough to slip inside, maybe he could find Izaiah and tear it open from within to get back to this world.

Sweat rolled down his face as he pushed himself far beyond his physical limits. It shouldn't be possible, but the adrenaline coursing through him knew no end.

As the rift fought him with dark and deadly surges of power, suddenly it gave up. The resistance stopped, and Kyleer let go to watch the rift roar open bigger than before.

Then from it…

Kyleer watched in complete awe and terror as a great black Phoenix emerged with an ear-piercing cry that rattled the stars.

The rift slammed shut. The force of it barreled into Kyleer, but he caught himself in the air with his wings. Then he beat them hard, chasing the black Phoenix.

Hovering in the sky, he watched as the Phoenix soared over the main battlefield, announcing its triumphant presence with another cry.

"He did it," Tynan said, floating next to him. "Izaiah became the black Phoenix."

Kyleer couldn't believe it. He wanted to yell at his brother for his reckless stupidity, yet all of that washed away under his incredible pride.

His little brother was brilliant.

Foolish, reckless, sometimes arrogant…but absolutely brilliant.

The black Phoenix landed in a gap that opened on their side. Everyone balked at the black Firebird as its shadows leaked around their feet. Izaiah's chest heaved, and people cried out, trying to scramble for distance.

Thick darkness rolled off his body and projected from his breath. It didn't harm any of the living. Kyleer didn't know much about the black Phoenix, but he tensed, awaiting the outcome of what its power could do.

To his amazement and complete fear…its breath affected the dead, not the living.

Kyleer landed on a mountain peak, stunned by what he was witnessing.

"It can animate the dead," Tynan informed him. "While Izaiah commands it, the corpses will fight for him."

It was a morbidly fascinating concept. As he watched the bodies of the fallen arise again, the tide of the war shifted in their favor. The numbers they were severely outmatched by evened out, and they would tip more in their favor with every enemy slain that Izaiah would temporarily resurrect to fight against them now.

The advantage was unparalleled.

Izaiah was alive.

His mind tried to soothe itself, but until his brother stood in front of him in his fae body, Kyleer couldn't let go of the terror of losing him.

Kyleer was about to go down and join the fighting alongside the black Phoenix, but an eruption of electricity and light cast his attention to his right. It was distant, wedged within farther mountain peaks on the fringe, but the sensation was unmistakable. The faint infusion of purple through the lightning attracted him like a moth to a flame.

Zaiana was in trouble.

His teeth gritted. Casting his sight back to Izaiah, he saw the Firebird and its army of the dead were dominating the battlefield, so he wouldn't be much of an impact. Tynan would go to him.

So Kyleer set his sights back on the anguish that was casting from his beautiful nightmare, and he went to her.

CHAPTER EIGHTY-SEVEN

Zaiana

W hen the surge of warriors charging forward became too much, Zaiana lost sight of Maverick and Reylan. Her heart raced, pushing through the crowd, trying to catch an opening large enough to splay her wings and chase after them.

He's going to kill him.

Zaiana should let Reylan have his revenge. Maverick had killed his mate right in front of his eyes, then he'd killed his king. Two unforgivable crimes that justified Reylan in his course.

She didn't know what it made her to abandon her station in pursuit of stopping Reylan in the vengeance he was owed. Would she be Faythe and Reylan's enemy again? She wouldn't blame them. She could live with that.

It was Kyleer who crossed her mind. The thought of having to flee as the enemy once more and leave him behind.

He'll get his memories back one day. Then he'll be glad for it.

The thought didn't make her heart ache any less.

Too much time was slipping by, and Zaiana grew frustrated at being smaller than most soldiers, pushing her way through like a fleeing child in an overcrowded market.

Finally, she'd made it back far enough to use her wings, and she shot up, scanning the ferocious battlefield for parrying strokes of blue. There were many. Firewielding was fairly common among the fae. Her attention darted from each fireball, but Reylan and Maverick had removed themselves from the thick of the fighting. Maverick's instruction would likely be to get the general as far away from aiding Faythe as possible.

Zaiana flew around a small, sharp piece of mountain. Several warriors fought in the smaller passages through the mountain fringe. The sound of war lessened the farther she got from the main field. Then she caught the unmistakable sound of Maverick's flame. It was unlike others, or maybe in all their years she'd become attuned to his particular sound of fire. *How strange*, she thought. It had never crossed her mind before, and she knew it was her panic tormenting her.

All she would do was make sure Maverick got away, far away, and that he would never come back. Zaiana justified her actions to defend Maverick by fairness. She'd been accepted by Faythe and her companions despite what she'd done...but the murders Maverick had carried out had come close to being her crimes. Even if he'd done it for his own gain, she couldn't let him die for acts that should have made *her* the villain Reylan targeted right now.

Zaiana's wings beat harder, flying around a tall, thin piece of rock.

She found them. Just them.

But she was too late.

Reylan stood poised, an arrow nocked in his bow, ready to release. A second arrow.

The first had already made its mark in Maverick's chest, and what was worse, as she flew closer, she felt the hideous sensation of the Niltain steel the arrow heads were made of.

She flew faster. Faster. Faster.

The second arrow fired, striking close to the first. Maverick fell to his knees, coughing black blood.

Reylan nocked again.

Zaiana dropped down in front of Maverick with a scream. "STOP!" Her chest heaved, staring off with the frightening loathing and rage of Reylan Arrowood.

"Get out of my way, or this goes through you both."

"Wait—please." *Gods*, she sounded pathetic, but her desperation didn't care.

"Move...Zai-Zaiana," Maverick said through labored breaths.

"You're a damned fool," she seethed at him, but it lacked its usual malice when she beheld the weakened sight of him.

The two arrows weren't in his heart—there was still a chance to remove them and find a healer to stop the Niltain poison from killing him. Nerida would do it.

"I don't want to kill you too," Reylan said, not yielding.

"We're fighting as one people," she said, scrambling to make sense. "You forgave me. I'm not asking you to forgive him for killing your king and Faythe, but just let us flee. We'll never come back to this continent again."

Reylan's eyes narrowed. "We?"

She swallowed hard. "I don't expect you to forgive me for betraying you like this. You're owed this kill, this vengeance, for what you lost—I know that. But I am asking you, as friends, if that's what we found in all the twisted treachery and battles we faced against each other, to let us go."

"What about Kyleer? You made him care deeply for you, only to abandon him for *that*," he seethed, his arrow finding a precise path to Maverick's heart this time.

"You know Kyleer deserves better than me. When he remembers everything, he'll know it too."

Zaiana didn't know what she was saying. What she was doing. The thought of never seeing Kyleer again was tearing her apart in places that had never been touched before. But so was the thought of Maverick dying.

Reylan's jaw worked, contemplating both their lives in the tip of his arrow. She listened to her heartbeats like they were a countdown to the last.

Then, to her immense relief, Reylan lowered his bow, and all the tension that had built in Zaiana's body deflated. "I don't do this for either of you. Mercy is not what I know for the crimes he committed. But Faythe does. It's because of her you live."

Reylan stood a moment longer, rigid and still furious. Zaiana held her breath, knowing he could change his mind in a second.

Only when a flare of light engulfed him and a white eagle took off, flying around the mountainside and out of sight, did she finally relax.

Zaiana's anger returned, however, when she turned to Maverick and kneeled to assess his wounds.

"Why did you do that?" he growled.

Her hands stopped just shy of touching him. "I just saved your gods-damned life," she snapped, incredulous at his tone.

"I didn't ask you to do that. It means everything was for *nothing*."

"What are you talking about?"

Their bickering and resentment was familiar, inspiring both comfort and irritation.

Zaiana reached for one of the arrows to pull it free, but he caught her wrist. Their stares locked, hateful and passionate.

"Leave me," he said.

"I hate you, Maverick. But I don't desire a world where I don't get to hate you. Not unless you leave it on my terms."

His black eyes flared. Their stare-off intensified until his grip loosened on her, and she reached again for the arrow.

Her next breath choked in her throat when he pushed her roughly. Caught completely off-guard, she lost her balance, falling hard onto her side.

Zaiana pushed herself up...and was met with the most world-shifting sight.

How hadn't she felt Mordecai approach? How had he gotten close enough to strike her in the back completely unaware? How had she been so slow to feel the Spellthief aimed for her heart...that was now plunged through Maverick's instead.

Zaiana *screamed*.

There was power in the sound the expelled from her. Waves and waves of unleashed lightning that blasted into the high lord, and she lost him in the violent waves of jagged purple lines.

Though she'd wanted to look him in the eye as she took his life, Zaiana hoped he'd burned to ash in the power of her lightning he tried to steal.

Maverick's groan snapped her attention to him. She gasped, lunging across the short space as he fell forward on his knees. Zaiana caught him.

Her heart slammed rapidly against his as it struggled to beat. Zaiana didn't know what to do, and it was strange what loose ends and silly questions demanded answers now time had turned to sand and was slipping through her fingers.

"What did you want to say?" she breathed.

When Maverick didn't answer, she pushed him off her chest to look at his face. She shook him when his lids fluttered, desperate to keep him conscious in her complete denial that there was no saving him.

"In the cave that night, do you remember? You wanted to say something, and I stopped you. What did you want to say?"

His trembling hand rose, barely grazing her chin before it fell limp to rest on her neck. "It wasn't just one night for me," his voice rasped. He was fading fast.

A sharp sob escaped her lips with a shake of her head as she gripped him tighter. "It wasn't just one night for me either."

Maverick tried to smile, but it was pained and short lived. She grappled his dark stare, the fear in them cleaving so deep within her.

"You once said we were the monsters that don't get a happy ending." His words were barely a whisper of gravel. Zaiana tuned out everything but him. The howling wind, the distant cries of fighting, the clashing of weapons. Like she'd done so many times before, Zaiana masterfully tuned it all out to catch every one of his last words. "I used to think there was no happy, only endings. But you showed me differently. You showed me...how to love again in this second hollow life.

Zaiana's emotions choked her.

"I know *you* feel love. I've seen it. My happy ending is getting to tell you that. Might we have met in a different time or realm, we would have met on the same side of the battlefield...but I'm glad in this life we didn't. I'm glad...you chose the right side."

It was only death—*death*—that could explode the vault of denial she'd sealed in her mind. *Death* that could grip every suppressed memory and feeling and drown her mercilessly.

"You can't die like this," she said through gritted teeth while his body fell into her again.

"I died a long time ago, Zaiana. More than once. The day they changed me. Then the second I stood before my own mate and didn't recognize her until it was too late and she'd died by my hand, I almost ended it all...until you.

"After the Blood Trials, you killed Finnian. And I knew that spiral that started within you. Love wasn't what either of us needed —it was hate. Something to deflect our self-loathing onto. I think you've known it too. Every time we battled, verbal blows or with steel, it was like attacking the person in the mirror. Unleashing all we felt about ourselves because we were one and the same. At some point, I suppose exhaustion took over, and I started to fall for you when I didn't want to. I knew you could never be mine. We would have both been stuck here, tragically cursed to never move on from our pasts."

Tears spilled over her eyes as she stared up at the night sky over his shoulder, holding him, listening to the broken countdown in his chest through all his confessions. Her throat was too tight; her chest swelled with agony. She thought she might die here with him.

He said, his voice slipping away with every word, "Please...let me die as Maverick Blackfair, but can you tell them to remember me as Callen Osirion? And tell Faythe Ashfyre...tell her it was all for you."

"Stop," she croaked, holding him tighter when he fell limp, the weight of him crushing her, but she didn't care. "Stop *dying!*"

It was too late.

That plea left her lips to be heard only by the wind Maverick's last breath carried on.

She captured his final heartbeat in her own.

Then he was gone.

Time...it no longer felt like an anchor to reality.

This wasn't how it was supposed to be.

Zaiana held him, wondering how this moment had come. Unable to find a reality that could imagine the days passing by without accounting for his presence. She didn't regret anything about their relationship. Not the hatred, not the malice, not the taunting, not the way she'd never realized...she'd been falling for him too.

"Zai."

Her name from Kyleer zapped through her as violent as her lightning. It snapped around her like a shackle to the present, and she looked down at the still form she held.

Maverick was gone.

"No," she said—a vacant word of denial. Zaiana frowned, shaking her head. "Get up."

"Zai—"

"NO!"

She held Maverick tighter as if Kyleer would rip him from her, and he was afraid to hurt him if he tried.

It can't be over. Not yet.

"Your life is mine," she said vacantly.

No—not anymore.

Mordecai had taken him from her.

"I'm sorry," Kyleer said gently.

Too gently. As if breaking the news she didn't want to accept.

Her arms began to loosen, the weight of Maverick's body becoming too much to bear.

"Me too," she whispered, looking over his still face.

She waited for his dark eyes to open. For him to say something insufferable.

A hollowness opened in her chest with every passing second. Something in her she didn't know had taken vital occupancy died slowly with her acceptance of the truth.

Died…with him.

Laying him down, he'd never looked so peaceful. As if he were just asleep.

He was finally free.

And for a second…Zaiana envied him for it.

A hand on her shoulder strapped her to this land. Zaiana shrugged it off to stand.

"You don't have to pretend you're not glad for it," she said, her voice cold like the death that lingered.

"I can't be glad for anything that causes you pain."

The smile that curved her lips was slow and villainous. Her grief sharpened her claws of rage and resentment, volatile to anyone in her path.

"You should leave," she warned.

Zaiana couldn't even turn to look at Kyleer. Anything kind and warm was a trigger to the loathing inside her that wanted to *hurt*. And when it became too much to bear within, the claws would come out, and they would make bright things bleed.

"I'm not going to leave you."

"I don't want you here."

"I remember." Those two words locked her spine. "I remember everything, and I'm still not going anywhere, no matter how many times you push me away."

She was so torn between falling to her knees in surrender or hurting him; doing whatever it took to make him leave if only to spare him.

"Then you're even more of a fool to be standing here."

"I want you," he confessed, edging closer.

"Stop," she begged.

"No matter how many times you fight me. No matter how long it takes for you to want me back. I'm not giving up on you."

How could he not know how desperately she wanted him already? Had she really been that awful to have not shown it enough to erase his doubt? She pulled him close only to push him away hard. He deserved better.

"I can't love you, Kyleer. This is what happens," she snarled, casting her hand toward Maverick, but she couldn't look down.

"I'm not afraid."

Zaiana mocked him with a cruel laugh. She was ready to unleash more of the ugly within her, stirring to hurt them both.

A flicker of movement caught her eye just over Kyleer's shoulder.

A flash of cobalt blue. Zaiana threw her lightning toward it in the same breath. Kyleer pivoted out of the way, shifting back until he was beside her.

She stared at the threat, utterly shocked and building with a rage so fierce and deadly she could split this mountain apart with it.

Mordecai still lived. Of course he did. But what racked her body with an acute, blinding vengeance was the blue flame in his hand. The Firewielding he'd stolen from Maverick with the dagger before it had killed him.

The cobalt flame mocked her grief. It was an insult to Maverick's sacrifice to save her, and Zaiana lost herself to raw anguish.

Her storm gathered in a lethal force, and she shot bolt after bolt at Mordecai. Though he'd only just been reunited with magick, his skill with it was so familiar. He moved like she did, in a dance of storms, displaying exactly where she'd inherited her powers.

Her teeth gritted, and her emotions chose the worst time to make her weak. Every flash of blue tore open her grief at the reminder of Maverick.

The distance had shortened between father and daughter, and when the last collision of amethyst and cobalt faded out, they stared off in a heated gaze of hatred.

"It's not the power I desired, but it is a close contender," he said, as if taking Maverick's life for it meant *nothing*. "You are every part my daughter, Zaiana. Every year that passed, I grew more certain your potential was a reckoning to this world."

"She's nothing like you," Kyleer snarled. Then a powerful blast of darkness hurtled for the high lord, striking him true.

Mordecai slammed against rock. Kyleer advanced again, but Zaiana stopped him with a hand around his arm. She wouldn't let him fight this battle for her.

As Mordecai peeled himself off the ground and targeted them with a vengeful stare, a colossal *boom* resonated over them.

Zaiana caught the flares of dark and light collecting in a devastating hurricane across the fringe. Faythe was battling Dakodas in a ferocious war that could destroy much of their land.

"Despite everything, you became more than I could have dreamed of, Zaiana Vesaria. I hope you find the will to use your potential. It would be such a waste for you to let yourself be overshadowed by these pathetic world saviors."

His words touched her like a goodbye, and she surged toward him, desperate with a shaking urge for violence to not let him get away with his life and Maverick's stolen power.

He threw a large ball of blue flame toward her, and she had no choice but to defend with a shield of lightning. When the magick dispersed, he was gone.

Zaiana snarled in frustration, scanning the skies to chase the coward, but she couldn't track him, and the blasts of world-shaking power coming from farther down the fringe tugged at her to answer like a call.

"Do you want to go after him?" Kyleer asked tentatively. He would follow her if she tried.

"He's nothing more than a rat who escaped with a new trick to play with. Dakodas is our real threat."

But a large part of Zaiana didn't want to fight anymore. She wanted to sink to her knees with grief. She couldn't look at Maverick's body, instead throwing her head back and closing her eyes to keep her eyes from spilling tears. They wouldn't help her. Nothing could help her.

She would avenge Maverick. She would make Mordecai suffer greatly for it.

In the darkness of her own mind, she knew what Maverick would say right now.

Get yourself together, Delegate.

Her eyes pricked more, but her resolve sharpened.

The war was still raging. Their enemies were still circling. She had to go on.

As Zaiana found the will to open her eyes, she grounded herself, facing the world that would always have an empty space now.

She sealed the vault on her heart that bled and grieved. It was the only way she *could* go on.

Zaiana turned her gaze and set her steel course of anguish on the sky, illuminated with light and dark.

"If we end Dakodas, we end the war."

CHAPTER EIGHTY-EIGHT

Faythe

Faythe Ashfyre had come for the one enemy to end all. Her heart had turned black, decaying in the wake of Jakon's death, and all she knew was that his sacrifice could be traced back to here.

Dakodas was the most cunning of them all. At least, the Spirit of Death believed she was, and she appeared so as the last one standing.

That is until Faythe arrived.

She didn't have any words, only vengeance, as she clashed power with Dakodas the moment she landed on the battlefield, and the two of them became a devastating blur of darkness and light.

Faythe clutched the Ruin Dagger, using it to build her power to contend with Dakodas. She was still aware of the innocents, her people, fighting on this battlefield.

So when Faythe got close enough that all it took was one reach, touching Dakodas, to drag them through Shadowporting, but Dakodas fought her for control within the void they traveled through, Faythe lost the power struggle within the shadows that answered the Spirit of Death over her.

While Dakodas landed effortlessly, it was like Faythe had been spat out. Her body rolled against the harsh ground, but she caught herself, pushing to her feet in the same breath.

Faythe didn't know how this battle would end, but after all she'd lost, if she had to go down in this fight, she was taking Dakodas with her.

"Your fight is futile, Faythe Ashfyre. There is no weapon that can kill me now—you made sure of that," Dakodas taunted.

They circled each other, charging with tension.

"I'll admit, it's impressive how you've been the true driving force of this war. For centuries, you let Marvellas believe it was all her."

"You killed my sister, didn't you? I no longer feel her heavy, insufferable plague in this world."

"You never cared for her at all."

"I am a Goddess. I do not attach sentiments that serve no purpose to my duty."

"How is this your duty? You are annihilating an entire species. Favoring another."

"No—you are. You send all these fae and humans to their slaughter in resistance to my new order."

"To keep humans as blood sources and fae as slaves."

"That is your narrative, your viewpoint, not mine. The one with the will to make the harshest judgments for the most efficient and powerful order will always be viewed as the villain. I am at peace with that."

There was no reasoning with an unfeeling monster. Faythe wasn't trying to change her mind, only buying time to recharge her magick. Even with the Ruin Dagger, Dakodas was too powerful an opponent, and Faythe was struggling.

She just had to get close enough…tap into the source of Aurialis's power that still lived deep within her, but for all her crimes, it was like it refused to open up to her.

A loud cry pierced the sky, and Faythe's head whipped around, believing she had to have mistaken the Phoenix call.

She hadn't.

Red Firebirds, perhaps a dozen of them, flew in a formation that painted a blazing horizon, heading their way.

Her heart beat full for the first time, in complete awe of the Phoenixes that flew over the battlefield, aiding their side.

Livia had made it across the sea…and it was true that the Firebirds lived on in Salenhaven. In all her grief and tiredness, it was truly a gift to watch history return in both the aid from their faraway western neighboring continent, and in the triumphant inferno of Phoenixfyre that lit up against the darkest hour.

In Faythe's distraction, she was vulnerable.

The attack of darkness that hit Faythe stole the air from her lungs and removed her from gravity until she slammed into something hard and fell to the ground.

The shadows animated before she could roll off her back, and they began flooding into her body.

The shadows surged down her throat, slithering like snakes through her ears, and her nose too. Her body arched off the ground. She could hardly feel with the force that was burning, but not like any flame she knew, and all she could think of was *Shadowfyre*. Darkness that scorched icily, expanding within her. Faythe silently screamed at an agony so overwhelming it took her from that realm entirely, placing her in an endless void of torture that only begged for death.

Death.

Death.

It was all she craved with the tiny slices over every internal organ that spilled blood freely, over and over.

In her misery, it broke only by small notes that kept her wanting to fight it.

Sapphire. Silver. Him.

Her losses made her want to let go. Maybe she would get to be with Jakon and Marlowe again and leave this world behind, like a nightmare they'd all escaped together.

Sapphire. Silver. Him.

Reylan was a light bright enough for her to want to stay despite the desolation. That kept her fighting to stay in a world that kept *hurting*.

Faythe thought she felt him, but her consciousness was hanging on by a thread.

In the depth of the shadows that devoured her internally, a sun burst to life. Faythe threw all her fading energy toward it, reaching back for it to pull her to the surface as the only way to survive.

The last essence of Aurialis was her only hope.

She touched it, then gripped it, allowing it to cast away the darkness, replacing the shadows with pure blazing light through her veins.

"Stay with me." Reylan's beautiful voice cut through her drifting mind, offering a thread for her to reach for and stay grounded through the raging vessel of power she became.

Faythe blinked at the night sky before she pushed up, coughing violently through her throat, which felt filled with ash and smoke.

Faythe clung to the warmth and safety that wrapped around her body, but panic thrummed in her chest.

Dakodas was here. Reylan was in danger.

That thought forced her back to full awareness until she found his deep blue eyes searching hers.

"Always," she whispered.

His brow flinched, and Faythe jerked at the sound of clashing power like wind and lightning.

Faythe stood slowly with Reylan's aid, and she couldn't believe what she saw.

Tauria and Zaiana were fighting Dakodas with an onslaught of wind and lightning. Nik rushed over to her, assessing her from head to toe.

"Sorry we took so long," Nik said, breathless and with a crooked smile. His eyes kept darting back to Tauria.

Faythe reached toward him, touching his cheek.

She wasn't alone. Never alone. Faythe still had friends in this world who looked out for her as much as she did for them, and she couldn't stop fighting to win.

"Let's end this," she said, and Nik's expression firmed to one of pure determination.

"Together," he said.

Faythe leaned off Reylan, exchanging a pained, fearful look, but they didn't need any words.

"I think I know what I need to do," Faythe said.

Reylan nodded, fierce but terrified.

That was all the time they got before they were pulled apart by the demand of their enemy pushing back against their friends.

Nik attacked with a bow on Tauria's right, while Reylan transformed into a large white lion on Zaiana's left. The four of them kept Dakodas's focus on defending herself.

Faythe held her palms out, giving herself over to the Ruin Dagger, which lay discarded. She didn't need the blade itself, only the amplifier that turned the touch of sun within her into a blazing core. Her golden tattoos lit up brighter than ever before. Her mind drifted away, retreating to allow the last piece of the Goddess of the Sun to take over…and end her sister once and for all.

Aurialis flooded her mind, and Faythe had to trust the Spirit.

"*You figured it out,*" Aurialis said to her thoughts, which Faythe was only a bystander to now.

"*Will you really sacrifice the last piece of yourself for this?*" Faythe asked.

Aurialis had control of her body now. When she'd broken the Death Ruin and watched Aurialis turn to smoke in a vision, Faythe had thought she'd lost the Spirit of Life then too. But while Faythe still lived, Aurialis could never truly die when her power was used to bring Faythe back. Just for this moment.

Aurialis said, *"Will you?"*

Once they pushed Aurialis's power into Dakodas, Faythe had long accepted that she would die without the Spirit's essence sustaining her anymore.

"It was all borrowed time, wasn't it?"

Faythe Ashfyre braced, ready to make her final stance.

Aurialis said, *"I wish it didn't have to be."*

Faythe looked at Reylan, but he wasn't there anymore. Not attacking Dakodas's front like Nik, Tauria, and Zaiana.

"Me too," she whispered.

Faythe ran. Her Phoenix wings cast out, shooting her into the air as she flipped over her friends. As Faythe reached for Dakodas, the Spirit called on a plume of shadow that engulfed her. Faythe fell into the smoke and would have been under the shadow attack again, but Aurialis's power formed a sphere around her. The light pushed out, and the shadows hissed, dissipating to reveal Dakodas in all her fury.

"Your band of saviors is nothing to me," she hissed.

Reylan, in his lion form, growled menacingly beside her. Faythe braced, but more darkness caught her eye—more so at the sight of the flesh stepping through several walls of darkness across the mountain fringe. Dakodas had brought some of her army to fight with her. Some hissed—savage dark fae. Others came running with war cries toward her friends.

The masses kept flooding through. Faythe gritted her teeth as the numbers quickly overwhelmed Nik, Tauria, and Zaiana.

"I have to distract her focus so she can't keep those shadow portals open," Faythe said to Reylan. "They need your help."

He roared, a sound of anguish and rage, but he lunged away from her even though it strained their bond to be separated.

Faythe honed her focus on solely Dakodas.

Her palm charged with light as Dakodas summoned shadow. When they raised their hands to each other, the force of magick that expelled from them both blast across the mountain. Faythe strained with the velocity of the attack until Aurialis took over. She shifted her stance, seeing nothing but golden light lashing in front of her, pushing against the darkness. Their collision of power shook the mountain and rattled the stars—a catastrophe that wailed with no victory, only destruction.

With everything she had, Faythe pushed hard enough to sever the dark, and her flare of light struck Dakodas. Using Shadowporting, Faythe appeared in front of Dakodas.

"Where's your ally?" Faythe taunted. Wrath and vengeance rolled off her as she paced, watching Dakodas peel herself off the ground. Her voice trembled with so much grief as she yelled. "Mordecai has left you, hasn't he? That's the difference between you and me. My friends do not falter and fear in the face of our enemies. Their loyalty does not waver for selfish ambition. We are one. We will fight as one and fall as one if that is our fate."

Dakodas used the wall as an aid to stand, and Faythe drove her blade through her stomach with a battle cry. She forced her arm to steady its hold on Lumarias. Dakodas's hands wrapped around the blade in her gut. Her head slumped.

Hot tears rolled down Faythe's face. She was so lost in her anger, in her mourning, that all she knew was violence. It kept growing even though she knew it would never bring back her two lost human friends.

The sound to reel her back in was chilling laughter. Dakodas was *laughing*.

"Did you really think you could beat me this easily?"

A chill broke over Faythe's skin when Dakodas lifted her head and those onyx eyes gleamed.

"The difference between you and me...is that I don't *need* anyone to fight my battles."

Dakodas's palm slapped the wall behind her, and a noise as powerful as thunder boomed. Faythe lost her balance when the rock beneath her feet shifted, releasing her hold on Lumarias. Her stomach flipped when her back didn't slam to the ground—she kept falling.

Dakodas had torn through the mountain deep enough to carve a chasm Faythe plummeted down. The sound of splitting stone and crashing rocks consumed her, and she tried desperately to summon wings, but she was flailing and falling too chaotically.

The shrill cry of a bird cut through the thunder, and Faythe caught sight of embers—only...she couldn't believe what she was seeing. Not until the black Phoenix caught her, and Faythe twisted, gripping fistfuls of feathers and swinging her leg to mount it as the giant bird ascended to take them out of the chasm.

"You did it," Faythe breathed, realizing it was Izaiah who'd saved her.

She couldn't wrap her head around how he'd managed to take this form. All she could feel was gratitude for his help and relief he was alive.

They soared out of the scar in the mountain, and Faythe leaned over to survey the battlefield. The dire sight made her heart pound faster. Dakodas's destruction continued to spread. The sides of the mountain fell away slab by slab, breaking off in an avalanche of rocks, crushing the people below. It didn't matter that Dakodas's forces were being slaughtered if her friends were among the blood-and-stone burial.

"We have to get them out of there!" Faythe cried to Izaiah. She scanned the devastation frantically but couldn't see any of them.

She reached within herself for her bond to Reylan, seeking him out the easiest. Then she saw him, shifted back to fae. He was fighting an onslaught of Dakodas's army alongside Nik and Tauria. To her horror, Faythe watched a large slab near the peak of the mountain to their right break off.

Izaiah circled around, and Faythe adjusted her position, summoning her Phoenixfyre wings.

"Rise the dead, Izaiah," she said—then she leapt off him.

She cut through the air as a stroke of flame, gathering her magick in the only way she could think of to stop the falling lethal rock. Faythe conjured fire.

When she was close enough, she released a blue flame with the force of all she was. It surged out of her like a God's breath as she suspended herself in the air. Her veins flooded with heat. Her golden tattoos flared so bright she became a piece of the sun. Her rays broke through the overcast gray sky her world had suffered, melting the snowfall before coming close.

She didn't know if fire would be enough to forge the falling rock back into the mountain, but she had to try. Without anything to cool it, she might only create a worse descent of molten rock that would fall when she released her magick.

Faythe's body trembled. Her skin was on fire. She had to let go, but she couldn't see if her friends were safely out of the way.

Then a wash of coolness battered into her fire just as Faythe let go. She watched in amazement as a colossal wave of water surged up the mountainside, but Faythe didn't have access to Waterwielding anymore.

She looked down to see Nerida, and Faythe's chest burst with pride. Nerida wasn't alone. Four others stood around her, their palms braced like hers, helping to command the flow that saved them all.

Faythe recognized some of them from Lakelaria—they'd crossed the sea at the call of their queen.

Faythe descended, letting go of her Phoenixfyre and almost doubling over, but she pushed through the burning ache of her body to search the battlefield for Reylan.

Behind her, Izaiah's distinctive cry rattled through the fringe. She winced, curling into herself, when a blast of Shadowfyre ripped through the air, curving around her to swallow the masses of enemy forces. Faythe's eyes struck a fallen body, a dark fae, with thrumming anticipation. Was the legend about their breath true?

Its limbs twitched after the Shadowfyre dispersed, and Faythe watched with grim fascination as the dead lifted itself off the ground, animated in stiff, horrifying movements. It looked right at her, and Faythe's magick became a dying wick, but she prepared herself to tap into it. With a second cry from Izaiah, the dead dark fae snapped its head in an unnatural way toward the opposing side. Then it took off in a frantic, terrifying run.

She spied many more racing in the same manner, and when she saw them launch into the enemy sides, she found Nik and Tauria relieved of their relentless fighting as Izaiah's army of the dead plowed through the front lines.

A sharp tug within her silenced her world.

Faythe's gaze instinctively swung toward the direction she'd felt it. Felt *him*.

Without missing a beat, Faythe sprinted, leaping over rocks, twisting through bodies. Occasionally, her magick cast out to eliminate anything in her way.

When Faythe rounded a giant rock, she skidded to a stop.

Dakodas was restraining Reylan on his knees, a hand gripped in his hair, pulling his head back, a blade already embedded dangerously in his throat. One second was all it would take for her to kill him. If Faythe so much as blinked, she might miss it. She noticed blood trickling down the sides of his mouth.

"He's not a royal by blood, but he's one of the chosen. Strength," Dakodas said. Her black eyes drifted up, and Faythe looked too...at the full moon. "I think he'll survive Transition just fine."

"No!"

Faythe's eyes flew wide, and she lunged as Dakodas's hand moved to kill him. She raced time, knowing it laughed with every feeble step she took.

Though it wasn't Faythe who screamed. It was Dakodas. The

A FLAME OF THE PHOENIX

blade clattered to the ground, and Faythe beheld the manacle Reylan had managed to secure. Her other hand released his hair, and her face twisted with such frightening wrath that Faythe braced for her attack.

It never came.

"Now!" Zaiana yelled. Having dropped from the skies, the dark fae secured the second Aetherbond around Dakodas's raised wrist.

Faythe's adrenaline roared to life at the opportunity as the Aetherbonds fully nullified Dakodas's magick. All at once, the power of a God flooded through her, and Faythe let it become her for what she had to do. To save the world. To save her friends, she *had* to do this.

Summoning the force of the sun inside her, Faythe's palms thrust against Dakodas's chest, and both of them *detonated.*

Waves of otherworldly power blasted through the mountains as Faythe drained every piece of Aurialis's power into Dakodas. It incinerated the darkness, torching the very fibers of what made Dakodas.

The light cancels the dark.

Marvellas had given her this idea to eradicate Dakodas when she'd told them of her plans to place the Light Ruin into the Temple of Darkness. Then, before she died...Marvellas had made sure Faythe understood it was possible.

Gods were prideful creatures—Death had told her that. Despite all Marvellas's wrongdoings and losing, she hadn't wanted Dakodas to triumph either after her betrayal.

Through the light and gales of wind, she saw Reylan as if Dakodas no longer existed between them.

"In every realm," she said to him.

Devastation stole his expression. Tears stood in his eyes.

"And every time," he answered.

He reached for her and when their hands clasped, Faythe's power climbed to a new pinnacle before she plummeted. The life drained out of her as Dakodas's skin started to crack. Piercing rays of light broke through. With a cry to defy Gods, Faythe pushed all she had one last time and felt something in her *snap.*

She lost her connection to Dakodas, falling back and not knowing what came next. Faythe didn't feel the ground nor any of the excruciating pain that had torn through her body at wielding that velocity of power.

Faythe was floating or flying—she couldn't be sure. Her body was weightless and her mind content.

Hands touched hers, returning a sense of gravity with a pull.

Faythe opened her eyes, which she didn't even realize were closed, and at who she saw she broke out in a sob.

"Marlowe," Faythe croaked.

She really was dead then. She had to be, but this was a gift with that miserable fact.

Marlowe smiled, floating with her in this void of white and misty silver. Her blonde hair weaved around her porcelain face, and those light blue eyes showered her with a love she didn't deserve.

"I've missed you," Faythe said, pushing to drift closer until she could pull her friend into an embrace.

"I've missed you too," Marlowe said gently. Her hug was so soft. It was peace.

"I'm so glad my death brought me back to you."

Marlowe smiled when they pulled away. Faythe didn't feel when it happened, but she was distracted by a compulsion to look down, wiggling her toes through fresh grass now.

Surveying their new surroundings, she realized they were in the Eternal Woods. A bubble of humor grew inside her. She hadn't escaped a fate tied to this place in the afterlife after all. It didn't matter. If this was where Marlowe's spirit now roamed, it was exactly where Faythe wanted to be too.

"Reylan knows what to do after your sacrifice. The window is very short, but he'll make it."

Faythe frowned, turning back to her friend. "Reylan?"

Marlowe walked to the wide lake by the waterfall. The yucolites chased each other, and Faythe missed the serene sight of them. With a skip in her chest, Faythe noticed only her own reflection cast in the water, but Marlowe was right beside her.

Tears welled in her eyes. "I have to say goodbye, don't I?"

Marlowe's arm looped around hers, and she leaned her head on Faythe's shoulder. "You have to live your life, but I'll always be here. We both will be."

Faythe sobbed. "Jak?"

Marlowe didn't answer.

"I failed you both. I miss you both so much. I don't know how I'll go on without you."

"Then you haven't failed us. We all paid prices in this war for the better world that is dawning now."

"Your price isn't fair."

"Nothing in life or death is about fairness. It's about choices.

Actions and consequences. Safety and risks. The beauty and fear of the unknown."

Faythe turned to her dear friend, reaching a hand to her delicate face. She felt so real Faythe couldn't stop her tears from pouring, wanting so desperately to stay here but also return to the living.

"Do I have a choice?" Faythe asked.

"You're making it right now."

She could hardly blink away her tears fast enough to cling to the image of Marlowe for as long as possible.

"I'm so sorry," she could barely choke out.

"It's time for your reign, Faythe. The world has been waiting for it. It's my privilege to have played a part in the history that will live on for millennia."

"You won't be forgotten. Never."

Marlowe smiled. "Then I am never truly gone."

Faythe felt the scene drifting away like a dream she held onto desperately.

Was it even real?

Faythe's mind would never be certain, but her heart was.

CHAPTER EIGHTY-NINE

Reylan

Dakodas was defeated, but he didn't take a breath of relief nor celebrate a beat of triumph.

Because Faythe had fallen too the moment the Spirit's body turned to black sand. Reylan caught her before she hit the ground, then the race against time began.

While Faythe had been giving everything she had into killing Dakodas, Livia had arrived before he was about to yell for help.

His cousin flew down on a Phoenix far smaller than Atherius, but Reylan was still incredulous as to how Livia had crossed the sea and made treaty with someone from Salenhaven to have come to their aid in this dark time.

"We need to get her to the Eternal Woods in Farrowhold—fast!" he yelled, letting Livia and Samara take Faythe from his arms.

Having to let her go and fly across in eagle form was the most soul-tearing thing he'd ever had to do. The distance felt endless even though he pushed himself harder than ever before.

Time mocked him, tormenting him that it had been too long since they'd left the fringe and landed in the fields before the woods.

Reylan didn't waste a single second. Faythe was back in his arms within a few breaths of landing, and he raced through the trees, bursting into the waterfall clearing.

He hoped he was right—that the yucolites in this pool would give her back the life she needed. Reylan slipped into the pool fully clothed, then he lifted Faythe in with him. He stood while the water helped carry Faythe's lifeless body.

Lifeless.

He had to shake his head to dispel the dizzying sweeps of panic.

"Please, please, please." He kept chanting, with his eyes darting from her stunning, peaceful face to the glowing orbs that floated around them. "PLEASE," he yelled desperately.

Gods, she looked so at peace, but he promised with everything he had that he would not let this world harm her anymore. If she just came back to him, he'd become whatever he needed to be to spare her from anymore pain.

Reylan brushed the tangles hair sticking to her face and rested his forehead to hers. "Faythe, my Phoenix, you can hear me. I know you can. After all we've been through, don't you dare leave now."

He kissed her cold lips and held her floating body, willing with every fiber of his being for life to be breathed back into her from this source of magick itself. She deserved this. Faythe Ashfyre deserved to see the world she'd saved. The world she would build now she'd rid the evil from it.

The yucolites gathered around her body, and with a jolt of relief, he watched as they attached themselves to her. They surrounded him too.

"Use me. Take whatever you need from me," he begged them. His life, his soul, his heart—it was all hers anyway.

The tiny prickles of magick grew over his skin, and Reylan closed his eyes, welcoming their presence. All he could do was hold Faythe and wait. There were no Gods to pray to anymore.

Her chest was so quiet it made every passing second grow with a misery he would never forget. Reylan knew this would come; that despite all she'd given already, it would come down to a sacrifice for her rid the land of Dakodas. He couldn't stop thinking of this place and the stories he'd heard of the yucolites. To restore life might be beyond what they were capable of, but they *owed* her this. The world owed Faythe her life back for all she'd sacrificed long before now.

If she didn't come back…Reylan feared what he would become in his grief.

Perhaps that was why Faythe had taken his memories before she died a long time ago. Not because he would follow her, but because she might have returned not to stop Marvellas but him, for the rage he would have poured into the world in his vengeance.

It made him no better than Marvellas, and for a moment, it was grim to acknowledge that there were no heroes or villains, only those who had reason to live and love, and those who had none at all.

The backs of his closed eyelids grew so bright he peeled them open to find Faythe glowing. She was so breathtaking. Ethereal. There were no yucolites in the lake anymore—they'd all absorbed into her.

Within, Reylan felt something snap, and he clutched her tighter with a horrified gasp.

Their bond.

"*No…*" he breathed. "You can't have her."

Maybe he'd been mistaken. Instead of bringing her here to save her…he'd brought her to her resting place, and they were taking what was left of her.

Absolute terror held him hostage. Frozen.

A sharp yank inside made him grit his teeth, and then…

He felt her.

He heard the gentle beat in her heart slowly growing stronger.

He saw…

Faythe's gold eyes fluttered open. Her hand rose to touch his arm.

"Reylan," she whispered. "Did we make it?"

A breathy, delirious chuckle left him, and he kissed her. Faythe managed to straighten and stand in the water with him, but he held her in a tight embrace.

"We made it," he mumbled into her neck.

"I thought…I thought I wouldn't. I don't think I'm supposed to be here."

"You're supposed to be with me."

Her weak arms tightened. Then she released him to rest her head against his chest. Faythe's fingers swirled over the surface of the water.

"The yucolites…"

"Know you belong here too."

He scented the salt of her tears as they mixed with his. He couldn't stop them. There were very few moments that invoked tears in him, but this joy was worth them.

Faythe stared into his eyes and he found the world in hers. Every day of misery, every hour of torment, it was all worth it to reach this moment with her.

Reylan braced his hands on her waist, lifting her out of the water to sit her on the edge. He looked up at her with the sun glowing behind her and the pride growing in his chest was a beautiful ache. She ran her fingers through his damp hair and the silence they basked in tender touches felt sacred.

"I love you," he said. "I love you more than those simple words could possibly convey. There isn't a language that translates what I feel for you."

Reylan lifted himself out the water and Faythe moved like they were magnets until she lay back and he hovered over her.

"There is," she said quietly. "There's a language that exists only between us that is louder than words."

Reylan's lips crashed to hers and Faythe's body arched into him as he pressed tighter to her. This was infinity. A vow to find her in every lifetime because what they had couldn't be lost or broken by time.

They might have won the war but their battles weren't over yet. He was ready to face everything that came next so long as he was by her side. To be whatever she needed him to be to begin to *live* the life she deserved.

CHAPTER NINETY

Faythe

Had the cost been worth the win? So much life was embedded in the wounds of a battle that would scar the land for ages to come. So many futures had become unreached dreams, so many faces existing now only in the memories of those left behind.

Faythe, battle-tired and devastated, walked like a ghost through the ruins of the outer town in High Farrow. She passed collapsed buildings, still smoking from extinguished fires. She took in the bodies buried under debris; the crimson stains over the cobbles. With so much tragedy in the wake of their triumph, there was no celebration to be had.

When she made it to her destination, it took everything she had left not to crumble as easily as the stone around her.

Because of everything that had collapsed in ruins…it still stood.

Right in front of her, wedged between two lost homes with their roofs caved in, the cramped hut of her childhood with Jakon still lived.

"Stubborn thing," she muttered, but her emotions threatened to flood all over again.

She was so exhausted.

The door creaked open at her push—a familiar sound that broke her first sob—and she paused, head bowing. For just a few seconds, she wanted to pretend he would be inside. That Jakon would be waiting for her to come home at that small benched kitchen table. She held onto that memory when his voice in greeting came so clearly in her mind she had to grit her teeth, nails drawing blood from her palms to keep back the tears—but it was no use. Her first tears fell, and she looked up into vacancy.

He wasn't coming back.

Faythe could hardly drag herself inside, but she did this for him.

The ghost of their memories played out in every abandoned corner. This place had never been vibrant in color, but it had been in joy. She'd lived out so much joy with him as her best friend.

In the bedroom, she hardly made it to his cot before she fell in her grief. Curling tightly into herself, she finally let go. Sobs racked her to agony, until she couldn't draw breath and nearly let darkness claim her. She buried her face in his pillow, and his scent...it was still there, so faint, but her fae smell could draw it out, and that only shattered the last piece of her heart.

She didn't know an end to this agony. How she would be able to go on when he'd left her here.

And that was all she was...left behind.

For hours, days—she couldn't be sure how much time she exhausted herself between crying until she thought it might kill her, sleeping, and lying there in a hollow detachment she couldn't climb out of.

She knew she wasn't always alone.

Most of the time, it was Reylan who stayed with her, sitting on the floor, because this cot was never even big enough for Jakon himself.

He didn't try condolences or attempt to pull her out of the void she was drifting in. She was grateful for it. Reylan's hand would brush through her hair or trace idly over her arm or leg. Sometimes he took her hand and just stayed with her, patient and mourning with her. He would fill the silence at times just to relay what was happening with everyone else outside these walls she couldn't leave yet.

She knew she would have to. That the world was moving on, and she would have to follow.

After a few days, she knew she couldn't deny her hunger any longer, and she was alone when she found the strength to sit up. She sat on Jakon's cot, hugging his pillow as a final farewell to him. This hut. This life. It would live eternally in her heart, and she was starting to accept what she'd lost.

Her mother. Her father. Caius. Jakon. Marlowe.

She repeated their names, stored them in her soul, and when Reylan returned this time, she felt enough stability to give him attention.

He hesitated in the doorway he'd ducked through, surprised to see her sitting. Faythe managed a small smile, and it was genuine. He was the rock that always grounded her. The fire that always blazed in her. With him, she would have the strength to live with her great losses.

"My Phoenix," he said, as gentle as a whisper across frost.

Reylan crouched in front of her, taking her hands and searching her eyes. Faythe fell into him like gravity demanded it. Her arms wrapped around his neck, and he held her with tight arms around her body. She listened to his heartbeat—the sound that kept her wanting to live. The sound she would always come home to across time and realms.

"We made it," she whispered, using her voice carefully for the first time in days.

Reylan's face burrowed more into her neck, and he breathed in deeply. "Yes, we did."

Faythe found the will to release him slowly, in no rush, but steadily climbing toward leaving this hut once and for all. She slipped a hand over his jaw while her head bowed with the weight of sorrow.

"How is everyone?"

"They're mourning with you in their own ways. Nik is grieving deeply, but he's still taking charge of his kingdom. We won the war, but there is always a battle to be fought for the survivors in the aftermath."

Faythe nodded. She knew how close Jakon and Marlowe had been to Nik and Tauria too. Their circle felt broken now, but between them, their heroic human friends would never be forgotten.

"She knew," Faythe said. Reylan's hand cupping her face forced her teary eyes to him. "Marlowe knew Jakon would die. He should have a long time ago, before I met him, by the same illness as his parents. But he was spared by Aurialis in the woods. My mother took him there. That was why Marlowe sacrificed herself, setting off her own chain of events to aid us toward victory. She wanted to be with him in the end, even in tragedy. Marlowe wrote it all and left it in the book I once borrowed from her, knowing I would come here at the end. It's my choice whether I let it be closure—that fate, no matter how tragic, could never have been fought—or let it fuel my resentment for that fact. It's unfair and cruel, isn't it, how the true heroes of the story never win? It simply cannot be."

Reylan's eyes filled with misery, sharing her grief.

"What do you choose?"

"I don't know yet," she said honestly. Her thumb brushed along his cheek while she swallowed her turmoil. "But I know I choose you. I feel selfish for it. That while you're still with me, I'm glad I'm alive."

His eyes closed briefly, like reprieve, before he lost his restraint to kiss her.

"You have no idea how desperately I've been waiting to hear that."

"I'm sorry I took so long."

Reylan shook his head. "Take as long as you need to grieve. I'll be right here. But know that from this moment I won't allow you torment in survivor's guilt. After all you've given, I swear my life to making sure you know how deserving you are to live this life to the fullest."

Faythe gave a broken smile of gratitude. He would never let her fall apart. They would return to Rhyenelle soon and begin the long road to healing their kingdom too. And for the first time since their victory, Faythe let the warmth of hope seep into her.

"Jakon and Marlowe won the war for us," she said quietly.

"They're two of the bravest people I've ever had the privilege of knowing."

She took a shaky breath, but she was ready to start carrying their legacy as they would want of her. "Me too."

Faythe rose and might have buckled from the shooting pain of her dormant muscles, but Reylan was right there, picking up every piece of her that crumbled.

He didn't let her go as they headed toward the front door. Faythe didn't stumble, she didn't stall, for if she did, she might never make it out. She kept walking against every tether that had wound around her from those days in the hut, tormenting her that walking away meant letting him go.

She would never. Until her very last breath, Jakon and Marlowe would stay with her in every step she took.

The air was clearer when she stepped past the threshold of the hut, but the heavy weight of sorrow still hung. Her eyes stung from the rays of sun that split the cloudy sky, but the light that warmed her face brought her peace.

At High Farrow's castle grounds, Faythe's walking slowed in her complete shock.

Three Firebirds occupied the courtyard, seeming so out of place. They'd had to cramp themselves around this space that wasn't designed for such large creatures. Faythe's heart ached with yearning for Atherius, who was almost twice the size as all these birds, but her joy was more prominent to see the species wasn't extinct after Atherius's death.

Their riders stood by. Livia was one of them, catching her eye amid talking to a beautiful, tall, dark-skinned woman. Lady Samara was also with them.

"Your belief was true then," Faythe said to her as they reached them.

"It was worth the adventure even if it wasn't," Livia said.

Their shared look turned to relief and gratitude before they embraced.

"We're thinking of going back to Salenhaven, actually," Livia informed her as they released each other.

Reylan folded his arms, emanating a protective aura. "Back to Salenhaven?"

"It's wonderful there. I know you'll miss me, cousin, but you'll have your hands full as the new King Consort of Rhyenelle." She winked at him playfully.

Faythe broke a prideful smile, and a giddy flutter broke inside her at the thought of him ruling by her side. "We?" Faythe tacked back to her, skimming her eyes over Samara.

A blush fanned across her pale cheeks when Livia's eyes fell on her. Then, boldly, the commander drew the timid lady closer with an arm around her waist.

"You get to bond a lot with a person over months crossing the sea to another continent," Livia mused.

Samara's face reddened more, but Livia kissed her cheek, then her mouth when it opened to speak.

Faythe smiled broadly, giving them privacy by shifting her attention to the woman beside them who'd come from far west.

"How many Firebirds live in Salenhaven?"

"Only two dozen or so. The Phoenixes come from a faraway island called Embercrest. I only recently learned they originate from your kingdom. It is not taught in our history books. My name is Rhiannon Garrikson. I was a supreme commander of the Phoenix rider academy on the island."

Faythe's mouth fell open in shock at hearing of the island.

A riding academy.

The concept sounded so wonderful she couldn't believe it.

"I would love to visit someday," Faythe said.

"It is very far. I hope you have wings."

Faythe smiled to herself. She didn't know if her Phoenix wings would stop being accessible someday without access to Phoenixfyre, but exchanging a warm look with Reylan, she knew they had other means.

"Thank you for coming to our aid," Faythe said. "We're indebted to you."

"Our high king wasn't convinced by the thought of risking great forces—it is why only a little over a dozen of us defied his order to come. Livia Arrowood made a very convincing case—I had to see the homeland of our beloved Firebirds. This is Ignisra." Rhiannon smoothed a hand over the feathers on her bird's wing, and it looked back on her fondly, with a vertical pupil cutting through a core of warm amber.

Faythe wanted to learn all the names of the Firebirds. It gave her a spark of hope for the future to get to see where they'd migrated to and how they lived on triumphantly.

"You're welcome to Rhyenelle any time," Faythe offered. Then she thought, "Do you know how the Phoenix eggs are hatched?"

"When they were wild beasts, we're taught they hatched sporadically, and some never did. It was like they chose when they wanted to come into the world. Since they've started bonding with mortals, they wait for a claiming. The egg stays dormant until it chooses its rider."

Faythe's eyes darted to Reylan's with hope for Atherius's egg.

"Faythe!" Tauria's voice sounded from the castle entrance.

The Fenstead queen ran toward her, and Faythe jogged to meet her. They collided in a burst of relief, joy, and sorrow. After all the separation, and with all the evil that had chased each of them on their own paths, Faythe squeezed the gift of her tighter, relieved they'd made it to this reunion in the end.

"I'm so glad you're safe," Faythe croaked.

"Oh, Faythe, I don't even know where to begin," she whispered back.

"One day at time."

It was the only way they would learn to move on with their losses.

She spied Nik over her shoulder. When they released each other, Faythe walked to him slowly. Her eyes pricked at the broken sight of him, though he tried so hard to wear a mask of bravery. It was like it all broke apart when they reached each other.

"Jak and Marlowe…" He trailed off, his voice barely audible.

Faythe couldn't speak, she fell into him instead. Nik's arms wrapped her tightly.

Nerida and Tarly were here too, and Faythe's burdens lightened the more people she accounted for from the battle.

She spun, scanning the courtyard twice. "Kyleer and Izaiah?" she breathed from the panic in her throat. "Zaiana?"

"Look up," Reylan said, slipping an arm around her.

Faythe threw her head back, and spying the stroke of darkness heading toward them stunned her as much as the first time she'd seen the black Phoenix.

The red Phoenixes cried and became restless. Faythe could feel their fear and distress.

"Is that a black Phoenix?" Rhiannon said in terror.

Faythe couldn't understand their fear. "It's not what you think," Faythe said, trying to calm them.

The other birds only grew more upset, knocking into statues and destroying garden beds. Izaiah must have noticed, because he shifted to a smaller bird to soar down lower before landing in a flash of light, revealing himself as fae.

"Am I really that frighting?" he commented.

Rhiannon stared at Izaiah in stupor. "How can you transform into a black Phoenix?"

"That is a grim story." When his eyes shifted to Faythe, assumption started swirling in her mind.

Faythe glowered at him, and he almost flinched away when she marched to him. She pulled him into a firm embrace. "You might actually be more insane and reckless than I am," she mumbled. "I'm glad you're alive, stupid choices aside."

He squeezed her. "Me too, Faythe," he sighed.

"The black Phoenix carries a dark legend," Rhiannon explained. "I always thought it was just a scary story we grew up with, but with the reaction of the other Phoenixes...well, I guess I'm just glad you're not a real one."

"What legend?" Faythe asked, her interest piqued.

"From the void, a black wing shall rise, and with its rider, unmake the light."

An eerie shiver broke over Faythe's skin.

Just then, a body dropped down behind her, and Faythe, still on edge from the battle, whirled with her heart in her throat. Her fright quickly changed to shock as her eyes landed on Kyleer, who tucked in his black feathered wings.

"I've had enough of legends and prophesies," Kyleer mumbled in response to Rhiannon's words.

Faythe almost fell into the demand to hug him, but his memories...

Kyleer smiled brightly. His arms opened. "Don't keep me waiting after the Nether we survived."

Faythe drew in a shallow gasp. *He remembers.* She whimpered as she jogged the few strides, and he lifted her off her feet in their embrace.

When he set her down, Faythe scanned him from head to toe. He was so changed, yet unchanged. His wings were beautiful, but he would have to carry them for the rest of his life against his choosing.

"Where's Zaiana?" Faythe asked, surveying the land and sky for her. She'd been there at the end to help kill Dakodas.

"I'm not sure. She took off after you got rid of Dakodas. Maverick...he's dead. Killed by Mordecai in the end."

"Mordecai is still alive?" Faythe breathed. Renewed panic of war and battle and bloodshed filled her chest, and she struggled to breathe.

Reylan's arms took her out of Kyleer's, and he soothed her senses through their bond.

"He has no armies. There are many dark fae who are loyal to Zaiana now—we just need to find her and hope she'll take her place as the Queen of Valgard. Mordecai is nothing without the Spirits, and they're gone thanks to you."

She tried to relax, but in the wake of their great war, it was like it was still reaching dark hands to everything she wanted to begin rebuilding.

Reylan took her face in his hands, and she met his sapphire eyes, glittering with such promise against the break of a new dawn. "We choose us now. We choose our happiness. We rebuild our kingdom and help rebuild the world from the war. There is nothing that can stop us."

Faythe's eyes flooded, and she nodded.

She repeated in a promise sealed between their souls. "We choose us."

CHAPTER NINETY-ONE

Nik

Nik stood on the balcony of his rooms, staring out over the kingdom of High Farrow with a fresh breath of perception. There was so much he wanted to achieve in his reign, and now he finally felt the freedom to begin to dream.

Tauria crept up, circling her arms around him from behind. He drew her around to his side, kissing the top of her head as she joined him in a silent moment of reflection and hope for their future.

"There's a lot to rebuild," Tauria said. "More so in Fenstead."

"We'll dedicate our time and forces to both kingdoms accordingly. The world knows we are the king and queen of both now."

"The path of healing will be long."

"So will be our reign."

Nik kissed her in promise, feeling the light of their future expanding in his chest. Asari rubbed herself around their legs as if she wanted to be included in their plans in either kingdom. Though she wasn't a beast native to either, he'd come to be glad for her unexpected, loyal companionship.

When a short knock came on their door, Nik called for them to enter. He warmed at sight of Nerida and Tarly, who joined them on the balcony.

Nerida slipped away from Tarly, talking off to the side with Tauria. Nik looked at them fondly, still in disbelief that they were sisters. But as they smiled and laughed, reaching for each other, it was a precious sight, and he couldn't be more delighted they'd found each other.

Katori nuzzled Asari in greeting—another uncanny sister bond.

Nik met Tarly's eye, and he was hit with a whirlwind of emotions he'd never gotten to express in the midst of all the war and chaos.

"Thank you," Nik said with all the sincerity he could, but it didn't feel like nearly enough. "You saved Tauria's life, and I can't ever repay you for that."

Tarly smirked, waving him off as if it were nothing and heading around him to lean on the stone railing. "I didn't really do it for you," he said nonchalantly.

"Still, it was remarkable what you did. All this time, you've thought yourself powerless when you were harboring the greatest ability of us all."

"Don't give me too much praise. It's weird."

Nik chuckled, leaning over the balcony with him and watching the sun set over the burning horizon. It made him think of Faythe, who would be heading home to Rhyenelle any day now.

"Will you be going to Lakelaria or Olmstone?" Nik asked.

"I'm not the heir of Olmstone. I can't explain how it doesn't feel right. But I know my sister will make a great queen when she comes of age, and I'll do whatever I need to until then."

"For what it's worth, I think you would make a great king."

"I hope to be...for her." Tarly's gaze slipped briefly across to Nerida, who now sat with Tauria on the outside chaise by the window.

Tarly was more selfless and devoted than Nik had bothered to see before.

"Nerida is claiming her throne then? I'm glad."

"There's going to be a lot to learn for both of us."

"You can call to us for anything. Anytime you need," Nik offered.

Tarly straightened, and his mouth quirked. "Let's hope that isn't too soon."

Nik hesitated, then he remembered the war they'd just survived and pulled Tarly into a firm embrace. "I mean it," he said.

Tarly looked stunned when Nik let him go, but to save the awkwardness, Nik turned toward Tauria and Nerida.

"Is it just me, or do they look to be conspiring?" Tarly mused.

Nik huffed a laugh. "Your hope of not seeing me too much too soon might already be thwarted."

As they got closer, Tauria's eyes sparkled as they looked up at him. She said, "We were just talking about how we want the world to know we share a father. Nerida is no less legitimate—there's no reason to hide it."

Nik's hand slipped over her shoulder. "I think that's a wonderful idea."

"The kingdoms of Ungardia have never been so united in bonds of blood and friendship. It's a new age for the people," Tarly said thoughtfully.

"It's the new age we all fought and sacrificed for," Tauria said, standing.

Nik pulled her to him with an arm around her waist as they watched the sun's fleeting rays. Nerida and Tarly stood beside them, with the wolves between them.

"I didn't expect to be a part of it all, but I'm so happy not to be hiding anymore," Nerida said quietly.

Tauria took her hand. "No more hiding. Now, we reign."

Nik found Faythe in the Eternal Woods. She kept her back to him, staring into the waterfall lake that no longer glowed with yucolites. They had been a beautiful sight, but much more so was the healthy and alive picture of his dear friend standing before him. The yucolites had always taken a liking to Faythe, and Nik was beholden to them for giving her their life force.

"Here we are," Nik said, sauntering up with his hands in his pockets. He watched the water ripple with their reflections. "The Phoenix Queen and the half-adequate king in the woods."

Faythe chuckled lightly, pushing into his side. "You've always been more than adequate," she said.

"Don't give me too much praise—it'll get to my head."

Her smile faltered, and Nik felt the weight on his own happiness too.

He said, "I'm going to make sure they're remembered. Jakon and Marlowe are High Farrow citizens who contributed immensely to the war. We wouldn't be here without them. So their statues will be built in the market square."

Faythe was silent for a moment. He scented the salt of her tears.

"That's a beautiful idea," she whispered.

They walked through the woodland in mournful silence. Faythe had planted a matching tombstone for Jakon next to Marlowe's. Nik wished he'd been here when they'd fought Marvellas... He was racked with torment, wondering if things could have turned out differently if they'd just had more help.

It was hard to accept the two fearless, gentle humans weren't coming back, but seeing their stones side by side, Nik wanted to believe their spirits lived on in these woods together.

"I want to come back as often as I can to visit them," Faythe said.

"You know this kingdom will always be your home too." His arm draped over her shoulders, pulling her into a side-embrace. They stood there for some time in reflective silence.

"You're going to make a strong queen, Faythe. It's always been in you, even before we learned of your heritage."

"I don't really know what I'm doing," she confessed.

Faythe hadn't grown up in court and around politics, but still, he had every belief in her.

"Just remember to always have Faythe," Nik mused.

Faythe's head angled back, hooking a brow of surprise at him. Nik smirked.

"Izaiah might have mentioned it. To live like death is a game, love is a prize, and danger is desire. It's a mantra he's taken on in full stride, coaching others by it."

Faythe rolled her eyes, but the lighter mood relieved some of their burden for a moment.

Her head rested on his shoulder. "I'm so glad you made it, Nik."

His arm tightened around her. "You can't get rid of me that easily."

"It's time," Reylan's voice interrupted gently from behind them.

As they turned, Nik playfully grabbed Faythe, pulling her into a crushing hug.

"You've had a mission to steal her from us since the moment you laid eyes on her. I don't think I'm ready for you to succeed."

Faythe was going back to Rhyenelle, and he didn't know when they would next meet again. She laughed, trying to wriggle out of his grip.

Nik let her go, tousling her hair as she batted his hands away.

"Rhyenelle is always a stop beside Fenstead," she said with a wink.

Nik smiled watching her leave with Reylan. He called one last time, "I'll await my coronation and wedding invite!"

Faythe's giggles as she leaned into Reylan settled in his chest before she disappeared out of sight.

Nik headed back toward the waterfall clearing, finding the most beautiful creature sitting by the lake, running her fingers along the surface of the water. Nik sat, tucking himself tightly in behind Tauria.

"Faythe is leaving," he said.

"We already said our farewells," Tauria said, with a hint of mischief that told him it might not be long at all before they saw her again.

"What's next for us?" he asked, eager to dream of the bright future that opened up for them. Nik swept her hair over her shoulder, planting tender kisses down her neck.

"We rebuild."

"Of course."

"We have two kingdoms to restore."

"Then...?" he prompted. "When the day comes that the lands are healed and we rule as normal, what do you dream of, my love?"

Tauria sighed, easing into him more. "A family, eventually."

Nik's spirit soared. He shifted smoothly until she was under him against the pristine grass. Tauria laughed, trying to playfully resist his allurement.

"I said *eventually*." Her smile brightened his world.

"Consider me very eager to practice until the time is right for both of us."

Though he wanted to take her here, Nik settled beside her. They watched the cloudless open sky with the freedom to paint their future on the canvas. So Nik did. With his hand in Tauria's forever, he knew their dreams were safe now.

CHAPTER NINETY-TWO

Faythe

They arrived on their horses just in time to watch the sun break over the horizon and spill over the city of Ellium from atop the hills. Faythe pulled her horse to a stop, needing a moment to take in the breathtaking sight of her kingdom alive against the rays.

"Do you think we should repair the inner wall?" Faythe asked, her voice reduced from the array of emotions that swarmed her.

She was home.

Without fear or wariness or uncertainty…Faythe Ashfyre had fought to come home.

"Whatever you desire. This kingdom is yours now," Reylan said fondly from atop his horse beside her.

"As my consort and leading general, I'd very much like your opinion."

Reylan cast a side-smile at her. She imagined him in royal finery, with a crown atop his head, but she had to expel it since she risked her emotions spilling down her face at how wonderful it was.

"We might have won our war, but in generations to come, there will be others. I don't view the wall as separation—it's security. They've long been a statement of Rhyenelle, and High Farrow was the first to follow our example and create their singular wall to have a stronghold in the face of an attack. It served well for them in this age, something that was built long ago. So for our future generations, I would rebuild it."

Faythe appreciated his insight. With Reylan by her side, the burden of a crown didn't weigh so heavy. "I agree," she said.

The red-peaked mountains shimmered under the sun's first light, as if awakening to greet the dawn. Shadows retreated down their jagged slopes, and a piercing cry split the tranquil stillness. Faythe looked up, her breath catching.

The Firebirds from Salenhaven soared triumphantly across the peaks, their wings ablaze with every color of a living flame—crimson, gold, and searing white. The air seemed to ripple in their wake. Their cries filled the air, a song of victory; of life undimmed by time or distance. For a moment, they drifted above the mountains, turning in perfect harmony, and the sunlight transformed their feathers into a blazing display that could have outshone the sun itself.

It was a sight so achingly perfect that she clutched her chest, unable to draw a full breath. The ache was bittersweet—half-awe, half-longing. She knew they would return to Salenhaven. Their home was far beyond these mountains. And yet her heart rebelled against the inevitable. What she wouldn't give for them to stay—for their fire to light these peaks forever.

Faythe waved back at two riders in particular. They were mere flickers of movement from this distance, but Faythe grinned wide at Liva and Samara riding together. Part of her envied their freedom for adventure as they would be flying to Salenhaven with Rhiannon and the others. But Faythe was determined to see the western continent herself someday. Maybe even farther, as she couldn't erase the stunning concept of Embercrest, which hatched new Firebirds and trained new riders.

She was too aware of the egg in her satchel. Maybe it was selfish, but she couldn't give it to Rhiannon to take to Embercrest, where it would await a claiming. It was a piece of Atherius she would keep close, even if it would never hatch for her.

Izaiah and Tynan caught up to them as they'd fallen behind on their horses. They could have flown to Rhyenelle from High Farrow and saved the weeks of travel, but she thought everyone was enjoying the mundane tempo of time. Embracing every moment, especially together.

"Now that's a sight I never thought we'd see," Izaiah marveled at the score of Firebirds.

Kyleer wasn't with them, but he would return soon. He'd taken off when they left High Farrow, in search of Zaiana. The dark fae had even left Tynan behind without a single word of explanation or goodbye. But they all knew her reasoning. She was grieving deeply for someone none of them could show sympathy for. Faythe understood her need for solitude. Kyleer wouldn't give up trying to reach her, however.

When they passed the outer-city wall, citizens emerged from their broken homes. Despite the wreckage, they were smiling. Children ran and people gathered on both sides of the pathway. Faythe smiled back at them, feeling their welcome, their acceptance of her.

She heard mutters of "Phoenix Queen" and whispers of her name.

After a moment, when the crowds grew thicker, reaching hands she wanted to touch, Faythe dismounted. She retrieved the egg from her satchel, wanting to share the precious gift with her people.

Faythe Ashfyre was the Phoenix Queen, and she would raise this kingdom from its ashes.

Her fingers skimmed so many, and she felt love in every spark. The walk to the castle seemed so much shorter while she lost herself in this moment, reuniting with her people and pleading her devotion to them as much as they did for her.

Faythe carried the Phoenix egg into the castle, right to the library. The glass case that had once held the large Phoenix feather of Atherius was gone, but the velvet bed for it was still there. It was Reylan who approached, bringing the new feather Atherius had left behind and placing it over the velvet. The first glimpse of restoring all that was tarnished.

She would replace the glass and add an extra measure of protection with her magick, but for now, she was content to leave it.

Dusk was falling by the time Faythe visited the Glass Garden. To her relief, most of it was intact. She'd prepared herself to find it destroyed by Malin's bitter wrath, but the perfect blooms of the white roses shone bright like a hundred moons under the falling night.

Her fingers skimmed the soft petals. Reylan's presence hung nearby, but he let her have a moment of reflective silence. This was her mother's garden, and her father had preserved it for decades in her memory. Faythe looked up at the darkening sky awakening with stars, and warmth spilled over her as though they were watching her, their spirits strongest in this shared space.

"Your Majesty," a castle guard interrupted.

Faythe turned to him, giving a nod to speak.

"I was wondering what you would like us to do with the body of Malin Ashfyre."

She tensed at his name for just a second, but then it dissolved into...sorrow.

"He will be commemorated in the catacombs with his royal ancestors," Faythe said.

She felt the guard's hesitation to question her about it. Most knew what he'd done, but Faythe was certain about where to place him.

"Of course, Your Majesty." The guard bowed and left.

Reylan approached her from behind. His arms slipped around her, and she leaned back into him. "Your heart is too golden for this world," he murmured.

"Malin did unspeakable things. I will never forgive it and I plan to forget him in my own history. He's been lain to rest because of Nyte. Though he didn't get to know his half-brother, he understood his spiral into evil in a way none of us could. So in Nyte's memory, I did it for him."

Reylan's lips pressed to the top of her head. "I think you made the right decision."

Faythe turned in his arms, taken by the picturesque sight of him as he always looked mesmerizing in moonlight. It turned his hair a brilliant white and lightened his sapphire eyes to shine more brilliantly that any diamond.

She ran her hands up his chest. "You really are stuck with me now, Reylan Arrowood Ashfyre."

His unguarded smile was a token of treasure.

"You're really so impatient," he mused.

Faythe was about to question what he meant, but he produced something from the inside of his jacket, and she gasped.

Reylan took her hand, slipping the cool metal around her marital finger. Faythe admired the ring: a gold band cradled a ruby diamond, simple but triumphant. "It was your mother's. She left it behind, and Agalhor kept it all this time. He wanted me to give it to you."

Tears welled in her eyes. "It's perfect."

"But I wanted you to have something that was just ours as well."

He took her hand again, slipping a second ring onto her marital finger. Her tears spilled over this time when she saw the delicate gold butterfly. Somehow, the bottom wings fanned perfectly around the ruby diamond behind it, as if the two rings were always meant to exist as a pair. It wasn't the same as the one she'd had before, but that was what made it even more special. It was a tribute to their past, but a hope for their future.

Faythe met his eyes with blurry vision. "You're perfect," she whispered.

Reylan took her face in her hands and kissed her with fierce promise. "I'm yours, Faythe Arrowood Ashfyre. Your best friend, your mate, your consort, your husband. This day...until the very end of days."

The End.

EPILOGUE ONE

Faythe sat in the presence of everyone she held dear at the grand round council table in Dalrune. Without a royal family, a year following their victory in the Darkest Hour War, the rulers of Ungardia had come to the unanimous decision that it would be a free land; a neutral ground. A lot of dark fae left without a home after the collapse of the Mortus Mountains had chosen to reside here. It would be a place for fae, dark fae, and humans to coexist under a governing body appointed by each of the rulers from the six surrounding kingdoms.

Their annual meetings to discuss kingdom and continent matters would be held right here, at this table, where they all sat as equals, on land that belonged to all of them and none of them.

At least…it had *almost* been unanimous. They were missing one ruling vote.

Kyleer entered inconspicuously through a side door, giving Faythe a solemn shake of his head.

Zaiana wouldn't come.

She'd refused her title as the Queen of Valgard profusely. The dark fae was grieving still, and though Faythe could harbor no sorrow for Maverick's death after all he'd done, she understood Zaiana's loss. Maverick wasn't her villain; he was her reflection, and in the end…for all that time he'd hidden behind wickedness…her protector.

Above that, Zaiana had gotten no closure for his death, with Mordecai still unaccounted for. There had been no sightings even though they'd all contributed efforts to try to track him. Faythe knew that was what kept Zaiana preoccupied too.

"We can't stall much longer," Reylan said close to her ear. He raised their linked fingers, kissing her knuckles.

Faythe smiled fondly at him, still giddy with butterflies in her stomach every time their eyes met so close. He was absolutely breathtaking in his royal black, gold, and crimson wears. A modest gold crown adorned his silver hair, and Faythe would never stop considering herself the luckiest person alive to have him.

"We can begin," she said, squeezing his hand before letting go.

Faythe glanced over the table, taken by love and pride at the sight of all her friends and allies gathered together with nothing but hope and joy to discuss. The others chatted among themselves, and she basked in a moment longer to watch their happiness.

Nik and Tauria leaned into each other, talking conspiratorially, with such bright grins and soft chuckles. While Nik wore his usual color of deep blue and Tauria had kept her emerald green gowns, they'd merged kingdoms proudly in the deep green sash Nik wore around his middle, and in Tauria's, which was blue. Their crowns matched, curving up into a subtle peak at the front like antlers. Their kingdom crests sat side by side as brass pins on their ceremonial shoulder cloaks.

Her dear friends were absolutely exquisite depictions of love and royalty.

Tarly and Nerida wore white and gold, appearing so ethereal it stole Faythe's breath when they first arrived. Nerida was known as Queen Amelie Da'Naid to her people but cherished her humble wanderers' name, Nerida, among her friends at this table. Tarly had stayed true to his decision, relinquishing his claim on the Olmstone throne despite Nerida's protests. The humble prince wanted to be hers —as her consort, nothing more. He'd given his throne to his sister, Opal, who was too young to rule alone, but her mother sat by her side, reformed and freed from her life by Varlas Wolverlon's cold side. Both wore the familiar wears of Olmstone in their color of deep purple.

Faythe's sight lingered on the vacant chair in front of Valgard's serpent crest carved on the table. The island that was condemned as the villain was no different to them. The citizens, mostly dark fae, wanted peace and connection with the mainland after so long in barren isolation. Their lands still didn't grow anything natural, and Faythe, along with all the others, was committed to helping them with trade plans. Without a monarch, things were uncertain for the kingdom, but Faythe hadn't given up hope that Zaiana might return and claim her birthright.

She'd wanted Zaiana to be a part of this day, but as Kyleer had tried to keep track of her, every time he made contact, it was not a welcome reception.

Faythe watched Kyleer make his way silently around the table to stand behind where Faythe and Reylan sat, joining his brother Izaiah, and Tynan who had seamlessly joined Rhyenelle military ranks after the war.

The table was a deep walnut, with the crest of all seven kingdoms burnished into the wood in front of each monarch. Faythe's fingers grazed proudly over her Phoenix emblem.

"I have a surprise waiting for you," Reylan murmured. His low tone broke a shiver down her spine.

"Is this you trying to hurry the meeting along?"

She turned her head to him, and he'd leaned his elbow on his armrest, lazily reclining as he watched her. His smile was devious. His fingers brushed her cheek.

"Absolutely."

Faythe needed no more encouragement. Her palm flattened over the large Phoenix emblem on the table, and her magick spilled into the lines, making it glow. In turn, the others around the table lit up one by one too.

In front of the owl crest of Dalrune, there was no seat but a statue. Faythe didn't see Maverick Blackfair when she looked at it—the dark fae who'd killed her, killed Agalhor, and killed many to spare the unforgivable deeds from Zaiana. Carved in royal finery, poised bravely, and wearing the crown of Dalrune...was Callen Osirion.

All seven kingdom emblems stayed glowing when Faythe settled her hand back in her lap, and they wouldn't burn out until the meeting was over.

It hushed the others into attentive silence.

Faythe drew a long breath, leveling her chin. "Before we turn grossly formal as monarchs to discuss kingdom matters, I have to say this..." She had to pause, swallowing the lump in her throat, the emotion of pure gratitude and love. "We fought through the Nether for these lands, and for each other. Ungardia has never been stronger, more united, than it is with us. I hope history remembers us not just as victors and rulers of the darkest hours our world has seen, but as the family we found in each other that kept us strong. That our bonds with each other made sure we could not lose. We all have our kingdoms to rule, but we are one land, one people, and a movement against one of us is a movement against all of us. The dawn of a United Ungardia starts here."

Nik's eyes sparkled with endearment while his half-smile turned up in amusement. "For one not raised into this role like the rest of us, you truly are a remarkable beacon of an example. You couldn't have done this without us, but we all needed you as much as you needed us."

Tauria sniffed. "You promised this wouldn't get emotional."

Everyone chuckled, and Tauria's eyes weren't the only ones glistening. It was difficult to release their breath and settle into their peace after so long fighting.

Tarly said, "I didn't think I'd be here. For a long time, I didn't even think I wanted to be. I found reason in Nerida, but I found acceptance in all of you."

The graying skin from his dark fae bite had never reversed, but he had full function of his arm and his hand. Though she didn't know him as well, Faythe was glad he'd survived it. Tarly Wolverlon was a hero as much as any of them for his tactics in the war.

"I learned how to grow vegetables!" Opal said excitedly.

Soft laughter echoed around the table. The young princess had kept safe on a farm on the outskirts of Olmstone, thanks to Tarly and his human friends who'd taken them in.

For the next two hours, they shared how their kingdoms were faring and what still needed to be rebuilt. They were committed to helping each other where they could with resources and workers.

When it ended, Reylan led Faythe away.

"Where are we going?"

"I found something you need to see."

They wound through the castle, which was still in a state of repair. Faythe stopped by a torn painting, her hand joined in Reylan's, straining with tension.

Faythe found herself caught in a moment of reflection. "After everything he'd done…he was never hoping for redemption, was he?"

Maverick—no, Callen's portrait was torn. Two scars across his face. Faythe made an urgent note in her mind to have it restored.

"I was almost the one to kill him…" Reylan trailed off.

Faythe squeezed his hand.

"It was like he was waiting for it. As if he knew I'd come and he'd already surrendered."

"The goal that kept him fighting was fulfilled," Faythe whispered.

She'd never expected to harbor any feeling for Maverick, but after hearing his final message, Faythe could at least understand him. He'd done it all for Zaiana. Faythe knew that kind of love. The kind that made villains out of people in its name. She'd sacrificed for Reylan and put the world at risk, and she had no regret.

"Except Zaiana rejected it all," Reylan said.

"Her place among us will always be open. When she's ready... she'll come back."

"I hope you're right."

Faythe turned to him, casting away the somberness with a grin. She poked his chest. "You've finally stopped pretending you hate her."

He rolled his eyes, grabbing her wrist and pulling her flush against him. "There's a kingdom that needs a leader before it falls to anarchy. I acknowledge she's important."

"You're always the first to see Kyleer and ask about her the moment he returns."

"I have to make sure he comes back with four limbs and two eyes after his dangerous monthly venture."

Faythe chuckled, and Reylan smiled before leaning his head down to kiss her. She wanted more after their long day of talking kingdom politics and catching up with their friends.

Before she could push him against the wall, Reylan pulled back, grinning at her look of protest. "After," he murmured, pressing his lips to hers once more before taking her hand and resuming their walk.

They headed down several steps, so Faythe assumed they were underground by now. She couldn't begin to guess what he might have found in his many scouts of this castle as they decided what to use it for and what needed the most repairs after the century it had spent overrun by the enemy dark fae with no order.

The room he led her into was dark, and she coughed from the dust a few steps inside. Stuffing her nose into her elbow, she surveyed the shelves, which appeared littered with trinkets and artifacts. Deeper within, Faythe saw something large leaning against the far back wall, covered in an old sheet. It was what Reylan let go of her hand to approach. When he pulled back the sheet, Faythe jumped at her own reflection.

It was a mirror...sharp around the edges, with no framing.

"Is that...?" Faythe couldn't be sure if she wanted it to be what she thought.

"A Dresair mirror, yes."

"How can you be sure?"

"Because my reflection *waved* at me when I first discovered it. Ask Kyleer—he almost ran out of here screaming."

Faythe snickered. "I'm sure he'd have a different account of that."

Reylan came back to her, resting a hand on her hip as they stared at their reflection together. "Last I was here, I saw a flicker of a familiar face."

Faythe looked up at him in confusion. Until color bled into the mirror—dark and glittering, like a night sky unfurling. It beckoned her to step forward; to soar into its endless expanse.

"What is this?" Faythe asked through a breath of wonder.

The midnight canvas cradling hundreds of constellations began to shift. It morphed into swirls of starlight before Faythe started to make out the shapes of buildings. A city that was born for the moon and stars with how brilliantly it shone under the night. Faythe took a step closer, mesmerized by the starlit labyrinth and the proud, glittering black castle.

Then the image changed again, and Faythe's spine curved back in shock.

"It's Nyte," she said.

Nyte didn't pay her any attention. Perhaps he couldn't see her. Nyte wore a smile she'd never seen before on him—one that unmasked every vicious part of him to reveal nothing but pure love and joy for the woman beside him. She was absolutely breathtaking. Her silver hair had strands that glittered when she moved, smiling with the same adoration at Nyte. They both wore finery fit for Gods, and what a picture of divinity they were.

"Astraea," Faythe said, recalling her name. Nyte's mate. The woman he'd chosen to return to rather than stay in this realm, where he was born.

Faythe's eyes welled, but she blinked to clear her vision, needing to capture this moment entirely. "He made it back to her," she said.

Reylan's arm tightened around her, and his lips pressed to her head. "It's happy endings like theirs and ours that are worth trekking through the Nether for," he said.

"In every realm and in every time."

"That is our promise. Do you want to prove it?"

Faythe couldn't deny she was tempted to step through the mirror if it could take her to that beautiful city. To exchange happier tales with the last family member she had left. But she had much more to see in this realm, and so, for now, she wanted to stay right here.

"Maybe someday," she said and let herself dream beyond the confines of her own stars.

Her heart swelled for Nyte's happiness, and she captured every last flicker of the night and the star who turned away from the mirror as it began to fade.

Before Faythe and Reylan headed home to Rhyenelle, Faythe had one last stop she had to make.

Staring up at the two figures that proudly stood in Farrowhold's outer-town market square, Faythe paid tribute to her fallen friends on one knee. It never got easier to see their faces carved in stone instead of having them by her side, but she was glad their bravery and sacrifice had been immortalized right here.

Jakon Kilnight and Marlowe Kilnight
Fallen Heroes of the Darkest Hour War

After, she found herself in the Eternal Woods with Nik. They parried lazily with their swords, talking mindlessly about court gossip.

"Asari has been particularly protective of Tauria recently. I knew it was only a matter of time before that wolf turned on me," Nik said.

Faythe ducked under his sword, twisting on her sole before lunging up and blocking his next attack.

"Doesn't Katori stay with you too?" Faythe asked.

Nik huffed, and a smile twitched Faythe's mouth at his pretend annoyance.

"Yeah. Apparently, she's miserable in the cold in Lakelaria. Now I have two oversized mutts I never asked for."

"You love them," Faythe teased.

She feinted left, and Nik fell for it, giving her the opening to disarm him with her fist slamming down on his sword hand. Nik hissed, shaking his tender hand with a scowl.

"I wasn't paying attention," Nik complained.

"Whatever helps you sleep at night," Faythe quipped, sheathing Lumarias.

"Speaking of, Asari has started climbing into our bed, and Tauria finds it *cute*."

Faythe giggled. "Maybe she's a better cuddler."

He shot her a scowl, which only made her grin wider. She missed Nik so much when they were apart, but it made these moments of reunion so special.

"We should head back if you want to get on the road to Rhyenelle before nightfall," Nik said, swiping up his sword.

Faythe strolled toward the ruins of the temple and sat on the broken steps. "I'm going to stay a few more minutes. Meet you at the castle?"

Her eyes skimmed over to the twin graves covered in bluedrops. Jakon and Marlowe's resting place was so beautiful.

Nik cast her an understanding smile with his nod, and she watched him walk away.

The silence of the woods only lingered for a moment.

"You still haven't told him you can see us?" The sound of Jakon's voice pricked her nose and eyes.

She turned her head, and the sight of him healed and broke a piece of her. "In his own way…he sees you too," she whispered.

Faythe didn't know whether Jakon was truly real or just a desperate figment of her imagination. She didn't have Aurialis's essence inside her anymore—the Spirit of Life was gone. But perhaps the essence of Marvellas, the Spirit of *Souls*, which she was born with, allowed her to manifest the image of Jakon and Marlowe's souls here.

Marlowe hooked her arm around Faythe's, leaning her head on her shoulder. The touch was barely-there—a seed of doubt that this was real. But Faythe cast her doubts away and chose to believe.

It was only here she could pretend they were still with her in flesh, but no matter where she was, they lived in her heart every day.

"Rhiannon has visited a few times over the past year, along with Livia and Samara and their Phoenixes. Rhiannon hasn't said outright, but I'm sure she thinks I'm selfish for not surrendering Atherius's egg for her to take to the island. If it hasn't hatched for me, then I'm only holding it back from finding the rider it was meant for instead," Faythe relayed.

It ached in her chest to admit that she wanted the hatchling to awaken for her so badly, so she could keep a piece of Atherius, whom she missed dearly.

"You won't be the last Ashfyre it may choose," Marlowe said.

Faythe's mind opened with the hope and yearning she'd harbored before in small kernels. Her hand hovered over her stomach at the beautiful thought of silver-haired Ashfyres. She didn't know when they would be ready for children, as there was so much she wanted to do with Reylan before then, but a smile bloomed over her face at knowing they had all the time in the world now.

Then, as though the key to that future could feel her joy, Reylan appeared through the trees ahead.

"Off you go then, Phoenix Queen," Jakon said playfully.

Faythe huffed a laugh, but she fought tears like she did every time she had to leave. She forced herself to stand, and Faythe didn't look back, too afraid her friends would be gone and the illusion would shatter. Instead she walked to Reylan with their presence still strong behind her.

"Ready to go home?" he said gently, reaching to tuck a lock of hair behind her ear.

"Yes," she said through her tightening throat.

Her hand slipped into his warm, waiting palm. Faythe had learned that the future wasn't a gift; it was a choice. And now, at last, it was theirs to make.

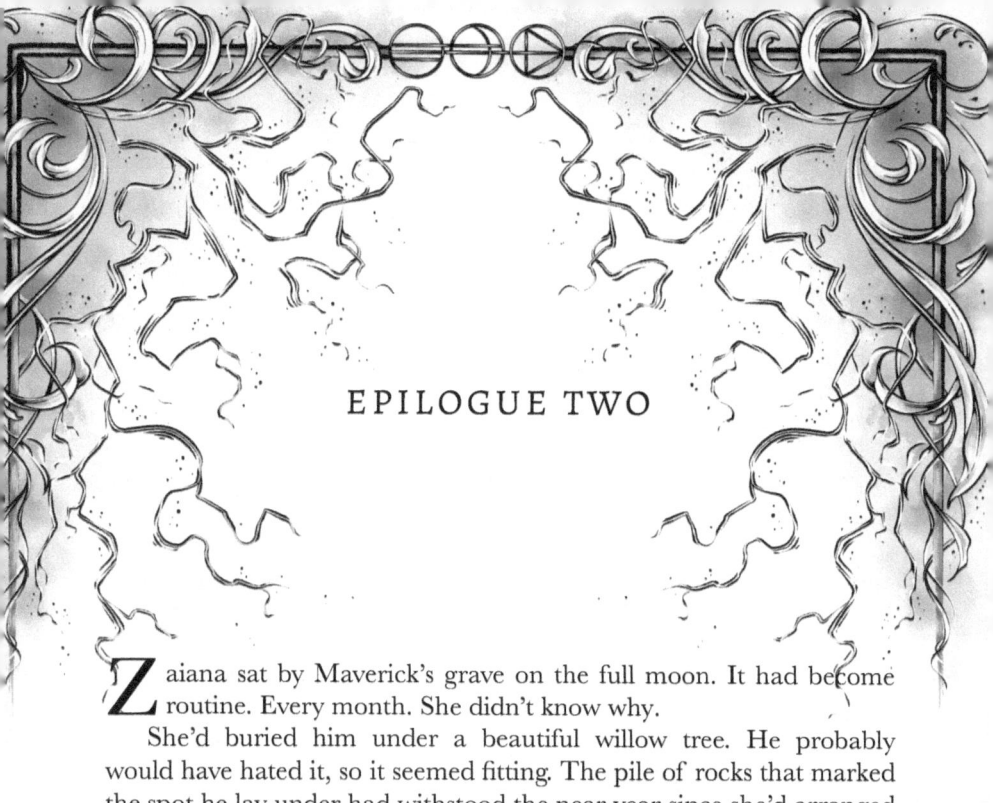

EPILOGUE TWO

Zaiana sat by Maverick's grave on the full moon. It had become routine. Every month. She didn't know why.

She'd buried him under a beautiful willow tree. He probably would have hated it, so it seemed fitting. The pile of rocks that marked the spot he lay under had withstood the near year since she'd arranged them. Not a single one had moved. *Stubborn even in the grave*, she thought each time she came here.

Zaiana sat in her solemn silence, hugging her knees to her chest, depleted of emotion. "I thought I almost found him last week," she told Maverick. "But Mordecai remains a snake in the grass."

Zaiana rested her chin on her knees, watching the glowing orb in the sky. She didn't miss anyone. Not even Tynan. Because she knew he was living a better life with Izaiah and the others than he would by her side. So she'd made sure he could never find her. She was very good at remaining hidden…

To all but one person.

She didn't miss Kyleer, because he'd stuck to his own routine of somehow finding her at least once a month despite her efforts to remain untraceable. Zaiana had come to consider it something of a game, trying to elude him every dawn after the full moon. When he would find her, it gave her a small distraction from her relentless pursuit of her father.

There had been little whisper of Mordecai, and she was beginning to suspect he'd fled the continent of Ungardia altogether. She just couldn't bring herself to cross seas yet. And she knew it was the damn stubborn pile of rocks next to her that felt like an anchor against setting sail.

The rulers of this continent were slowly gaining the trust of the dark fae. She'd noticed some roamed freely on the mainland, welcomed as citizens in various new kingdoms.

They'd tried many times to convince her to take over leadership of Valgard, where most dark fae had chosen to stay or return. She refused to take that throne. Their king still lived, and until he was dead, the clutches of his ghost would always cling to her.

Besides, the idea of a crown on her head and a title of *queen* was just laughable. Her whole life had been hidden, a companion of the shadows. She wasn't born to lead the dark fae into the light.

Faythe and the others had taken over Dalrune, *Maverick's kingdom*, and she resented it. They'd invited her there for their monarchs' *meeting*, as Kyleer last relayed. She couldn't bring herself to step into the castle of Dalrune.

Until she killed Mordecai for killing Maverick, she couldn't rest.

In truth, Zaiana feared when that day would come, for after she'd achieved her goal…she didn't know what would become of her.

There was nothing left for her to do in this world, and maybe it would be better off without her in it.

Kyleer would be better off. She really believed he would have given up by now, since every time he'd tried to touch her frozen heart she'd lashed out with icy bitterness.

He didn't deserve it. She despised herself for hurting him, but he kept. Coming. Back.

The longest he'd left her alone was two months, and she'd believed then he'd finally let her go. Then, when he appeared in the midst of her killing a string of savage dark fae, her heart might have been glad for it, but her mind resented him for splitting it open anew.

Zaiana sighed, wincing from the ache of her dormant muscles as she stood. The first rays of dawn spilled over the horizon—her signal to leave.

"I will find him," Zaiana said to the ghost of Maverick that followed her steps of vengeance. "Next time I come, I'll have killed him."

She spoke that vow every time, even though not once had it been true.

An hour later, Zaiana crouched on a high rooftop, her hood drawn and a covering over the lower half of her face. She waited, wanting to catch Kyleer before he caught her.

When she detected a presence across the roof behind her, Zaiana spun, bracing to lunge for him, as their regular greeting always exploded in violence.

Except this time, every muscle in her body locked against movement. She was sure her heart had ripped out of her chest and landed in the clutches of her intruder. He smiled, and it was so uncanny it jerked Zaiana straight, even stumbling over her own feet with her backward step.

"Maverick," she breathed.

"Zaiana, I presume? I've been looking for you for quite some time."

Only when he spoke did she snap out of her trance. It wasn't nearly the same accent or deep tone. Still, a lump had formed too thick and fast, and Zaiana couldn't swallow past it.

Her next words were barely a squeak. "Who are you?"

"My apologies," he said. The longer she stared and the more he spoke, the more she started to notice how very different this male was to Maverick. "This must be a shock to you. My name is Theron Osirion. Callen was my older brother."

His hair was longer, brushing past his nape. His eyes were a similar shape but a plain brown. The way he spoke retained the sense of regality Maverick had let fall to cold depression. Then, behind him... Zaiana had been too stunned to notice the small Firebird on another rooftop, watching them carefully.

"Maverick never mentioned you," Zaiana said, coming back into herself and raising her guard.

"Maverick was not my brother," he answered with bitter notes of resentment.

Zaiana's teeth gritted at his disgust. "Then you've been looking for the wrong person. Find Faythe Ashfyre if you want the Dalrune throne."

"I don't. And I have found the right person. For not long before he died, I received this letter..." Theron retrieved a parchment from inside his jacket. "Signed by my brother, Callen. I want to believe there was a part of him still in the monster he became, and so I've come to help you."

"Help *me?*"

"Find Mordecai and kill him. You may seek retribution for Maverick, but I'm owed justice for my brother, my parents, and my country he destroyed."

"Your country is being restored. You're the rightful heir and should focus your efforts there."

Theron unfolded the paper that looked so thin now, as if he'd read the letter many times. He read it to her.

"Fate may have stolen my mate, my family, and my life, but it has not stolen justice. You know who did this. You know what must be done. Do not let my death be the end of this story—let it be the reason Mordecai never knows a moment of peace. Find Zaiana Vesaria. She is the only one I trust to serve adequate justice, but you should be a part of it too. She's violent, headstrong; she's the shadow that lingers even in the dark. Please, brother, as my last wish, protect her. For she'll try to take this path alone, and I fear this is one too dark for her to make it back to the light when vengeance is had."

The wind blew over a wet trail Zaiana hadn't felt rolling down her cheek until Theron stopped speaking. She was grateful for her hood and her face covering to disguise her slip of emotion.

"Maverick would never write something so…*heartfelt*."

Theron's smile was a partial wince as he folded the letter again. "Callen would. That's why I've come to honor it."

"If you cared so much about your *brother*, then where have you been?" Zaiana yelled. She ripped her mask down to spit her emotions violently. "Where were you while he died in *my* arms! Believing he was *no one*. Believing he *had* no one!"

Misery fell over Theron's face. "I've been in Salenhaven. After the Great Battles…I barely escaped with my life. I don't recall much of who helped me, nor how I made it across the sea beyond Lakelaria. All I knew was that I wasn't Theron Orison anymore. I couldn't be. If I was to survive, I had to start again, and I believed my whole family was dead. Until this letter. I don't know how Callen knew I was alive and where I was… I guess I'll never know now, and it kills me. I failed him. But you…you saved him."

Zaiana's vision flashed with a white-hot rage. Her hand shook, clutching a blade she'd unsheathed to parry with Kyleer. "Saved him?" she said, her voice as sharp as a blade. "He's *dead*."

"That wasn't all he said about you in that letter. He's never spoken about anyone that way who wasn't his mate. Callen died, but his heart lived on in Maverick…only for you."

It was like he was giving her praise, and it crawled over her skin so treacherously she wanted to rip off her own flesh to be rid of it.

"You know nothing," she said coldly.

Nothing of how cruel she was to him. Nothing of how many times she'd hurt him. Betrayed him. And then let him die.

"You're right. But I want to know everything. You're the only one who carries the story of Maverick Blackfair. The real story of the monster everyone saw, who had a heart so deeply buried that only you could reach it."

"Only to tear it from his chest," Zaiana spat. She may as well have.

"I don't believe that."

"I'm not interested in sitting down by a fire with you to exchange tales about the *monster* your brother became. You've wasted your time."

"You're looking for Mordecai. I want vengeance against him as much as you. He slaughtered my family and destroyed my kingdom. And I know where he might be."

Zaiana was about to dismiss him again until that final sentence.

"How could you know?"

"Because he has no allies nor reputation in Ungardia anymore. Trying to conquer here would be foolish with the new alliance of the continent and the acceptance of the dark fae. Someone like Mordecai will seek the next highest power that aligns with his vision, and there's been a tyrant on the throne of Salenhaven's capital for too long. There's been whispers of a new ally in his court, but no one has seen them. It might not be him, but it's a good place to start looking."

She considered everything he said, torn between wanting to cast him away and resume her mission in solitude, but if she were to go to Salenhaven…she knew nothing about those lands. Theron did.

Zaiana turned away from him to consider this new venture. Leaving Ungardia…she'd dreamed of it before. When this continent felt damned and beyond redemption, she dreamed of flying far, far away. Perhaps beyond Salenhaven, to discover uncharted lands.

But now this continent was saved, and its prospects were bright. Zaiana didn't want to flee to escape its terrors. She felt compelled to leave as she was only a dark stain on these lands that were moving forward while she was stuck in the past.

"Fine," she said at last, turning back to her unlikely ally. The resemblance he bore to Maverick punched her in the gut again, but she focused on the differences that soothed her aching chest. "But I warn you, I won't be kind, and you're just a means to an end."

"Understood." Theron smiled, and Zaiana wished Maverick had smiled that way. So genuine and *happy*. Nothing had given him reason to.

With the distraction of Theron, Zaiana had completely forgotten she was scouting for another irritating presence. Until he found her first.

She hissed when a body dropped from the skies behind her and a blade rested against her throat. Kyleer's warmth seeped into her, and for a second, the threat of the blade was insignificant. His scent filled her nostrils, and she breathed it in. She would spend every month firming her denial that she ever wanted to see him again, but every time he came, it took seconds to obliterate those efforts.

Steel sang, and she found Theron braced with his sword, pinning Kyleer with a lethal look. The Firebird stirred too, its wings flaring and embers skittering off its feathers.

"New friend?" Kyleer said in her ear in a low, seductive tone.

"I thought it was about time I find better company," she said.

Zaiana hooked her foot around his leg and grabbed his wrist holding the knife. In one swift movement, she slipped out of his hold, and Kyleer stumbled but didn't fall.

"Who is that?" Theron asked from behind her.

Kyleer's gaze narrowed on Theron. "Who are *you*?" Kyleer said it like an accusation. But then his face relaxed, realizing... "Elaina and Ragnar Osirion had two sons...but you...you're supposed to be *dead*."

"I'm glad I'm not."

Kyleer rubbed a hand over his face. "What is going on?"

"He thinks he knows who Mordecai might have turned to for an alliance," Zaiana explained.

That shifted Kyleer's entire demeanor. He straightened, and his face firmed, tuning in to the commander as if Theron had just announced an impending war.

"Where?"

"Salenhaven," Theron said.

A muscle in Kyleer's jaw worked, and his eyes shifted to her. "When are we going?"

Zaiana shook her head. "You're not coming with me."

"Like shit I'm not."

"Ky—"

"When. Are. We. Going?"

"It sounds like you two have to work this out. I'm going to find a tavern to sample Ungardia wine after all this time away," Theron said. "Find me when you're ready, Zaiana. My Phoenix, Azarra, should be easy enough to spot."

When he left, Kyleer wore a calculating look as he stared off to the side.

"It's been getting rather dull around here anyway. Rhyenelle is doing well. Faythe and Reylan have had little instruction for me. They'll understand my leave for a while."

Her teeth ground. "I don't *want* you to come with me."

Kyleer tried to hide his hurt, but she saw it. However negligible, she always saw his pain and felt it as if it were her own. Though he was a master of pretense.

"I'll save you the torture of admitting you *do* want me with you. I've been dying to see Salenhaven after discovering the Phoenixes have migrated there and beyond. Faythe is going to be so jealous."

Internally, she groaned. Zaiana knew there would be no dissuading him, and maybe...

Maybe she wanted his warm company for one last perilous quest. For when the wrath of two storms would meet, only one would make it out alive. Father or daughter.

HAVEN'T CAUGHT UP WITH NYTE'S STORY YET?

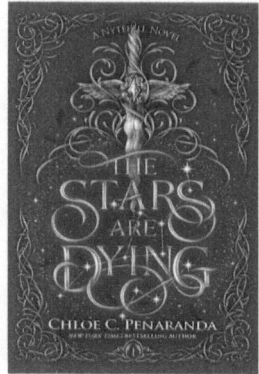  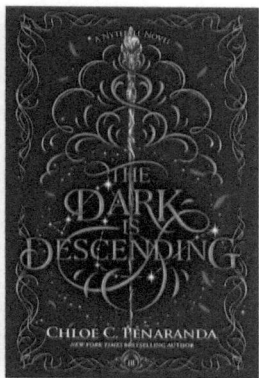

THE NYTEFALL TRILOGY

A STARCROSSED VILLAIN X SAVIOR ROMANTASY

THE STARS ARE DYING: SYNOPSIS

THE BRIGHTEST STAR NEEDS THE DARKEST NIGHT.

In a world abandoned by the celestial guardians and left to suffer a tyrant king's reign, all Astraea knows is safety in seclusion. With fragmented memories of only five years of her life, she's determined to discover more about her past, even if that means fleeing the cruel arms that hold her safe from the wicked vampires rumored to roam the land.

But when Astraea stumbles upon the mysterious Nyte, she soon realizes determination alone isn't enough to guard her heart. He lingers like the darkness that expands between the stars, and soon she discovers her captor's wicked means of control weren't based on a lie to keep her under locks after all. In her desperation, Astraea accepts Nyte's help before she can decide if she might have sold her allegiance to one of the bloodthirsty beings the people of her world fear.

Once their bargain is struck, Astraea's chance to escape comes in the form of accompanying her best friend Cassia to the King's Central. There on royal territory it's the centenary of the Libertatem, a succession of trials hosted by the king in which five human lands compete for a cycle of safety from the vampires seeking blood, claiming souls, and savaging after dark. So when tragedy strikes, Astraea must decide if taking the place of a murdered participant for the safety of her kingdom is a ruse is worth dying for, or if protection—and the answers to her past—really are her strongest desires.

For fans of From Blood & Ash and Shadow & Bone. Star-crossed hearts bleed and the first sparks of war ignite in this dark romantic fantasy loosely inspired by the Greek myth of Astraea and the fall of the Golden Age.

AUTHOR NOTE

Dear reader,

I can't thank you enough for taking this journey with me, Faythe, and co. It's bittersweet to be ending the story that started everything for me.

Before writing An Heir Comes to Rise, I didn't know where I existed in the world. I'm a quiet soul, a fractured heart, and for the longest time I didn't belong anywhere. I wrote book one in my living room couch on an old iPad, in a council rental apartment where I could hear what my upstairs neighbours were having for dinner. I lost myself in the pages sun up to sun down and knew by the end, when I had the story complete, that there was so much more to come, and I wanted so passionately to share it with the world. This was how my small voice could roar.

Fast forward to today, I can't believe how far we've come. I started this journey with no expectations, no social media following, only a dream in my soul and joy in my heart. I lead with passion and loved every minute of creating little TikTok videos and sharing my life on Instagram.

I found all of you, and you found me. I strongly believe you can achieve anything when you lead by passion, charge on with delusion, and sometimes be fueled by spite. You are unstoppable when you choose to say "fuck you, watch me" every once in a while. Because there are always people who will try to keep you from moving forward. Don't fight them, work in silence and celebrate loud.

Like Faythe, I came from nothing, and I hope to keep rising to everything I once thought impossible. More so, I hope YOU have found inspiration through these books and my journey to pursue your own greatness.

I see you, I hear you, I believe in you.

Here's to you, to us, and to endless adventures together.

ACKNOWLEDGMENTS

It's the end of an era. First and foremost I have to thank my readers, those of you who have been here since book one, or two, or three, or wherever you picked up this series. If you're reading this years from now, April 16th 2025, THANK YOU. This is my debut fantasy series five years in the making which will always be so close to my heart. I lived, learned, and laughed through these pages. I cried, grieved, and fought with these characters. And I hope you did too.

To Lyssa, I'm so grateful these books brought one of the best friendships into my life. Thank you for being you, and always being there for me no matter what since the very beginning.

To my mum, thank you for believing in me and my dreams. You've always supported me and let me be exactly who I am. You're the strongest woman I know.

I wouldn't be who I am without my immediate family: my dad. My two brothers, Marcus and Jason. One sister, Eva. Five nieces, Chiara, Alicia, Eliana, Harley, and Katie-mae. I have so much love for you all.

To Bryony Leah, I thank my lucky stars for finding you. I couldn't imagine a better editor for these books. You've always understood these characters and this story, and been such a big supporter. It's been a long road and I hope it's not the end. Thank you for all your patience, passion, and hard work.

To Alice Maria Power, Team Rocket has done it! These six phenomenal covers are so iconic. Thank you so much for lending your incredible talent for these books. But don't think you're rid of me.

There's so many individuals from my street teams and general social media over the years that I can't possibly name you all in this one space. I think you know who you are. I see you, and I hear you. Thank you endlessly for reminding me why I love what I do, for keeping me going through all the hardships and celebrating so hard with all the triumphs. I hope you know how much your comments, posts, DMs mean to me, because words can't begin to express.

Until our next adventure.

ABOUT THE AUTHOR

CHLOE C. PEÑARANDA is the *New York Times* bestselling Scottish author of *The Stars Are Dying* and *An Heir Comes to Rise.*

A lifelong avid reader and writer, Chloe discovered her passion for storytelling in her early teens. An Heir Comes to Rise has been built upon from years' worth of building on fictional characters and exploring Tolkien-like quests in made up worlds. During her time at the University of the West of Scotland, Chloe immersed herself in writing for short film, producing animations, and spending class time dreaming of far off lands.

In her spare time from writing in her home in scenic Scotland, Chloe enjoys digital art, graphic design, and down time with her three furry companions. When the real world calls...she rarely listens.

www.ccpenaranda.com
@chloecpenaranda

www.ingramcontent.com/pod-product-compliance
Lightning Source LLC
Chambersburg PA
CBHW031727180726
48283CB00005B/1402